✠ THE WORLD ✠
IS NOT ENOUGH

✠ THE WORLD ✠ IS NOT ENOUGH

by

ZOÉ OLDENBOURG

Translated from the French by Willard R. Trask

CARROLL & GRAF PUBLISHERS, INC.
NEW YORK

Copyright © 1948 by Pantheon Books, Inc.

First Carroll & Graf edition 1998

Carroll & Graf Publishers, Inc.
19 West 21st Street
New York, NY 10010

Library of Congress Cataloging-in-Publication Data
   Oldenbourg, Zoé, 1916–
     [Argile. English]
     The world is not enough / Zoé Oldenbourg ; translated by Willard
   R. Trask.
       p.   cm.
     ISBN 0-7867-0489-6
     I. Trask, Willard R. (Willard Ropes), 1900– . II. Title.
   PQ2629.L4A813   1998
   843'.914—dc21   97-17488
                                        CIP

Shall the clay say to him that fashioneth it,
What makest thou? or thy work, He hath no hands?

ISAIAH 45:9

CONTENTS

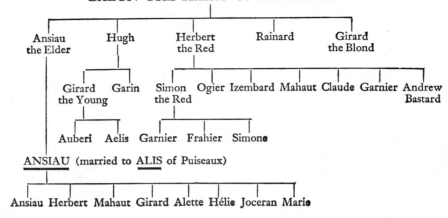

GALON THE HAIRY OF LINNIERES

Ansiau the Elder — Hugh — Herbert the Red — Rainard — Girard the Blond

Girard the Young   Garin   Simon the Red   Ogier   Izembard   Mahaut   Claude   Garnier   Andrew Bastard

Auberi   Aelis   Garnier   Frahier   Simone

ANSIAU (married to ALIS of Puiseaux)

Ansiau   Herbert   Mahaut   Girard   Alette   Hélie   Joceran   Marie

★

HERBERT OF PUISEAUX

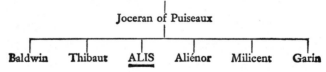

Joceran of Puiseaux

Baldwin   Thibaut   ALIS   Aliénor   Milicent   Garin

MARRIAGE

THERE HAD BEEN RED WAX CANDLES.

And everywhere in the church—on the altar, against the pillars, in the windows—flowering branches of hawthorn and apple.

And a pair of rings made of Syrian chased gold.

The two of them, standing there, were moved, as two children must be who have just been washed, dressed, lectured, and left at the altar by their parents in front of all the guests, their brothers, their sisters, their uncles, their playmates.

They were so little alike. He a boy and she a girl.

At Christmas time their parents had settled the amount of the dowry and the other details. The bridegroom's father was old and he wished to see grandchildren of his race and lineage. That was the reason why tonight Alis of Puiseaux would have to go to bed with a boy.

At Castlehervi, on the border of Champagne and Burgundy, the ponderous square church dominated the village and its inns. In King Robert's time, it was told, the relics of a saint had been found there—a certain St. Thiou, whose story was unknown. The church had been built on the spot; it was called St. Mary's-of-the-Angels. And the name of St. Thiou had become a common countryside oath. The palatine road from Troyes to Tonnerre ran through Hervi, and the counts of Champagne owned a forest there.

In this year of grace 1171, when King Louis the Young reigned in France and Henry the Openhanded held Champagne, Linnières, in the southern part of the Pays d'Othe, was a manor neither better nor worse than any other, believe me—it was just as muddy and just as smoky. From Hervi, you took a narrow by-road which ran through a forest of beech and birch. Here and there the road was crossed by a little brook, and at such places dry branches and half-rotted planks had been thrown across. Today, in honor of the bride, the crossings were strewn with new withies, yellow as down. The forest was luminous and gray, with barely a beginning shimmer of green. Great dark birds flapped their wings high among the branches.

At the small square gray watchtower of Seuroi, with its barricade of uneven palings, the procession drew rein. They were still two good leagues from Linnières Castle, the bridegroom's home. It was noon. Beyond Seuroi the road became miry; here the forest of Linnières was broken by vast green spaces where no trees grew, where rushes disputed the ground with straggling shrubs and clumps of young willows. The forest was dank and abounded in game.

Alis was fourteen. Her blond hair, tirelessly washed in camomile water, would darken as she grew older. Full lips that were still soft; heavy eyebrows; blue-gray eyes, small but unflinching; a longish face with very pink cheeks—Alis was considered pretty, and she knew it. Tall, slender, strong-muscled, she always seemed ready to leap, to run, to stretch like a cat. She had learned all the things that a girl of noble blood must know: she sewed and spun and embroidered; she could dance and sing, ride horseback, draw a bow, train hawks.

And now it was good-bye to Puiseaux. Alis felt quite sure that she was in love with her bridegroom, as she was in duty bound to be. Last Christmas at Puiseaux—that time on the big chest behind the curtain, when they had been playing hide-and-seek—she had let him slobber her lips and squeeze her breasts between her dress and her shift. Those were courtesies which she had already granted to other boys; but this boy was more ardent than the others, his face grew red and tears came to his eyes. But she had known enough to beware: the strange creatures would weep and wail at you over nothing—worse than girls; and everyone said that they became harsh once they had their will. For Alis, to be married was primarily to sleep with a boy—until now she had always slept with her sisters on the pallets in her father's vast bedchamber.

Alis had four grown sisters, so her standards of masculine beauty were very definite: there was no doubt of it, her bridegroom was not handsome. Yet she had thought him charming as they came out of the church; he was sixteen (and said to be a virgin), he was tall, square-shouldered, and had been knighted a week ago. But no, he was no St. George for looks: a heavy brown mop with reddish highlights, a big head, a perfectly obvious face running to width, with flat cheekbones and a low forehead—big horse eyes and an enormous smile which exposed heaven alone knew how many teeth. He had no beard yet, and didn't prick when he kissed. His best point was the way he threw back his head to get the long fringe of hair out of his eyes—it reminded her of a restive colt. Then the fringe would tumble back, and he would try again.

His name was Ansiau—rather a commonplace name. But his father was named Ansiau too, and his first son would bear the name in turn, everyone said, because the grandfather wished it. Alis had passed close to the elder Ansiau—the grandfather to be—on the church square. He had kissed her and pinched her left breast—he was fat, huge, with a scanty beard, pockets under his eyes, eyes that were as yellow as a sparrow hawk's. He said: "In nine months, eh?". . . and winked.

Brown and muddy on ordinary days, today the courtyard of Linnières was strewn with branches and sheaves of straw. The bridegroom's uncles and cousins dismounted and welcomed the bride and her family, shouting and clapping their hands. Six girls in light dresses were standing by the well, and when Alis' foot touched the ground, they opened a great basket and set free a flock of pigeons, which rose in a whir of wings amid the joyous cries of all the company.

The castle of Linnières was spacious and dark. Little daylight filtered through the narrow windows. Two sheep and a calf were roasting on spits in the huge fireplace, not to mention various kinds of fowl. The great, dark, smoky hall combined the functions of reception room, kitchen, and chapel—the latter being separated from the rest of the hall by a curtain. Above the high table the whitewashed wall was decorated with lances, pelts, and long, crudely painted shields. All the long, narrow tables were covered with white cloths, the floor was strewn with herbs. Along the benches and between the pillars hung garlands of wildflowers.

Washed and refreshed after her journey, the bride was led to the high table. Her beautiful hair, which she usually wore braided, hung down over her back and breast in little regular waves; it reached to her knees. Her head was covered with a veil of red silk, held in place by a silver circlet set with rubies—a crown which each of her older sisters had worn on her own wedding day. By contrast with the intense red of her dress and veil, the little bride's face looked as pale and translucent as a flower. She came slowly forward, surrounded by her attendants. It was a charming sight, that procession of slender young girls who for all their grace were as hard as young colts; as they walked, they swung their hips, making the muscles of rump and thigh play visibly, and the ends of their long girdles danced and clashed.

Even an ordinary dinner meant hours at the table; the benches for the bridal couple's relatives and the distinguished guests were strewn with cushions and pelts. The water in the wash basin, into which all the men dipped their hands in turn, grew dark and greasy: there were so many guests. The women took their places beside their husbands—cautiously, for fear their long, gold-embroidered veils would be disarranged.

Seated on a high-backed double chair under the great blazon of Linnières, the bride and groom were the focal point of the assembly; from every table, from every bench, the guests turned and craned their necks to look. The men wiped sauce from their beards, the women loosened their girdles; wine after wine, viand after viand, the banquet pursued its course, and only the bride and groom in their places of honor barely touched the dishes which were offered them—for so custom decreed. The handsome boy, all russet and brown and red in his wine-colored, gold-embroidered garments, bent his awkward head, and his large, round, restless eyes flitted over his bride's white hands. Those hands, dutifully crossed over her abdomen, made him think of things which he was in a hurry to learn—his forehead, his ears, even his neck grew red, and conscious that he was blushing, he blushed even more—he did not like the feeling that people were looking at him, he wished that he could leave the table. Alis, who was more patient, concentrated on showing the guests a calm and smiling face; she sat straight and stiff, with lowered eyes. She was hungry, and regretted that she was not allowed to eat more heartily.

It was all as if they were two young, highly bred animals which had to be successfully mated—and as such, indeed, they regarded themselves, for they were not proud. It was a serious matter: their parents had had to choose a good day, calculating it carefully in accordance with the phases of the moon and the bride's menstrual period; to make sure that it was not a Friday or a Wednesday, and wait until the lilacs had gone out of bloom and the wild parsnips had budded. And the evening before, Alis' lady mother had ducked her in a tub of rain water caught near the chapel of St. Anne-in-the-Forest—St. Anne-in-the-Forest protected the female population of the countryside for five leagues around and made mares and heifers and married women fertile, without distinction. The girl was very young—and everybody knew what an old father-in-law who expects heirs is like.

When the sunlight had all ebbed out of the courtyard the old master of the house decided that it was time to conduct the bridal pair to the nuptial chamber, and he made a sign to Lady Adela, his sister-in-law, who rose and approached the bride. Alis stood up, all rosy, and stretched her numb little hands. Amid a thunder of shouts: "Noël! Long live bride and groom!" the two drank a cup of wine to the guests; then her attendants surrounded Alis and led her by the hand past the tables while the varlets pushed the swarming dogs and children out of the way.

The groom hardly dared to follow her with his eyes—he was in love and was afraid of showing it. Calm and unbending, he smiled at his companions' jokes with regal good grace; at sixteen he already had the natural dignity which uncommon height and great physical endurance confer. He had a fine body: his waist was so slim that he wore his white leather belt doubled around it, and his long, thickset legs seemed to spring directly from his waist. His magnificent square shoulders had set many a girl of noble blood and many a village maid dreaming; but he preferred his horse and his javelins; women to him were simply men who wore skirts and had no beards. His answer to his companions' coarse jokes on the subject of his virginity was a laugh—they did not trouble him—he had said such things himself to his friends when it had been their turn to be married. He would rather have been killed on the spot than to let anyone see that he took this thing seriously.

The bathhouse at Linnières was a small square building of chalkstone and yellow clay; it stood opposite to the stables and on ordinary days was not very different from them in appearance. But that day the door and the two windows were hung with garlands of marsh marigolds and forget-me-nots; all the way from the keep to the bathhouse, planks had been laid to bridge the mud in the courtyard, and the planks had been strewn with straw and fresh grass. Built only some forty years earlier, the little bathhouse was the scene of all the great events in the lives of the family—marriages, child-births, purifications—because it was the only part of the castle where it was sometimes possible to escape the eyes of the entire household.

A low, wide couch stood in the center of the little room, which had been thoroughly scrubbed. The walls were covered with tapestries. Along the sides of the bed and around the pillows there were bunches of dried lavender, violets, and lilies-of-the-valley. Gradually the room filled with guests who were glad to leave the table for a time and stretch their legs; an odor of sweat and undigested wine made the air unbreathable, and the noise of voices was so loud that no one could understand what was said.

Seated close to the bed in the place of honor, the two fathers wiped their foreheads and wondered how soon the bride would be ready. In a corner of the room Alis' attendants were undressing her and braiding her hair for the night; the younger girls had made a circle around the older ones and were holding up two large woolen cloaks as a screen. They were all chattering viva-ciously. "Are you coming to fish for carp at Plassis, Berengaria?" asked one, and another groaned: "I think I ate too much stuffed guinea fowl."—"Oh, Milicent, will you put this little stick down my throat and make me vomit?" —"Hi! Girard!" This exclamation was addressed to a little page who had slipped his dark head between the two halves of the improvised screen. The bride's attendants drove the indiscreet intruder away with a volley of slaps and kicks.

A wild shout rose from the back of the room. Alis dropped her arms with a look of disgust: "Just as I thought! Baldwin has drunk one cup too many again; he might at least have waited till I had been put to bed."

"Is he dangerous when he drinks?" Brigitte of Le Plassis asked.

"I should say so! At Hermenjart's wedding he almost stabbed the groom's uncle, and it was just when Hermenjart was undressing—you can imagine if she was terrified of being left there like that!"

The girls laughed loudly. "God, Alis! how white your body is! What do you do to get rid of fleabites?" Alis had the very beautiful body of a young girl who is later to be a strong woman—no fragility, no pretty-prettyness, a classic and already fully developed figure, long limbs, bold hips. Her long, fine linen shift, which she was not to take off until the candles were put out, was so transparent that it could not conceal the warm flush of her shoulders and breasts, rosy with heat and emotion. They led her to the bed and seated her with her back against the pillows; her younger sisters arranged the folds of her shift on her arms and chest.

Ansiau sat down beside her and stretched his long legs under the gray woolen coverlet. Blushing and placid, both lowered their eyes; they knew that it would be a long time yet before they had done with answering the greet-ings and congratulations of all their kindred. Old Lady Adela, sister-in-law to the master of Linnières, brought them a great beaker of wine mulled with mint leaves and parsnip, which are reputed to excite love between man and woman. While they drank, groomsmen and bridesmaids clapped their hands and sang:

Ansiau and Alis do love each other well;
Ansiau loveth Alis, Alis doth love Ansiau.

Meanwhile the room was gradually emptying and through the open door the cool night breeze entered and set the candle flames trembling; the ladies of Linnières plugged the windows with slabs of wood and deerskins. The two fathers, Joceran and the elder Ansiau, both a little drunk, inspected every corner of the room together, looked behind the bed curtains and under the pillows, to make certain—and to prove to each other—that no deceit was possible. They were the last to leave the room, and old Ansiau double-locked the door.

Left alone together, the two did not yet dare to raise their eyes. Two tallow candles were spluttering behind them on the headboard of the bed. From the keep, drunken cries and songs rose ever more loudly to the health of bride and groom, and at the door of the bathhouse there was stifled laughter, a sound of shoving—people were trying to look through the keyhole and the edges of the door. A cracked voice chanted: "Cockadoodledoo!" Alis felt like crying and wanted to call her mother. She was trembling. Ansiau, abashed, caressed the ends of her long blond braids. Then he took her by the hips. "Put out the candle," she said.

They were in darkness, lying side by side. Three times Alis refused to take off her shift, as her mother had sternly warned her to do the day before. And the fourth time she stripped, threw her arms above her head, and lay motionless. Around her, over her, that great boy was twisting and panting like a pack of hounds around a wounded stag. And afterwards she cried, and he fell asleep—that was what always happened the first time, her elder sisters had said.

That morning Ansiau woke late for the first time in his life. It was pitch-dark in the bathhouse. Threads of sunlight seeped in around the edges of the door. Ansiau thought that, for all he knew, it might be noon. Outside, hens were clucking, grooms were shouting at horses—Ansiau felt a bunch of faded violets against his cheek, and he smiled. His damsel was there beside him, she was breathing gently like a little child, in the darkness he could make out her braids, lying across the pillow like two heavy ropes, and the chain with a cross and amulets which she wore around her neck; and then the great dark stain of her half-open mouth. To lie there so peacefully, in a bed with sheets, with flowers and a damsel—for a boy who had never slept on anything better than straw it was paradise. For three days they would be allowed to have this bed, these sheets, this quiet, so that for all their lives they might remember that God had united them to found a new family and a new line.

The door was unlocked, the windows were opened, and the elder Ansiau with Alis' parents, Joceran and his wife Hodierne, came in first to wish them good day. Alis, dazzled by the light, rubbed her eyes and could not seem to remember what her mother had told her she must do on the morning after her wedding. Now her sisters and her cousins were around her, putting on her shift, combing out her hair; tired and dreamy, she turned her head toward Ansiau. He was still lying there, he gave her a wide, blissful smile, as if he were only half awake—and she knew then what a fine and simple boy he was, and it touched her, and she sighed.

Ansiau was soon carried off by his groomsmen, and she did not see him again all that day, for no one seemed to be paying any attention to him now. He went hawking with his cousins and he said no more about his wife than if he had been merely a groomsman at the wedding. It was the first time, and he felt ashamed. The mere thought of the girl set hot lead flowing through his veins and made him dizzy, and he tried not to think of her before nightfall.

In the bathhouse Lady Hodierne of Puiseaux and the ladies of Linnières were examining the sheets and the bed and questioning the bride: they wanted to know at what hour the act had taken place and how long it had lasted, so that they could determine whether the girl had conceived or not—Lady Irma, Alis' sister-in-law, was convinced that she had done so, and insisted that she must fast until noon and rest all day, for the fruit would still be very frail. "It is not as it is with us older women," she said. "We should be glad to get rid of it the first day if we could. But if the first fruit is spoiled, the others will never be perfect."

Alis had great respect for Irma's wisdom, because Irma was said to be something of a sorceress. She listened with interest while the ladies complacently described their own wedding nights and their daughters'. She thought of the night to come and of what, now that she knew him, she would say to her Ansiau. She would not be tongue-tied, as she had been the night before—he must not think that she was stupid. She would say: "I come of noble lineage, and you must not scorn me. I am your peer and your equal. I will love you if you will love me. But it shall be for all our lives, forever, and you shall not forsake me for serving-wenches, even when I am pregnant, even when you are at war; and you shall see how well I will serve you, and how well I can wash your feet and scratch your head and bandage your wounds—for I have been taught all those things," (and her eyes grew moist when she thought what an accomplished young lady she was), "and I know how to train hawks too, and to throw a javelin, and embroider and spin, and dance and sing—you will never be bored in my company."

In the keep the rejoicings were still in full swing, and the knights showed little interest in the bathhouse—it was the women's business now. So the bride and groom had a quiet evening. The ladies withdrew early. Ansiau had spent all day in the forest and had managed to return too late for supper. But it did not matter whether he was there or not—his father, the old lord, received the congratulations of the guests in his stead. Besides, the boy had been in such a hurry to join his young wife that he had not even gone up to the keep. Seated on the floor beside their bed, he pressed his cheeks against his damsel's cool, smooth knees. Timidly she ran her hand through his hair. He had thick, curly, tangled hair. Alis took a comb from the headboard and began untangling it, lock by lock. And she said none of the things she had planned to say. Instead, she reached under the pillow for a piece of honey cake which she had hidden in her sleeve at supper. She gave it to him, and he devoured it without a word, in two bites, so fast that she felt afraid. Then he began to caress her—roughly, like a boy who does not know how to go about it—and Alis pushed him away, filled with shame. And he said: "I love you so much! So much! If only you knew! It is so good to be with you. I will do anything, I will be your varlet." And Alis thought how much she would have loved him if he had been quieter, less rough, less hot, and she said to herself: "Ah, men!"

Ansiau had never known his mother—she had died when he was nine months old. His foster mother had died when he was two. He had lived the rough-and-tumble life of a castle, among a crowd of cousins and squires. For a boy became a varlet as soon as he reached four if he had not a hot-tempered mother to protect him. Everyone was rough with him, pushed him. "Ansiau, my knife! Ansiau, my belt! And hurry up!" Slaps and pinches rained down on him; his older companions often snatched his piece of bread out of his hands. Then came his training—riding, archery. As a child, Ansiau was a little brute so accustomed to blows that no one thought he felt them. He was very strong. From seven to ten, the skin of his buttocks and back was always torn and bleeding—the result of paternal switchings. It was the old lord's way of bringing up his son. When he saw that the boy was not first at sports or archery, he switched him. "The lord of the castle must be strongest," he would say. "Do not forget, you bitch's son, that you will be castellan after I am dead." Ansiau did not know what "castellan" meant, and he did not particularly care. He was very much a child: his ambition did not extend beyond owning a horse; horses were his passion, he dreamed of them even when he was awake.

The blows which were his daily fare had given him strength; pain never made him hesitate or retreat. Nor did he ever feel angry with anyone who struck him, because he considered it quite natural to be struck for no reason— life was like that, and children were made to be beaten.

Then came six years of service at Troyes, in the household of his god-father, the lord of Nangi. It was hard. The child was made to do a man's work because he was big and never refused any sort of task. He was always lighthearted, he liked listening to minstrels and storytellers at night after supper; he laughed and cried easily over noble tales, but he had never once cried over his own troubles. He adored tournaments and had been allowed to take part in them at an early age, to carry lance and spear, sometimes to fight. It was his life. No one knew horses and arms better than Ansiau of Linnières. He had friends; he loved his lord, William of Nangi—a god-father-in-arms was so much more than a father; he loved the fields, the woods, hunting and battle. He was not a demanding boy, not he!—and now suddenly this thing had happened to him which made him richer than a king, and he had neither asked for it nor deserved it!

It had happened all of a sudden, at Christmas, when he had come to Puiseaux with his uncle Herbert, to exchange engagement rings with Joce-ran's daughter. He had no notion of it then—oh, no! He thought that she was a girl like all the others, and not too pretty at that; and then, in a game of hide-and-seek, they had been alone together on a chest behind a curtain—and the girl had said she did not want to be kissed, had said it so decidedly that he had taken up the challenge. And then it had come, he had felt his legs grow weak and the blood had sung in his ears until he could hear noth-ing else. He did not know what was happening—under his lips, very far away, a little drowned voice was saying: "Stop, you are hurting me." He had wanted to possess her wholly, there on the chest; but she had said and sworn that she would not permit such a thing before their wedding night—she was of too good lineage, and she would never bring that shame upon her family. Ansiau had found himself thinking that everything she said was beautiful. He adored her; he adored her father, the lord of Puiseaux, and his wife and sons and daughters. In public he was formal and dignified as always, and he never talked about his betrothed—that was the proper way for a knight to behave.

And then had come the moment when his father and the lord of Puiseaux and the priest at Hervi gave him his damsel all washed and adorned, with a ring on her finger and a red dress, and said: "There, take it, it is yours, it is all for you, and for you alone, and for always—take as much as you want, surfeit yourself, you are the master." Ansiau had not waited to be told twice.

As soon as the days of celebration were over, he had moved back to his old pallet beside his father's great bed. And for the first time in his life he found the straw prickly, the ticking wrinkled, and the smell of the blankets sour and oppressive. His cousins and the squires were making too much noise, the dogs barked too loud. He would have liked to give his damsel a square tower with a beautiful bedchamber and a garden—to have been left alone together for three nights was so little. They had a tiny corner where they were alone, a hollow in the big pallet—Alis hunched herself together and did not move, her thin, cool arms were around his neck and she talked very low.

"You know," said Ansiau, "when my father is dead I shall be castellan, I shall have my father's bed. And all the quilts. And the sheets. We shall have room to play and do whatever we like. You love me? You aren't too homesick?"

"Oh! I am!" she sighed. She could not lie to Ansiau. She wept as she thought of her mother and sisters.

The first weeks were always hard—that she knew, Lady Hodierne had said so. Alis was brave; she entered her new family with her head high and with good weapons in her hands. She was not a nobly born girl for nothing, she had learned how to behave. She made an effort to be sweet and kind to everyone; with the jewels of her dowry she gave gifts to all her new aunts and girl cousins; she kissed them and called them "sister" and "friend"; she went into ecstasies over their children if they had any—even the ugly ones. In general, she admired everything: carpets, chests, silver, horses, dogs. She said: "What a lovely carpet! What a lovely bed! What a lovely horse!" with the look of perfect conviction that she invariably assumed when she was lying. (She was far from admiring everything, and she thought there was nothing really beautiful except at Puiseaux. She had no one with her from Puiseaux except her foster sister, Catherine, and the two girls secretly exchanged grimaces and ironic looks when they saw that at Linnières the spiced wine was prepared in a different way from what they were used to at Puiseaux.)

Alis was a lively, hot-blooded girl, and quick-tempered. But the caresses of the big boy they had given her for a husband had, for the time being, calmed and softened her. She had so often been told that love was a good thing. At table she let him press her hand or pinch her waist and she turned white and red with the pleasure of it. All day she waited for night, for the game that made her head swim so. "That is what love is," she thought. And yet there were at least three nights a week—Fridays, Wednesdays, and the eves of feasts—when women had to sleep apart from their husbands—especially the younger wives. Lady Adela made them go to bed in the lefthand corner of the great bedchamber, behind the curtain with the unmarried girls. Once, on a Friday night, Alis had yielded to her husband's entreaties in spite of her fear of sinning. She had gone to him behind a settle near the great hearth—and she was properly punished for it, for in the darkness she stumbled against a stool and hurt her back. And the following evening old Lady Adela came to tell the old lord that his new daughter-in-law had blood-stains on her shift. The old gentleman was terribly angry, for he had thought that she was already fruitful; he boxed her ears and ordered her to take better care of herself—at fourteen, other wives were mothers already. Until that happened he had been kindly to her, but now he turned hard.

The old man sat from morning to night in a great armchair under the window, with his enormous gouty feet resting on two pillows. His eyelids were heavy, he was very tired. Too much wine, too much meat, too many women—and nothing else except a long life of warfare and hunting, enough to kill you with boredom. Was it any pleasure for an intelligent man to have a great lout of a son with no more brains than a rabbit? God knew that he did not love his son, but what was to take shape and grow in the body of his new daughter-in-law—that made his heart beat faster, because it was his own flesh.

The old man was impatient. Two months after the wedding day he was already calling his daughter-in-law vile names and reproaching her with her poverty. "I tell you, your father gave me only thirty marks for you, and my son could have had the heiress of Bercenay, but she is not yet ten. I took you to get heirs, and you do nothing." And he threatened to send her back to her father, or to breed his son to a serving-wench so that at least he should have bastards. Alis did not yet know that her father-in-law's bark was worse than his bite, and at night she wept in Ansiau's arms—he, at least, no more wanted to be a father than he wanted to be a bishop, and he consoled his beloved by saying: "The old man has not long to live."

The forest of Linnières. The meadow in front of the castle. The heat of July, and the mown grass spread on the ground. The blue of the sky was heavy, dark, unbroken: not a cloud. The sun's rays fell vertically, beating like hammers on the meadow and the warm hay. There on the hay Ansiau and his beloved came to sit after their noonday nap—Alis looking like a little peasant girl, in her linen dress with only a plain white kerchief over her head. They could hear the grasshoppers singing in the buckwheat field, the soldiers hailing one another on the ramparts. The hot air was heavy with the odor of mint.

A light breeze stirred the runaway strands on her forehead. Her face was all bathed in blond light, and her nostrils dilated so slowly, she looked so happy and so peaceful, that Ansiau was overwhelmed. "She is beautiful"— why were there no other words but those, which everyone had always heard and known? But there were no others. That day Ansiau stayed dreaming beside his wife for a long time, he caressed her arms and smoothed her eyebrows, he studied her teeth, he felt her all over as if she were an object—so great was his astonishment at suddenly finding this new beauty, this beauty which was too much for him. And after that day he could never think of a woman's fair skin calmly again.

They had been married almost three months—she had grown accustomed to him, she loved him. She would say: "God! what beautiful eyes you have!" and "what a beautiful mouth!" and then "your beautiful hands!" and "your beautiful hair!" and "your beautiful nose!"—to her, everything about him was beautiful—she overwhelmed him with kisses and sudden and awkward caresses and forgot all her mother's good advice. She waited on him like a little page. She thought herself very happy.

That month Lady Adela and Lady Richeut, her daughter-in-law, counted the days on their fingers and said: "It begins to look likely now." Alis was made to eat leeks until they choked her, because leeks were reputed to make women pregnant; she said novenas at St. Anne's-in-the-Forest: "St. Anne, good lady, make my father-in-law content with me." On Assumption Day she fainted in the chapel, and from that day on her father-in-law was content with her. He sent for her, he made her stand near him and looked at her for a long time, his chin in great folds, his lips trembling. "There," he said, "there, there! No foolishness now—and make it a boy, eh?"

Ansiau was hunting that day and did not come home until late in the evening. His cousin Mahaut told him the good news, and Ansiau gave a sigh of relief and thought: "At least the old man won't pester my sweet any more." And he went to the upper chamber to see Alis. Sick and miserable from too many potions and too much nursing, she had for once been permitted to share the bed of old Hugh and Lady Adela; she was resting, stretched straight out at the very edge of the bed; old Uncle Hugh was already snoring with his face to the wall. Ansiau sat down on the bed, and his big black dog jumped onto the quilts and rested his head on his master's thigh. Alis, lying with her hands under her head, looked at her husband sadly and seriously.

Ansiau smiled at her: "Everything all right?" Alis made a face. "All right," she said. "You don't know what is to come. I shall start swelling up like a cow that's eaten green clover."

Ansiau thought the comparison very funny, and burst into a loud laugh; Alis was a little put out. "Do you think that's amusing?" she said sulkily. "What if I die in childbirth?"

"Nobody dies in childbirth," said Ansiau, fondling the dog's ears.

"They don't, don't they!" Alis cried indignantly. Then, in a milder voice: "And what are we going to name the baby?"

"Ansiau, after my father, I suppose," said her husband.

"And if it's a girl?"

"Don't fret," said Ansiau. "If it's a girl, father shall not hurt you—I will protect you."

The next morning the young women of the household rode to the Armançon to bathe; it was a very hot day. But the old castellan announced that his daughter-in-law was not to leave the castle; it was no time for her to be riding horseback and bathing—not in her condition. And Alis had such a longing to go bathing, there was not a breath of air in the castle, the courtyard was foul with the smell from the latrines. "No, no, I won't have it. The others will get cool in the river, and I—" It was too unjust to be borne; none of the others wanted to bathe as much as she did. She threw herself on Ansiau and clung to him. And Ansiau lost his head at the sight of her tears. He ran to the old lord at his window—his wife was his wife, she had a right to bathe if she pleased, it was none of the old man's affair, let him go and get married himself instead of meddling with other people's wives. It was the first time Ansiau had ever said such things, and he was not even conscious of it, because what was uppermost in his mind was Alis' great longing to go bathing. And to everyone's amazement the old man did not become angry, he merely knit his brows wearily. Then he said: "Go see Lady Adela, she will explain it to you."

It did not take Lady Adela long to break the young man down. She said that water snakes instantly sensed the presence of pregnant women and drew them to the bottom, and that a woman carrying a child was weakened and therefore more susceptible to the evil eye and to spirits; she must not pass through a forest, especially in summer after Assumption Day, nor ride horseback, because an evil spirit might make her horse rear. Of all this, Ansiau understood only one thing—Lady Adela and his old father wanted to keep Alis from going bathing, and if she would not obey them they were ready to threaten her with water snakes and spirits and God knew what mysterious catastrophes. For the first time in his life he felt weak and alone in the presence of a world full of beings stronger than himself and utterly incomprehensible. And what was the use of having a wife if he couldn't even prevent other people from making her cry? It was his old father's fault if Alis was big-bellied—that was what came of eating too many leeks! As for himself, he would as lief she stayed thin all her life.

Alis said: "I hate your father. He hit me in the face. He called me vile names. I thought he would grow kinder when he saw that I was carrying a child. And now he wants to shut me up in the castle. And he won't let me sleep with you. Not for seven more months. I have known nothing but misery since I entered this house. And the child will kill me—you'll see. Just as I killed my own mother."

"My father can be sure of one thing," Ansiau said. "If you die in childbed, I will kill the child; I will throw it down the well."

"Oh no," Alis said. "No! What a fearful sin! Promise me that you will not!"

The air of the castle was heavy and acid, the courtyard smelled of manure and rotting straw. Flies and mosquitoes lit and clung everywhere. Whenever he climbed to the roof of the keep, Ansiau saw white clouds piling up in a bright blue sky, saw the forest about the castle quivering in a bluish mist. The air was dead, the stones of the parapet were white and burning. From time to time the soldiers on the top of the keep hailed those on the ramparts, then all was still again. And the crickets chirped in the scorched grass of the meadow, and the sound was so incessant that Ansiau finally thought it was his own blood humming in his ears. A new temptation had come to him—one that he had never known before. Gisela, the huntsman's daughter, was white-skinned and blond, and she was always brushing against him in the stable or when he passed between two benches in the hall. One day, when they had met each other on the rampart behind the keep, she said: "You may do all your will—come. No one can see us." And she lifted her gray skirt and showed her legs and her white thighs. Ansiau spat in her face and passed on without even touching her. The girl irritated him; he thought that a girl who offers herself is like a merchant who is too anxious to sell his wares because he knows that they are worthless. He put himself on his guard. But Gisela was always there, she left the neck of her dress unfastened to tempt him the more, and let her hair show under her white bonnet. Until one fine day, instead of spitting at her, he threw her on her back by the palisade, behind the barns. But afterwards he felt ashamed—he saddled his horse and rode off without a word to anyone.

No one had ever taught him that a man should be faithful to his wife: that article of the marriage contract was for the woman alone. It was not proper for him to look on another man's wife as a woman—but a girl was there to be taken, like a ripe apple or a fresh loaf of bread. So far as Alis was concerned, he felt no remorse because he saw no comparison. But he knew that he could have Gisela ten times a day if he wished, and that was precisely what disgusted him with the girl and with himself: it was too easy.

Along the road all was still. Only the grasshoppers sang in the dry grass. And the sky was blue, blue, blue. Ansiau rode until noon without feeling either hungry or tired. After buying a piece of bread in Bernon village, he entered the forest. That part of it was very wild, without roads or paths, and he was already thinking of returning the way he had come when tracks in the moss and a line of broken branches told him that there was a boar about. The beast had gone by only a few minutes earlier, Ansiau could still smell its rank odor—his nose was as keen as a dog's. He had no arms but a knife and a lance no thicker than a man's finger. But he saw the boar's tracks and he did not stop to reflect. He thought that he might possibly surprise the beast while it was taking its midday sleep, and he followed. The tracks circled, disappeared again, quite fresh—but no boar.

Ansiau searched so long that he had to spend the night in the forest, perched in a tree. He slept badly; the forest was full of sounds. His horse, tethered to the foot of the tree, began to tremble convulsively when it heard the howling of wolves.

At dawn Ansiau sought in vain for the tracks which had led him to the tree. Look as he would, he saw only unfamiliar places, strange little glades, impenetrable thickets, old trees with tortuous branches; the farther he went, the surer he became that he had never passed that way before. Dismounting, he climbed a huge larch. From its upper branches he saw nothing but a motionless, irregular sea of treetops stretching away in every direction, threatening in their stillness. Two buzzard hawks cut the air with hoarse cries. Ansiau climbed down and began to walk aimlessly, leading his horse and praying to St. Christopher.

He was hungry. After finding a glade where he saw no noxious herbs and thought he could safely pasture his horse, he began to look for something to eat himself. He succeeded in finding a fine thicket of whortleberries and picked as many as he could—afterwards his pouch and his hands were black from them. Water he could not find. At times he thought he heard the sound of running water, but it must have come from underground.

He spent another night in the forest. His thirst and the heat made sleep impossible. He sensed a hundred stifling breaths around him—he did not know if they were animals or spirits. Even the trees seemed to sigh. When he woke, the sun was beating down on his head. He felt a vague pain in his temples. He could hardly climb down the tree, hardly untie the reins; he did not want to ride his horse for fear of exhausting it, but he could scarcely walk himself. It was getting on for noon, he thought, when he came to a great glade rank with tall grass. Huge white stones lay in the center of it—so white under the merciless sun that they hurt his eyes. Ansiau knew that he was in the Fairy Glade, the place where in times past the pagans had come to worship their idols. Those white stones had been set up by the pagans, they had been thrown down long since, but spirits still haunted the glade.

A few crows settled heavily on the arid whiteness of the stones. The air was motionless and fiery, not a grass-blade stirred. Ansiau felt as if a band of red-hot iron were being tightened around his temples. Exhausted, he lay down in the grass, without even thinking of protecting himself from the sun. It was the first time in his life that he had felt so ill, and he believed that he was going to die there on the spot. Strangely, he felt neither fear nor regret. He liked the yellowish, dry grass stalks which tickled his cheeks and swayed against the sky above his head—he liked the fleckless sky, vast, and suddenly so near—the crows filled his ears with their cawing, and in the incessant sound there was such peace and warmth that Ansiau felt happy; he no longer thought of death, he was no longer conscious of himself; his consciousness was filled by the sky and the tufts of grass.

How long he remained in that state he did not know. He saw the grass part and a naked woman bending over him. First he saw her breasts, standing out against her yellowish body like two white balls surmounted by two brown buds. Black hair hung down in regular locks on either side of a round, white face, and the black and very brilliant eyes had an oily, dulled gleam—they made him want to sleep. Fascinated by those eyes and breasts, Ansiau did not stir; he felt certain that it was the fairy, but he was not afraid. He thought her beautiful and good. He said it—or at least believed he had said it—the woman did not understand, she made curious signs, with her hands above her head; it looked as if she were tying and untying threads which only she could see. And then she drew away, and Ansiau raised his head and saw her mount one of the white stones and raise her arms. Then he saw nothing more. When he awoke, the fairy had vanished.

He was so sore that he could scarcely stand up. His horse was gone. The grass around the stones was trodden and crushed, and upon the stone on which the fairy had mounted there were bloodstains and crows' feathers.

The sun was already below the treetops when at last Ansiau emerged from the forest. Before him he saw a hamlet—twenty hovels at most; girls were washing clothes at the stream. They sprang to their feet, shrieking, "A man! a man!" But since the man did not look very terrifying, they remained where they were. Ansiau told them that he had seen a fairy in the great glade, and they cried out and crossed themselves.

Ansiau said that he wanted to stay there by the stream, he could go no farther. He lay down in the damp grass and was seized with violent attacks of vomiting which did not stop until nightfall. Terrified lest they should see him die, the girls had gone. One of them had charitably put a damp cloth on his head.

Ansiau opened his eyes once more. It was night. The sky was very clear, the air warm. His horse was there, a short distance away, grazing in the meadow; he heard its bridle bells tinkling. Ansiau dragged himself to the stream, wet the cloth, and replaced it on his head. He did not move again. He felt sick, broken, mortally sad. At dawn the girls came to look at him—they were sure that he would have died during the night because he had seen a fairy. Finding him alive, they cried out with joy and offered him bread and garlic. Ansiau managed to eat a little and asked where he was. He learned that the village belonged to the lord of Vanlay and that it was three leagues from Linnières.

Ansiau had never been ill. Or if he had, he had been unaware of it—he would spend two or three days in the straw without eating, a fellow squire would bring him water to drink from time to time, then he would get up and go back to his duties. But it seemed there was a difference between being a bachelor and being a married man. Alis nearly went out of her head when she saw him come home with hollow cheeks and burning hands. He said that he was tired and lay down on his pallet; he wanted only to rest. But Alis came and sat beside him, she rubbed his temples with mint leaves, made him drink herb teas, and massaged his hands and feet to drive the tiredness out of them. Little used to such treatment, he was restive at first and said that it was not the duty of a lady like herself to look after a sick man. But after a time he felt better, and he fell asleep with his head resting against his wife's body; light fingers stroked his forehead soothingly, making him forget the pain that was torturing him, and once he drew one of her little hands to his lips and kissed it, humbly, as a man kisses his master's hand, and Alis blushed a little, drew her hand away, and said: "Stop being silly."

Five days later, when he got up and went to the window, Alis looked hard at his face and exclaimed, ruefully: "God! You are getting a beard. There, on your chin—and there too—oh, no! it's too ugly, I don't want you to have a beard." Ansiau said that he was no minstrel to shave his face, and that, being a man, he must one day have a beard. Alis shook her head: "Oh! I liked you better before. I don't want you to get old."

To hear old Ansiau tell it, Alis was the only woman in the world who had a chance of becoming a mother. And the child she was expecting would be emperor or pope. He overwhelmed her with counsels and care—she must not swallow too fast, she must not stoop, she must not eat pork, she must not run. And then came the hundred-and-one old-wives' remedies—potions extracted from herbs and the entrails of animals. (They were compounded by Flora, the witch at Fairymount, and old Ansiau sent his squire Lambert for them secretly, without Lady Adela's knowledge or the chaplain's.) When Alis drank one of these strange beverages she felt mortally afraid that she would poison herself or make God angry with her, but she did not dare to disobey her father-in-law.

She could not take a step without the old man's interfering: she must not look at such-and-such a thing, she must not turn in such-and-such a way; if she looked at knives the child would die the first day, if she looked at dogs it would be born deformed, if she sat on the left of a monk it would be born dead. It seemed that whatever she did was wrong. She began to see evil omens everywhere herself, to be terrified of everything; she did not know what her father-in-law might not do to her if anything happened to the child. Furthermore, she did not feel well physically. She grew pale and thin, her hair began to fall, she pulled out handfuls of it with her comb.

And Ansiau got angry because she refused to go walking in the meadow with him or help him train hawks. He said: "You were much nicer before, you know," and again: "You know it won't do you a bit of good just to sit there on that bench—you're growing as ugly as an old woman."

Alis looked at the fire burning on the hearth, at the great logs crumbling, and let her sewing drop into her lap; tears came into her eyes, and all she could see was a red mist. "Come, my fair niece," said Lady Adela, "if that is how you work, your child will go bare. Do you expect the maids to do your work for you?" Alis went back to her work, but never before had she sewed or embroidered with such distaste.

And then—Ansiau was always plaguing her; he got angry for no reason, and his caresses were too sudden and too rough. There were times when he could not take her hand without squeezing her fingers until they cracked, or kiss her without biting her, or touch her hair without pulling it. Alis bore it all with tolerable indifference and resignation, saying to herself: "All men are like that." They still met—secretly, of course—at night, in a corner behind a great wooden chest; but Alis no longer felt any desire, she went only out of pity for Ansiau, because he said: "I shall die if I don't have you tonight." Yet at heart he was growing restless. Autumn and the hunting season were over, and in the bad weather of winter Linnières was as dreary as possible. The courtyard was a lake, the forest roads were streams, ponds, bogs—the castle was so damp that the palisade on the ramparts rotted away every year, and in the rooms water ran down the walls in steady streams and all the furniture smelled of mold. Ansiau felt that he would like to go back to Troyes, to his godfather's. He had been a knight for eight months and had not yet had an opportunity to try his arms; and his one thought was spring and the tournaments at Eastertime.

Five days before Christmas it began to snow. The forest turned black and white like a magpie's plumage. And the stream with its willows stretched like a narrow black ribbon between pure white banks. Inside the castle it was almost light, there was so much whiteness everywhere outdoors. In the great hall the squires and the kitchenmaids were already beginning to prepare for the Christmas Eve banquet. Fowl and rabbits scuffled in the cupboard where they had been shut up, and the maids fed them to bursting with grain and herbs. Others polished the copper dishes with ashes from the hearth; the little pages sharpened knives by rubbing them against each other.

As the cold became intense toward Christmas, pilgrims and travellers turned aside to beg shelter in the castle, the smoke of whose chimneys rose from behind Seuroi Wood. They were allowed to enter. Old Ansiau did not like it—he said: "All these beggars bring nothing but sickness and mud."

But Lady Adela ruled the house as an absolute monarch. "It is very easy," she said to her brother-in-law, "to sit and warm yourself by a good fire and let poor folk perish of cold. They're worth more than an old sluggard like you. All you do is eat and drink and kill, like the wild beasts. Are you so tired of not killing men with steel that you want them to die of cold?" The old man said: "Let me alone, let me alone."

The pilgrims would come in and sit on the floor in the great hall, fighting among themselves for places near the fire. They were nearly always poor, ill-clad people—travelling monks, petty townsmen, simple peasants. Lady Adela would give them a little bread and money for their journey, and would ask them to pray for her to the saints whom they were to visit.

Alis was brought to bed toward the end of Lent, in March, when the rainy season is at its worst, and in the very room where she had spent her wedding night eleven months earlier. Irma, her sister-in-law, had come from Puiseaux to help her in childbed (Irma took every opportunity to get away from Puiseaux and her husband Baldwin), and with her Alis felt a little less frightened—she did not like the ladies of Linnières. The old castellan, in his chair by the hearth, sent a varlet every few minutes to ask if the mother-to-be was making any progress; the door kept slamming in the high wind; the courtyard was a sump of liquid manure, and varlets and maids ran back and forth between castle and bathhouse, splashing themselves with mud to the eyes.

She lay on the bed, and Lady Adela, Lady Richeut, Irma, and two midwives bustled around her, red with exertion and fear—the child was coming badly, Alis was too narrow in the hips. Lady Adela, bulky and strong, was holding her by the shoulders to keep her from thrashing about. Alis was screaming at the top of her lungs; during the moments of respite she shrieked: "Let go of me, I hate you, you want to kill me," then she sobbed: "Mother! Mother! come, it hurts me," and she tried to catch old Lady Adela's hands in her teeth and bite them. Then the pain rose and rose—rose to suffocation, rose to a supreme, astonished "Ah!", rose to insensibility. All the struggle had gone out of her—it was death.

Irma finally drew the child out with her hands; and Alis stopped screaming, bewildered to find herself still alive. Between Irma's long, thin hands something pink was fidgeting: Alis had never seen such a pure and lively pink, it was a completely new color. And the pink thing was crying like no cry of man or animal. How gray and dreary and lifeless Irma's hands and the

26

women's faces looked—they did not know what it was to have been delivered, to be at peace, to live—dazzled, she shut her eyes. It was too beautiful. She could not believe it. She rubbed her cheek against the cool pillow which Lady Adela put under her head, and never had she experienced such pleasure as the touch of that fine linen against her sweaty cheek. She loved the pillow. She wanted to kiss it.

She thought that a long time had gone by, she opened her eyes—the women were still there, they were washing the new little thing and it was still crying. Alis thought: "They will hurt it," and her heart turned over. Only now did she realize that they were talking, only now did she understand what they said. They were saying that it was a boy, thank God, and that he did not look strong, but that he would live. "Yes," said Lady Adela, "and hereabout we always rub them with salt water, it makes them stronger." Irma was swaddling the baby in long fine linen bands. "I think he will be blond," she said, "he looks like his mother." "Is the chapel ready?" Richeut asked. Then Alis understood that they were talking about carrying the child away to be baptized, and instantly she saw the rain, the wind, the drafts, her old father-in-law's big hands (he would be godfather), and she was amazed how terrifying those things suddenly became—it shattered her. And when Lady Adela took the child in her big, calloused hands, Alis said: "Be very careful!"—God knew where she found the courage, because she was afraid of Lady Adela. But Lady Adela's answer put her in her place: "I am fifty-five and over, and I have borne twenty-two children, by God's grace, and I have always taken care of them myself, to say nothing of my nephews and grandchildren and grandnephews, and it was I who received your husband when he came from his mother's belly. You may well believe that I know more about taking care of children than you do." There was nothing for Alis to do except to keep quiet, but she was mistrustful. She had to be held down to prevent her from getting out of bed and running to the chapel where the baptism was to take place.

The old grandfather was so proud that he looked ten years younger. He stood there in his best green tunic, which had become too tight for him, and he held the little swaddled doll as he would have held the crown royal on a golden cushion. "I always knew," he said, "that the daughter of such a house could not but bear a fine boy," and he asked his brother Hugh: "Do you think he looks like me?" Ansiau was not at the castle: two days before Alis was brought to bed the old lord had sent him to Bernon, a village he owned on the other side of the forest, to settle a dispute with the mayor. In reality, the old man believed that a husband worrying and fretting himself into a panic would bring bad luck to a woman in childbed. When Ansiau came back from Bernon, it was to learn that he had a son already three days old. The child had been baptized Ansiau, but his grandfather called him Ansiet to distinguish him from his own son.

Ansiau was amazed at the change which had taken place in his absence; he had almost despaired of ever seeing his beloved thin and pretty again.

Now that she was rid of the child, he thought she would be his as before. He found her in the bathhouse sitting on her bed, dressed in her beautiful red dress, her hair neatly braided, her cheeks rosy. He ran to kiss her, but she pushed him away and told him that they must wait until after her churching—Lady Hodierne had said so. Then, in a completely changed voice, and with a wide smile, she asked: "Have you seen the baby?" The baby was long and all beswaddled, with a round head covered by a white bonnet. Ansiau thought its face rather commonplace, in fact ugly. But Alis seemed to be in heaven. She put the little thing on his knees and smiled at it with such a happy and tender look that Ansiau could not keep from smiling himself. "He is so beautiful," she said. "I have had him three days and I can't stop looking at him." She raised her eyes to her husband's face, trying to divine what he thought of the baby—at that moment Ansiau was nothing to her but a new visitor to whom she could show her little boy. But Ansiau's face expressed so little admiration that she felt disappointed and turned away.

During Holy Week, old Ansiau prepared himself for death. He had done so toward the end of every Lent for almost ten years; it was the effect that fasting had on him. This time, however, he was sadder than usual. He said: "Ah! soon now I shall die in all my sins. Better that I had died when I was a child! Does anyone believe that these mangy priests can help us to salvation? They will be the first to go to Hell, for making people believe that they can save them when they can do nothing." Then he announced that he was dying. He called for his brothers and nephews and commenced asking them to forgive him for the wrongs he had done them—but he scowled so fiercely and talked so haughtily that it seemed more as if he were giving them orders. Next, he made them swear that after his death they would obey his son—the boy was old enough now. Then he dictated a long list of the several bequests he wished to make by way of reparation to villages he had pillaged or to the families of men he had killed.

After that he stayed in bed for two days, depressed and sad. Then he began eating and drinking again, as if it were not Lent. Lady Adela was indignant, but he only shrugged his shoulders: he was sick, a sick man was not obliged to fast; he did not want to die.

Ansiet was a very blond, very rosy baby, with round eyes and a big delicate mouth. He was a curious sight, as all small infants are when you look at them closely. He rolled his eyes, wrinkled his forehead, opened his mouth like a hungry nestling, rubbed his cheeks, which were covered with nearly white down, against the sides of his bonnet. Alis was lost, drowned—she saw nothing but those two little dark eyes; she died each time her baby cried, she dandled it, she gave it the breast thirty times a day—Lady Adela's advice and reproaches had no effect—and yet her breasts were so sore that she gnawed her lips every time she gave suck; she almost enjoyed it, she was

proud that her little boy had such strong teeth. He was no ordi[...]
no! he was the grandson of Joceran of Puiseaux, the great-grandso[...]
of Marseint, and the heir to Linnières; one day he would hold the[...]
domain, from Hervi to Flogny—Seuroi and Bernon and the forest and[...]
fields; Alis was proud of the castle and domain of Linnières now. And th[...]
old castellan, more impotent than ever, made her come to him with the child
and said fondly: "Anyone can see she comes of good stock. Look at the fine
boy she has made for me! Come here, my beauty, give me your cheek so I
can pinch it." Very soon, however, he began to fret: the child was not growing, the child cried too much, the child did not eat properly. He was very
superstitious, and everywhere he saw plots against his grandson's health. His
own blood.

Ansiau of Linnières the Elder had always been a gloomy man. God knows
what tormented him. He was brave, he was astute, and clever at taking
money wherever he found it. Even during his father's lifetime he had held
the domain; he was twenty-five when his father took the cross to go to
Palestine with the count of Champagne's troop. King Louis of France had
taken the cross after the burning of Vitry. Many knights had set out for that
war, and they had cause to rue it, for few were those who came back. Galon
the Hairy, of Linnières, had taken all his grown sons with him and had left
Ansiau, the heir, to guard the domain. Galon had come back an invalid, two
of his sons had died, the other two were safe and sound, but afflicted with
an incurable longing for travel and adventure. And Ansiau the Elder had
remained embittered all his days because he had been left like a dog to guard
the house.

He had never loved a woman. He had married four times. He wanted
sons, his wives had borne only daughters, he hated his daughters, and had
disposed of them as soon as he could. He was forty when his third wife,
Laurence of Le Mahiet, gave birth to a boy. It had been his only son. Laurence had died soon afterward, and her successor, Agnes of Vanlay, had
produced five stillborn daughters. Ansiau had repudiated her after the fifth.

In the great nest of Galon the Hairy, several successive broods had been
brought up in the mysteries of arms and hunting, and of this family there
were still five sons living—not to mention the daughters, who had gone to
other castles to bear other knights. Of the issue of Galon's first wife, there
remained Ansiau the Elder and Hugh, both nearly the same age and alike
in their height, their corpulence, and their blondness; but Ansiau's eyes
looked even older than his body whereas Hugh, at fifty-five, had one of
those faces on which wrinkles and white hair look like make-up, a deliberate
deception; his eyes were young and blue, his smile vivacious, he resembled
his older brother only in his incurable laziness, and he had a great weakness
for women and wine. Married at fifteen to the virtuous Adela, who was two
years his senior, he had allowed her to govern him in all things ever since,
as much from indifference as from good nature.

Herbert and Rainard, sons of Galon's second mar-
s Hermeline of Jeugni, of a noble house in the neigh-
h her sons were most proud. Herbert was a red-head,
peculiarities had given them their nicknames. Shorter
lf brothers, lean and sinewy, they had long noses and
gave them a vague resemblance to wolves or boars.
eyes and a florid face, his hair and beard were a violent
say that his face blazoned blue and red, the colors of
k and gaunt, with his hobbling gait, his watery, dull,
shifty eyes, his thin beard, had lost all his front teeth in battles and brawls;
two black, decayed eyeteeth stuck out of his mouth, completing his resemblance to a wild animal.

Herbert had fought in the Crusade. He had been a great frequenter of
tournaments, not only in Champagne, but in Burgundy and France as well.
He could sing and recite poems, he dressed richly, had a reputation for courage and deserved it—and was attractive to women though not handsome. He
never stayed at Linnières for more than two weeks at a time; he was restless
and nervous, vain and curious, and a great skirt chaser; but now he was
forty-one and was beginning to feel tired. He had almost given up travelling
and went no farther than Troyes, where he always had lawsuits to fight and
debts to pay.

His brother Rainard was the black sheep of the family. He lived apart
from his brothers in the little watchtower of Seuroi, two leagues from Linnières. He never appeared at merrymakings or public gatherings, but on the
other hand he often ventured on to his neighbors' lands and onto the palatine road, where he robbed merchants and other travellers with insufficient
escorts. He indulged in unnatural vices and practiced witchcraft to further his
dark plots. As a result he was more or less excommunicated—not officially,
but he would never have dared to show himself in church. He dressed in
rags, or nearly. He had a mirthless laugh, half chuckle and half whinny, and
he was always laughing. Yet he was a good brother and loyal to his kindred.

The only representative of Galon's third family was Girard the Blond, a
handsome man of thirty-five. He had been his father's favorite and had remained a spoiled child despite his age. Women liked him, men disliked
him, his brothers did not love him.

The brothers accounted for quite a numerous household. For if Ansiau,
the eldest, had only one son, Hugh had six full-grown and three still boys;
Herbert had four, of whom two were knights; Girard had three; and Hugh's
eldest sons had big boys of their own. The daughters, as usual, did not
count—even the eldest had little enough hope of making good marriages,
the others would have to put up with squires or poor knights in the pay of
some castellan in the neighborhood. The profession of arms cost more than
it brought in, and of the five brothers only old Ansiau knew how to get and
keep money.

And the old man died.

It had happened in the evening, on a Saturday—the Saturday before the second Sunday after Easter. He died unprepared, in all his sins, stricken with apoplexy after a hearty meal—the usual death of knights who had not got themselves killed at an earlier age. His face blue and purple, his eyes bloody, his hands stiff as hands made of wood. Six men could hardly carry him to his bed. He lasted three more days, but he never recovered consciousness. His brothers and Ansiau sat up with him by turns, as if they were watching a corpse. For three days his throat rattled; the huge body disintegrated with terrifying rapidity; the whole back and the folds of the skin broke out in festering sores, the eyes grew hollow and swam in a yellowish humor, the dry and swollen lips split. And still the warning, monotonous rattle sounded on. Ansiau had never loved his father; since his marriage he had only too much reason to wish him dead, he wanted to take his place. And besides he knew that for days the old man had been tormenting Alis because the child was not putting on weight, and Alis could think of no possible way to escape the old man's wrath. A squire's wife, Haumette, had offered to nurse the little boy sometimes, and the child digested her milk even less well than he did his mother's; Alis was in terror lest her father-in-law discover the ruse and accuse her of trying to poison the child.

And now Alis no longer had anything to fear.

Now everything was being solved in the simplest way possible. Too simply, in fact—Ansiau could not comprehend it. Because he had drunk a cup too much, the old man was no longer the old man, he would become a corpse and rot, and his soul would go God knew where—probably not to Paradise; and nothing could be done now, nothing could be altered, not for all eternity. Vulgrin, the clerk skilled in medicine who periodically bled the whole household at Linnières, had said that the patient could not recover consciousness: the heated blood had begun to boil and had risen into the brain, with the result that brain and blood had become mingled and the brain had been destroyed—if the patient still breathed, it was only with a remnant of his former life. However, it was necessary to wait for actual death before burying him.

At the end of the third day the old man finally gave up the ghost. He stopped breathing, his mouth fell wide open. Vulgrin tied a linen band around his face, and old Ansiau's mouth became fixed forever in a disdainful grimace; the lower lip protruded as it had never done before.

The body, washed and dressed, was carried into the chapel and laid in an open coffin which had been set on the great oak high table. Never had he looked so tall and so stout. The coffin, which was longer than the table, seemed to fill the whole chapel. The chapel was divided from the hall only by a linen curtain, and the slow, plaintive voice of Father Arnoul, chanting the Office for the Dead, reached even the kitchen, where the funeral feast was being prepared. Little by little the courtyard and the stables filled with kinsmen and friends of the dead man; they came with their horses, their wives, and their servants and counted upon staying at Linnières for at least a week: it was no small thing, the death of a castellan, especially of an old man, a man who had ruthlessly held his lands for twenty-five years. The young man, the heir to the domain, must now make people feel that there was a new master at Linnières.

Dressed in his dark-red tunic, his only ceremonial garment, Ansiau stood in the hall under the shields, between his uncles Hugh and Herbert, and returned his kinsmen's kisses and embraces with good grace. He did not weep, but he wrung his hands and beat his brow most conscientiously when he went near the coffin—so custom demanded. He feigned no grief, and no one was surprised; he had too much to gain by his father's death.

The instant the old man had stopped breathing, Ansiau had become castellan; he felt it from the tips of his toes to the roots of his hair—he was not the man to be unmindful of his rights. So long as he had been only one nobly born youth among many, he had never tried to take more than he was given. But now he was the master, his uncles had sworn fealty to him, and a knight's word is no light thing.

First he ordered two beeves and three calves slaughtered, together with a good half of the poultry, and had three barrels of wine brought up; then he opened the old man's chests so that he might give each of his guests a present—a garment, a jewel, or a piece of plate. The body was buried from Hervi Church, and Ansiau had copper pieces, large and small, distributed on the church square to the poor and to all the peasants who had come from the surrounding villages for the funeral—he wanted to be sure that they would pray for his father's soul. Then he announced that anyone who wished to come was invited to the funeral feast—young or old, rich or poor—his house was open, and everyone would be fed to his fill. For two days long lines of poor peasants and vagabonds trailed over the roads which led to Linnières, and in the castle courtyard the squires and the younger boys moved back and forth through the crowd with round loaves of dark bread and quarters of roasted meat. In the keep the guests sat at table for three days in succession. Ansiau, seated in the place of honor, gave orders to old Lady Adela, who—red, breathless, and exhausted—scolded the varlets and supervised the preparation of the dishes. Alis, seated beside her husband, a gold-embroidered ribbon about her brow, looked dignified and severe, as befits a funeral repast; but everyone could feel her pride at being mistress of the castle at last. And Ansiau glanced at her from time to time with a blissful smile; he was proud to show her to his kinfolk.

He knew that at least he would not be reproached with failing to honor his father's memory worthily; half of his wealth had gone—in money, garments, and things of price. Lady Adela said: "If you go on at this rate, your children will be sleeping in the hay ten years hence." But Ansiau thought to himself that money came and went and was not made to be kept locked up in coffers—the thing a man must keep was his land and stout arms to bear good weapons. With weapons a man could always get money.

In Hervi churchyard old Ansiau slept in the white, chalky ground beside his old father, and his brothers who had died before him, and three of his four wives. A week after the funeral no one gave him a thought, except perhaps his brother Hugh, who told himself: "It will be my turn soon." But it was not to be as soon as he thought.

It was in June that the men of Linnières received orders to assemble at Paiens with the other vassals of the castellany; from Paiens they would be led to Troyes by Viscount Arembert of Reuilli. The count was going to the wars; it was said that he would join the king's army—the king was at war with the duke of Normandy, his vassal, and had summoned Count Henry to help him.

Ansiau knew that he must go—like his uncle Herbert and Girard the Young, who was replacing his father Hugh, too old now for the wars. Ansiau had his arms and his hauberk brought out and put in condition—he was not sorry to leave the castle and see something of the world. He had heard much talk about Henry Plantagenet, king of England and duke of Normandy, and the war promised well. "King Louis," Herbert said, "is not worth the king of England's little finger, and it is a great pity that the count of Champagne is his man. I would give a finger of my right hand to see King Henry fight."

Ansiau, who had inherited his father's great bed, spent a last night with his lady; he was sad at leaving her for so long. They had been married thirteen months, and he could not imagine life without her. He was jealous of their child—he wished that he could take his lady with him: he would carry her behind him on his horse, and hold her in his arms every night, under his field tent; so fresh she was, so smooth, it was so good to bury himself against her—and to take her into his heart (no one else had ever looked after him; she, his lady, did it perfectly simply, just as she ate and drank). Ansiau saw the world from those blue eyes of hers, straight and unflinching between stiff lashes. Hers was the first face he had ever thought of looking at squarely—just like that, for no reason, simply to come to know it better.

On his departure he left his lady the great bed (with permission to share it with anyone she wished, provided it was a woman), and told Lady Adela to take good care of his young wife—for Lady Adela was still the real mistress of the castle.

At earliest dawn the horses were saddled, the hauberks ready and carefully packed in their boxes. Five squires and ten soldiers accompanied the knights. Those who were to go said good-bye to their families. It was half dark in the courtyard, the air was cool. Alis had come down with the other women, holding her child in her arms. Her head was bare, her small face pale and puffy with sleep. Ansiau kissed her several times on eyes and lips, and then suddenly, not knowing why, he kissed the child's cheek.

The three men mounted—Richeut, Girard's wife, was crying; Alis cried too. But when the child in her arms began fretting she quickly dried her tears and hummed a lullaby. To her husband's wave of farewell she answered with the look of obstinate indifference she so often had for. everything except her child.

And Ansiau rode through the gate. Once outside, he felt his sadness wear off little by little. The rhythmical. gait of his horse and the coolness of the early morning made him happy to be alive, and he broke into a gay refrain.

Paiens. And then Troyes, and helmets in hundreds and painted shields and pennons floating in the wind and war cries sounding from every direction. Then came long days on horseback, each indistinguishable from the last. No familiar country now. New roads, new forests—but all alike because they were not the roads and forests of Champagne. Fields stretching over gentle slopes, and more fields, and forests, and castles, and more forests. And the slow, peaceful current of the Seine. And the road, winding and climbing, always the same, and the horizon still before them, now bordered with trees, now blue and vague and vanishing in the gilded mists of twilight.

It was tiring, monotonous travelling. Time seemed to stand still. The heat was intense and their thirst matched it. But Ansiau felt no desire to complain; he was neither sad nor tired. He rode beside his uncle Herbert, lulled by the rhythmic gait of his horse, and because his eyes saw the same forests and the same trees day after day, they saw nothing.

From time to time, a stone cross. He crossed himself. The others too. The sky was very blue, the road empty, the cross white. From time to time a stone bridge over a stream with low banks. And after it the road ran on, curved, climbed—endlessly. And Ansiau felt that at the end of the road God knew what adventures awaited him, God knew what battles, what splendid swordplay. And he thought nothing. And his face began to put on a mask of indifference and proud hardness, like many another, like so many others. And still the road stretched away to the horizon.

Over the roads and hills and valleys of the Ile-de-France dragged the great host with the fleur-de-lis upon its banners—particolored, formless, endless. The horses followed the road, two by two; footmen and munition carts encroached widely on field and meadow; and when the road became impassable, whole troops poured out into a field, furrowing it like a gigantic harrow. The rainbow has fewer colors: first came the French king's blue and white banner with its golden lilies, then the blue and silver bars of Champagne, then the arms of Orléans, of Brienne, of Dreux, of Beauvais. The highroad ran through Chartres and Paris, the other road, to the south, led to Melun. Leagues to the rear, files of wounded, pilferers, and laggards made their way. The sky was gray, forests cast in lead stretched out of sight, bordering the fields of the Beauce; the immense cathedral of Chartres with its heavy square towers, long left behind, still dominated the horizon, motionless and ever-present like the sun.

Horses' hoofs sank fetlock-deep into the mud, spattering armor and shields. The horsemen's bodies were numb and chafed by the shirts of mail they had worn for so long, and the dust encrusted on their faces had become as much a part of them as their skins.

King Louis, in blue flower-embroidered vest over travelling armor, moved his stiff fingers and rubbed his right eye with his ungloved hand. Before him, in their gold-embroidered trappings, swayed the cruppers of his standard-bearers' horses, and the knight banneret who carried the fleur-de-lis standard turned his head from left to right, making his silvered helmet gleam. On the upright lance the banner hung like a rag. Then the wind stirred it.

The sky darkened, and the gray masses of the forests became even more leaden. Behind the king his first squire was leading his white Arabian charger; it sniffed the air, snorted, and exchanged whinnies with the squire's horse. Its battle armor glittered with plates of gilded iron. Three other squires led three more royal mounts behind it.

A train of munitions and tents followed the knighthood and soldiery of France. The heralds and King Louis' standard-bearers were already deep in the forest when the colors of Champagne appeared on the horizon and moved slowly down the road under the fine gray rain of the Beauce. Twenty knights bannerets came forward, riding at a walk and followed by their squires; next came the arms of the seneschal and the count, then all the seneschalsy—knights, and squires leading their chargers. Count Henry of Champagne, tall and stout on his enormous mount, his gilded helmet ringed with rubies, rode slowly forward, his heavy silvered gauntlets firmly holding his silk-fringed reins. His eyes were dark and tired under his bushy blond brows. Behind his squires marched his household, a long procession in parti-colored tunics; and the suck of hoofs in the mud, mingled with the creaking of harness, the click of weapons, the oaths of the varlets, formed an indistinct uproar whose echoes were prolonged for leagues along the road down which the troops were moving. It was a retreat.

The castellany of Paiens came on under the banners of the viscount. After the viscount's household, which was followed by some hundred men-at-arms armed with short lances, came the castellans, in troops distinguishable from one another by the colors of their shields and banners. Riders were scattered over the fields along the road as far as eye could see, squires hailed one another, horns sounded, hundreds of well-shod hoofs struck the earth rhythmically. Heavy horses carrying heavy knights in campaign attire, upright in their saddles—their tired eyes stared through the round or square apertures in their helmets. The yellow, red-striped shields of Puiseaux followed the green crosses of Monguoz, then came Linnières' blue wolves on a red ground, and the two black bears of Breul.

As at their setting out, the troop from Linnières still numbered three knights and nine horses, with fifteen footmen; Rainard's little company was lost somewhere in the rear guard, they had not seen him for ten days.

Ansiau rode at the head of his men; this tenseness in the loins, this spread of the legs had become so natural to him that he felt cramped when he was not on horseback. This monotonous swaying to the rhythm of his mount had stupefied him until now he thought that it was the horizon which swayed. Through the square aperture of his helmet his face was visible from forehead to mouth. His eyebrows were bushy, his eyes large and wide and set close to the surface, like a hawk's. His nostrils were strong and mobile, and he had a fine mouth with big, firm, soft lips; a sparse brown mustache had already appeared on the upper lip and extended to the cheeks, where it joined the short beard which framed his face. Dust had lodged in the lines of his eyelids, in the curve of his nostrils, at the corners of his mouth, and was forming wrinkles. Wind and sun had tanned his face until it was the same swarthy brown as all the others. His magnificent brown eyes were expressionless. But they could be terrible on occasion, as anyone who ever looked at him knew well.

War had not brought him what he expected from it. Endless riding, tiring and ineffectual—unimportant skirmishes with little bands of the English, the siege of Gisors where the English king's men had forced King Louis' army to beat a hasty retreat over hill and dale, to the great indignation of all the men of Champagne. During the retreat there had been villages sacked and pillaged, quarrels between the king's men and Count Henry's. They were bringing back neither booty nor prisoners. There had not even been any good fighting. Money and strength had been spent for nothing. Ansiau was not tired, but he was disillusioned. There was a growing void in his heart; and at night when, despite the stiffness of his body, he lay down to sleep on the ground under his field tent, a secret, suppressed anguish, insidious as a gnawing worm, grew and grew in him until he hated life. Then little by little it dissolved in sleep, and by morning it was gone.

A night halt in the forest, around the fire: the darkness, and the crackling flames painting black shadows and oblongs of light on the tired faces lost in dreams or sleep. Through half-closed lids, Ansiau studied Girard the Young —his nose, his big, true eyes, his beard half lost in the shadow of his collar; and Herbert's red head, in shadow too; and Joceran's broad face with the firelight falling on it from below: from an affable face, the huge scar, the bushy eyebrows, the nostrils in full light, the black shadows under the eyes and on the forehead changed it to a face of pain, of despair. Something gleamed in front of Ansiau's partly closed lids. He was half dreaming; he did not rightly know if what he was seeing and hearing was actually taking place. Tongues of fire licked up and climbed the trees, tufts of foliage began to flame, leaves in black masses swept down on them to put them out. Girard's and Joceran's heads were part of the conflagration. A roar of rage— "God! God!"—put an abrupt end to the play of flames—again Ansiau saw the bonfire, the trees, the dark forms of the sleeping men.

"By the body of St. Thiou, my uncle, I would not wish you on anyone as a bedfellow!"

"Why not? The ladies think highly of me," said Herbert. "This thing that troubles me is like a sort of sickness—I do not always have it. Your father had it sometimes too."

"What is the use! Oh God, what is the use!"—since he had been sleeping beside his uncle, Ansiau had grown accustomed to that monotonous plaint, which found an echo in his own heart.

"Say a rosary to Our Lady, my uncle, and it will pass."

"I have tried, a hundred and a thousand times," said Herbert, "but I can no more pray than if I had a stone for a heart. Is this war a war? It is good for nothing but to make a man sicken like a carp out of water. At this rate I prefer a tournament—you spend less and profit more. Lord God! This trouble empties my heart until there is nothing left in it. A fine thing to ride all day and not be able to sleep at night!"

"Do you know what causes it?" asked Girard the Young.

"How should I?" Herbert flung his red mane back on the saddle which served him for a pillow. "It comes, and it grips your entrails, like a colic. It is sadness—does anyone know what causes sadness? It is because life is not what it used to be. The fine wars we fought when Count Thibaut was alive! But nowadays men are not allowed to make war as they would."

Joceran of Puiseaux rose and went to the fire to warm his hands. "Everyone has his turn," he said thoughtfully. "It comes on some men because of a woman, and on others because of the fear of God."

"Ah," said Girard, "it would be no bad thing if many men had such a fear of God."

"I used to know Osmond of Buchie," said Herbert. "He sold all his property to make a pilgrimage to Jerusalem. They say he died on the way."

"And his sons are serving as squires to men not as good as themselves," Baldwin of Puiseaux said suddenly, in his usual aggressive tone. Joceran lay down by the fire, his eyes fixed on the flames.

"When I lost my comrade Guy of Marseint," he said, "such a sadness came over me that I no longer wanted to live. I would not eat unless someone made me, the only way I could sleep was to get drunk. True—I was young then."

"Sometimes a comrade is more than a brother," said Herbert.

"I tell you," Joceran went on, "it is not right that two comrades who love each other so dearly should be parted. And why did he have to die when he was still so young? God! I tore out half my beard; I rode through the forest like a madman, I called to him, I talked to him. I could hardly see for weeping."

Recollections assailed him, all the more powerful because he had never before called them up in the presence of others; and a long-forgotten past suddenly awoke in their slow-moving, weary memories. And Ansiau's past was only the white body and the blond hair of his beloved, and he shut his eyes so that he might see them better.

The road led to Paris. The next night they slept in their tents in a field. Herbert invited Joceran of Puiseaux and his son Baldwin, and Geoffrey of Monguoz and his nephew Mathis, to spend the evening in the Linnières tent. There were too many for the space, but by crowding they managed somehow to find places on the trusses of straw set in a circle along the cloth wall. In the middle, beside the tent pole, Herbert had placed a small oil lamp, and his squire served hosts and guests a Spanish wine which Herbert wished to share with his comrades-in-arms. It had been given him that same day by Rainard. Rainard had rejoined his kinsmen laden with spoils whose source was obscure and which he had no desire to advertise to the world in general. Two skins of the Spanish wine were included in his booty, and, like a good brother, he gave them to Herbert. Furthermore, he did not make his appearance among the guests assembled in the tent; humility was one of this strange knight's few virtues; he did not want to have his presence bring shame upon his brother and his nephews in the eyes of neighbors who knew him all too well.

For nearly ten days not one of the men had tasted wine. The roads had been unfrequented, the villages poor, they had skirted Chartres to the south, and only the king's men had been permitted to stop there. To make up for it, the wine which Rainard had brought was excellent, and the cup passed from hand to hand, perpetually refilled by the squires.

Ansiau chattered with his squire Thierri. Thierri was charming; no one could help liking him. A year younger than Ansiau—he had just turned sixteen—he was already stout and tall; dark-skinned, and with a turned-up nose, he had a wide, sweet smile which lighted up his tanned and heavily freckled face. Old Ansiau had known what he was doing when he chose Thierri for his son's body servant. Thierri was an unfailing comrade and servitor, and as attached to his master as a dog. Nor was Ansiau slow to return his devotion: his rages, his sulky spells never included Thierri, and he would rather have been cut to pieces than let anyone harm his squire.

"You know," he said to Thierri, "there are fairies in this field. Everybody says so."

"It looks so to me," said Thierri dreamily. "When I was putting in the tent pegs, I thought I saw white shapes of women in the mist over the brook."

"Be careful, Thierri. Don't ever go close to them." Thierri turned his head toward the tent door. "Listen to the grasshoppers," he said. "They don't sing like that at home."

Outside, the triumphant and strident song of the grasshoppers rose from the withered grass. Neither the voices and laughter of the knights in the tent nor the vague noises of the sleeping camp could drown that sweet and piercing chant. Listening, Ansiau all at once forgot the war and his cumbersome armor, his uncle and their guests—he longed to walk out of the tent and set off across the field, across field after distant field filled with that song which was as immense and overwhelming as night. The stars in the sky, with their blinking lights, were singing like so many grasshoppers. Herbert's voice, Joceran's voice, were lost in the distance, dulled and empty.

After carrying a cup of wine to Baldwin of Puiseaux, Thierri returned to his place at Ansiau's side. Wine and fatigue sank him in a delicious torpor. The pale flame of the oil lamp flickered and cast shapeless shadows on the tent walls. The knights' faces were half in darkness. Their voices grew more excited as the wine flowed from the skin.

"All day," said Joceran, continuing his story, "I held them off with my sword. I had the wall at my back, but my shield was cut to pieces. They would have had me if Guy of Marseint had not come to my rescue."

"There are no men like Guy of Marseint nowadays," said Geoffrey of Monguoz. "When he made a pledge, he would rather have died than break his word."

"What do you mean by that?" said Baldwin of Puiseaux quickly. His voice, which was always menacing, had grown even harder because he had been drinking. A tall, handsome man of twenty-five, Baldwin was the terror of his family and his friends.

"Calm yourself, fair son," said his father. "Lord Geoffrey did not mean to anger you. Has any friend of yours ever broken his word?"

"Never," said Baldwin. "But I don't like his saying it."

In Baldwin's presence the air seemed to grow heavy and big with lightning, as on a stormy night. Herbert knew him, and he hastened to change the subject.

They talked of King Louis and Henry Plantagenet and the countess of Champagne—people who could not possibly irritate Baldwin's susceptibilities. Herbert could not forgive King Louis for having caused the failure of the Crusade. "The king," he said, "wasted his time praying when we should have acted, and acted when he would have done better to keep quiet and pray. The idea of his attacking the king of England! A rabbit might as well attack a boar!"

"Speak no evil of the king," said Herbert's nephew Girard the Young. "You must not forget that we are his men."

"We swore no allegiance to him," said Herbert. "If Count Henry wanted to serve the emperor tomorrow, we should be the emperor's men."

"I prefer the king of France," Girard said. They were on the verge of a quarrel. Herbert was partial to the king of England, whom he considered a model king and a model knight. He never tired of hearing tales of his exploits; but above all he admired him for being a redhead. "If we were in the service of such a man," he said, "we should never have been beaten."

The Crusade was one of Herbert's favorite subjects; he still saw it with the eyes of his fifteenth year. "Ah," he said, "no one who did not see it could even imagine it. At Constantinople the sea is like a great sapphire set between gold and enamel banks. And when the sun shines on it, it is like molten gold trembling and flowing. And all the ships with their red and white sails—so many that you cannot count them. I have never seen anything so beautiful in my life, and never shall. The sky there is bluer than cornflowers. And when the sun sets, God! it turns so red that you would say the sea was on fire. I shall never forget it so long as I live. We crossed the

Bosporus when the sun was low on the horizon, and the sea was as red as vermilion and our sails were like a field of tents made of gold and brocade. All our flags flapped in the wind like the wings of birds; and the squires blew horns and trumpets until it was a joy to hear them."

"How well you tell it, friend," said Joceran dreamily. "God knows, I was there too—and I see it again as if it were yesterday when you tell it."

"You went through Constantinople, my lord knight?" asked Mathis of Monguoz. His deep black eyes were alive with curiosity.

"Indeed we did. But we did not stay there long."

"There is not a more beautiful city in the world," said Joceran.

"Nor a richer. The houses are built of stone so white that it hurts your eyes. And the church spires and domes are gold. And inside the churches— there is no such beauty in all Europe, no, nor anywhere in Christendom. The shrines are all of pure gold and precious stones, the images and the crosses are so thickly set with gems and diamonds that they shine from far off with countless red and yellow and green flames. And the vestments are woven with gold and embroidered with flowers and crosses, and they are so beautiful that it makes you faint to look at them. And the choirs sing like the angels in Paradise, some high, some low, and it is such beautiful music that I have never heard anything like it since. . . . I used to know some of it by heart, but now I have forgotten how to sing it. They sing in Greek, and we cannot understand them."

"And the men and women go dressed like kings and queens," said Joceran, "in long robes all embroidered in fair colors."

"And the women go veiled like infidels. And the men shave their mustaches and beards. And there are wonderful fruits like scarlet apples, and the trees on which they grow are such a dark green that they look black—and the fruits are big, like big apples, and when you bite into one it tastes bitter; but if you peel them they are so good to eat and drink that you feel neither hunger nor thirst after one mouthful. We called them fruits of Paradise."

Joceran sighed: "God knows we did not taste them often. Outside Damascus what we had to eat was very different."

"My brother Garin died there of a malignant fever, God rest his soul," said Herbert. "But for the king's stupidity, we should have taken Damascus, and every man of us would have been rich for life."

"If the king would take the cross again," cried Mathis of Monguoz, "I would go as if I had been summoned to a feast. I would kill so many infidels that I would finally carve myself a barony in the lands of the Turks. In Champagne a man's hands are tied. He has to swear so many allegiances that he cannot turn around without having count, viscount, or seneschal on his neck."

"Softly, my nephew!" said Geoffrey of Monguoz, who felt that the young man had drunk too much and was speaking too freely.

"I do not want to die without seeing Jerusalem," said Ansiau suddenly.

"To tread the ground on which Our Lord walked! It must make a man weep for wonder."

"You are right," said Herbert, "there is no place on earth more holy, I think. Not a man of us but wept when he saw the Holy Sepulchre."

"But God knows that not all Christians lead holy lives there," Joceran remarked with a laugh.

"Did you see Queen Eleanor, My Lord Herbert?" Thierri asked suddenly in his soft voice; then he blushed at his own boldness and hid his face in his sleeve.

"Certainly I saw her," answered Herbert, with a long sigh in which regret and admiration were mingled—it was very easy to set him talking. "I saw her at Mainz, where we had gathered to salute the king and queen. By St. Thiou, she was a beautiful woman in those days. She stood in front of the church, beside the king, and raised her hand in greeting to each knight. I can see her as if it were yesterday—I was not thirty paces from her. Such a fair young woman. Eagle eyes. And a pink mouth like a hawthorn blossom; and hands like two white doves, and she moved them so gracefully that it was beautiful to see. She wore a white dress interwoven with gold, and on her mantle there was a great red cross. Not a man but fell in love with her that day."

"Is it true," asked Girard the Young, "that she slept on rose petals, at Antioch?"

"I do not know, I was never near her bed. But we heard it was so. And we heard many other things." Herbert broke off, remembering that Queen Eleanor was the mother of Countess Mary of Champagne. There was a momentary silence. For an instant the picture of a marvellous woman—all perfume, joy, nobility, splendor, pride—hung in the minds of these humble, petty knights, and a fugitive fire gleamed in Mathis' little hard pupils, flickered in the wide brown eyes of Ansiau, touched Thierri's boyish face. Girard the Young scratched his beard, Herbert bowed his head and toyed with a ring on his finger.

Troyes was surrounded by ramparts of pale stone and chalk. The rain had stained them with dark lines and blotches. Soldiers on the towers hailed one another through the morning fog. Over the great gate the arms of Champagne, protected from rain by a narrow cornice, were sunk in shadow. In the city the horses floundered on the slippery chalk, their hoofs sank into the puddles, splashing houses and knights. The streets were so narrow that two men on horseback could not pass through side by side, and the advance of the knights was slowed to the pace of a hay wagon which, drawn by a strong red ox, moved deliberately on, brushing the house walls. Two deep ruts full of brownish water stretched behind the squeaking wheels. The soil was yellow with manure, the street stank—the smell of mold, of dampness, of privies was overwhelming at first, then they became used to it. The wizened houses, jumbled together higgledy-piggledy, were built of yellow and gray stone, and had little square windows curtained with leather. Ansiau knew Troyes from his days in William of Nangi's service. The gayest place in Troyes was the great square with its market—you could hear the noise of it right across the city, as soon as you entered the main gate.

Herds of cattle and horses came and went through Troyes, cloth merchants and vendors of arms and leather and jewelry, troops of strolling players and bands of gypsies. Ever since his boyhood Ansiau had cherished a wonderful memory of the Noah's Ark and Tower of Babel which was the great market place—full of cries and colors, bawling, plunging, squalling, mooing, eloquent and joyous. Monkeys in red, tinselled coats; dancing bears with iron rings through their noses; jugglers in striped costumes, twisted into circles or stretched into rails; dwarfs, giants, hunchbacks, gypsy women with brass necklaces and bare arms.

Even today, under the ceaseless drizzling rain, the market place had its old look of perpetual carnival. Merchants lolled under cloth tents, their wares displayed to catch the eyes of passers-by. Horses whinnied and plunged. Cows mooed, licking their calves. Froth dripping from his muzzle, his feet in chains, a huge bull tethered in a pen by a hook through his nostrils puffed and snorted, rolling bloodshot eyes; women crossed themselves and clung to their husbands when they passed. The gray sea of sheeps' backs looked even grayer under the rain. Rivers of brown and yellow mud flowed and spread around the animals; narrow planks were laid here and there for folk on foot; the women raised their skirts as high as modesty permitted.

Ansiau was so fascinated by the bird market that he almost rode down the goose seller; beyond the smooth backs of geese, black swans and white moved their countless graceful necks and red bills—it looked like a strange dance of snakes. Some slept, their necks turned back over their wings; others searched for food in the mud. Farther on pheasants glittered in the reddish gold of their tails and crests, peacocks arched their iridescent breasts and spread their tails. The countless heart-shaped eyes in their tail feathers—blue, green, gold, bordered with black—gave Ansiau the same dreamy ecstasy he had felt as a boy.

They passed wild beasts in iron cages—two black bears, two huge monkeys. Such crowds of women and children stood around the cages that it was difficult to get through to the quarter of the cloth merchants. There the market became quieter. Varlets armed with cudgels chased beggars and idlers away from their masters' stalls; the crowd was less dense, the planks were wider and covered with carpet here and there. Affluent burgesses strolled by with their wives, who wore dresses of colored wool. Here and there knights had stopped at the booths and were bargaining for lengths of wool or linen. After the displays of gray and unbleached cloths came stalls bright with all possible colors. Finally the three riders reached the shop of a tailor who dealt in mantles and tunics made of wool or silk, trimmed with braid or gold lace or even with precious stones. The shop was a good-sized tent where clients sat on cushions to examine the merchandise. Herbert and Ansiau dismounted and left their horses to Thierri. Herbert had promised himself that he would buy new clothes with some of the money Rainard had brought in. Their field outfits were anything but elegant—old tunics of coarse unbleached wool, already much frayed and patched.

Uncle and nephew seated themselves on two of the high white woolen cushions which were scattered about the tent, and the merchant—a stout, clean-shaven man—showed them a number of woolen mantles and linen tunics. Herbert wanted a bright-blue mantle because blue brought out the color of his eyes. He was very vain of his eyes, and in fact they were still such a bright blue that they looked like the eyes of a young man. Though Herbert had never been handsome, he was as proud of his face as if he had been Apollo. His copper-red hair and beard were his especial pride, and now that age was beginning to dull them he had them tinted with henna.

He finally chose a blue mantle embroidered with gold in an intricate design representing birds with women's faces and lions with the heads of birds. There were little red crosses scattered everywhere among the figures, for Herbert was always careful to go armed against evil spells. He would not have bought the most beautiful clothing in the world unless it bore some sacred symbol, either woven into the cloth itself or represented in the trimming.

Sitting next to Herbert and Ansiau was a tanned, strongly built knight whose long hair hung down over his shoulders. His strange pronunciation and his guttural voice attracted Herbert's attention. "Your pardon, sir knight," Herbert said, "may I ask your birthplace? Are you not from the Empire?"

The man, who seemed bored, was delighted to find someone to talk with and smilingly answered that in fact he was from the Empire and that he had been born in Westphalia, where his brother held a castle.

"I have a great admiration for your emperor," said Herbert politely. "I am sure that you must serve a noble baron, for it is clear that you do not lack for money. Should I be discourteous if I asked how you chance to be here in Troyes and what your name is?"

"Not at all," the German answered, "I am very happy to have made your acquaintance, for you are well known in this land. I shall hide nothing: my name is Walter of Trauenburg, and I serve the count of Lorraine. I am here for the tournament which the count will hold after the Nativity of Our Lady."

By the time they left the shop the three men were good friends, and Herbert invited Sir Walter to spend the night with them at the "Crimson Goose" inn, for he liked nothing so much as to hear of foreign lands, and he expected that his new friend would have some interesting stories of adventure to tell him. Before going to their inn, however, the knights stopped at the bathhouse, for they had not bathed since they left Linnières. Herbert had difficulty in obtaining admission, the bathhouse was already overcrowded. But since he patronized the place two or three times a year, he considered that he had acquired a permanent right to enter it as lord and master. He stormed and scolded so vehemently that at last he and his two companions were allowed to enter. In the great hotroom, the wooden floor of which was covered with coarse woolen carpeting, the steam was so dense that they could see nothing; in the damp, oppressive, burning heat, they were vaguely aware of a stirring and breathing from innumerable relaxed, perspiring bodies; a penetrating smell of sweat mingled with the odors of musk and lavender and scented oils. They heard laughter, songs, the slap of hands against wet backs, the splash of water running into basins. Through the suffocating steam Herbert led the way between the seated and reclining men who occupied most of the floor; at last he found the master of the establishment and demanded attention for himself and his friends. As Herbert's tone was too peremptory to permit an answer, the master asked the man he was massaging to excuse him for a moment and hurried off; he returned with two varlets to rub and bathe them and a woman to wash their heads.

When he left the bathhouse some hours later Ansiau felt resurrected—having his body clean and white and perfumed again was a positive joy. His hair had been washed and combed and oiled; it fell in regular waves over his head and down his neck. His hands were so white and clean that there was no dirt even under his fingernails.

At the inn Ansiau, his uncle, the German knight, Thierri, the two barons of Chalmiers (friends of Herbert's), and two merchants from Lorraine were given one fairly small bedroom, where they were expected to make the best of two shaky and flea-ridden beds. Both of Herbert's friends were extremely fat, so they slept three in a bed with one of the merchants; the remaining three knights and the second merchant took the other bed. Their varlets unsheathed their knives in case of an alarm, and disposed themselves at the foot of either bed and close to the door. It was a dark night and the heat made the stench of wine and the fleas more intolerable than ever. Thierri opened the window, but it was so small that it produced little effect on the air in the room. Outside, rain swirled down the gutterpipes and the night watchmen marched back and forth across the square.

Jammed between his uncle and the snoring merchant, Ansiau sank into a blissful state between waking and dreaming. Listening to the hard, guttural voice of the knight of Trauenburg, who was telling Herbert the story of his life, he lived through incredible adventures. He saw himself carried over the sea in a round-bottomed boat; the sea roared; the infidels brandished glittering swords; the sun shone down on immense white-and-gold castles and on ships with yellow sails. Rich Venetian lords moved past, clad in green, red-flowered mantles; black-eyed and beautiful Saracen ladies looked at him over the white veils which hid the lower part of their faces.

Walter of Trauenburg had seen infidel lands. He had been shipwrecked on a voyage to the Holy Land with his lord, the count of Mantua. He had been sold as a slave to a rich emir of Alexandria, had escaped on a Venetian galley and served as a sailor for five years on a Venetian merchant ship.

While on a pilgrimage to St. Magdalen of Provence, to expiate the murder of a comrade, he had made the acquaintance of a rich old widow; he had lived in her house for a year and she had given him money to buy arms and a horse. Later he spent some time in Aquitaine, in the service of the English king. Having killed an Aquitanian knight in a quarrel, he was obliged to flee. After many more adventures he had settled down in the service of the count of Lorraine, with whom he now made a good living from plunder and tournaments.

Herbert listened to his companion avidly and asked him numberless questions concerning life in Venice, the customs of the Alexandrian Moslems, the wars in Aquitaine. "It is good to meet a man who has seen the world," he said, "and who has news of it to tell. We are bored to death in Champagne. You are young, you cannot have known the glorious life we led there in former days." Walter in his turn was curious to learn of his companion's adventures and exploits; and he did not fail to hear them, for Herbert the Red loved to talk. It was late—the bells had long since rung matins—when Herbert noticed that Walter was snoring. He felt a little disappointed, but he was tired too—he closed his eyes. Instantly, the old malady began to gnaw at his soul, and he wondered how the wine he had drunk and the lateness of the hour could produce so little effect.

Too weary to make the effort of waking his companions, he moved his head from side to side to drive away the throbbing anguish which held him fast. The rain still poured down the gutterpipes; somewhere quite close by, he thought, water was dripping on stone—one-two-three-one-two-three-one-two-three—and the sound became so exasperating that he felt he could bear it no longer. The two barons of Chalmiers were snoring in chorus, one of the varlets was talking in his sleep. The air was heavy and weighed on his chest like a stone. How could God so utterly abandon a Christian? Little by little Herbert saw his sleeping companions disappear, sink into the ground, and he remembered that he had heard of inns built directly over Hell—inns whose floors opened and precipitated the slumbering guests into eternal flames. One thing he knew—he was alone in the room. Around him there was emptiness. No living thing, no human being to succor him. Now pitiful wailings rose on every side. Frozen to the marrow by an icy terror, Herbert lay, not daring to stir. "Alas, Lord Jesus, St. Michael, St. George, my patron—only save me from the pit, and I swear that I will neither kill nor drink nor know a woman all the rest of my days. On the site of this inn I will build a chapel and I will serve in it as sacristan, barefoot, dressed only in a shift, with a rope around my neck. Holy Virgin, may I see Thy fair face that I may be freed of all my sins. Lady, crowned Queen, if Thou canst show Thyself to me, let me see Thee and implore Thee to deliver me. Ah!" With a loud cry Herbert woke and sat up in his bed, jostling Walter of Trauenburg. He saw a white square of light, and finally understood that it was the window. The sun was rising. Ansiau, wakened by his cry, painfully unglued his long eyeslashes, heavy with sleep. "Thierri," he said, in a thick voice, "Thierri, is it day?"

"It must be past prime," said Herbert, slowly returning to his surroundings. He was happy to know that one more night was past.

"Let us leave here, my nephew," he said. "This is an evil place. I think that I shall not visit Abner today, I have had as bad a night as ever Christian passed—it is not the right moment to visit a Jew."

After dressing in their new clothes and taking leave of Walter of Trauenburg, uncle and nephew went to Mass, which was sung very early that day. Ansiau amused himself by looking at the assembled knights and the noble dames in their long red or white veils; but Herbert for once prayed with fervor, beating his breast and kissing the straw-strewn flagstones. "Lady, Empress, Noble Queen," he prayed, "succor me, assist me, sinner that I am; I will build for Thee a stone chapel with windows of painted glass. I will have the doorway decorated with capitals carved in leaves and flowers, like those at the church of St. Peter. Good Lady, Thou who hast power with Thy Son, save me, for well Thou knowest that never have I sworn a false oath by Thy name. Well Thou knowest that always I have prayed to Thee and honored Thee."

And as he prayed he seemed to feel a great peace flood his heart, and little by little he grew certain that his prayer would be granted. But after leaving the church and eating dinner he quickly forgot his pious exaltation. He even suggested to Ansiau that they should spend the evening with prostitutes; he knew an inn at Troyes, he said, where the wenches were beautiful and even clean. Ansiau had an innate distaste for women of common blood.

"In two days we shall be at Linnières," he said, "I am not in such haste that I cannot wait two days more."

"It is clear that you are still too young," said Herbert, shrugging his shoulders, "and that you do not know life. Are you a peasant, that you should be content with only one woman? You can have as many as you please. Your lady will lose nothing by it, and you will gain much."

Alis had reason to be proud of her lineage: her maternal grandfather had been Guy of Marseint. Twenty years after his death his name still awakened smiles of affection and regret. No, said those who had known him, neither this country nor any other would see his like again—such a comrade, so loyal, so just, so good. He had been but a petty knight without land or wealth, in the service of the viscount of Saint-Florentin, but when men spoke of him they said "the noble Guy of Marseint," and noble he had been, as noble as any count or marquess. And old Ansiau, when he had been looking for a daughter-in-law of good stock, had not hesitated: Guy of Marseint's granddaughter would give good knights to the house of Linnières. Guy of Marseint had died young, leaving only a daughter. On his deathbed he had entrusted her to Joceran of Puiseaux, his brother-in-arms.

Joceran was married and had three sons and four daughters by his wife, the daughter of a vassal. And later, when little Aubrey of Marseint reached twelve, Joceran saw that she was pretty and made her pregnant; then he repudiated his wife and married Aubrey. It was not for long, Aubrey died in childbed. But her child had lived and grown strong, a daughter, Alis.

Three months after Aubrey's death Joceran took another wife, Hodierne of Hervi. She was not beautiful, but she was a rich heiress and of a good house. It was she who had taken the place of a mother to Alis; she had her own children too, one every year, but only the first four lived.

Hodierne's mother had been a lady of Provence: in the course of a pilgrimage her father, Boemond of Hervi, had met and loved a daughter of the house of Tourves and had carried her off to Champagne. Hodierne of Tourves had been a beauty, but her daughter had inherited only her brown hair, her black eyes, her thinness, and her excessive piety. Joceran of Puiseaux thought that he must have married a nun. At Puiseaux Hodierne was considered a saint—everyone loved her. She was short and wizened; because of some intestinal disease her skin had grown almost black. She moved through the castle quickly but unhurriedly, kept an eye on everything, gave orders, checked linen, dealt out supplies; one of her hands was always on her bunch of keys, the other on her ebony rosary. No one could understand how she found time to do all that she did, for she spent half her days in the chapel. She did needlework too, making chasubles, stoles, altar cloths for poor churches—it was her one great diversion, she was never happier than when she was finishing a beautiful piece of embroidery. "One more house of God beautified," she would say. "The saints and angels will rejoice."

Never had lady loved God more fervently: when she entered a church or merely saw a cross her face grew younger and her eyes lit up. She could not contain herself, she went down on her knees and kissed the flagstones and the ground and the foot of the cross. She fasted four days a week, and, daring her husband's anger, fed three poor people at her table every Sunday.

Alis had soon come to understand that her stepmother was not happy. No woman can be happy who is always pregnant, ill, overwhelmed with work, and who bears a child every year only to see it die a week or two after it is born. Hodierne took little part in bringing up her living children, she had better things to do—she prayed for them. She was not the kind of woman who could whip or slap her daughters. The serving-women saw to that, and—later on—Joceran. Alis adored Lady Hodierne, and though her stepmother had never struck her, she obeyed her instantly. And Lady Hodierne never caressed her—she had only to look at her with her great black dark-rimmed eyes and Alis forgot all her troubles.

And Alis loved her father too. When she was with him she felt safe from all the ills of life. What should a girl fear who was the daughter of Joceran of Puiseaux? Joceran was reputed the strongest man in the castellany, as well as the shrewdest and the most favored by women. He profited as much from his successes with ladies and townswomen as he did from his skill at tourneying. No one knew whether Lady Hodierne found this distasteful or not. But when he decided to make a kitchen maid her rival and took the wench to sleep in his own bed, Hodierne uttered no word of complaint—she merely grew thinner and blacker than ever, and tears flowed from her eyes while she worked and she was powerless to stop them. Though Alis was only twelve at the time, the sight of such resignation made her blood boil.

"My lady and mother," she said, "you should not bear this shame. If I were you, I would have the wench stripped and whipped in the middle of the courtyard, were my lord to kill me for it."

"If I were you," said Lady Hodierne, "I would not talk about matters which do not concern children."

Alis protested: she was not a child any longer, she had received Communion. She knew that a noblewoman must not let herself be supplanted by a serf. "You should revenge yourself," she said. "The wench has spit in your face; it is as if she had boxed your ears a hundred times and more—that is what she has done to you."

Then Lady Hodierne stiffened and her lips narrowed. "It is because I have deserved it," she said. "Do not speak of this thing again."

Alis saw that her hands were trembling more and more violently. She thought that her lady mother was greatly to blame. But she did not pass judgment on her father.

With his tanned face almost split in two by his celebrated scar, with his blue eyes under bushy brows—big and heavy without being fat, accurate and quick in his movements but never losing his calm—her father was one of those men who take what they find without even asking themselves if they have a right to it; he had every right, he was Joceran of Puiseaux, of the castellany of Paiens, liege of the count of Champagne. There was a saying that Joceran would lie down in God's own bed if he went to Paradise. At the same time he was a modest and a kindly man, so affable that even his enemies were forced to smile when he talked to them. And Alis, a little girl who played with his beard and his earrings, adored him and never even wondered whether he were right or wrong—he could not possibly be anything except what he was.

Like every girl brought up in a castle, Alis had passed through a hard school before her marriage. Women's work was not always easy to learn, but Alis was proud, and she was sure to respond to an appeal to her pride—her future mother-in-law and sisters-in-law must not say that the girls at Puiseaux did poor work. Then too, Alis had sisters and brothers, sisters-in-law and girl cousins. She did not like her brothers. Baldwin, the eldest, was regarded by the household as a sort of mad bull—not to be approached, and likely at any moment to break loose. He was too ready to play with his knife, yet on the whole he was kindly. Of her other brothers, Thibaut and Arnoul, Alis knew only that they had tormented her when she was a tiny child. Later they had gone to Troyes, and Arnoul had died there as the result of an accident. Thibaut had come back and had married. From her sisters-in-law Alis learned that, for a woman of noble blood, married life was a bitter thing. Irma, Baldwin's wife, lived on drugs and philters, gave them to her husband to put him to sleep and to other men to keep them awake. Alis knew it, and considered that it served Baldwin right.

And then she had reached the age when boys began trailing after her skirts. Alis knew how to keep her skirts down, because she had a boundless fear of being shamed; but she did not know much about protecting her lips and the neck of her dress. Her blood was hot, it began tormenting her when she was no more than twelve. How many boys had kissed her and held her and tickled her Ansiau could not know, he thought that he was the first. Alis swore it to him, at the same time whispering a faint "no"—besides, kisses did not count.

Fair am I, fit and fair, and I will love.

At very dawn of day, from bed I rose,
To my father's orchard went, where many a flower grows,
And how I wished that my true love were there!
Fair am I, fit and fair, and I will love.

My true love will I love as he me prayed,
Such courtesy and gentleness should be repaid.
Father and mother may rage, I shall not care.
Fair am I, fit and fair, and I will love.

My song, to all good lovers I you send.
Like me, may they love on and on and never end.
Of all false-speaking tongues let them beware!
Fair am I, fit and fair, and I will love.

After her milk failed and Ansiet was given to Haumette to be nursed, Alis felt at a loss and did not know what to do with herself. Her beloved had gone to war, she was surrounded by strangers. And now that her child was taken from her and she no longer dreamed over his eyes, was shattered when he wept, she felt changed beyond all possibility of recapturing her former life.

Monotonous and burdensome the summer days passed. No festivities, no hunting. Day after day there was nothing to do at the castle but to walk on the ramparts or lie down in the hall or the bathhouse when the weather grew too hot. As formerly, Alis spent long hours with the falcons—it amused her to train them and tease them. She was more than willing to sew and embroider dresses and coverlets for her baby, and she was making a braided girdle as a gift for Ansiau on his return. But all these things did not occupy her as once they had done. She sometimes grew absent-minded and forgot her work—it had never happened to her before.

Finally she became aware that she had changed even physically—she had grown a good inch taller since her marriage and had been obliged to lengthen all her dresses. Now when she bathed she began to take pleasure in looking at her white arms, her long tapering legs, her rounding breasts. She would be sixteen that winter.

In her father's castle she had felt sheltered from all the ills of life. She had liked nothing so much as terrifying stories—tales of massacres, conflagrations, rapes, torture—but it had been precisely because she had felt herself so strong that nothing could touch her or frighten her. Only death frightened her; but she knew that death was far distant, and she preferred not to think of it. Of course she had seen her old uncle Gervase die, and a varlet disembowelled by a bull, and her cousin Raymonde, who had died in childbed—but she felt certain that none of it concerned herself. They were differently made, that was all; they were made in such a way that the blood could grow cold in their veins, that they could become white and stiff and leaden; they had allowed corruption to lay hold on them and the earth to cover them. She, Alis, was made of flesh so full of life and light and heat that the like could never happen to her—or it would happen at a time when she herself would have become a different Alis.

It was a year now since her marriage. The brutal misery of her wedding night had already taken away something of her fine pride. Then had come her pregnancy, and her fear that she would die, and childbed, which had been almost a death. And now, with all that storm passed over, Alis found herself alone with herself in a life which she no longer recognized, among strangers, in a strange house which was to be her home to her dying day.

Alis was often bored and passed her time in endless conversations with Catherine. Catherine was expected to know everything and to have an answer for everything—otherwise Alis became angry. And Catherine was an intelligent girl and played her double rôle of oracle and confidant well. "Catherine, my girl," said Alis with a knowing look, "if you take my advice you will never marry. It is much more fun to remain a maiden. I would give two fingers from my left hand to be a maiden again and live in my father's castle."

"And your baby?" Catherine asked. "Would you want him gone?"

Alis thought for a moment and suddenly began to cry. Tears filled her eyes and overflowed and she could not stop them. "He loves Haumette more already than he does me," she said. "All these women put a spell on me to make my milk dry up. It is not right to have carried him and brought him into the world and then not be able to look after him."

"Bah!" said Catherine, shrugging her shoulders. "You will have more. You are freer this way. And it makes a woman ugly to give suck for a long time, it draws all the juices out of her body."

Alis sighed and dried her eyes.

"Holy Virgin, it is sad! I must look on the bright side of it, I suppose. But what is the use of my being pretty and amusing myself? Before I was married that was all I thought of. But now I am getting old."

Another day they both practiced throwing darts at a circular piece of wood hung up in the courtyard. Two pages and Mahaut, Herbert's daughter, were playing with them. Alis was disgusted to discover that she was much less skillful at the game than she had been at Puiseaux—Mahaut hit the target every time, and she, Alis, missed it two times out of three. Finally she flung her darts on the ground, ran to the palisade, and sat down on a bench.

"What is it, my cousin?" Mahaut called. "Are you angry because I am winning? If that displeases you I will miss as many as you like and we shall have the same score."

Alis was touched by so much courtesy.

"No, my cousin," she said, "that would not be fair play. Win as many points as you can while you are a girl. And God grant that you lose fewer than I when you are married. I see that games are no longer for me."

"My fair cousin!" exclaimed Mahaut, who had a good heart. She sat down on the bench beside Alis. "Really, you have no cause to be sad. All our ladies envy you for being married to the castellan—that is why they are unkind to you."

"You are kind, Mahaut," said Alis, and looked thoughtfully at her cousin's broad, homely face. Its pallor was accentuated by a halo of wanton coppery curls. With her small, blinking eyes, her thick lips, her broad scrawny shoulders, Mahaut was no beauty, but she had a look of gentleness and frankness which made her attractive. Until now Alis had always disdained her for her lack of grace and her noisiness. Today she felt a new sweetness in her heart because of Mahaut, and she smiled.

"Mahaut," she said, holding out her hand, "will you be my friend? I think I will love you faithfully if you will love me."

Mahaut smiled, showing her large, pretty teeth, and took Alis' hand.

"By St. Thiou, I will and gladly, my fair cousin. You are noble and of good lineage, and anyone might be proud to be your friend. And I am the daughter of a noble father too, and you can rely upon me."

"I promise to be as nice to your brothers and your sister as I can," Alis went on, in her new humility.

"As to that," Mahaut cried, laughing, "you may do as you please. I am no fonder of Izembard and Ogier than you are, and for all I care you may tell them so. Simon is nice, and so is Andrew, but they are always away."

Alis seemed to have forgotten her husband. During the months of her pregnancy and the weeks which had followed the birth of her child she had been almost unaware of Ansiau's presence, he had disappeared from her life. And after her churching her response to his caresses had been purely automatic. Now she was sleeping with Catherine and Mahaut—the latter had come to share her bed from the beginning of their friendship. And Alis rather regretted that this state of things would not continue permanently. With women, one was so much freer and calmer. And she had become genuinely fond of Mahaut; never before had she felt any tenderness for a girl of her own age—her relation with her sisters had been a stormy and defiant comradeship, and Catherine, her confidante and intimate friend, was as much a part of herself as the dress she wore every day. But Mahaut, born of another family, Mahaut, the daughter of another line, Mahaut to whom she was not accustomed, was a new being for Alis, a discovery—she wound her friend's wild curls on her fingers, she gazed into her eyes to decide what color they were, admired the whiteness of her skin —there was fresh delight every day. At night they held each other close and caressed each other like lovers, for when Alis loved it was with all her heart. She told Mahaut frankly that she wished her husband would be kept at the war another six months. "With a man, my cousin, it is always a sin and there are always children; women are much more restful. I never knew that there could be a beautiful and courteous friendship like ours."

Mahaut was forever admiring her: "God, my fair cousin, what beautiful needlework you do! God, my cousin, what lovely hair you have!" Her motions were sudden and rough, and often she nearly knocked Alis down when she clapped her on the back, or deafened her with loud, hearty laughter. But she was much less violent and hot-tempered than Alis, and she frequently laughed at her friend's rages. Independent yet not proud, humble yet not servile, Mahaut was a girl one could not help liking. But their friendship was not to last long: Mahaut married before the year was out, and died in childbirth ten months later.

It was the day on which the knights were expected home. Alis and Mahaut stood on the roof of the keep side by side. Mahaut's gray eyes burned with impatience; Alis' eyes were dreamy and a little sad. Before them the miry road ran on, following the valley. In the forest blotches of yellow already showed here and there among the grayish green of the leaves. Brown fields alternated with black. Down the road came the knights, and their red, blue, and green garments shone in the sunlight like flowers in the grass. Behind, two mules drew a baggage wagon.

"That is my father in blue," said Mahaut. "Can you pick out your husband?—your eyes are better than mine."

"He is in front of your father, and beside him I see your brother Andrew, and Thierri a little way behind." Alis sighed. "We shall not be sleeping in the same bed any longer. And we were so happy together."

"You will be even happier with your lord," said Mahaut.

"I don't know," said Alis and rubbed her cheek against her friend's. "I feel freer with you. There is never any way of knowing what a man wants."

When the knights, horns sounding, entered the courtyard, the ladies were waiting by the well; on the well coping there was a vat of wine, and Robert, the old squire, stood ready with a cup in his hands. The well was decorated with leaves and apple branches bearing fruit. The courtyard was strewn with green hay.

After a brief contest in courtesy between uncle and nephew, Herbert dismounted first. Ansiau dismounted immediately afterward, and together they advanced to greet the ladies. Lady Adela took the cup, which Robert had filled with wine, and handed it to her brother-in-law, who emptied it with a bow and handed it to the squire. Robert refilled the cup, and now it was Alis' turn to take it and present it to Ansiau, while the other knights noisily dismounted and the court began to ring with a joyful bustle.

"Drink, my lord." "Not before I have touched your lips, my sweet." "How she has grown," thought Ansiau, as he bent to the full red mouth she offered him. Her calm blue eyes looked at him with the half-savage frankness he knew so well. Never, he thought, would he tire of looking at those eyes, so rightly placed, so deeply set in their sockets, so well protected by their wide thick blond eyebrows, so frank and brave—never would he tire of coming home to them, kissing them. How could he forget that face—the only real face in the world, the only face he truly knew? Yes— he knew how she blinked in the sunlight and the way she licked her lips with the tip of her tongue—he knew the little mole on her underlip, the golden down on her cheeks, the little triangle of hair between her eyebrows, and the thousand colors of her eyes, changing with the time of day, her dress, and her changing humor.

After drinking and handing the cup to Robert, Ansiau used the few free minutes left before dinner to talk with his wife. They sat down together on the edge of the well. They could find nothing to say. Alis twisted the ends of her girdle between her fingers, a little embarrassed, and yet happy despite herself to feel her husband's heavy hands on her shoulders.

"You have grown taller and more beautiful," Ansiau said at last, humbly.

"Not at all! You are making fun of me, my lord. I am badly tanned from the sun."

"Is your baby well?" asked Ansiau, remembering how worried Alis had been when he left for the war.

Alis lowered her head and blushed. Must Ansiau choose this moment to remind her that she was not even able to raise her child, that she had been obliged to entrust it to another woman? Yet was it not perfectly natural that he should want to hear about his son? She was so ashamed at the thought of admitting her incapacity that she did not answer her baron's question and tried to free herself from his arms. "I . . . I will go get him," she said.

"Oh no—don't go. You will not have time. Look—all my cousins have drunk, and now we must go up to dinner."

Alis, her head still hanging, gnawed the end of her girdle and hummed the tune of a round dance to herself.

At table Ansiau was served first at each course, but he did not begin to eat until he had offered the best bit to his lady. So that evening Alis felt that she came first in the castle, which was no small satisfaction to a girl who, at home, had always been made to sit at the foot of the table among the crowd of her sisters and cousins.

She sensed that her cheeks were flushed and her eyes bright, she smiled and showed her teeth and gestured with her hands and shoulders. She knew that Ansiau was not the only man to admire her that day; and when he offered her his cup of wine before putting it to his own lips she smiled at him, indifferent and radiant, her eyes darting sparks, her mouth trembling— he had never seen her so before. And she laughed so gaily that even Uncle Hugh, roused from his torpor, smiled at her out of his white beard; but when Herbert's blue eyes rested on her, burning and hard, Alis, meeting them, turned quickly and looked at Ansiau.

. . . This tall, thin, broad-shouldered knight—tanned, bronzed, almost bearded—was someone she did not know. Her memories of tenderness and desire were centered upon the boy who had grown up too quickly, with his big eyes like a startled child's, the golden down on his cheeks, and his warm, mobile lips. The newcomer brought only traces, fugitive signs, of the lover she had known; his wide eye sockets, the impatient way he tossed his head to throw the curls back from his forehead. But it was not enough to restore Alis' old confidence, to bring back the abandon of her first days with him. He to whom she must give herself tonight was a stranger, and the thought brought her a vague disquiet mingled with curiosity. "Shall I love him?" she thought, and looked at him covertly, screwing up her eyes so that she should see better. "He looked nicer without a beard. And he is drinking so much he will be drunk by the end of dinner. He will go on laughing and singing and there'll be no stopping him. I shall certainly get no sleep tonight. Ah, men!"

Although she was resigned to what must come, her husband's drunkenness frightened her: his eyes shone, his mouth looked hard, his voice was hoarse. "Holy Virgin, what have they done to him? He is so changed—it must be because he has grown used to killing men. If he is drunk enough to forget me I will arrange to sleep with Mahaut."

But she was not forgotten. She had to go upstairs with him, and he held her hand because he feared she would run away from him. He was quite drunk, the steps and the walls of the chamber rose and fell and the lighted oil lamp at the head of the bed danced like a will-o'-the-wisp.

Their bed, the largest and finest in the castle, stood in the warmest corner of the room, not far from the fireplace, and the wall around it was panelled in wood. It was huge, as wide as it was long. Two old swords, crossed over a bearskin, hung on the wall at the head of it, and at both head and foot it had risers which could serve as tables or clothespresses. With the help of Catherine and two serving-maids, Alis had spent two hours making it ready

—spreading the sheets smoothly, putting the big pillows, the coverlets, and the furs in place, laying bunches of mint and lavender between the sheets, polishing the woodwork and the candlesticks. Alas—it was so white, so cool, it smelled so good—why could she not have it all to herself tonight when she felt so tired?

It was a sultry night. In the dark chamber she could hear Uncle Hugh's noisy snoring alternating with Lady Adela's; the mutual recriminations of Izembard the Red and his wife Agnes; snores, sighs, a child's crying—that was Richeut's little girl, who had an earache. "Alas, my Ansiet is sleeping with Haumette!" Alis wanted to get up and go to the servants' room where fat Haumette slept with her husband and her children. Ansiet's little gentle voice which could not yet form words, his lovely round clear eyes, his frail small fingers—Alis' heart became so full of love for her child that she thought she could not bear it. She was sitting on the edge of the bed, she swayed forward; she felt stifled. Oh! if she could have him there, in her arms, on her knees, if she could feel his little lips against her breast—yet God knew he had hurt her. "Never," she thought—"I never can. What good will it do me to have other children when the child I love is mine no longer?" She clenched her fists, she wanted to beat her skull against the head of the bed. "I want him, I want him, I want him. Nothing else."

Her husband, lying asleep there, sprawled almost across the bed, his arms flung wide, his breath coming hoarsely—he was too difficult to love. He smelled so of wine. He felt so hard when she touched him. Yet she had been obliged to put him to sleep like a child, rock him, smooth his hair. "There, there, don't get excited, my dear, all is well, I am not going away, I am here, just close your eyes." His head was so heavy, his breath so harsh, he was like a great river carrying you in a little boat, tossing you among rapids and whirlpools. The tenderness he had awakened in her seemed something foreign to herself, she felt that she had become a part of him, so helpless, alas, so humiliated for him, so sad. Why was he not a little child she could take in her arms and teach and protect? He was too big, too ponderous—a rock hanging over her head.

Sadly she remembered her father, her brother Baldwin, her cousins at Puiseaux, and she thought: "Men are always so! Poor me! And he is only seventeen."

Meanwhile, she could not get to sleep. The bed was so big that four could lie in it, but Ansiau had found a way to take it all up—he was sleeping with his arms spread like a man crucified, and Alis had only a little corner to herself, where she curled up as well as she could, wrapped in the covers. Her feverish longing for her child had subsided a little, she tried to lie still and think of other things. Her temples were covered with sweat, her eyelids burned. "Thierri," she said softly, "Thierri." The youth had accustomed himself to waking instantly at the sound of his name, even when it was only whispered. "Here, my lord," he said. "It is I, Thierri—I, Alis.

Listen, Thierri, could you go and get me a little water to drink, from the jug by the door? I must have eaten and drunk too much this evening, I cannot get to sleep."

"At once, lady." He set the full goblet on the edge of the bed and lay down on the floor again. Alis drank a few swallows and moistened her forehead and cheeks.

"Thierri, are you there? Talk to me a while, if you will. It is dark, I feel afraid."

"Afraid of what, lady? Our baron and I are here to defend you. There are none but friends in the room."

"Everyone is asleep," sighed Alis. "It is the darkness that makes me afraid. Tell me, Thierri, did you see any fine country during your campaign?"

"It is always the same thing, lady—forests and fields. No better than here."

"But you must have gone through some fine cities," she said dreamily.

"Yes, we did. Paris is a fine city."

"Tell me about it, Thierri."

"There are houses. And there are churches. Like Troyes."

"Thierri, tell me, did you see my father?"

When he woke, Ansiau realized that he had drunk too much the previous evening; it was a thing he did not often do. Alis said: "God keep you, my friend. Have you a bad headache?"

"No worse than a man deserves who has finished five cups of wine the night before. I am sorry that I got so drunk, my sweet," he added in a low voice. Alis appeared not to hear him. She had slipped on her shift in a flash, and sitting on the edge of the bed was combing her long hair. Ansiau dreamily passed his fingers over the even, silky waves; she went on combing without looking at him, sometimes starting when his fingers dug too deep. "Enough, my lord," she said. "I am in a hurry. It is late."

She kept to the same tone of courteous indifference she had used toward her husband since his return. Later that day she confessed to him that she had been obliged to entrust her child to Haumette. "Someone must have bewitched me," she explained, "for I had plenty of milk all through the first three weeks—you know that yourself. And Haumette is a very good nurse, we could not find a better anywhere." (It cost Alis an effort to praise Haumette, for she was jealous of her.) "And besides, her own baby died, so she can give all her milk to ours."

"A very good arrangement," said Ansiau, "at least he won't be in our way."

Alis had not expected such an attitude toward a subject which caused her so much grief, but she thought it better not to argue: after all, it was right that Ansiau should not scold her and call her a bad mother since she was in no way to blame for what had happened.

The following days she was calm and good-tempered; she enjoyed going hunting again with Ansiau and her cousins and lived in expectation of Mahaut's wedding, which was to take place after All-Hallows. Mahaut was marrying a certain Geoffrey of Chesley, whom she barely knew and whom she did not love. "Because I am ugly, my fair cousin," she said with her usual simplicity, "I cannot expect much in the way of a husband. He is not too old—I shall have children. And then Chesley is not far away; we shall see each other from time to time."

"God," Alis sighed, "I shall be unhappy without you."

And then there befell her a thing which she did not expect. One day, among other gossip, Catherine told her that her baron had amused himself with camp wenches during the campaign in Normandy. Alis had been resigned to such things in anticipation—when a husband spends half his time away from home he cannot always remain faithful to his wife; everyone had always told her so. But when Catherine said that Gervase, Herbert's squire, had seen her baron with a debauched woman nicknamed "the Yule Log," Alis was as stunned as if she had been struck on the head with a hammer. She blushed all over, rose from her bench scattering skeins of wool in all directions, and before she knew what she was doing struck Catherine on both cheeks and knocked her off the bench onto the ground.

"Trollop," she screamed, "trollop, trollop!"

"You have gone mad," Catherine shouted. "Let me alone, I haven't done anything to you. Go and beat your baron if you like."

Somewhat sobered, Alis passed her hand over her forehead. What had happened? Then she remembered what Catherine had just told her, fought her way through the women who had gathered around her, and flew downstairs to the hall, where the men were sitting around the hearth.

She flung herself on Ansiau with such a wild look that he thought something must have happened to their son. She dropped on the bench beside him, too breathless to speak, and put her hands on his shoulders, devouring him with her eyes. Steadily she stared at him, as if she were searching for something in his face—like a mother scanning the face of her child for symptoms of illness. She was so lost in her thoughts that she had forgotten what she wanted to say to him. Ansiau, seeing that everyone was looking at them, finally asked: "But, lady, what has happened?"

"I . . . I will tell you," she murmured breathlessly. Little by little she was coming back to herself. There were so many things she wanted to say, and she did not know how to say them. She said only one of them—a perfectly simple thing, but a very foolish one too: "Is it true," she asked, "that you lay with women during the war?"

Her question aroused loud laughter from the entire company, from old Uncle Hugh down to the pages. Alis paid no attention. She dug iron fingers into her husband's shoulders, shaking him and repeating: "Is it true? Is it true? Tell me, is it true?" Infuriated with her because she was making him ridiculous and hurting him into the bargain, Ansiau brutally seized her wrists to break her grip and cried: "Of course it is! Stop bothering me!"

Alis put her hands to her temples, stared at him for a moment open-mouthed and mindless, then rose quickly and fled from the hall amid the mocking laughter of the company.

She ran to the door, scrambled down the wooden ladder which led to the courtyard, passed the stables, the poultry yard and the cowshed, climbed the broken section of wall behind the keep, ran along the rampart—then stopped, exhausted. She did not know what she feared nor why she was running. The blood throbbed in her temples until she felt that her skull would burst; red circles opened and closed before her eyes like bloody tongs. She had but one thought—not to be followed, not to be found, to be alone. On one side rose the back wall of the keep, separated from the rampart by a narrow, stinking kennel in which sand and broken stones were mingled with all sorts of rubbish and refuse. On the other side the rather high wall overlooked the orchard, and behind the orchard was the palisade, surrounded by a moat more than twice as wide as a man's best jump. Suddenly Alis made up her mind; she unlaced her shoes and dropped them into the orchard. Then, tucking up her long skirt to her waist, she set to work climbing down the rampart. She was as agile as a squirrel at climbing walls, and this one was not very difficult to get down—it was not perfectly perpendicular and there were jags in it. Slowly, clutching at tufts of grass and clinging to cracks, she managed to reach the ground. At the foot of the wall there was a thicket of nettle and brambles. Her dress soaked and torn by the thorns, her legs scratched and stung by the nettles, she managed to make her way out of the thicket and sat down on the grass, exhausted. She did not know where her shoes were, she did not want to look for them among the brambles. It was suppertime, the orchard was empty. It occurred to her that, barefooted and with her hair down as she was, she might easily be taken for an orchard marauder if a soldier should see her from the top of the keep. Yet after all, she would not care—if Ansiau had done shameful things, it was fitting that his wife should be dishonored too; even if they were to expose her naked in the middle of the courtyard, they could not make her feel ashamed. No, she must not stay here. She must get out of the orchard, go on—where? No matter. The orchard gave onto the forest; Alis knew a place where the moat was filled with rotten straw and chalkstone—it was cleaned out only in the spring. She slipped between two stakes of the palisade, sank her bare feet into the mud and chalk, and crossed the moat. God, how it stank! Her feet were black and sticky, she cleaned them as well as she could on the grass, and began running through the forest toward the path which led to the Vanlay road.

She ran on until she reached the stream and there she stopped to reflect a little. She sat down at the foot of a tree, rested her head on her hands, and closed her eyes. Why didn't she have Catherine to tell her what she was thinking? When she was alone her thoughts became all confused; and she was afraid to speak aloud. What had happened? How? Why? Trollops. No doubt, it was a sin. But it was allowable in time of war. Well then? That other woman, "the Yule Log"—now she too knew what his face looked like when he woke, and his way of sleeping with his arms flung out. She too knew how he said "My sweet," and how he muttered in his dreams. "But tell me, Catherine, how is it possible—such a thing? How could he talk to them? How could he smile at them?

"Those things happen. My father has done much worse. But Lady Hodierne is old, she is used to it. If I were old too . . ." Joceran, Lady Hodierne, Baldwin, Thibaut, Herbert passed before her eyes, and she let herself sink into a dull reverie. Then, because her feet were cold, she raised her head and looked around. The sun would soon be setting. Somewhere between the trees there was a patch of red sky. The stream murmured and whispered over its stony bed. What was she to do now? Her first idea was to go back to Puiseaux. By following the streams, she could easily reach Vanlay, and from Vanlay there was a direct road to Puiseaux. But she knew that Joceran, kindly as he was, could not possibly approve of such an escapade and that she was certain to be sent back to Linnières after a good whipping. And to go back to Linnières herself, with her skirt torn and her feet filthy—she had not the heart for it.

And then again her thoughts returned to Ansiau, and such anguish seized her that she had to bite her lips to keep from screaming. No, no— she could never see him again—she must go, shut herself up in a convent, no matter where; die and be buried. "If I die he will take another wife. I don't care if he does, now that he has had other women. Catherine, listen, Catherine!—I am going mad. Catherine is not here."

Alis became aware that she was bruising her head against the trunk of the tree under which she sat. She lay down on her stomach, buried her face in her arms, and lay motionless, trying to quiet the nervous fluttering of her heart. But quiet did not come. Her eyes were closed now, and in a red mist she saw pictures which made her blood boil. She saw Ansiau's face bending over her—not her old Ansiau, but the Ansiau who had come back to her from the war. He showed his teeth as he smiled, and his eyes glittered. He said: "My sweet, open your beautiful eyes," but she knew it was a cheat. It was not to her that he was speaking. She felt that she herself had become another—one, two, three others. It would drive her mad. And he was bending over all those others, with his big brown eyes and his wandering curls. Unless she killed those trollops she would have no more peace as long as she lived. But that would not help, because there would always be others still. She could never kill them all. In a horrifying vision she saw herself transformed into a horde of debauched women, ugly and painted, and Ansiau was kissing them all on the lips. "No," she cried, "no, no. I won't. I won't." Roused by her own voice, she sat up again and looked at the sky. It was white, and the forest was growing black. From the direction of the castle a horn sounded an alarm. "They are looking for me," she thought.

Squirrels leaped from tree to tree, throwing acorns to the ground. There was a sound of flapping wings from the nests of crows. A snake glided through the dry leaves. Alis, suddenly afraid and shaking with cold, stood up and began to walk along the stream. "After all, it is better they should find me," she reasoned. "The forest is full of brigands and I have not even a dagger with me. And if I stay here too late I may meet a spirit, and I should die of terror if I even saw one." She wandered along the stream for a time, exhausted, her feet sore and bleeding; she felt hot tears running down her cheeks. "Holy Mary, St. Thiou, St. Catherine, St. Michael," she repeated over and over, but she could not call to mind the words of a prayer. She was so tired that she no longer felt anything. Her head and her heart were as empty as clapperless bells. Frogs croaked in the reeds.

The notes of the horn came nearer and nearer. But Alis had not even the strength to walk faster. The sound of footfalls made her tremble—a hundred paces away—or nearer. "It is not a boar," she thought, "I do not hear him breathing." Half dead with fear she hid behind a tree, and just in time—the man was coming straight toward the stream, pushing his way through dead branches and brushwood. As he passed close beside her, Alis recognized Ansiau; his hair was dishevelled, his lips were taut, his brows bent. It was not until after she had let him go past that Alis realized his mortal anxiety. Then she came out of her hiding place and called his name.

He turned with a terrible movement, then, after a second of hesitation, threw himself toward her with a cry like an animal's—or a sob. Alis clung to him with both hands. Ansiau spoke in furious anger, his voice shook: "You are trying to kill me. You have lost your mind. You are mad. I'll have you locked up in the cellar. What have I done to you? You are stupid—you are idiotic—I ought to turn you out."

He accompanied his words by a storm of kisses, and Alis, weak and dazed, made no resistance; she pressed against him and returned kiss for kiss with trembling lips. They returned to Linnières together; Ansiau carried her in his arms most of the way. When they reached the castle he made her sit down in a great chair by the fireplace, brought her hot wine and white bread with his own hands, and forbade Lady Adela to breathe a word of his wife's escapade in his presence.

When at last they found themselves in the bedchamber, where everyone was already asleep, Alis, a little drunk, lay close beside her baron and wept hot tears. "How could you?" she asked. "How did you look at them? What did you say to them? I would have borne anything from you and never complained. I have been as courteous and true as a woman can be. But I will not let you love other women."

"Then you love me?" he asked, happy and softened.

"Do I love you!" she said. "I have nothing else on earth. I love you more than my life."

Thus did Ansiau win his wife's heart again. She forgave him his fault so completely that on the morrow it was utterly forgotten. And he haughtily declared that he would not tolerate the least allusion to the incident of the previous evening, even from his uncles. He was obeyed.

Alis was not hard to disarm. She abandoned herself wholly and with no reservations—it was as if she wanted to make up for the time she had lost by her mistrust. Ansiau was never to find again the sweetheart he had known in the early days of their marriage—like her body, her heart seemed to have grown and ripened. She seemed to have forgotten how to laugh and chatter— now she often sighed deeply, sank into long silences, looked at him with a tensity and a tenderness that it was difficult to bear—so a mother would look at her child if it were threatened by death. It seemed that she could never have enough of looking at her lover: she would take his head in her hands and stare at him endlessly, devouring him with her eyes, wordless, serious, intent, uneasy.

Sometimes she would turn away and sigh, and sigh again, as if too great a weight lay on her heart. If Ansiau asked what troubled her, she shook her head as if she had lost the power of speech, and at last said that it was because she loved him too much. And for two weeks Ansiau was happier than ever he had been in his life. He was in love. He was calm, and sure of himself, and asked nothing of anyone. The union between himself and Alis was so deep that they no longer needed words, or even looks, to understand each other; everyone was astonished by his sudden kindness and gentleness, by which all the inhabitants of the castle benefited, from his uncles to his dogs. At night he forced himself to sleep with his arms crossed, or even to stay awake, in order not to trouble his lady's repose. Listening to her sleep with her head on his shoulder, he felt himself the strongest and happiest man on earth. And he never forgot that he owed his strength and his happiness to Alis.

Autumn was advancing, the days grew darker and shorter. It was the season for hunting wolves and boar—the men spent the greater part of their time at Seuroi, which was nearer to the big drives than Linnières. Poor Alis suffered greatly at being separated from her husband, but Seuroi was no fit place for a lady. Ansiau, too, was unhappy at their separation and his cousin Andrew, who was really fond of him, did not fail to tease him. "One would think," said Andrew, "that your wife's arms and legs and the rest are not the same as other women's. Is she made of gold or silver?" Ansiau was no less fond of his cousin and took his teasing calmly. Besides, hunting was very much on his mind, and after a time he thought of his wife less frequently.

And soon Alis knew that she was pregnant once more. Even the first time it had frightened her, and then she had not known what it would be. Now she was utterly terrified. To think that every winter she would have to go through these months of sickness, and that every spring she would risk dying —no, what a life, what a life! Better never to have married. She told no one but Catherine, and together they searched their imaginations and their experience for some means of producing a miscarriage. But the weather was too bad for horseback rides or bathing in the river; hot baths and tumbles from ladders proved ineffectual and Alis emerged with nothing but a black-and-blue spot on her left leg. If only Irma were at Linnières!

So Alis could only resign herself to admitting her condition to her baron when he returned from Seuroi. He was not overpleased, but he was generous enough to offer her the consolation of saying: "After all, it is not your fault." And for the first time in her life Alis regretted the loss of her old father-in-law—he, at least, had not thought of the child she was to bear as a useless burden, a mishap; for him, at least, the news would have been a joy. Whereas now no one cared about her, or her health, or her future child. She felt so alone, so forsaken, and she did not even have the courage to reproach Ansiau with his indifference—she loved him too dearly for that.

Ansiau found himself further and further from her. It was not intentional, but he preferred spending his time with Andrew and Thierri and Simon, and with his uncle Rainard, whom he had at last begun to like. This unsavory person, the shame of his family and the scourge of the countryside, had yet a certain charm of manner; he was Herbert's blood brother and the fact told. Lame, toothless, hollow-eyed and with a straggling beard, he managed to look like a thoroughbred and wore his patched dirty tunic as Herbert wore his silks.

From Seuroi, drives for wolves and boar were held all winter. After the day's hunting everyone slept on straw in front of the great fireplace. This house without women suited Ansiau perfectly, for he was feeling a growing inclination for disorder, idleness, and the simple life. He was perfectly satisfied with meals consisting of nothing but a great chunk of bread and garlic, and went for weeks without taking off his leather jerkin or washing his face. And when he went back to Linnières, Alis wrung her hands: "My God, what a state you are in!" And she washed him and combed his hair as if he were a child, despite the effort it cost her to move—she was too jealous to leave such tasks to other women. And at night her unborn child turned and kicked so often that she could not sleep. She began to think of it tenderly, and to say to herself: "He will be a fighter."

KINSMEN

I. THE BRAND OF PUISEAUX

In the fields outside Troyes, where camps and paddocks stood in readiness for the sports, more tents were being pitched, colorful against the gray grass. The growing crowd of knights and their servitors, spectators, merchants, beggars swarmed through and about the camps and over the lists. The noise carried for a league around, the gossip too. The inns and taverns of Troyes were full of revellers in gay clothing, the courtyard of the count's palace was illuminated all night.

The first three days were spent in ceremonial visits between relatives and friends who had not seen one another since the last festival. Truces were made, lawsuits begun. Gamesters crowded around dice tables and chess tables, others made bets on the coming jousts. There was even greater excitement when the fighting began—first single combats, then combats between small groups, and then, on the third day, the real battle, in which all the knights still able to fight took part, divided into two opposing camps.

Through the crowd of men with beards combed or curled, with white girdles cincturing their bright-colored tunics, Ansiau walked with his head high, sure of everyone's esteem and ready to accord his own to any who deserved it. He knew by sight and name a good half of the knights who had gathered for the tournament, and was no less at home here than at Linnières. Having no brother, he had finally adopted his uncle Herbert's family as his own, and he was seen everywhere with his cousins, especially with his close friend Andrew.

A portrait of Herbert:

He went everywhere, always accompanied by his four sons—Simon, Andrew, Izembard, and Ogier. He was very proud of his offspring, and he had cause to be, for they were strong, well-built youths, all taller than himself, proud in bearing and brave-hearted. His red hair waving in the wind, his bright-blue mantle thrown over his shoulder, he walked through the camp with his four graceful sons in their long tunics of blue and red wool (and Ansiau the fifth, the tallest of them all), and every lady turned to look after them, and every man greeted them with respect. All Herbert's sons were redheads like himself, except Andrew; in his case, his mother's flaxen hair must have lightened his father's copper-red by a few shades, and his hair and beard looked like fine gold. Although a bastard, Andrew flattered Herbert's fatherly pride more than any of his other sons—growing more startlingly handsome every day, good at arms and hunting and gaming, as clever as he was brave, as gay as he was loyal, Andrew was indeed a son to be proud of. Herbert may have loved him more than his other sons, but he respected the rights of his legitimate children and, in agreement with Andrew himself, with Simon, Izembard, and Ogier, and with Hugh of Beaumont, their uncle, he had settled it that after his death his son Simon should receive his arms, his clothes, and his great chest; Izembard and Ogier should inherit two other chests which he kept at Linnières; and Andrew should inherit nothing. In compensation, Herbert gave Andrew more of his affection and confidence than he did to any of his other children; and such was Andrew's charm that his half brothers were not in the least jealous.

Herbert at this period was trying to solve the difficulties of the barons of Chalmiers, to whom he had taken a liking. Herbert often took sudden likings. They never lasted long; but it must be said that once his friendship was won he rarely changed.

The barons of Chalmiers were bent upon retrieving their father's estates, which they considered had been usurped by their stepmother. But their step-mother had persuaded the viscount to recognize the rights of her son and had done homage in his name. Her rights were questionable, and everyone accused the viscount of partiality. The two brothers were poor. But Herbert of Linni-ères had taken up their cause with the fervor he always put into other people's business. He was on good terms with the Jew Abner, one of the rich usurers of Troyes, and together with several of his friends he had undertaken to stand security for a loan for two months at 1.5 per cent per day.

As soon as they received the money, the two brothers abandoned the tourna-ment and went to Troyes for arms and men. They counted on taking their stepmother's castle by surprise and putting her out of it before she had time to order the gates closed. Unfortunately for their plan, one of her brothers, Robert of Lorgi, noticed their absence and sent a squire to Chalmiers to warn his sister.

Edith of Lorgi, widow of the baron of Chalmiers, was still a very young woman and the greatest beauty in the countryside. Married at fourteen to the lord of Chalmiers, who was then sixty, she had been widowed four years later; and as her husband had quarrelled with his sons and turned them out of the castle, she had taken advantage of the opportunity to have her own sons seized of the domain to the detriment of her stepsons. Herbert had first seen her when, frail under her white widow's cap, she had come to beg help of Viscount Arembert—it had been during the festival at Paiens at which Her-bert had arranged the engagement of Ansiau and Alis of Puiseaux. For Edith he felt the violent desire which he always felt for beautiful and much ad-mired women; and if she had known him better, she would doubtless have decided to be kind to him for a few hours, or a few days at most, for Herbert had promised her that he would be discreet. But she was young, daring, and inexperienced—she laughed in the face of a suitor who was too sure of him-self, and thus made him a mortal enemy.

Ansiau did not share his uncle's hatred of the beautiful Edith, whom he had never met; but it was enough for him to know that his uncle had taken sides with the two brothers—their cause became his own.

The tournament brought Ansiau a series of unexpected successes; after months of idleness he was sure that he could not fight as well as men who had spent their time practicing at Troyes or at some great castle; furthermore, his hauberk was already rather worn, it had become too tight, and he did not have money for a new one. Nonetheless he attracted attention by his skill and particularly by his spirit, which served him so well that in the three days of the tournament he overthrew ten knights. As he had no ambition, he was always the first to be surprised at his successes; and he loved fighting for its own sake, not for profit or glory. With Andrew's assistance Ansiau fixed the ransoms of his prisoners and spent a very pleasant evening in their company; he served them wine, brought them the leftovers from the feast at the count's castle to eat, dressed their wounds, and did his best to be an agreeable host. He gave them three months in which to pay their ransoms and undertook to furnish each of them with a horse and a cloak for his homeward journey.

That evening the camp was half buried in mist; torches flared among the gray tents, and to the music of bagpipes and oboes circles of young men and women sported in the field, singing farandoles. The sky was limpid, and through the mist which rose from the valley the stars looked fresh washed. The forms of the dancers ceased to be red or blue or green and little by little became white and gray. Gradually their cries and laughter ceased. A joyous uproar rose from the tents.

Lost in the crowd and the mist, Ansiau trembled each time he caught sight of a long-haired woman, thinking that it was Alis. But he found her nowhere; it was the eve of a feast day and she was spending the night in her sisters' tent with her girl cousins.

It was a large square tent. Ansiau stopped at the curtained entrance, listening to the fresh laughter of young girls, piercing cries, then laughter again. He was not forbidden to enter, yet he felt afraid to go in, for it was a world which he did not understand and which he considered hostile and strange. "They laugh at so many things that a man would not laugh at," he thought, "and they talk about love and lovers, and dresses and ribbons, and they make fun of you when you have done nothing wrong." The days when he used to treat them like boys were long since passed. He was there, waiting for the only one of them all who did not make him feel afraid. Summoned by the waiting-woman she came to talk to him through the narrow entrance.

"You may not come in, my sweet, for all the damsels are naked."

"Lady, I want to see you."

"I cannot, my sweet—I have already undressed."

"Lady, you can throw a cloak over your fair body and come outside. It is not cold."

"I will come, my sweet," said the low, gentle voice, with a sigh. Swathed in her woolen cloak, straight and slender as a candle, she stood before him—an armless statue which suffered itself to be caressed without responding, motionless and unresisting. For three weeks she had been pretty again, for now she had another little boy on her pillow, a bald something that cried incessantly. Alis thought him even prettier than his elder brother; his name was Herbert.

"Sweet, have I made you happy?"

"I am more than proud—all my friends are jealous of me."

"Listen—I will buy you gold brocade with my ransoms."

"Oh." She laughed with delight. "But it will not make me love you either more or less—you know that. What I want most is for you not to look at other women—they will all be making eyes at you now."

"Then come for a walk in the fields with me."

"No, my sweet, it is a sin." She kissed him, tore herself from his arms, and vanished into the tent.

Alis was delighted to be again with her younger sisters Aliénor and Milicent, and proud to show them her two beautiful babies. "And if you knew how much my baron loves me," she said; "there is nothing in the world he would deny me—ask me anything you would like to have him do, and you'll see he will do it."

The two girls burst out laughing, and Aliénor said: "Ask him to go to the count's castle naked." But she was soon to repent her words: the next morning she came upon Alis talking to Andrew, Herbert's son.

In all the castellany there was no handsomer man than Andrew, bastard son of Herbert the Red. He was tall and broad-shouldered, with a slim waist and powerful chest. His features seemed to be carved in white marble, his large eyes in their broad sockets sparkled under golden lashes, like two perfect sapphires: they were an intense blue, inclining neither to violet nor green, but blue like cornflowers and periwinkles, and they were so alive and so bright that they seemed to shoot sparks. But Andrew's greatest beauty was his hair, which fell to his shoulders in waves, like shot silk the color of ripe wheat and molten gold. A straight part divided it on the top of his head; it hung down on either side of his face, making delicate ringlets by his temples and waving at the ends. His short, heavy beard was tightly curled like a sheep's fleece and gleamed with reddish-gold and tawny lights. Dressed in a simple gray woolen tunic girt with a leather belt, Andrew carried himself more nobly than any count. He held his head high and lowered his eyes to no one.

Andrew had been on his way back from the field where the men were practicing archery, and had leaned against the wooden scaffold on which Alis and several other young ladies of the viscounty were sitting; Aliénor came running up to tell her sister that a marketwoman had arrived with a big basket of strawberries—then she stopped, opened her mouth, and grew as pale as death. Andrew threw back his golden fleece and said: "Greetings, fair cousin, may

God preserve you in your beauty." Aliénor said nothing, and her pallor became a deep blush. Andrew bowed to the ladies and walked on.

Alis burst out laughing at the sight of her speechless, wide-eyed sister, and said: "Have you seen a ghost?"

Aliénor clutched her arm: "Fair sister, in God's name, who is that knight?"

"He is Andrew, my baron's cousin. The son of Uncle Herbert the Red. He is a bastard."

"Is he married?"

Alis laughed again: "Andrew? No."

"My fair sister, my life, my white pearl," said Aliénor, clinging to her sister, "make that knight mine, and I will love you and serve you all my life."

Alis knit her brows: she was thinking. At last she said: "You must not think of it, fair sister. You will not be happy with him."

Instantly Aliénor became aggressive.

"How do you know?"

"He does not love women."

"What!" cried Aliénor disconsolately, "does he love men?"

"Oh no! I don't know. I only think that he does not love women of noble birth. He laughs at the women who love him."

"I don't care about that," said Aliénor, "if only I can have him."

"No, no," said Alis, "you must not think of it. He would make you weep too many tears."

"Very well then," the girl cried, "I shall say that you are afraid to ask it of your baron. All your boasting meant nothing. You cannot arrange for me to marry him, and so you tell me not to think of it. I know very well that if your baron orders his cousin to marry me, he will."

Alis said: "Father must consent."

"I know father—he will consent if your baron asks him."

"But it is too silly—I do not know how to ask my baron for such a thing."

Aliénor cried: "Boaster, liar! I know very well that you can do nothing. And if you do not get me that man for a husband, I shall go and give myself to him as I am, and that will bring shame on all our family."

Alis said: "God, no! God preserve you from such a thing. I will speak to my baron. I will do what I can. Anything—rather than have you do that!"

That evening she arranged to meet Ansiau in the meadow under the elm and said that she had a great favor to ask of him: "If you will not do it, I shall think that you do not love me."

Of course he said: "I will do anything."

"Swear it."

"I swear it."

"And I, my sweet, swear that you shall not touch me until you have done it."

He made a wry face and said: "We shall see. Is it something that takes very long to do?"

"No," she said. "It is only to make Andrew promise that he will do a certain thing that I shall tell you."

"Andrew is so fond of me," said Ansiau, "he will do anything to oblige me. I am sure of that."

"Well then—but you must not tell anyone except Andrew—my sister Aliénor is very much in love with him and wants to marry him, and he must ask my father for her. My father will not refuse you both."

Ansiau said: "The Devil! Your sister has good eyes. But if Andrew consents it will be to oblige me, for I do not think he is in any hurry to marry."

"She is very pretty," said Alis, "much prettier than I am, even if she is dark—and she comes of good blood. Andrew can be proud of her."

Ansiau had reasons of his own for wanting to get the marriage arranged quickly: he talked to Andrew, he talked to Joceran. Andrew consented at once —why not oblige a friend? And Joceran was very fond of his son-in-law and not in a mood to refuse him anything. Andrew was a bastard, but he was a dazzling young man; many women would envy Aliénor. The engagement was celebrated before the end of the tournament, and the handsome Andrew put a ring on the finger of the slender dark girl who devoured him with her eyes so hungrily that she saw nothing of what was in front of her. Aliénor was beautiful rather than pretty—she had a very delicate, very regular face, a small mouth, large brown eyes, and two long thin black braids. But she was not to Andrew's taste—as a betrothed, he was cold and formal, although perfectly friendly. Aliénor was left to think up her love story by herself, and she had imagination enough for two. For Lady Hodierne's eldest daughter was a hot-head—her grandmother's southern blood ran strong in her veins. During the short ceremonial visits Andrew paid to the ladies of Puiseaux, Aliénor solemnly recited her catechism of gallantries to him and accepted the handsome knight's least smile as a gift from heaven. With men, Andrew talked freely and well, but he could not say three consecutive words to a young lady; with women, he was habitually coarse, for he had spent three years in a monastery—his father had thought of making him a priest.

Their elders had decided that the marriage should be celebrated at Pente-cost—the claim of the barons of Chalmiers had to be settled first. And Aliénor grew paler and thinner as she waited for the great day. After the tournament she had to return to Puiseaux with her sisters, and she took leave of her knight in Joceran's tent; she pressed her forehead and cheeks against Andrew's chest—he was much taller than she—and begged him not to forget her. "Of course not," he said, "of course not." She said: "I shall die waiting for Pentecost." He laughed: "Come, come!" "And whatever may happen," she said, "I swear to you on my cross that I shall never give myself to anyone but you." Andrew was certainly not the man to swear as much in return.

The barons of Chalmiers well knew that it was impossible to put their step-mother out of her castle by force. So it was unanimously decided to bring the lady to reason by threats and promises—she was to cede to her stepsons, if not the castle, at least half the revenues of the fief, and they would consent to serve her if she wished. "Once inside the place," said Auberi of Chalmiers, "and we shall know how to set about paring her claws."

Edith's castle, which was known in the region as the castle of Javernant, was only two leagues from Puiseaux. So Joceran invited the barons of Chalmiers and of Linnières to his castle, and from there they proceeded to the village of Chalmiers which was on the border between his domain and Edith's. There they pitched their tents in a field and sent a messenger to the lady of Javernant: if the lady would leave the castle and pitch her tents at the other end of the field, they would come to her and attempt to find a solution for their quarrel. The knights of Linnières and Puiseaux would stand security for the good faith of the barons of Chalmiers.

And Edith came, with an escort of armed men; and presently her opponents saw three blue-and-white striped tents silhouetted against the elm wood—on the tallest tent Edith had her red-and-white standard raised, and she sent a knight to say that she was awaiting her stepsons for a parley. Whereupon Auberi and Walter loudly declared that they would not go—it would be putting their heads in the lion's mouth—she would have them stabbed in the back. Let the barons of Linnières go and speak in their names. Herbert said that he would not go—he hated the woman too deeply, he did not want to lay eyes on her. It was far better that Joceran of Puiseaux should go—he was Edith's neighbor and had nothing to gain in the matter—he would make the best spokesman. Joceran said: "I am willing. Here is my cross. I will take ten armed men with me, and I leave you my two sons as hostages—if I do not act becomingly, you shall keep them prisoners."

In Edith's tent there were woolen cushions striped red and white. Edith sat in the center of the tent. She wore a long white veil, her eyes were cast down, her hands clasped, she was as motionless as a statue. Beside her sat her two brothers, Enguerrand and Robert of Lorgi, and behind them stood the lady's vassals.

"Do you bring us peace, my lord knight?"

"If you do our will, lady."

Edith made Joceran sit at her right and asked him to set forth her stepsons' demands. "I rejoice," she said, "that they have sent me their message by a baron so noble, so renowned and so brave." Joceran straightened his back, puffed himself up, and stroked his beard to display the glittering rings on his fingers. His nostrils palpitated and the corners of his mouth turned up. And Edith's eyelids fell, but they could not hide the brightness of her eyes.

One by one Joceran began to recount his warlike exploits under the watchful eyes of the barons of Lorgi, but his laugh spoke of other things than swordplay, for he saw the lady's white breast rising and falling faster and faster under the delicate white hand with its many rings.

When Edith rose to terminate the audience and dismiss her brothers and her guests, Joceran allowed the barons of Lorgi and their vassals to precede him and then let the curtain which closed the entrance to the tent drop behind them. With a laugh Edith threw off her veil, the cloak which covered her shoulders, and her heavy girdle. For a second Joceran was so thunderstruck by the beauty of her face that he did not dare to stir—he stood in his tracks, openmouthed. Then he threw her on the cushions.

The following day, in the presence of the barons of Lorgi, Edith, and Joceran of Puiseaux, Edith's clerk put into writing an agreement by which Edith undertook to recognize her stepsons as heirs in case her own sons died, and to pay them twenty marks apiece every year. For his services as intermediary Joceran received a good horse and thirty silver marks.

But when the document, signed by Edith, was read aloud in Ansiau's tent by Edith's clerk John, Joceran was the first to perceive that matters were far less simple than he had thought. Auberi of Chalmiers said: "Are we beggars? What good are her twenty marks to us? We borrowed ten times as much from Abner." And his brother cried that, short of going and killing Edith's bastards in the castle of Javernant, there was no way in which they could inherit from her.

"By the body of St. Thiou, friend," cried Herbert, astonished, "what did you swear on your cross?"

"Were you drunk, my father-in-law, that you betrayed us in this fashion?" Ansiau burst out. The word had been spoken, all the knights were on their feet in less than an instant. Joceran, red as a beet, put his hand to his girdle and said: "Who, pray, permits himself to offer such insults to his guests in his own tent?"

"Come," said Herbert. "Explain yourselves, both of you. You are close kinsmen, do not speak without thinking. Fair nephew, you are young—what you said you did not mean."

"By the body of Our Lady, I do mean it!" said Ansiau, pushing his uncle aside. "Either he let them fill him with wine till he had no more mind than a brute beast, or he betrayed us willingly and knowingly. Such things are not done."

There was an explosion of angry voices and shouted threats, followed by an affray in which Joceran and his two sons had to defend themselves against twice as many knights. Baldwin, white with fury, threw himself on Ansiau and, forcing him back against the tent pole, ripped open his right nostril with the point of his dagger, saying: "There, bear—there's a brand for you!" The men of Linnières seized Baldwin by the arms and were just getting the upper hand of him, when Joceran and Thibaut, plying their fists and their knives, managed to free him, and together the three backed out of the tent with bared daggers, calling to their men for help.

The same day, Joceran and his followers went over to Edith's camp.

The men of Linnières, forced to retreat through forest and swamp, pursued by Joceran's men and the men of the barons of Lorgi, spent the night in a thicket around a heap of wet branches that would not burn. The drizzling rain gradually soaked their clothes, and they had neither time nor room to spread their tents.

Ansiau, lying on the ground, his face buried in green leaves and wet grass, wept burning tears of rage and shame. Over and over he repeated: "I'll castrate him. I'll castrate him." His wound had become infected and painful, and his tears only irritated it the more.

Alas! It was all over—never again would he have the right to look anyone in the face. Women would turn their eyes from him and laugh when he passed. Never again would he be handsome—and he was only eighteen! Men when they saw him would say: "A stronger man than he put his mark on him," and they would laugh at him and shrug their shoulders, saying: "It is the brand of Puiseaux he bears on his face." Even now Baldwin would be boasting to the lady of Chalmiers and his brothers; he must be saying: "The baron of Linnières will not forget me as long as he lives, and whoever looks at him will think of me and my dagger!"

Joceran, meanwhile, was leading a joyous life at Javernant, where, in fact, he was lord and master. He made Edith's nieces wait on him when he bathed, dressed in silks and brocades, gave his vassals and soldiers the oldest wine in the castle cellars to drink, slept with the lady and did not disdain her waiting-women, and kept the candles burning day and night. Edith was so much in love with him that she let him do anything and never wearied of admiring him and approving all his extravagancies.

Enguerrand and Robert of Lorgi, indignant at their sister's shameless behavior, had tried to make her listen to reason. She only laughed at them. Then one day when she was at table with Joceran, Baldwin and Thibaut in her little tower chamber, Robert sought her out and showered her with vile insults—he was drunk. Red with fury, Edith rose from the table, caught up the basin of soup which was being kept hot by the fire, and, before Joceran could stop her, poured the boiling liquid over her brother's head. At the scalded man's cries of anguish Enguerrand came running with his son and his vassals; Robert was carried off unconscious, and the same day the barons of Lorgi left the castle with all their men as well as some of Edith's vassals who were indignant with their lady. Robert, swathed from head to foot in bloody bandages, was carried across the courtyard of Javernant on a litter. Standing at the tower window, Joceran watched the mournful procession draw away, and tears came to his eyes at the thought that Robert of Lorgi had been one of the handsomest men in Champagne. When Edith came to embrace him he spat in her face and said: "Who could love you, you hussy, after what you have done to the son of your mother?"

"I would do more than that for you, my fair love. Come—I like your spittle better than other men's kisses. When you have left me, you will have the right to boast that you have made Edith your slave. No other man in the world can say that."

Joceran of Puiseaux spent a whole month at Javernant without giving much thought to the danger which he was running. The men of Linnières thought of nothing but revenge and were preparing to fall on his castle, which he had left unguarded—they had already come to an understanding on the subject with their neighbors, the barons of Hervi. On the other hand, Robert of Lorgi, disfigured, blinded, covered with wounds, had himself carried from castle to castle to arouse the knighthood of the countryside against his sister and Joceran.

However, Joceran was beginning to tire of Edith—he was not greatly pleased to be the lady's tenth or twelfth lover and to have been preceded by vassals and grooms; furthermore, he disliked living in a state of open adultery. One day he announced to Edith that he was obliged to return to Puiseaux.

"Ah yes," she said, "I have done you harm, I will not deny it. Go, and may God keep you." And she burst into tears. Touched, Joceran kissed her on the eyes for the last time and went to see to the saddling of his horses. He left the castle the same day with his sons and his vassals, bearing a rich booty of precious stuffs, gold, and furs—Edith's parting gift.

The return of Joceran and his followers to Puiseaux was celebrated by a great feast: Joceran distributed Edith's gifts of jewels to his wife, his daughters, and his nieces; and each of his men, down to the lowest churl, received a present from him. Lady Hodierne sat at his right, wearing a bandeau of coral and pearl—one of Edith's pieces—on her brow. Her face was darker and pastier than ever; her cheeks were the color of earth, and the blackness under her eyes spread over half her cheeks.

The very next morning Joceran took his son Thibaut and a score of armed men and went to visit his neighbor Fromond of Buchie, whom he wished to engage as an ally. Joceran found him in the courtyard of his castle; he had a wooden cup in his hand and was drinking the blood of a bull just slaughtered. Fromond, at thirty, was strong-bodied and red-faced; he had a bristly blond beard; a great scar cut through the middle of his left eyebrow.

"Are you willing," Joceran asked him, "to serve me in the war I am fighting against Ansiau of Linnières? He has defied me several times, and I expect to see him on my land at any moment. He has made an alliance with the men of Hervi. And they must pass through Courtelon to reach Puiseaux, and Courtelon belongs to your niece."

"I have no desire to harm you," said Fromond, "but neither do I wish to harm myself. What recompense do you offer me?"

"I am your friend," said Joceran. "I think no man your equal in hardihood. As warranty I promise you the hand of my favorite daughter, Aliénor—if you wish, she shall be yours before we set off to war."

"True enough," said Fromond, "I am in need of a wife—mine died three weeks ago. But I thought that your daughter Aliénor was already betrothed."

"She is so no longer," said Joceran calmly, "since I have fallen out with Linnières. I have sworn to give her to no one but the bravest knight in the castellany; I would rather see her enter a convent than marry a coward."

Two days later Joceran returned to Puiseaux accompanied by Fromond's entire garrison; Fromond brought with him his nephews, ten men-at-arms, his vassals, some thirty soldiers, horses, and arms. For his entrance into Puiseaux

Fromond had put on his finest clothes; he wore a long red woolen tunic and an embroidered cloak. Joceran ordered the candles in the chapel lighted and the nuptial chamber in the lefthand turret of the keep prepared.

"You are going to marry our Milicent to him?" Lady Hodierne asked.

"Milicent can wait. I have promised him Aliénor. They will tear out their beards with rage at Linnières."

"It is a sin, baron, you must not do it."

Joceran paid no attention to his wife. He returned to the courtyard, helped his guest to dismount, and took him up to the hall.

Aliénor was in the bedchamber with her sister; looking out the window she had seen the arrival of her father with Fromond and his soldiers. "Milicent," she said, "there is a handsome knight for you. I would wager that he is dressed for a wedding."

Milicent, who was only thirteen, crossed herself in terror and shook her brown head.

"God grant he is not," she said, "I feel so frightened. It is Fromond of Buchie."

"If I did not love another," said Aliénor, "I would not say no: I have seen him fight."

Then she saw her father enter the room and come straight toward her. "Come, pigeon," he said. "Don't be afraid. I will tell you all about it, come."

Aliénor felt her heart grow heavier than lead. She followed her father without a word.

In the middle of the hall she saw Fromond of Buchie, all red and gold, surrounded by his nephews and vassals. "Here is my daughter," said Joceran. "I defy you to find a nobler and more beautiful girl in the castellany."

Fromond, who had been red, turned crimson, and showed his fine white teeth.

"By St. George and St. Michael," he said, "I will have her."

He could say no more. But his big yellow eyes stared at Aliénor, empty and ruthless.

"My father," said Aliénor, greatly troubled, "I see none but men here. Permit me to return to the upper chamber."

"Do so," said Joceran, "and put on your prettiest dress for supper."

"Well," said Fromond as soon as the girl had gone, "is the priest ready? Will there be time to marry us before supper?"

"I think not," said Joceran. "The sun is very low. Better put it off until tomorrow. There is no hurry."

"Curse the sun," said Fromond angrily. "My comrade, my brother, if you will give me your daughter, I will serve you as long as need be and for nothing."

The following morning a boy covered with blood came running to the gate of Puiseaux Castle and clung to the bars. He was the son of the miller of Bercy, a village which Joceran owned and which lay over toward Hervi. "They killed my father," said the boy, "and sacked the mill, they threw the millstones in the water and smashed the sluice gates. They put my father's head between the millstones."

"The dogs!" Joceran cried. "Let us go and hunt them down before they reach here."

"Brother," said Fromond, "it is just that I should remind you of your promise. You promised to give me your daughter before we set out."

"What I have promised I will keep. We shall set out tomorrow at dawn, and we will celebrate the wedding tonight."

The castle rang from cellar to roof with the clang of iron—hammers striking against battered helmets and dented shields. The women hurriedly patched and stitched jerkins, horsecloths, and surcoats, reinforced the buckles on belts and furs.

In the little chapel two altar boys and the priest set out white candles and covered the stalls with green branches.

Joceran was here, there, and everywhere. His hair was rumpled, perspiration beaded his forehead, he was on edge, and alternated between gaiety and rage: "Is that the way to mend a shield, you fool? It will be worse than before. James, if the veal isn't on the spit yet, I'll spit you. Lady, have benzoin burned in the round chamber and don't forget to put lavender between the sheets."

The marriage was performed about the hour of sext, without much ceremony. Aliénor, pale under her red silk veil, stood before the priest and gave her hand to Fromond, who wore a scarlet cloak and whose cheeks ran through the entire gamut of reds. He never took his eyes from his bride's face and could not answer the priest's question properly.

"Alas, my lady, my mother, can I do nothing to escape from him? My soul is sick and my heart is ice. Save me, tell my father that I am ill."

"My daughter, they are waiting for you downstairs. I will go and tell them that you do not feel well. But I fear they will not believe me."

"Try, try—tell them anyway." Aliénor fervidly kissed her mother's lips and hands.

Downstairs the uproar was increasing.

"Lady!" It was Joceran's voice shouting. "The bride is wanted. Bring her here."

Lady Hodierne's wan figure appeared in the door of the hall.

"Baron, noble lords, my daughter cannot come down. She feels unwell and begs you to excuse her."

Instantly Fromond, his nephews, and Joceran sprang to their feet, knocking over their stools.

"Never!" Fromond shouted. "You do not keep your word, brother."

Joceran reddened with rage.

"I? You shall soon see. I am going upstairs—I will bring her here if I have to force her."

"For the love of God . . ." Lady Hodierne implored, and tried to hold him back.

"Hands off, lady. If that girl dares to insult me in this fashion before my guest, I will soon punish her."

"I will go with you," said Fromond. "She is my wife, and I have my rights too. I will permit no one to insult me."

When she heard their steps on the stairs, Aliénor thought she would go mad with fear. She ran and hid herself behind her brother Thibaut's bed—then, because she could not stay there, she ran to the window, and then to the ladder which led to the servants' quarters. And suddenly a great red light illuminated her and her despair ceased. With a sort of somber joy she went to Irma's chest, which stood beside Baldwin's bed. In this chest Irma kept all manner of herbs and plants and cosmetics, ingredients which she employed on the most various occasions. Opening the chest Aliénor began swallowing anything that could be swallowed: a black liquid, a red cream, powders, a blue root with a penetrating odor—then, hearing the door opened by a smashing fist, she shut the chest and stood up.

Joceran and Fromond were before her, red and panting.

"Never, my fair lady!" Fromond cried. "Do you think I am easy to hoodwink?"

"Come here," said Joceran, "you must have forgotten what a whipping feels like. I promised you and bestowed you before the priest, and I will have no nonsense."

Aliénor put her hand to her stomach and said: "I am dying," then fell to the floor in convulsions. Fromond picked her up and carried her to the window; her girlish face had turned completely blue, her hands were icy. Joceran, much alarmed, cut her girdle and the neck of her dress with his knife and ran for water and the waiting-women.

For several hours Aliénor hovered between life and death. All night she vomited blood and writhed in convulsions. Joceran and Hodierne watched at her bedside. As for Fromond, Joceran had managed to persuade him that it was a case of the evil eye and that Aliénor's sudden illness was not serious; and he gave him the pretty daughter of one of his serfs for the night, in partial compensation for the loss he had suffered through his bride's illness.

"I am sure the child took something to make herself sick," said Lady Hodierne, "and if she dies it will be your doing."

"How could I foresee that?" Joceran growled. "Fromond is a handsome man and of noble blood."

At dawn of the following day Joceran of Puiseaux and Fromond of Buchie, with their garrisons and their arms, set out from the castle to meet the enemy on the Bercy road. Aliénor, still very weak, had insisted upon going down into the courtyard to say good-bye to the knights. She was afraid of inspiring Fromond with a hatred of Andrew, so she smiled at him with as much good grace as she could muster.

"After all," Joceran said to his son, "the child acted wisely. Fromond will only desire her the more, and I shall have all the better hold on him."

The men of Linnières and of Hervi had already reached the forest of Puiseaux when Joceran fell on them from behind, forcing them toward the forest and thus cutting off any possibility of their retreating. The men of Linnières were fifteen knights in all, counting Rainard and the two brothers from Hervi, and they had a hundred armed men, part horsemen and part footmen. Joceran had only ten knights and sixty men; but he was well armed and had managed to take his enemies by surprise. It was a hot fight, especially around Baldwin, Ansiau, and Fromond.

Ansiau wanted to unhorse Baldwin at any cost, but to cut through to him he had first to unhorse Fromond's two nephews, who were attacking him from above with their lances. The hill rang with cries and blows, and the folk of the neighboring villages were hurrying to the castle with their flocks and provender.

With a sudden leap Ansiau freed himself from the clutches of the two barons of Buchie and attacked Joceran from the side, in order to rescue Herbert, who had lost his lance and shield. Joceran barely had time to parry—the blow had been so hard that his mount stumbled and a lighter and less skillful man would have been unhorsed. He turned to see who was attacking him and recognized his son-in-law by his helmet, painted blue and red, and by his broad shoulders.

"So it's you, Noseless!" he shouted, bringing his lance to bear on him. "A good thing you put down your nose piece—you won't raise it after tournaments any more."

Ansiau parried his thrust and made his horse take a backward leap to give himself room to charge. Joceran, parrying all Ansiau's thrusts with his shield, laughed louder and more mockingly.

"You've forgotten how to fight, boor," he shouted. "The little brains you had must have dropped out through your nose."

Ansiau gave him a blow which shattered his own lance and sent Joceran's horse reeling back several paces.

"A lance, a lance!" Ansiau shouted, "and I'll get the traitor, the stinking fox! I'll spill his guts and his brains on the ground."

"This time I am not laughing," said Joceran. Leaning well forward he rode straight at Ansiau and, putting his whole weight into it, gave him such a blow that horse and rider went over and rolled down the hill, legs in the air.

Three of Joceran's vassals rushed at Ansiau to pick him up and bind him. But Andrew and Haguenier of Hervi came up in time to rescue him.

A week after the battle a varlet came to Joceran's camp to tell him that a messenger from Paiens was waiting for him at Puiseaux: he must assemble men, arms, and horses and go to Paiens; the count was sending his army against the king of France and was summoning the knights from all the castellanies in the neighborhood of Troyes.

"Alas! Am I to leave my fields and my vineyard to these swine?" Joceran exclaimed. "I shall wait until they have gone—surely they must have been summoned too. The viscount would not do me such treachery."

The men of Linnières and Hervi did not receive the news until three days later. Ansiau sent a man-at-arms to Joceran's camp to ask for a truce until they should have finished their service with the army, and to negotiate the exchange of prisoners.

In the army of the castellany of Paiens friends and enemies met once again, their arms refurbished, wounds more or less healed, shields repainted, flags flying. Their faces were so effectually concealed by their helmets that no one knew whether he was with allies or foes. One by one they marched past the church. The barons of Chalmiers were there, and the barons of Lorgi; and the barons of Breul, of Hervi, of Monguoz, of Buchie, of Puiseaux, of Baudemant, of Linnières, and many more—all the knighthood of the Pays d'Othe.

During that short summer campaign there were many who died of sunstroke or fever, many who sickened from having drunk over-cold water. The long march was hard. Thunderstorms burst on them. In the battle the count's men were outnumbered by the king's, and the men of the castellany lost many prisoners but gained a few minor successes in skirmishes.

Camp was pitched for a few days' rest outside Reims. Many a man, lying by the fire in that scorched field, remembered his own fields, his forest, the smoky hall of his castle. Many thought of quarrels or lawsuits which must be fought out when they had reached home again. Some dreamed of other, more distant campaigns, other, greater armies, oceans of tents, campfires stretching to the horizon—the blue-green sea with its foaming waves—the sea which few of them had ever seen with their own eyes.

A multicolored crowd of knights and soldiers sitting by the fire in the red twilight of an autumn evening. The sky was overcast. The camp smelled of smoke and roast meat. Here and there a juggler did tricks and told ribald jokes—around him an echo, a circle of guttural snickers, of clear loud laughter, made a bright patch in the gloomy silence of the bored, weary, sodden multitude.

Andrew the bastard was there, his helmet resting on his knees, his fair golden head flaming in the sunset glow and the flickering light of the camp fire.

"It is strange and wonderful, brother, to think that Our Lord lived and died under that very sun. He looked at it with His human eyes just as you are looking at it now. Can it be that He walked the earth just as you and I walk it, and that neither the earth nor the sun nor the moon were changed?"

"I know not, brother. But if I could see the ground on which He walked, I think I should never sin again all my life long." Ansiau sighed and drew his long curls out of his iron collar. "Why do we stay here when there are still so many infidels on earth? Why do we who are Christians fight among ourselves, why do we burn our own churches? And why burn the fields of France when there are lands far richer than France—lands where the walls of the houses are fine gold set with gems? The king and the count and the king of England should make peace and go together to fight the infidels."

"The king sees nothing, my nephew," said Herbert. "If the count lets him have his will, there will be no more freedom in the land. Far better that we keep our land of Champagne as it is, frank and free, with no seneschals and provosts sent by the king to put their noses into our affairs."

"Bah," said Ansiau. "At that, they are better than the count's, because they see nothing. So long as they aim only at the count and the county, they let the barons alone."

"You are mad to say such a thing," his uncle answered, shocked. "Though you are Burgundian by your mother, you come of the best stock in Champagne, and we have all sworn allegiance to the count."

Herbert professed an intense loyalty to the count. It went no further than words—but in words, at least, he was extremely strict on the point.

Farther on Joceran had found a place for himself and his family, together with the barons of Buchie and their uncle, and the barons of Chalmiers, with whom he had made peace so that he might better defend himself from the men of Linnières. Ever since they had become enemies they had ceased to talk, they even tried to avoid seeing each other—there could be no question of starting a private war in the middle of a campaign. But such was the force of habit that there, under the tent and banners of Champagne, quarrels and ill will lost their meaning. Memories of old campaigns were reawakened, memories of other quarrels, and of peace made, and joyful feasts of reconciliation.

For Herbert, Joceran was still the crusader, his old comrade in more than one tournament, in more than one fierce battle. Herbert's hatred was aroused by men, not by their acts. He had never hated Joceran of Puiseaux, and his heart could not change with every sudden change in his old comrade's humor. He had never loved Joceran either; but he esteemed him as a good and clever knight, as a great fighter, and as a man of the best blood in Champagne. Even when making war on him, he was ready at any moment to make peace.

Ansiau was of a very different temper, and he talked of nothing but murder and shattered skulls and entrails dragging on the ground. His first humiliation had gone to his head, he could not accept it, it made him ill, he must avenge himself at any cost. For Joceran, he said, death; for Baldwin, castration; and death for Fromond of Buchie too, for he had taken Andrew's betrothed. Andrew, however, was the last to worry himself over that particular form of insult—he asked nothing better than to be relieved of a useless and irksome task.

Andrew had no notion of love or jealousy—he gave away his women as he gave away his clothes, his arms, and his horses; everything slipped through his fingers. He had been known to buy a cloak at a fair and give it to the first comer the very same day. He never grew fond of his horses and was always ready to exchange his charger for another he liked better. He dressed with the utmost carelessness, forgot to change his clothes when they were dirty or torn, and blushed like a child when his father called his attention to the fact. His one vanity was his hair and beard; he had them washed and perfumed regularly and combed them twice a day.

Ansiau idolized his cousin: Andrew, with his perfect kindness, his perfect courtesy, his perfect wisdom, seemed to him the pattern of a knight. Andrew was so intelligent, he spoke so openly; he seemed to be free from the most unavoidable faults—he never flared up, he never got drunk, he never became deeply involved with a woman.

"In the matter of love," Andrew said, "women—noble or peasant—are all alike. If noblewomen are more faithful, it is because they are afraid of being shamed. And at that I know more than one who is less honest than people suppose. We are all made from Adam's rib, and we shall rot in the ground just like the peasants—no woman is better than another, and it is madness to believe that there is only one in the world who can please you. I swear to you that if tomorrow night I were to bring you a tall, thin wench with plenty of long hair and tell you it was your lady, you would not know the difference.

"An animal knows his master from a stranger by scent. But in love we are not equal to the beasts, for I tell you that the queen of France would not know the difference between the king and the king's groom if the groom bathed and perfumed himself like the king. Why, I once knew a woman who was mad about me and begged me so urgently that I grew sick of it. I sent her Garin, my squire. And when she saw me the next day she said she would never have believed that I could be so gentle with a woman. You can imagine if I had a good laugh."

"Just the same," said Ansiau, "you might at least have sent a knight in your place. That is no trick to play on a noblewoman."

Andrew laughed heartily. "Why not? They both enjoyed it. Garin won't boast about it; she is a married woman."

Toward the middle of September the army passed through Troyes, from whence it would scatter over the roads of Champagne. It happened that a great tournament was to be held at Troyes for the feast of the Nativity of the Virgin, and those who were returning from the war arrived just in time to take part in it. Although they were tired and their armor was not in the best of condition, many knights decided to stay and risk their luck.

There was no more room at the inns, so the men of Linnières pitched their tents on the field, and fell to mending their hauberks and repainting their shields. All still had good horses and had suffered no serious wounds. Ansiau, who was considered a very good jouster, hoped to profit from the fighting— he needed money to carry on his war against Joceran.

The field was surrounded by stands on three sides, on the fourth it followed the city wall, where townsmen and idlers came to admire the combatants. The stands were covered with tapestries and strewn with flowers and red silk canopies had been set up over the seats for spectators of high rank. The flags of Champagne, of Troyes, and of the other large cities in the county flew above the barrier. At the foot of the stands minstrels played hurdy-gurdies and oboes and sang battle songs. Heralds dressed in blue and yellow walked up and down the field, their trumpets to their lips.

When the tournament was over, those who had not once been thrown to the ground marched, happy and tired, past the stand which faced the rampart and in which sat the count, the countess, and the ladies.

In the stand a woman stood laughing—among other women as tall perhaps and as richly dressed, but no one seemed to notice them. So purely white was her face that beside it all other faces looked lusterless; so bold the curve of her eyebrows that men thought they saw two wild falcons swing from their eyrie; so clear her laughter that it rang like the sound of a spring shower on spring leaves. Under her fine white dress, embroidered in green and gold, she was as straight and slim as a poplar. Her golden hair fell to her knees in long tresses, and danced like two snakes when she moved or turned.

She was so beautiful that the knights as they passed drew rein despite themselves and could not take their eyes from her.

Ansiau and Andrew, riding side by side, stopped openmouthed before her and forgot to salute the count. Then they rode on and quitted the field like the others.

Ansiau had taken five prisoners, Andrew three, Herbert four. They were resting in their tent before the festival began. For the first time in his life Andrew was lost in a dream, wide-eyed, wondering. "By the body of St. Thiou, what a woman! Ah! By the body of the Virgin, by the womb of the Virgin!—James," he said to his page, "go find out the name of the lady who stood under the shield of Reims, at the count's right."

"I know her," said Herbert, entering. "She is from our castellany. You have heard of her often, she is the lady of Chalmiers."

"Edith!" Andrew exclaimed in surprise. "Then I forgive Joceran all the follies he committed, if it was to win such a woman as that. By St. Thiou, I would have my beard shaved, I would walk naked on my hands to get her. She is still a widow, I hope?"

"No woman could be more a widow. No husband, no brothers, and no uncles. However, don't go too near her—it is dangerous."

For the first time in his life, Ansiau saw Andrew brushing his clothes, smoothing his eyebrows, looking at himself in the blade of his dagger, and perfuming his hands and feet. Then he disappeared and was not seen again all that evening.

The next morning Ansiau was wakened from a sound sleep by a hard hand shaking his shoulder. He opened his eyes and saw his friend sitting beside him—radiant, his hair uncombed, a faint smile on his lips.

"What is the matter?" said Ansiau, who was still half asleep.

Andrew threw down a green ribbon and a purse embroidered with the arms of Chalmiers.

"The lady of Chalmiers?" Ansiau exclaimed. The news had troubled him strangely.

"Her very self. I spent the whole night in her tent. I didn't sleep a wink. Ah, brother, what a woman! Ah! by the body of St. Thiou, by the soul of St. Thiou!"

He picked up his trophies and began staring at them as if bewitched.

The day before Ansiau had thought the lady of Chalmiers so beautiful that he had not even dreamed of desiring her. It does not occur to a man to sleep with the sun. But now, looking at the green ribbon and the embroidered purse, he seemed to see a sudden vision of a tall, slim body, white as snow, and wound around it were two tresses as shadowy and tense as two live snakes. And he saw himself mingled with that body and master of all that beauty. And suddenly he felt that there was only one true sorrow in the world—the pain of not possessing the lady of Chalmiers.

He could say nothing to Andrew about these feelings, and congratulated him on his success. But for him the sky had grown black, the air pestilential, food bitter. He wished to see nothing and no one, pretended that he had a violent stomach-ache, and lay down in his tent with his face to the ground.

His vision did not leave him, and others came to him, bright and terrible as bolts of lightning. The eyes, the lips, the hands of the lady of Chalmiers.

"What!" he thought, "others have possessed her. And I—is it written that I shall never be happy? There is no other woman in all the world. Is it my fault if Andrew loves her too?"

But he told himself that he would rather die than wrong Andrew. "Since there is no other way," he thought, "I will die. There is no life for me without her. Even if I live to be fifty, even if I take twenty prisoners in every battle, what good will it do me if I cannot have the one joy I desire?" Alis had vanished from his mind as if she had never existed.

The next two days and nights he remained lying in his tent, refusing food, only drinking a little water. Andrew was too preoccupied with his conquest to worry over him; he only came to the tent night and morning to ask how his friend was faring.

But by the end of the third day Ansiau could hold out no longer. He called for bread and wine, combed his hair, washed his face and hands, and told himself that he was really too young to die.

Andrew, stopping in to see him, was delighted to find him up and looking so well.

"Good!" he said. "Can you fight in the second battle, day after tomorrow?"

"Yes, I think so." Then, as Andrew rose to leave, Ansiau said: "Brother."

"What is it?" Andrew asked anxiously. "Do you feel ill again?"

"Brother, I can bear it no longer. Let me go to the tent of the lady of Chalmiers in your place. I shall die if I cannot have her."

Andrew bit his lips and stood motionless for a moment. "Very well," he said. "There is not a woman in the world who can come between two friends. Go when it gets a little darker. Her tent is the third on the left side of the enclosure. You go round behind it and draw apart two planks. There is a slit in the cloth, you slip in—and be careful, because the tent is full of birds."

"Of birds?"

"Birds of all colors. She loves them."

He was in such haste that he almost let the two planks drop, almost tore the tent, almost fell as he entered. The tent was as dark as an oven, as odorous as a spice coffer, and full of beating wings, and breathings, and sighs.

"At last," said a clear voice. "You come very late."

He slipped onto a couch so soft that he thought he would drown in it. He touched two heavy tresses, lying like a barrier between them. He began to speak, he stuttered: "My joy, my happiness, my only beloved, my heart, my soul—"

Edith, her voice trembling with fury, said: "Who are you? How did you get here?"

"Enough, my beauty, do not ask me. I am dying for love of you."

"I am waiting for Andrew of Linnières, son of Herbert the Red. Surely you are not he. Who are you?"

"Have no fear, I am not less than he. I am his cousin Ansiau, the castellan."

"A charming family," said Edith, "one of you is as good as another. Was it you whose nose Baldwin slit?"

"Do not mock me, my lady. You do not know me. I shall revenge myself—and afterwards it will not be Ansiau of Linnières at whom men will laugh!"

"My friend, I have seen you fight. I like you well enough, I will take you. You can imagine that if you had not pleased me I would have had my men cut your throat. I am not a common trollop. But I love to be loved. Say something sweet to me—Andrew never said anything."

Through the gaps in the cloth the sun sent narrow rays, lighting the carpet, the cushions, the feather bed, the bright wings of the parakeets which were tied by the leg to an iron rod in a corner.

"Holy Virgin!" said Edith, waking with a start. "It is late. Go quickly— I hear no one about yet."

"No, lady. I have you and I shall keep you. I have but three more days at Troyes. I want to enjoy you for all of them. Since I please you, be mine alone."

"You are very bold," Edith sighed, stretching. "Stay then. I will say that I am ill, and let no one in except my waiting-woman, who will bring us food."

That day Ansiau took every advantage of the lady's favors, and Edith lent herself to all the fancies of her strange lover, whose hungry eyes seemed always to be lost in some distant beyond, who seemed always to embrace something greater than herself. He talked less than he had the night before—he only said, over and over: "How beautiful you are, how beautiful you are." In the evening he stretched himself at her feet, tired, silent, humble. By night he was better able to speak. He talked with his head on her lap: "It is this way. You would never want to marry me. Nor would I want it. I have my uncles and my cousins and my land. I love you to madness. Do you think it will ever end?"

"Men do not know how to love," said Edith. "Men always have uncles and nephews and lords and vassals—for them, you will go to your death. But from a woman all you want is your pleasure. You will forget me as soon as you leave me."

"You would not be willing to love only one man?"

"No, my friend, I am too fond of my freedom. Marriage is not always an easy thing for a noblewoman. So long as I am free, I love any man who pleases me, I make war on anyone I want to, I need render an account to no one. So long as the viscount does not force me to take a husband, I prefer to remain a widow."

"If you were my wife, I would kill you. Tell me—did you love Joceran of Puiseaux?"

"More than my life."

"Yet he is old."

"Young men are not the only ones who know how to make love."

"And Andrew—did you love him too? More than me?"

"Andrew is handsome. But he is as hard as rock. No, my friend, today it is you whom I love best."

"I have two days left to love you. I want to glut myself with you—take all I can. Afterwards, I shall ask nothing of you."

From Edith he learned that there were women who rubbed their teeth with herbs to make them bright, who perfumed their hair with Arabian essences, who washed their faces and bodies in milk and oil and wore knots of sweet-smelling herbs between their breasts. Edith twined threads of gold and strings of pearls into her hair, she wore embroidered shifts of white silk, she spent hours whitening her hands and arranging her hair. In those hands of hers, with their clean white nails, Ansiau saw for the first time a real silver mirror, and the reflection of her face in it was so true that he could have believed it the living Edith. "Alas, if it could always keep your image and I could take it with me! Why cannot you stay in it?"

Ansiau even forgot that he was missing the second battle. At the end of the third day he kissed Edith on lips and eyes, on forehead and breast, and said: "Give you thanks, my lady, I have loved you greatly."

"And I have loved you too, lord castellan," said Edith, laughing. "Are you going to make war on me when you reach home?"

"I shall never make war on you."

"Shall you boast to your wife that you have had Edith of Chalmiers for your mistress?"

Ansiau thought, not without regret, that he would not dare to make such a boast in Alis' hearing. With regret, but without desire, he looked at Edith's beautiful shoulders and softly rounded cheeks. All the same, she was beautiful. All the same, she had been his.

"Lady, if ever you have a child by me—"

"And how would I know he was yours?" asked Edith, breaking into a laugh. "Do you think he would be born with a slit nose?"

Ansiau reddened in anger, then shrugged his shoulders.

His kinsmen had not been much worried by his disappearance, for Andrew had explained that he was with a lady. "It cannot be anyone but Edith of Chalmiers," said Herbert. "Much good may it do him. Best take what you can get from her—it is the only thing she will ever do for anyone."

Herbert had lost even the memory of the passion he had felt for Edith two years earlier. He thought so highly of himself that in his opinion the woman who had disdained him was worthy of nothing but hatred and scorn. He hardly remembered that Edith was a woman, it even astonished him to see his comrades or his nephews fall in love with the lady of Chalmiers.

At Troyes uncle and nephew paid a visit to Abner.

His house was the house of a rich Jew—dark and humble outside, but furnished luxuriously with sofas and silken cushions and rich Persian rugs. Vases and cups from Arabia and Persia, carved or damascened, stood on low ebony tables. Abner was a fine-looking man between forty and forty-five, tall and strong; he was dressed in the Jewish fashion in a long violet surcoat elaborately worked at the neck and wore a richly embroidered turban. His long black beard, in which there was a scattering of white hairs, fell on his chest in regular ringlets. His large, dark, heavy-lidded eyes were cold and penetrating. He had a hooked nose and a full lower lip which gave him an ironic and slightly disdainful look. With Herbert and Ansiau of Linnières Abner appeared to be servility itself—to judge from his words, which he spoke in a beautiful low singing voice with a strong Mediterranean accent. But, looking at his face, you would be more inclined to think that it was he who barely condescended to speak to his guests, and that, if he was a poor Jew, they were certainly even poorer Christians.

Seated on cushions before a small, low table on which Abner's servant had set a bowl of exotic fruits candied in honey, uncle and nephew spoke of the loan they expected to receive and of the sureties they would be able to give. Abner, standing before them, listened, his eyes half closed.

Abner might be a Jew, but Herbert enjoyed his company—there was a strange mixture of disdain and esteem in their relationship. Abner was intelligent and had seen the world. In expansive moments the two men conversed in Arabic: Herbert had learned a little Arabic during the Crusade and never lost an opportunity to improve his knowledge of the language; Abner spoke it as if it were his native tongue. Ansiau, hearing them exchanging strange and meaningless sounds, yawned and began to eat the candied fruits, one after the other.

A veiled woman in white trousers and a green velvet jacket—a slender, delicate silhouette—moved aside the door hanging; Ansiau saw two big black eyes above the veil; then the hanging fell back.

The luxurious furnishings, the odor of musk in the airless room, the thick carpets, the necklace and bracelets of gold coins around the veiled woman's throat and wrists, the diamond aigrette on Abner's turban—Ansiau found himself harboring strange thoughts of loot and arson and rape.

"That dog of a Jew," he said to his uncle when they had left Abner's house, "he despises us."

"He is of another race," said Herbert, "he has his laws, foul though they may be. He is a good Jew, and even a man of his word."

"Bah! the word of a Jew . . . Meanwhile we must bleed ourselves white to pay him."

On his return from the war Fromond of Buchie went directly to Puiseaux for his wife. To tell truth, Aliénor had lost much of her beauty as a result of her illness on her wedding night. Pale, hollow-cheeked, her neck so thin that it bent under the weight of her long hair, she looked a little like a starved animal. Her eyes roved anxiously, her mouth was drawn and sad. The thought of Fromond's return plunged her into a distress which would not let her sleep—she was terrified of breaking her pledge to Andrew, every night she prayed: "St. Michael, let Fromond be killed in the war!" And she secretly hoped that when Fromond saw how ugly she had become, he would not want her.

But Fromond was not the man to give up a woman who had been bestowed on him before a priest. Had she gone blind or bald, he would still have insisted on his rights. Besides, thin and gaunt and hardened as she was, Aliénor still made his heart beat faster—he was a man of dogged desires. Wanting to please her, he had bought her a pair of silver earrings and a length of red silk in Troyes. As soon as he saw her he began to kiss her with long, devouring kisses which hurt like bites; Aliénor's lips and cheeks were blue and sore afterwards.

But the very day on which the knights returned Aliénor found an unhoped-for cause of delay—Lady Hodierne had another miscarriage, and everyone thought that it could not but be her last. Joceran was obliged to put off the wedding festivities until a later day. But Fromond, not without reason, declared that in the eyes of the Church the girl had been his wife for six weeks; he did not want any wedding festivities, he wanted to take his new lady to his own castle. "I cannot deny it," said Joceran. "There is no doubt of your right. Do whatever you think best."

Aliénor said to Fromond: "My lord baron, you can see that my lady mother is dying. I love her with all my heart: I want to remain with her. When she is gone I shall never see her again—these are the last days I can ever be with her. As soon as she dies I will follow you to your castle."

Fromond took her gently by the shoulders. "I have a mother too," he said. "I will let you stay. But the day after the funeral you must be at Buchie, or else you will learn what my anger is. And that I hope you will never know."

That death could be so hard after so hard a life was incomprehensible. Lady Hodierne's body, so frail that it seemed to be made of spirit instead of matter, resisted more tenaciously than many a young body full of sap and life. Livid, with staring eyes and open mouth, the dying woman's face was a terrifying sight. No one had ever before seen those delicate lips lose their mild, sweet curve. But now the veil was rent; there was no Lady Hodierne in the castle now. Nothing remained but a human soul which had already renounced its title and its rights, had laid down its arms. Aliénor did not know that gaping mouth, that lolling head. But she had never loved her mother so greatly before. She had lost her old fear of sickness and death— with her sister Milicent she watched by the bedside day and night.

Joceran had waited two days for his wife to die. Then, because he must meet the attack which the men of Linnières were ready to make on Bercy, he said farewell to her and set out with his sons and his garrison. Those seventeen years of life together were coming to an end at last, and Joceran could hardly believe it. "Alas, my lord, I have loved you so dearly!" So women loved him—even she, she whom he had loved least, the ugly one. Well, she could have kept her love—he had not needed it. And now that she was gone, who would keep house? He must think about that later.

For the first time in her life Lady Hodierne dared to speak to God aloud. It was a shrill plaint, a litany: "Lord, Lord, have mercy. Alas, I have sinned so many sins. Foul creature of corruption that I am! Have mercy!" Again she stiffened, fingers and toes tense, twisted—a horror. "Lord Jesus, remit my sins that I may go free! Our Lady, intercede for me—may I not blaspheme! Ah, Lord Jesus, King of Glory, may I receive Thy most sacred body and be healed. Take me while yet I am strong to give myself. Lord, my heart fails, have mercy!"

After a week of suffering she became quiet. Her face, dark as smoke-yellowed wax, delicate as the head of a bird, stood out against the white pillow. No one had ever seen her so young. A newborn child has eyes less clear, less full of wonder, lips less humble and pure. Despite the lines of pain under the eyes and the cheeks there was springtime in her emaciated face—it was hard to believe that such simple, natural serenity had ever known a beginning, it seemed that Lady Hodierne had always been what she was now, that she could never have been anything else.

"My lady, you are better, you will recover."

"I am happy. My fair daughters, my doves, my pearls. I love you so. Tell my Garin that I love him. My lord whom I loved so greatly and who never loved me—God grant he will be happier with his new lady. Tell him—to love her, to respect her—she is so young. . . . And tell Baldwin to be gentler, for love of me. Aliénor, my first-born daughter, you will soon have a husband—love him. Think of me—love him above all things—let him be to you father, mother, brother, son. Alis, my orphan child, child of my heart, God keep you—Milicent, be gentle.

"Call all my waiting-women and varlets. William, Bernard, bring my oak chests here. Take all that I have—to each his share. There's my gray fox. There's my red dress—unfold everything. There's my embroidered cloak. It is a pity I was so small—my dresses will not fit many. There's my silver necklace, and my inlaid necklace. My gold girdle. Let each of my maids take something. The silver pieces are for the men. The cup is for little John the Lame. I want today to be a feast day for you as it is for me. Keep that in memory of me.

"Don't cry, you silly creatures. I leave you to go to Our Lord Christ's Paradise. With Him I shall have nothing to fear. He has never lied to anyone. I am only sad at leaving you, and my daughters, and my son and my lord—all of you, tell him how much I love him. I have never had anything to reproach him with—believe me.

"My voice fails me—Lord, I come—my prayer is for him, Lord, not for myself, for him, Lord."

Lady Hodierne's head dropped back. She seemed to be still trying to speak. She was praying. Then she was seized with convulsions, but only for a few seconds. She died without much struggling, and the thing that lay there on the bed was so frail, so small, so insignificant that those who were about her could hardly believe that it was the body of Lady Hodierne. The corpse looked shrivelled; already it had lost the appearance of humanity. The tangled strands of brown hair seemed to have been stuck about the temples at random, and behind those closed lids there had never been eyes.

Still Aliénor could not believe that her mother was really dead—something, of course, had happened, something strange—she had been very ill after her miscarriage, then she had seemed to be getting better, she had received Communion and extreme unction—but after that—no, it was not true, they were all wrong, her mother had somehow gone away, hidden herself. Where was she? How to find her? How tell her all the things she had not had time to tell her before? Aliénor watched four varlets carry a small black coffin into the vault under the chapel. Garin sobbing, Milicent sobbing, Irma . . . and tomorrow, Aliénor suddenly thought, I must be at Buchie. And she wished that she too were dead.

Joceran and Fromond succeeded in stopping the men of Linnières just as they were entering the domain of Buchie. The brand bearers had already accomplished their mission; the wheat was burning, fire licked the apple trees and raged through the vineyards. The air was black with smoke.

"What now, you wolf, you wild boar!" shouted Fromond, when he saw Ansiau standing with his men on the farther side of the field. "What have I done to you that you should enter my land and fire my wheat? Did I ever in my life defy you?"

"Fromond of Buchie," Ansiau shouted back, making a trumpet of his hands, "you have allied yourself with my enemies, and I have sworn to punish you. You have taken a wife who was betrothed to one of my blood, and I shall not sleep in a bed until I have avenged the wrong."

"You will never sleep in a bed again," shouted Fromond. "My friends and yours be witnesses, and we shall see which of us is the better man."

Ansiau took his shield and lance from Thierri and rode into the medic field beside the burning field of wheat. Fromond too armed himself and rode to meet his enemy.

"Tell your people not to come near us," he shouted. "My troop and the men of Puiseaux will stay where they are."

Gathering speed, the two men bore down on each other. Ansiau bent over his saddle just in time; the lance only grazed his helmet. Fromond was carried to the farther end of the field before he could rein in his horse. Ansiau, lance pointed, head lowered, sped straight toward him, resolved not to let his enemy escape. Fromond spurred his horse so hard that blood spurted from its flanks; he drove forward, peering over the edge of his shield. The last thing that he saw was a red-and-blue helmet and the point of a lance—then a blinding light. There was a terrifying crash, a dull thud. Helmet, face, and skull smashed open, Fromond of Buchie sat his trembling horse for an instant—a trunk clad in a hauberk and holding a lance; his teeth had been knocked to splinters, his face was gone, blood flowed in torrents over his beard and the collar of his hauberk. Then he dropped forward in his saddle like a sack. Ansiau cut his stirrups and let him fall to the ground. Into the open skull he plunged the butt of his lance; the brain splashed out over helmet and grass.

When he saw Fromond fall Joceran took his lance and rode into the field, followed by his sons and Fromond's nephews. Seeing them, Herbert, Andrew, and Rainard rushed to Ansiau's assistance. Greatly outnumbered, the men of Linnières had much difficulty in extricating themselves from their dangerous position; they fell back into the forest, where they succeeded in making their way to an unfrequented road and shaking off their pursuers. After vainly seeking their enemies through all the forest of Breul, Joceran and his men returned to the field where they had left Fromond. Before the mutilated corpse of his son-in-law, Joceran began wringing his hands and tearing out his beard.

"Alas! The guilt of this calamity lies on me! And his mother is alive! And we have not yet avenged him!"

"What are you waiting for?" said one of Fromond's nephews, Galeran of Buchie. "Ansiau's cousin Simon the Red is a prisoner in your castle. We shall soon make him pay for his baron's crime."

"I go," cried Baldwin, putting his hand on his sword. "He shall not live a day longer than Fromond."

Baldwin and Galeran of Buchie set off at a gallop in the direction of Puiseaux, while Joceran arranged for a tent to be set up in the field and sent to Buchie for white sheets. He resolved to watch by the body himself with the dead knight's kinsmen.

In the white tent stood an improvised bier, decorated with green boughs. Fromond's lance, sword, and shield were disposed around the body. They had managed to wash the blood from his hauberk. The hands and feet had had to be tied. The head was concealed in a new helmet. Sitting at the foot of the bier, Joceran gave himself up to lamentation, tearing his hair and beard.

Baldwin and Galeran arrived at Puiseaux about nightfall and rushed into the hall, crying that they had come to kill Simon the Red to avenge Fromond's death. Simon was imprisoned in the cellar. Drawing their swords, the two men ran downstairs, and they would have killed him if Irma, Baldwin's wife, had not thrown herself between her husband and Galeran.

"In God's name," she said, "do not kill this defenseless man; it would be a shame upon us all and a sin upon your own souls. I will shield him with my own body until you surrender your swords; it shall not be said that you kill your prisoners. Who will surrender to you if you do this thing?" Their anger somewhat cooled, the two men handed their swords to Lady Irma, and Simon's life was saved. It was not until he returned upstairs to the hall that Baldwin learned of his stepmother's death. He went to the vault where her body lay buried and wept over it for a long time, striking his forehead against the flagstones.

Vengeance is sweet to the heart of a free man—Ansiau had tasted it when he plunged his lance into Fromond's skull. But it was an imperfect pleasure, for Fromond was not even kin to Baldwin, and Ansiau's mutilated nose would run blood until Baldwin had been castrated. However, Fromond had taken Andrew's betrothed—he had earned his death. Ansiau felt no regret for what he had done.

But his youth took its toll. To have fallen upon a man—and a man he knew—and have made him into that thing of horror, that sort of quintain with a seething face—he could not yet believe that it had been so easy. He sometimes thought that Fromond was not wholly dead, that he would come to him and protest, demand back his face and his brain; somewhere, surely, that bleeding soul so suddenly driven from its body was calling for vengeance upon the assassin. At Buchie Castle a mother was mourning and praying God to punish the slayer of her son; and a mother's tears are stronger than offerings and vows. He, Ansiau, had no mother to pray for him. Sometimes in dreams he saw Fromond come to his bed and sit on his chest—ah, that bleeding, faceless head! Then he would waken Alis and take her in his arms. Sleepily she would ask: "What is the matter, my lord?"

"My sweet, I am sad."

"You drank too much, your stomach is troubling you."

Reassured by her voice, he would huddle against her, and she would caress him as if he were a child, stroking his hair and his forehead. "There, there, my love, I am here, all is well."

Often during the long winter evenings he would go out into the courtyard and climb the rampart and walk, his eyes fixed unseeingly on the yellowish fog that closed the horizon. The forest was gray and icy, the howling of wolves could be heard even inside the castle. It was a drear winter. The mere sight of that foul sky and the naked forest froze his heart.

It was at such a time that he discovered in the castle a thing so warm that he was never cold again as long as he could keep it with him. A little thing that had been in his house for twenty months—but he had never paid much attention to it. Alis was always looking after the youngest child, and the little thing which was the elder had been turned over to Haumette and no one seemed to think of it after that.

One day Haumette brought the child to the baron to tell him that it had cut its sixth tooth. And its father was astonished at the sight of the big doll with its swaddled legs and dimpled arms and blond curls.

"There," said Haumette, holding the child up, "my boy is going to smile for the baron, he is a very good boy."

The little round face was rather pale and marked with pink spots from fleabites. The big round blue eyes were laughing and surprised, the soft pink lips parted a little. Clumsily, Ansiau took the little thing in both his hands, which suddenly seemed enormous. The child gave a chuckle of pleasure and then began to coo and pull at the gold ring in the baron's ear. Ansiau blinked and laughed, rather bewildered.

When his nurse wanted to take him back, the child put his arms around the baron's neck and pressed his warm cheek against his father's face. Ansiau broke into a laugh of admiration and pride. He was conquered for life.

"Haumette," he said, "do you think he likes me?" He unfastened his earring and gave it to the child, then gave him the buckle of his cloak too; he listened, rapt in adoration, while the child cooed and gurgled. "I want him to sleep downstairs," he said, "beside the great bed; you can put your bed beside ours." All that evening he plagued Haumette with foolish questions: "Is he fond of horses? Would he like some toys? Does he understand French? Does he look like his father or like his mother? Will he have a steady hand and a good aim?"

Alis finally became jealous of Haumette and told Ansiau to leave her in peace: "He is my child, not hers."

From the moment of that first caress, which had gone to his heart and soul, Ansiau had unquestioningly accepted the strange little white and gold creature with the bulging forehead. He loved his son as an equal. The child had become fond of him, and he was as proud of its fondness as he would have been of the friendship of a count. He spoke of him as he would speak of a man: "He wants this, he likes that." And Andrew, for whom children scarcely existed, thought that his friend might just as well have fallen in love with a sword or a horse.

Women have a language for children, but a man who has never spoken to a child in his life must talk to it either in the language of grown men or not at all. The conversations between this father and his son were always very serious. The father spoke little, and chiefly made plans for the future— "When you're big enough, I will teach you to shoot a bow . . . When you're big enough, you shall have Courante's second foal . . . When you're big enough, we shall go to Troyes and joust together." The son spent most of his time playing with his father's hair and beard, pulling the rings off his fingers, playing with his daggers. He had a way of kissing with his mouth wide open which made Ansiau's cheeks and nose wet. He laughed and gurgled endlessly; Ansiau sometimes teased him with little taps on the nose and forehead; but he was so gentle-handed that it never really hurt.

When Alis told him that she was expecting a third baby, he said nothing and she was offended. "You ought to be glad to have more children," she said. "You know now that my children are handsome and strong."

"The eldest is enough for me," said Ansiau. "I need no more. I shall not love them."

"It is not good," Andrew said to him one day, "to become too fond of a young child. You cannot be sure that he will live."

"Do you wish me harm, brother? Why say that he will not live?"

"That oak there may bear a thousand leaves and a thousand acorns every year. Not ten will take root, and not two will grow to be oaks. There are many children born who have not the seed of manhood in them—out of fifty, are there twenty who reach eighteen? A child is not a man, brother. There are children who grow to be men, and then is the time to love them. But what use is it for you to say: My child will be this or that? Are you God, or a prophet? Leave him to the women."

Herbert, seated at table at the viscount's right, spread his long thick red beard over his blue silk tunic; then, in his drunkenness, he put his right arm around the waist of a young and beautiful girl clad in a clinging red dress. Long green ear pendants hung down beside her white neck. Two white greyhounds, sitting in Herbert's lap, licked at his plate.

The viscount had said: "Herbert of Linnières delivered me from the hands of the French king's men, wherefore I vow to make him my companion and my brother; he shall eat at my table and sleep in my bed. I give him my silver cup and my pelisse of fox and sable and the best of my hauberks. I enfeoff him of the revenues of all the forests in the castellany for the year to come, and he shall live with me at Paiens for as long as he pleases and whenever he pleases."

A last youth for Herbert of Linnières, who was getting on toward fifty and growing fat. Even now there were bluish pockets under his eyes, his nose and cheeks were a network of violet veins, his beard was becoming dull despite repeated dyeings, and his eyes had lost their luster and looked like faded violets. He was beginning to suffer from pains in his intestines, headaches behind the eyes, and spells of dizziness.

At Paiens, where he had the right to use or abuse the viscount's hospitality, he took a bath every day and was served by beautiful girls—not noble, of course, but all under fifteen. He dressed in silk and fine linen, wore golden earrings and jewelled finger rings. He had bought two pure-bred Arab horses, and when he went into the country to hunt, everyone marvelled at his white greyhounds and his golden falcons.

Unless he got drunk, he could not sleep at night. The anguish that tortured him became more poignant night by night, the vice clamped tighter every day. Was it fear of having committed a sin for which there was no forgiveness? Or sadness at never finding pleasures violent enough, deep enough, lasting enough to satisfy him fully? His minutes, his seconds of pleasure and forgetfulness were becoming shorter and shorter, the edge was wearing off, the terrible day must come when every charm would have lost its power. His soul at bay saw itself driven from all its refuges, all its lairs, stripped and cast out into a vast waterless desert. On hunting evenings Herbert sometimes took a wolf or a fox which was still alive and drove his dagger into it again and again until there was not an unpierced spot in its body; he was rich enough to allow himself the luxury of spoiling a pelt.

During five or six months of the year—spring and summer—Herbert brought his whole family to live with him at Paiens: his four sons, his nephew Ansiau, his two sons-in-law, his younger brother Girard the Blond. During the hunting season the viscount's castle was crowded with people, the air was unbreathable, from cellar to roof there was a perpetual uproar.

Ansiau found life at Paiens very much to his taste. He hunted all day, or practiced archery or casting stones. Every night there was a gay banquet— wine, songs, blazing candles, glittering plate, bright cloaks embroidered in gold thread. Alis was always ready to welcome him into the great bed, where they were somewhat crowded since they shared it with Andrew, Simon, and Simon's wife. Alis now had three children: the two boys and a girl, Mahaut. All three slept in a big cradle beside the bed and at night when the baby cried Alis got up and gave it the breast.

At twenty-two, Ansiau of Linnières was one of the handsomest knights in the castellany of Paiens. He was strong-bodied and thick-necked, with arms like iron bars. The curve of his back, the way he carried his head, gave him a haughty air—his hips were narrow, and his long heavy legs supported him firmly; in hand-to-hand fighting he had never staggered or fallen back so much as an inch. A short but luxuriant brown beard covered his cheeks and chin, and his strong eyebrows met over his nose. Sometimes a dreamy gentleness came into his eyes, then again they would grow hard. Despite the ugliness of his mutilated nostril, his face was not unpleasant to look at, with its deep tan and high color, its ardor and its seriousness. But still the brand of Puiseaux was on it—four years, and Baldwin still at large! But Ansiau was not the man to let an insult go unpunished—he was only waiting his chance; and afterwards, if Alis wanted to cry—why, let her!

For four years little Ansiet and his father had loved each other dearly, with a love so gentle and so courteous that people were astonished to find such delicacy of devotion and such loyalty in a mere child's heart. Ansiet was always happy to serve his father at table, to unlace his boots and gaiters at night; he brought him the lizards and May bugs he caught, the birds he shot; whenever people gave him delicacies he wanted to share them with his father. Ansiau set him on the front of his saddle and took him with him hunting or when he made the rounds of the guard posts—in rain or snow he sheltered him under his great woolen cloak. The boy had a round head and blond hair—flax-blond, almost white. He had a slender neck, eyes that seemed always to be asking questions, a wide mobile mouth perpetually ready to laugh or cry. He was graceful, and a little frail—"born of too young a mother," as Lady Adela put it. He took after his father only in his wide, radiant smile and his habit of tossing his head to throw back his hair.

Lady Alis could not help being jealous of her baron's preference for his eldest son. When Ansiau sat down on the bench beside her and took Ansiet in his arms, she never failed to put Herbert in his lap, and when he kissed the elder she always saw to it that the younger should receive an equal number of kisses. "He hasn't lice or the itch," she said, "he is your son as much as his brother."

"Lady, I love his brother and I do not love him."

"What, baron! I carried him for nine months, I bore him in pain, I fed him with my milk, and you will not make an effort to love him? I have not deserved this insult; he is no hunchback and no fool."

"Then I will love him to please you, lady."

But little Herbert was hardly more to him than the children of his cousin.

Yet Herbert was a fine boy. He was big and strong for his age and promised to be stronger than his elder brother. Very blond and very white, he had a big head and a round face as pale as the moon; his full red lips, little cushions swollen to bursting, and his large, steady, unblinking eyes gave him a sulky look. He was always standing in corners, hands behind his back, round belly protruding, blond head bent, and big eyes staring straight ahead under his bulging forehead. He was obstinate and willful, talked little and badly, never laughed, and almost never cried. He seemed slow-witted, but Alis knew better: those eyes of his saw everything, noticed everything, judged everything. In his rages he became quick and sure of himself, at once powerful and agile. "No one will match him in guile and strength," Alis thought, "nor in beauty." Meanwhile, he was a ferocious little beast who came out of his torpor only to bite and scratch and claw and kick and scream. Yet he loved his mother; first he had been jealous of his father, then of his little sister Ala who lived only two months, then of Mahaut, who clung to life more tenaciously—Alis nursed Mahaut for thirteen months.

As flax-headed as her two brothers, Mahaut had brown eyes, she was merry and pretty—she was only two, but everyone in the castle admired her. The baron was very proud of her. And Lady Alis thought: "Ala would have been even prettier," but only she knew it.

Joceran had a father's heart. When he had seen his favorite daughter at the viscount's castle, sitting at table beside her baron, he had felt his anger and rancor melt. Moreover, he had recently quarrelled with the lady of Buchie and saw no reason for continuing to bear his son-in-law ill will. He accosted Alis as she was strolling in the castle courtyard with other ladies— she was carrying her little girl in her arms, and her two boys were clinging to her skirts.

"What, children, no greeting for your grandfather?" Joceran said. "By my faith, they take more after me than after Ansiau. Your youngest son, my daughter, looks just like Baldwin did at his age."

"I am afraid so, my lord," said Alis, happy to see that her father was not angry with her. "He is so bad and noisy and quarrelsome that I don't know what to do with him. Even Baldwin must have been easier to bring up."

"It means he will be a good fighter. You have changed, my pigeon. You are taller and prettier.—There—I see that I shall have to make peace with your fool of a baron since you are so fond of him. Besides, he has many kinsmen, and he is so strong and so brave that I could be proud of such a son-in-law. Tell me—what would he ask for security?"

"I am afraid that he will not agree to anything," sighed Alis, rubbing her head against her father's gray beard. "He has nothing against you, but he hates Baldwin, because of the brand he put on his face. If Baldwin falls into his hands he will have him castrated. All that I can do is to warn you."

"Baldwin will come to a bad end one way or another," her father growled. "What a punishment from God to have such a son! In all fairness, I can understand your baron's attitude. But I cannot disown Baldwin before my family."

Since Lady Hodierne's death the housekeeping at Puiseaux had gone from bad to worse. Even Joceran was aware of it, and he vaguely regretted his dead spouse, the only one of them all who had put up with him long enough for him to become accustomed to her. Irma, Baldwin's wife, managed the house, but she could not make herself respected. When Joceran was at the castle he and Irma spouted torrents of insults at each other while Baldwin, somber-eyed, sat in his great chair, ready at any moment to throw himself on his father with a knife or a stool. Baldwin was not a bad son, but his love for Irma turned his head. He was thirty and Irma thirty-three—worn out by two husbands and eight confinements and God knew what spells and infernal practices, for she was full of such things. She was faded and sallow, she had never been beautiful. But she had so bewitched Baldwin that for him she was the most beautiful woman in the world and the best.

For years father and son had been on terms of grudging and slightly scornful friendship.

"Are you not ashamed to change your mind like a weathercock?" said Baldwin.

"If an angel came to take you to Paradise," said Joceran, "you would begin by sticking your knife into him. That is all you know. You never change your mind because you have no more brains than a boar."

Ansiau and his uncles were at Paiens when they were summoned to Troyes by the Court of Peers, for the lady of Buchie had finally found a champion who had offered to challenge Ansiau and accuse him of murdering Fromond. Until now no one had dared to do so, for it was generally known that Fromond had been killed in a fair fight and before witnesses. But Fromond's old mother wanted revenge at any price and had offered all her possessions to a poor but brave knight in the neighborhood, Walter of Chaource, if he would defend her cause before the count—she maintained that her son had been taken by treachery.

When Baldwin of Puiseaux heard of it he flew into a rage and showered his father with reproaches.

"Now what will people think of you," he said, "you who promised to avenge Fromond? You pledged your word before his body was cold. And now you let someone else avenge him. Did you not say that you would allow yourself to be called coward before the whole castellany if you did not avenge him? And you sit by and watch while another openly takes vengeance away from you."

"He was neither my uncle nor my nephew," said Joceran.

"He was your son-in-law. And that was why Ansiau killed him—as you very well know. Do you want it said that you are afraid of Ansiau and his uncles? I shall go to Troyes at once and challenge Walter of Chaource and fight Ansiau in his stead."

"I forbid you to do it," said Joceran. "We cannot take on so many enemies at once—we are already at war with Breul. Better that you should wait: if Ansiau proves strongest in the trial, you can attack him without having to challenge Walter of Chaource."

"Very well," said Baldwin. "Ansiau will have to pass through Puiseaux on his way home, I shall lie in wait for him at Chaource crossroads, and Fromond will be avenged one way or the other. We have waited long enough."

For many hours Ansiau sustained a hand-to-hand battle so desperate that several times he believed he could fight no longer. His lance was shivered, his horse killed, he had nothing left but his good sword. He swung it in both hands, bringing it down, now right, now left, on the sword of his opponent. Walter was thirty-five, stockier and heavier than Ansiau and agile in all his movements. Time and again the edge of his sword grazed Ansiau's helmet. Time and again the knights around the lists thought that Walter of Chaource was winning, and Herbert the Red began to tear his beard in grief while Arnelle of Buchie shouted for joy: "Walter, Walter, quick, that I may see his brains and his guts!"

"Alas, must I die? I can do no more. My soul is leaving me, I am so weary and wounded in body. God, God, I am innocent, help me!" He hardly knew how it happened, but his sword suddenly came down with a dull splintering sound. Walter, his right shoulder fractured, tottered and fell.

Ansiau flung his sword on the ground and made a great sign of the cross. He turned toward the line of knights along the lists, toward the judges and the witnesses.

"My lords," he said, "I would have you know that God came to my aid; and if this knight can fight no longer, it is not my doing, but a miracle, for I had reached the end of my strength. Judge, then, if I have not proved my cause. More than that I want not from him—neither from him nor from the lady of Buchie."

He was at once surrounded by his squires and cousins; they led him from the field and helped him to take off his armor; he was bruised all over and covered with black-and-blue spots. By the judgment of the peers Walter of Chaource was sentenced to have his right hand cut off for calumny and false accusation, and the lady of Buchie paid a heavy fine to save him from undergoing this punishment.

Some days later Ansiau's kinsmen left Troyes, but Ansiau himself was imprudent enough to remain with only Thierri and two men-at-arms. He said that he wanted to rest for a time in the house of his godfather, William of Nangi. But it was another reason which kept him in Troyes—he had heard that the lady of Chalmiers was there, and he wanted to see her once again. He was well punished for his evil intent, for he found her gone and he ran into grave peril on his homeward journey because of his insufficient escort.

At the crossroads, on the road from Troyes to Chaource, Ansiau suddenly saw two blue-and-yellow shields before him, two armored horses, the points of two lances. "Traitor, defend yourself! Remember the brain of Fromond of Buchie!"

"Judas," cried Ansiau, recognizing Baldwin's voice, "you can well see that I am unready. Let me put on my armor, my soldiers have it here. And my horse is not trained for battle."

"I grant you time to take your shield and lance: a man who knows how to fight needs nothing more."

Baldwin's horse was wounded in the eye and went down; at the same moment Ansiau's horse reared and threw its rider. Ansiau was vainly summoning strength to rise when he saw Baldwin slowly closing on him. His sword was raised and he was panting and grunting like a wild boar. Ansiau had just time to lift his shield above his head. And suddenly hate flooded through him, so burning and so painful that he felt a sort of spasm in his heart and soul and believed that he would die. He picked himself up, still covered by his shield, and slowly retreated until he had his back against the trunk of an oak. Over his head he saw a lance swaying, the lance of Baldwin's companion, who was still mounted.

"Hola, Baldwin of Puiseaux, who gave you leave to attack this man on our land?"

The barons of Breul came up at a gallop—one of their soldiers had told them that there was a battle at the crossroads. Baldwin was so enraged that he almost threw himself on them with his sword. But they were more numerous than his party. They rescued Ansiau and helped him to find his horse. Ansiau and his men reached Linnières in pitiful plight, for they had been obliged to travel by forest paths to avoid another attack.

Man-hunt. In the forest of Puiseaux, Baldwin was hunting the stag, never suspecting that he himself was the quarry for which a stalwart band of poachers lay in wait. Hidden behind a hazel thicket, Ansiau, Herbert, Andrew, and Simon reined in their horses and listened: there were the notes of a hunting horn growing ever more distant, there were the thudding hoofbeats of a heavy palfrey carrying a heavy rider. Dead branches cracked, and the echo rattled among the tree trunks. "He went through here, Robert. The dogs have lost the scent." Baldwin appeared in the open glade. His hair was dishevelled, his face red and sweaty, his coarse unbleached linen tunic soaked with rain and dew. His squire Robert followed him, carrying his hunting lance and shield.

"My horse just shied—there must be a bear about," said Baldwin. Then, riding toward the thicket, he saw four men's heads emerging from the leaves.

Very pale, Baldwin turned to his squire.

"Robert, ride for reinforcements—fast. The men of Linnières are here, I recognize Herbert's red hair."

But Robert did not have time to turn his horse—a javelin found its mark between his shoulder blades.

Then Baldwin whirled his horse around and struck into the path to Puiseaux. Riddled with javelins, his horse snorted, reared with pain, then stumbled into a tree. Baldwin had barely time to leap clear. Ansiau was not ten paces away.

Gasping, Baldwin crawled through the underbrush, sending hares and partridges scurrying in every direction. Wet branches struck him in the face, thorns tore his clothing. Just behind him branches cracked, leaves parted with a whistling hiss—it was Ansiau following his track, gasping, sniffing the air for the scent of his enemy. Through the branches Baldwin saw two red heads —Simon's and Herbert's.

Dagger in hand, Baldwin slipped on through the grass, stopping at the slightest sound. The trees became scarcer, the thickets less dense. Fearful that he might become bogged in the swamp, he stopped and crouched in the grass, listening. In every direction he heard the crack of trodden branches. Andrew —his was the blond head—stepped out of the bushes and looked about, seeking his enemy's track. Baldwin stood up, brandishing his dagger, and walked toward him—their blades crossed. "I have him, I have him!" Andrew cried. "This way, father, brother!" Beset on all sides, Baldwin defended himself like a wounded bear. His knife was torn from his hands, he fought with his fists and elbows, and so effectively that more than once he shook off and drove back all four of his enemies, as a boar throws off a pack of harrying dogs. He was the heaviest and strongest man of them all.

But he was alone against four and his strength gave out. He was seized, bound, hoisted onto a horse, crosswise over the saddle. The horse moved with difficulty under his weight. The road was long, Baldwin's hanging head filled with blood and turned purple. Through the red circles that spun before his eyes, he saw the smoking belly of the horse, the dust and stones of the road; the world appeared to be upside down—the sky was below him, over his head the ground and the horse's hoofs.

The riders reached the tower of Seuroi after a half day's journey over forest roads. Baldwin was carried into the hall amid shouts of joy; varlets tied him hand and foot to the four corners of the bed and there he was castrated by Rainard and Edme, Rainard's horse dealer, in the presence of Ansiau, Herbert, and Herbert's sons.

"Now," said Ansiau, fingering his nose, "everyone will be afraid when he sees my scar. No one will want to laugh at it again."

Rainard wiped his bloody hands. In a tense, heavy silence broken by Baldwin's pitiful groans, Herbert mopped his forehead, for it was a stormy night and the air in the room was stifling. Through the open door a pallid dawn fell on the blackened straw with which the stone floor was strewn. A torch cast its reddish light on the pale faces of the men standing around the bed, on Baldwin's white, hairy expanses of flesh.

The first moment of triumph passed, Ansiau stared in astonishment at the white, drawn face of his enemy—eyes closed, forehead beaded with sweat, mouth frothing, hair glued to his temples, Baldwin had nothing now to arouse hatred, to set the blood boiling. Ansiau felt something that was almost pity.

"After all," he said thoughtfully, "he is punished enough. He has paid his debt to me, and I wish him ill no longer. Uncle, I want to give him clean clothes, and I shall ask you to let me have some old wine from your cellar for him to drink. Tomorrow I will have him carried to Puiseaux Bridge on a good litter, so that he may never say that I ill-treated him when he was disabled."

"You owe him that," said Herbert. "By my faith, he was a brave man. His kinsmen shall learn what it costs to insult the men of Linnières."

The following day the soldiers who guarded Puiseaux Bridge found a litter covered with wolf skins on the road, and on the litter lay their baron's son, wrapped in a woolen cloak. With cries of grief they carried him to Puiseaux.

When Joceran saw his son thus mutilated and dishonored, he roared with grief and began to tear out his hair and beard. "Ah! when will I have done with that man! Alas! Baldwin, my first-born son, that I must mourn for you while yet you live! What have I done to that wolf that he seeks to wipe out my house?"

Stretched on the bed, pale, his eyes closed, Baldwin for the first time in his life seemed heavy-hearted and hopeless. "I am done for," he said. "My life is over, I can only die. I am your eldest, be just to my sons."

Seeing him so sad and so softened, Joceran felt his heart swell. "By my beard," he said, "I shall not leave you unavenged. May God curse me if I do not pay Ansiau back all that he has made you suffer. You shall outlive me and you shall hold the fief after my death as if you had remained whole."

"How should I dare to show my face before other knights," Baldwin mourned. "Better that I die."

"By the body of St. Thiou, I will deliver him to you bound hand and foot," roared Joceran. "Weep not, my fair falcon, my blood, my pride! You break my heart. I swear to you that you shall have satisfaction, or I am not a Christian. Within a month from this day Ansiau and his uncles shall be more to be pitied than you."

Ansiau had good reason to believe that his revenge would not escape notice in the neighborhood and that he would have to answer for it in one way or another. "If I come safely out of it," he said, "I will be feared through all the countryside."

He summoned his uncles and his vassals and barricaded himself in his castle.

When Alis learned what he had done to her brother, she began to weep and lament. "Ah, Baldwin, son of a noble father! Unmanned, degraded! Alas, my wretched sister Irma! Alas, my poor nephews!"

"Lady," said Ansiau, "is this your loyalty? You promised me that you would renounce your family. You told me that you did not love Baldwin."

"God! Could I know? Have you not spilled my own blood? See—I have his mouth and his eyes, and can you look me in the face? Why did you not send me back to my father? You do not love me, you hate me, go away, you shall no longer sleep in my arms."

"I shall do so as often as I please, lady, and well you know it. Let me hear no more of your complaining."

A month later Ansiau and his kinsmen received a message from Troyes summoning them to appear in court again to answer for outrages and mutilations inflicted upon the body of the count's liege man and loyal knight, Baldwin of Puiseaux.

"That is Joceran," said Ansiau scornfully, "he does not know how to take justice into his own hands—he appeals to the count, like a townsman." He sent an answer to say that he was ill and would not come. He was sure that he would be ambushed on the road if he went.

If Alis had not come of good blood, she could have forgotten the shame that had been put upon her father's son. Baldwin's mother might be Blanche of Montméjart—nevertheless he was the heir to Puiseaux. Many times a day she went white and red when she looked at her husband's uncles and cousins, for before her eyes there floated the hideous picture of her brother's naked body mutilated by their hands. "Can they see me without boasting to themselves that they have dishonored my kindred? Must they not think me a light woman who allows her family to be insulted and says nothing? The shame is upon me," she thought, "and my baron had no pity on me and my blood. What can I do to justify myself in the eyes of his kinsfolk and the whole countryside? People will say: 'She sold and betrayed her own lineage to sleep with a man.'"

Yet, God knew, Ansiau could not live all his life with Baldwin's brand on his face.

"Men," Alis thought—at night when her little girl cried, or by day when the flames danced on the logs in the hearth. They were always so. They must always be hurting one another, always be wanting to stab or hack or disembowel one another—they were all one-eyed or lame or scarred, one had lost a hand, another two fingers. Baldwin was the last man to let an insult go unpunished. And how could she help loving her fair falcon ambushed by such hardy sparrow hawks?

Had she ever had anything to reproach her husband with during these six years of their marriage? Never had he failed to give her gifts, weekdays as well as holidays; never had he struck her, even with the flat of his hand; never in her presence had he turned his eyes on another woman. Even Catherine had to admit it—he was as good a husband as a man could be. If he sometimes lost his temper with others, to her he was always sweetness itself. There was no shame in loving such a husband, particularly when he was her first, the man who had taken her at fourteen.

Alas, what ailed them, every one of them? Was life like that? Must they always be cutting into flesh—and always into her own flesh, her father, her brothers, her husband—her sons, when they grew to be men?

Alis dreamed red dreams—always red—a chaos of painted shields, men's entrails, mutilated heads, and blows, endless blows—she woke with a start, thinking that a lance or an ax had struck her. No, she no longer liked war, it was too painful. Now she liked winter, despite the cold and the gray short days, because in winter she could keep her beloved by her and take her pleasure of him—God, how avidly!—who knew if she would have him long? Her two sons were little, she could cover them with her body, warm them, hide them within her as if they were still inside her womb. But her baron, alas! was so big that she grew weary of counting all the vulnerable spots in his body. Carefully she went over his arms, his helmet, his hauberk, his shield, and thought that after all they were only iron and wood—dead things. And she stuffed them with amulets, magic roots, holy symbols. But there again—who knew but that the enemy had charms stronger than hers?

Lady Adela died that winter, a few days before Christmas, in a state of sin; she had not had time to confess or to receive the sacraments. Suddenly she had turned dark red, almost purple, her tongue had lolled out of her mouth. From the bench on which she sat she fell to the ground as heavy and lifeless as a sack of flour. Carried to her bed, she lay there, snoring horribly, her eyes bloodshot, her legs and arms flung wide, her fat heavy hands dangling, the fingers spread like a baby's.

Neither bleeding nor cold water restored her to consciousness. She died during the night—rigid, impenetrable, more terrible than ever in that implacable dumbness which nothing could break. All night candles burned in the bedchamber where two waiting-women and Richeut washed the body, discovering that Lady Adela had been a woman too, wiping the sweat from her enormous marble breasts, and combing her gray hair, long concealed under a white cap.

She who had ruled the castle for so many years was laid out in the chapel on a long table, and her daughters-in-law, waiting-women, and varlets had perpetually to remind themselves not to run to her and ask: "Lady, what is next to do? How much wine shall I draw? What hangings will be used for the funeral?" Black, bloated, and threatening, Lady Adela's face seemed to say: "Shift for yourselves. I have worked through my day."

Old Hugh, seated in a chair beside his wife's body, remained motionless for hours on end, only sniffling from time to time, or swallowing the tears which ran down his cheeks in two thin trickles—his white mustache was wet with them. He had lost the power of speech, and could only moan like a deaf-mute in answer to anything said to him.

Alis inherited the old dame's bunch of keys, as well as her scolding voice and her rough hands, quick to strike. At twenty, Alis was a strong, robust woman, tall and still slender; she had round high breasts which moved like two waves when she walked, for her walk was swift and decided. She had a narrow waist, long legs, slim ankles; and her head, set high on her round white neck, steadfastly bore the weight of her two long braids, which swung against her rump and hips when she walked. When she entered the hall, clad in her red woolen dress and tightly girt with a heavy, embroidered girdle, anyone who saw her for the first time said: "Truly a noble woman, and one to bring forth fair issue. If her husband dies, she will not search long for a second."

By spring the men of Linnières were forced to leave the castle, for they were without hay and wheat. Their fields had been burned by the men of Puiseaux, and there was famine at home, the bread was made from bran, and even so it was scantily doled out. The villagers, who did not even have bran bread, dragged themselves to the castle gate. Ansiau let them come in, and Alis let them take what was left of the pig feed and horse fodder; on Sundays she doled out bread too. It became necessary to slaughter, one by one, all the pigs, the beeves, the sheep—men-at-arms are great eaters. As for hunting, it was not safe to go beyond Linnières marsh, the men of Puiseaux were prowling all about.

Ansiau resolved to throw himself on the count's mercy—he had revenged an insult which he had carried on his face for four years; no one could accuse him of having taken his enemy unawares. So long as a freeman in a Christian country had a right to vengeance, the count's laws could reproach him with nothing. The ride through the country, however, would be dangerous, for the men of Puiseaux were prowling about the forest and keeping watch on the roads. They must go in a body and well armed—Ansiau had no desire to be castrated in his turn, still less did he wish to get one of his cousins killed. So the watchword was: Let no man stray from the troop. Ansiau's plan was to reach Chaource by way of Bernon, and from Chaource make his way to Troyes, enter the count's presence barefoot and wearing only a shift, explain his reasons for having refused to come the previous year, and clear himself of Joceran's accusation—at most he would be forced to pay a fine for not having appeared before the court. In any case, at Troyes he had friends. He had Abner to lend him money, he could have his men's hauberks put in order, and buy wheat at Chaource on his way home.

Yet some men must be left to guard the castle. Ansiau and Herbert decided that no one would risk entering Linnières marsh in springtime—it was enough to guard the tower of Seuroi, which stood at a crossroads just opposite Hervi. His lady could guard it, they would give her ten soldiers, that was enough, the tower was small and solidly built.

Alis was four months gone with child, but she bore up well under her pregnancies. She resigned herself as well as she could to leaving her two boys and Mahaut to Haumette, and followed the men to Seuroi.

The little troop stopped at Seuroi for the night. Uncles and nephews warmed themselves before the great fire of branches which Rainard had ordered lighted in a hearth as black as hell. Alis, seated on a bench close to the fire, warmed her numb hands. Outside, gusts of wind set the yet leafless treetops creaking—the men crossed themselves; on such nights the souls of men who had perished in the forest lamented and wept. Rainard himself, who had been suffering from a bad cough since fall, gasped and spat into the fire. "A bad season," he said, "a bad season," and he shivered and wrapped his old greasy rags about him.

That night it rained in torrents. It seemed that all the water in the sky was being poured down on Seuroi Tower through a vast funnel. Alis, huddled against her husband, heard the rain streaming and cascading down the walls —outside it was flowing in rivers through the courtyard and the moat; every other sound was blotted out by the noise of water pouring into water. "God, the children!" she thought. "The castle is so damp! And they will want to go wading in the courtyard—if only Haumette won't let them!" And then she thought that the men might be set upon on the road between Bernon and Chaource, and who knew what Baldwin would not do to Ansiau if ever he caught him? Life was not happy.

Dawn was as dark as night—they heard prime rung from the church of St. Mary's-of-the-Angels, far away, they yawned, sleep was just beginning to be sweet despite the fleas and the prickly straw. Alis rose and stretched her numb arms. She must help her baron to wash and comb his hair, he was in haste and nervous. Herbert and Rainard were laced into their hauberks by their squires. Andrew inspected his stirrups—at Seuroi, men and horses bedded in the same room, the horses were led down into the courtyard over a cleated plank.

The courtyard was strewn with tangled yellow reeds floating slowly toward the black palisade whose stakes were deep in mud. One by one the men gave their lady a farewell kiss and went down the plank with their horses. Ansiau held her longer than the others.

"Lady, if I do not come back—"

"Do not say that," she said.

"Lady, if I die, do not go back to your father. Marry one of my cousins."

It was almost light in the courtyard when the varlets opened the gate and threw planks across the brimming moat. Limping painfully, Rainard approached his strawberry horse, when a sudden fit of coughing seized him and he fell to the ground spitting blood. Two squires helped him to rise. Gasping, Rainard took another step toward his horse, and caught at the saddle to keep from falling.

"Brother," he said to Herbert, "I shall stay here."

In the confusion, Herbert had not been aware of the weakness which had come over his brother; his squire was fastening his gauntlets at the wrists and he was patting his horse. And Rainard's voice had been so stifled that Herbert had not understood him. "What?" Herbert said, without turning. "Speak louder."

"I shall stay here," Rainard gasped.

"What? God in Heaven! What is the matter with you?"

The sick man smiled weakly, as if to excuse himself.

"I will let Bernier take my horse. Have him lengthen the left stirrup."

"Let them put you in the saddle," said Herbert. "You will soon feel better."

"No. I am going in. Farewell."

Herbert said "Farewell," and Rainard dragged himself to the plank which served as a stairway and sat down. For an instant, Herbert's blue eyes became misty, he blinked and sniffled, then it was over. He had already mounted and was picking his way carefully along the muddy road when the image of his old brother and comrade, collapsed on the stair like a crushed toad, once more passed before his eyes. He thought he should never see his brother again.

Alis was far from pleased to learn that she was to share the bed with Rainard—Rainard had castrated Baldwin with his own hands (aided by Edme, it was true). It was Ansiau who had ordered the thing done, but the blood was on Rainard's hands, and if Baldwin ever caught him alive he would cut off his hands as if he were a peasant. But the man was Ansiau's uncle, and Alis could not but treat him as a kinsman.

To serve her she had brought only a little girl of twelve, whom she kept by her day and night. Rainard's ten soldiers, who made up the tower guard, did not inspire her with much confidence. For her protection the baron had also left a young squire from Linnières, named Milon of Le Cagne. Seventeen years of age, Milon was strong, quick, and nimble; he was a cousin of the baron's squire Thierri and deeply devoted to the house of Linnières.

As soon as the knights had left, Alis decided that Rainard must be put to bed and made to drink red wine to replace the blood he had lost. The sick man had managed to drag himself to the hearth—there he lay on the flagstones and from time to time gave a plaintive groan. At first he refused to go to bed—he was cold, he wanted to stay by the fire. Alis said: "I will have stones heated for you. You will be better off in bed. Your wine is ready now, but I shall not give it to you until you are in bed."

The old fellow raised his head and gave her a strange look—it was as if he wanted to laugh.

"You're a beautiful woman, aren't you?" he said in his lifeless voice, and his two long eyeteeth reappeared in the corners of his mouth.

Alis raised her eyebrows—it was the first time she had ever heard Rainard trying to be gallant. She shrugged her shoulders, and Rainard, who had felt touched and had wanted to say something pleasant, closed his eyes. In the end he let them put him to bed, cover him with wolf skins, and surround him with hot stones.

"And now drink this," said Alis, "but not too fast, it might give you a shock."

Rainard said: "What a fuss you're making. Let me die in peace."

"There. Don't talk any more. You had a bad night, that's all."

Rainard gave another mocking laugh, and finally lay still.

Seeing that he had fallen asleep Alis went to the captain of the Seuroi guard, Rainard's bailiff, Florimond. She told him that she wanted to keep the keys in her own hands. Florimond said: "I am a man, and I can keep them better than you." To which Alis replied that she had a good knife in her girdle and, furthermore, Milon of Le Cagne was there to protect her. "When the barons return," she said, "I will speak to them for you if you obey me."

Florimond handed her the keys, with a smile which plainly meant: "I know I can get them back whenever I want."

Florimond was a man from the south and his past was wrapped in darkness. It was known that he slept with Rainard. He was not an unattractive fellow, with a pale face, a very black beard, and very red lips. Alis disliked him because he was insolent to her. He was always trying to play the master. He said outright that the baron and his uncles would certainly be thrown into prison at Troyes and lose their heads for having disobeyed the count. "And then you will have to depend on us to defend your brats," he concluded. For Florimond, there was not a man on earth who was not in imminent danger of losing his head—all it took was a summons to Troyes to answer an accusation of this or that and, biff! the block—if not the wheel and the rack. Alis usually refused to listen to him, yet she began to feel somewhat uneasy—two weeks passed, then a third, and still the knights had not returned. The stock of food was diminishing, and men from Puiseaux and Hervi prowled around the tower and tried to climb the palisade; now no one dared go out, and there was no way of communicating with the castle.

One fine April morning Alis could not find Mabile, the little girl who waited on her; in vain did she call—Mabile was nowhere to be seen—she was not on the roof, she was not with the horses. But that evening Alis was looking from the top of the tower, and she discovered a little white body mired in the mud of the moat. For the first time she felt afraid. The child in her womb stirred and stretched gently. She asked herself if she would live to bear it, and her heart sank—never before had she so desired the life of a child. She told Milon what she had seen. And thereafter she never left Rainard's bedside— at that, it was the safest place in the hall.

Alis finally became accustomed to Rainard because he was the only man at Seuroi to whom she could talk as an equal. She nursed him as well as she could, for she was not a woman who could not bear the sight of blood and convulsions. And Rainard looked at her out of his strange, ironic, resigned eyes and sometimes said: "I thank you, my fair niece." He knew that his men would have let him die like a dog. He was prepared for that. This woman was interfering in matters which did not concern her. But because she was his niece and the daughter of a noble father, he did not send her about her business. The fact was that, despite everything, she succeeded in lessening his sufferings.

He suffered without complaining, as he had always suffered, like a beast which does not lie down except to be devoured; he had held out to the last, knowing that the first manifestation of weakness would be the signal for the end.

The end had come for him, and Florimond and the soldiers knew it so well that they considered him dead already and no longer asked how he was doing. But Alis was too kindhearted to let her husband's uncle perish like a beast. She spent hours mending the cloth and the embroidery of one of Rainard's old tunics—so that she could at least bury him decently, she said.

"It is shameful, there is not a garment in your chests that is not full of holes and filthy. It is easy to see that you have lived without a woman. And to your own great harm, I must tell you, for you know that God hates no sin so greatly as the sin against nature."

"Bah," said Rainard, yawning. "What need had I of bastards?"

Many a time Alis thought that he would die in her arms, but he lived on. Day after day she grew used to hearing his strange confessions, for he became talkative when he was roused with wine. God knew whether it was to relieve his conscience or to remind himself that he had lived after all, but he freely related his unhappy past. He had a good memory. Alis heard him without horror or pity, with dignity, like a confessor. Now and again she would shake her head and say: "An ugly thing." "Why yes," Rainard would answer tranquilly, "it is not pretty."

His stories were not such as can be put in decent language, for they were almost always so crude and obscene that the Devil himself could hardly have invented worse. Rainard was famous for his cruelty, but how far it could go no one but himself knew. That he had tortured men, women, and children for the pure pleasure of it Alis knew, but she had never heard the details. Rainard had so little shame and told it all so calmly that Alis never found herself blushing—the man was speaking a language which was not the language of humankind. Nerves laid bare, muscles stretched or cut, breasts torn off, monstrous couplings of men and beasts, refinements of torture by false hopes, false promises, bloody spectacles enacted before the victim's kindred—Rainard had conscientiously tried everything. He was supposed to be dull-witted, but in this department no one could have shown more imagination.

"And in the end, my fair niece," he said, "it doesn't amount to much. I say it again: it doesn't amount to much. It doesn't even make you feel warm. To hear people talk, you'd think it would do something to you. But no—as I said, it doesn't amount to much." And, in fact, though he told stories fit to make anyone's hair stand on end, everything he told was intensely boring and flat. His way of describing things was so trite and dull that the crudest words lost their meaning and Alis frequently yawned while listening to his infernal tales. "If it doesn't amount to much, my uncle, why have you laid such a great weight on your soul?"

The question was too complicated for Rainard's intelligence.

"A great weight," he said, thoughtfully repeating her words, "a great weight . . . yes, I suppose I have. Everyone wants his pleasure, doesn't he?"

In any case, Alis decided, Rainard must be a hard man to please: he cursed and criticized everything. According to him, not a baron in the castellany was worth two pease, and Count Henry of Champagne was not worth much more; the king of France was an utter imbecile, and the king of England, though a brave man, was an imbecile too; neither of them was worth a worn glove. As for the two popes, one was as much an impostor as the other; they ought both to be locked up or, better still, hanged. The only man he spared was his brother Herbert. "Herbert is a man, there's no denying it. And a good brother." Rainard also had a few favorites among soldiers and squires. "So-and-so," he said, "is a wonderful hand at training a greyhound. So-and-so is a good archer. Yes, he is a man too, he's a good archer. And Florimond? Florimond is an idiot, he doesn't know enough to come in out of the rain. You wouldn't think it to look at him. But he is not worth a moldy bean."

Rainard knew that Alis was pregnant, and she could not keep from talking to him about the child. "If it is a boy, I shall name him Girard. Perhaps he will look like my baron . . . strange that none of our children take after him."

Rainard yawned and said: "He's not very handsome, your baron." He said it with no intention of hurting Alis. She realized it, and did not become angry.

"And a child doesn't amount to much either," said Rainard thoughtfully. "You think it is going to be something—you're a lady, it's in your belly, and when you bear it everyone congratulates you. I cut open a woman who was carrying a five-months' child, and it was damned ugly, like a frog with a big head, all curled up and sticky; I threw it to the dogs—yes, threw it to the dogs." Alis thought of her Girard and shuddered.

"You would have done the same to me," she said, shaking her head— the picture of the unborn child thrown to the dogs troubled her.

Rainard did not understand. "You? Of course not. I never dreamed of it. Besides, one doesn't cut open noblewomen. Except those who sleep with varlets. They have to be killed because they corrupt the race."

Alis shuddered with disgust: "They ought to be flayed alive."

One day when the sick man seemed weaker than usual Alis exhorted him to give some thought to his soul.

"There is no priest here," said Rainard.

"Let me send a man to fetch the one at Hervi."

"No one would go. And the priest would not come for me. They will be only too happy to let me die damned."

"But I have a piece of consecrated bread—it is sewed into a little bag and I wear it around my neck. Take that for a host."

"It is more than twenty years since I received Communion," said the dying man. Alis crossed herself.

"And you are still alive? But you must know that if you go to Hell it will not be for a year, or for two."

"I know, I know." He coughed feebly and let his head fall back on the pillows. There was neither fear nor pain in his green eyes. He had been dying for five weeks. He had had enough of it. He had heard all about Hell. He did not expect that it would amount to much either.

That evening, as he seemed to be sinking, Alis made him swallow the consecrated bread—he spat it up at once, with a rush of blood that soaked the sheets. Alis considered it a bad portent. The hollow chest, covered with long black hair, began a continuous rattling. The face, blue and contorted, was so dreadful to look at that Alis ran to call Milon and Florimond. When she returned, the sick man had opened his eyes again. They were staring and expressionless; his nose had grown thinner and he seemed to have swallowed his lips.

"High time," said Florimond. Rainard appeared to have heard him; he raised his eyebrows with a look of reproach. Then he stretched, his neck fell back, his mouth opened. The adam's apple projected from his fleshless neck like a second chin.

"A peaceful death," said Florimond, and crossed himself almost against his will. Alis and Milon followed his example.

Washed and clothed, the body was laid out on a table in the center of the hall; three candles burned at its feet. Alis had managed to send a man to Hervi for the priest, but it turned out that Rainard had been right—the priest refused to come. Furthermore, he forbade them to bury Rainard in consecrated ground, to light candles, and to pray for his soul. Alis lit the candles notwithstanding—not to have done so would have been putting too grave an insult upon her husband's uncle—and she resolved to watch the body herself. Some other priest would absolve her from her disobedience.

Rosary in hand, Alis watched the body. In a corner of the hall the drunken soldiers were swearing and throwing dice. Florimond sat apart on a bench, chin in hand, apparently sunk in thought. He looked dangerous—when Alis met his eyes she shuddered.

Rainard's head stood out white against the black cushion. There was a bluish shadow on his translucent, yellowed eyelids, the nostrils were pale violet, the lips brown; the temples were gray, sunken hollows, and the whole face had already taken on the tints of a thing no longer human, subject to its own laws. The corners of the mouth were drawn back, displaying the long black eyeteeth in a last laugh, derisive but no longer hideous.

Never in its human life had the body of Rainard of Linnières owned this strange beauty—a beauty not born of feature but, as it were, lighting the face from within—everything seemed rightly placed to compose a perfect harmony. The low forehead was relaxed, the hollow cheeks and the thin lips were drawn into a smile which no longer expressed joy or sorrow, but a peace beyond all understanding. And Alis, looking at that face, thought that God must know better than men. One by one the beads of the rosary slipped through her fingers: "*Ave Maria.*" She had never learned the prayers for the dead. "*Sancta Maria, Mater Dei*"—never yet had Christian so sorely needed prayers.

And then the face became terrible, and she covered it with a white cloth.

Rainard was carried to his burial on a litter and let down into a grave dug a hundred feet from the tower, at the crossroads. Later, a great square stone was set up there, and the place bore the name of Rainard's Grave ever after.

Ansiau was returning from Troyes in good spirits—he had succeeded in exonerating himself before the Court of Peers and now had nothing to fear from that quarter. True enough, he had been obliged to spend a whole month at Troyes, to sue to the viscount and the seneschal, and to promise his services to the bishopric of Troyes. But he had established his innocence, and the court had declared that Joceran had no claim on the count in the matter—if he wanted justice, he must seek it himself. After buying wheat at Chaource, Ansiau prepared to cross the danger zone again—the men of Puiseaux had not mustered numbers enough to attack him the first time.

This time, however, the blow fell, for the men of Linnières, emboldened by their success at Troyes, were less cautious than they had been six weeks earlier. Auberi, son of Ansiau's cousin Girard the Young, left his companions to ride after a stag. And he did not return. The troop had reached Seuroi, and Auberi's father sent men searching for him all through the forest. The following morning the young man's body was found before the tower gate. Auberi was twenty-three. He was two months older than Ansiau, and Ansiau was deeply fond of him—they had played together as children. But Auberi was a humble youth who had never left Linnières and never worn anything more solid than a leather vest. The body bore the marks of ten lance thrusts—the throat had been cut by a dagger.

Girard the Young was a stolid man. But at the sight of his dead son he flew into a passion and accused Ansiau of having caused the boy's death. "He was killed for your quarrel," he said. "You have redeemed yourself at the price of his blood. You are a coward—you had no right to castrate that mad dog if you cannot defend your friends."

Ansiau said: "Fair cousin, forty days from today you shall have full recompense."

Girard shouted: "Braggart! You waited four years to revenge the brand on your face. By St. George and St. Michael I will no longer serve such a man as you, and I shall tell everyone what profit a man gains in your service. As sure as I live, until my son is revenged neither my brothers nor my nephews will serve you; we will go to Hervi this very day, to your great shame, Ansiau of Linnières. Go hide your face—you will not dare show it before our good knights now that you have paid your debt with the blood of my son."

Ansiau mastered his anger and replied: "You do not know what you are saying. Calm yourself. Go serve whomever you please—I shall know how much to count on your loyalty hereafter. But if you are not avenged on the fortieth day, then call me a coward."

And Girard the Young did as he had said—he left with his three brothers, his second son, and his nephews. Ansiau was in such a fever to act that he thought he would die before the term was up, but he did not dare attack the men of Puiseaux before the end of the forty days stipulated by the law—he had had trouble enough justifying himself for the castration of Baldwin. He knew that he was innocent—it had not been his fault if Auberi had not stayed with the troop. Yet he felt himself dishonored. "Who can respect me," he said, "if my family no longer trusts me? If I cannot protect my own kindred, let me rather die."

He returned to Linnières, bringing his wife with him from Seuroi—a doleful and weary woman after the trials she had undergone in his absence. And he gave her but a poor reward for having faithfully held Seuroi Tower for six weeks—he seemed almost to have taken an aversion to her, he could not forget whose blood ran in her veins. He said: "What can my nephew's death mean to you? He was not of your blood."

And the fortieth day after Auberi's death he took Herbert's sons and rode at full speed to Puiseaux, hoping that Joceran had not yet had time to make ready for an attack. And in fact, at Vanlay crossroads, the riders came upon several men of Puiseaux led by Garin, Joceran's third son. In two minutes Garin was thrown from his horse, then his men scattered to seek reinforcements. Garin lay motionless and Ansiau was already preparing to cut off his head, but Andrew cried: "Stop, perhaps he is still alive." Ansiau's answer was to prick his enemy's cheek with the point of his sword; Garin opened wide eyes of terror—he was seventeen, not very tall, and with ways almost like a child's. Ansiau did not dare hurt him now; he picked him up and said: "Your father killed one of my nephews. You know it." Garin bowed his head and tears streamed down his cheeks. Andrew and his brothers started laughing. "If he is crying," said Simon, "it must be for Auberi."

"Look at the brave knight," said Izembard. "How well he defends himself! Surely he is no son of Joceran's."

And Ansiau said scornfully: "What a face! My cousins are laughing at you, and well they may. Answer me: Do you know that your kindred have killed one of my nephews?"

Garin raised his head and fixed his beautiful, tear-filled brown eyes on Ansiau's face. A smile, half confident, half fearful, flickered on his lips—it was the baron's voice, not his words, which had reassured him. And Ansiau, who had been ready for anything except to see the boy smile, bit his lips. "By my beard, I believe he is an innocent," he said. "I am sorry, my boy, but I shall have to turn you over to my cousin Girard. If he lets you go, that will be your good luck, and you can burn a fine candle to Our Lady."

He put Garin back on his own horse, and the whole party rode straight to Seuroi, where they barricaded themselves. From Seuroi Ansiau sent a varlet to Hervi with a message for Girard the Young: "I have the goods you want, come to Seuroi and take them."

Garin, who had partly recovered from his terror, dried his tears and laughed at his own weakness. As lord of the tower, Ansiau felt under some obligation to keep him company; he massaged his arm, which had been dislocated by the fall, and gave him wine to drink. Garin chattered with feverish animation. "It is not that I am a coward," he said, "I just can't help crying. But I am not afraid."

Ansiau scolded: "A good thing you told me! No one would know it. At your age you should have more self-control."

"Tell me," said Garin with something of a tremble in his voice, "what do you think your cousin will do to me?"

"How should I know?" Ansiau growled "Your kindred did not spare his son. You must know that."

"It was because he fought like a boar," said the boy. "Father only meant to castrate him." Ansiau threw him such a scornful look that Garin blushed and said no more.

Toward nightfall Thierri came down from the roof and said that he had seen Girard the Young galloping down the road with all his family. Garin crouched in a corner, his hands clasped before his chest, his teeth chattering. Ansiau rose, went to the door, and said to Thierri: "Go out to meet Girard and tell him to dismount and come to me on foot and ask my pardon; otherwise I will not let him in."

Girard, when Thierri had repeated Ansiau's words, reddened with anger, but he did as he was told, for he was in haste to be revenged. He entered the courtyard on foot, and climbed the ladder. Ansiau had seated himself on his bench by the hearth and did not even raise his head to greet his cousin.

"So you have come, my fine cousin," he said. "Are the barons of Hervi more generous than I? Do they treat you better? No doubt they have already avenged you?"

"You cannot have sent for me to mock me," Girard cried. "Remember, I have lost my son for you."

"You acted disloyally to me."

Girard did not hear him. He was burning for his revenge.

"You have taken Joceran's son. I want him. You promised him to me."

"And what are you going to do with him?" the baron asked.

"What they did to my son."

Involuntarily the baron said: "He is only a child."

Girard answered brutally: "Everyone knows that your children are safe enough."

Ansiau regretted that he had not cut off Garin's head as he had intended. He turned to the boy and said: "Get out of that corner and come here." The boy rose, took two steps toward them, and burst into sobs.

Girard, who was not hard-hearted, felt a surge of pity. He sniffled loudly and turned away.

"I have sins enough upon me," he said, after a brief silence.

"My cousin forgives you, boy," said Ansiau. "Kiss his hand and thank him. It is no small thing he has done for you."

Spontaneously Garin knelt before Girard the Young. "My lord, if you will, I will serve you all my days in the place of your son who is dead. It is great goodness in you not to harm me."

Girard stroked the boy's brown head.

"Blood for blood," he said. "Your father shall give of his blood to make mine good: you shall live with us. On such terms, your kindred will not dare to do us harm."

Though still a little hesitant, the boy said that he was willing. And to bind the agreement, Herbert, who was skilled in medicine, made an incision in the vein of Girard's left wrist and another in Garin's and tied the two arms together with the incisions against each other. When time enough to say three Paters had passed, Herbert untied their arms and quickly bound up the cut wrists. "Now you are one in blood," he said. "Exchange crosses and embrace."

After they had done so, Girard said: "I will no longer seek to harm your father nor your kindred, provided that you serve me faithfully. He whom I have lost was my trustiest friend." Tears came to his eyes. "Never forget what I have done for you."

And now Baldwin and his father quarrelled more than ever. Baldwin said: "You sold me to save Garin. He is a damozel, his blood is better than mine, I know. You have never loved me."

"Fool, must I have the boy killed for your sake? Was not Auberi's blood enough for you?"

"So long as I live, I can never look Ansiau of Linnières in the face. And you make peace with him as if it had been a quarrel over a flour mill. By the body of the Virgin, I would have defended you better if I had been in your place."

"Nonsense!" his father scolded. "Who told you that I have made peace? If I can get Garin back from them, you shall see Ansiau's son castrated, though he is my own grandson."

"What do I care for Ansiau's son? It is Ansiau I want."

"And you shall have what you want," cried Joceran, losing his patience. "But I must get Garin out of their claws."

Baldwin shrugged his shoulders: "A fine excuse for doing nothing. They will never let him go. I would never make such a fuss over a little coward who saved himself at his brother's expense. If I am not avenged before Easter I will hang myself."

Joceran was frightened by this threat, for Baldwin was a man of his word.

"Better go say your prayers and ask God to forgive you," he said. "It is not good to talk of such things."

Baldwin had borne up under his misfortune better than anyone could have expected. He was not without greatness of soul, and he held his head high despite everything—he went to the count's court at Troyes, hunted with his friends and neighbors, and no one dreamed of laughing at him. But when Joceran met his eyes—like the troubled eyes of a beast wounded to death—he wanted to tear his hair. He racked his brains for a way to free Garin. But other days, unable to bear it longer, he showered his son with reproaches: "Mad boar that you are! I always knew that you would not be like the others. It is your own fault you are paying for, not mine. And because of you I cannot sleep nights. Ah! to think—to think that I had a bonfire lighted on the day of your birth!"

"You will light one on the day of my death," answered Baldwin morosely. "For I shall not live long—soon you will sleep peacefully again."

His father roared: "Idiot! Hold your tongue. Misfortune is never far off."

Forcibly detained at his father's castle by the hard winter weather, Baldwin was as restless as a captive bear. Spring, he thought, would bring him some relief—at Troyes he was sure to find Ansiau, and he would not let pass the opportunity to challenge him. Meanwhile his head was busy with other thoughts: he had become so jealous of his wife that he almost went mad. Day and night the great upper hall of the castle rang with their quarrels. Irma screamed at the top of her lungs, rolled on the floor, flung herself down the stairs howling for help to her father-in-law, her cousins, and the varlets. She had a stock of oaths which horrified even Joceran, and swore to her conjugal fidelity by so many saints male and female that it seemed impossible there could be room for them all in Paradise. And Baldwin, whose love appeared to have turned to somber rage, pursued his wife armed with a bench or an iron bar, and Irma took refuge behind Joceran at the risk of bringing Baldwin's blow down on his father's head.

Baldwin's jealousy was not without foundation, for Irma was on the prowl for every young varlet in the castle. She daubed herself with white and red and wore all her jewels—desiccated and thin as she was, she looked more than ever like an embalmed corpse. But she had the keys to the storerooms and the wine cellar, so there were fellows brave enough to run the risk. Yet the attractions of a bountiful repast were less powerful than the threat: "If you refuse, my fine fellow, I shall tell my lord that you seek my harm, and we shall see which of us he will believe."

Joceran, who saw through Irma's maneuvers, said: "Beware, lady—if you get yourself killed, you will have no kinsmen to avenge you."

And Irma answered brutally: "Isn't it enough that he has made me the laughingstock of the countryside? I have suffered too much on his account, and on yours, my father-in-law. A capon should not crow like a cock."

"Beware," Joceran answered. "I'll stick you like a sow if ever I catch you in the act."

One bright April morning—the weather was growing warm—Joceran was washing his hands in the great tub set in the corner of the keep to catch rain water. It was time for dinner and the smell of roast meat drifted out into the courtyard. Suddenly Joceran saw a man's body reflected in the tub, a body so big that it could only be Baldwin's.

"Hurry, son," he said, "so we can go up—I am hungry."

Baldwin's big white hands were stained with blood, they shook so violently in the water that he could not bring them together. Joceran raised his head in astonishment, his mouth fell open, he could not utter a word: Baldwin's face was ashy, his cheeks had sunk in, there were dark blotches under his eyes, his jaw hung loose.

"Baldwin, for the love of God, what is the matter with you?" Joceran cried at last. Baldwin's shaking hands were still splashing in the water. In a toneless voice he said: "I have killed Irma."

Joceran crossed himself: "God! It was bound to happen. Come, man, in God's name, get hold of yourself. We'll go up and drink some wine, you'll soon feel better."

Baldwin let himself be led upstairs, let himself be given a cup of malmsey heated with spices, let himself be settled on a bench in a dark corner of the hall. But he did not come out of his stupor—the blotches under his eyes grew darker, his face more ashen.

The bodies of Irma and her lover were found behind the stables by a boy who came running in terror to tell the castellan. It was a pretty piece of butchery: the half-naked bodies had been cut to bits with an ax. Irma's head, suspended from threads of muscle, still had an appearance of life: her eyes wide open in terror, her mouth gaping, she seemed about to cry out. Joceran shuddered and turned away. He became aware that he was wading in blood—it had not yet sunk into the clayey soil. It seemed as if ten men must have been slaughtered, there was so much blood on the gobbets of pale, earth-soiled flesh. "I want that picked up and buried before it begins to stink," said Joceran to his varlets.

His squire Bernier said: "It should be buried decently, she was your daughter-in-law."

Joceran spat. "I want none of that filth in my vault. Not another word!" And he went into the castle.

For three days Baldwin neither spoke nor ate—motionless, openmouthed, glassy-eyed he terrified all who saw him. His children did not dare to pass by him. In other respects he was as gentle as a lamb and allowed himself to be led from his bed to his bench, from the hall to the chapel, silent but unresisting. And one fine evening, seeing his two youngest children, Berta and Bernier, clutch each other and hide when he passed, he sat down on a rung of the ladder, plunged his hands into his hair, and burst into sobs. Joceran found him and told him to find some better place to cry in. Then Baldwin went down to the hall and took refuge in his corner.

His father consoled him as well as he could: Irma was not worth weeping over—she was a woman of no account, he had always known so. "You are neither the first nor the last to undergo it. Any other man would have done as you did. It was a tooth that had to come out: now you'll be easier."

"Easier?" cried Baldwin. "I cannot live without her."

Joceran shrugged his shoulders: "You ought to be ashamed of yourself."

Baldwin was never to recover from his grief. However, he gradually began to eat and drink again, and little by little to look like his old self. Indeed, he soon became fatter than he had ever been. He spoke little, and showed no interest in anything. He avoided his children and seemed to have taken a dislike to his father and brother. He no longer thought of his schemes of revenge, and the name of Ansiau of Linnières roused him to nothing but a feeble smile of scorn.

"At Pentecost, when we go to Troyes, I shall put myself in the service of some baron on the other side of the Seine," he said to his father. "I have had enough of the castellany. If I stay here, I shall kill myself."

"A change of air will certainly do you good. But you must at least wait for the marriage of your daughter Ida."

Baldwin shook his head. "I don't belong at a wedding; you will do better without me. She would not be proud of her father."

"Come, come," said Joceran, "you mustn't let people think you are ashamed to look them in the face."

"But I am ashamed. Let me go. In any case, I cause you more pain than pleasure."

Joceran could not but agree. He sighed. He was weary of living with this perpetually bleeding wound and he thought with relief of the day when he should be rid of it.

II. HERBERT THE RED

It was something more than a great tournament that the knights who had gathered at Troyes saw in the forthcoming festival. Rumors of the disasters in Palestine were becoming more and more definite: the king of Jerusalem and his barons were sending messengers into the West to ask for help against Saladin.

Ansiau and his kinsmen, with their tents and horses, had halted by the bank of the Seine, not far from the lists which the count's carpenters and masons were busily building and decorating. "I'll stake my horses on it," said Andrew, "something new is brewing this time. See how big the lists are, and how many pillars and canopies they are putting up. Looks like at least a bishop—perhaps two."

"The viscounts of Provins and Coulommiers are here," said Ansiau. "I saw their people."

"The count would not put up canopies for them," said Herbert, his blue eyes lighting with joy.

"Didn't someone say the duke of Burgundy would be coming?" asked Simon the Red.

As they were entering the city to perform their devotions, their neighbor Haguenier of Hervi joined them on the road. He was smiling broadly. "Neighbors, something is brewing in Champagne."

"Whatever is brewing, we shall know it before we are many days older," said Ansiau of Linnières.

Enguerrand, Haguenier's brother, shook his head with a knowing look and showed his broken eyeteeth. "The sooner the better. I count on you, neighbor, to attack that party which gave us so much trouble at last year's tournament. From Bar-on-Aube, I think they were. If I find the man who had two yellow crosses on his shield—"

"Speaking of crosses," said Andrew, "I think we shall soon see some which are not yellow."

"I don't know what we shall see," said Haguenier. "But we must suppose that Count Henry is as good a man as his father was. We are lucky to serve such a man."

"Ah, youth!" sighed Herbert, rubbing his hands. "I knew Count Thibaut, and he was brave, and good to his barons. But Henry is his equal in everything."

They took a childish pleasure in talking cryptically of something that they all awaited, that they all knew was imminent. Count Henry would not die without following his father's example and doing his Christian duty toward the City of God.

The throng of knights and men-at-arms which flowed in and out of the churches of Troyes was full of feverish faces and glittering eyes and fists shaken at the infidels. Herbert and Ansiau went to see Abner, whose services they required only too often. They had to buy new lances for the forthcoming tournament. Herbert counted, too, on Abner's telling him what was afoot, for the Jew had friends and relatives almost everywhere and was always reliably informed.

Abner had been born in Acre, where one of his brothers was a banker. From this brother he had long since received the worst possible news of the Holy Land, and he was convinced that Count Henry would take the cross. The count was awaited in Jerusalem, Abner said, because the affairs of the kingdom were at their lowest ebb. Saladin had occupied Damascus and Aleppo, and he and his emirs were besieging the Frankish cities under the nose of the king, who was powerless. A man must be found to hold the kingdom, for the king, the word went, was a leper and had not long to live.

The chief concern at the moment, then, was to make a good marriage for the king's sister, who was a widow and the mother of an infant. The barons of the kingdom were considering the duke of Burgundy—so Abner said—and Count Henry was expected to negotiate a marriage between the duke and the king's sister during the course of his pilgrimage to Jerusalem.

Herbert had always been curious to learn what was going on in those distant courts. The intrigues and parties of Jerusalem and Antioch, of Poitiers, Toulouse, and Rome, were almost as familiar to him as the most. trifling events at the court of Count Henry.

The hope of seeing the Holy Land for the second time brought back his youth and gave his eyes and his smile a new radiance. "If the king of France," he said, "can think of nothing but picking a quarrel with the king of England, we will do without him. Our brothers in the Holy Land shall soon see that there will always be men among us ready to go to their aid."

And Ansiau, chin in hand, fixed his wide empty eyes on the rich oriental rugs that hung on Abner's walls. Their brothers in the Holy Land, the barons of Ultramar, left him indifferent. He thought of all that he had heard about the blue sea, and white-sailed ships, and the wealth of Eastern lands. His zeal for the sacred cause was to be awakened later, amid flags and trumpet blasts and the singing of the *Te Deum* in the vast enclosure before the assembled barons and bishops.

Count Henry was there with the countess and his sons, and his brother, and the duke of Burgundy, Count Henry's nephew, and Peter of Courtenay, son to the king of France, and the bishops of Beauvais and Troyes and Meaux and Langres. From their place in the crowd, the men of Linnières could see little but the count's blue and silver canopy and the high, gold-fringed banners floating in the breeze against a soft gray sky. The throng of knights and men-at-arms which crowded against the stands and filled the vast lists swayed like a field of wheat—a field of heads blond or dark, bared before the cross and the relics which the bishop of Troyes had sent to his brocade-hung tent. Amid the babble of voices, shouts and sobs went up from the crowd on every side—it was difficult to understand what was going on, and the count's criers, in their blue silk livery, pushed their way from end to end of the lists through the gathering of knights, announcing in monotonous and thunderous voices what was taking place under the tents and the canopies of the nobles.

"The count, with his brothers and his barons, and Count Peter of Courtenay, announce to their knighthood, their vassals and vavasors one and all, their decision to take the cross and travel to the Holy Land to adore the Holy Sepulchre.

"Baldwin, king of Jerusalem, asks the barons of the West to come to his aid to fight the Saracens, who are sacking the Christian cities of the Kingdom and killing pilgrims.

"If among the knights of the count of Champagne there are men desirous of assuring their salvation and serving God, they are free to take the cross instantly, to go and adore the Holy Sepulchre, and to aid King Baldwin.

"The bishop of Beauvais will himself attach the red cross to the count's shoulder, and the count will then swear on the relics of St. Peter to accomplish his pilgrimage to the end."

Every hand rose of itself, touched forehead, breast, the left shoulder and the right—as one man, the knights crossed themselves at the instant when the count, kneeling on the carpet before his tent, received the cross from the hands of the bishop of Beauvais. And when he rose, every hand went up and every voice joined in acclaiming him. Among all those men, not one in ten could afford a pilgrimage to Jerusalem, and many of them had no idea of cutting their lives in two for love of the king of Jerusalem. But at that instant each one of them took the cross in the person of his suzerain, and they were one in the gratitude and love they felt for him. It lasted while the criers were announcing that the cross was being taken by the bishop of Beauvais himself, by Peter of Courtenay, by the count of Dreux, by the barons of Brienne and Ramerupt and Bar-le-Duc—then, as name followed name, the excitement increased, changed its object, and in the noise of voices the criers were no longer heard. At the four corners of the stand, priests in violet stoles were blessing those who came to them to receive the cross.

No doubt those who came forward were far more numerous than those who would really go. But as they returned to the company of their kinsmen and friends with the red cross on their shoulders they all bore Jerusalem in their hearts. Ansiau moved toward the stand, pushing his way through the crowd of onlookers and of those who, like himself, were going to take the cross. Something had happened to him—he did not quite know what. These unknown men—he was a head taller than most of them—they seemed so close to him, he could have embraced each one of them and called him brother. No doubt he was too excited to reflect. When he had seen the count take the cross, he had felt a cross of flame burn into his own shoulder, and everything had gone black before his eyes. What until then had seemed vague and distant had suddenly become near and necessary—at that moment he knew no distinction between himself and the count and his barons and the other men of good will who were to offer themselves to God that day.

His emotion had almost subsided when he knelt to receive the priest's blessing on his bent forehead and touched his lips to the golden cross. The movements he had to make freed him momentarily from the enthusiasm which had overwhelmed him. Now he knew perfectly well what the cross was and why he was taking it and why it was necessary to follow the count and his barons to Palestine and defend the Holy Sepulchre. He let himself be carried by the current. For the first time in his life he saw clearly what it was needful to do for God—it was perfectly simple, the road lay plain before him. When he took the oath he thought of home just enough to tell himself that he would not miss it. His life had been nothing but piling sin on sin. Suddenly a way of escape had opened, so close that he could touch it with his hand—the cross, which promised happiness and salvation to all who would follow it. He knew that, as castellan of Linnières and liege man to the count of Champagne, he could not love God rightly.

He was a good Christian on high holy days—so were most of his comrades. But he knew God well enough to regret not knowing Him better. God was so beautiful that no human countenance could ever equal His beauty. On the humble wooden crucifix in Hervi church, the formless, rudely sculptured face shone with a light that was not of the flesh—those protruding cheekbones, those slanting eyes, those lips like fillets revealed miracles of beauty to him who looked at them humbly, simply, as a man looks at the sky and the sun.

He was ignorant enough. He believed that there might still be folk old enough to remember the Virgin and the Apostles, believed that God had been put to death by the Saracens. Concerning Jesus Christ Himself, he knew but three things—that He had been born of a Virgin, that He had been crucified, and that He had risen again. But as he was one of those who know how to pray and love to pray, he needed no intermediary between himself and God except monstrances, crucifixes, sacred images, and the Host. He felt for God the staunch affection of a vassal who thinks it an honor and a joy to die for his lord.

For these men, with their perpetual thirst for novelty, the taking of the cross was an event which would be talked of for two whole weeks, in the city, on the roads, in the castles. All the rest of that day the knights moved through the streets of Troyes in processions, singing, and shouting insults at Saladin—"Noël!" was their refrain. "Noël!" and "Holy Sepulchre!" Night fell, and the city was bright with torches. Such of the knights as had found lodging in the inns or with townsmen invited their kinsmen and friends who were camping outside the city to share their temporary quarters, and all night in the low-ceilinged inn parlors, lighted by tallow candles, guests came and went, discussing the great news and downing huge cups of wine to the health of the count, the bishop of Troyes, the duke of Burgundy, and King Baldwin of Jerusalem.

The men of Linnières had decided to leave in a body—the more so since the men of Hervi were leaving too—it was a safeguard for the future, for neither party wanted to leave their lands at the mercy of their neighbors. Once off their land, the barons of Linnières and Hervi became good friends again, and planned wars and marriages together.

—"Know well, my brothers, that he who loses his life for love of Our Lord will save it to all eternity. Our Lord said: Sacrifice all things for the Kingdom of God. Therefore those who now go to defend the Kingdom of God shall find pardon for all their sins, great and small.

"Let those who have sworn to go look to it that they keep their oath. For once a good work is begun, to turn back is a grievous sin. Let not your zeal be like fire in straw; be not distracted from your good resolve by impious quarrels, by hate between brother and brother, and know that God hates nothing so much as vengeance, for He has commanded you to forgive your enemies.

"Lo, Saladin (may God look upon his infamy and bring him to shame!) —Saladin is at the gates of our free and Christian cities and promises to sack our churches and trample the Holy Cross under his horse's hoofs. And you, meanwhile, you scheme to slay and maim your brothers; and the infidels look at you, and well may they say that you are not God's servants but the Devil's. And because Our Lord said that a kingdom divided against itself cannot stand, you will go straight to your perdition, for you think of nothing but turning your arms and your wealth against one another, like fools hacking their own bodies with knives . . ."

It was not Ansiau's nature to reflect and hesitate for long. There on the square before the cathedral, where he had listened to the bishop's sermon the morning after he had taken the cross, he knelt at the feet of Baldwin of Puiseaux, who was coming out of the lefthand portal with his father and brother. The crowd of knights jostled them, then gathered around them. The bells were ringing in full peal, drowning the noise of voices and filling ear and heart with their jubilant din.

Confronted by that huge, pale, puffy-faced man, Ansiau felt no more rancor, no more rage. He forced himself to think that God bade him humble himself before his enemy, and in the effort he almost forgot Baldwin's presence.

"What does he want with me?" Baldwin asked his father. "I will not speak with that man."

"Baldwin, brother," said Ansiau, "I am at your mercy. I have wronged you, forgive me. What you have done to my house, I forgive you." The impossible words seemed easy to him at the moment. All his life had been turned upside down, all his values were changed—he would joyfully have knelt not only before Baldwin but before a beggar covered with sores. It mattered nothing by what means he was humiliated, since his humiliation was for God. But a lingering fear of what people might say forbade him to raise his head.

Baldwin's first movement had been to put his hand to his hip and feel for his dagger. But he restrained himself. His pale face went red, then pale again. Joceran and Thibaut looked at one another in silent astonishment, wondering how to react. Baldwin buried his face in his hands.

"Ah, traitor!" he said in a broken voice, "save that God commands it, never would I forgive. Forgive I must but it is hard indeed."

And now at last, as Ansiau raised his head at the sound of that shrill, mournful voice, pity and remorse overwhelmed him. That huge, bent, stooping man had been a young and handsome knight only two years ago. Ansiau had never been so close to him since. He was horror-stricken. Accustomed to judging the harm he did by the affront he had to avenge, he had never stopped to imagine the suffering he might be causing. Now he understood that it was harder for Baldwin to forgive him than for himself to beg forgiveness. Humbly he said: "I thank you, brother. If you want reparation, I will grant it—ask whatever you will."

Baldwin looked away and said: "I want nothing from you. Go."

A crowd had gathered around them, but it soon melted away. Each man returned to his own affairs, his prayers or his pre-occupations. It was not the first such sight they had seen. What God had caused these two men to do on this day of repentance and pardon was not exceptional.

When they reached home the women would have to be told what had taken place at Troyes. The news of the countryside always came to Linnières belated—there behind the forest and the marshes they were safely shut off and cared little what happened in the world outside. But when the squires rushed into the hall and broke the news that they were to go to the Holy Land, Richeut fainted at her wheel and Odette, wife of Herbert's son Simon the Red, began to wail aloud. So the knights arrived in the midst of a general uproar, and Ansiau had to shout when he ordered the women to hold their tongues and set the table, for he was hungry after his journey.

All during supper Alis did not dare to question her husband. Yet she was on fire to learn what this talk of the Holy Land might mean and timidly hoped that her baron was not concerned in it. It was hot. The evening set in fair. After supper the baron and his wife sat on a bench under the window for a breath of fresh air. Out the window they could see a patch of black wall and a patch of sky white as pearl, with a star twinkling high up. Alis sighed because she was expecting a calamity—yet just to live was so good! And because Ansiau could not quite bring himself to speak, she opened her nostrils wide and shut her eyes. She was in no haste to hear what he had to tell her.

"Sister, sweet," he said, "I have made peace with your brother and your father. I am sure that must make you happy." Knowing that he was going to hurt her, he wished to prepare her, to soften the blow. Alis raised her head in surprise.

"Indeed? How did you go about it? You are making fun of me."

"You know," Ansiau went on, speaking softly as if to a child, "that the count has taken the cross and is going to the Holy Land. It was very beautiful. If only you could have seen it! All the high barons were there in their embroidered cloaks, and the count had a tent of silver brocade. When he took the cross it was a noble sight. He vowed to go to the Holy Land and adore the Holy Sepulchre."

"No doubt he did well," said Alis. "But tell me about yourself and Baldwin."

Ansiau, who had lost the thread of his thoughts, opened his eyes wide. "Yes, of course . . . Well, Baldwin was there. I offered him reparation."

Alis frowned and looked into his eyes. "Surely," she said, "you are trying to tell me something else."

"True, lady. I am trying to tell you that I took the cross—I and all my family. When the count goes, we go with him."

Alis had prepared herself for this news—nevertheless it came as a blow. She wanted to faint, but she could not. She put both hands over her heart—it was beating wildly.

"What!" she said. "We have not been married eight years, and already you want to forsake me? Are you weary of me?"

"No, no, beloved, it is not that. But I have bound myself by an oath."

"And who forced you? No one is a liege man for the Holy Land."

Ansiau remained silent. He did not know how to explain the reasons for his sudden decision. A man, he thought, would have understood him without words. But with a woman even words were useless. He only said: "You know that I love you dearly."

"No one would think so," said Alis bitterly. "What have I done to you to deserve such an insult? No one forces you, and you bind yourself to go God knows where and for God knows how long! You cannot have thought of me."

"Sweet," said Ansiau, "surely it is a beautiful thing to go and adore the Holy Sepulchre. You know that the count and the bishops are leaving their lands and their friends to go. Jerusalem is the holiest place on earth."

"And I?" Alis demanded. Ansiau was getting tired of this way women had of harking back to themselves. What had she to do with it? Alis pressed against him and took his face in both her hands. Surely—she said—he loved her too well to wish her death. He had not reflected. And after all, to bind oneself was not to go. He did not even have money for his equipment. And why need he go to the Holy Land to worship God when he could just as well worship Him at Hervi or Troyes?

"Lady," said Ansiau, "all this is beside the mark. You are talking of things you do not understand." He thought that she had a poor little brain which could see no further than Troyes or Hervi, whereas *he* knew that worshipping God at Jerusalem was a different and a better thing than worshipping Him at Hervi.

"I know as much about it as you do, my friend, and I am as good a Christian. And I tell you it is a sin to forsake wife and children to seek your fortune God knows where. If you do not come back, your sons will be servants to the barons of Hervi or Jeugni."

For the first time Ansiau felt troubled. "Lady, if God wills, I shall come back. Besides, the men of Hervi are going too—you will have nothing to fear from them."

"Sweet, sweet, Jerusalem is so far! God! God!" she suddenly cried, and her head fell on Ansiau's knees. "And I am still so young!" And she began to sob with such desperation that Ansiau's heart sank for pity and he thought of nothing but how to console her.

"My sweet, my sister, my dove, I did not mean to hurt you. Come, dry your beautiful eyes. You will grow used to it, you are not the only one. Besides, it will not be tomorrow. We certainly shall not leave before next year."

"God, God!" Alis sighed between two sobs. "A bitter year it will be for me! How shall I live without my love!"

The news had indeed brought panic to the women at Linnières. But with time everyone became accustomed to the idea. Herbert returned to sitting by the hearth and recounting his memories of Palestine and the siege of Damascus, improved by embellishments in which his own imagination combined the various details, veracious or otherwise, which he had managed to collect on the subject of those distant lands. The men—especially the younger men—listened to him breathlessly, burning with impatience to see the fair land of God with their own eyes. And the women, less susceptible to the magic of adventurous tales, and more sceptical by nature, shook their heads. They knew well enough that those evergreen trees and fabulous fruits and burning sands, those infidels who could not speak French, would never exist for them except in tales—what matter whether they were real or not? And some of them began to look forward, not without secret relief, to life without a master. But Alis, who loved her husband, was sincere in her affliction.

She was loyal by nature, and proud of it. From the day when she admitted to herself that her lord was to go to the Holy Land, she ceased to reproach him and even tried to find excuses for him. He would gain the respect of every knight in the countryside by such a manifest act of piety. And perhaps he would bring back a rich booty—valuable stuffs or precious relics. After all, he was a knight of prowess and he must not stay forever tied to his wife's apron strings. Yet in her inmost heart Alis could not but feel that there was no glory or profit in going away to conquer infidel knights whose names and prowess were utterly unknown in Champagne.

Alis' secret torture was an anticipated jealousy. The fact that it had no foundation in reality only made her jealousy the more painful. It was in vain that Ansiau had promised and sworn to remain faithful: he could not know the future. The campaign would take a year, perhaps two, perhaps three. And poor Alis, to whom her husband was the pattern of manhood, believed that the ladies of Palestine would no sooner see him than they would try to seduce him. He was young. If he should happen to meet a rich and beautiful woman who offered to marry him, who knew if he might not choose to abandon Linnières and stay with his new wife? Alis had a high opinion of herself, yet she perpetually feared for her husband. For her, the world was full of blond, slender, beautifully garbed women who dabbled more than a little in magic —she believed in love philters and charms which could make a man forget even the name of his old love. And Saracen land must be fuller of such perils than any other.

Preparations for departure were the great business of the year. For a minor castellan of no great wealth like Ansiau of Línnières, it was a very complicated matter. He had already gone into debt for the tournament at Pentecost. Now he must borrow ten times as much again to complete the equipment of his men and horses and to pay for the sea voyage, for which the count's wage would not suffice. Alis, who would hold the fief during the absence of the knights, had to go to Troyes with her husband and Herbert. They explained to her what had been done and what was still to do—she knew almost nothing of loans and interest and crossed herself in terror at the thought of talking to a Jew. Husband and wife made the rounds of the bankers of Troyes together. Ansiau borrowed on his land, his forest, his vineyards, even on his furs and his wife's jewels. As he expected to be in the Holy Land when the loan fell due, Alis had to sign the agreement in his stead and personally swear to pay the creditors on the appointed days and with the stipulated interest. She did it grudgingly. Ansiau, more used to dealing with men of low condition, was affable and accommodating. But Alis heartily despised bankers and Jews and barely condescended to speak to them. When she took the oath her eyes narrowed, her mouth became hard, and she thought of nothing but how to lengthen the term and pay less than would be due. Once the men were gone, where was she to find money to repay the loan? Ansiau did not bother his head over that—the great thing was to go, the rest was none of his affair.

In his fever to be off he passed all his time with Haguenier of Hervi and Giles of Monguoz, crusaders like himself and, like himself, clients of Abner and Master Simon Brézier. He grew more and more impatient. The day of departure was still in the indefinite future—the negotiations with the duke of Burgundy dragged on, no more news came from Jerusalem. Everyone except the crusaders themselves had forgotten the Crusade—and even some of the crusaders had discovered that they had business more important than King Baldwin's war against Saladin. Alis went loyally on, helping her husband in an enterprise from which she had nothing to gain, and let him lead her from usurer to usurer to serve as surety.

On her return from Troyes she suffered a painful miscarriage as a result of the fatigues of the journey. She took it deeply to heart—the child was a boy, and she had been pregnant for five months. Ansiau, who was the most indulgent of husbands, did not dream of blaming her, and she was grateful to him. The rains and frosts of November again shut Linnières away from the rest of the world, and Alis fell asleep at night thinking that another winter she would not have her beloved beside her in their great curtained bed. But he thought of nothing except Palestine and Holy Sepulchre, and counted the weeks until the day of departure, which had at last been set for the second Sunday after Easter.

Of them all, Andrew was by far the happiest and the most excited at the thought of going—he had changed beyond recognition—he looked ten years younger and went about the castle singing at the top of his lungs, laughed at everything and nothing, teased the dogs, and could not keep still an instant for joy. Such childish gaiety was touching in a man nearing thirty. For all his love of subtle argument he had a simple heart, and the prospect of a magnificent adventure dazzled him so that he was incapable of serious thought. He for one was determined not to miss a single beautiful woman, a single good meal, or a single place of pilgrimage. He already knew all the holy places by name—he had the memory of a learned clerk and was forever talking of saints and miracles with calm assurance. Things sacred and things profane were almost alike to him. Yet he had a lively faith, and the thought of setting foot on the ground which God had trodden moved him deeply.

He told Ansiau the stories of the Holy Sepulchre and Golgotha and the Mount of Olives and the Sea of Galilee, and was amazed afresh: "Can it be, brother, that our own eyes will see the wood of the True Cross and the marks of the nails? Surely, on the day that we see it, we shall not need to fear death, for all our sins will be forgiven us—far less would be enough. And do you know what happened at Emmaus, three days after God was crucified? I learned of it from the clerks who taught me to read, and it is a wonderful story, both to hear and to tell. And they say that the place has become so holy since that day that all who go there—Christian and infidel alike—are cured of their sicknesses, whatever they may be. And to tell of all the miracles which God performed in that land would take a man's whole life, I think. It was on the shore of the Sea of Galilee that he multiplied the five loaves and two fishes. . . ."

Ansiau listened avidly, his eyes shining. Though he had never heard these stories told, he felt that he had always known them. They fed his love of God—by them it grew through the long idleness of winter evenings and months of waiting. Since the day when he had renounced his own will before Baldwin of Puiseaux his life had become an acceptance of God. It was a state wholly new to him and it filled him with joy and astonishment. Sometimes he would spend hours praying in the chapel, staring so long at the crucifix that when at last he turned away he saw only crosses wherever he looked. Yet he had no visions, and he asked for none. It was more than enough for him to know that he would see Jerusalem and Holy Sepulchre with his own eyes. Next spring's great tryst to which God had called the men of Champagne was incomparably more real than acts of piety performed in ordinary life—it was no hypocrisy and no trifle, that prayer stretching four thousand leagues and filling two whole years.

"Brother, we have never made any promise or sworn any oath to each other," he said to Andrew. "That is well, for now we can take our oath before the Holy Sepulchre, which will make our comradeship surer and holier than any other." Andrew agreed that such an oath would bless their friendship—no, they would not exchange crosses before they had seen Jerusalem.

The end of Lent and the approach of Easter made the great day of departure present and real—they had waited so long that they had almost ceased to believe in it. Alis had secretly hoped for some sign from heaven which would forbid the count to take the cross, but no sign had come—at least they had not heard of any at Linnières. During Lent she had suffered another miscarriage, brought about by a fall from horseback. And this time Ansiau had not concealed his displeasure—she was no longer fifteen, she ought to know how to take care of herself by now. Here she was, with little Girard still her youngest, and he already eighteen months old. Never before had a baby claimed her for so long, and all the affection which she would have given to the two miscarried boys was transferred to little Girard. None of her children had ever seemed so intelligent, so bright, so affectionate. And her baron's departure would leave her sterile for years—perhaps forever, for she had no thought of remarrying if she should be left a widow. So she spent her days mourning with little Girard, saying: "My joy, my love, soon I shall be left alone with no one but you to console me."

Ansiau was exasperated by her excessive affection for her youngest child— now that she was no longer nursing him she should pay no more attention to him than to the others. "Believe me," he said, "you are wrong—he is no better than his brothers. It is high time you stopped saying your rosary over him." He who was such an ardently partial father expected Alis to be justice itself—he thought of mother love as a tangible and palpable substance, which a mother owed to her children as she owed them her blood and her milk, and she had no right to give more of it to one than to the others. Whereas he, being a man, was free to love as he chose.

The boy would be seven in May. He had long since been taken away from the women; and though he was tall for his age he looked as frail and delicate as a bird when he straddled his legs across a saddle. He had big gray eyes with long lashes, and the smile of a very young child, a smile which expressed a joy out of all proportion to the object which aroused it. And his father's heart quickened when he saw that smile.

On the eve of their departure Mass was celebrated in the chapel of Linnières and all the men received Communion. The evening meal was eaten in unwonted silence. All the women's eyes were red, the men who were to go felt their hearts swell at the thought that perhaps they were eating at that table for the last time. Only Herbert was as cheerful as ever—he joked and drank even more than usual. Of them all it was he who had least to lose. He had given up struggling against age and had stopped dyeing his hair, but he still was a fine-looking man. After years of an idle life, the Crusade promised him new pleasures. No doubt they would be his last.

That night for the first time Ansiau weighed the sacrifice he was to make

—he was so accustomed to his lady that ordinarily he thought of her no more than he thought of himself. Now he felt that it was from himself that he would part. He was not a man who could live without a woman. Palestine was famous for beautiful ladies, yet he thought of them without anticipation. For four years he had been faithful to his wife, and he sincerely believed that she was the best of women. If he did not often reflect upon love, it was because he lacked occasions—he was too enveloped in it to think of it. Now that he was to leave his lady he found himself as much in love as a young bridegroom, and he overwhelmed her with promises and prayers. This time it was Alis who stayed silent. His departure had been imminent for so long that she had grown used to the thought of it. Instead of grief she felt only a sort of stupor. She knew that she had many more things to tell him, but she had forgotten them all. Later, when she remembered their last night together, she was to reproach herself for her coldness: "What a memory of me he will carry with him! He will think that I do not love him."

And in the morning it was farewell. The forsaken wives were weeping and wailing in anticipation, beating their breasts and tearing their hair. Alis would not be outdone by the others—she loyally tried to do all that a noblewoman should on such an occasion. And Ansiau, drunk with the joy of departure, had eyes for no one but Herbert, Andrew, and Thierri—he kept going down into the courtyard to see if the horses and baggage were being properly attended to.

Lady Alis brought their four children to her husband and asked him to bless them in case he should not return.

"Remember," said the baron, "that it is Ansiau, the eldest, who is to inherit the fief and the castle. Until he is of age, you are to hold the land and let no one else have it." Then he took Lady Alis by the shoulders and kissed her lips and eyes. "Sweet, farewell. Keep the domain. Do not forget me. Wait for me seven years, as is right."

Lady Alis hung on his neck, weeping. But he gently put her away—he knew that if he let her cry she would never stop.

"I have this to say too, sweet. If I die, marry again, but look to it that your husband does not wrong my children. Take a rich man who has his own lands and will not want ours."

"I will never take a husband," said Alis. "If you die, I die."

Ansiau did not pay much attention to this—he knew that women always say such things. "Keep your wits about you," he said. "Take good care of yourself. And do not grieve."

"Do not forget me with the ladies of Palestine," said Alis, weeping.

He laughed. "I? You don't know me. You will forget before I do."

He kissed her again, several times—quickly and impatiently. "It is time to go, sweet. Farewell."

He knew that the worst was to come. She clung to him, followed him down to the courtyard, caught at his stirrup, at his horse's mane, at his cloak.

At the final moment she could not bring herself to let him go. And he was thinking of nothing but the time when he should be on the road—at last.

This gathering had an atmosphere unlike the other days of departure which Ansiau of Linnières had known, an atmosphere of freedom and unconcern which pervaded the army, from the embroidered tents of the bishops to the humble camps of the sergeants. These men had taken leave of life for so long a time that they considered themselves free from every restraint. More than one of them had no sooner reached Troyes than he spent all the funds he had raised for the long journey—he could borrow again, or take service under some richer crusader. Tents and inns were loud with song, and everywhere there were bright-colored garments, garlands of flowers and leaves. Kinsmen were taking leave of kinsmen, friends of friends, old comrades were meeting again and welcoming one another. Among those who were to go Ansiau encountered his father-in-law, and the two men accepted each other's friendship as if nothing had ever come between them. Joceran came to drink and talk with the men of Linnières, and every man of them asked himself: "How the Devil could we have picked a quarrel with him?"

Joceran was going with his nephews and his vassals; his two sons were to remain in Champagne. The day after the taking of the cross, Baldwin had gone to serve the viscount of Chantemerle for a term of three years. Since Irma's death he could not bear the sight of Puiseaux—his one wish was to avoid his family and his friends. And since that left no one to guard the domain and the castle during the crusaders' absence, Thibaut had perforce submitted—it was obvious that Joceran, as the elder and more sinful, had the greater need to go. Joceran was more than willing to atone for his sins, which his confessor had convinced him were many. His beard was now wholly gray, his eyes almost colorless, but he still had his fine presence and the smile that stirred so many women's hearts. One of the few survivors of King Louis' Crusade, he was indifferent to the wonders of the country he was to revisit. Joceran hardly remembered the adventure from which Herbert of Linnières had returned full of burning fervor and uneasy dreams. For such things he had no need. He had his scar to prove that he had gone, and he asked nothing more. And Herbert, now that the memories of the earlier Crusade had taken on reality again, loved his old comrade-in-arms for the sake of that distant past. And Ansiau thought of the first days of his marriage and of Joceran's broad face beside the delicate face of Alis, as he had seen them then. And because Joceran's smile was as beautiful as his daughter's, Ansiau could feel nothing but kindliness for his father-in-law. And other men still remembered the great friendship which had united Joceran and the noble Guy of Marseint of blessed memory, and they said: "The man who had such a friend cannot be evil."

Freed from the burdensome presence of his eldest son, Joceran felt that he was himself again—boon companion, soldier of fortune, adventurer.

War had never meant anything to him but opportunity to lead the free life of a camp, and this departure for the Holy Land promised him at least two years in the field.

Edith of Chalmiers was at Troyes too. She was not going on the Crusade, but she had thought it well to send one of her vassals in her place, for never did soul have sorer need of forgiveness and atonement. At the moment her zeal for the sacred cause took the form of a great love for its future martyrs, and she freely gave herself to men whom she wholeheartedly admired and pitied.

The army was to move on the second Sunday after Easter. On Thursday Herbert was stricken by apoplexy after a too copious repast at Count Henry's table. Frequent bleedings restored him to consciousness. But he was paralyzed and had lost the power of speech. His sons had carried him to the house of a cloth merchant to be cared for. He lay there in a huge bed, groaning and gasping, trying in vain to make himself understood. He had but one thought —to recover before the army moved. And he demanded Masses, relics, healers, to the consternation of his sons who could not understand what he was trying to say.

The doctor who had been called to attend him said that he could not possibly get up again for two or three weeks. Ansiau at first considered putting him in a covered cart and bringing him along with the baggage. "If we leave him here he will die of grief," he said to Herbert's sons. "Better that he should risk the journey." But Simon the Red, Herbert's eldest son, sided with the doctor, who affirmed that the jolting of the cart and the exhausting effect of the journey would certainly kill the patient, and that in any case he would never be able to ride again. And Girard the Young said: "We cannot drag an invalid to Palestine. If he must die on the road, it is better that he should lie at Linnières with his kinsmen." Ansiau was obliged to give in to their arguments, but his heart was heavy. Herbert's illness was a bad omen for the journey. He was almost tempted to give it up entirely—the thought of leaving his uncle behind gave him such pain. For six days he had been living in Troyes, waiting for the second Sunday after Easter, drinking and amusing himself like everyone else. The time to which he had so long looked forward had come—and he found himself all at sea and deeply disappointed. Not a sign of fiery swords or trumpeting angels in the sky—rain soaking the red cross standards and sluicing away the roads. And now he must abandon Herbert—his second father, his best comrade—as a man leaves an old horse whose days of usefulness are over.

When the matter was decided at a family council, Andrew, in a sudden burst of self-sacrifice which he was later deeply to regret, said that he would remain with his father. He was a bastard—if he had grown into a man, it was only by his father's will; he could not be ungrateful; as long as his father lived he would stay at his side. His legitimate brothers thanked him heartily. And Ansiau wept, but he said: "I cannot stop you from doing your duty." And he insisted that their decision must be announced to the sick man. However, none of his sons had the courage to do it. Saturday evening Herbert appeared to be better and was able to speak a few words. He asked if the count were ready to leave (he was hoping there would be some delay in the preparations).

Ansiau answered him: "We leave tomorrow at dawn, after Mass." Then Herbert closed his eyes and threads of tears trickled down his cheeks onto the pillow. Ansiau's heart sank, and his voice was so broken by sobs that he could say nothing. Then Andrew, who stood beside him, knelt by the bed and said: "Father, I will stay with you." The sick man gave a weak smile of disdain—did they take him for a child who can be consoled by a toy!

"As soon as you are better, uncle," Ansiau said, "you can rejoin the army— we are sure to be kept at Marseilles for a time waiting for ships." Herbert opened his eyes again and said: "No." He knew that he would never be fit to make the journey and was only waiting for the moment when he might peacefully resign himself to death. Age and his illness were gaining the upper hand again; he wanted nothing but to rest.

But not yet—he must wait for that, he knew, until the crusaders had left the city. Meanwhile, he felt that he was the object of a respectful and affectionate pity, and the feeling restored a little of his strength. He began bidding them all farewell with as much solemnity as his condition permitted. And when his three sons knelt beside him and asked for his blessing, he understood that he would never see them again in this world.

And now, for the first time in his long, feverish life, he condescended to look at them attentively, at the three sons who had been his companions and yet were his inferiors, a sort of honor guard necessary for his prestige— his issue, his heirs. Now that their lives were to be severed from his forever, he became aware that they were also his friends—or could have been so if he had deigned to notice them. With a lucidity intensified by his state of weakness he studied those wolf faces, pale and framed in reddish beards and bathed in a light which proceeded, he knew, from his own soul, not from the candles burning by the bed.

He saw them as they had been—turbulent boys, ungovernable youths, fairly steady young men—as he knew them now, even to the darkest corners of the souls they hid so well. Izembard, the youngest, with his low forehead and mobile mouth—violent and obtuse. Ogier, the second, big and hairy, with his shifty, perverse, wily eyes. And above all Simon, the eldest—the best of them, the most like himself—a man now, thirty-two, neither handsome nor brilliant, but like those strong straight oaks which, even in midwinter, send the living, straining sap up to their uttermost buds. Simon looked at the world straight and reflected on what he saw, his mouth was firm and noble, he carried his head proudly. Herbert knew that he was intelligent and alert—no, he would not be wasting his time in Palestine, he would make his way, he was not like those who can only pray and drink and fight. Herbert was fifty-two, and never before had he stopped to reflect what was to become of his sons. To Simon he yielded his own place in life. In the emotion of a last farewell, he was glad to leave him his private heritage of ambitions and dreams and plans. Some day men would know the name of Simon of Linnières, son of Herbert the Red.

The solemnity of the occasion—a father bestowing his last blessing upon his sons as they set out on the Crusade—somewhat consoled the old knight for his unhappy plight. But his tongue would not obey him, he could not speak the words which would have been appropriate, and for that he was never to find consolation. But he summoned the strength to turn his eyes to Andrew and say: "My hand—bless—" Andrew finally understood what he wanted and took his father's left arm and laid the heavy, swollen, lifeless hand on Simon's forehead. Simon bent his head and crossed himself, then he rose and kissed his father's hand as if it were a relic. His eyes filled with tears—a sign of intense emotion in a man so reserved. Then Andrew repeated the gesture for Ogier and for Izembard.

Ansiau said: "Brother, I never supposed that a day would come when we must part. But it is true that we promised each other nothing and that your father is closer to you than I."

"You do not know what it means," said Andrew. "I had not a rag to cover me and my grandfather beat me from morning to night. He was ashamed of me because of my mother. I had scabs and bruises all over my body. When my father took me to the castle my elbows and anklebones had worn through my skin. And he was not ashamed of me."

"You never told me." Ansiau was aghast at the thought that Andrew had ever been a whipped, half-starved boy.

"Brother," Andrew said softly, "no doubt I am not what you think me. But you will never have a better friend than I. Since we cannot make our promise before the Holy Sepulchre, we can at least exchange crosses. You shall wear my cross to Jerusalem."

"Amen. It will guard me on the road. Let me be dishonored, let me see my sons die, if ever I fail you in loyalty. Whatever you ask of me I will do. God does not intend to part us forever—I shall come back, or else you will journey to the Holy Land."

Andrew sighed. "Not so long as my father lives."

"Since you are to stay," said Ansiau, "I entrust my lady to you—be good to her. I shall be easier knowing that you are here. I would not say it to anyone except you, but she is very young, and I shall be gone a long time. Above all, see that she does not marry again until she is certain that I am dead."

"Count on me," said Andrew.

And Ansiau went on: "Naturally, if I die I should not ask a better husband for my lady than you—if you were willing. I hoped you would marry a princess of Ultramar—but my lady—well, she is a lady of great worth. But if you do not want her, at least look to it that she does not marry a man of evil life or a fortune hunter. And when you see her, tell her that I think of her always."

Another day of departure. Slow and cumbersome, the army began its march—over roads that ran between vast fields, green or black, bordered by leafless forests downy with young green. Men on horseback with crosses sewn on their garments, painted on their armor, carrying tall white banners marked with the red cross too—the peasants who saw them pass crossed themselves, hardly pausing to wonder what these strangers were setting forth to do in a strange land.

And looking now at the sky, now at the backs of his comrades, Ansiau forgot Andrew, forgot Herbert, forgot his lady. His past life was already behind him. Ahead were roads and mountains and rivers and ports and the blue sea. And the great cross which men adore in Jerusalem.

During those first days Alis wept often, as was seemly—she already regarded herself as a widow or a woman abandoned. She thought it hard for a woman of her age to live without a husband and she could not help feeling resentful toward the man who had so cruelly forsaken her. No one can weep forever, so she finally resigned herself and returned to supervising the household as before. But she often climbed to the roof of the keep and gazed down the road until it was lost in woods and thickets beyond the stream—she still hoped that some last-minute obstacle would oblige her baron to return to Linnières.

Finally, about the end of May—the fields were bright with flowers and the forest was growing a darker green—poor Alis from her post on the roof of the keep saw three riders coming over the hill which lay toward Seuroi. Ansiau was not among them. But Alis had good eyes and she recognized them perfectly: they were Herbert the Red, Andrew, and Gervase, Herbert's squire. She needed no witchcraft to divine the reason for their return—Herbert's horse was moving slowly, the rider fell back into the saddle like a sack at every step and looked thin and exhausted. Andrew rode at his side, ready to catch him if he should lose his balance. Alis hurried down to the hall and announced that Lord Herbert was on his way back to the castle. Claude, Herbert's unmarried daughter, clapped her hands for joy and sent two waiting-women to gather field flowers to decorate table and walls. And Alis became aware that there was a wine stain on her dress and that she had not combed her hair for three days—she ran to the upper chamber, blushing at the mere thought that Herbert might have found her in such a state.

For six weeks Alis had felt lost, changed—she did not know herself. Ansiau's love had been like the warmth of a great fire all about her, like a high mountain hiding sun and sky and mankind from her eyes. He had left her so suddenly. Now there was no one to admire her hair, her arms, her feet—no one to give her presents every Sunday, to serve her the choicest morsels from each dish—no longer need she wear beautiful dresses, or perfume and massage her body which her baron had always wanted white and smooth; and when she bathed she sighed over so much wasted beauty. Ansiau had made her so used to thinking of herself as a garden of delights. And the doglike devotion of a Milon of Le Cagne could not even flatter her—what was it to her that a varlet loved her?

Not even her little son Girard could console her any longer. She was pregnant again, for the ninth time—her fear of losing this child, too, made her almost overcautious, and Girard was becoming too heavy to be carried. She did not know how to approach her older children—Ansiau had so monopolized her, so imprisoned her in his cloying affection that she had hardly had time left even for her youngest. Once weaned, a child must no longer compete with its father. And, really, no child could require more care, more watching, more affection than a man like Ansiau. No other woman, he thought, could equal Lady Alis at bathing him, combing his hair, massaging him, helping him dress, holding his stirrup; she had to make braid for him and sew it on, make his girdles, serve him at table if he was in a bad humor. Whenever he went to tournaments at Troyes or Bar-on-Seine he took her with him. That, however, she rather liked. But as for the children—it was all she could do to snatch time to make the sign of the cross over them in the morning, or to say: "Stop making so much noise in here!" When they were ill she said the rosary at their bedside and sprinkled them with holy water. She knew that they ought to be whipped, and hardened to cold and hunger, especially the boys. But there, too, her baron would hardly ever let her do what she thought she should; she was a woman and could not possibly know how to bring up men. Now he was gone, but the boys were still his, entrusted to squires, already promised as pages to William of Nangi—future strangers.

As she combed her long blond hair Alis felt something like fresh waves of blood rising to her cheeks, flowing to her fingertips. Her idle, formless thoughts concentrated, took shape, she became all impatience to learn the story of the crusaders' departure, to hear news of her father and her cousins; perhaps Andrew would bring her some last farewell from her baron. Herbert was a good talker, and she was sure he would give a minute account of all that he had seen and heard at Troyes.

When the three riders entered the courtyard Alis, Richeut, Claude, Odette, and the other ladies were standing by the well, ready to greet them. Herbert, weak to the point of exhaustion, was half carried up the ladder and seated in Ansiau's great chair by the fireplace. He was shivering despite the warmth of the day, for repeated bleedings had taken too much of his blood. His face was earthy. Alis saw his long sinewy hands grip the arms of the chair. When she knelt to offer him wine he looked down at her; his eyes, clouded with sadness and fatigue, still had their old kindliness. Strangely enough, it was just their kindliness which she found difficult to bear, and she looked away. Herbert had always rather frightened her because of his amorous past, his knightly achievements, his fine manners—above all because of his arrogant bearing, the proud curve of his back—a prince or a count could not look loftier. In eight years she had not become intimate with him; yet he loved her, and she knew it.

"Fair cousin," she asked Andrew, "did my lord give you no message for me before he set out?"

"Indeed he did. He said that he thought of you always."

Alis sighed—really her baron had no imagination, it was just like him to have sent so poor a message.

Alis was mistress of the castle, and she made it a point of honor to see that her husband's uncle should want for nothing. And very soon Herbert became master and lord of Linnières.

He had never tried to interfere in the management of the household. But he insisted on being well served. At all hours varlets and waiting-women were on the run for him, now bringing him hot stones, now a fortifying wine, now a toothpick. To regain his strength he was drinking the blood of live birds, and he would touch none but the blood of falcons and buzzards, which was extremely costly—and Alis often went hunting wild kites herself in order to save her own favorite hawks. In addition Herbert would not eat or drink at set times. The fire burned on the hearth from morning to night, and at all hours the cooks were stewing fowl or roasting quail or simmering broths of bones and medicinal herbs. Every day Lady Alis' waiting-women had to massage him, rub him with unguents, scratch him or whip him with green walnut twigs to stimulate the circulation. In short, the old knight managed to fill the entire castle with himself and his whims. And Alis did everything to please him, as much out of respect for him as because it was the proper thing to do. Andrew was a good nurse. No one but he knew how to quiet his father and reason him out of his headstrong whims, and Alis was duly grateful to him.

Slowly the sick man's strength returned. One morning in June—St. John's Day had passed—he had his horse saddled and rode out hawking with Andrew, Alis, and his daughter Claude. He cast a falcon admirably, and the two young women cried out their admiration as they watched him. Claude said: "I have never seen a better falconer than my father. If I were not his daughter, it would be he I would choose to love." And Alis said nothing and thought: "After all, his temples are gray and he has a great long nose." The thought pleased her, God knew why.

Herbert drew her thoughts now—naturally, as a magnet draws needles. It was for him that she smoothed her hair over her temples and rubbed her hands with lemon juice. For him she sat on a bench in the chimney corner with a girdle or a shift to embroider, keeping her eyes on her work to show that she was an industrious woman and clever at needlework. For him she

called her sons to her and caressed them and talked to them about Ansiau—
to show that she was a good mother. Her vanity, which Ansiau had satisfied
so well, resumed all its old exigency and became tyrannical. She would have
done much to win or to keep the esteem of Herbert the Red—he impressed
her as no man had ever impressed her before; he had been the companion
of her father and of her grandfather, the famous Guy of Marseint, he knew
so many things, such splendid things, and she never dared look him in the
face, for she believed he could read her thoughts. "Your father," she said
to Andrew, "is a most noble and most wise man—no one could ever tire of
listening to him." And Andrew thought: "There is one woman with good
sense."

Alis gave birth to her sixth child without mishap. On Christmas day she
brought a girl into the world. Richeut was the child's godmother, and she was
named Alis, after the little elder sister who had lived but two months. And
Lady Alis, whose heart had not forgotten her little Ala lying white and cold,
called her new baby Alette. She had gone through a difficult labor and after
it she felt completely happy and hardly thought of her husband's absence.
Or if she thought of it, it was to say, "How glad her father would have been
to see her," or "The baron little thinks that he will have five children when
he comes home from the Holy Land—he will bring no present for you,
Alette." And since it was a bitterly cold winter, she spent her time in the
chimney corner beside Herbert's chair, holding her new baby in her arms.

Herbert finally recovered almost completely. Under Andrew's uneasy eye
he hunted and drank as he had done before his illness. Nine months had
passed since the departure of the crusaders, and the old knight had reconciled
himself to his disappointment and had even begun to dye his hair again.
After a life spent in travelling from city to city, from tournament to tournament, he began to find that he was no more unhappy at Linnières than anywhere else. The castle was small, dark, and mean, but he knew that here
he was absolute master. He was the head of the family, and among all these
women and children and varlets he felt himself cock of the roost. He did
not deign to concern himself with the details of the castle economy—it was
Alis who paid the soldiers, had the hides tanned, the grain ground, the cloth
bleached, it was Alis who scolded the servants and kept count of the candles
and spice boxes. But Herbert lived in the belief that all these things were
done solely to satisfy his needs and his whims—he had only to ask for what
he wanted. The forest, the horses, the hawks grew and increased for the
pleasure of Herbert of Linnières.

During the long winter afternoons Herbert served as a welcome substitute
for the minstrels who came all too rarely to the castle, for he was never
tired of telling tales of war, of singing himself and setting the young men
and girls to singing in chorus. He had a good memory and the remnants
of a pleasing voice. He sang everything—war songs and crusaders' songs,
lays, ballads, dawn songs in the language of Provence, sacred canticles in

Latin. And Lady Alis, listening, put little Alette in her cradle and wiped away the tears that streamed from her eyes.

Alis was completely devoted to the old knight. She was only astonished that she had never known before what a wonderful man he was. Naturally she accepted all that he said as gospel truth. And he, though no braggart, knew how to put his best foot foremost and show himself to advantage in his memories of war and pleasure. Alis listened with a light in her eyes, and Herbert saw her cheeks go white and red and her breasts rise and fall under the sheer linen of her dress. Herbert, on his side, did not remain indifferent to such intense admiration, and Alis pleased him greatly—he valued her for her good blood, her bravery, her loyalty, and above all for the esteem in which she seemed to hold him. He even said to Andrew one evening: "If Ansiau does not come back from the Holy Land—which God forfend!— I will take his wife."

Andrew innocently asked: "What will you do with her?"

"What does a man marry a wife for? I shall be master of the domain as long as the children are not of age. And besides, she is of good blood."

"Of good blood and well brought up," Andrew agreed. "A braver woman does not breathe and no one ever equalled her at managing the domain— not even our lamented Lady Adela."

"And to think that it was I who arranged their marriage," Herbert went on thoughtfully. "I could quite as well have had her myself. It was just Ansiau's luck to get such a woman without taking any more trouble than going to bed with her."

Andrew, uneasy at seeing his father infringe on Ansiau's rights, even though it were only in words, hastened to change the subject.

Alis had recovered all her joy in life. She sang over her spinning, ran about the hall like a girl, pinched her children and smothered them with kisses whenever they came within reach. And toward the end of Lent she began to watch the thawing snow stream away past the stables and the palisade, and great drops falling everywhere so swiftly and steadily that they seemed to be chasing one another. The cawing of crows filled her with delight and pain, the air was so clear that she could distinguish the black and gray branches of birch and ash far away in the forest and the smoke from the hearths of Bernon village. She felt such a love for the forest and the fields and the muddy courtyard that she was amazed to think she had ever loved another house and another stretch of earth. What remained to her of her first nest except the memory of her parents and her pride in being the sole descendant of that noble Guy of Marseint whom Herbert so often praised? Now she was prouder of the lineage of Linnières than of her own, and when she said "we" and "our kindred" she thought of the brothers and sons and nephews of Herbert the Red. As for Ansiau, she had made a beautifully idealized image of him and she conjured it up every night before she fell asleep. But she would not admit to herself that she felt freer and happier than she had when he was with her.

Alis had always been vaguely excited by Herbert's kisses. But that year at Easter the vapors of spring and twelve months of enforced chastity had such an effect on her that she almost fainted when Herbert pressed his hard brown lips on her half-open mouth. After that she began waiting for the next time he would kiss her as she would wait for a feast day. She did not reproach herself—it was an innocent pleasure, and Ansiau must be tasting much more real ones at Jerusalem or elsewhere. And since Herbert was accomplished in every respect, it was only natural that he should kiss better than other men.

Herbert was not the man to resist temptation—but first he must be tempted, and in this case he was not. For one thing his taste ran to unripe fruit, and a woman of twenty-three could hardly excite him. For another, to dishonor his nephew was in his eyes to dishonor himself—he no more desired Alis than he desired his daughter Claude. All this did not prevent him from thinking of her as a possible wife, love and marriage being two quite different, and even opposite, things. He admired Alis, he considered her intelligent, noble, superior to the run of women—in short, an ideal wife for a knight, loyal and chaste as St. Margaret. But he was beginning to persuade himself that his nephew did not deserve such an accomplished woman; Ansiau might well take service under some baron in the Holy Land —he was young, at his age a life of adventure was the natural thing—castles and firesides and marriage beds were the prerogative of elder men, men who had earned their rest.

"Ansiau is a fine lad," he said to Alis. "I would say nothing against him to you—he is your lord and you should love him well. But he has the makings of an excellent groom."

Alis was rather annoyed by this remark. But she could not believe that anything Herbert said was untrue, and the halo with which she surrounded Ansiau began to grow a little tarnished.

Another day Herbert took it upon himself to tell her that after the war in France Ansiau had seen the lady of Chalmiers and had fallen so madly in love with her that he had spent three days and nights in her tent, thereby missing a tournament. It was a complete surprise to Alis. "If anyone but you had told me," she said, "I would not have believed it. He always swore to me that he had loved no one else."

"I shouldn't advise you to put your hand in the fire on the strength of a husband's oath," said Herbert, laughing. "It is no dishonor for a man to be well treated by a beautiful woman."

Alis sadly agreed, because she could no longer hold any opinion that was not Herbert's; but she felt unhappy nonetheless. Her trust in Ansiau was rudely shaken, and now she felt certain that he had long since forgotten her with the beautiful ladies of Palestine.

"Is the lady of Chalmiers really so beautiful?" she asked Herbert some time later.

He shrugged his shoulders. "So they say. Your father would know more about it than I do, I imagine. She has gone through so many hands that there's not much left. But in her day she was pretty enough."

Alis bit her lips, mortified to hear Herbert say that any woman except herself was pretty.

No one suspected the love which bound Alis to her husband's uncle. Even Andrew thought that she showed good sense in seeking the friendship of a man so noble and so brave—he never supposed that she was in love. And Herbert thought of her with more tenderness than he was accustomed to feeling. She was so pretty, he had never seen her look like this before, with cheeks flushed and eyes alight. She trembled when he took her hand, dropped her lids when he looked at her. But he saw only modest reserve in these signs of her embarrassment, and they delighted him. He loved her with a chaste love, for there were two or three village girls who regularly shared his bed— he could hardly do without them—and if he had married Alis a dozen times over it would have made no change in his habits. But she stirred him precisely because he thought her as chaste as he was not. He was astonished to find himself so much attracted by virtue in his old age.

It was on a dark, rainy June day that a stranger wrapped in a gray cloak knocked at the castle gate. His horse, his clothes, and even his face were covered with mud. "You have nothing to fear," he said to the varlet who let him in and helped him to dismount, "not even death or the Devil will come looking for you here." Then he asked if the good knight Herbert of Linnières, surnamed the Red, was still alive. "Is he alive!" said the varlet, smiling at the traveller's ignorance. "If he weren't, it would not be long before everybody knew it! He has been out hawking all morning." Then Garin of Linnières and two of Girard the Blond's sons came to ask the newcomer into the castle—their lady, they said, had a good hot bath and a feather bed ready for him in the upper hall, for she had guessed that he was a knight.

He went upstairs, and the waiting-women took off his boots and cloak and carried them away to dry. Alis came up to welcome him and turned pale when she saw that his skin had the dark tan of men who have been in hot countries. The knight, who had a strong Lorraine accent, said that his name was Philip of Wassy and that he had a message for Herbert the Red. "By St. Thiou," said Alis, "you are my guest and you shall do nothing before you have bathed and rested. My lady cousins will bring you fresh clothes. My lord, too, is on his travels, he is far away in the Holy Land."

The knight came down to the hall that evening. Herbert was awaiting him with an impatience which can easily be imagined. "Surely," he said to Andrew, "he brings news of our kinsmen. And I fear that it is bad news."

138

Alis made Philip of Wassy sit in a cushioned chair beside Herbert's, and Claude put a pillow under his feet. The knight drew from the bag he wore at his waist a small copper plaque encrusted with amethysts and put it into Herbert's hand. "Look," he said, "this medallion belongs to your son Simon of Linnières. He gave it to me to show you who I am."

Herbert crossed himself and Claude gave a great cry. Andrew leaned over the back of his father's chair. And Alis fixed astonished and unbelieving eyes on the man who had seen their kinsmen who were so far away—had he seen Ansiau too?

The news that Philip of Wassy brought was bad news for Herbert: Simon sent word to his father that his two younger brothers, Ogier and Izembard, had been carried off by fever as soon as they reached the Holy Land. They were buried at Acre. Simon himself had taken service under a baron of Palestine descended from one of the noblest families in the kingdom and brother to the Baldwin of Rames who had wished to marry the king's sister. Simon did not expect to return to France, and he ordered his wife to go back to her parents; his children were to be entrusted to Ansiau's lady. He, Philip of Wassy, had made Simon's acquaintance at Jerusalem, where he had gone on pilgrimage.

Death, and especially death so far away, was a commonplace accident which came as no surprise, and Odette, Simon's wife, felt quite as much widowed as the wives of Izembard and Ogier. Herbert, however, suffered great grief, as was seemly, and tore his clothes and even plucked out a few strands of his hair. Alis shared in his sorrow—she put herself in his place. "If Ansiau were to lose his sons," she thought, "he would go mad."

Herbert had himself bled for fear of a second attack, and spent the following day in bed. Having thus performed his duty as a father, he got up, unable to resist the attractions of a new face and recent news.

Philip of Wassy had little to tell concerning the other crusaders from Champagne. He had seen some of them at Jerusalem. Count Henry had been pointed out to him as he was leaving Holy Sepulchre after praying there with the king. He knew, too, that the army of Champagne had camped with the king's near Tiberias (or some such name) but there had been no battle. "Ah," said Herbert, "the king is too young or he has bad counsellors. Then or never was the time for a battle—it is not often that he has so many of our good knights of Champagne with him."

"True," said Philip, "but he has had few of his own since the battle he fought at Mongesard, near Saint-Georges, where so many of his best knights were taken prisoners."

Count Henry of Champagne and his barons, together with Peter of Courtenay, had left the kingdom soon after Easter, making their way northward toward Antioch. As Simon had explained to Philip of Wassy, they expected to return to France by land, either because the cost of sea transport was too high or because the count had a secret mission to the emperor.

"If I envy them," said Herbert, "it is because they will see Constantinople.

There is not a fairer city on earth—it is Paradise. Why, simply on the archbishop's robe I saw more jewels than are stored in the count's treasury at
Troyes. Beware," he said, turning to Alis, "your baron will stay there, he
will never want to come home."

"I do not blame Simon," said Alis, "it is his own concern. But if my lord
did as he has done, I would wish him covered with sores and scabs, with
every sore eaten by worms and flies."

Herbert said that a good wife should desire her husband's honor and
profit. Simon was no fool and he knew what he was doing. At which Philip
began praising Simon—never had he known a wiser or more courteous
knight. He had seen him at Jerusalem in the train of his new lord—he was
living in great luxury, he had six squires to carry his lances, and wore ostrich
plumes on his helmet. And at the wedding of the king's sister he had worn
a cloth-of-scarlet tunic which must have cost half his wage for six months.
Herbert sighed enviously. "Ah, if I were his age! And did he tell you who
his friends are? Is he well lodged? Is his lord well disposed toward him?"

Philip of Wassy professed the greatest admiration for Simon. Simon had
decided to remain in the Holy Land for the most estimable reasons, Philip
said—first, because he wanted to be near the tomb of his brothers, and then
God Himself had commanded him not to leave a country so full of infidels
and in such grave peril—he had come to Jerusalem at thirty-three, the age
at which Our Lord had suffered martyrdom, therefore he would spend his
life fighting the Saviour's enemies and worshipping Him in the land where
He had lived.

"And wearing cloth of scarlet," said Alis without raising her eyes from
her needlework. Philip of Wassy barely shrugged his shoulders, but Herbert
was angered and answered in a hard voice: "Silence, woman, mind your own
affairs."

Tears came into her eyes and she wished that the ground would swallow
her. Herbert did not speak to her again all evening and hardly condescended
to look at her when she offered him the wine cup during supper. It was not
that he was still angry—he was too busy talking with his guest and had
forgotten her very existence. But Alis thought that he bore her a grudge.
She heard no more of Philip's tales or Odette's lamentations. She lay awake
all night trying to think of some way to justify herself in the old knight's
eyes. The next day she humbly asked his pardon for having spoken foolishly
—she had not meant to blame Simon, but she had felt so sorry for Odette.

"Not at all," said Herbert. "I took no offense." And he turned to his
guest again, and Alis felt even more deeply hurt and wanted to say something cutting to him.

Philip of Wassy spent ten days at Linnières and left on the eve of Burning
Martinmas—which this year did not live up to its name, for the day was
cloudy and cold. Alis presented her guest with a gray cloak and a carved
wooden cup and asked him to visit her sister Hermenjart of Rumilli at Troyes
—which would save him the expense of a hotel—and also to have a Mass

said at the cathedral for Ansiau and his kinsmen. Life at the castle grew dull after Philip left. Herbert's old longing for adventure had come upon him again and he was bored to death. To divert himself in his terrible attacks of melancholy he threw knives, using a live dog for a target, or plunged into shameless debauchery which he made no attempt to conceal. Alis thought: "It is because of his grief for his sons," and her pity was stronger than her anger. And she, too, began to suffer from boredom, even little Girard could no longer distract her. She let her women do their work unsupervised, wandered from the courtyard to the hall, from the hall to the courtyard, or went down to talk to Milon who was always at the stables.

She was less proud now, and it pleased her to see a young man turn red and white when she came near him and stammer when she looked him in the face. Those were the ordinary and unmistakable signs of love, and Alis thought more and more often of love, and particularly of a love of which she should be the object. At least she could be sure of Milon. She sometimes let him kiss her hand—he would kiss it too long, she would laugh, and he would grow sad and shamefaced and begin to talk to his horses—indeed he talked to horses far oftener than he did to men.

Then came the day when Alis saw that without borrowing further she could not pay her soldiers. And to borrow, she must first repay her old debt to Abner, or at least pay the interest—she had already managed to have the term extended for a year, and she had thought that the year would never end. But the year did end and still Ansiau had not come home. One of Haguenier of Hervi's nephews had stopped at Linnieres to report that disquieting rumors had reached Troyes—it was said that the count and all his men had been taken prisoners by the Turks. Herbert maintained that such rumors were more likely to be false than true, yet he was troubled. And Lady Alis, though she did not yet understand all the significance of the news, understood that if Abner believed it he would not lend her another penny. However, she decided to go to Troyes to see what could be done.

"If it is being talked about in Troyes," said Herbert thoughtfully, "there must be some foundation for it. News is scarce. But surely, if they had reached Constantinople we should have heard of it one way or another."

Alis, sitting on a stool beside him with her head in her hands, was trying to think what more she could pledge. If she could find some way of redeeming the land without paying—if for example she went to Troyes Castle and threw herself at the countess' feet, if the countess ordered Abner to remit her the interest—and the interest amounted to at least three-fourths of the sum originally borrowed—but even then where was she to find money to repay the loan when she had to begin by borrowing . . . ?

Herbert took pity on her.

"It is not easy to find a way out, my fair niece," he said.

Alis said: "They ought to hang every Jew in Champagne."

"Don't fret," said Herbert with a smile. "At your age people take things too much to heart. Something can always be done. Listen—I will go with you. I can make Abner come to terms."

Alis was suddenly seized with such terror that she let her embroidery frame fall from her knees; the skeins scattered over the flagstones, and her hands shook so violently that she could not pick up her work. Little Simone, Simon's daughter, ran after the skeins and put them back in Alis' lap.

"You are shivering, aunt," she said. "Are you ill?"

She was answered by a slap. Alis rose, not daring to look at Herbert, and went upstairs. There she plunged her hands into a jug of water and then rubbed them over her forehead and cheeks. The waiting-women, who were spinning under Richeut's supervision, looked at her in astonishment. She went to a window, leaned on the sill, and put her hands over her eyes.

To make the journey to Troyes with Herbert. To be with him hour after hour, under his eyes, hearing his voice. The very idea made her thoughts and her legs as heavy as lead. What would the reality do to her? Could she be with him from morning to night and not betray herself? All that time alone together—what could she say to him? How would she dare to look at him, when even now she could not force herself to open her eyes, simply because he had said that he would make the journey with her?

Once at the inn, she thought, once at Troyes she could not resist offering herself to him, and then he would despise her, or . . . Was she in love then—she, Alis of Puiseaux, daughter of a noble father and a noble mother? In love? She had been so afraid of falling in love—love, for a crusader's wife, could bring nothing but sorrow and shame. No, Ansiau should not come back only to learn that she had betrayed him, like the wife of a common sergeant.

Yet it would have been marvellous to love Herbert of Linnières. A man so noble, so brave, so wise. If his ceremonious kisses gave her such pleasure, what would his amorous kisses be? He was not old, for he still loved women —why should he not love her? She was no uglier than the women he had loved. No, he was not old, for he was the only man in the world. He was her master, she his slave. She would go to him, kneel to him, tell him— perhaps he would take pity on her. Yet was it possible that he did not know it already, he who understood everything, knew everything? But then she felt the blood rush into her face, and she knew that not only could she not offer herself to Herbert, she could no longer even see him, she felt such shame. He was the last man in the world to whom she could speak of love.

Ever since her childhood Alis had been told that love was a sickness, and she did not dream of resisting it. She sincerely believed that she was in love for the first time in her life; her love for Ansiau had been something utterly different, and she thought of it now as childishness. Never in Ansiau's presence had she felt this strange fear, never had her heart beaten so wildly, never had her blood so swiftly rushed to her face or so suddenly drained back. She lived now in a world whose center and axis was Herbert of

Linnières. She hardly dared speak to him, yet her need to see him was so great that she managed to be wherever he was. She lived in the hope that he would finally divine her love for him, yet she, dreaded that he might and woke every morning terrified at the thought that today she would be led to commit irreparable sin . . . Then nothing happened, and at night she wept in frustration and sorrow.

Herbert the Red was not without vanity, but he had long since given up playing the lover. This granddaughter of the noble Guy was a piece of goods he would have liked to lay hands on but which would have lost all its value if ever she became a woman like other women. Their relation had changed—he did not even know why. He did not admire her as he had done. He wanted to go to Troyes to see people and pick up news of his kinsmen, and Lady Alis did not seem to want to make the journey—now the weather was too hot, now she felt unwell. Herbert thought: "A young woman who doesn't know her own mind." Finally he said that he would go alone. He would do the best he could with Abner. Alis knew that he was extravagant and irresponsible, but in him these were only added virtues; Herbert of Linnières was not a usurer or a merchant. She freely gave him the power to pledge and borrow in her name. But on the eve of his departure she was terrified by the thought that she would not see him again for weeks.

It was an extraordinarily beautiful day. The meadow in front of the castle was covered with white daisies. Women and girls wandered over the slope, gathering nosegays to decorate the chapel for Assumption Day. Herbert—in a good humor for once—was strolling through the tall grass with Alis and Claude. Claude kept stooping to pick flowers, Alis was pulling the petals from a daisy. They reached the brook and the shade of the willows. Alis sat down in the grass to rest, and Claude set off down the brook looking for forget-me-nots.

Left alone with Herbert, Alis sat motionless with downcast eyes, listening to her heart pounding against her ribs. She felt intensely sad—how long would it be before she saw him again? But when he sat down on the grass beside her she threw a desperate look at Claude in her blue dress vanishing among the willows and hazels.

Herbert could appreciate a beautiful woman, and the woman beside him was charming—fresh from the bath, she wore a white, very sheer dress, she had long white hands with pink fingernails. In love, it would never have occurred to him to make a distinction between words and acts—so he could not talk of love. But he felt a sort of tenderness which he tried to put into words.

"If ever you become a widow, fair niece, I know one who will need no urging to take you," he said with an embarrassed laugh. Alis answered that she had no desire to become a widow.

He smiled. "I know. You are a good little wife. But a second husband may match a first. Anything can happen. Mind you, I say nothing—I love

Ansiau, he is of my blood. But—I think I love you more. First of all"—he rose and began hacking at the trunk of a willow with his knife—"first of all because you were good to Rainard. Any other woman would have treated him like a leper, poor fellow. But you are not like other women. You never forgot that he was a knight and came of good blood. It is the stock. The stock is stronger than ourselves—you could not do wrong even if you wanted to."

Alis shivered and looked at him. He was smiling kindly—she had never seen just that expression on his face. She opened her mouth to speak and could think of nothing to say. Besides, Herbert was talking enough for two.

"And you are good to me too. Andrew told me that I have been troubling you with my little trollops—now you can have peace for a while. I could see that you didn't like it." He cut two willow branches and began swishing them through the air, striking them against the tree. "It's too bad you are not coming with me tomorrow. I am very much afraid that Sales of Hervi may have been telling the truth the other day. I want to get to the bottom of it."

"How could the count's whole army be taken?" Alis asked. "It is impossible. It must be a false rumor."

"Don't be too sure. The infidels are strong—may God damn them! I want to get to the bottom of it. Fair niece, have I offended you? You seem not to feel as you did toward me."

"Not that I know of, my uncle."

"No—you don't want to say it, but there is something. I can't help it—I am old, I have troubles. I am sick, I haven't long to live. Ask Andrew if I can sleep nights—the thoughts that come to me make my hair stand on end. There are nights when I would rather kill myself than wait for morning. My time is out. You are young, you cannot understand."

Alis began to weep for pity, softly she wiped away her tears with her fingertips. Herbert paced up and down like a caged beast, slashing his willow branches. Claude's clear voice came from the distance: "Father, father!" Herbert started, then called back to her.

"Yes, I would have given a great deal to be in Simon's place. But it is all over. And you are young and pretty, and all you think about is children and debts and land. You can just as well do that when you are fifty."

"And what should I think about, my uncle?"

"How should I know? You could go to Troyes, see what is going on, dance, sing, wear your jewels. It would be no loss to Ansiau."

"Fine advice!"

"Better than you suppose. You need distraction. It is bad for you always being shut up here."

Just then Claude—scratched and dishevelled and laughing—came up with a great bunch of forget-me-nots. She threw herself on her father's neck and began sticking flowers into his beard, behind his ears, in the clasp of his collar. "They make your eyes bluer," she said. "I am going to make you a crown of them. Stop wrinkling up your nose." Herbert said: "Silly!" and stroked her hair. And Alis looked at them and bitterly regretted that she was not in Claude's place.

The sky was a pale yellow over the keep, and the walls and the palisade cast a shadow as far as the stream. Alis was walking slowly beside Claude; Herbert preceded them, his back as straight as ever. And Alis saw the red sunset light touch his long fluffy hair and transform it into a fiery halo around his beautiful shapely head. And she thought that perhaps there might be a love nobler than the love she had felt for Ansiau—a love without embraces and without pregnancies, a love in which a woman could spend her whole life looking at the man she loved, asking nothing of him but his presence. And she kept remembering that tomorrow he would not be there and she knew that she had only to speak and she could go with him—he had almost asked her to come, he would be glad to have her. But at the last moment her courage failed her; she did not dare to say that she had changed her mind, she was sure that Herbert and all the household would know the reason at once. Herbert set out the next morning—excited, rejuvenated by the thought of regaining his old liberty, by visions of roads and inns and Troyes. Yet to show himself in Troyes with the beautiful Alis of Puiseaux on his arm would have flattered his vanity—ah, women were always full of whims. He said good-bye to her coldly. Andrew, who was always ready long before his father, was pacing up and down the court, fussing over the stirrups. He felt uneasy and said to Gervase: "We must see that he does not drink too much. He forgets that he has been ill."

After three long gray leaden weeks of waiting, Alis saw them coming back. She had been so prostrate, so indifferent to everything, that Richeut had finally said: "You seem very sad now that Andrew is gone." Alis had answered: "You had better find some other story to tell the baron when he comes back. Andrew will never betray him." But she seemed so happy at the knights' return that Richeut clung to her idea.

The news Herbert brought was as bad as possible. The count had in fact been taken a prisoner and not one of his men had escaped—all had been captured, killed, or sold into slavery. A knight of Champagne returning from Constantinople had confirmed the news to the Countess Mary. The count had sent messengers to the emperor and the king of Jerusalem, and the emperor had himself dispatched this knight to Champagne with an escort, to reassure the countess. The emperor promised to do everything in his power to free Count Henry and his barons. But Herbert had not been able to learn whether the men of Linnières were with the count or had been killed. One thing was certain—Joceran of Puiseaux was dead. His head had been thrown into the prisoners' camp a week after their capture, and a half brother of Fulk of Rumilli had recognized it. The emperor's messenger, who knew Fulk and his wife Hermenjart, had told them the news. There was every reason to suppose it was Joceran's head, for no other crusader had a scar like his. The rumor in the camp was that Joceran had been taken by the Turks while he was looting a Saracen village, and that he and his men had been flayed alive on the spot because they had refused to abjure their faith. Baldwin, recalled from Chantemerle by his brother, had come to Troyes and received the fief of Puiseaux at the countess' hands—Herbert had seen him just after the investiture. "He is fatter than he was, but he can still ride. And I must say, my fair niece, that I should not have liked to be in his place —he did not look happy. His eyelids were red and swollen, I could hardly recognize him. I tell you, my niece, a man suffers when he loses his son but it is even worse to lose a father. I have not yet forgotten the day when I lost mine. A man can always beget more sons, but a father gone leaves a void forever."

Alis wept, yet to her surprise she felt less grief than the occasion demanded. Already she had almost forgotten that she had a father. It had all happened so far away, it all seemed so strange—she only half believed it. Sometimes she would remember how, as a little girl, she had stolen bits from her father's plate, or had put her little arms around his neck and fallen asleep. And she could not comprehend how that same father of hers could have been flayed by the Saracens, how his head could have been thrown into the latrine of a prisoners' camp. She knit her brows and shook her head. If she could have laid hands on those Saracens she would have torn out their eyes and their hair and beards, she would have thrown their babies into the flames. Mercy was not for such folk. And she began to understand why men were afire to fight the infidels.

Herbert said: "Be of good cheer, my fair niece. More than likely the good emperor will save our kinsmen. A nobler knight than the Emperor Manuel has never walked the earth. He is wise and courteous and he is friendly to the French. He will ransom the count and his men, and your husband will be home before New Year's."

Alis was weary. She wished that she were in Ansiau's arms again, crying her heart out—she had always been so at peace with him. Herbert was so baffling, so strange, he made her suffer so much. Sometimes she felt sure that he loved her, then he became curt, almost scornful—she did not know what to make of him. No man had ever been such a stranger to her—he was so distant, so superior. She could not bear to go on suffering for no end. She told herself that if Ansiau came back she would love him all over again.

And one evening Herbert did not return from hunting. When Andrew brought his own horse back to the stable he saw that his father's horse, Noradin, was not in his stall. Yet he had been sure that the old knight had returned with Gervase and young Garin. He went to the castle, questioned Gervase—Gervase had thought that his master was with Andrew and Girard the Blond's sons. No one had seen him. A little groom, nephew to Milon of Le Cagne, said that Lord Herbert had followed the dogs toward the boar's lair. "He said: 'Go tell Gervase that I have found the track.' And I couldn't find Gervase or anyone, and I can't remember where I last saw Lord Herbert." Boiling with rage, Andrew whipped the boy till the blood ran and sent the huntsmen to search for his father. All night at the castle they heard the horns calling and answering in the forest, and Alis, standing at a window, watched the torches moving up and down the road along the stream. It was a clear night but cold, such a night as comes early in October. The wind drove moon-white clouds over the forest.

Herbert did not know how he had lost his dogs. He was exhausted from his long ride, the blood throbbed in his temples, he had been obliged to loosen his collar and stop. Then, his faintness passed, he had tried to follow the boar's track—walking slowly, leading Noradin by the reins. Then the track had vanished in deep mud. He was in a part of the forest he did not know. The clumps of reed became scarcer, the ground drier; grass and moss were strewn with freshly fallen leaves, yellow and red. He came to a little glade and mounted again. His legs hurt, the effort it had cost him to reach the saddle had exhausted him so much that everything went black before his eyes. Noradin crossed the glade, sniffing the wind and looking to right and left. There was no opening, no path. Glancing at the sun, Herbert decided to go north, where he thought that he heard horns sounding. He wanted to blow his own horn, but he had not breath enough. Noradin picked a way between the birches and ashes, avoiding the underbrush. Feeling that he was about to faint, Herbert drew rein. The horse stopped suddenly. Herbert, who was leaning sideways, struck his head against a tree, lost his reins, and let himself slide to the ground head first.

Blood ran over his forehead, dripped from under his ear, soaked the hair at his temples. But the violent bleeding had done its work—he had recovered consciousness and was beginning to be aware of the trees above him and to feel intense pain in his left leg and right arm. The blow on his forehead had dulled his mind, but the suffering from it was not unpleasant. The pain gave him a feeling of being alive. The flowing blood was freeing him from the burden of sickness, from all the ills of the body. He closed his eyes. The sun was setting, and somewhere far away through the branches the sky was red.

God knew how long he had been there. Hours—days. The pain in his arm must be from a fracture, it was growing so intense that he had to bite his lips to keep from screaming. His arms and legs were like lead. The stones and dead branches and roots on which he lay were beginning to eat into his body like fiery wounds. Between the trees the sky was a smoky gray now, with only one thin streak of red low on the horizon.

Noradin stood leaning over his master, trembling, tossing his head—from time to time he gave a little appealing whinny: "What is he waiting for? Why doesn't he get up and go?" A hunter for forty years, Herbert believed in spells, in herbs soaked in toad's blood, perilous to horses—there were spells to bloat their bellies, spells to blind them, others to make their hoofs drop off. Herbert had never allowed a horse of his to graze in a strange place. So now he would not let Noradin leave his side. "Steady there, old boy," he said, "they will find us in good time." But he no longer felt very sure of it himself. He tried to raise his hunting call, "Ho-ho-ho-hoi," and his hoarse, feeble voice broke in his throat. Night was falling. The sky had grown white, the tree trunks black.

"That's Andrew looking for me." Far away the notes of horns roused the echoes—now sustained, now hurried, anxious, plaintive. Noradin raised his head and shook himself nervously, and Herbert laboriously raised his left hand and stroked his horse's muzzle. "They'll find us. They're coming now. Make a noise, Noradin, call them. Come on, call them." But nothing answered the long uneasy whinny. Once more the horns drew away. Herbert tried to take a position in which his bruised and broken limbs would pain him less, but he had to give it up—the pain became worse and worse. All night he spent his strength sending his long hunting call into the vast emptiness of the forest—"Ho-ho-ho-hoi." His racked throat, his thick tongue would no longer obey him. Each time he called the wound on his forehead bled and pained. At dawn—chilled, numb, soaked with dew—he felt almost too weak to breathe. When he opened his eyes he saw a cold, unfamiliar sun rising behind a network of half-bare branches. Sky, sun, and trees were all strange to him. And now he knew that what had come to him was not a hunting accident. It was death. He would never see a human face again.

Then fear bathed him in cold sweat and made his heart sink in his breast. He shouted: "Simon, Andrew, Simon!" and the sound of his own voice, thick with fear, brought him back to himself. He closed his eyes and tried to think. Call again. No. The horn. It was slung to his saddle. Noradin must turn sidewise and then lie down. It took time to explain to the animal what he wanted it to do. Then, over and over, Herbert tried to catch hold of the saddle and reach the horn—his left arm groped in the air and dropped back, the right was causing him such pain that he nearly lost consciousness each time he moved. Herbert had never known that the world of matter was so heavy and so inert. His bones were stone, his muscles lead, his swollen fingers did not know whether they had attained the goal or not, the saddle was slippery, the thong from which the horn hung was so thick and rough that his hand could not hold it—his clothes, wet with sweat and dew, stuck to his body and pained him at every movement.

He spent three hours trying to reach the horn, with such concentration that he thought of nothing else. Finally he fell back, panting, exhausted, whimpering like a child. Not for anything on earth would he have raised his arm again. But Noradin's warm breath brought him back to reality. He hated to send the animal off, perhaps to get lost, to eat some poisonous plant, to become bogged in a swamp, to fall among a pack of wolves. But it was his last chance and he must take it. "Noradin, old fellow, go find Andrew. Go on, old fellow. Bring Andrew here, don't come back without him." And as the horse hesitated, looking at its master with great loving eyes, Herbert made an effort to smile and repeated: "Go. That's what I want. Go quickly." The horse pricked up its ears, sniffed, whinnied, and started slowly away. Herbert heard it leave him with a painful pang; for a long time he tried to catch the last faint sounds of breaking branches and rustling leaves which still testified to Noradin's living presence. Then there was silence.

A new life began for him.

There was no anguish in his heart now, only a cold certainty—he would not be found alive.

He had always imagined that his death would come to him in some scarlet tent on a night after battle—drums throbbing, trumpets calling, shields stuck with arrows, hauberks red with blood. . . . Or in the great hall of the castle, on a pompous bed—candles burning, friends and relatives weeping, priest and deacon reciting the prayers for the dying. Confession, the gilded chalice and the shining white host, the warm oil of extreme unction, Masses said and Masses sung for his departing soul. With all that to help him, he might well find the hard passage not too painful. Never had he thought that it would befall him to die alone, without the sacraments, in a slime of his own sweat and blood and excrement, like a fox in a trap. He had not deserved it.

But since he must needs prepare himself for death alone, he closed his eyes and made an effort to forget the pain which racked his entire body. Softly he said his *Pater*, his *Credo,* his *Ave,* then repeated them a second time and a third.

But the prayers, so familiar and sweet in the castle chapel or at Hervi or St. Peter's at Troyes, were as empty now as clapperless bells. They had no music. A confusion of strange words whose meaning he could scarcely understand. Behind the network of branches, behind the crowns of the birches swinging threateningly above him, behind the heavy clouds, endlessly flying, flying, behind the unknown sky—there was no Father.

In everything around him now he saw only a vast Absence—the trees were hollow, the leaves ready to sink into dust. The pheasants, the squirrels skipping from branch to branch, were only skeletons clothed in fur or feathers. The corruption which was already devouring his body was only an extension of the black soil, the wet moss, the flies, the gnats, the ants. God was where there were men. What madness ever to have felt unhappy in a good warm bed, or before a good fire, with a fine white-and-golden woman at his side!

Already she was so far away. On her bench by the hearth, with her little girl in her arms. On the grass by the brook, in a white dress, with her pink cheeks (they were always pink), and her eyes full of pity. Linnieres was farther away than Jerusalem now. Was it indeed he, Herbert, who was dying? Was it not rather that the castle of Linnières had sunk into an abyss? Troyes was no more—nor Tonnerre, nor Dijon—nor Jerusalem. Ansiau's wife, Andrew, Gervase, Noradin, they had all sunk into a past which made them equal with the dead. Was Simon in his cloth of scarlet more alive than Joceran of

Puiseaux who had gone, men said, to Paradise? Ah, Joceran had outwitted death and the Devil and, dying, had won a martyr's crown. Herbert tried to make his thoughts follow his old comrade into a Paradise which seemed as far away and illusory as all the rest of the world.

All of them—all turned to dust and ashes, as well he knew—passed before him. They said: "You too. Are you made of other flesh than ours?" Joceran the Scarred, his companion in the Holy Land, bad friend, good comrade—and beside him the noble Guy of Marseint, dead for thirty years, the knight without land or wealth, who, dying young, had left his smile in the hearts of all who had known him. And after Guy of Marseint came John and Ogier of Linnières, sons of Hermeline of Jeugni like Herbert himself, his blood brothers, so long forgotten, Ogier killed at twenty in a tournament, John disembowelled by a boar in the forest of Linnières—on his deathbed his face had been like a child's, diaphanous, almost blue, too beautiful for a mortal. And his other brother, the lame one, who had outlived them to his own small gain, Rainard, the hardened old sinner, damned from the first, Rainard with his cavernous cough and his perpetual sneer—had he ever been young? Of course —Herbert saw him as he had been in the days of his service at Paiens, a boy like all the others, a little silent perhaps, a little cold. He too had been beautiful on his deathbed, or so Ansiau's wife had said. Then another dead man rose before his eyes—there was the catafalque in the chapel of Linnières with old Hugh lying on it blue and swollen, with his white hair that was turning yellow at the temples—and his wife Lady Adela, a few months before him, just as blue, just as swollen, hard, menacing; and before her Ansiau, the oldest of the family, a heap of marble flesh—before he had died his throat had rattled day and night, his soul had fled, but still for three days his body held out—yet in the end it had gone to rot in the tomb like the rest.

Then Galon, his old father, came—with his red hairy face, and the empty yellow eyes that were like old Ansiau's. Herbert had been barely twenty when his father died. Losing his father was always a hardship for a younger son without money or land, and the old man had loved his crusader son for his ardor and his courage—he called him "Cockscomb" because of his red hair and his love of fighting. Ah, thirty years had passed since that heavy hand had rested on Herbert's head and the broken voice had said, "Cockscomb." And now it was Herbert's own turn to pass to the other side, and he felt no whit the wiser than he did on the day old Galon had bade him farewell. And after his father, his mother came and bent over him—not the Hermeline of Jeugni of whom he had been so proud, but the mother of his memories, a forgotten mother, tall, very tall, like a column in a church—he had to stand on tiptoe to reach her waist, her hand covered his head, her mouth covered his hand. In her arms it was like being rocked in a boat, it was as warm as a big feather bed. O mother! Was she dead too? Lying in the graveyard at Hervi with Galon's other three wives? Oh—not she, not his big, warm, real mother! And closing his eyes Herbert became a child again, and he wanted to tell his mother about the thirst that was parching his throat, the pain in his arm—if only someone would drive away the flies that were swarming in his beard, in the wound on his forehead, behind his ears, trying to crawl up his nostrils and under his eyelids.

But already his body was growing numb, already it had ceased to struggle. Only his thought lived on, in a strange indifference to everything that had been his life until now. A great accounting with an unknown God who had no name in any Christian language. A sinner, he did not know what was sin and what not—unless he were to regard his whole fifty years of life as one long sin against God. But now Hell itself, with its boiling pitch, its flames, and its pincers, had been left far behind—it was as meaningless as Troyes or Toulouse. The world was reduced to the immense struggle of a carnal body laboring to bring forth another life; the pain in his arm and his wounds had ceased, and in a last effort to live, the thing that was Herbert the Red opened its eyes and saw nothing, opened its mouth to breathe an air that was not there—the last pulse of his blood just echoed in his ears. And suddenly there was a light in him and he knew that what had been flesh, corruption, dust, was leaving him forever and he had no more part in it.

The last thing that he saw was a great burst of brightness, fountains of white light so powerful that they shattered his sinews, his heartstrings. His head fell back. Consciousness drowned.

The crows were already beginning to scatter the swarming flies—they were fighting among themselves with beak and claw.

III. INTERLUDE

Herbert's body was found three days after his disappearance. His flesh had been torn to shreds by the crows; the fragments of his face still wore a mournful smile formed by the two rows of bared teeth. Andrew wrapped the body in two great woolen cloaks and helped his men to lay it on a hastily made litter of branches. Swarms of black flies hung around the horses, the air was so pestilential that the varlets held their noses. Andrew rode beside the litter, his broad shoulders shaken by sobs.

Alis saw the slow procession from afar—the strange, long, shapeless bundle lying on the litter, Andrew's shaking shoulders—and understood it only too well. Just as she was, she ran into the courtyard, out the gate, and down the road. Weeping and frightened, Claude and Richeut and the other ladies followed her. And when Alis reached the riders and the litter-bearers she fell on her knees and clung with both hands to the cloak that covered the dead man's face. And when she saw that nameless, eyeless, featureless face she found the strength to look at it for two long minutes—until Andrew lost patience and ordered a man to take her by the shoulders and tear her away. The bearers moved on and Alis followed them without a word, open-mouthed and empty-eyed. Claude was sobbing and tearing her hair. But Alis did not have the strength to lament as became a niece of the dead man.

And before the closed coffin she blasphemed in her heart and called God a traitor and a churl and swore that she would never again pray to Him or serve Him—He was too cruel, He had no right to punish her so. And she thought that she had no more desire to live, now that the best man on earth was dead.

And three days after the funeral Andrew came to tell her that he was going on pilgrimage to St. James of Compostella—his father had asked him to do so. "He died without the sacraments, and I must go to pray for his soul. He wanted to go himself, but he had not time."

Alis said: "Andrew, brother, stay here until spring, do not leave me alone in the castle. My task is so hard and I am so unhappy."

But Andrew answered that his duty to his father came first; he must not put off his pilgrimage a single day, so long as his father's soul was suffering torture in Purgatory. Alis let him go; she was weary, her heart was empty. She could not sleep because of Herbert's fleshless face—it haunted her as soon as she closed her eyes at night. "Why did I not speak?" she thought. "Perhaps he would have loved me. Perhaps he would not be dead." Surely she would have been able to hold him back, to follow him, to prevent him from losing his way. . . .

And then time passed and she thought of him no more, for she had too much to do. But she had grown thin and had lost her beauty—she was un-recognizable. Young Milon of Le Cagne followed her with great eyes full of tenderness and pity, and sometimes he said: "You are overtiring your-self, lady." And toward Lent pilgrims coming from the south brought news that Count Henry was on his way home—but which of his barons he was bringing with him no one knew. Then there were feverish days of waiting at Linnières, varlets and pages continually out in the road, going as far as Tonnerre, asking news of every traveller they met.

Two days before Shrove Tuesday Herbert's son Garin came to tell Alis that the men of Hervi had reached Champagne two days since.

Alis was standing by the hearth; when she heard the news she fell at full length on the flags. The hall was filled with shrieks and sobs, the women rolled on the floor and clawed their faces. If the men of Linnières had not come with the count it was most probable that they were never to return.

As soon as she had recovered from her faint Alis went down to the court-yard, ordered horses saddled, and set off for Hervi through the wintry weather to ask for news of her husband and her kinsmen. She found her neighbor's castle alight and rejoicing. Haguenier of Hervi was celebrating his return to Champagne—of all his troop only two men were missing, all the rest had come back safe and sound. But when he saw Alis—thin, haggard, her face reddened by tears and the cold—Haguenier felt ashamed. He invited the lady of Linnières to join in the feast and set her in the place of honor. But Alis could neither eat nor drink, and her heart burned at the sight of all the happy faces around her. Haguenier did his best to console her: he could tell her nothing about the men of Linnières, but he had not heard that they were dead. He did know that, since the day that they were captured by the Turks, Ansiau and his followers had not been with the count—where the infidels had taken them God alone knew. Perhaps it would be possible to communicate with some Frenchmen in Ultramar. Perhaps Simon of Linnieres could discover if his friends were prisoners and arrange to ransom them. Alis heard him out, gloomy and unconvinced—she clearly saw that Haguenier thought that nothing could be done. The knights who had remained with the count had been ransomed by the emperor and had returned by way of Constantinople. Those who had not been ransomed were as lost as grains of sand on a sea beach—where were they to be sought? In what market places, what deserts, on what roads, in what fields full of vultures and crows?

"Neighbor," said Alis, "it is not seemly for you to rejoice when there are widows and orphans not two leagues from your house. Surely my lord would not have done the like, if it were you who had not come home. But I tell you, though he never comes back, it will profit you nothing. I shall not let you take an inch of the land that is my children's."

Haguenier forgave her, for he could see that she was in great grief. He respectfully escorted her on her homeward road as far as Seuroi. And Alis returned to Linnières and wept over her children, calling them orphans and fatherless.

When spring came Alis had to go to Troyes, for Count Henry had died and service for the fief must be done to the young count, or rather to the countess, who was to rule Champagne until her children were of age. Despite the evidence Alis could not believe that Ansiau was dead—he must be only a prisoner, he would manage to escape somehow, he would come back, he would show Haguenier and the rest that his children would not be left fatherless. At Troyes she bargained with Abner and succeeded in obtaining the countess' permission not to pay interest—she was the wife of a crusader and her husband had disappeared, she was too poor to pay all her debts. Her business affairs kept her in Troyes for over two months.

She stayed with her sister Hermenjart of Rumilli. Hermenjart often advised her to remarry—it was almost certain that Ansiau was dead; even if he were alive he would never come back. "You know how the infidels treated our father, why should they treat your baron better? Even if they leave him his life, a man who has been long in those lands will never come back to France. Perhaps, to save his life, he will even take service under some lord of Ultramar. You know that he has done much harm to our family—you would be wrong to cling to him when you have such a good excuse for breaking away. You are young, you need a husband, you need someone to hold your land." Alis answered that she would never remarry without being sure that her lord was dead. How could she look him in the face if ever he came back and found her married? If that should happen she could only kill herself.

Yet at Hermenjart's house she made the acquaintance of a young man who let her know that he greatly desired to marry her. He was a young crusader who had returned with the count, a very good jouster, and famous for his successes with women. Hermenjart said: "Every woman would envy you such a husband. And ever since he first saw you he has been a different man—he was never so much in love with any woman before." The young man's name was Erard of Baudemant, and he was handsome enough to damn the saintliest of women. Alis felt flattered to see him so much in love with her. He was younger than she and very ardent—he swore oaths to her, wept, threatened to kill himself. And one evening, after a tournament in which he had fought for her, she became aware that he attracted her more than she wished. They were in Hermenjart's chamber, two candles were burning. She let him kiss and caress her for an hour, but she would allow nothing beyond kisses—she was too afraid of becoming pregnant. Later she told Hermenjart that she would marry Erard of Baudemant if her baron had not come back within a year. Then she set out for Linnières. She felt confused, she was not at all sure what she wanted.

It promised to be a hot, quiet summer.

LADY ALIS

A N August morning at Linnières in the year of Our Lord 1182. Freshly whitewashed, the keep is blinding in the intense sunlight. The flag of Champagne and the blue-and-white standard of Linnières float from the roof.

The forest is still. It lies breathing the hot air of noon through all its leaves, its grasses, its reeds, its thousands of mosquitoes and dragonflies and green frogs and chestnut-brown toads, of quails and curlews and hares and squirrels —through all its serene and swarming soul—in brushwood and coppice and the great groves where the trees stand so thick that their tangled branches have grown together, twisted and tormented like wrestlers' bodies. There for decades no ray of sunlight has touched the black, soft soil, made from the slow decay of rotted branch and fallen leaf. Deep burrows slant between sprawling roots. Here from a hollow tree a lynx cautiously puts out his dusky head crowned by brush-tipped ears. There, with soft heavy steps, a bear lumbers into a glade to warm his hump in the sun. A forest of red foxgloves and heather and giant nettles covers the clearing, burying the trunks of fallen trees, from which, here and there, barkless branches rise into the air, like hooks to catch the sailing crows. Where the sunlight penetrates there is a ceaseless humming and buzzing. In the shade, beyond the coppices and the marsh, a fetid stench and armies of flies mark the great lairs where the wild boar is master and king. In the black mud where they lie to bask—inert, huge, imposing—they breathe the superb indifference of creatures who have nothing to fear; above them hangs the sky, bounded by the motionless treetops and scored by crows. Here the note of the horn comes muffled, and the hunter's voice is barely distinguishable from the buzzing of flies.

The forest stretches beyond sight, dwarfing fields and castle. The yellow road runs on—two ruts filled with water, and between them deep-sunken hoof prints. Yet the yards, the stables, the palisade around the castle look imposing compared to the clay-and-wattle hovels which make up the village of Linnières. Behind the castle, to the southward where flows the Armançon, there are fields of rye and barley, then come meadows, and again the vast forest once more. But there the dry chalky soil begins, the paths are white, and the forest is all beech and birch.

Such was Linnières, a small domain on the outermost edge of Champagne— a house of freemen, answerable only to the count through his castellany of Paiens.

The three pilgrims who were travelling the clayey road to the castle were barefoot and bareheaded. They carried staves in their hands. One after the other, or all together, they livened the way by singing—war songs whose subjects were Nureddin and Saladin, or the brave companions of brave Renaud, or the fair city of Troyes in Champagne. Joyous or sad, the tunes were all alike—charming and wild, monotonous as incantations, with a long quavering end to every line. God knows when, how, and by whom they had been composed; the pilgrims sang them in their own fashion, spontaneously, to beguile their weariness, their griefs, their joys. Their legs were bare, their feet as horny as hoofs, and the dark tan of their faces was the tan of southern countries.

Two of the three were young. The other might be forty or fifty, his hair was growing gray, his long nose drooped over his mustache, his knotty fist was tense on his staff. But the other two bore only such marks as a sword bears which has passed through fire—blackened, the guard charred to bits, but the blade intact. There was a far-away look in their eyes, and something like a mirrored image of burning cities and skies too blue and fields of carnage—it was as if their eyes were covered with a film of varnish. They were no longer the clear eyes of children which accept whatever they see—they had an inner flame, stiller and more concentrated, whose seat was those grave mouths and the depths of those quiet pupils.

Such on that August day, at the place where the road began to skirt the forest, were Ansiau of Linnières and his two companions—all that remained of the troop which he had led to the Holy Land. Two years earlier he would have been ashamed to come home to his castle on foot and barelegged, like a beggar; but now the thought did not even enter his mind. He saw the walls of Linnières and was astonished to find them so small. Yet at each tree, each turning, his heart leaped—after so many unknown roads here at last was one whose every stretch he knew—ford, sheep pond, iron cross, the bridge.

Alis was sitting in the hall by the window, teaching two of her nieces an embroidery stitch. On the floor at her feet the bright-eyed girls eagerly followed the clean, precise movements of her white fingers. The women of the castle—eight damsels and half a dozen waiting-women—were singing together at their spinning. And when Lady Alis' swift blue eyes looked up from her work a moment to scan the spinners' hands and lips, not a hand dared cease turning the spindle, not a pair of lips dared break off singing. The field hands, the huntsmen, the tanners had long since learned to know that look, and no lord of Linnières had ever ruled the domain so strictly as Lady Alis.

She was a grown woman now, slender, tall, and strong, youthful, yet fully ripe. She had a high color, and under the transparent skin of her fine full lips the red blood beat, ready to spurt out if she bit them in one of her rages. Under her straight, heavy brows her eyes were steady and as blue as two aquamarines—they could nail you to the ground with a look of anger, and even when they were mild and calm they were hard to face. Because she wanted to be obeyed, and because she wanted to hide her sorrow over her loneliness, she had come to seem haughty. Waiting for an absent husband—and he had been gone for more than two years—was not easy for a woman with the hot blood and hard head that marked all the race of Puiseaux. No woman is so virtuous that she cannot feel temptation, and sometimes Alis thought with regret that she had been more strict than need be when she sent away Erard of Baude-mant, and she lived on the memory of his kisses as a poor man feeds for a week on the leavings of his Sunday dinner. To marry Erard would have been a good solution for her difficulties—it would not have made her any the less mistress of the castle. The children were growing, and they needed a man to bring them up. When she thought of her baron it was almost with rancor—what did he mean by going so far, by staying away so long? That he was not dead she was certain; all her prayers, all her vows told her so, every presage, every sign, the gypsies at Troyes and Flora at Old Village. When she looked at the sun she thought: "He sees it too." But when she closed her eyes and thought of him, she no longer knew whether the man she saw was Ansiau or Erard.

Hearing a noise in the court she had gone to the window, and at the same moment Robert, the captain of the soldiers, came running into the hall.

"Are the servants quarrelling again?" she asked.

Robert said: "Lady, the baron has come home."

She went white. "If you are trying to trick me," she said, "I will have your beard torn from your face, and your face rubbed with pitch. How do you know he has come home?"

"He is in the courtyard."

Alis said: "You lie. I have heard no horse come into the courtyard."

"He came on foot. With My Lord Girard and Thierri."

Without waiting to hear more, Alis rushed into the courtyard. The blood pulsed so violently in her temples that her mind could grasp nothing. She saw a crowd of huntsmen, dairymaids, soldiers around the well—some had fallen to their knees, the children had climbed on their parents' shoulders.

She shouted: "Stand back!" Instantly the crowd fell away, and she found herself face to face with a tall sun-blackened man in rags.

He straightened and his whole body trembled when he saw her. From his throat came a great, hoarse, heart-rending cry: "Lady!"

He did not know what he was doing. With the bound of a wild beast he dove forward. His face was pure joy.

Instantly Alis found herself swept from the ground—two iron arms held her up like an offering before an altar or a child at the font. Her head lay against a hard shoulder—she could feel the heat of it through the coarse linen sleeve. She blinked and tried to see her baron's face. In spite of everything she could not help feeling rather scandalized at such an assault upon her prestige.

She was aghast because so often, in imagination and in dreams, she had lived through this instant. And now he had come, and his coming upset every-thing, and she hardly knew him.

But he was filled with a joy almost painful to see—the joy of a pauper. He clasped his burden as if it were a piece of booty won in fight. And Alis closed her eyes and involuntarily turned from his fierce kisses. He bit her like a starving man who finds food and tears his share away by force. He could not even see her reluctance—and what did it matter now that he was holding her, body and soul, in his arms and against his face? A stuttering flood of words she had never heard before: "Oh, my very own, my little one. my only love—my only lady, mine. . . ."

How he had changed! His neck looked thicker, his beard coarser, there were wrinkles about his eyes; and the dark-brown skin of his cheeks and forehead, glossy over cheekbones and temples, looked as hard as tanned leather—a face all dark except for the whites of the eyes and the white teeth—the face of a gypsy. Where was the handsome lover of her nightly dreams?

But it was he after all—even if his joy was a little ridiculous, it touched her—and she buried her head against his neck and burst into sobs. Then he said gently: "Silly! Is it anything to cry about?" And he stroked her hair and the back of her neck. And the fatherly gesture only made her cry the more. She said: "I cannot bear it. What a way to come home!"

"Sister, sweetheart, don't cry. I have frightened you. And I have changed too. Tell me—the children?"

She gave a proud smile. "All alive, thank God. You will see no finer children anywhere."

"God be praised! I knew that my lady's children would be hardy. This is the greatest day in my life, lady. If you knew! We could have gone through Mahiet and borrowed horses and clothes from my uncle. But it would have been a long way round. I was so near—I could not resist. When a man has a beautiful woman waiting for him at home he loses his head. Isn't that so, Thierri? Oh—you haven't seen Thierri yet, lady—or Cousin Girard. There are not many of us, you know—" The baron's eyes dimmed with tears. God must have taken pity on us and brought us safe home. Go kiss them."

Leaving the baron's arms, Alis found herself clasped by Girard the Young and Thierri in turn. And as she returned their kisses she wept with emotion, and with sorrow for those who had not come back. "Thanks be to God you are safe home, fair cousin, the Virgin keep you. Thierri, your freckles have all disappeared, my friend—I should never have recognized you."

"And Andrew?" the baron asked. "Is he hunting?"

"He has gone on a pilgrimage," said Lady Alis. "It was his father's dying wish."

Ansiau crossed himself and remained silent for a time. Everyone in the courtyard fell silent, except the weeping mother of Eudes the Stammerer, of Linnières. More than one of the women envied Richeut and their lady that day.

"Enough!" said the baron. "And now a good bath for all three of us. We have earned it. I do not want to see the children yet, I should frighten them. Are the boys good riders, lady? Are they as blond as ever? And now go see to dinner. You are master here now, my fair golden falcon. I do not know what may be afoot."

He kissed his lady on the mouth, laughing with admiration and pride and a boundless gaiety which could not seem to find words and gestures enough to express itself.

"Haumette, put the children in their white dresses with the red borders and comb their hair nicely. Be on your best behavior, my sweets, today is a great day and a great festival."

"What saint's day is it?" asked little Mahaut.

"Silly," said Ansiet, her eldest brother. "Don't you know that the baron has come home?"

"And if you are not nice to him, I shall be angry," said Lady Alis.

Ansiet asked: "Did he bring us some pretty things from the Holy Land?"

"Certainly not," said Lady Alis. "He guessed that you hadn't deserved them."

Ansiet began crying and Herbert stared at the floor and scowled and pouted. "He promised me some Turkish arrows," he said.

Lady Alis boxed both boys' ears and called them bad sons. Then she took little Girard, her favorite, in her arms and began kissing his pale, round cheeks.

"You won't ask your father for anything, will you, my treasure? Haumette, you've let the dogs lick him again. Don't touch him, I'll change his dress myself, you'll disturb his bandage. By the blood of Christ, that woman knows no more about taking care of children than a German soldier. Heaven knows I have enough to do without looking after them too."

Lady Alis ordered dinner, then she went to the bathhouse to wait on her lord herself in his bath, as custom and courtesy demanded. It was an honor she owed to Ansiau—Erard would never have seen her at his feet, if he were three times her husband!

Ansiau was lying on a bench over which a piece of linen had been thrown, an old waiting-woman with hands as rough as brushes was rubbing his body with lavender and scented herb waters. "So, Lizarde, you seem happy to see me back."

"By Our Lady, I am! We are all happy—all but a very few."

"We were fifteen when we set out, and we have come back but three. That makes many widows."

"Widows who'll soon be married again, take my word for it," said Lizarde. "And it is a good death, to die in the Holy Land."

Just then Lady Alis entered the bathhouse, followed by two girls carrying a white linen shirt and an embroidered tunic.

As she bent over her lord's heavy, black, calloused feet, washing them and rubbing them with unguents, Alis felt that now she was indeed a servant again —but so great was her need for love that she never thought of complaining. When the baron was dressed she inspected him once more and thought that he looked handsomer than he had in the courtyard—the red tunic gave his dark skin and short hair an unexpected elegance; what he had lost in looks he had gained in bearing.

"What, lady," said Ansiau, "am I seeing double? Are there four of them or five? Who is that? Not Girard, is it?"

"No, it is a girl, my fair lord. Her name is Alette. Come here, my beauty, don't cry, the baron won't eat you. She will be twenty months old on Assumption Day."

"God, what a smooth skin she has. . . . Take her, I frighten her, look how she is crying.

"And is that Girard? And is that Mahaut, my big girl? You don't remember me, Mahaut?" The pretty blond child hid in Haumette's skirts, stealing sidelong looks at her father with a coquetry which her five years made touching.

"How could she remember you? She was much too young," said Lady Alis. "Stop being silly, Mahaut, and come and kiss your father. If you knew how she behaves every time I have to show her to a guest! Come here this minute if you don't want a slap, naughty girl."

But Mahaut knew in her bones that there would be no slaps that day, and she wriggled to her heart's content. "He's too black, I'm afraid," she whined, but her eyes were bright with joy. Then, to escape her mother's hands, she wound her slim little arms around the baron's legs.

She was beautiful, with the delicate beauty of an unopened bud in which lies the promise of a splendid flower. Her eyes were too big, her profile too babyish, her skin was so translucent that her nostrils and the lobes of her ears seemed diaphanous and turned golden in sunlight. The baron admired her, dazzled and a little intimidated, for he did not know what to say to her—in his mind his eldest daughter was the future wife of a rich and noble knight, and this little laughing-eyed creature had many years to live before she could bind the red veil of a bride over her golden hair.

His sons were another matter—with them he knew where he stood. One nine, the other eight, they were both big boys, still very blond and a little uncomfortable in their best clothes. Herbert had scraped most of the skin off his chin, Ansiet had a bump on his forehead. The first question the baron asked them after he had kissed them was: "Can you ride a full-size horse?"

Herbert, who was still thinking of his Turkish arrows, remained sulkily silent, but Ansiet was easier to tame. "I can even gallop standing on the saddle," he said, "and I can make the strawberry mare's Gaillard jump the sheep pond. My lady mother said that I could have Gaillard for my own after Christmas."

"He is yours today," said the baron, and the boy clapped his hands, almost weeping for joy. "My Gaillard, my Gaillard! He's so pretty! Oh, baron, come look at him—you'll see. He loves me so much that he laughs when he sees me."

The baron was ready to follow the boy to the stables, but Lady Alis stopped them. "In your clean clothes!" she said. "And the bell will ring for dinner any minute. Stay where you are, Ansiet. You can talk to your father just as well sitting on the bench."

Ansiet had put his long thin arms around his father's neck and was chattering on and on—about how handsome his Gaillard was, and about his withers and his hocks, and then about a live hare he was raising beside the dovecote, about a hedgehog, about a snake Robert had killed with an ax. "Are there snakes where you were?"

"I saw a few," said the baron.

"They say the Holy Land is a beautiful country."

"The most beautiful in the world."

"When I grow up I will go there too. How many infidels did you kill while you were there?"

"Three," said the baron.

The boy's face fell.

"That's not many. When I go I will kill three score, or three hundred. I can already kill a flying crow with a stone. But he"—his eyes turned to his younger brother—"he's better at it than I am."

The baron looked at his son's thick ankles and heavy fists, and knew that they promised height and a powerful frame—but strength could come only through exercise and training.

To the baron the boy's simple immature face with its big candid eyes was the image of perfect beauty; two years had not changed him—a little more filled out at most, and ennobled by the daily pursuit of fatiguing and even dangerous activities. Ansiau felt that probably he alone saw and understood the beauty of soul which delighted him in the boy's every gesture and look.

He would have remained lost in contemplation, if his lady, as usual, had not seen to it that each had his due. She took little Herbert under the arms and stubbornly set him on the baron's free knee. "You have looked at his brother long enough."

Though neither taller nor broader than his elder brother, Herbert weighed more—it almost seemed that he was made of denser matter, that he had more blood in his veins. He was, however, a handsome boy—like his mother, he had a very fair skin and very pink cheeks, and his curly hair was so blond that it looked almost white. The baron smiled at him, but it was not easy to make Herbert brighten up. He sat there awkwardly—pouting, refusing to raise his eyes, as if he were saying: "If I am here it is because I was put there, and I am too polite to go away."

The baron said: "Has the cat run away with your tongue, my fine son?"

The boy shook his head solemnly.

"Then why don't you say something instead of letting your brother do all the talking?"

Herbert bent his head and muttered something between his teeth. "What?" asked his father, and Ansiet hastened to explain: "He said, 'I want Valiant!' " Herbert bent his head even lower and began cleaning his fingernails.

"Who is 'Valiant'?"

"The black foal Courante had by Mandor—he'll soon be fifteen months old," said Ansiet.

"Well, my boy, you shall have your Valiant," said his father, "since your brother has Gaillard. There! Does that make you happy?"

Herbert raised his head and said deliberately: "Thank you, baron." But as for being happy, few had ever seen any happiness in Herbert's face—his eyes would light up for an instant, then the light would go out of them, that was all. However, during the course of the evening his blue, empty pupils sometimes rested on the baron and his companions with a strange expression of wondering curiosity and envy.

At dinner the three travellers were given the place of honor under the shields and Lady Alis poured wine for them herself—for Thierri just as she did for the baron, and the poor squire blushed with embarrassment and did not dare to ask for more—he would much rather have been filling their cups himself and talking to the kitchen boys. In a few hours he had put on his old life again like an old coat, and two years of adventure had dropped from him like a dream—he hardly remembered them. But the baron would have been ashamed to separate himself from his comrades on such a day.

"You have nothing to blush about, Thierri," he had said. "What is right for me should be right for you. I didn't come home on horseback, and you didn't come home carrying my shield."

Girard the Young seemed too tired to speak or even to eat. His wife Richeut, sitting behind him on the bench and digging her sharp chin into his shoulder, urged him to eat everything on his plate. "Just that drumstick! I had it dressed with capsicum sauce especially for you."

After the second dish of meat, when the spiced wine had been brought up from the cellar, the baron rose and stood on his bench to speak. The sound of voices and the clatter of dishes ceased.

"Friends, brothers, hear me. Tomorrow early we shall set off for Hervi, my lady and myself and my two friends, and any who wish to follow us on foot or horseback. We are going to Hervi to have Masses sung for our friends who died in the Holy Land. And to render thanks to God for those who are yet alive. And I ask you especially to pray for a knight named Walter—it was he who payed our ransom.

"If there is anything you want to ask of me, you may do it when we come back from Hervi. If anyone is being punished in the vaults, I forgive him. If any of our young men want to marry, they shall have what wives they please. We will celebrate the weddings on Assumption Day. And on that day everyone—young and old—shall have new clothing from my coffers."

Lady Alis thought: "There he goes. He has drunk too much." And one by one, like beads on a rosary, the difficulties which her husband's outburst of generosity would cause her passed through her mind: the pilgrimage interrupting the work of the tanners and the repairs to the palisade—marauders given a chance at the vineyards and orchards again—weddings during the height of the work season—and her chests and the baron's emptied. "Ah, men," she said to herself, "men!"

Now at last husband and wife were alone together behind the drawn curtains of their great bed. Alis had set the little oil lamp on the oak headboard and was braiding her hair for the night. She sat there like a young bride, silent, her eyes downcast—after the two years she had spent waiting for this moment she would have liked to hear caressing words. (Oh, how well Erard could speak them—he had practiced them on women enough!) And her baron seemed to have nothing to say. Propped on the pillows, he was patiently waiting for his wife to finish braiding her hair—then he would put out the light. He would not allow himself to hurry her—he did no more than stroke the very ends of her braids or brush her waist or her neck lightly with his elbows; but he did it with the naive complacency of a man who knows that at last he is going to have his fill and feels satisfied that he has deserved it.

"I have changed in two years," Lady Alis said at last, and sighed. "Look— my hair is not as fair as it used to be."

Ansiau said: "You are more beautiful."

Alis shook her head thoughtfully. "I shouldn't be. These years have been hard years for me, my dear."

Gravely he said: "I know, lady." Then, after a moment: "You know, I was afraid I should find you married again."

Tenderly she said: "You know very well that I would never have married again, sweet." Her reward was a look so full of confidence and admiration that she blushed.

He said: "There is not another woman in the world to match you."

She sighed again: "Still, I do not believe you thought of me very often in the Holy Land."

He said: "Yes, we had other things to think about. We had our share of troubles."

Vexed, Alis turned away and said that she did not want to put out the lamp until she had hunted for fleas.

Ansiau answered: "I can see that you are not as eager as I am. What makes you so distant?" As there was a reproach in the gentleness with which he spoke, Lady Alis smiled and made up to him again. "It has been so long since I saw you, sweet. Let me look at you."

"How beautiful you are. How white you are. You will not believe me, lady, but it has been more than a year since I touched a woman—yes, that's right— it was last Easter Week."

Alis shrugged her shoulders: "So you say."

"Do you want me to swear to it? It is simple enough—we came all the way from Marseille on foot, and if we had stopped to amuse ourselves with wenches we should never have made it in forty days." He moved closer to her, his voice grew low and hoarse: "I thought of you every step of the way."

Alis tried to avoid his eyes. Their ardor hurt her, for she knew how much brutality lay under the mask of gentleness he was forcing himself to wear. Each time he came back she wished him different from what he was—more curious, more jealous, more subdued perhaps—something, she did not quite know what. . . .

The next morning they had to be up before dawn. The cocks had not yet crowed. The forest was so lost in mist that the world might have ended just beyond the palisade. In the courtyard horses pawed the ground and shook themselves, the dogs were barking in the kennel and jumping at the door—they thought that a hunt was preparing.

Ansiau waited while two squires led out the finest horse in the stable for him—a big Spanish black named Mandor, so fiery and bad-tempered that no one rode him. The beast reared and danced like a cockboat in a stormy sea, throwing back his head and shaking his long, ribbon-braided mane. Alis stood close beside her husband, pressing against him—she had no wish to go, for the first time in years she would have liked to sleep late, dally over doing her hair, take Girard and little Alette into bed and play with them. But the baron was not the man to change his mind about going to church. Standing with his arm around his wife's shoulders, he was admiring Mandor's fine lines and gleaming coat. "By the blood of Christ," he said, "he has had good care."

Then Lady Alis freed herself and knelt to hold his stirrup. The horse was so restless that both squires had to help her. Mandor reared, and Ansiau, who was out of practice, had difficulty in controlling him. Lady Alis mounted her gray palfrey, Girard the Young his chestnut. One after the other the riders crossed the bridge and turned down Bernon road in the direction of the forest.

At Hervi the party from Linnières heard Mass at St.-Mary's-of-the-Angels. Ansiau had taken the front-row chair which he had occupied ever since his father's death, and he watched the same fingers of light move with the sun across the white capitals with their carved vines. Nothing had changed.

Girard the Blond, of Linnières, knight. Ogier the Red, of Linnières, knight. Izembard the Red, of Linnières, squire. Eudes the Stammerer, of Linnières, squire. Garin of Linnières, son of Hugh, squire. Garin of Linnières, son of Girard, squire. Garin of Puiseaux, squire. James of Le Cagne, sergeant. Ansiau of Beaumont, sergeant. All dead in the service of God, at sea, in the Holy Land, or in Turkey. God save and protect them!

Except for old James of Le Cagne, who died at Galilee, and Herbert's two sons, not one of them had Christian burial. So Ansiau decided to have a monument set up at the left of St. Mary's altar—a stone slab bearing a large cross, with nine small crosses around it, in memory of the men of Linnières who died in Count Henry's Crusade in the year of Our Lord 1180.

It happened that Haguenier of Hervi was riding through the village carrying a falcon on his wrist, and followed by his son and three squires—he stopped by the church to pray just as Ansiau and his party were coming out the door. He flung himself on his neighbor with the delight of a man who finds a fellow countryman in a foreign land. The two men embraced like brothers. Haguenier, who had come back with the count, still bore traces of the Mediterranean sun on his broad face.

He was delighted to find his neighbor safe and sound, and at once asked him to come and stay with him for as long as he pleased—he would be only too happy to receive such a guest.

Haguenier had guests already—his brother, who had been in the Holy Land too, and a relative of his wife's, Manesier of Coagnecort. Ansiau and Girard the Young (who was young no longer) spent their time in the orchard or hawking. All of them enjoyed recalling their long journey and their days in Palestine.

"If the barons send an army to the Holy Land, I shall take the cross again," said Ansiau.

"If I were your age . . ." Haguenier sighed. "No. No more of it for me. I shall never leave my manor again. I have seen enough."

Ansiau said: "There is much left to see. You remember the day we went to worship at the Holy Sepulchre? My cousin Simon the Red was beside me—no farther than I am from you at this instant. Well, he was crying so hard that no one could stop him—and you know he is not given to crying. I thought he was crying out of pure devotion, because there was not one of us whose eyes were dry that day. And that evening he said to me: 'What this country needs is fewer prayers and more men. For our sins, the dogs will take Jerusalem from us.' And he cried so much that I began crying too. It was then he told me he had decided not to go home."

"I should never have thought it of Simon," said Manesier of Coagnecort.

Ansiau said: "It was God's will. I was so sure of it that I did not try to hold him from his resolve. He said: 'Linnières is only a filthy little swamp, and here we have all the glory of Christ our Saviour.' And he said: 'My path lies clear before me. My two brothers are dead and my father is old; I shall not see him alive again; I have no one left in the world.' And he asked me to stay too. But I did not want to deprive my sons of my fief."

"Did he become a Templar?" asked Haguenier.

"No, he entered the service of the baron of Ibelin. It is a rich and generous house. Baron Balian's brother married the widow of the king of Jerusalem. The king of France has nothing in Paris to match their palace at Acre."

"Yet it is a strange idea, leaving wife and children to seek his fortune God knows where," growled Girard the Young, and Ansiau straightened as he said: "He knew very well that I will not wrong his children."

"A man ought to go there," said Haguenier, "just to see how many infidels there are left on earth. If I had not seen it, I never should have believed it."

Ansiau said: "It is a shame and a curse. From here no one can realize how strong they are. And never forget that the king of the country is a leper. You will see that he will bring misfortune on his realm."

"So they say," sighed Haguenier. "Yet he is a tall handsome stripling and he knows how to lead an army."

"And it is a crying shame too," Ansiau went on, "to see Christians living like infidels and dressing so that no one can tell a Frank from a Saracen. And —God forgive me—I believe they are on better terms with the infidels than with pilgrims from our lands. To see castles and camps crawling with such vermin, you would think you were in Saladin's camp."

"By St. Michael," said Haguenier, "I have been told of men—I will not name them—who accept gifts from Saladin and are in his pay."

Ansiau thought he saw an allusion and was instantly offended. "Never believe it of the Ibelins," he said. "There has been no such talk about them." In his inmost heart he was a little displeased that Simon had chosen such an exotic master; but he was loyal to his cousin, and the princely house of Ibelin had taken a place in the sanctuary of his loyalties; no one had a right to touch it.

Ansiau was telling his story:

"When we were taken prisoners, the emirs chose the viscount of Saint-Florentin, Raoul of Arci, William of La Ferté, and Ansiau of Monfélis for their share, because they saw that they were men who could pay. The rest they sent to Aleppo with the caravan.

"There were nine of us knights, I think. But with the squires and sergeants we made up a good hundred men. We were herded along like sheep. Our hands were tied behind our backs. When a man fell to his knees the overseer rode up and tore open his face with his horsewhip. And because we were bareheaded, at least thirty of us died from sunstroke on the road. That was how I lost Garin of Puiseaux, my brother-in-law. And Eudes the Stammerer, my nephew, and Ansiau of Beaumont. Girard of Arrentières died of sunstroke too, I think, but I did not see it, he was in the rear, at the other end of the caravan. God! what a journey! We were so thirsty that our tongues cracked. When we saw the horses watered we thought we should go mad. At night we dreamed of water lapping against stones.

"God grant we never undergo anything worse. As I was telling you, the dogs took us to Aleppo, to the slave market. There they shaved us. And there we remained for a good two weeks. Infidels came to feel our flesh and look at our teeth as if we were horses. Some of us felt ashamed. But the rest thought that it is no shame to suffer for God. The thought gave us courage again.

"At Aleppo a slave merchant bought us and took us to Damascus, then to Damietta, and there he sold us to the captain of a galley. By us, I mean we three here—Girard, Thierri, and I. My cousins Garin and Eudes died of dysentery, but we three, by God's grace, were stronger and recovered, though it was a long fight. I must admit that the merchant had us cared for. He gave us food and drink, but he was a hard man, and his overseers were even harder. Yet I swear to you, once we were on the galley, we regretted them.

"We had almost lost hope of ever getting home. We were on the galley for eight months, until the day when we were taken by Turkish pirates. They sank us, and a good half of the rowers were drowned. But we three were in the right spot—near the bow, which did not go down till last. The pirates fished us out of the water, they must have thought they could sell us again. And then God showed me what to do.

166

"You remember the knight of Trauenburg whom I brought to our tents when we were camping under the walls of Jerusalem? The knight who wore a white-and-gold turban—except for his blond beard you would have taken him for a Turk. However, he is a knight, and God alone knows under how many barons he has seen service. I saw him joust at Troyes once, and it was there that I made his acquaintance. He is a German by birth, but he told me that he never speaks his language now except when he talks in his sleep— awake he could hardly say yes or no in it.

"Well, in Tripolis he married the widow of a rich Venetian merchant, and there he lives now, and luckily I thought of him when we were on the pirate ship—God put the thought into my head.

"I asked to see the captain, and he had an Armenian with him who spoke French. I managed to make him understand that I had a friend in Tripolis who would ransom me and my two companions. The captain said that if my friend would pay twenty bezants' ransom apiece for us he would take us as far as Latakia and let us make our way ashore in a cockboat. I tried to get better terms, but he would not listen. He gave me money for my journey and told me that if I did not come back with the ransom money in two weeks my two friends would be sold and sent to the galleys.

"Well, three days later I was in Tripolis. But finding Walter was another matter. I did not know his wife's name, and no one in the city knew his. I knocked like a beggar at every door in the Venetian quarter—you should have seen the reception the porters gave me, for I had all the earmarks of a man escaped from the galleys. And the astounding thing was that in the end I did find Walter's wife. But Walter himself was not at home. Well, she was neither young nor pretty, but she had a kind heart, as you will see—she said that she would not dare give me sixty bezants without an order from her husband, but she felt so sorry for me that she sent ten varlets through the city to find their master and ask him to come home at once. And the varlets brought Walter back two days later; he was amazed to see me. Instead of sixty bezants he gave me eighty, so that we could pay for our journey home, and asked me to have a Mass said for him at the church of the Two Marys in Camargue. He has a special devotion to the Two Marys.

"And when I had found my captain again on the coast of Cilicia, he said that he would keep his word and he sent us off to Latakia with some of his men in a small sailboat. Only he took the whole eighty bezants instead of only sixty. His men put us ashore on a rocky beach north of the harbor. By nightfall we were in the city."

Over Ansiau's face flitted the reflection of a great joy and a great weariness. He fell silent, carried away on a stream of intoxicating memories—the leap from boat to rock, the bath on the sunny beach, the sea shining blue and gold; the roofs of Latakia white against the gray of olive groves, the dark groves of lemon and orange which ringed the city; and sails, white, red, and yellow, swaying in the harbor, against the green water; the far-away blue mountains drenched in sunlight, shrouded in a golden haze—liberty. All that world was his, was theirs—a world where there were no guards, no chains, no whips, where they could eat and sleep whenever they liked. The joy of kneeling in a church at last, of once again touching statues of saints and holy crosses with his hands and lips and brow, feeling the holy water on his face and the cool flags, made holy by the prayers of Christians, under his knees and feet. To be once more in a city where there were crosses everywhere, great and small, tall or square, of stone, or iron, or gold—crosses raised to protect and bless.

The three pilgrims were without money, and they hired out as sailors and porters on a Genoese ship bound for Marseille, for great was their haste to be home once more—in their thoughts the skies of Champagne were always clear and mild, the forests swarmed with game, the women's faces shone with tenderness. They were nearing home, they forgot everything else, they did not even know that they were hungry and tired.

The days went by and Lady Alis began to find time hanging heavy on her hands at Hervi, the more so as she did not much like Marsille of Coagnecort, Haguenier's wife, with whom she was obliged to spend most of her time. The baron was always very much in love with her at night, but by day he seemed to forget her; he even seemed to have forgotten that he had a house of his own only three leagues from Hervi. But Lady Alis did not forget it, for she knew that in her absence the work would be done neither thoroughly nor seasonably.

In the evening she would say to Ansiau: "I hope you don't think that Richeut is capable of supervising the waiting-women," or, "All these varlets could be making themselves useful if they were back at the castle. Here they have nothing to do but play at pole-vaulting."

The baron would answer: "Bah! What does it matter? We shall be back well before Assumption Day, in plenty of time to prepare for the feast. I intend to invite the men of Hervi and Coagnecort and Hugh of Baudemant with his brother—Manesier tells me that he is a first-rate jouster. Our courtyard will be big enough for all the sports. We haven't a hauberk left, so we shall only be fighting for fun, you'll have nothing to worry about."

Lady Alis thought: "You would suppose he had brought back Saladin's treasure from the Holy Land," but she knew better than to say it and merely pointed out that she had not yet sold the pelts and that she had already mortgaged the vineyard to the monastery at Hervi.

The baron answered: "We can still mortgage Bernon."

Lady Alis said: "Mortgage our children too while you are about it!" Seeing that she was angry, Ansiau took her in his arms and covered her with kisses and said that he would do nothing against her will. Finally, a week after their arrival at Hervi, Lady Alis said to her husband, half in earnest, half jokingly: "When people see that you are in such little haste to go home they will think that you do not like it there, and I will be blamed for it." Then Ansiau promised that they should leave the next day, for he was just as willing to go as to stay.

Again it was Lady Alis who had to see to the preparations for the festival. At night she went to bed tired and cross. The heat and the mosquitoes prevented her from sleeping. But the baron's skin was too tough for mosquitoes and he had seen hotter days than ever came to Champagne; so he was always cheerful and always far too much in love with his lady. However, now that the fever of the first days was over he began to be aware that Lady Alis was not as happy as he. Yet he had been faithful to her, both in heart and in body —he had desired her so greatly, he had been so patient and so gentle with her —what more could he do? It was the first cloud in his sky. But his cheerful humor triumphed. He spoke to his lady: "Sister, sweet," he said, "I see that you are not pleased with me. You are afraid that I will mortgage more than I can pay back. You think I do not know what I am doing. But listen: money and possessions are always to be had. What counts is friends—you'll see—I am the last man on earth to leave my children landless."

Lady Alis could only say: "You are right," for what he said was reasonable. She was sorry to lose the authority she had acquired, she felt out of her element now that she had to take orders instead of giving them.

And there was another thing: she wondered why he had invited the two brothers of Baudemant—she had no wish to see Erard again. Now that she was her baron's once more, she believed that she had no feeling for the young man. But he might still have some feeling for her—he might betray her—and, after all, she had come very close to yielding to him: he could whisper words which made her heart flutter and sent the blood rushing into her face. Her good common sense told her that Ansiau's presence made succumbing less of a danger. But she had no wish even to be tempted.

The guests were to arrive two days before Assumption Day. Alis spent all the preceding evening at her toilet table. She had her hair washed and touched up, she rubbed her skin with lemon and bacon grease to make it white and smooth. She intended to dazzle the guests—particularly Erard. She did not want him too quickly to console himself for losing her.

Hall and chapel were decorated with bunches of grapes, sheaves of wheat, and foliage. On the table was a red cloth embroidered with white. The two great escutcheons of Linnières had been thoroughly cleaned and gleamed in red and blue on the wall opposite the door, above the seats of the knights. There was nothing on the spits because the eve of the feast was a fast day, but freshly baked bread—still hot—had been set out for the guests, together with cheese and grapes. Father Aimeri was rehearsing the children in the choruses they were to sing.

Ansiau had gone to meet the guests himself, escorted by four of his young cousins. Even in fair weather the road to Linnières was wretched; it ran through the forest, and on the driest days of summer the mud was so deep that no carriage could get through. It was by far the worst road in the countryside, for the clayey soil ended at Bernon and Hervi, just on the other side of the great forest. But the lords of Linnières had no thought of leaving a dwelling which was so well and solidly protected and where they were so thoroughly at home.

To make it possible for his guests to pass without too much difficulty, Ansiau had branches cut and strewn on the road as far as Seuroi. There, not far from the hewn stone which marked the grave of Rainard, he stopped and awaited his guests. From Seuroi it was only half a league to Hervi, which lay on the farther side of a wood intersected by many streams. The two neighbors had wrangled in court over that wood for four generations—it abounded in partridge, wood grouse, curlew, and wild duck.

Horns sounded in the forest, and Ansiau replied by a welcoming fanfare. Soon the barons of Hervi emerged from the forest, with their wives riding pillion behind them, their dogs, and their hawks. Manesier of Coagnecort and the two brothers of Baudemant followed close behind. Ansiau greeted them all with a delight which was certainly unfeigned. He was still overflowing with love for his fellow men, provided only that they were Christians and countrymen.

Haguenier of Hervi was a dark, stocky man of thirty-five. Outspoken and uncomplicated, he made an attractive companion. At the moment his principal concern was pleasure—he felt that he was entitled to it after his long, toilsome journey from the Holy Land. Manesier of Coagnecort introduced young Erard of Baudemant who came riding up behind his brother, his eyes fixed on his horse's ears. Hugh of Baudemant had been married to one of Ansiau's sisters, Ala (she had died two years earlier)—so Ansiau treated him as a kinsman, though he had never liked him. Hugh was almost an old man. He had a long gray beard, he was short and skinny (Ala had been twice his size), had the reputation of being a miser, and was on bad terms with his brother. Born of a different mother, Erard was twenty-five years younger than Hugh— he had come back from the Crusade a grown man and a knight, and was demanding his share of the inheritance. Ansiau had never seen him before, though he had heard enough about him from Manesier of Coagnecort. He was very unlike his brother; though not tall, he was a fine figure of a man and he displayed his fresh young beard and his strong wolfish teeth with a vanity which was almost insolent. Ansiau, who knew men and the world, was struck by the young man's graceful carriage and clear eyes and sinewy hands. "I imagine he's a good fighter," he thought. Erard seemed rather more reserved than he might have been, but Ansiau attributed his lack of amiability to the presence of his elder brother.

"We never met in the Holy Land," Ansiau said, "because you were with the viscount of Provins. But I have heard such high praise of your jousting at Troyes that I was determined to make your acquaintance. I hope that we shall cross lances."

Erard answered that it was true he had not yet met the baron of Linnières but that he knew Lady Alis quite well—he had met her at Troyes. Ansiau said: "So much the better. You will feel more at home with us," but he considered the young man's remark uncalled for—men should not talk about women, especially about noblewomen, unless there was some very good reason for it.

Dressed in her best, Lady Alis received the knights in the castle courtyard and offered them barley wine, assisted by her lady cousins. She was all graciousness, and the slight trouble she felt only heightened her beauty. She smiled at Erard as politely as at the others. He thought he would choke with fury when she handed him the cup—he nearly threw it in her face.

After a light repast the entire company assembled in the chapel for vespers. It was a beautiful evening. When the guests had gathered in the hall again for a supper of bread and roast fish the choir of children sang more hymns to Our Lady. And the grooms currying their horses in the stable and the squires spreading straw for beds stopped their work and their chatter and listened while the pure crystalline voices glorified the Blessed Virgin whose body never knew corruption. The little golden stars appeared one by one in the pale sky. Beyond the palisade a mist rose out of the black forest, owls wailed and stags belled far away. The dogs in the kennel growled in their sleep.

In the half-light of the castle there was a perpetual joyous coming and going, punctuated by stifled laughter, whispered words, and sudden oaths. The varlets —both those whom the guests had brought with them and those who belonged to the castle—slept on straw in the hall. All the beds were taken by the knights and their families, and even so there was a good deal of crowding—for the most part the beds were merely straw pallets without coverings. The baron himself gave up his bed to Haguenier and Manesier and their wives, and found a place for himself and his lady in Girard the Young's bed. But Girard and Richeut wanted to sleep, whereas Ansiau and Alis were not sleepy at all. They talked until matins, happy because they had guests, happy because tomorrow would be a feast day, happy, too, because they were a little crowded and uncomfortable in Girard's bed. Alis was excited by the knowledge that Erard had not forgotten her, and she was pleased to be able to tell herself that she preferred her baron. And Ansiau made plans—they would joust with light lances in the courtyard or perhaps on the meadow; they would get up a great beat for boar; and afterwards he would give the black greyhound to Haguenier and the red bitch to Manesier, Erard should have the pearl-gray falcon, Orgival, and Hugh of Baudemant—what could he give to Hugh of Baudemant?

"You can think about that later. Haven't we talked about them enough? Tell me—did I look pretty today? Did you like my white dress?"

"I felt very proud. Compared with you, all their wives are ugly."

She laughed softly. "You shouldn't say that. And it is not true."

"Do you want me to swear it is true?"

"Better not. Ouch! No—don't touch me. This is the eve of a feast."

"One swallow doesn't make a summer."

But Lady Alis would not be persuaded—principally on Richeut's account, for she did not want to be reproached with not observing her feast days properly. And besides, it was one more point gained against the baron.

The midday meal was bountiful, there was an unusual variety of dishes, and they were prettily served. There was game in abundance with sauces highly spiced. The baron, as head of the house, carved the meats and kept an eye on the service; he was so busy keeping his guests supplied that he ate nothing himself. Never before had he been so affable, and his neighbors thought that his two years of adventure had done him good—before he went away he had the reputation of being touchy and easily offended, now he was simplicity itself. And Lady Alis frowned a little when she saw him constantly getting up to give an order at the hearth or simply to sit for a moment beside one or another of his guests. "You do not honor your guests, baron," she said at last, "by disdaining to eat with them."

He said: "You are right, lady," and, picking up the leg of a kid, he began biting into it where he stood, without interrupting his orders to the cook—then, before he had finished it, he handed it to his little cousin John, son of Girard the Young. Then, wiping his hands on the skirt of his robe, he sat down beside Haguenier and asked him if the sauces did not remind him of those they had tasted in the Holy Land on the day they had eaten at the table of the seneschal of Jerusalem? For both men it was a memory full of humor, for the seneschal's sauces had burned their tongues—theirs and many another knight's—to the point where they had been unable to swallow again for three days. Haguenier half choked on the piece of meat he was eating. But Ansiau's reference to Jerusalem and the Holy Land almost precipitated a quarrel. For Hugh of Baudemant at once asked: "Is it true that your cousin Simon has turned Templar?"

"No, he remained in the Holy Land in the service of Balian of Ibelin," Ansiau answered.

Then Erard raised his voice: "True—it is dangerous to be a Templar. They are always first in battle and they are never taken prisoners; the infidels cut off their heads."

Ansiau raised his eyebrows and sat up straight—there was an embarrassed silence. But the baron of Linnières restrained himself, for he had drunk almost nothing and he reminded himself that the man was his guest. He answered rather sententiously that a man did not need to be a Templar to fight, and that anyone who did not want to be taken prisoner had only to refuse to surrender. Erard had the good sense to realize that he was beaten; but Lady Alis had gone very red.

The meal went on for three good hours, from sext to nones, and toward the end of it most of the company could neither move nor speak—half asleep, their girdles loosened, they leaned on the table or against each other. Lady Alis herself was slightly drunk—she pressed close to her husband and said unsteadily: "I feel sleepy, sweet—excuse me to the ladies."

Ansiau and Thierri were almost the only men still steady on their feet—they had eaten and drunk very little. They undertook to conduct the male guests to their beds for a nap. And poor Lady Alis had willy-nilly to do as much for the ladies—she was having a hard struggle to keep from vomiting, but she managed to smile and look pleasant. She was only too glad when at last she could lie down on a pallet covered with red tapestry beside Marsille of Hervi —her head was spinning. Suddenly she was afraid, she trembled—she could feel Erard's look on her neck, her shoulders. She opened her eyes and saw no one but the ladies of Hervi and her own cousins.

When the heat of the day had passed, pages and varlets rekindled the fire and spitted boars and sheep for the evening meal. The flagstones of the great hall were strewn with fresh greenery, planks were laid for dancing in the courtyard and benches set out by the well and covered with tapestry. The ladies seated themselves on the benches and the baron's two sons brought them water mixed with honey to drink, serving them in turn, beginning with the mistress of the castle. A minstrel seated himself at Lady Alis' feet and began playing dance tunes on his bagpipe, and the girls sang with him, clapping their hands to the rhythm:

> *Renaud and his lady*
> *Ride away,*
> *All night they ride*
> *Till break of day.*
> *The joy of love*
> *Soon turns to pain. . . .*

Erard of Baudemant was the only knight without a wife, so Ansiau gave him Claude of Linnières for a partner, a skillful singer and dancer if ever there was one. Alis danced with her husband, but she could not keep her eyes off Erard and Claude. Herbert's second daughter Claude was tall and slender —a highly bred girl of nineteen with milky skin, red hair, and rather small eyes. Alis gnawed her lips with rage as she watched the girl's pale face run through the whole gamut of pinks and reds under Erard's bright eyes. "The fool—she believes everything anyone tells her," Lady Alis thought. And the baron asked her if she was not suffering from stomach-ache.

For the next figure there was a change of partners. Alis let the baron take Marsille of Hervi's hand and gave her own to Erard. It was the first time he had spoken to her since they were at Troyes, and now she was so angry that she had forgotten everything that had happened since.

Between refrains she asked him if he found red-headed women easier picking than blondes. Erard said: "I prefer them."

Lady Alis laughed: "You won't be the first lover she has had."

Erard made no answer, he smiled as he watched Lady Alis clapping her hands in time to the refrain. Then, when she had finished, he said: "You wanted to be in her place."

Alis reddened with rage: "What a lie! No one but you would believe that."

He wheeled about her in time to the music, like a vulture wheeling above its prey, and she felt herself caught in his magic circles—she could not escape from them, she could not even raise her eyes. But for the next dance she gave her hand to Manesier of Coagnecort, and Erard started off with his brother Hugh's wife.

After the dancing, which left them all hot and rather breathless, knights and ladies seated themselves on the benches and on mats spread on the ground. The younger women unhooked their collars and cooled their cheeks against the discs of metal or enamel which hung at the ends of their long girdles. The smell of roasting meat issued from the open door of the hall, mingling with the odors of mint and herb-benjamin with which the dancing floor was strewn.

Erard had found a place on the ground at Lady Alis' feet. In something of a temper, she said: "You had better go find my cousin Claude."·

But she already knew Erard's trick of never answering what was said to him. He did not even appear to have heard her, he simply said: "Have you noticed the beautiful buckle on my collar? A lady gave it to me in Constantinople."

Alis bent to look at the buckle, and their heads almost touched. Then Erard spoke quickly in a low voice. He said that Lady Alis no longer had the same reasons for not giving herself to him and that, being mistress of the castle, she must know of some place where they could safely meet.

Alis said: "Stop. I have no wish to listen to you."

He stared at her insolently. "Oh, it is not that you do not want to. You are afraid of the baron, that is all."

"Not in the least, my friend. I love him."

"A man you have had for ten years!"

Alis felt sure of herself now—she liked nothing better than arguing with Erard.

"I love him all the better for it," she said.

"Impossible. Anyone will tell you so."

"Believe me, my friend, true love is love for life."

Erard laughed and said that he knew nothing of such love. "Besides, you cannot possibly love him. In the first place, he is as wall-eyed as a horse."

Lady Alis laughed, struck with the accuracy of his observation, and decided to remember it to tease the baron with some day.

"How about yourself?" she said. "What are your eyes like?"

"That is for you to say, lady."

She looked at him from under lowered lids and thought that he had very beautiful eyes—very beautiful when she saw them so close—as she had at Troyes; the memory troubled her so much that she could think of nothing to say.

"Anything new is better than anything old," said Erard. "We eat fresh eggs and fresh fruit and fresh meat—and once they get old they rot and are fit for nothing but to throw away. Try a new love, and you won't want the old one any longer."

"No, fair sir," said Alis, smiling. "Love is like wine, the older the better."

Erard said: "New wine is more intoxicating."

"Perhaps. But it is only fit for soldiers."

Alis was delighted with her own wit and with the turn the conversation had taken. But their *tête-à-tête* did not last long, for now Claude of Linnières, her brother Garin, and Erard's sister-in-law Bertille joined their discussion on the subject of love.

Claude said: "There is nothing pleasanter than talking of love. And this honorable knight is a master on the subject, I hear."

"Far from it," the young man answered. "But give us your opinion—from which would you receive greater pleasure, a new lover or a lover you had had for ten years?"

Claude blushed and said that, since she was not yet married, she was not in a position to judge. And Bertille gave an unhesitating vote for the new lover.

"As for me," said Alis, "I hold that the old lover is the best, because everyone prefers a faithful lover to an inconstant one."

"My lady cousin is right," said Claude, clapping her hands.

Erard would not concede defeat and said: "Here comes the baron of Linnières. Let him decide." Claude burst out laughing at the idea of her cousin Ansiau's deciding a point of love, and beckoned to him with a white finger. "Come here, cousin, we need you."

Ansiau gave them one of his wide, radiant smiles and asked how he might serve them.

"Tell us, cousin, which is best—an old lover or a new."

Ansiau answered unhesitatingly: "A new."

Lady Alis pouted and threw her husband a reproachful look. "You have put me in the wrong, baron," she said. "And they are all against me. But I still maintain, sir knight, that the old lover is best."

Ansiau said: "As you please, lady. I know nothing about it. Talk of love is for the young."

And he hurried to join Haguenier and Manesier, who were describing the capture of a bear in the forest of Othe, not far from Buchie.

"There you are," said Erard to Lady Alis. "You have no choice but to surrender."

Alis answered angrily: "Let me alone. I do not like this game."

Erard rose and sat down beside Claude at the other end of the bench. Then Lady Alis was ready to weep for rage and jealousy, and for the moment it seemed to her that Ansiau was the newcomer, the intruder, arrived from God knew where to part her from Erard. He had abandoned her, he had been unfaithful to her God knew how many times, and after two years and a half, when she was beginning to forget him, he had come back for her as if she were something he owned, his horse, his dog. She found it so hard to hold back her tears that she told Bertille she had a headache. "So have I," said Bertille; "I ate too much too."

Just then the chapel bell rang for vespers. Lady Alis rose and began to readjust her collar, which she had unfastened because of the heat. She was standing with her back to the bench and she knew that Erard must pass behind her. She felt him stop. She felt his beard touch her cheek.

"I am sick. Why will you not cure me?"

"Go tell that to Claude."

"I love no one but you. You know it well. Tell me where I can meet you."

Lady Alis said: "In Hell," and joined the baron, who was walking toward the keep.

And all through vespers Alis, her head duly bowed, racked her brains to think of a place where she could meet Erard that night alone. Everyone would be a little drunk after supper. She would go up to help the ladies into bed, then she would say she wanted a breath of fresh air. She would go out by the little north door which gave onto the wall. From there she would make her way to the small inner garden. Erard could enter the garden only by climbing over the stable roof, but when the varlets were all in the hall after supper no one would see him. Leaving the chapel she leaned on the baron's arm and such a dizziness came over her that she feared she would fall. Cold sweat stood on her temples and her eyelids, her terror was so intense that she thought the ground would open up and swallow her. Ansiau asked: "Are you ill, lady?" "I am very tired." "Poor thing! It will soon be over—supper won't be as long as dinner."

But supper was a long and boisterous affair. The candles were lighted, for it was dark in the hall though it was still daylight outside. The wine cup hardly stopped, the squires had barely time to refill it. The knights made it a point of honor to empty it at a draught after offering the first mouthful to their ladies. Toward the end the baron himself was rather drunk. The songs and jokes became more and more gross and the ladies rose to go up to bed. Erard rose at the same time on the pretext of going out into the courtyard; he crossed Lady Alis' path and stopped in front of her. In the half-light his eyes shone yellow like a cat's, his pale face looked beautiful. He appeared to be suffering and Alis was touched.

She said: "Good rest to you, sir knight," and added softly: "The little garden behind the stables. Climb onto the roof and you will see it. At once." His eyes lighted up, his nostrils expanded. And thinking of his pleasure Lady Alis forgot her own fears.

It was pitch-dark in the bedchamber when she returned, and more than once she stumbled into the body of a sleeping varlet. Two oil lamps burned on the cornice of the cluster of pillars in the center of the room. Lady Alis slipped into bed beside Richeut, gritting her teeth to keep them from chattering.

"Where were you?" Richeut asked. "I looked for you everywhere."

"I felt sick, I went out on the wall for a breath of air."

Richeut said: "If your baron had better sense, I would tell him all about your going out to take the air."

Alis did not have the strength to argue with Richeut that night. She lay face down on the bed with her head in her arms and did not move. She heard the men come noisily in, and listened for a long time to their drunken singing, their oaths and laughter and horseplay, wondering if the room would ever be quiet again. The baron's voice was enough to tell her that he had drunk a good deal and that he would soon be asleep—for the moment she asked nothing more.

The baron lay down beside her and asked her rather thickly why she was shivering. She said: "I am tired. Let me alone," and soon she heard him snoring. But Lady Alis could not shut her eyes all night. Most of all she thought of the risk she had run and of the danger to which she was still exposed. Erard might do something rash, and he had her ring. He would not kill the baron, but he was perfectly capable of challenging him and causing him all sorts of trouble. She asked herself: "What shall I do? What shall I do?" Yet she thought with a smile of pleasure of the low, urgent voice of her lover.

She felt no remorse, for her fear of dishonor was stronger than her fear of sin. The baron must never know what she had done. She, Alis of Puiseaux, must never be accused of adultery, as Irma had been, or Adela of Bercen who could not wait for her husband. Richeut and the other women had only to hold their tongues. She was and would remain a woman without reproach; she would swear it on the cross, on relics; besides, she believed it herself; it was true. It could not be that an hour's pleasure changed an honest woman into a whore. She was no worse today than yesterday, her face was not dirty nor her body covered with scabs.

Such were the things Lady Alis told herself while she watched the windows grow gray, then white, and at last heard the first cock crow.

In the courtyard and stables squires were calling back and forth, horses pawed—the hunting party was to rise at dawn. They were not many that morning. With Manesier of Coagnecort and Erard of Baudemant the baron was one of the first to be up. Then Garin, son of Herbert, Girard the Blond's two sons, and Thierri appeared in the courtyard, where the two packs of hounds were shivering with impatience, sniffing the air and waving their sterns. The mist had not lifted; the sky over the forest was pink; the same pink touched the walls of the keep, but the shadow of the palisade was still so long that the men and horses were lost in it—only the riders' heads emerged from it, radiantly.

The horn sounded, the heavy gate creaked on its hinges. "God be with us," said Ansiau, crossing himself. "I wish you all good hunting, my lords. I hope that my forest will do you honor."

As a courteous host, he waited for Manesier and Erard to precede him. Slowly the young man rode forward on his dapple-gray, erect as always. He turned to Ansiau and gave him a long straight look in the eyes—a look whose mocking and hostile insistence surprised the baron. He was tempted to say: "Have you never seen my nose before?" but he restrained himself, he did not want to be rude to his guest. On the road, however, he said to Manesier:

"My brother-in-law Erard is a valiant knight, but he seems not to have much fun in him. I don't like the way he looks at people."

Manesier, who was fond of Erard, replied that the young man led a very difficult life with his brother, enough to sour anyone. Old Hugh gave him neither clothes nor horses and was seeking by various means to have the viscount deprive him of his share of their inheritance.

"A bad brother," said Ansiau. "But I am surprised that Erard should take it so to heart. He is unusually handsome—he will certainly make a rich marriage."

"If only the women were to be consulted, he could have them all," said Manesier. "But there are their kinsmen and the viscount. And to get a rich heiress from the viscount you have to begin by giving him presents, as everyone knows. And poor Erard hasn't even enough money to keep his horse in fodder."

On their way back, a little after nones, the hunters stopped by the sheep pond. Ansiau asked his two guests how they had enjoyed the day's hunting. "I killed so much game you would think it had been put there on purpose for me," said Manesier. And Erard smiled broadly. "It is a great pleasure to hunt in my brother-in-law's preserves," he said. "There are none better." And again Ansiau felt uncomfortable, there was something provocative in the young man's vibrant voice.

During dinner Erard was gay and animated and the baron thought: "He is not unpleasant—quite the contrary." Yet he lost his composure whenever those blue eyes rested on his face, as they did from time to time. He seemed to read scorn in them—what did the man mean?

That morning Alis had risen exhausted and mortally sad. She knew it—the house had been turned upside down, the varlets were still drunk and asleep, the women were not doing their work, the cattle were untended, and God knew how much of her flour and spice and raisins had been wasted and stolen because she had relaxed her vigilance. A single day's rest—and this was the price she must pay for it.

Was it she, the lady of Linnières, who had run madly to the little garden and thrown herself into the arms of a guest of her husband's? She, the daughter of Joceran of Puiseaux, the grand-daughter of Guy of Marseint—a woman so noble, who had so strictly guarded her virtue while her baron was away—and now that he had returned, gave herself to another as if on purpose to show her scorn of him?

Seated on a tapestry-draped bench under the windows of the hall, she entertained the ladies of Hervi and Coagnecort by showing them the needlework she had done during the past year. She had taken a vow to give a gold-embroidered chasuble to St. Mary's-of-the-Angels if her baron came home safe and sound, and to hasten the effect of her vow she had gone to work on the chasuble at once, so now it was almost finished; the ladies admired it greatly, for neither of them could do such fine embroidery. Alis had always been proud of her skill. That day she thought that she was the noblest in everything; and yet this foul thing had happened to her. It was a great pity.

Yet had these women never committed the sin of the flesh? Of course they had—why should they be more steadfast than she? Somewhere in the past of each of them there must have been a squire or a minstrel or a chance-met knight (and more than one, perhaps). It took an Irma to make herself talked about. No one talked about the others, and no one should talk about her—only she and Erard would ever know—and she would take good care not to confess her sin to the canon of St. Mary's at Hervi. She must look out for some priest passing through on pilgrimage, and she would give him a gold bezant for his church. Then her sin would be carried away to some monastery in Lorraine or Languedoc, and no one would ever hear a word of it. She was resolved not to be weak again. Erard had taken all his will of her, and already he despised her—for he had gone hunting without seeing her. She would say to him: "Fair friend, I have shown you that I loved you; now I shall show you that I am a noblewoman. I will not wrong my lord again." The words gave her a glow of self-satisfaction. Thinking what pleasure she would take in hearing herself speak them to Erard, she almost forgot her regrets and her grief.

During dinner Lady Alis did not dare to look in Erard's direction very often, but she was charming to the baron—first because she really intended to be faithful hereafter and to right the wrong she had done, and second because she wanted to make Erard jealous.

After dinner there was dancing again. The knights and their ladies danced first, to the singing of the unmarried girls and the squires, who sat on the ground or the benches. There were six couples, and it was a figured dance, a very complicated one, with figures for couples and squares. The baron was the best dancer of them all, the most skillful and the most spirited—he clapped his hands and snapped his fingers and moved with surprising agility for a man of his build.

It was a charming picture they made there under the warm shadow of the two lime trees by the well—the couples circling and meeting as the music bade—the ladies in their pale dresses, the knights between in their long bright tunics—the baron in red, Erard in blue, the brothers from Hervi in red striped with green. All changed partners at each new stanza; it was like a bright wreath perpetually woven anew.

The baron had resigned Lady Alis to Erard and was dancing with Claude. The two cousins made a fine pair, for Claude was as enthusiastic a dancer as Ansiau. Claude finally announced to any who would listen that her cousin was the handsomest man in the company. Ansiau burst out laughing and said that she must be trying to make her lover jealous.

The girl answered: "I have no lover."

Her cousin asked: "Then why is your face so red?"

She said: "Because I am hot."·

The baron said he knew what had made her hot and that his brother-in-law Erard no doubt had something to do with it.

"Oh, I wouldn't waste my thoughts on him," said the girl. But her eyes kept seeking the young knight's blond head.

When Alis and Claude came together again Alis winked and said: "Beware!"

"Of what?" she asked.

"Of my brother-in-law. He is a mighty hunter."

"And I'm better at running than he is at hunting," said Claude with a laugh.

"Don't be too sure. You know I never joke about such things."

Claude made an angry little face and said: "You know who my father and mother were."

Now Lady Alis and Erard were dancing together, and she forgot all her unhappy thoughts and gave herself up to the pleasure of the moment. She said no more than that, when a knight has won his lady's love, he does not go off hunting the next morning. Erard answered that he had done it to avoid arousing suspicion. "I know you, you can always find some excuse," said Alis. Then she gave her hand to Manesier, and Erard danced with his sister-in-law Bertille. Now Bertille was only eighteen, she had a charmingly slender waist, and she seemed to be smiling at Erard far too often. So, when it came Lady Alis' turn to dance with Erard again, she assumed a reserved and distant air which quickly froze the bright, conquering smile on the young knight's lips.

"Lady, you do not look at me as you ought."

"I owe you nothing, sir knight."

"Lady, if you have changed toward me, may God punish you—I have not deserved it."

Alis answered nothing, intent on the figure she was dancing.

Then, when she turned to give her hand to her partner, she met such a hard look that she was terrified. He said: "If you have changed, I know who is the cause."

Lady Alis said: "You can say nothing against my sworn lord."

Erard bent forward and said almost into her ear: "Judas."

Alis was going to pull away her hand and strike him, but she mastered herself and merely pinched the palm of his hand as hard as she could. He revenged himself by crushing her fingers so that she almost fainted. In a loud voice she said that she was too tired to dance any longer.

Then the squires and the damsels had their turn to show their skill at dancing. The baron seated himself on the bench beside his lady and said that he would give a cup of claret to the couple who danced best. He was excited, happy at having spent such a pleasant day, and when his eyes fell on his lady and he saw her flushed and warm, with her wide lips open like a flower to the sun, he asked himself what more a man could want from life. "How much more beautiful she has grown," he thought, "she never looked like this." And he put his arm around her shoulders.

Alis shuddered in spite of herself. His possessive gesture made her uncomfortable—involuntarily she turned to Erard, who was sitting cross-legged at Claude's feet. She saw that his face was pale and tense, like the face of a man suffering from a violent toothache, and she forgave him whatever she had to forgive. Gently she freed herself from Ansiau's heavy arm, saying that she felt quite hot enough as it was. The baron looked at her out of the corner of his eye, somewhat surprised by her lack of courtesy. But he said nothing and, resting his elbows on his knees, returned to watching the dancers, clapping his hands in time to the music, and singing the refrain in his deep voice which sounded a little out of tune with the others.

It was a hot, bright night. Guests and hosts climbed to the upper hall to rest on beds sprinkled with lavender water and strewn with bunches of fresh herbs. The noise in the courtyard gradually ceased and the singing of the grasshoppers began to well in through the windows, smothered now and again by snores, the creak of a bed, a growling dog.

Alis was thinking that, of the two men, Erard loved her best because he was jealous, and that she had good reason to love him. And when she had to respond to the baron's caresses she did it with great reluctance; but she did not dare to defend herself for he was a little drunk. But afterwards she felt so unhappy that she could not hold back her tears; and the more she cried, the more the tears came—her face grew wet, she wiped it with her hands and her hair, and still the tears flowed. Ansiau finally became aware that she was crying and asked her why. She was too upset to think of a plausible reason; she said she had no idea. Then Ansiau became anxious: "Lady, no one cries without a reason. I can feel that your cheeks are covered with tears. You should tell me everything, you should hide nothing from me."

"No, baron, no—it is nothing, I swear it."

"Sweet, you are wrong to distrust me. I am here to protect you. If anyone has harmed you, you must tell me. You must not be afraid of me."

"No one has harmed me, baron."

"Is it because of the children then? Is one of them ill? You would be wrong to hide it from me—anyway, I should find it out sooner or later."

"What a thing to say! You must not say such things. No one is ill, thank God! If I tell you I am crying for no reason, it is because I am crying for no reason. I am not in the habit of lying."

"Lady, I am sure that someone has troubled you. If it is someone you wish to spare, I promise you I will not harm him. But you must tell me or I shall not sleep."

"Let me alone, baron. You can see that I am not crying now. I felt very tired, that was all."

And she buried her head in the pillow and did not move, biting her hand to keep back the choking sobs. The baron did not wish to question her further. Yet he was grieved by her lack of confidence in him.

He sat on the edge of the bed, plunged his fingers into his hair—too thick since it had been shaved—and began scratching his head like a man at his wits' ends. Here he was—he had come back safe and sound out of pure Hell, he had found his castle and land in good condition, his wife and his children in good health, his men faithful and devoted, his neighbors full of courtesy. . . . And for all that his lady managed to be unhappy—she had never wept in this fashion before the Crusade. He had thought himself as happy as a saint. And into his mind there came the stale, the oft-told story of the knight who stays so long in the Holy Land that he loses his lady's love.

It had been his wife's duty to wait for him seven years. Yet he saw unmistakably that she did not love him as she once had. Furthermore, he admitted that he deserved it. A woman so excellent and so nobly born, he thought, could have found a better husband. He had never tried to please her—he had taken her. Here he was—blackened by sun and wind, his body hardened by the lash, calloused until it was impervious to insect bites. That body which had been dragged through slave markets and the galleys still had a clean white bed to welcome it, and in the bed was a lady with a body as white and soft as a flower, bathed and smelling of lavender—noble and spotless and clean. Now he reproached himself for having thoughtlessly exercised his rights. She must feel less than proud of a husband who had come home barefoot and bareheaded—if he had thereby gained forgiveness for his sins, it did not follow that he had gained his lady's love. Without too much complaining he had endured hunger, stripes, the blazing sun—misery is no humiliation if it is borne for the love of God. But he did not believe that a woman—even a noblewoman—could understand that. It was perfectly natural that she should feel humiliated to have a poorer husband than other ladies, to see other ladies better dressed than herself—she was proud and wanted to be first in everything.

And for the first time in his life Ansiau bitterly regretted that he had come home empty-handed, when Ultramar was such a treasure house of silks woven and embroidered with gold, of muslins and orphrey work, of transparent veils, of rings and fillets. In the shops in the trading quarters of Acre and Jerusalem he had seen things so beautiful that it had hurt his eyes to look at them—embroideries in which beasts and flowers were mingled with bright foliage and golden threads; ear pendants of sapphire and amethyst which would so beautifully bring out the color of his lady's cheeks and eyes. And how much respect can a woman have for a man who cannot even buy himself a hauberk?

She lay still, her breath came evenly like the breath of a sleeper. But Ansiau knew real sleep from feigned. He said: "Lady." She did not answer. He did not urge her further, for he felt that he had been at fault. Yet at the same time he felt that she was being unduly harsh.

"What can I do," he thought, "to win her love again?" It was not seemly to take a noblewoman by force, against her will. Yet he did not see what he could ever do, for to be displeasing is the most difficult of all faults to amend. And why—by St. Thiou!—should she be crying as if her heart would break? Women, he thought, are hard to understand—they are much too delicate for men.

At dawn they all went hunting. Riders and dogs raced down the meadow before the castle and scattered over the roads toward Seuroi and Bernon. Fearing to soil their dresses, the ladies chose the Flogny road, which was less muddy than the other—it would take them to the chapel in the old forest and from there they could join the beat later. Erard of Baudemant, Garin of Linnières, Haguenier's son Renaud, and two squires offered to ride with the ladies, and Ansiau said to himself that their troop was more suitable company for Erard than the others. In his tight-fitting tan leather vest, with his blue cloak thrown over one shoulder and his blue falcon on his left glove, Erard capered and strutted before the ladies, displaying his horsemanship by sending his mount over the bull-pen hedge, bringing it to an instant halt, and plucking oak twigs at full gallop. Ansiau was so irritated by the young coxcomb's display that he found it hard to keep from insulting him. He had never before so thoroughly despised anyone. "What a mountebank," he thought, "going to all that trouble to show the ladies that he has a fine body." A provocative note in Alis' admiring laugh made him stiffen and prick up his ears, like a horse at the approach of a bear. But he was so far from any thought of jealousy that he merely said to himself: "If the coxcomb dares to touch Claude I will cut off his ears."

The two troops soon parted company. The ladies and their escort rode through fields diversified by clumps of birch and elm. They progressed very slowly, casting falcons, constantly turning back, much more interested in gossiping than in hunting. Only the younger ladies were out—Manesier's wife Lucienne, Bertille of Baudemant, Claude of Linnières, and Lady Alis. Alis, as usual, thought herself the prettiest of them all, but she knew that Claude and Bertille were slimmer than herself and that she was now twenty-five. Usually she paid strict attention to the hunting, but that day she had eyes only for her Erard—she hardly knew where she went and did not once cast her falcon. He was so handsome! And the other women seemed to look at him so tenderly! And he smiled at them, showing his white teeth, just as he smiled at her.

"What a hussy that Bertille is," she thought. "She will not let him alone. She's a married woman—she ought to be ashamed of herself." And suddenly, from the quiet impudence with which Erard took his sister-in-law's arm, Alis realized that he was already on intimate terms, that he had long been on intimate terms, with his elderly brother's young wife. She saw red. She rode close to Erard and said to him: "You are having a very pleasant morning, my lord knight."

He answered that, on the contrary, he was having a very unhappy one because he was not alone with her. Lady Alis stiffened: "You shall never be alone with me, upon my honor. I decline to discuss it."

"But I want to discuss it with you! Give me one good reason!"

"My lord pleases me better than you, that is all," she said and gave the reins to her horse, which sprang forward.

She was certain that she had touched Erard to the quick, and the knowledge gave her a bitter pleasure. She wondered what he would do now to punish her.

He punished her by not speaking to her again until the party halted near the chapel to rest and refresh themselves. One of the varlets had a sack of provisions slung from his saddle—bread, cheese, salted meat—and two cups which the young men hurried to fill at the brook. After they had eaten, the ladies said that they wanted to stay a while to digest their food, and they loosened their girdles and settled themselves comfortably on the unmown grass. Then Garin of Linnières, Herbert's son, asked if the knight of Baudemant would not tell a story to pass the time, and the ladies clapped their hands and said that Erard was a wonderful storyteller. Erard did not consent without further urging, as was seemly. Then he ran both hands through his hair to smooth it, looked round the circle with his usual provocative glance, and began:

"This is a true story from beginning to end. I had it from a friend of mine who has travelled far and wide. Here it is:

"Once upon a time there was a damsel at Toulouse, a rich and most courteous damsel. Her father was butler to Count Richard of Poitiers, the son of the English king. And when this damsel was old enough to marry, her father gave her to a noble knight of Toulouse, and they loved each other dearly, as is right. But it came about that the lady's husband went to the Holy Land and the lady was left alone for three years and she had no news of him; and she was sad and sorry and she began to fear that he was dead. And because she was so bad, her father took her to the court of Count Richard, where at that time the greatest barons in the land were gathered and the most beautiful ladies too—Queen Eleanor, and our noble lady Countess Mary of Champagne, daughter of King Louis, and many more whom it would take too long to name. But of them all the lady of whom I am telling was the most beautiful.

"Now among Count Richard's knights there was a noble and brave young man whose name I do not know. But what I do know is that he saw the lady and fell in love with her so much that he could neither eat nor sleep. This knight was a handsome man and his good fortune was such that all the ladies whom he desired came to him of their own free will. But after he had seen the lady of whom I am telling you he wanted to see no other woman, for all other women had become ugly in his eyes."

"What a liar he is!" Alis thought, but she felt flattered.

"Well, the knight went to see the lady and asked her for her love most courteously and becomingly. But the lady was cruel and proud and said that she would remain true to her lord. The knight was greatly grieved, for he well knew that he could not live without the lady. So, seeing that he must die if he could not have her love, he continued to beg and beseech until at last the lady would listen to him without anger. But still she would not love him.

"Now at Troyes—I mean at Toulouse—there was an English knight who appeared at every tournament and who was so big and strong that no one dared to fight him in single combat, for the blows he gave with his lance were so powerful that anyone he struck was either killed or crippled for life. He did not intend it, but he could not help it—so great was his strength. He was not a bad Christian and he beat his breast and repented each time he killed a man, but the poor knights were nonetheless dead for all that.

"And one fine day the beautiful lady said to her knight: 'Fair friend, bring me the arms of that English knight and you shall have my love.' She was sure that he would refuse, for the English knight was twice as heavy as her knight and he was forty years of age while her knight was only twenty-five. And indeed it is great folly to ask such a thing of a man merely because of a woman's whim. And the knight would have done well to refuse. But he loved the lady so greatly that he could not bear it, and he did not want to pass for a coward. So he prepared his arms and confessed and communicated and prayed to God and Our Lady for victory, well knowing that if he were taken prisoner he could never ransom himself, and if he were killed he could hardly expect to go to Paradise.

"And at the tournament, when the English baron rode into the lists, the knight of whom I am telling you threw down his gauntlet and challenged him, to the great surprise of everyone present. Whether the lady feared for him or not I do not know. Twice the Englishman struck him and broke his shield in two. But the third time, with God's help, the knight rode so well and struck so hard that the Englishman was unhorsed and fell to the ground and lay motionless. It took more than an hour to revive him.

"Then everyone praised the knight and he rose in all men's esteem, and he was glad, but gladder still because of the lady. That very day he took the Englishman's arms and went to her tent. It was a tent of red silk, filled with tapestries and cushions. The lady looked so beautiful that he almost fainted. And so far as receiving him goes, it must be said that she received him well, for she knew that he had risked his life for her. But, being the woman she was, she granted him everything except the one thing he most wanted. She was ashamed, she said, because of her kindred. It seems to me that she should have thought of that before she promised. But the knight thought otherwise. And she begged him so hard to spare her virtue that he fell into the trap and loved her better than he loved himself. And now hear what this lady asked of him as a proof of his love: she asked him to leave her and not to see her again for six months—if he were true to her for those six months she would grant him her love and marry him, provided that meanwhile her lord had not come home."

"I am sure," cried Claude, "that her lord came home! That is what always happens in stories."

"And in life too, the more's the pity. Well, as I was saying, the knight was trapped by the lady's fine words like a fly in honey, and he went home to his manor. And I leave you to imagine if the time passed slowly for him. Night and day he suffered torments, he could neither sit nor sleep. But still the six months had not passed. And now the lady's baron came home from the Holy Land. When the knight heard of it he fainted for grief. His sorrow was so great that he lost his wits. But since he must die if he could not win the lady's love, he managed to think of a plan: he went to visit a kinsman of his who knew the lady's baron well. And he asked his kinsman to take him to see this baron—of course he did not name the lady or even speak of her."

Here Erard stopped and asked one of his squires to bring him water to drink. Alis, sitting a little apart from the rest, was weaving a garland of buttercups and daisies—she did not dare to move or to raise her eyes. Memories of Troyes came flooding back, she smiled with happiness at the thought that after all poor Erard had really loved her—even though she felt certain that he had never fainted with grief. It was just like him to talk such nonsense. But because, instead of going on with his story, he was sitting silent, she raised her head. Slowly he drank, and handed the cup to his squire.

"Aren't we going to hear the rest of your story?" asked young Renaud of Hervi.

"You are too curious, young man. It is time we set out, the sun is high."

Bertille of Baudemant said that he must finish his story first.

"If the lady of Linnières asks me, I will finish it," said Erard.

Alis had gone back to weaving her garland; she said nothing.

"Oh yes, Cousin Alis, ask him," cried Claude. "Come, Garin, tell her to ask him. Please, cousin!"

Alis looked up and said softly:

"Why consider me, fair sir? You can see that all these other ladies want to hear your story."

"Very well," said Erard, throwing back his head. "You shall have the end of the story, then, but briefly, for it is late. Where was I? The knight went back to Toulouse and there he found the lady with her baron. And the very morning he arrived he worked to such good purpose that the lady granted him a meeting in a fair garden of cherries and roses where they could be alone together. And there they had great joy and pleasure, as you may well imagine, and I assure you that the happiest of the two was not the knight. So he thought himself sure of his lady's love.

"But the lady was disloyal and a liar, as you shall see for yourselves. The next day she told the knight that she loved no one but her baron—though, in my opinion, she had taken a strange way of proving this the day before! Now as for the baron—I do not know what he was like but I do not believe he was much of a man; for his lady had been true to him while he was away and yet could not deceive him fast enough after he came home. And as for the knight, others will say that he was wrong to bother his head over such a changeable woman. But I believe that he should not have borne such an insult without complaining; and perhaps he was too much in love, which was not his fault. So he tried to win the lady back. And now tell me—which of the two had a better right to this lady's love, the man who won her or the man who could not keep her?"

Alis felt like a criminal in the pillory; she could hardly keep back her hot, stifling tears of pity and remorse. Bertille of Baudemant was the first to break the silence: "A good story. But still unfinished."

Erard said: "I leave it to you who have heard it to finish it."

Then Garin of Linnières laughed and said that since neither of her lovers had satisfied her, the lady had only to take another, who would perhaps be more successful. This solution aroused much merriment, but the ladies found it too daring. Renaud of Hervi declared that the knight alone was to blame— he should submit to his lady's will and try to win her by patience.

"No," said Claude, "it is the lady who is wrong. People should not change their minds so lightly."

And Bertille added: "Very true. The young man had won her fairly— and, as the proverb says, 'never refuse the harness after you give the horse'."

"I see," said Alis, letting her garland drop into her lap, "that I must say my say too, for it is not courteous of you ladies to lay the blame on the woman. What we do not know is whether the knight was as faithful and as unhappy as the story says. If he had been noble and loyal, he would not have allowed himself to blame his lady." Bertille glanced at her out of the corners of her eyes, doubtless wondering if Alis was not the lady in question—but suspicions of that sort were better left unspoken, and poor Bertille had only too many reasons to be discreet.

The company rode through the tree-lined road toward Seuroi, scattering through the glades and paths. Lady Alis soon managed to join Erard, and this time she did not give him a chance to speak.

"Infidel! Liar! What have you to complain of? Do you wish to ruin me? Have I not proved my love for you enough? What more would you have? Do you want me to go down on my knees to you? Do you want me to come to your bed?"

There was anger in the young man's eyes. "You told me that you love your baron better."

"And are you such a fool that you believed it? I—who was mad enough to let you have your will of me—I who cried all last night because of you?"

"Perhaps—but you did not come to the little garden. I waited for you there."

Lady Alis stared. "But I could not come. It is too dangerous."

"It is you who are too cowardly."

"It is not for myself that I fear."

But words were not enough—he insisted that she should show her courage by parting from the company and riding with him to the Fairy Glade, where she knew that none of the hunters would venture. They tied their horses to the ancient oak and Alis looked in terror at the great white stones rising threateningly from the high grass. It was here that Flora still came to dance naked and summon demons. Flies buzzed, crows cut the air in slow, laboring flight—their long, hoarse calls seemed to come from very far. Lying in the grass, clasped, mingled, bound mouth to mouth, the two beings of flesh had become as grave and simple as the stones, the grass, the torrid air. The forest lived its eternal life, paying them no heed. Sometimes the note of a horn sounded toward the marshes—and that was all.

". . . The man who won you, or the man who could not keep you?" The hoarse voice was intoxicated with satisfied pride, with unashamed joy. Alis answered him with many kisses.

"The man who has won me. I am your slave forever. I ask you but one thing, my lover, my brother—one thing for the love of me. Swear to me that you will not speak another word to the ladies who are here."

"How could I do that without arousing suspicion? Impossible."

"I know my baron. He will never suspect anything. Every time you smile at a lady you turn a knife in my heart. As you pity me, stop it. Or I shall be unkind to you again—it is stronger than I am."

"I promise you. Whatever you wish. I care nothing for any of them."

She stroked his forehead and his hair. "I love you so much. And yet—I know that you have been the lover of your brother's wife. I could see it."

Erard spat with disgust and shrugged his shoulders.

Lady Alis laughed and said: "Beware that you do not spit on me like that one day. I shall hear of it. And I shall avenge myself."

"Oh, you . . ." He was lost in admiration—it was the first time she had ever seen him so forgetful of everything but his emotion. He had grown younger, his eyes were deep and dark. "If you knew how I despise her. She threw herself at my head, and now she runs after me like a bitch. Even though I have no love for my brother, it makes me feel sorry for him."

"Perhaps. But she is younger than I."

"That makes no difference to me. You are my first true love. I have never felt anything like this with any other woman. And of course you have a husband already! Yet what has he to do with it? Tell me—is he a leper, is he impotent? He could not hold you—that is neither my fault nor yours. He should have kept his eyes open."

Alis said: "I do not want to talk about him."

"Yes, he should have kept his eyes open. When a man is a man, he defends himself. If he doesn't, he can't complain. True, he can hardly boast of his looks. But if we ever come to blows, you'll see that I will relieve him of the rest of his nose."

"I will not have you say that."

"Why? Why? Why? If you love me, you ought to detest him. You are not loyal to me."

"My God," said Lady Alis, seeing the dull gold sun touching the treetops, "they must have started home by this time. What shall we do?"

Erard turned pale. "We must catch up with them as soon as possible. I hear horns over toward Bernon."

"Those are the baron's and Girard's horns," said Lady Alis. "Go join them, and I will ride straight to the castle. God! oh God! They are sounding the end of the hunt—they are starting back. Listen—you have a long way to go. Take that path there and ride straight toward the sun till you come to a clump of birches. There you turn to the right and follow the valley and when you come to the old willow, you take a boar path that leads toward Bernon. Above all, don't bear to the left or you will be bogged. There you can sound your horn, they will answer you. Tell them that you lost your way—but not a word about the Fairy Glade. And hurry."

"Yes. Come to the little garden tonight."

"I will."

"See that you do not keep me waiting for nothing."

"No, my sweet love. Haven't I a head on my shoulders? Somehow I shall find a way. Hurry. God keep you."

Erard spurred his horse and rode off without looking back. He felt uneasy and wondered whether he would be in time to rejoin the hunt. If their absence together were ever noticed, he could not imagine how he would extricate himself. He was never afraid of an honest fight, but the thought of dishonor and a court of justice made his heart sink. He followed the narrow path with difficulty; more than once his horse was nearly bogged in the marsh and he had to dismount to help the beast regain his footing on firm ground. He arrived covered with mud, red-faced and dishevelled, and was received with mocking looks and bursts of laughter, which he had to swallow as best he might. He said that he had followed a stag and been led into the marsh—which was not hard to believe. "Next time," said Ansiau, "take a squire with you who knows the forest. There are places here where you can get bogged and never come out."

That evening Ansiau waited so long for Lady Alis that he almost dozed off. Girard and Richeut had long since gone to sleep, the vast chamber had fallen silent, and still Lady Alis did not come. He was beginning to be uneasy when he heard a swift, light step and felt her slip into bed beside him. She was panting a little.

"You are not asleep, baron?"

"No. Where the Devil have you been? Everyone is asleep. I thought you were dead."

"I was with the children. Girard would not go to sleep."

"I have something to say to you, lady. Do not be angry with me, but I think you are too fond of Girard. It is wrong to favor him above the others. I think you are not always just to Mahaut and Simon's sons. And it is bad for the boy to spoil him so much."

"You are quite right, baron, quite right. I feel sleepy."

"I am not surprised. A little more, and you would have been with Girard until matins."

Lady Alis did not answer. It was bright day under her closed lids. There were lips upon her lips—his eyes, his hands—she was full of Erard—she had forgotten the baron, her children, God, herself—nothing mattered but Erard's beauty, his beautiful eyes, his beautiful teeth, those beautiful hands she had kissed so many times. She wanted to laugh.

"You are acting very strangely, lady. Something has happened to you."

"No. I am only sleepy."

He thought to himself: "Perhaps I have drunk too much and am imagining things." And once again, as if in the presence of danger, his body stiffened. The acrid, sourish odor of an unknown man hung close by in the air—but he thought he must have been dreaming, for there was no man near but his cousin Girard.

In the morning, watching his wife dress, Ansiau suddenly asked: "Where is your pink pearl ring? I have not seen it for two days."

"Holy Virgin," Lady Alis cried, "it is gone. Yet I know I didn't take it off, sweet, I know it. I must have pulled it off with my glove, out hunting. Oh God, I was so fond of it!"

"My uncle Herbert gave it to me," said Ansiau. "A beautiful ring it was, made in the East. It would be a shame to lose it."

"Do you think losing it will bring me bad luck?" asked Lady Alis uneasily.

"Of course not, lady. Think no more of it. People lose all sorts of things and are none the worse."

That day there were sports in the courtyard. Alis did not even watch—she was thinking that the sky looked very black over the forest and that there might be a storm that evening which would prevent her from going to the little garden. And the fear left no room in her mind for any other thought. But after the pole-vaulting, the stone-casting, and the shooting, the knights made their appearance on horseback. Then Alis clapped her hands for joy because she could admire her lover.

For a moment the sports seemed likely to end badly. Erard, instead of crossing lances for fun, as they had agreed, gave the baron a hard thrust in the loins. Ansiau, who was not expecting anything of the sort, was thrown from his saddle into the mud. Erard calmly said that he had not done it on purpose. Nor did he make a move to help his adversary rise—he pretended to be controlling his horse.

"Well, brother-in-law," said Ansiau with a wry smile, "if you can thrust like that without meaning to, you are the man to kill Saladin. But you should learn to control your strength."

Erard said that he had learned all he needed to know.

"No one would think so," said Ansiau with an insolent stare. Then he remembered that he was speaking to his guest. The sports were resumed. But the baron could not take part in them because his side was so painful that he could hardly move. He sat cross-legged at Lady Alis' feet, took her left hand and laid it on his head. Lady Alis gently withdrew her hand to scratch the back of her neck. She felt rather ashamed of admiring her knight's strength and skill despite what had happened. And, to console herself, she rehearsed the reproaches she would shower on him that evening under the cherry tree.

Meanwhile, Ansiau was under no misapprehension as to the blow he had received—it had been given on purpose, and given in a masterly manner. He wondered what the man could have against him. And after the sports he followed Erard to the mew. He wanted to talk to him alone—his patience was at an end. Erard, busy playing with two rust-red falcons, did not even look up to greet the baron of Linnières.

Ansiau said: "It is clear that you are a falconer. Those birds like you."

"Others do too," said Erard, still very much absorbed in his birds. He stroked their beaks and chirruped at them as if he had been alone with them. Then he raised his hand, and one of the falcons let its droppings fall on the baron's sleeve. The baron drew himself up and flicked the bird with his finger.

"You are clumsy," he said to Erard.

"Perhaps."

Ansiau forced himself to control his anger. "Listen, brother-in-law," he said, "I do not like your manners. You take me for an idiot. At your age, a man should know better than to mock people to their faces."

Erard turned white and said: "What do you mean by that?"

"I do not want to offend you," said Ansiau in a milder voice. "You are my guest. But tell me—have I ever harmed you or wronged you?"

"No," said Erard curtly.

"I believe that you did not love my lamented sister Ala. Have you a grudge against me because I was her brother?"

Again Erard said: "No."

"Then what have you against me?"

"Nothing," said Erard, in the same cutting voice.

"Your way of speaking to me is not what it should be," said the baron. "Why?"

He was master of himself now, and it was with disdain and surprise that he saw the young man's fine nostrils dilate and contract and the corners of his mouth twist with hatred. His eyes were like the eyes of a wildcat at bay.

"What is the matter with you?" asked Ansiau.

Erard roared: "I do not like you."

Ansiau fell back a step, rather hurt by such a frank avowal.

"I do not ask you to like me," he said. "I did not bring you here by force. And I am not forcing you to stay."

"Are you sending me away?" said Erard.

"I am not forcing you to stay. You may do as you please. I shall give orders to have your horses saddled and ready tomorrow morning."

Erard bowed his head and said: "It is your house."

Ansiau was expecting further insults and felt a little humiliated by so much mildness. But he did not want to alter his decision, because he could not look at the man without disgust—he did not understand it, but the feeling was too strong for him to resist.

In a wind that was already bringing the first drops of rain Lady Alis stood waiting, wrapped in her cloak. The man leaped from the stable roof, landed on both feet, and strode across the beds of lavender.

"Lady, I leave tomorrow. Your husband has sent me away."

"You are dreaming. You cannot leave tomorrow."

"He talked to me. He told me to go."

Alis began to understand. Her head swam.

"He told you . . . ? Because of your lance thrust? He has no right. He cannot send people away like that."

"What do you want me to do? It is his house."

Lady Alis could bear it no longer. "He has no right. It is cowardly. I shall go and tell him so. I shall make him ask you to stay. By the body of the Virgin, he thinks that he is sole master here. But it is I who hold the domain, do I not? All he can do is get into debt. He shall not insult you in this fashion so long as I am here. You shall stay."

Erard said: "I shall not stay under his roof one more day."

Lady Alis clung to him. "And I? Do you want me to die? Are you tired of me already? After three days? I cannot live without you. You know it."

The young man shook his head. "I will no longer eat his bread."

"It is my bread. My house. Can you not humble yourself a little for my sake? You mean to go now?—not to see me by daylight again? You do not love me!"

With his two strong hands Erard angrily unclasped her fingers and pushed her away. "You are mad. He must suspect already. Do you want to betray us completely? I must go, and I am going—that is all. It is time for you to get back."

She sat down on the ground and began to weep. He knelt beside her and threw her brutally on her back. This time he took pleasure in humiliating her.

"That will do for him," he said, "the great hog without a snout—I've branded him where he won't like it—I've dirtied him so that water won't make him clean, or perfume either. He is very proud of you, isn't he? I have won my right to laugh at him."

"Don't think about him," Alis begged. "You put shame on me. Talk to me as you used to. It will be so long before I see you again. Listen: when the baron goes to Troyes to take back his fief I will go with him. I will find means to see you."

Erard shook his head. "No. I shall not stay in Troyes. I shall go to Provins, to my mother's house. Her husband has just been made seneschal of the viscounty. Perhaps he will find a wife for me."

"And you tell me that! You are cruel."

"No, lady, you do not understand. I shall always love you. I shall never forget you. Other women are dirt to me. If I marry, it will be for a dowry—since I cannot marry you."

She cradled his head against her breast and rocked him as if he were a baby. "No—I know you, my fair friend. You will find other women, more beautiful than I. You will say: What a fool she was to betray her lord! To think that I shall never see your beautiful eyes again! Do not go yet. No, he suspects nothing. . . . I am so happy here with you."

But he was already freeing himself, shaking himself, a little annoyed by her babying him. "Come, lady, we must say farewell. Why linger over it?"

"But there are so many things I want to tell you. And now I have forgotten them all. No—stay a little longer. Here—" From among the crosses and medals on the chain she wore around her neck, she unfastened a silk bag and put it into his hand. "Here—there is a thread from the Virgin's cloak sewed inside it—a real one—my grandfather brought it back from Palestine. Wear it always—it will protect you from foul blows. Kiss it when you say your prayers at night, and say three extra *Aves,* it is a very holy thing. And here is a buckle—feel it—the stone is an amethyst, it will protect you on your travels and keep your mind clear when you drink—I have tried it. And take this embroidered girdle too, it was a present from my father—wear it against your flesh and think of me. And be sure not to give it to anyone! Oh, I have money in the chest beside my bed—if I had known, I would have brought you some. You need another horse."

Erard took her by the shoulders and shook her. "You must go in! It is beginning to rain."

"Yes. Let me kiss you. There. On your eyes. And your lips. And your hands—left, and right. Yes, I am going. And keep my girdle. Do you promise?"

"Yes. Go quickly." He almost pushed her toward the stairs. It was very dark. She opened her eyes wide, trying to discern her lover's features in that dim gray blotch. The rain began to fall in great drops, and at last she forced herself to climb the stairs and go in.

Tired, disgusted, almost glad to be going, Erard took shelter in the stable. "They are all alike," he thought, "they never know when to stop." Yet this woman he loved. He had known so many. Young and old. The lady of Linnières was not old, only two years older than himself. But she had been married very young—that aged a woman. All the same, he would have been very happy to have her if she had been free.

Alis noiselessly turned the key, opened the little door, and entered the vast, pitch-dark chamber. She did not dare go to the baron at that hour. She decided to spend the rest of the night with Claude and Girard the Blond's daughters. Claude made room for her without asking any questions. Perhaps she guessed something. But as the daughter of a knight, she had such a fear of the sin of the flesh that she could more easily have committed it than have thought about it. If some other woman sinned, there was nothing to do but shut your eyes and stop up your ears, for fear of being an accomplice. Such things did not exist, or existed only in romances. And—no accusation, no guilt.

Meanwhile, the baron had finally sent Thierri to look for Lady Alis in the corner where the children slept. She was not there. Then the baron thought that she must be with her cousins and he asked Thierri to send Mahiette, Claude's waiting-woman, to find her. Rather frightened because her husband had sent to look for her in the middle of the night, Lady Alis slipped on her shift and followed Thierri to Girard the Young's bed, where the baron was waiting for her in a very bad humor.

"You are trifling with me, I think, lady. When you intend to sleep elsewhere you should send me word. You are making me ridiculous."

Lady Alis sat down on the edge of the bed and dropped her head on her knees. This was too much! Not only had he driven away her lover, he must annoy her and scold her over nothing too! She could bear it no longer! She burst into sobs.

"Lady! What is the matter with you? Lady! Stop crying so loud. You will wake everyone."

Lady Alis cried out that she did not care. She had had enough. He did nothing but humiliate her. He had gone away, leaving her there like an old woman he had tired of, with his fief to keep and his debts to pay; he had come back and turned the house upside down without even asking her advice; he had let himself be unhorsed before all their guests by a man younger than himself; and now he had sent all over the castle looking for her—he had done it on purpose, as if she were a wanton, a concubine. And burying her face in her arms, she began to weep again even more wildly, quite carried away by her own feigned anger. Little by little the memory of Erard's caresses returned, and then she thought that she would go mad. She forgot all restraint. They were tearing out her heart. And she was supposed not to show that it hurt her. She was supposed not to cry. The baron should see that she was not easy to crush.

Her storm of sobs, broken by hoarse, terrible cries, confounded Ansiau. He was torn between pity and embarrassment—he loathed drawing attention to his family affairs, his guests would be sure to think that he ill-treated his wife. Richeut and Girard waked and offered Lady Alis cold water and a stone to quiet convulsions. And little by little she ceased to cry and fell into a doze.

And sitting there beside her, shamefaced and repentant, Ansiau was aware of one thing—that he was not the husband Lady Alis would have chosen, and that she had changed too greatly in the last two years, as no doubt he had also.

Ansiau rose early to see Erard off. Lady Alis had finally fallen asleep. She was moaning, her face was drawn and swollen, her eyelids were red. Frowning, Ansiau bent over her for a moment, trying to read the secret of her unhappy face. It was not wounded vanity which had made her sob so bitterly. And for an instant he felt a suspicion which sent a shudder through the core of his body—but he dismissed the temptation instantly. Lady Alis was an honest woman. She could no more commit the sin of the flesh than she could bathe in a cesspool—there were things which such a woman did not do. He might have foul thoughts—who had not had them?—but he must leave his lady out of such things.

Ansiau went down into the courtyard—he intended to ride as far as Seuroi with Erard. He had Mandor saddled, and the two men passed through the gate, followed by their squires. The horses' hoofs sank into the boggy clay. Ansiau rode ahead to show Erard the best part of the road and the adjoining paths and broke off the wet branches which sometimes overhung the way. All through the journey neither man opened his lips.

Swaying rhythmically to the wary tread of his horse, Erard stared at the broad shoulders, the narrow waist of the baron of Linnières. The fellow, he thought with a mixture of bitterness and disdain, could still please his wife—women found consolation much more quickly than they admitted. Well, the baron could now pick up what was left—even that was too much for him.

He was cured of his passion. He no longer wanted to kill the husband in order that he might marry the lady—he knew he would not marry her now if she were a widow ten times over. He had wanted to enter Lady Alis' bed as lord and master, not to take her in secret like a thief. But she was like all the rest—she had not been able to resist. He regretted it, because he loved her more than he had loved any other woman.

It was not his fault, nor hers. The only culprit was the man riding ahead of him, riding so calmly, with his head high and assured—the man who had dropped in out of a blue sky when he was no longer expected or wanted. Dubbed and married at sixteen, he already had ten years of knighthood behind him; he had been given time to show his prowess, to father five children, to fight in two wars and a Crusade—what more did he want? He had had his day. He ought to make way for other men. He was outstaying his time. After losing soldiers and arms and horses he had come back to his fief to fatten like a hog in its pen.

Why had he not known enough to die in the Holy Land, when he would have gone straight to Paradise? He, Erard, would have been there to replace him—he would have become Lady Alis' husband and lord of the fief until the the children were of age. He, Erard, had loved Lady Alis loyally, as a widow and a free woman. And the fellow had come back to oust him from the place he had rightfully won, and turn him into an adulterer. And poor Lady Alis—Erard was not tender, but his mouth twisted at the thought of the relic he wore on his breast—she deserved a better reward for her nobleness and goodness.

At Seuroi, where the roads to Hervi and Chaource crossed, the riders stopped. The bells of St. Mary's-of-the Angels were ringing terce; a pallid sun was breaking through the clouds and the morning mist that hung over the forest of Linnières.

"Let us have no hard feelings, brother," said Ansiau. "We shall meet again at Troyes."

Erard made no answer—disdainfully he turned away. If his life had depended on it, he could not have spoken respectfully to a man he thought his inferior. He shrugged his shoulders.

"I am going to Provins," he said.

"Then God keep you and give you a good journey."

Ansiau put out his hand and Erard did likewise, but without taking off his glove. Ansiau reddened, picked up his reins, and made his horse wheel. The man had no manners, he thought—never in his life would he speak to him again. But as he neared the castle he felt that a great weight had been lifted from his heart. The man was gone—now everything would be decent and peaceful again, life would become what it ought to be. There was something queer about the fellow—it had irritated him like an ill-tuned string in a lute. Ansiau wished neither to understand him nor to judge him. He was gone—good riddance.

That morning Lady Alis had waked in a cold sweat. She had not fallen asleep until shortly before dawn, and now she did not know whether it was day or night—she did not know why she was in Richeut's bed nor why she was alone and had only just waked when everyone else was already up. Her eyes hurt, she had cried so much the night before—she remembered a great sorrow—Erard had left her—who was Erard? Her lover, who had lain in her arms. He was gone forever, in three days he had had enough of her. She would never see him again—not tomorrow, not day after tomorrow, not in a week. And all the misery of her situation was suddenly clear before her, as if she had waked from a dream.

She had dishonored and soiled herself with a man who no longer wanted her and who would despise her. She had let the honor of her baron be thrown to the dogs—she was like Irma, like a bitch in heat—she who had always so despised the sin of the flesh. She did not accuse Erard—he was pure gold, she was ready to worship even his vices. But herself! A woman of such high lineage, a woman so respected by all the castellany! And she had given away her relic, and her girdle, her father's gift, and her beautiful clasp—and she had cried all night long like a madwoman—and if the baron should suspect what she had done—if she had betrayed herself? If she had talked in her sleep? Surely she had—Erard's name came only too easily to her lips. Then her anguish changed to terror—what might await her she did not know, she did not dare to think.

The pain that gnawed at her heart, the blood that hummed in her ears made her incapable of reflection. She had but one thought—to quiet the nervous trembling which set her teeth chattering, to pretend to be asleep. She buried her head in the pillow. Crouched and motionless like a hare ringed by hounds, she clasped her hands and prayed and promised. "Blessed Virgin Mary, Mother of God, stainless and sinless, crowned Queen of Heaven, Lady of us all, Queen of glory—no longer have I your holy relic, he who has it needs you too—Lady of goodness, I have sinned in my folly, but if you will take pity on me I will burn a candle on your altar night and day as long as I live. St. Peter, St. Mamas, St. Thekla, St. Margaret—let my baron know nothing, or I will kill myself and be damned forever." Her baron must not know. She would deny it. She would swear on her children's heads. She would go on talking until she made him believe her.

Then in the murmur of voices around her she distinguished the word "baron" and trembled. It was Claude who was speaking. "Here is the baron coming back already. He is covered with mud from head to foot. What weather, Holy Virgin! And I wanted to go hunting today!"

The baron no sooner reached the castle than he went up to the bedchamber to inquire into his wife's condition. He was told that she was still sleeping. He went to the bed, and when she heard his step Alis stiffened in feigned death, the last resource of a hunted beast. She no longer knew how or why he had come or why she feared him so. He sat down beside her and laid his hand on her shoulder. And his touch sickened her, for she remembered other hands, lighter and swifter. But from the way his hand rested and lingered on her she understood that he knew nothing, and would never know. A great weakness, in which there was a certain vague sense of delight, came over her. She stretched and said in a plaintive voice: "Do not touch me, baron, I feel sick." He rose and left the room.

Then Lady Alis recovered her wits and reproached herself with having dreamed a danger which had never existed. And the pain of losing Erard came over her again implacably—no escape, no hope, life was over. She tried to ease herself by imagining that the baron would take her to Troyes and that Erard would be there, but she knew it was never to be. Young and ardent as he was, he would soon forget her. How could she live with this shameful wound in her heart?

Ansiau was surprised to find that time had begun to hang heavy on his hands. Three weeks earlier he had been convinced that to a man who lives in his castle surrounded by his friends, who eats when he is hungry and makes love when he feels like it, life can hold nothing but happiness. And he, Ansiau, ought to be happier than anyone else, because he had the best wife in the countryside and a fine brood of children. He had thought he had only to go to bed with his wife and she would love him—and now he saw that she had forgotten him, that she no longer cared for him. He felt like a stranger in his own castle. His household loved him, he knew, but he saw that they had become used to taking orders from Lady Alis. With Haguenier, Enguerrand, Manesier—even with Hugh of Baudemant—he felt more at ease. Among men of the same castellany there was a common past of wars, tournaments, lawsuits, and quarrels, which made for instant understanding. True enough, Manesier and Hugh had not gone on the Crusade, but they had brothers and cousins who had been in the Holy Land. However, a man could not spend his life talking about the Holy Land. Ansiau of Linnières had experienced more than his share of adventure and hardship, but an hour had been enough to tell it all. The rest—the blue sea, the olive- and cypress-covered hills, the cloudless sky, the blazing sun—for all that he had no words. Sometimes in dreams he would be back on his galley bench, dreading the whip on his raw back. Only his companions could know what a Hell it had been. The fetid odor from the hold, the festering sores on thighs and feet, the raw palms staining the heavy oars with blood, back and loins straining so painfully that it drove everything else out of his mind—and, worst of all, thirst. And after all that, to sit by the old gray stone hearth, smelling the odor of roast meat, in the fine castle of Linnières—and not to feel happy! Man was a creature of ingratitude.

On the road from Marseille to Tonnerre, stumbling with weariness, jeered as a beggar, he had been happy. Stronger than his companions, he had sawn wood or carried water in return for a loaf of bread and a pan of milk. He had washed shirts and breeches, because Thierri had always refused to fill the office of laundress—as a squire, he had his pride. And Ansiau, as leader of the little troop, was bound to supply all their needs. He had done it cheerfully—he was not embittered like his cousin Girard, he was young. And the reward which awaited him made him forget hunger and weariness. Now, because he was neither hungry nor tired, he had nothing much to look forward to.

Without realizing it, he tried to put off the moment when he would have to drop back into ordinary daily life—if there was still such a thing as ordinary daily life. Every day he hoped for something new. He began to long for Troyes, for the river bank, the count's castle mirrored in the Seine, with its battlements and its banners, its sentinels wearing short blue tunics over their armor. He could see the streets of the merchants, the horse market, the great flag-hung lists under the ramparts, and the peaceful flow of the Seine at Paiens, the grassy bank and the wide palatine road over which shepherds drove their flocks. At Troyes he would see his godfather-in-arms, William of Nangi, who must now have more than one white hair in his curly beard, and his son Manesier, and Mathis of Monguoz, and many another knight doing guard duty at Paiens.

His guests, he thought, would stay till the end of the month and he would leave with them—in time to spend the feast of the Nativity in Troyes, for he was anxious to pray in a cathedral and receive the blessing of a bishop. He had little respect for bishops as men, but much for their rank and office; and he wept each time he prayed in Troyes Cathedral.

On the evening of the day on which he had so highhandedly dismissed Erard of Baudemant, the baron finally found himself in Girard the Young's narrow bed beside Lady Alis. Lady Alis had been bled twice and felt weak and somewhat calmer. She upbraided her husband, but more gently than the night before—she was so tired, she felt so unwell, she could not bear any more of this perpetual uproar, these guests who filled the castle from cellar to roof. Every day there were elaborate meals to be served, work was neglected because the waiting-women had to dance attendance on the ladies instead of spinning, she could no longer keep track of anyone. The children were getting entirely out of hand and soiling their best clothes. And she had a strong suspicion that some of the squires from Hervi were debauching the serving-wenches, and she could not say a word to them. Worst of all, they would have to mortgage Bernon, and God knew when they would be able to redeem it. The baron thought of everything and everyone except his wife, and then expected her to show him a happy face.

"Lady," said Ansiau, "you know whether you are dear to me. I will do whatever you say. If you wish, I will see to it that they all leave here tomorrow."

Lady Alis was really touched. "What, my friend? That is impossible."

"Wait and see. Shall it be said that I cannot do what my lady asks of me? I would do far more to make you happy again. Now shut your eyes and go to sleep. You shall see—I shall be able to arrange everything."

Lady Alis went to sleep unhappy but resigned—she had nothing to fear from the baron, which was a great relief in itself.

The baron kept his word. The next morning he undertook to persuade Haguenier to go hunting in the forest of Hervi, where an unusually old and large stag had been seen by his squires. Haguenier and his brother, as well as Manesier, caught the infection at once, and it was decided to leave for Hervi immediately. The baron of Linnières himself saw his guests off, after giving each of them a present, and Lady Alis exchanged jewels with their wives. It was settled that Ansiau should remain at Linnières for two days to set his house in order, after which he was to join the other hunters at Hervi.

Alis was most grateful to her husband for this hurried departure, which spared her the torture of conversing with Bertille and entertaining the other ladies. Quiet descended on the castle, much to the disgust of the young people. And on the evening of the same day Alis became nearly certain that she was pregnant and told the baron. He said: "Already?"

"Oh, I know what it is like by now—I am not apt to be mistaken."

"Then take good care of yourself and rest. No wonder you have been looking ill."

As this was her ninth pregnancy in eight years, he was beginning to be used to it. The first weeks were always difficult—afterwards things went much better. After all, perhaps this was the explanation for his lady's strange behavior—how was he to know what women were like inside? So he set off for Hervi without her—he would not be back until about the middle of September, he said; he must go to Troyes about his fief and to see his godfather and his friends.

And Alis, lady of the castle once more, soon had things running in their usual orderly way again. It was a joy to her to resume her place in her great bed, where she felt so much at her ease. She had it all to herself now, as before the baron's return. She wanted to rest, to recover her breath, her head was still dizzy from her sudden fall. So she must grow accustomed to life as a woman dishonored—she who had always thought herself safe from any reproach, who had been so sure of herself. Yet she had not lost her honor—for no one would ever know her shame except the man who shared it. She would never do it again. Erard had possessed her four times in all—it was so little, it could hardly count.

For a week she wandered about the hall, the little garden, the courtyard like a lost soul, pale, her hair uncombed—everywhere her eyes sought the face of her absent lover—his face as she had seen it in the Fairy Glade, at the dance, in the hall when he had lain at her feet—above all as she had seen it in the little garden, by moonlight, radiant with pride and joy. And who could blame her for not having resisted such a man? For a week Alis was sick with love, she was tortured, torn apart, and she asked herself how it was possible that the man who was flesh of her flesh should be far from her, in an unknown city—with other women perhaps. He had made her a part of himself, and then had left her like a stranger. It was against nature, such things should never be. If he had really wished it, could she not have met him in Troyes?

Then gradually the ferment in her blood died down, reason returned, and she began to be grateful to the baron for having sent Erard away—the danger, by God's mercy, was ended, all was over. If the thing had lasted longer God knew what she might not have done or where she would be now. Thanks be to God, she had not dishonored her lineage, and her children would not be called bastards. Thanks be to God, she would not have to go through a court of justice—frieze shift, shaven head, the convent. Thanks be to God, she was still mistress in her own castle and no one could question her virtue—if anyone dared, the baron would soon make him swallow his words. Her blood was too hot, it had served her an ill turn, but now she would be on her guard against it—she was cured of her lechery, all she needed was to receive absolution from a priest and then stop thinking about it. There was nothing to be gained by thinking about it. Men were all the same. Perhaps she would end by loving her baron again.

He came back to her in September, and the yellowing forest rang to the notes of horns and the barking of dogs. The rains had almost washed away the road. Wet, muddy, and happy, Ansiau looked his old self again. And as she watched him drying his boots at the hearth Lady Alis remembered their younger days and sadly asked herself: "Why did he have to go to the Holy Land?"

And Ansiau was well satisfied to be back at Linnières. He had made good use of his time in Troyes. He had borrowed money from Abner on Bernon, bought saddles and hunting gear, and also—it had been far from sensible, but he could not resist—a carved gold ring for Lady Alis. The stone in it was an opal with yellowish lights and Ansiau had rather hesitated about buying it because it was clouded. But the jeweller had assured him that it was just the thing for disorders of the blood and the humors and would make a lady be kind to her lover, and Ansiau thought that was exactly what he needed. A good third of the money had gone for it.

William of Nangi had received him well and taken him into his house. The two men rarely saw each other, but there was a great love between them. William was big and blond, as tall and square-shouldered as Ansiau, so that they were often taken for father and son. William was a placid and restful being, a man to whom you could talk about anything, say anything—he never answered you, he took it all in, he was no giver of advice. He knew armor and swords and harness, and loved tournaments. In his household everything was simple and clear, and under his influence Ansiau began to think himself the only man on earth who had family cares, and to laugh at his own weaknesses. William of Nangi was poorly lodged in a townsman's house in Troyes, his lands were mortgaged, he lived on what he could borrow, and the countess still paid him a wage which allowed him to maintain his horses and arms. His present wife, the blond Beatrice of Chesley, dressed like a countess or a marchioness, and no one suspected what this last love of William of Nangi's cost him, in money and worries. His son Manesier and his daughter-in-law lived with him, together with a whole household of grooms, kitchen boys, laundresses, to say nothing of poor relatives and pilgrims. It was rather crowded in the baron of Nangi's house, but everyone in it felt at home.

Ansiau talked about his two sons—next spring he would bring them to Troyes and Lord William should take them into his service. Already they were fine young men—they could ride and shoot and hood a falcon. It had done them no harm to be without their father for over two years, Lady Alis had supervised their upbringing and had not tied them to her apron strings. It was time they saw some real fighting and were initiated into a life of service. "I like the elder best," he said, "and I make no secret of it. People say he takes after Guy of Marseint, Lady Alis' grandfather."

Seated on her bench, Lady Alis continued to spin with her women and did not raise her head. So Ansiau went to her and asked her to make room for him beside her. It had been so long since he had seen her.

He still remembered that she had given him to understand that he was displeasing to her. And he was not the man to beg for what was his by right. He remained silent, waiting for her to deign to speak to him.

"What is the matter, baron?" Lady Alis asked, raising her eyes at last, "are you angry?"

"No more than you, lady. Is your health restored?"

"Yes, thank God. Did you have a good journey?"

"The roads are bad at this season."

Lady Alis returned to her spindle. If he wanted to talk to her, he was free to do so. She would wait. Erard would never be at a loss for something to say to her—and at the memory she shook her head to drive away the images that rose in her mind. She expected to feel the baron's arm around her waist or her shoulders. Then expectation became desire—she was never reluctant to receive a caress. But Ansiau sat there formal and unbending. He seemed to have forgotten her. Impatiently she rubbed her shoulder and knee against him. Then he took her in his arms and the spindle fell from her hands. She laughed. "Now pick up my spindle." He obeyed without further ado.

For a moment Lady Alis listened absently to the monotonous singing of the maids and the hum of the wheel. She felt so peaceful and so safe that she did not want to move or speak.

Ansiau laughed and said: "You seem to be feeling better again."

"Better?"

"You are not going to say no this time, are you?"

A little ruffled, Lady Alis shrugged her shoulders: "Go away—you are keeping me from working."

The baron took her left hand in his two horny palms and began caressing her long fingers one by one, absorbed as a child in a game.

"You never found your pink pearl ring," he said suddenly. It was so unexpected that she started.

"How should I find it?" she said sharply. "I told you that I lost it hunting."

The baron looked at her in surprise.

"I meant no harm, lady. Why be angry?"

"I am not angry. What an idea!"

Rather taken aback, Ansiau thrust his hand into one of his capacious pockets, which were always stuffed with the most miscellaneous objects, and finally extracted a green silk purse which he untied with the help of his teeth. From it he took the opal ring he had bought, and returned the purse to his pocket.

"There," he said, "I think that will look well on the same finger."

And he put it on her finger himself. Lady Alis cried out with delight and admiration, for she knew gems. She raised and lowered her hand, letting the opal display its fires, and revelling in the new beauty which it shed on her fingers.

"It will make up for the one you lost," said the baron.

Equally touched and ashamed, Alis looked at him. Then she could hold back no longer—she kissed him loudly on either cheek and said with a laugh: "Baron, there is not another man like you!" The baron looked at her in surprise—he did not think that he deserved such praise.

That night when they went to bed Lady Alis turned her new ring back and forth in the lamplight. It was by a ring that husband and wife were bound together—a link in the chain which encircled her finger, and her hand and her arm and her whole body. Of all the rings which the baron had given her, this was the most beautiful and the heaviest.

"Sweet, it was wrong to spend so much money for a ring when we have so little."

"Bah! I shall always be rich enough so long as I have you, lady. A ring is a small price to pay for you."

Alis, who liked nothing better than making fine speeches, answered gently: "Sweet, never think me a woman to be bought and sold. I am a noblewoman, and I love you for the faith I vowed to you at the altar, and not for rings and jewels."

Ansiau liked hearing fine words, but he could answer them only with smiles.

Lady Alis remained pensive. "Do you think this ring has a virtue?"

"I do not know, lady. Do you love me?"

She sighed: "I suppose so."

"You are not going to cry at night, sweet, like before? Tell me, sweet, did you never think of taking another husband? I thought you did not want me any longer."

Lady Alis flared up—how could he dream such a thing? She would like to know how, with the domain to keep and five children on her hands, she had had time to think of another man? And where would she have found him? And who was she, that she should want to take a man while her husband was still alive? If he loved her, he would never have asked her such a question!

Ansiau knew her too well to feel reassured. "I do not ask you to name him," he said. "I only want to know one way or the other. There are plenty of handsome knights hereabouts and you are young. If it is true that you are fond of some man, I shall not be angry with you. It was my own fault for going away."

Then Lady Alis began calling Heaven to witness that never in her life had she desired any man but her baron, and he was an oaf and a boor to suspect her.

"Will you swear it to me, lady?"

"By whatever you will. Here—I swear it on my cross. Take my hand—feel there—see if I am not holding my cross. There you are. I never thought of any man but you. Now are you satisfied?"

"I suppose I must be."

She said: "Baron . . ." She felt afraid, her heart was racing. She tried to cling to him, to stop his mouth with kisses, and he did not resist for long.

Afterwards he had no desire to ask further questions. He was very tender, as he always was when he thought himself the stronger. And Alis, in a languishing voice, asked: "Sweet, will you never love anyone else?"

"Erard," she thought, "Erard;" and she heard his hard reproachful voice: "You are disloyal. You are cowardly . . . We must say good-bye. Why linger over it?" No, he would not be as easy to hoodwink as the baron. She shook herself and stretched: "Tell me, sweet, are the ladies of Palestine as beautiful as people say?"

In the morning—he always woke earlier than Lady Alis—Ansiau opened the bed curtains a little to watch her sleep. She had let him undo her braids— a favor which she granted him only under exceptional circumstances—and her long hair covered the pillows like a great net. She looked very young.

But his tenderness vanished with the dark, to be replaced by a tranquil, reasonable good humor—Ansiau of Linnières was something of a Moslem in one respect, he could not imagine Paradise without a lady in his bed. His lady was night. When day returned it was time to think of the day's business. His lady was night, diversion, relaxation—whatever consolation there was for the ills of life—by day, memories of the night became embarrassing. He had looked at her long enough, he called Thierri and began to dress—he wanted to set out early for Seuroi—he must see the bailiffs and the guards. And he wanted to take along "the boy," as he called his eldest son—his pride as a father would not be satisfied until he had seen Ansiet mounted on a full-sized horse and riding beside him like a man. "And go quietly, Thierri, so that you will not wake Lady Alis. I don't think she and I got much sleep last night."

The baron ordered Mandor and Gaillard saddled and said to Haumette: "I am taking the boy with me. Lady Alis is not to worry—I'll look after him. We may spend the night at Seuroi."

Lady Alis had trouble combing out her hair that morning. Melancholy filled her at the thought that it had not once fallen to Erard to take down her hair. God knew, he had never had anything but the crumbs from Ansiau of Linnières' table, and he had been only too well aware of it, poor fellow. What he had been able to take from the baron was not much.

Father and son rode side by side, followed by Thierri. With an expert eye Ansiau admired the sober elegance of the boy's motions. Tall for his age, he was one of those boys who seem to know everything instinctively, without practice. There was never a superfluous movement, never a gesture which was not precisely right. He did not even seem conscious of his skill—he simply became one with his horse, his falcons, his bow, his javelin. But no sooner did he have nothing to do than he was transformed into the most irresolute and changeable of creatures, a spoiled child—and his father was far too intelligent not to know it.

It was a fine day, and the riders halted at a clearing beside the brook to lunch and rest their horses. From his saddlebag Thierri took a round loaf of bread and a strong-smelling cheese, and the baron made a cross on the loaf with his knife and began cutting it into slices. Ansiet ran to the brook to fill the mug which Thierri had unhooked from his saddle.

The ground was strewn with red and yellow leaves, and Ansiet amused himself by heaping them together and then hitting them with his whip, making them fly in all directions. The baron, lying on his stomach in the grass, watched him with a smile.

"Can't you keep still a minute?" he said at last. "At your age a boy should have outgrown such foolishness."

The boy dropped his whip and sat down beside his father. Leaning back his head, he stared at the spires of the firs swaying slowly against the luminous sky. He sighed. "Tell me, baron, is it true that Garnier's father is not dead?"

"He is not dead if God still guards him. He stayed behind in the Holy Land."

"What for?"

"To defend Holy Sepulchre, fair son."

"And why must it be defended?"

"Because there are very many infidels all about it."

The boy raised dreamy and astonished eyes. "All about it? Tell me, is Holy Sepulchre very holy? Tell me, baron, what is Holy Sepulchre?"

Puzzled, the baron scratched his head. He thought that everyone ought to know what Holy Sepulchre was, but he could not explain it himself. "It is where God died. It is a big church," he said at last.

The boy was satisfied—he knew what a big church was, he had passed by St. Mary's-of-the-Angels at Hervi, it was a big church and it had a great door with columns carved with oak leaves; you could hear the bells of St. Mary's all the way to Seuroi—they rang for the offices, ding-dong—and he saw his uncle Simon standing in front of the church, shield over arm and sword in hand, and the infidels drawn up around the church like a palisade. For him the infidels were beings resembling the animal-headed demons who peopled his nightmares. He sighed again and shook his head. The air was warm. Not a grassblade stirred. At a distance they could hear a squirrel throwing pine cones to the ground—in the intense silence all the breathings of the forest became perceptible and almost oppressive. The boy flung himself down and put his ear to the ground.

"Oh! I hear him," he said suddenly, intensely excited. "Baron, listen a minute. There! Don't you hear something?"

"What should I hear?"

"The stag. Listen hard. Ding! ding! ding! It sounds like silver because his hoofs are enchanted."

"What stag?" his father asked, amazed. "I have heard of no enchanted stag hereabouts."

"I'll tell you." The boy's big eyes opened wide and he moved close to his father. "I saw him the other day when I was riding Gaillard over toward the old chapel. And he spoke French as well as you or I."

The baron raised his eyebrows. "Indeed? And what did he say to you, fair son?"

Ansiet dreamily passed his hand over his forehead. "I've forgotten. But he spoke. His voice was as beautiful as Uncle Andrew's. And on his chest there was a shining golden star—oh, how it shone—and all around it there were little shining arrows. God, it was beautiful!"

"And what did you do then?" the baron asked gently.

The boy blinked, opened his mouth, hesitated. But he was used to having his imagination run away with him. "I dismounted and fell on my knees to worship him. That is what I did. Then he turned and started away. And I ran after him. I did. Oh, how I ran! He kept turning to look at me as if he were calling me. And then we came to a great copse, the trees were blue, the moss was blue, everything was blue. And in the moss I saw a red flower that blossoms every ten years. It is redder than a poppy and as tall as a lily. And it was so beautiful that I shut my eyes." He shut his eyes, rubbed them, and tossed his long hair.

"If you pick it on the night of the full moon," he said solemnly, "you are sure to find treasure within the week. You hold the flower in your hand, and when it bows toward the earth, that is the place to dig. You know, there are a good dozen buried treasures between here and Aumont and Jeugni, they were buried in the days of the infidel gods. And when the infidels were killed, here in the forest, their blood flowed into the ground, and since that day a red flower springs up every ten years—it is their blood coming back to earth. And that is why the flower is drawn by treasures."

"There is too much about the infidels in your story," said his father. "It is an old-wives' tale—you should not believe it."

"Oh no, it is true. Everyone knows about the flower. At least my brother does, and Garnier. But the trouble is I have never been able to find the way again. As for the treasure, I'll give half of it to my brother and the other half to Garnier."

"What about yourself?" said his father, laughing.

"Oh, I'll take another half still. The great thing is to find the way again. Oh!" The boy sprang to his feet, caught up his whip, and ran to his horse which he had tied to a young oak and which was browsing peacefully. "Stop that! Dog! Swine!" Ansiet seized his horse by the bridle, pulled up its muzzle, and gave it five or six quick, hard blows with the stock of his whip. Quivering, the beast plunged back, pawed and reared, but the boy would not let go and finally mastered it. Giving it a parting blow on the muzzle, he went back to the baron, his eyes sparkling with rage, his face red from exertion. "The dog! the churl! He knows perfectly well that I don't let him eat by himself! I'll teach him." He was panting.

His father stole a look at him—it had cost him an effort to let the boy handle his horse himself—and he felt proud of him. But he did not wish to let his pride be seen.

"You must never hit a horse on the muzzle," he said. "It makes him timid and spoils his looks."

"Really? Oh, baron, you can teach me what to do. You must know, because you are a knight—at least you know more than Robert does. . . . I want him to learn to obey nobody but me. You can tell me how, but I want to train him all myself. That's why I won't let him eat anything but what I give him.

A horse is soon ruined if you don't look out for him. And there are poisonous plants . . ." And suddenly Ansiet flung both arms around his father's neck. "Oh, if you knew how much I love my Gaillard! Will you let me take him to Troyes?"

"We'll see."

The boy opened his eyes wide. "Does that mean yes or no?"

"Yes—if you are a good boy. Up you get—we're off."

At Seuroi, where the three riders stopped for the night, the soldiers of the guard made a rough bed of straw and covered it with unbleached linen. There was no table in the hall, and the men sat down on the floor by the hearth. Ansiet, though tired from his day's riding, carved the meat and kept running to fill the cup for his father and Thierri and Girard, son of Girard the Young.

"Fair son," said the baron, "it is time you learned that you must smile when you offer the cup and do it graciously. A boy who does not know how to serve will never make a good knight. That we are seated on the floor is no reason for you to let yourself be slack—it falls to king and count to sit on the floor."

When the baron had finished eating and had wiped his mouth he allowed the boy to sit down and take a slice of bread and a piece of meat. But Ansiet, as excited as he was tired, ate almost nothing. The low, dark hall—like a big stable—looked strange; he had never spent a night away from Linnières. The fire on the hearth threw huge shadows of the seated men onto the straw-strewn floor. Behind the wooden partition the sleeping horses pawed and stamped. Suddenly Ansiet threw his bread into the ashes and burst into sobs.

"By St. Thiou," cried his father, forgetting to guard his speech, "what ails you, my boy? Are you ill?"

The boy sniffled noisily.

"It's Gaillard . . ." he sobbed. "I hurt Gaillard. I hit Gaillard."

Ansiau stroked his hair, trying to soothe him.

"There, there, it is over and done. No use crying about it."

"Oh, baron, let me go and see him. I'll give him my bread and salt to make up for it. I won't be long."

The fire had died down, the soldiers were long since snoring in the straw, and Ansiet was still behind the partition with the horses. The baron lit a pine splinter and went to look for him, shielding the flame with his hand so as not to startle the animals. Ansiet was asleep, stretched on the ground with his head on Gaillard's saddle. His father hesitated a moment before he waked him. He could carry him to bed as he was, without rousing him. Then he thought of all the sudden awakenings, all the painful nights of watching, all the hardships of a soldier's life which the boy would have to bear uncomplainingly. Better that he should become accustomed to them early. "Get up, my son. Thierri is asleep. It is your turn to wait on me tonight."

The boy whimpered. "Where am I? Haumette! Why, it is you, baron!" He stretched. "Oh, I was having such a good sleep. I'm coming. Wait, I must kiss Gaillard. Good night, Gaillard."

He followed his father and helped him to unlace his breeches and shoes—his little fingers were not very skillful, he had to give up on several knots and leave them to the baron, who undid them with plenty of oaths. "Where shall I sleep, baron? At the foot of your bed, or beside you?"

"Beside me, boy. You would be cold on the floor. And what about your prayers? Don't you say your prayers?"

"Oh no, never, baron."

"You ought to. You are old enough."

"I don't know how to say prayers." Ansiet shook his head in perplexity.

"But you chant them in chapel, don't you?"

"I know how to chant them, but not how to say them."

"I will say them for you. You need only answer Amen."

Together they knelt down beside the bed. The baron was not always so strict about his religious duties, but he wanted to teach his son proper behavior. So he said a *Pater* and an *Ave* and named a round dozen of patron saints before getting into bed. Ansiet cuddled against him—he was cold. "You must teach me to say prayers the way you do," he muttered sleepily, "I like praying."

The next morning there was a high wind, clouds drove across the sky, hiding and revealing the sun; in the forest the trees swayed and cracked and mingled their branches, yellow with green—the blast blew out the riders' cloaks and Ansiet laughed aloud when he felt his long hair whipping about his temples.

"Oh look, baron," he cried suddenly. "Rainard's grave is all covered with moss."

Ansiau looked earnestly at the peaceful gray stone flecked with green. Soon it would be a landmark on the Hervi road, and nothing more—no place was ever less haunted.

"Baron?" the boy said in a dreamy voice.

"What, fair son?"

"Baron, tell me—who was Rainard?"

No sooner had they returned to the castle than Ansiau began thinking of leaving for Troyes. The countess was to preside over a tournament toward the end of September, and he did not want to miss the opportunity to acquire some armor, although a hauberk big enough to fit him was not easy to find.

Lady Alis received him rather coolly—what reason had he to spend the night at Seuroi and leave her to sleep alone? What was the use of her being married if she must live the life of a widow? The baron laughed and said: "Bah, you will love me all the better today. We will make up for lost time."

"God, God!" said Lady Alis. "Do you think time lost can be made up?

And the two winters and three summers you have left me here alone—do you think I shall forget them? I shall never forget them. Never!"

Ansiau's answer was to put his hand between her shoulder blades, as he liked to do, and let his palm slide over his wife's strong and muscular waist—it was not the slim waist of the Alis of three or four years since, but he loved it as it was.

When, at the supper table, the baron announced his decision to leave the following morning for Troyes, Alis turned white with anger but she said nothing. That evening in bed she asked if he would not take her with him.

"No, my sweet, I cannot provide you with a decent place to live in at Troyes. At my godfather's house I shall sleep on straw with the men. You know I haven't a sou. I do not wish to put you to shame."

"It was hardly worth travelling fifteen leagues to spend only two nights! Why must you go to Troyes?"

"Sweet, if I do not take two or three rich prisoners we shall not be able to feed the horses this winter. Out of what I win I will bring you back a fine piece of cloth-of-gold for a dress."

Lady Alis sighed, thinking that such a promise should close her lips. But she felt sad. "You cannot love me very much if you are going to leave me so soon. You will see beautiful ladies in Troyes, and—I know—you want to be free to pay your court to them. After all, I can sleep on straw as well as you."

"Truly, my sweet, it would not be decent. And you have much to do here at the castle."

Ansiau had meant no harm by this remark, but Lady Alis became thoroughly angry. Was she a servant that she must work at the castle while he went to live a gay life at Troyes? If he was tired of her, he had only to take back his ring and give it to some other woman—no doubt that was just what he wanted.

"My sweet, do not be angry. If you want so much to go, I will take you."

Before such a sudden surrender Alis felt a little taken aback and almost disappointed—now she was not sure that she really did want to revisit Troyes after her adventure of the previous spring. Besides, when all was said and done, the thought of making her appearance there as the wife of a poor man was humiliating. But her fear of leaving the baron defenseless against the enterprising ladies and wenches who would gather for the tournament quickly decided her and she resolved to go.

Travelling with Ansiau of Linnières was not what she could call a pleasant experience. She was too used to being her own mistress. Why, he stopped anywhere and everywhere, now to talk to a soldier encountered on the way, now to pray in some village church—again and again he forsook the direct road, for he had a habit of picking up pilgrims and giving them a ride on the crupper of his horse or Thierri's, and if it happened that the pilgrims were bound for Bar-on-Seine or Estissac, they would take them a good part of the way merely for the pleasure of hearing their tales of distant countries and miracles. She would have thought that he must have had his fill of travels and miracles by now. But Ansiau, rather naïvely, supposed that other men's pilgrimages must be stranger and more edifying than his own—he had had the bad luck to be sold as a slave and to row in the galleys, it was to be hoped that other pilgrims had encountered adventures better worth the telling. Some of the pilgrims were on their way from Spain, others from Rome, others only from Vézelay or Langres. Alis felt nothing but scorn for such serfs and their tales—they must be lying, for what could induce people of naught to tell the truth? No one vouched for them.

"At this rate, baron, we shall be in Troyes for Christmas."

"Come, lady, it is four days before the tournament begins."

Yet if he had wished it she would have ridden down the highroad with him, side by side and hand in hand. There had been so little time for her to talk to him. She would have liked to tell him of the sorrows of her two years' widowhood, the pains of her last childbed, her attacks of fever, her quarrels with Richeut—all that he still did not know about her life—and then to talk to him about Herbert, his last months, his death in the forest, and all the fine tales he had told her. Herbert, at least, had not disdained to speak to her, had not preferred the company of pilgrims to her own. Yet he was as good a man as Ansiau. Now more than ever she cherished a deep devotion for the man who had not desired her. But Ansiau would never turn to her if he wanted to hear anything about his dead uncle—so she spent her time casting her falcon at crows and rooks, or galloping full speed down the dusty road and listening to the wind whistling in her ears.

They reached Troyes on the day of the tournament. Ansiau had barely time to stop at William of Nangi's house and put on his godfather's hauberk. It was too large for him and he wrapped a length of woolen cloth around his waist to make it comfortable. This time he could not let himself be beaten, for William of Nangi had no other armor, and to redeem it, Ansiau thought, he would have to mortgage all of Linnières—without counting his ransom, which he would never be able to pay.

He had the luck to take two prisoners—one was a certain Imbert of Potangis, whose imposing height promised Ansiau a hauberk that would fit and whom he had picked out at a distance among the troop of knights from Sézanne. The other was Fulk of Rumilli, whom he had detested ever since the castration of Baldwin of Puiseaux—Fulk was the husband of one of Joceran's daughters and he had done all that he could to prejudice the viscount against Ansiau. Fulk, who lived in Troyes, payed his ransom the same day. As for Imbert of Potangis, Ansiau took him to his godfather's, to the latter's great embarrassment—his small house was filled on tournament days, in fact it was so crowded that his guests had to sleep almost on top of each other on the floor. Alis had finally found a place in a comparatively comfortable bed with the wives of William and Manesier of Nangi and a certain lady prioress, a kinswoman of Manesier's mother.

Imbert of Potangis was a big man of thirty, red-faced and short-winded. He consoled himself for his defeat by swallowing cup after cup of the red wine with which William generously supplied his guests. Apparently Imbert had a strong head, for he did not get drunk. Ansiau sat down beside him and, according to custom, asked him who his kinsmen and godfathers and comrades were—perhaps they had friends in common? Imbert was in service at Sézanne and was only stopping at Troyes, he was poor and had counted on the tournament to pay his debts. He had, he said, a great weakness—his passion for dice, which had ruined him, for he never cheated, having taken a vow to that effect to Saint Mamas after a serious wound from which he had almost died. He had been known to stake his shirt and even his breeches and to wrap himself in a sack some varlet bestowed on him in charity. Ansiau burst out laughing at the picture of a man of such corpulence trying to hide his nakedness in a sack, and Imbert laughed too—it had not been the worst of his adventures.

"You will not be able to pay your debts this time," said Ansiau, still laughing, "but I will let you off your ransom—what I wanted was your hauberk and your horse and so on, as you no doubt know. Do not take it amiss—it is our good old custom here in Champagne."

"Will you not play dice with me for them?" asked Imbert, looking up pitifully.

"By my beard, no! I do not play for what I have already won."

Alis had other business to attend to in Troyes—it was not without apprehension that she looked forward to All-Hallows, the day on which the entire household of Linnières received Communion. She had no desire to make a false confession, consequently she must get rid of her dangerous secret as soon as possible. So she asked the ladies of Nangi what friars were frequenting the churches of Troyes, and Lady Oda, Manesier's wife, told her of an Augustinian famous for his sanctity, who was soon to go on pilgrimage to St. James of Compostella in fulfillment of a vow. "If you wish to obtain a grace or some special favor, this is the moment to go to him. He will pray to St. James for you when he gets to Compostella." Conducted by Oda, who hoped to find out the reason for her new friend's devoutness, Alis went to see the good father in the church of St. Pancras. But she would only say that she was going to confession.

She did not approach the confessional without some tremors—the devils who would hear her might at once begin preparing the appropriate punishment for a lecherous woman. But Hell was far away. So, neither justifying herself nor accusing herself, she confessed her misdeed point by point—she had committed the sin of the flesh so many times, in such and such places, with such and such a man—she had repented, she wished to receive absolution. The monk must have been a stern man—he told her that a wanton woman could receive absolution only after she had shaved her hair and shut herself up in a convent. Alis took it very ill and replied with some heat—

she was ready to swear that he had never said as much to his own mistresses, it was shameful that the wife of a knight should be exposed to insults from a black cowl.

She left the church in anger. Her first thought was to go to Ansiau and complain, but she soon realized that this would be dangerous and hardly sensible. After some reflection she found herself thinking that the monk might really be a holy man after all, in which case God would be angry with her for her insolence to him. So she went back and humbly begged the Augustinian's pardon—she was a free woman and not accustomed to being insulted, but if he would absolve her from her sin she would give him a golden bezant for his monastery and submit to whatever punishment he prescribed. The monk was not hard-hearted; he finally give her absolution on condition that she would make a pilgrimage to the cathedral of St. Mamas at Langres—she must go herself, and go on foot. Alis protested, saying that she could not possibly go on foot—and besides, what sin would people think she had committed? It would bring scandal on all her kindred.

The good man consented to let her go on horseback—but she must go before Christmas.

Now that he had a hauberk and a second horse, Ansiau was not much inclined to revisit Linnières.

"Suppose we go to Provins?" he said to Lady Alis. "What do you think, my sweet? They say it is a fine city."

"To Provins?" cried Alis, frightened. "What for?"

"Can't you guess? I have a strong desire to break two or three of my little brother-in-law's ribs."

"Which brother-in-law, Holy Virgin? We have more than one."

"Only one who lives in Provins. Erard of Baudemant. I shall never rest until I have made him bite the dust."

Lady Alis instantly protested: "He never harmed you. Let him alone. It would be wearing out your horses for nothing."

"Not for nothing, my sweet. There is to be a tournament at Provins in a week, on St. Remy's Day. You will see some fine jousting."

Alis said shortly that she would not go to Provins. She wanted to go home. It made her unhappy to be away from her children for so long.

"Bah! We'll be back well before All-Hallows."

Alis flew into a rage. No, no, no—she would never go to Provins. She did not want to miss the hunting season. She had work to do at the castle. Oh, what it was to have a husband whose only thought was to wander over the countryside with beggars he picked up on the road!

Puzzled, Ansiau scratched his beard. "What now? I cannot let you go back without an escort, and I need my men. However, I can manage with Thierri; then the two others can go back with you."

"What? You mean that I am to go home without you?"

"It cannot be helped, my sweet. I am too anxious to setttle accounts with our ill-bred friend. My hands are itching already. Do come with me—you'll see how I will handle him!"

Ansiau was astonished at his own words, for he was not in the habit of boasting beforehand.

Lady Alis stamped her foot. "No, I will not go. Stop pestering me."

"As you please, lady." Ansiau accepted these inexplicable feminine whims without protest—he took them for a law of nature. He fitted Lady Alis out for her journey the same day, gave her his two soldiers as an escort, and husband and wife parted good friends. Alis made him swear that he would not touch a woman until after he returned from the tournament, and wished him good luck. But in her heart she hoped that he would not harm Erard.

Ansiau went to Provins with Manesier of Nangi and took part in the tournament, though he did not take any prisoners. Nor did he encounter Erard of Baudemant—the young man had entered the service of the count of Brienne and had gone to Flanders with his lord. Ansiau sighed. He would have liked to travel to Flanders—the country was said to be rich and full of brave knights; but he had no money and the hunting season was already far advanced. Besides, he had promised Lady Alis that he would not touch another woman, and he did not want to risk his word on an absence of many weeks. And he remembered that his son had only one more winter to spend at Linnières.

Despite the cold the hunting continued until the first days of December. Alis remembered her pilgrimage only a fortnight before Christmas. She was terrified—suppose she had not time to reach Langres! The roads were bad and crowded with pilgrims as the Christmas season approached.

She told the baron that a holy monk at Troyes had ordered her to make a pilgrimage to Langres because of a grievous sin she had committed, and if she did not make the pilgrimage before Christmas her sin would not be forgiven.

Ansiau cursed. "Can't these shavelings mind their own affairs! You don't mean to set out on a journey in weather like this?"

"I must, baron, I promised." She sighed, thinking of her belly which was beginning to be cumbersome—who knew what might happen to the child if she failed to keep her promise?

"Let someone go in your place," said the baron. "You cannot travel in your condition."

"On the contrary," said Lady Alis. "I must be freed of my sin before I am brought to bed. I promised to go myself, there is nothing else to do."

"But after all, my sweet, a woman cannot commit very serious sins. You have not sworn falsely?"

"I have a man's death on my conscience," said Lady Alis, and she was not lying. "I had a thief beaten the day before Martinmas and he died under the rod."

Ansiau shrugged his shoulders. "Bah! a villein. Your monk has no more brains than a rabbit. By my beard, you shall not stir from here until after you are brought to bed."

But, vowing that she could neither eat nor sleep until she had performed her penance, Lady Alis talked so long and so well that the baron finally yielded. She had been quick to realize all the advantages that her act of piety could win for her, aside from forgiveness of her sin: prayers said during a Christmas Mass at the cathedral of Langres were infinitely more efficacious than ordinary prayers, and the whole household had great need of the help of Our Lady and St. Mamas. There were new arms to be blessed, Masses to be sung for the dead, to say nothing of a Mass of thanksgiving for the baron's return. She prepared for her departure in a fever of joy, she was filled with pride at accomplishing such a meritorious work—all the baron's kinsmen loaded her with commissions—she was to ask St. Mamas to cure an illness, to revive a dying love; she was to bring back holy water and boxwood from the cathedral. The baron gave her his big fox cape and all the money he had left, and the children looked with trembling wonder at their mother who, for the first time in their lives, was going to celebrate Christmas far from them, in a holy place.

Lady Alis took Silette with her and two men-at-arms for an escort. The baron rode with her as far as Coussegray, a league to the east of Linnières. They stopped at the crossroads. The wooded hills of Tonnerre stretched before them in a frigid mist. Banks and branches were covered with hoarfrost; the sky was gray and still. Lady Alis wrapped herself more closely in her great cape and blew on her fingers—they were already stiff from holding the reins.

The baron put his hand on her shoulder. "God keep you, lady. But if anything goes wrong with this child, it will be your own doing."

Alis crossed herself. "Don't say such things. Nothing will go wrong. Farewell, my friend."

Ansiau returned to the castle, sat down by the hearth, and began counting the days until Christmas. Twelve days. A long time. He wondered if he ought to fast—Lady Alis was very strict on the subject of fasting and abstinence, but she was gone and he felt freed from such obligations—he had fasted more than enough in his lifetime. He was not a great eater, but cold weather, and particularly inaction, inclined him toward the pleasures of the table, and he had a great desire to taste roast kid.

Night fell early. And it would be endless. In the closed, heated bedchamber the air was stifling, despite the cold outdoors. For the first time since his return Ansiau found himself alone in his great curtained bed. And since he had never been able to think of his bed without Lady Alis at his side in it, he felt lost—it was as if half the bed had sunk into the earth; he feared that if he fell asleep, he would drop into emptiness. Sleep would not come, the old anguish of his nights in the field when he had fought in France came back to gnaw at his marrow and his brain; it was years since he had been alone—always there had been a comrade at his side—even in the galley it had helped him to see a back and a head in front of him. But now Ansiau regretted that he had not stayed in the Holy Land, where there was always a chance to fight the infidels. Simon had made the better choice. He had not stayed here to rot in this forsaken house in the middle of the marshes; there were no more wars in Champagne, and at tournaments you spent more than you gained. Andrew was God knew where—perhaps he had died on the road—perhaps he had taken service under some baron in the south. If only day would come and drive away the anguish that was tearing at his heart. But the night had only begun. Ansiau decided to wake his squire.

"Thierri."

"Here, baron."

"Thierri, I am so sad that I cannot bear it. If you could find me a woman to sleep with. I shall never sleep otherwise."

"What woman, baron?"

Ansiau thought for a moment. "A tall one—and not too dirty."

Monotonously the short, dark days wore on—the nights were long and cold. With Lady Alis gone, the servants took advantage of the freezing weather to neglect their work and crowded into the hall, warming themselves at the hearth and listening to Christmas legends told by a pilgrim from the Holy Land whom the baron had brought home from the hospital at Chaource. The approach of the holidays created an atmosphere of idleness and rejoicing such as had not been known at the castle for many years. Their lady's absence had something to do with it, as well as the thought of the benefits which her pilgrimage would bring to them all—it was not every year that one's lady went on pilgrimage at Christmas. And the baron obviously considered that his wife was praying enough for two, for he let himself go as he had never done before. Lady Alis' departure had caught him unprepared. When she was there he was lord and master of the castle and knew perfectly well what to do and what not to do, but now he felt himself relegated to the ranks of the stable boys and could find no occupation but looking after his horses. He did it very well—it was one of his gifts that he could sense an animal's needs by looking at it and touching it. But time hung heavy on his hands, and he wondered how he was to get through the winter months which still lay ahead. He scanned the sky for snow clouds—snow would make it possible to get up a beat for wolves.

Lady Alis made slow progress over the frozen road—the woods on the horizon rose and fell rhythmically before her to the steady gait of her mount. The hoofs of the four horses struck the ground with ringing thuds which were echoed by the empty forest. Not far from Tonnerre the travellers entered the highroad, and thenceforth they were never out of the slowly moving crowd of pilgrims on foot and on horseback—indeed they made such slow progress that Lady Alis, who was never particularly patient, began to feel that she was standing still. The crowd laughed, swore, or chanted hymns—

there were monks in brown cowls, poor men in rags, townsmen in ample woolen capes, prostitutes, and penitents travelling barefoot and bareheaded despite the cold. At long intervals there was a group of three or four knights —those who appeared to be of sufficiently high rank did not hesitate to whip the humble folk on foot out of their road. At night at the inns the mob crowded around the doors and into the barns—a fire was lighted in the courtyard and there they toasted their slices of black bread. The lady of Linnières could afford a place in a bed, where at least she was warm. The fleas and the stenches prevented her from sleeping. Every evening there were brawls; the inn would ring with drunken shouts; from the courtyard rose songs and laughter which did not stop all night.

The journey took ten days and Alis grew rather tired. More and more she gave herself up to her pleasurable sense of the light burden which made her hold her back straight and prevented her from bending forward. As she sat, she felt it there against her thighs, safe and warm under her woolen dress and her fox cape, safe and warm in her womb, in her blood, next to her heart. It did not cause her pain, but she was beginning to be full of its presence. She lived through her old pregnancies again—except for the first two, none of them had been painful. Again she found the great peace of body and soul which had been denied her for two years. At last the baron had relieved her of that forced sterility which had made her languish and burn and behave like a madwoman. Once more she was what she should be—everything was right again.

At most she had only five months to wait. Her baby would be born after Holy-Rood Day, in May; the forest would be green and full of the singing of birds. How big Girard and Alette would look then! How warm its little head would be, how fine and smooth its skin, and so soft that already she longed to touch it. Its delicate round mouth would cover the nipples of her breasts, which were already swelling with milk. It had been so long since Alette was weaned—thirteen months, yes, over thirteen months! And now there was another coming, another to reach out with eager little lips and cry in its hunger and slowly fall quiet as its mouth filled with milk. Of her children it was always the new baby that she loved the best—as they grew, they were alienated from her. The baron merely lent her the race of Linnières for five or six years—the girls a little longer—just time enough to clothe them with bones and flesh and skin, to teach them to walk and talk, to bring them to the point where the baron could make them into the men he wanted. But this child, this child who was with her now, needed nothing from the baron or from anyone else. If it was a boy she would name him William— she had chosen that name for her next boy long ago, after Alette was born, and she had dreamed of it ever since. Because of Duke William Curtnose, of whom the ballad tells, and of William the Bastard, duke of England, and of Duke William of Aquitaine who had made the beautiful songs that Herbert had sung to her. As she thought of these things Alis sighed and murmured "William"—a name so sweet that it was like a caress.

At last the pilgrims caught sight of Langres, with the massive silhouette and square towers of its cathedral overlooking and crushing the town. Despite the cold the streets and squares swarmed with people. Bewildered and lost in the crowd, Alis could hardly keep up with her travelling companions. She finally drew rein before a secluded inn which was less crowded than the others. Like it or not, she had to share a bed with two women whose husbands were burgesses of Auxerre. The next day would be Christmas Eve and a great Mass of Pardon was to be sung at the cathedral. Alis put on her Lenten clothes and, hand in hand with Silette, followed the crowd of pilgrims and penitents which flowed slowly through the narrow streets, trampling the muddy snow. The warmth of fires and the smell of roasting meat poured through the partly-open doors; inside there was a cheerful clatter of pots and the oaths of cooks. The crowd pressed steadily on toward the cathedral. More and more urgent, more and more tangible, the sound of bells filled air and streets and ears and hearts—agonizing, monotonous, like a summons and a warning. The immense nave of the cathedral, the side aisles, the square itself were filled with the faithful in penitential garb—bare heads strewn with dust, frieze shifts, naked shoulders torn by the scourge, black veils, ulcers covered by rags.

Glittering with candles, swathed in black and violet cloth embroidered with silver and pearls, the high altar dominated the crowd, crushing in its severe purity; the choirs thundered, supplicated, groaned; and before the majesty of the Office nothing was more paltry than that crowd of men and women with their poor little ugly sins—sins so little and so ugly that they could hardly be remembered. Towering with raised arms above the kneeling penitents, the bishop of Langres pronounced the words of absolution; and hundreds of eyes were fearfully lifted to the man who was clothed and enveloped and marked and sealed with the grace and power of God, to the glittering miter, the amethyst ring, the gilded crozier and the delicate white hands transmitting the pardon sent down by the Most High.

Supporting herself against a cold pillar, Alis knelt, seeing only, far away, the reflection of the candles on the shields and oriflammes behind the altar. And with all those others who were abasing themselves and suing for pardon she wept aloud, and in the chorus of sobs and sighs she could no longer hear herself and she was not afraid to give her sorrow vent. Her tears were not tears of remorse—she had felt no remorse—but tears of regret and tenderness for the man who had loved her as she desired to be loved, the man who was so like herself in body and heart, her brother, her true friend, whom she had not the right to see again. She asked nothing; there was nothing now that she wanted; she was resigned. It was the last time she had the right to think of him—before the final pardon which the bishop was even now sealing above her head. And now it was over and done. Alis rose slowly as, rank by rank, the crowd stood up. She bowed her head, feeling the burden of the pledge she had given to God. No more sin. No more Erard. There had been nothing. She had never been anyone but the wife of

Ansiau of Linnières and the mother of his children. When, one in the fervid and joyful crowd of forgiven sinners, she went to kiss the foot of the statue of St. Mamas, Lady Alis was thinking of William, and it was her child whom she dedicated to the saint, because she believed that she no longer had the right to pray for that other.

The daughter of a petty castellan, Alis of Puiseaux had never celebrated Christmas anywhere but in her parish church. And it would be long before she would forget that midnight Mass lit by a thousand candles, the vast cathedral hung with cloth of gold and silks red and white, the chanting of the choirs, the presence of the bishop, and all that crowd of worshippers, such a crowd as she had never seen before, even at the greatest tournaments. Wonder drove every thought from her mind—openmouthed and wide-eyed she stared at the white candles, whose wavering, sputtering flames shone like immense stars melted together; the choirs, the deep voices of the men alternating with the boys' high treble in a chant that was ever triumphant, announced that the joy which is given to the saints in heaven is worth all earthly joys a hundred times over. And for once Lady Alis believed it in her heart and had no thought but to rejoice with the saints and the angels. She exchanged the kiss of peace with the women around her so often that she knew them and loved them like sisters; she caught Silette in her arms and laughed for delight. Like most of those who had come from a distance, she remained in the cathedral all night, watching and praying.

When she came out into the square the icy air pierced her to the bone. The sky was dark. The square and the streets were lighted by smoking torches and red lanterns which swayed above the crowd like ships on a stormy sea. Alis noticed that she had become separated from her two soldiers; she clung to Silette's arm. In the great houses the garrisons had been feasting and making merry since soon after midnight, and cries and songs poured into the streets; bands of drunken soldiers and prostitutes and minstrels rushed out shouting, tumbled in the snow, fought with passers-by. The sky above the rooftops was turning a sickly gray. The heavy black silhouette of the cathedral stood out against the sky, towering over the houses. It was visible from everywhere—the painted windows glowed with light, the bells were already ringing prime.

How it happened no one knew. First there was a great shout, then a cloud of white smoke rose from a lighted torch somewhere in the mass of pilgrims on their way back to the cathedral. The smell of smoke spread through the still, frosty air, someone shouted "Fire!" In two seconds the wave rolled down from the cathedral square toward the market place and the cloth hall. Alis saw something red, the smoke was blinding her, she jumped back and tried to run; and suddenly all she could see was backs, shoulders, chests pressing on her from every side, crushing her with their weight. The first shouts of surprise had been succeeded by a low moaning—she felt something soft move under her feet, she almost fell, she fought furiously, striking out with her elbows, pushing with her shoulders, receiving curses and kicks. No more smoke was rising, but the impulse once given, the wave could not now draw back—the grills and doors of the cloth hall were broken down, startled soldiers poured out, grasping their lances and wondering what could be the matter. Alis began to lose hope of ever extricating herself from the crowd; her strength was failing, her heart gave great irregular beats which seemed to draw all the blood from her arms and legs; everything went black before her eyes. Her baby. These swine, these sacks of offal, these fools, rushing God knew where. She felt her foot slip, terror gripped her, and she caught at the mantle of a man whose massive back was crushing her. She heard herself give a long cry: "St. Mamas! St. Mamas! Help!" Then everything stopped. She saw no more.

It was almost broad daylight when she came to herself—she was sitting on a bench at a corner of a street which gave onto the market place. Two women were rubbing her temples and hands with snow. Alis first put her hand to her belly, as if to assure herself that her child was still safely there. She wanted to speak, and could not find the words she wished to say. Her lips were trembling so much that she could not open her mouth. A woman in a brown cape was bending over her—Alis thought she knew that face and tried to remember where she had seen it. Yes, Silette—it was Silette. She realized where she was, and rose and went into the inn with Silette. For two days her body was racked by chills and she could not collect her thoughts or speak an intelligible sentence.

Lady Alis remained at Langres for three weeks; the weather was so bad that she did not dare set out for Linnières. Rain mixed with snow alternated with silver thaws. And she felt weak and ill. She feared for her William and thought how angry the baron would be if she returned to tell him that she had suffered a miscarriage. After all, if she had heeded him she would still be at the castle, warm and free from care. She had almost forgotten why she was at Langres and why it had been so necessary for her to obtain forgiveness for her sin. She saw a bad omen in the accident which had befallen her on Christmas morning—she was sure that something would happen to her child. Day and night she waited for the sudden little thumps which revealed her William's presence, and each time she murmured: "Thank God, he is still alive." But the movements seemed so tremulous, so weak, so unlike the movements of her earlier infants, that her heart sank—yet she did not know why.

She longed to be back in her baron's arms—nowhere in the world was there a sweeter or surer refuge. She remembered him as he had been when she had carried her other children—he valued his offspring because he knew they came of good stock. He knew how to take care of her—it was part of that unfailing breeder's instinct of his. On the frozen road, under the wind and the rain, Alis thought of his hands. They were always burning, but now that she was so cold their fire would not trouble her.

It was a hard winter at Linnières. The marshes froze, the ice-covered roads were deserted, lost all resemblance to roads—nothing could be more desolate than those shapeless stretches of gray or grayish-yellow, with the black and stony forest pressing in on them from either side. Crows dropped out of the air, frozen in flight. In the castle as in the village life seemed to have stopped. After Christmas the baron had most of the horses brought up to the great hall, for he feared the effects of the cold on his Spanish stock and his colts and two-year-olds. The fodder began to run low, it had to be mixed with straw to make it last until he could send to Hervi for oats—Haguenier had bought so much that he must have some left over to sell. Thus half of the hall was transformed into a stable, and room was found for the poultry yard too— the fowl picked about among the horses' feet. The soldiers of the guard, the tanners, and the huntsmen never stirred from the hall, where they kept up such a riot that the women no longer dared enter it and finally shut themselves up in the bedchamber. There they spun, ate, and gossiped between two spinning songs. The baron was pleased with this arrangement—he felt very much at his ease in the hall now that it was full of noises and smells which reminded him of the barracks in the castle of Paiens and the camps he had known with the army of Champagne.

When Lady Alis returned to Linnières about the end of January she received an unpleasant surprise, which was quite understandable. The horses were still kept in the hall and, as a result of the thaw, the straw with which the rooms were strewn had rotted—fresh straw had been added, but the old straw had not been removed, ostensibly for the sake of warmth. The smoke from the green logs and the steam from the kettles made a thick fog; the soldiers were swearing by every saint over a game of dice in the chimney corner. The smells of men and animals forced Lady Alis to hold her nose when she entered.

The baron came to meet her and took her in his arms before she had time to see much more through the fog. She was too tired and too angry to abandon herself to any such conjugal outpourings; she said in a pleading voice: "Please, baron, let me warm myself and change my clothes." Then she threw her gloves on the floor and said that she would not stay another minute in a stable. She mounted the ladder, followed by Silette and the baron.

The moment she reached the upper chamber Lady Alis was besieged. Her cousins flocked around her, her children clung to her skirts, her women stared admiringly at their lady who had been to visit St. Mamas. Poor Alis' head whirled, her legs shook. The baron curtly dismissed the women who were pressing around her, and for once she was not displeased by his lack of manners. In two minutes she was seated in an armchair by the fire, with cushions under her feet and elbows and a bowl of hot milk in her hands. The baron had furze faggots thrown on the fire to revive it and ordered ten candles lighted. Lady Alis thought: "What a waste," but the soft warm light flowed around her; she felt happy, she wanted to smile and close her eyes. Ansiau might not know how to manage the house, but he did not lack presence of mind when it was needed, and he knew how to cheer her spirits. She could not be angry with him.

Sitting on a stool in front of her, he helped her to hold her bowl of milk and blew on it to cool it. She closed her eyes and drank slowly, then set the bowl on the floor and lay back against the cushions. Ansiau sat there before her, taking his ease and admiring her, and the childish joy that burned in his great dark eyes set her smiling. He had changed in less than two months; he had grown much thinner, with the result that the scar on his nose was more apparent and gave his whole face a fantastically irregular look. He must have neglected himself shamefully during those six weeks—he was wearing a greasy black tunic, torn in several places; his hair and beard, fuzzy and tangled, seemed not to have known the touch of a comb for weeks; and the dirt of ten days lay in black streaks along the lines in his cheeks and under his eyes. His big, calloused, cracked hands had black, broken nails half an inch long, and instead of a bracelet an open, festering wound ringed his right wrist. Ansiau appeared unaware of his neglected state—at any rate he was in high good humor and wore the smile of his best days. He questioned Lady Alis about what she had seen at Langres, and her two sons, standing behind him, stared at their mother with great bright eyes full of timid wonder.

"But baron, you have a wound on your wrist. Let me see it."

He laughed. "What an idea! It is nothing."

And in truth he had known far worse things. But Lady Alis was already examining the wound and scolding him. "You're wasting your time looking after horses if you don't even know how to look after yourself! What an example to set the children! I must put some of my serpent grass on it—that guards against malignant fevers. There. . . . Berta, go find it in my chest— here is the key. Herbert, go with her and see that she doesn't take anything else."

The baron laughed heartily, amused to see Lady Alis take a little scratch so seriously.

"It is no laughing matter," said she. "Come here, I want to look you over. Your hair is in a pretty state, my friend. Do you have to have a professional bath woman to wash your head, as you did in the army? Couldn't you ask Lizarde to look after you? Or Haumette? It is shameful to let a man get into such a state—I shall have a word or two of my own to say to them later." She drew a little iron comb from her sleeve. "Bend down. Come, let me do your hair—I know you enjoy it. By St. Thiou! look at all the lice on you! You must have been itching horribly, my poor friend. Don't move—I'll soon have it unsnarled for you."

Skillfully she cracked the lice between two fingernails and, one after the other, combed out the stubborn locks. Gradually the familiar occupation brought back memories of all the many years she had lived at his side. Memories of those same locks when they were longer, lighter, softer under her fingers—memories of that same hot, heavy head resting against her thigh

—her eyes wandered among images so far away that she was astonished to find that she could still recapture them—their first kisses on the coffer at Puiseaux, and the first night, the heady wine, the smooth sheet, fear mingled with joy, the overgrown, excited boy, as ignorant as herself, and trembling with happiness and amazement—she could not believe that that boy and the baron of Linnières were one and the same.

"There, my friend, now you are all combed and handsome. Unless you would rather have your beard parted in the middle—it looks very well too, your uncle Herbert always wore his that way. And tomorrow you can have the bathhouse heated, for I imagine it has not been used for a long time. Really, my friend, the castle is a poor place for you when I am away. You need a nurse."

"I have been very unhappy without you, my sweet."

In the baron's eyes she was more beautiful than ever, now that her face was a little pale, a little puffy, subdued and still, now that her eyes were mild and her lips without desire. She was sweeter, more womanly when she was pregnant; he felt that she had been brought closer to him by the child which filled her as water fills a cup, as sap swells a bud. He loved to be served and tended by her during her pregnancies; he felt that her fingers were gentler, her hands warmer, her gestures more maternal. Thank God she was one of those women who do not lie fallow long, and he was in little danger of lacking heirs.

To please her, he promised to have the horses taken down to the stable and the hall cleaned, and he let her put a dressing on his wound. Lady Alis was touched by so much gentleness and felt a desire to say caressing words to him, as if he were a child.

"Come here, sweet. Sit down beside me. But don't squeeze me too tight. Talk to me. You never say pretty things to me."

"You are laughing at me, sweet."

"Long ago you used to talk to me. But now you are too proud. Ever since his lordship came back from the Holy Land, he won't say an unnecessary word for fear of wearing out his precious tongue."

Ansiau's only answer was a laugh.

"Come now," said Lady Alis, "you complain about my finding fault with you. Well, it is your turn now. Don't be bashful—reproach me with anything you please. I will listen and not say a word."

"And what do you think I have to reproach you with?"

"That is for you to say. Come—surely I must have faults. Surely you must have something to complain of. You are too polite to speak out."

He laughed again. "No, sweet."

"Think hard. You must be able to find something. Tell me—where have I failed you? How have I wronged you?"

"Nowhere and never. How odd you are!"

"Think hard. Have you really nothing to say? Think now, so that you will not have to take it back later."

Ansiau said: "Lady, will you never have aone? I do not love by halves. For me you have no faults."

Lady Alis laughed and put her hands on his shoulders. "Look at the lucky man—he has a wife without a fault! I wish I could say as much in return." She shook her head and sighed: "Yet I have loved you well."

He leaned over her and said: "Aielot."

Alis trembled, because it had been years since her husband had called her by that name. She thought that he must be very excited that day to permit himself such intimacy. Ansiau was always very chaste in words with his lady, so much so that merely uttering that one pet name burned his lips— it seemed indecent because it was so intimate. That pet name, which no one had ever called her but himself, stripped her of her dignity and set her on a level with the Guiones and Bertas, made her into a thing which belonged to him. That day, because of the new gentleness in her voice, he knew that she was at his mercy. She welcomed him to her arms, accepting him as the first and eldest of her children, the one who lived again in all the others, their source and their image, the one of them all who would need her longest. The next morning she knew that she was afraid of seeing him turn from her, and she thought of her age and her condition.

THE HOUSE OF LINNIÈRES

For the first time in her life Lady Alis had an extremely difficult labor. She had been carried to the bathhouse; there she moaned hour after hour, too weak and too exhausted to scream. Two days after the first onset of pain the child was not yet born, and Richeut, who was acting as midwife, told the baron that she feared for Lady Alis' life—it was taking too long, she did not know what to do, they must call another woman, Flora or someone else. She had heard that Flora always knew a remedy, perhaps she could do something. The baron at once sent a man for Flora, with orders to bring her back by fair means or foul.

He was frightened. He was not prepared to become a widower. Candles had to burn in the chapel day and night and he ordered all the ladies of the castle to take turns saying litanies and novenas to Our Lady. But he could think of nothing to do himself—he wandered from the bathhouse to the hall, from the hall to the bathhouse, from the chapel to the stables, found to his amazement that he could not recognize his own horses, bumped into pillars and forgot his varlets' names. His head whirled; and hearing Lady Alis' terrible moaning, he could neither eat nor speak.

And when he went to her, she received him badly. She said: "This is no place for a man." Or: "You are not the one who is suffering—there is no need for you to look so woebegone." And when the pains came too strongly she cried: "Why did you ever come back? It is all your fault. You are killing me. Stay away!" And Ansiau felt that he was a murderer in very truth.

The third day Alis lost her courage and thought that she was dying. She asked to see a priest and receive the sacraments. She had but one wish—to die as quickly as possible. She was suffering too greatly. She sent for the baron and clung to him, digging her long jagged nails into the palms of his hands. As her body hung from his hands, he felt it grow steadily warmer and heavier.

"Baron, I swear to you. Baron, listen, I swear to you. No other man has ever touched me. That is the truth."

"I know it, lady. No more of this."

She tossed her head back and forth on the pillow in the obstinacy of delirium. "No, you do not know. I swear to you. It is the truth. I am not lying. It is the truth. Baron, all my strength is gone. Do not leave me."

And she began to scream again—long animal howls alternating with whistling moans. Then the screams grew weaker and weaker—now nothing issued from her parted, swollen lips but a hoarse panting. Ansiau had been present at so many deathbeds that he felt no fear of her labored breathing and her changed features.

Heaven was dark and God was ugly. The baron was not a man to bear sorrow tranquilly. He freed his hands and began pacing up and down the room —but it was no use, he could not stupefy himself. He stopped at the door and began knocking his head against the iron latch, each time with increasing violence, and he thought that he would like to spend the rest of his life there, beating his head against that oaken door. But habit soon rendered him insensible to the blows. And his grief returned, and to escape the threat it brought he stretched himself on the floor face down and lay motionless, holding his breath. He had ceased to know either who or where he was.

Then someone touched him on the shoulder and said that Flora was in the courtyard. And suddenly his sorrow was gone—his sorrow, which had long been vainly seeking a way of escape, had found it now—it was Flora. Instantly he was on his feet. As he entered the courtyard all his thoughts were concentrated on the one being who could save him—Flora should cure his lady. It could not be otherwise.

Flora was standing by the stables, with all the folk of the castle, masters and servants, gathered around her at a respectful distance, watching her with a fear which was spiced with admiration—the great thing was not to irritate her or offend her, for her evil eye was terrible. Ansiau himself had never seen her before. He was not afraid of the Devil, but the sight of one of the Devil's minions intimidated him nevertheless—he was not quite sure what etiquette it was proper to observe with a witch.

He was a little surprised to see before him a woman of middle stature, rather fat than otherwise. There was nothing striking in Flora's appearance. She was of indeterminable age and quite without beauty; her face, which looked amiable enough though rather puffy and formless, was extremely pale, as white as her linen coif. Between her blinking lids her great owl eyes shone like two black diamonds. She seemed distracted, lost in her thoughts. It was said that she paid dearly for her dealings with the spirits—often they beat her and left her for dead by the roadside; sometimes she was seized by convulsions and cried out in a language no one could understand; and she was almost always hearing voices and was quite unaware of what went on around her. The presence of the lord of the fief seemed hardly to frighten her. She did not even look at him.

He said: "Woman, do you know why I sent for you?"

"I see a blond woman," said Flora in her monotonous, drowsy voice—she was like a blind man groping to find his way—"on an oaken bed. Her back is to the sun. There is a male child within her. But the hour has passed, the child cannot come out. I see death close beside her."

"Bitch," the baron cried, "I know all that myself! Do something, quickly!"

"I can do nothing," said Flora. "We must trick death. I need a white ewe or a white she-goat. And a white sheet that has never been used. And a basin of rain water."

Then she went into the bathhouse, and Richeut and the other women who were tending Lady Alis crossed themselves when they saw her enter. Flora shivered and said shrilly: "Let no one make the sign of the cross in my presence." Then she laid her hand on Lady Alis' forehead and Lady Alis stopped screaming. Flora took off the necklace of relics and crosses which Lady Alis wore around her throat and put it on the ground at the foot of the bed. Impressed and frightened, the women watched her.

When two of the waiting-women had brought her the things she had asked for, Flora demanded to be left alone with the patient. Richeut, although she felt mistrustful, consented to leave the room, and Flora told her to wait outside the door.

Like a bird fascinated by a snake, Alis followed the woman's movements with her eyes—she knew that it was Flora and dared neither speak nor stir for fear of displeasing the "fairy." Flora seemed not to be paying any attention to her. It was as if her eyes were fixed on invisible objects which absorbed all her thoughts. She moved slowly around the bed, as cautiously as if the floor had been strewn with unsheathed knives. Slowly she unfolded the white sheet and covered Alis with it. Alis lost consciousness.

Standing at the head of the bed, Flora executed a series of strange contortions, stretching out her arms and swaying her body rhythmically. Then she took the white she-goat by the horns, tied its four feet together, and held its head over the basin of rain water. Catching up a knife, she cut the beast's throat. The blood spurted out in torrents and poured into the basin. Still holding the goat's horns with one hand, Flora took Lady Alis' wrist with the other. The beast's body was shaken by dying throes. The blood flowed, the water grew redder and redder, and Flora continued to sway from side to side, chanting incantations in a guttural and monotonous voice which seemed to come from somewhere outside her body. When the goat ceased struggling and, after a last convulsion, grew stiff, Flora gave a great cry and fell backwards onto the floor, writhing like a trodden worm. Her cry was answered by a piercing scream from Lady Alis.

Richeut was only waiting to hear that scream. She entered, trembling, and ran to receive the infant. The other women followed, crossing themselves in terror at the sight of the dead goat and of Flora lying unconscious on the floor.

Lady Alis, weak and breathless, but already herself again, smiled wanly when she heard her baby's first cry. "A boy?" she whispered.

"A boy," said Richeut, dropping the baby on the bed. "God, but he is ugly! My cousin, the baron will never forgive you for making such a child. Do you want me to drown him? I will say that he was born dead."

Suddenly Alis' strength returned.

"What! My baby? Bitch, whore, give him to me this instant. Don't you touch him."

Richeut protested. "What a fool you are. As if I cared! I only wanted to help you. There—take your miscarriage, I wash my hands of him."

226

"Miscarriage! Indeed! We shall see what you give birth to when St. John's Day comes around!"

"He can't help being handsomer than yours!" Richeut cried. "And I know very well who you conceived yours with."

"Go tell my baron if you know so much about it. You're not the woman to talk about miscarriages. As if I didn't know that your daughter Mainsant had three miscarriages last year!"

Richeut could stand it no longer—she plunged her hands into Lady Alis' hair, and Alis would have lost a lock or two if the other women had not intervened. Richeut spat and vowed she would no longer live with such a woman. And Alis, lying with her cheek on the pillow, looked sadly at the poor little creature who had cost her so much suffering and who was being so ill received. A puny body, thin and twisted, with a huge, soft, swollen head, and big eyes wide open in a sort of stupefied terror.

Lady Alis' heart sank. Yes, her poor William was ugly, and she would have a hard time getting him accepted.

"Swaddle him up well," she said to Lizarde, who had come to wash the baby. "If you'll put something over his head he will look better."

The baron was in the hall with his cousins. He had already been told that his wife had brought forth a living son, and he had ordered the chapel decorated for the christening and a banquet prepared. Though his hands still shook and his lashes were still wet, he had quickly recovered from his emotion and was serving wine to his friends. The cup passed from hand to hand to the health of the fortunate mother.

In the bathhouse the women were washing the floor and making Lady Alis presentable. When the room was ready Claude ran to call the baron and his cousins, and Lady Alis, dropping her arms on the coverlet, leaned back against the mound of pillows, ready to receive the usual congratulations. Framed in red silk and embroidery, her face looked gray and bloodless. To the baron she seemed thinner and younger, and his heart overflowed with tenderness and gratitude—he had not lost her. Henceforth he would take care of her, protect her, spoil her, never again would he cause her pain.

When Richeut came to congratulate him she thought that she ought to prepare him: "The baby is not quite perfect, you know—he was so long being born—it did something to him." And when Lizarde presented him with the swathed doll she lowered her eyes contritely.

The sight of the child clouded the baron's good humor. He was too intelligent not to see that the child was incurable—if it lived at all, it would be an idiot. Ansiau frowned and said outright that it was senseless for a woman to suffer so much only to bring forth a monster. Then he turned away and went to greet his lady.

He kissed her on the forehead and she looked up at him. There was a frightened question in her eyes. He divined what she was thinking and gently stroked her hair.

"Don't fret," he said, "I will not hold it against you. An accident may happen to anyone. You will do better next time."

Alis sighed, for she was not yet thinking of the next time. Her thoughts were all for her William. Who would ever love the child if his own father did not want him?

That night, after the christening, there was a great banquet in the hall, and the baron, who did not wish to seem ungrateful, made Flora sit in the place of honor under the arms of Linnières and had his sons and Claude serve her. He was not a man to haggle over details—the child had turned out badly, but Lady Alis was safe and sound, that was what mattered. Flora's face remained placid and indifferent, she ate greedily, like a peasant, and paid no attention to anyone. She was often well treated in noble houses, and quite as often beaten—sometimes both. This time her reward was the dead she-goat, two hens, and a sack of flour. She left at dusk, for the baron did not want her under his roof at night.

Three days later Lady Alis was still in the bathhouse, and the baron went there to talk to her. She was recovering rapidly, he no longer need fear that he would tire her, and what he had to say was urgent. He found her nursing her child and frowned. When she saw her husband come in Alis took William from her breast and handed him to old Lizarde, who put him in his cradle. Ansiau sat down on the foot of his wife's bed—in spite of himself his eyes sought the little whimpering creature which Lizarde tried to hide from him. That swollen head, those round eyes, that shapeless mouth nauseated him—he loathed poor quality.

"Why are you looking at him like that?" Lady Alis said at last. "Speak to me. You haven't even asked me how I feel."

Ansiau looked at her and smiled. "You are enchantingly beautiful," he said. "You know i like you thin."

She pouted. "You may as well say you like me ill and be done with it. It is not good for me to be thin."

"I love you however you are," he said. "Don't be angry. Listen—I have something to tell you."

Alis sighed, divining beforehand what it would be. "I feel tired this morning, baron."

"It won't take long. Listen, my sweet. This house is not a hospital. We have no place for such a child. If you like, I will have Thierri or someone else take him to Chaource tomorrow and leave him at the gate of the Monastery of the Trinity. The good monks will surely take care of him."

Lady Alis was not prepared for so sudden an attack. Tears sprang to her eyes.

"Don't cry, sweet. Am I not right? Listen to me. The child is only three days old. If he is taken from you tomorrow you will soon forget him. It is a bad moment to be got through, that is all."

Lady Alis answered that she would not abandon one of her children, even if he were a leper.

The baron scolded: "You do not know what you are saying. In any case, the child will not live long, and as long as he lives he will poison your life. I do not want to see you spend your strength and your health for nothing."

"But baron," Alis pleaded, "after all, he may get better. I will take a vow. I will have Masses said. I will go to Reims on foot if need be."

"You will go nowhere for that child. I tell you there is nothing to be done. Tomorrow he will be gone."

Lady Alis pressed her hands against her temples, seeking for arguments which would convince the baron. "It is a sin to abandon our child," she said hesitantly.

"Not when a child is so ill-made. No one will blame us."

"But baron, listen—he is not so terribly ugly. His mouth is quite pretty. And his eyes are just like yours."

Now the baron was angry. "That would be the last straw. Next you'll say that it was I who made him the way he is."

Alis answered bitterly: "I didn't conceive him by the Holy Ghost."

"Better not say more," said Ansiau. "You know very well that it is your own fault. There was no need for you to go to Langres at Christmas."

Lady Alis shrugged her shoulders. "That is not the reason. It is the evil eye."

"The evil eye has nothing to do with it, lady. When you put your hand in the fire you get burned. I warned you. I was a fool to let you go."

Seeing that he was losing his temper, Alis buried her head in the pillows and began to cry bitterly. She was still so weak, she had suffered so much, she had nearly died—and he had nothing better to do than to come here and reproach her!

Instantly the baron became all tenderness and tried gentle persuasion. Certainly he did not want to cause her pain, especially after the hard time she had gone through. What he wanted was her own good. She was a woman, she could not understand certain things, her love for her child had turned her head—she could not see that such a child could bring her nothing but pain. Better to spare herself from the beginning. In ten or eleven months she would have another, healthy and well formed—this time he would not let her take any risks. But Alis was not interested in another child—there in the cradle beside her bed lay William of Linnières, sprung from the flesh of Joceran and Guy of Marseint, her own blood and her own flesh for all those months. In comparison, the child's beauty or ugliness was of no importance.

When she saw that her husband clung to his idea, she changed her tactics and said that she was willing to obey him—all that she asked was a few days' grace—time to gather herself together a little; she did not want her milk to sour in her breasts. Ansiau, rather shamefaced because he had made her cry, consented, and promised not to dispose of the child without her knowledge. And Alis hoped that as time went on he would grow accustomed to her baby and begin to love it.

To say that Ansiau did not love his second son would not have been quite true. His benevolence extended to whatever, in any sense of the word, belonged to him, from his feudal lord to his dogs. Herbert of Linnières, a fine healthy boy and his second son, born of a noblewoman, had unquestionable rights to his affection. And when he studied the boy he was forced to admit that he would make a good knight. Indeed, a very good knight—one had only to see the assurance with which he drew his bow and hit the target at the first try, without blinking or fidgeting or wasting time over sighting. A very good knight, his father thought again, as he watched the hard plump little hands gripping the reins and guiding the horse as expertly as the hands of a grown man. But each time that the thought came to him, Ansiau felt a sort of regret, an unavowed jealousy. In justice, God should have given Ansiet that sure eye, those strong arms; the younger boy had no use for them—they would not profit the house of Linnières.

The boy was like a thorn in Ansiau's flesh. At times he could not control the irritation he felt; then he struck hard. He believed he had every right to do so—it was his own flesh and blood. The boy had precisely the defects he most detested: he rolled on the ground when he bumped himself or caught a colic, and he was always catching colics because he stuffed himself with apples and sweets. Abstemious by nature and habit, Ansiau could not comprehend greediness. He called the boy "swine" and "cur." Indeed, Herbert heard few other names from his father's lips—he quickly grew used to it.

Herbert was afflicted with a disastrous resemblance to his uncle Baldwin. In Lady Alis' opinion it was this which had turned his father against him. A sort of unspoken complicity had grown up between mother and son, for Alis felt somewhat to blame for having given the boy so much of her own blood. When he had been too naughty Herbert would hide under his mother's bench or behind her skirts; and when he was punished by being deprived of food she would secretly bring him bread and cheese. The boy did not even thank her. He was not at all demonstrative, it was as much as he would do to speak to his mother—often the baron pulled his ears and said: "Cur! that will teach you to greet your mother properly." Then Herbert would salute his mother, feeling not at all certain what it was his father wanted of him—his mother did not demand respect, she was something warm and good, something created to nourish and protect him, a bed, a covering, a nurse—he had not yet forgotten the breasts he had sucked. And Lady Alis was not deceived: of all her children it was Herbert who loved her best. But she no longer knew what to say to him, now that he was out of swaddling clothes. She had no more rights over her sons than a brood mare has over her colts after they are taken from her—she felt rather like a hen who has hatched a clutch of duck eggs. Boys must forever be fighting, covering themselves with bruises and scratches, until the time came for more serious injuries—Alis had resigned herself in advance and preferred not to think about it.

In the trio composed of Ansiet, Herbert, and their cousin Garnier, Simon of Linnières' son, Herbert was the youngest but the most respected. Children see things differently than their elders, and for his friends Herbert was a hero. The enormous quantities of bread and meat he could consume aroused their admiration, his silence before his elders was a proof of his dignity; in addition, he had talents unsuspected by his parents and the master-at-arms, he could catch flies with his mouth and give perfect imitations of the manner of speech of the baron and Father Aimeri and Milon and Girard the Young and many another. He had knowledge which children usually do not have, and God knew where, at nine, he had acquired so much experience; in his case it seemed to be due to precocious maturity rather than to viciousness. Both Ansiet and Garnier were gentle and cheerful by nature, Herbert rather overawed them. In their games he dominated, at meals he took the best place—the two others let it pass, it did not occur to them to make comparisons.

The three boys lived in their own world and paid no attention to the world of their elders. They hardly knew that Ansiet was the baron's favorite son and Garnier an orphan with no heritage; Herbert himself was unaware of his father's harshness toward him. The two brothers had no reason to believe that their rights were equal in respect to the tall, ponderous, bearded being whom they must address as "My Lord." Ansiet loved the baron, and Herbert did not. But as they never talked about him to each other, it was as if they had two different fathers. Among themselves, they had other things to talk about.

Ansiet was a great seeker after treasures, a great inventor of fabulous countries; he dreamed extraordinary dreams filled with fairies and werewolves and diamonds with magical powers, and often enough he did not know where his dreams ended and reality began. He had great faith in the power of holy water and the sign of the cross, which he regarded as the most effective instruments in the search for buried treasures. His vivid imagination had caught at fragments of tales told by Herbert the Red or by some casual guest; in his mind they glowed with all the colors of the rainbow, were shrouded in blue mists; he interpreted, arranged, and rearranged everything in his universe—its center was Linnières, but it stretched on out of sight until it was bounded by Hervi church with its painted windows and its beggars—then, at regular intervals, came Troyes, Toulouse, Jerusalem, Tintagel, white and luminous, full of knights whose helmets were painted blue and red like the baron's.

Garnier, who was eight months younger than his cousin, was the eldest of Herbert the Red's grandsons, but in the third generation the red had lost some of its virulence and Garnier's hair was the color of a hazelnut—only the heavy copper freckles under his eyes betrayed his origin. In addition, he had a turned-up nose and black eyes, and bore not the least resemblance to his father, Simon. Ansiet and Herbert had become friends with him simply because he was their cousin and their own age. But he was a charming boy besides—active, standing up for his rights, always ready to laugh. As a child, brought up in the great hall among a crowd of cousins and varlets, the successive departures of his father and mother had left him almost indifferent—he hardly knew his father, and his mother had always been occupied with the younger children. But he knew that his father had taken the cross and had remained in the Holy Land—and the boy finally built up an image of him not far removed from his image of God. He would say: "When I am a knight I shall go and find my father." And his two friends seconded him in his project, for they believed that they would never part— together they would go and help Garnier's father split open Saracens and carve earldoms out of the land of the infidels. Garnier's father became a legend to them, a personage like Roland or William of Orange. The baron's prestige paled beside that of Uncle Simon. And Herbert, the most practical of the three, said to his brother: "Ask the baron if the Holy Land is far away, and how to get there. We don't want to lose our way."

At Pentecost Ansiau was to take his two sons to Troyes. He was a little apprehensive over the forthcoming separation—he judged Ansiet's feelings by his own. "Above all, fair son, do not be too unhappy at Lord William's. It is no use longing for home." With his fingers he smoothed the long tangled locks which fell over Ansiet's forehead. He felt for him a tenderness so great that he did not dare to show it—sometimes he was frightened by it himself. The boy was too handsome, too perfect, his father would have to pay for possessing such a treasure, something was bound to happen—ah! if he should fall from his horse or be shot in the eye by an arrow, if he were crippled, if he were killed . . .

"Pure as a host," Ansiau thought, and he could not have expressed it better—he alone knew to what an extent the boy, for all his rough manners, was untouched and naïve—in his mouth the most obscene oaths, the spiciest stories lost all meaning—he did not understand the first word of them. It was not ignorance, it was a basic incapacity to see evil—never had Ansiau noticed in his son a trace of those curious looks, that embarrassed laughter, those sudden blushes which reveal evil thoughts. He was a boy who had nothing to hide.

Ansiau of Linnières, third of the name, was not what could be called handsome. He had a big mouth, a wide, flat nose, and straight, coarse hair which was always in disorder. And his mother, who considered curly hair a necessary part of masculine beauty, would say with a sigh: "My poor boy, the ladies will never love you for your looks." Herbert, on the other hand, had a real fleece of tight curls of which Lady Alis was very proud, but every second or third day, when Haumette combed them for him, he set up such howls and stamped so furiously that Ansiet blessed his own straight hair.

Ansiet did not consider himself handsome and cared very little whether he was so or not. But he was winning; he had a charming smile and white teeth. His body was tall and thin, a little lymphatic, with rather big joints; he had the clumsy grace of a newborn colt. He had always grown too fast, and he tired easily because his mind was so active. He never complained. At ten, he astounded everyone by the indifference with which he bore pain—when he was hurt he did not even frown; when he was ill he did not moan. It was as if the thought of complaining had never entered his mind, he did not seem to suspect that such a thing as complaining existed.

His younger brother Herbert, though stronger and tougher, was far less long-suffering. The baron would say to him: "Cur! aren't you ashamed! A man never cries." Herbert would scream: "No, I'm not ashamed, no, I'm not ashamed." "Your brother never cries." "Nothing hurts him." The baron thought the boy's answer absurd. Yet it contained an element of truth. Ansiet's impassivity was rooted in an almost complete disregard of pain: his thoughts were so busy elsewhere that he did not deign to be aware of his body. One day he had quarrelled with Garnier over a copper medal they had dug up in the meadow—Garnier had thrown it into the fireplace among the coals—without a thought Ansiet had plunged his hand into the fire, and his delight at recovering the medal was so great that he was unaware that he had burned his fingers. Another day, toward the end of Lent, Ansiau came upon him in the courtyard stark naked despite the cold—he had taken off his clothes to wrap up a litter of puppies he had found on the manure pile. "They're still alive," he had said, "I'll soon have them warm, and they'll eat milk. I'll train them." Training animals was one of the boy's passions. He adored animals and made little distinction between his brothers and his horse Gaillard, which he loved with a violent, tender, and confiding affection. He was ten years old, and the laws and bounds of life were not yet clearly marked for him. He would have much to learn at William of Nangi's.

Though she had prepared herself for it, the moment of their departure was a solemn one in the life of Lady Alis. The first of her children were trying their wings, leaving the nest—in four or five years it would be Girard's turn, then Mahaut's, then—who knew?—William's. . . .

How big they both looked! To her eyes, accustomed again to the tiny limbs of an infant, their square, hairy heads, their strong, tanned hands assumed gigantic proportions—and they were not through growing, the day would come when she would have to raise her head to look them in the face. Already they received her kisses and her tears with the impassivity of men. Ansiet, the less excitable of the two, looked about him with those clear, slightly astonished eyes of his and wiped his cheeks, wet with his mother's tears. The boy who cried when his horse picked up a stone could be as insensible as a block of wood when he had something on his mind—the thought of his departure absorbed him so that he had dreamed of nothing else day or night—and the lamentations of the woman who knelt before him affected him no more than the other preparations—if Lady Alis was behaving like that, it was because she had to. "My beautiful boy, my fair son, my first-born, my fair white falcon, my fair dove, my soul, my joy." His affection for Lady Alis had little filial tenderness in it. He thought her beautiful, she was the woman the baron loved, she was the person who actually ruled the castle. His real mother was Haumette, who had fed him with her milk.

Herbert, though far more affectionate than his elder brother, did not know how to express tenderness. Bowed head and swollen lips were his greatest signs of grief. From time to time he sniffled noisily and wiped his nose with the back of his hand.

What really touched the two boys was parting from Garnier, who was to remain at Linnières—Ansiau had promised that he would bring up Simon's children himself.

Seated at the foot of the great oaken table beside William of Nangi's grandsons, the two boys opened their bright eyes wide and forgot to eat. Everything astonished them—the big terra-cotta oil lamps, the round pillar in the center of the room, the shifting shadows on the walls, and the dark corners, which were so different from the dark corners at Linnières, because they could not guess what might be hidden in them. The baron, seated beside William, was laughing and talking loudly. As long as he was there the boys felt safe, sure of themselves, and the strange faces did not frighten them.

Herbert, his eyes on pretty Lady Beatrice, William's wife, stared at her with a lustful expression which did not become his round pink face. And Ansiet saw nothing, for he was thinking of the peacocks and monkeys he had glimpsed on his way through the fair.

By the end of the week the two brothers were so deep in their new life that they hardly noticed their father's departure; they embraced him hurriedly, impatient to have it over, for Manesier of Nangi was going to take them to see the barges on the Seine.

When the boys had left, Ansiau sat down beside William on a stone bench in the little galleried courtyard. Gray and white pigeons trailed their round black shadows through the sunlight, sparrows picked at straws. Ansiau followed their motions with unseeing eyes—he felt sad. Vaguely he sensed that this day marked the end of his youth.

The two men did not speak. Their friendship was made up of long silences; they were always happy together. William was holding Milicent on his knees. His only child by his last and best-loved wife, Milicent was four, a frail, gentle little thing, a mere wisp in her full red dress with its embroidered collar. Her head was a trifle too big, she had large eyes and a thin neck. An affectionate child, she rubbed her pale little cheek against her old father's hairy hand. Ansiau was fond of all children, but little girls in particular filled him with wonder—he felt lost, as if in the presence of beings of another species, strangers to him forever. Gently, like a child reaching for a butterfly, he let his fingers run down her long soft curls, and Milicent raised her large gray eyes and smiled at him with the rather vague and very happy smile of a dreamy child. Touched by so much trust, Ansiau smiled back and said: "You have a beautiful daughter there, god-father."

Old William answered with a sigh. Ansiau understood only too well what his sigh meant—that he would not live to see his child grow up; that he was on bad terms with his son Manesier; that he had reached the age when a man is useless and despised. And Ansiau, resting his elbows on his knees, stared at the flagstones and saw Mahaut, his slender, blond, black-eyed daughter, and his two big sons who were leaving him to become men—and he reckoned the number of years they would remain in service—eight years, nine perhaps; service was hard and arms were heavy. And those two must not be given their heads too soon, especially Ansiet, the wild colt, who asked nothing better than to break his neck. And Ansiau pictured what his house would one day be—those two, so ardent and so ruthless after pleasure, more eager perhaps to take his place than to serve him. And once again he regretted Jerusalem.

At seven, Milicent of Nangi passed for a tomboy. She was tall for her age, a little too thin, but agile and lithe. She had fine blond hair, which she wore in a black ribbon down her back. Her clothes were always torn and covered with chalk stains. Her mother, the young Lady Beatrice, was a magnificent blond beauty, but even at seven Milicent promised nothing out of the ordinary. Her features were irregular, expressive, and delicate, and Lady Beatrice thought that her daughter would never prove a very redoubtable rival.

As happens to little girls who are neglected by their mothers, Milicent was ignorant and disorderly; she had never learned how to hold a needle or how to hang up her clothes properly. Her mother, who was always beautifully dressed and perfumed, she had come to regard as one regards a shrined madonna—she adored her. She observed that her old father did everything in his power to please Lady Beatrice and that he smiled at her, despite his attacks of gout, whenever his lady deigned to turn her eyes on him.

Milicent's old father had been her universe, he enclosed her as a shell encloses an egg; she had known her first joys, her first illnesses in his arms. He was so big she could hardly realize that the enormous limbs onto which she climbed were parts of a single body. She knew that there was the gouty foot which must not be touched, which had to have cushions under it—on the other foot, which was much smaller, she was allowed to sit and cry "Gee-up, gee-up!" She had learned to tell the angry lines from the kind ones in the old man's broad brown face, and she cried when she saw the angry lines appear between his eyebrows—but no matter what had made him angry, as soon as she cried old William grew calm. Before she even knew that the sun was good she knew that her old father's smile was the best thing in the world. At the age of four Milicent was already so experienced in love that, all her life after, she was to learn nothing new about it, she was merely to remember lessons it seemed impossible that she could ever have forgotten.

When she was five a new being had entered her life, a being of the same flesh as hers and fashioned like herself, only taller—so tall, indeed, that she hardly came up to his waist. But he had not acquired the stupidity of grown-ups, who seemed to regard a child as a little animal to which they must speak in a special kind of voice. His name was Ansiau. He had long blond hair and his hands were always dirty and covered with scratches. From the first day Ansiau had taken possession of her, as a falconer takes possession of a bird he intends to train. He was very serious—he made her recite her prayers, chant hymns, and when she made a mistake he made her stand in a corner with her arms up. And such was Milicent's respect for her young master that she stood there motionless, with aching arms, and swallowed the tears of pain she could not hold back. From Ansiau she learned that there was a God in the sky and a countess at Troyes; from him she learned to tell a horse's age and to know the time of day from the sun; she learned that the earth was full of buried treasure, that it was only a matter of digging in the right place; she even learned that such treasures bring happiness to those who find them—she did not understand why, she believed it because Ansiau had told her so.

No one had ever talked to her so seriously about serious things, or laughed so heartily with her when she wanted to laugh; it was not like her father, whose eyes were sad even when he smiled.

On winter evenings Ansiau would come in all pink and chilled from the courtyard or the stables, panting because he had run too fast, and courteously salute old William in his chair by the fire. Of all the varlets and squires in the house, Ansiau had the noblest bearing and the noblest manners. Milicent, child though she was, could see that. And she would say to her old father: "I love Ansiau well, he is the handsomest."

"You would like to have him for a husband, wouldn't you, little one," the old man asked, and caressed her chin.

Milicent hardly ever left the house except when she went to see a procession—Isabel would lead her by the hand through the narrow streets which swarmed with common people, and Walter, Isabel's husband, would escort them, careful to see that no one brushed against "the little lady."

Women as they passed went into ecstasies over the child's red dress and pale blond hair, and Milicent vaguely understood that the praises were addressed to her and she felt proud of herself, like a little white dove among ducks and hens; she was very sure of her nobility and treated Isabel and Walter as inferiors without even being aware of it. When the procession passed, Walter would lift her onto his shoulder and she would sit far above the crowd—then the houses and the streets had a very different look, she could see the window sills, people looked fatter and shorter, and instead of seeing skirts and breeches, she studied hats and coifs and took great delight in watching the sun shine on bald heads.

Then the procession would pass. It was delirium, but a silent delirium. Her eyes wide open, her lips tense, Milicent breathed and drank the spectacle with her whole being—the embroidered, gold-fringed harnesses of the horses, the great cloaks with flowers red and green and winged beasts and golden crosses on a black ground—the rich furs, the white ermine of the countess' mantle, and the young counts, Henry and Thibaut, blond, pink, and grave in their heavy mantles of red velvet. Thibaut seemed about Ansiau's age, but he had a much handsomer face, and to Milicent he was like an angel from heaven.

And then the bishops would appear, with their golden miters bordered with rows of precious amethysts and rubies, and their long mantles of purple velvet and of satin iridescent in the sun—then the deacons and the choir boys bearing the cross and banners with the insignia of the Virgin and St. Peter. And Milicent, in ecstasy, sang with the choir: *Salve Regina.* The bystanders turned at the sound of the little silvery voice coming from above their heads.

Her special amusement was finding Lady Beatrice among the cortege of the ladies of Troyes. Each one was dressed in silk and glittering with jewels, but Milicent hardly looked at them, so great was her impatience to see her mother with her shining blond hair barely concealed under a white muslin veil. How well the rows on rows of pearls looked about her white neck! How prettily her blue silk dress with the little pleats fell from the heavy gold girdle set with pearls! Milicent could not help being proud that her old father had married such a beautiful wife.

On the nights after processions Milicent always had a fever and could not fall asleep. And the next day she would go back to her monotonous little life, a bird in a cage. As her father never left Troyes, she had never seen a meadow or a field or a forest except at a distance.

Ansiau was the first to tell her that a forest was the most beautiful thing on earth—the forest of Linnières in particular. In the forest you met stags with golden stars on their foreheads, and naked white fairies dancing over the glades in the vanishing mist—you could walk and walk endlessly, always seeing new trees and new glades—in the marshes the will-o'-the-wisps lured hunters into bogs—and whoever died in the forest without receiving the sacraments was certain to be damned and to become a will-o'-the-wisp himself. "When we're both big," he said, "I will take you to Linnières and you shall see the forest and the meadow and the brook. I'll find you a kite's nest." He often sighed for his forest. The great hunts got up at the countess' court, in which William of Nangi had to take part, did not console him for his long rides in the forest of Linnières where he had been as free as the wind. Here, reduced to the rank of a little squire among so many others, he was allowed to do hardly anything but skin and cut up the quarry and look after the dogs.

From the very first months of their stay in Troyes the two brothers began to grow apart, like two trees from the same root bending each its own way. No one any longer spoke of them as the two sons of Linnières; they were Ansiau and Herbert, and there was no danger of anyone's confusing them. The strong bond of their common friendship for Garnier was broken. They had different tastes. Already they could not understand each other—which did not prevent them from adoring each other. Herbert took no interest in little Milicent, it would never have occurred to him to do anything with her except put his hand under her skirt—what could you do with a girl anyway? And Ansiet loved the child with all his heart because she was blond and gentle and trusting; he was so noble that he was not afraid of being laughed at—he had his fists to defend his right to behave as he wished.

A squire's duties were often very hard, and with the years the boys became rugged, uncouth, and narrow-minded. They had forgotten their quest for treasure, the forest fairies, their uncle Simon—now their great concern was the shooting matches at the count's castle, grooming horses, and the tournaments at which they must carry Manesier's lance and shield. A passion for tournaments took the place of their old dreams and projects, Garnier was supplanted—and the baron, who came to Troyes each year for Pentecost, each year found them simpler and more nearly of the common mould. At least they appeared to be so. Herbert no longer howled over attacks of colic, and Ansiet did not strip himself of his clothes to wrap up puppies.

Milicent admired the baron of Linnières because he was the only man who could match her father's stature—other knights who were admitted to the old man's table looked short and narrow-shouldered. Small as she was, Milicent regarded them disdainfully from the vantage point of old William's imposing height. The baron of Linnières had big, dark, frightening eyes, and eyebrows that met over his nose; but Milicent thought him very handsome, the handsomest man she had ever seen—even his dark complexion and his missing nostril seemed to her to be evidence of his nobility. She had not yet learned the world's idea of good looks; she saw that the baron of Linnières had an unusual face. Besides, he was Ansiau's father. And Ansiau had told her so much about his father that she had come to believe the lord of Linnières was the most valiant knight in all Champagne. He rather frightened her—she would no longer let him caress and kiss her as she had done when she was a little child. When he sat down beside William she perched on the old man's knees and, hiding her face in the folds of his tunic, peeped out at the marvellous knight. And he sometimes surprised her maneuver and laughed heartily. "Look at her—she knows how to wink already! She is charming," he said to William, "you will have no trouble finding her a husband. If only my little girl were as gentle!"

"She is too good for me," said William. "All my other daughters have long been married and have forgotten me. But you won't forget your old father, will you, little flower?"

Milicent looked at him with her lovely candid eyes. She wondered what her old father could mean.

That year the two boys received their first Communion—Ansiet was fourteen, Herbert thirteen. Ansiau had wished to be present at the ceremony and had come to Troyes in Easter Week, accompanied by Andrew and Garnier. He brought the boys two beautiful, well-trained greyhounds, not to mention the pastries and honeyed preserves which Lady Alis had prepared. Separated from them, he had grown used to the idea that he had two sons, and he no longer discriminated between Herbert and Ansiet, at least not visibly.

Combed and washed and dressed in light-colored garments, the two tall boys made a fine appearance and Ansiau felt very proud. When he saw them return from the altar, excited, dreamy-eyed, their faces pink with emotion, he took them in his arms and drew them to him, but his first kisses were for the elder. They were both so tall already—the same height—they came up to his shoulder. Anyone would take them to be fifteen.

Herbert seemed the happier of the two, but it was chiefly satisfied vanity —he felt very proud of being a man at last, of wearing fine clothes and having people notice him. He entered upon his new dignity as a Christian with an almost insolent assurance—he ran to kiss all the saints' images, constantly took holy water, and offered it on his finger tips to his brother, to Andrew, to the baron; he crossed himself ostentatiously and refrained from oaths with exemplary patience.

William of Nangi was afflicted by a disease of the heart which made his legs swell and turned his arms blue. He suffered from terrible pains in his feet and joints, and he moaned aloud, to the great dismay of Milicent, who shook him and sobbed: "Father, father! Please don't be ill! Don't be ill or I will kill myself!"

That day the two communicants were given the place of honor, and Milicent, who was already a big girl of eight, served them wine and kissed them on the lips to honor them. Afterwards Lady Beatrice and Lady Oda, Manesier's wife, withdrew from the hall, and Isabel took Milicent away. Then William said to Ansiau: "My fair godson, I have business to discuss with you. Help me from the table to my bench. Let the boys amuse themselves for the rest of the evening, it is a great day for them.

"Fair godson, I have not long to live. I shall lie under the ground before

Christmas. God knows I do not complain, I have lived long enough. I have had what I wanted in my lifetime."

Ansiau remained silent, and William sighed and recovered his breath.

"My godson, of all the boys who have borne my arms, I have loved you best. I say nothing against Manesier. He is a good son. But there is his wife. He has children of his own. It is hard, being an old father who is good for nothing. Better to be dead." He sighed again.

"My fair godson, you must not forget that I made you a knight. At your age a man still remembers, but if you forget it in ten years or twenty, you will be doing a dastardly thing."

"Godfather, I do not understand what you mean. You know if I love you."

"Now I must go and leave her alone," the old man resumed. "God, God! If only I might live to see her grown. Fair godson, this is what I ask of you—do not refuse me. I shall leave my daughter half of her mother's dowry and what lands I still own about Birenne. I have watched your eldest son during the four years he has been here. I believe he loves the child, and she will love him too."

"By St. Thiou, godfather," cried Ansiau, "I have often thought of the same thing myself, but I did not dare to be the first to speak. I want no other wife for my boy."

Then William sent for Manesier, and together the three men discussed the terms of the projected marriage. The old man wanted to marry his daughter before he died, which annoyed Manesier somewhat, for he considered that his father lacked confidence in him. "Nonsense," said William, "you will have worries enough after my death, and I am sparing you this one. It is a large dowry, and when Beatrice marries again her baron will want to get his hands on it, if the child is not already married." They agreed to celebrate the wedding after Pentecost, when Ansiau would be back in Troyes again.

Alone with his godson once more, William continued explaining his plans and his projects. Though habitually so chary of words, and weakened by his sufferings, he talked on and on about Milicent's future—between Easter and Pentecost the women would have time to make a part of her trousseau and her wedding dress—the lady of Linnières would undertake the rest. "I have plenty of fine linen and wool and braid—it is only a matter of hiring the seamstresses."

"At Linnières the women do all such work themselves," said Ansiau.

"Far better that they should," the old man sighed. "In my day it was always so. I have a great love for your lady, though I have seen her only once; she is sensible and good and she will be a mother to my child."

Out of courtesy, Ansiau suggested leaving Milicent with her mother until she should have reached puberty. But William sadly shook his head. "It is not right to encumber a newly-married couple with the child of a former husband. She will be better off with you. You will be a father to her, you love her already."

He let his thoughts stray where they would. The child was looking a little pale, she was not having enough fresh air—at Linnières she would get a fine color, she would play in the meadow with Ansiau's daughters and gather flowers and berries in the forest; Lady Alis would teach her the things a young lady should know; Lady Beatrice had hardly had time. "Your lady will find her very ignorant, the poor child—but warn her not to beat her too much, she is delicate. God! I had her too late. She needs careful watching, but I promise you that once she is formed she will be a fine woman. Poor child. She loves me. It will be hard for her to leave me."

Ansiau protested. There was no question of that! The child should stay with her father as long as he lived. He must not inflict such a sacrifice upon himself, he should see her on his deathbed. The old knight hid his face in his hands.

"I want to take my leave of her while I am yet a man," he said. "She shall not see me infirm or disfigured. A sick man is too ugly a sight."

Ansiau answered: "Godfather, there is no use thinking about these things, it is too saddening. Cheer up—we shall have a fine feast at Pentecost, and you will still be as good as the next man, you'll see." William's eyes lit up again and he began to talk about the details of the wedding.

The next morning William had a red carpet spread in the hall, and on the carpet he had a bench placed and covered with skins. He seated himself on the bench and made his wife and Ansiau sit at his either hand; then he had the whole household summoned to the hall, family and servants.

"Milicent," he said, "and you, Ansiau my boy, come here and stand before me.

"Ansiau, fair son, you have served me for four years and I have always been content with you. Together with your father, I have decided to give you a gift which should make you very happy, for to me it is the best thing in the world. Guard it well, fair son, for to none but you would I have entrusted it." He began wiping away the tears which were trickling down his cheeks, and the two children looked at him in surprise, wondering what it could all mean. Despite his fourteen years, Ansiet did not grasp things quickly, for his mind was usually wandering.

"Come here," said William, "give me your left hand. Milicent, my lovely lamb, come here. Ansiau, look at her well. She is still a child, but in five years you will be a man and she a woman. She will serve you and obey you, and you must love her well, for she is the daughter of a noble mother, and I am your lord. Take her hand."

Ansiet, at last understanding what his lord wanted, blushed crimson and lowered his eyes. His childish embarrassment was amusing to see in a big boy, almost as tall as a man—yet at the moment he looked very handsome, with his long lashes and the smile of naïve pride which he could not keep back. Speechless, Milicent looked at him. Obediently she held out her little hand and Ansiet took it in his hard fingers.

The old man drew his daughter to his knees. "Milicent, my little flower, I have never talked to you of marriage, because you are still too young. But now, before all this company, I shall tell you something, and do you remember it well. Here is Ansiau who shall be your lord and who will love you and take good care of you. You and he will be together always. You will eat from the same dish, sleep in the same bed, you will be his beloved and he your lover. You must love him well and be loyal to him. You must obey him as you would obey me, and never say a harsh word to him. Soon he will be all that you have."

Milicent flung herself on his neck. "Father! You are crying! Father!"

"No, my lamb, I am not crying. By Our Lady, I thought you loved Ansiau well. Come, give him a smile. See—he hardly dares to look at you."

Father Dude, Lady Beatrice's brother-in-law, came and seated himself on the bench beside the baron of Linnières. The preliminaries to taking the oath were arranged. Then the children were conducted to the church of St. Pancras, where the two fathers swore in their names to respect the terms of the contract, not to covenant with anyone else, and to have the marriage performed on the Sunday after Pentecost.

Dwarfed by her tall betrothed, little Milicent looked around and yawned, hoping that it would soon be over so that she could go back and play. Ansiet felt flattered by the honor he was receiving, he blushed with pleasure and gnawed at his nails. The elder Ansiau was thinking that perhaps the little bride was rather too young. Six years made a great deal of difference at their age. Thin and spindly, she barely came up to Ansiet's chest—she seemed made of finer matter than the men who stood about her. Her thin blond silky hair fell over her shoulders and back, so light and fluffy that the least motion of the air stirred it, and it seemed to cast a radiance on her pale, fresh little face.

The two exchanged rings provided by their parents, but the grown-ups' rings were too big for their fingers, and Milicent dropped hers when she forgot to hold up her hand. Lady Beatrice took the rings, tied them together with a golden thread, and put them away in a jewel casket, saying that children were not to be trusted with such fine things—they should have their rings back when they became husband and wife for good and all.

After the betrothal banquet Ansiau took his son aside and gave him all sorts of advice—he must be proud of his godfather's choice, the old lord would not have given his favorite daughter to the first comer. "You must love her well," he said, "and keep and protect her. You have sworn an oath this day, and he who breaks his oath is a dastard. Her father has not long to live and I shall surely die before you. You must remember your oath and never forsake her as long as she lives."

Docile and a little absent-minded, the boy listened. He did not understand what all these solemn words had to do with himself—the baron seemed always to be hovering over great gulfs of the past and the future. Ansiet had long known why he must love old William and how oaths should be kept, but he thought he still had time before he need put such things into practice.

"At Pentecost," said the baron, "I shall come with Lady Alis and the whole family, and after the wedding I shall take little Milicent to Linnières—that is her father's wish."

"But you say she is my wife," Ansiet remarked. "Why take her away? Suppose I don't want you to?"

"Know, fair son, that a boy does not think of women before he becomes a knight. Once knighted, you may do as you please. Meanwhile, it is I who shall decide what to do with the girl, and it is to me that her father has entrusted her."

A little disappointed, Ansiet frowned. He was beginning to have had enough of being a child.

William's choice had awakened Ansiet's heart to a tenderness of which the boy himself was hardly aware. This frail, sweet girl—so delicate, so pale—had been given to him, he could do as he liked with her. Oaths and promises had made her his for life—she would be beside him always, with her big eyes and her sweet smile. He had never thought of it before, but now that it was done he was as happy as he had been on the day his father gave him his Gaillard. He hastened to take advantage of his new rights as Milicent's betrothed and lectured her on their duties to each other—actually, he merely repeated his father's words, for he lacked imagination on the subject. Despite the difference in their ages, he took her perfectly seriously. "You know," he said, "that your father knighted mine, and that is why I am taking you. It is an honor for me, because you are pretty. I must keep you always, which is what I want to do anyway. If your father dies, I shall be your lord."

Milicent smiled at her friend's simplicity: "My father will not die."

"He is very old. Listen: I will love you as the baron loves Lady Alis. You'll see—my mother is more beautiful than Lady Beatrice. But you will be even more beautiful. I shall take you to tournaments. God, if you knew how fine it is to see the lances splinter!"

One day he made Milicent sit in a window niche on the stairs and fell to kissing her lips and cheeks. He was astonished how soft her smooth, fresh skin felt. He liked the new game so well that he went on and on, and Milicent's cheeks grew red and hot. "It takes too long," she said at last. "Why do you kiss me so often?"

"Oh, this is nothing," said Ansiet. "When we are married I shall kiss you even more. People always do. It's very nice."

He blinked, delighted with his new discovery. Milicent leaned pensively against the window niche and smiled that rather absent and very sweet smile of hers which Ansiet liked so well. He wondered what she could be thinking. He began to study her face, which four years had taught him to love. He was amazed—he had never noticed that she had a high, rounded forehead and that her eyes were gray, flecked with gold, like the feathers of a wild buzzard. People said she was not pretty—but he saw in her all the nobility of a marchioness; he would have whipped any boy who said she was ugly. Gravely he kissed her eyes again, ruffling her long, golden lashes a little, then he kissed her forehead once more, and her temples, and her hair. It was sweet to know that already she was almost his.

And then, suddenly, he felt ashamed, as if he had done something wrong.

"You must never tell your father about this," he said. And when she looked at him in surprise, he instantly found the one argument which would convince her: "He would be angry with me."

But he could not long keep the secret of his first love, and old William, seeing him pensive and absent-minded, smiled in his beard. As was the custom, he teased the boy and said to Milicent: "Look at that great booby mooning after you." And Ansiau blushed and covered his face with the back of his hand.

He had become steadier and quieter—even to Milicent he did not talk much. He was thinking. Certainly, since he had been entrusted with the most precious thing in the world, he was no longer a child. With an intense and tender pity he thought of her frail little childish body, of her lips which turned blue when she ran too fast, of her dresses which would never hang straight. With him, she should never want for anything. He would fight more fiercely than the bravest, and make the world know that Milicent of Nangi was his love. He said little about his feelings, but he could not help asking Herbert what he thought of his betrothed. Herbert thought she was too young. Ansiet merely raised his eyebrows, wondering what connection there could be between Milicent's virtues and her age—if she were only three it would make no difference in her.

Herbert, though he was a good brother, could not but envy his senior. Everyone in the house thought only of Ansiau. Lady Beatrice's seamstresses were making him a splendid wedding coat of linen embroidered with golden roses. And he, Herbert, must be content to appear at the wedding in a plain blue silk tunic—a mere groomsman. Herbert wanted to be the bridegroom at every wedding.

As Pentecost approached, Lady Alis began packing her finest clothes in her travelling coffers. It was four years since she had left Linnières, except to go to Hervi. Indeed, since her pilgrimage to Langres, she had never travelled. It was four years since she had seen her boys.

God! What a long chaplet of troubles and illnesses and fears those four years had brought!—the boys had gone the year William was born—yes, that was it—and after William there had been the twins, two fine boys—ah, people had chuckled over that; they had meant no harm—but Alis herself never doubted that the thing had been a consequence of her sin, a sign that she had known two men—truly it was a bad omen. The two boys had been named Garin and Geoffrey, both of them were as healthy as crickets; and the next year she had borne a boy who had lived only two days; and on the second Sunday after Easter—just three weeks ago—she had buried her newest baby, Peter, born on

Good Friday—and oh, this constant pain in her breasts, the cracks, and the perpetual bleedings—her arms and wrists were still blue from them!

William was four now—he still had the same swollen, almost bald, blond head. Alis had made vows and taken him to Flora, but he could still neither walk nor talk, and the baron was nearly at the end of his patience—he would not have a monster in his house, why, the mere sight of William would make Lady Alis bear other such children. And Alis wondered how much longer she would be able to keep her William.

In two years it would be little Girard's turn to leave her, like his elder brothers—he was eight now, he rode horseback and shot a bow, and Lady Alis felt her heart sink when she saw him go down to the stables. And more and more she clung to Mahaut, her big girl—she at least would be her mother's until the day when she must be given to a man. When Mahaut hurt herself or was unhappy Lady Alis took her on her knees and made a game of drying her tears with kisses. "There, child, you will have enough to cry about when you are grown." At ten, Mahaut was becoming a beauty. She had her father's large dark eyes, and golden hair which was becoming more and more coppery —her mother, horrified at the thought that it might grow red, washed it in camomile water every Saturday. Mahaut had a keen mind and a mocking and changeable humor—she was like no one else in the family. Her mother seemed to be the only person she respected, for the baron himself did not always escape her malicious remarks (which he often did not understand)—he said: "She is certainly not what a young lady ought to be. She would do well to model herself on my godfather's daughter at Troyes—Milicent is younger, but she has much better sense." And now the time had come, and Lady Alis was looking forward without the slightest pleasure to the arrival of the strange girl who was bound to deprive her children of a share of their father's love. For her, Ansiau's marriage was a piece of business, but meanwhile it was herself who would be called upon to pay the costs. And why burden themselves with a child whose parents were still alive? "After all," she said to Ansiau, "why not leave her with her mother? Bringing her here is an insult to the woman."

Was this thin, wizened woman the beautiful Lady Alis of their childhood? Ansiau and Herbert hardly recognized their mother. How little she had become! They were as tall as she now. Her cheeks still had their old, lovely color, but already there was something frail and sad in her beauty, so soon to fade. Lady Alis was almost thirty. In her family the men grew stouter with age, the women thinner—and Lady Alis was in the habit of saying she feared she would melt away like a candle, and she ate large quantities of bacon and cream.

In her gray, dusty travelling clothes she really did not look her best. And Ansiet regretted having told Milicent that his mother was more beautiful than Lady Beatrice.

She kissed them both twenty times over, laughing with admiration and surprise—she felt their hands, their arms, their cheeks, as if to assure herself that they were really made of flesh and blood. "Indeed I never knew that I had such handsome boys, such handsome young men! Oh, Herbert my dear, you have not changed—but Ansiau has! He will soon have a beard. Oh God, to think that you have already received Communion!" And with a distracted smile she moved from one to the other, hardly knowing what to say to them—she was more bewildered than happy over this meeting which had no tomorrow, this meeting before a parting as long as the last. Not without bitterness she was thinking that her sons no longer needed her.

Milicent, on the contrary, against whom she was prejudiced in advance, instantly drew her—the child was like a fledgling fallen from the nest. And though she was to be the bride, no one paid any attention to her in the bustle of preparations for the wedding: her dress was ready, and the time to put it on had not yet come. Lady Beatrice was too busy with her own clothes, and Lady Oda had her own children to mind. It was Alis who undertook to look after the little girl—she made her wash her hands and face and combed her hair and found her a place to sit in a corner of the ladies' chamber, beside Mahaut.

"Kiss each other," she said, "you will soon be sisters and you will sleep in the same bed. Today you may play together, but don't make any noise."

The two girls looked at each other curiously. Mahaut, the elder by two years, smiled protectively and asked nothing better than to offer her friendship to her new sister. Milicent, less docile and a little suspicious, dropped her eyes and gnawed the end of her girdle—perhaps she had caught a mocking light in her pretty new sister's dark eyes.

Mahaut asked: "Can you sew?"

"No."

"Can you embroider?"

"No."

"Not even the Turkish point? Or the Cordovan point? Or passementerie?" Milicent did not answer.

"Then do you know how to hood falcons? Or how to dance and to sing carols in honor of your father?"

Then Milicent raised her head and looked Mahaut straight in the face—little yellow flames burned in her eyes.

"No, I don't know anything!" she shouted. "And I don't want to know anything, and I never will know anything!"

Mahaut drew back, rather surprised. Milicent crouched in her corner, hanging her head—she felt like crying and was making a great effort not to let it be seen.

For a long time both remained silent. Finally Mahaut spoke—gently, as she had the art of doing: "I'll teach you, shall I? It will be great fun—you'll see." And since Milicent answered not a word, Mahaut spoke again: "Will you be friends? I'd like to be friends with you."

Milicent burst out sobbing.

In St. Peter's cathedral, where she had gone to say her prayers with Oda of Nangi, Alis was almost brushed against by a man wearing a short frayed coat; she raised her eyes and turned round, but the man was already at the door. Yet something in his appearance had struck her, her heart beat faster. And just as she turned the man turned too, and she recognized Bos, Erard of Baudemant's squire.

All through the office of Lauds Alis could not follow the responses or once cross herself. At every moment she thought she saw Erard walking down one of the side aisles—or no, there he was in the front row, among the other knights who were attending the service. Every blond man dressed in blue bore a sudden resemblance to Erard—he could not be far away because Bos was there. The previous year, through Hugh of Baudemant, Alis had learned that Erard had finally married a young and rich heiress, that he had two children and lived in great luxury on his wife's income. Yet Bos's shabby clothes seemed to indicate that his master's affairs were not in a brilliant state—Alis could make neither head nor tail of it all. "Even if he is ruined," she thought, "it is no concern of mine. It will be a good lesson for the woman who married him."

Finally she had to yield to the evidence—Erard was not in the church. How ugly and insipid they looked—all those men who were not he! Leaning on Oda's arm, she walked sadly back to old William's house through the dark, narrow streets, between buildings which seemed bent on crushing her. Oda of Nangi, a pretty brunette, rather retiring, and the best-hearted creature in the world, was complaining about her husband and her father-in-law—as she saw it, Manesier sacrificed her to the old man's whims, whereas William maintained that Manesier let his wife lead him by the nose.

"You are lucky to have a husband like yours. I never saw a man with better manners—he is as courteous to his varlets as he is to a duke or a marquess. I will wager he is not forever calling you whore and bitch."

"Is yours harsh to you?" Alis asked.

"Oh, he loves me well enough—it is all because of the old man and that Beatrice. Oh, God! what a snake, what a plague of a woman! It is not enough for her to leave me with the whole house to look after, I believe she would take my baron away from me if she could."

"Not really! Have things gone that far?" Alis exclaimed, rather curious.

"You are a lucky woman," Oda sighed again. "At least your baron is true to you—no one has ever seen him wear a lady's colors, at Troyes or anywhere else. Yet he would not have far to seek."

The lady of Linnières remarked, not without self-satisfaction, that in such cases the credit was always due to the wife. "You do not know him. If I did not hold a firm hand, God knows what he might not do."

"As for me," said Oda, "I have stopped thinking about it. If we had to cry over such things, we would never have done. I have worries enough already, what with the children and the house."

"I know how it is. I have been brought to bed eleven times," said Alis.

"And I seven. There you are—I am younger than you, and I don't look it. A dreary business—always a big belly, cradles, swaddling clothes—year in and year out it never changes. And time passes. It would be pleasant to be able to think of something else—we only live once."

Alis had no intention of encouraging confidences which she did not wish to hear. She said calmly: "Something else? There is nothing else."

The next morning after Mass Lady Alis let the baron and their hosts leave the church, and remained behind herself with only Silette and Milon of Le Cagne. She did not think that she had any ulterior motive—she wanted to pray a little longer. But she was not surprised when a young fellow of fifteen approached and asked her if she was not Lady Alis of Linnières.

"I am," she said. "What do you want?"

"My master," said the boy, "asks you to accept a present from him."

"I do not know your master and I cannot accept presents."

"Lady, do not be angry. He knows very well that you will not accept it, but he asks you to look at it. It is all he asks."

Rather suspiciously, Lady Alis opened the oaken casket which the boy handed her. Never had she been given a stranger present—in the casket lay a bunch of lavender, a cherry twig, a white stone, and a ring—her ring with the pink pearl. And the memory of that night in the little garden at Linnières, under the cherry tree and down among the lavender, came over her with such force that she almost dropped the casket, her hands were trembling so. She set it on her knees, took out the little blue bunch of fragrant lavender and raised it to her lips; then, remembering that the boy was watching her, she put it back in the casket; tears poured down her cheeks and she did not try to stop them. That white stone—the Fairy Glade, the sun, the crows, the warm grass . . .

She did not know how many minutes had passed. She was there in her seat, nothing had changed. The boy, still kneeling before her, appeared to be waiting.

"My God!" she sighed. "And where is your master? What is he doing?"

"He is at Monguoz, at the castle. He was taken prisoner by Baron Giles after being wounded in the leg. He is very ill."

"Ill? Wounded?" Alis cried. "Is it serious? Tell me everything, keep nothing back."

"He has a high fever and his wound is infected. But I think he will recover."

"God! God!" said Lady Alis, twisting her fingers. "To think that I have herbs to cure wounds and that I left them all behind at the castle. Baron Giles is having him looked after at least? Has he a bed, sheets?"

"Oh yes, he is well looked after." Alis did not grow calm until she had asked the boy every possible question about his master's health and learned that his condition was not really serious.

Then she asked: "And how does he know that I am at Troyes?"

The boy answered that his master had learned it from Bos only the day before. His master had not dared to send Bos, for fear of arousing the suspicions of enemies who would try to prevent him from communicating with Lady Alis. He sent word to Lady Alis that he thought of her always and that he was in great misery, a prisoner, sick, and without money—he needed ten marks for his ransom and he did not know where to turn for them. He implored her, in the name of their old friendship, to advance him this sum—it would set him free at once, and he was tired of captivity.

"God!" said Lady Alis, "how well that he thought of me! Certainly I will do everything to free him. I am not rich, but I have jewels of my own. Here, my friend," she said, stripping off her silver necklace, her two bracelets, and her earrings. "Take these and sell them. They will fetch more than ten marks —twelve perhaps." She put them into the casket, took out the pink pearl ring and slipped it on her finger—God, how thin and scrawny her hands had become! She wanted to ask the boy further questions about Erard, but pride restrained her. She replaced the ring in the casket and said: "Go quickly and sell them today. And tell your master that he must not try to see me again. But if ever he needs me, let him send some trusty person with this ring. He can always count on me."

The boy hid the casket under his shirt, kissed the hem of Lady Alis' dress, and left the church.

It was almost dark in the side chapel where Lady Alis had been saying her prayers, but Milon and Silette, kneeling five paces away, might have seen the stranger talking to their lady and their lady stripping off her jewels and putting them in the casket. So Alis made them swear that they would never breathe a word of it to anyone—the boy was a page who had been sent to remind her of a debt of honor about which the baron knew nothing. She did not trouble to explain why her eyes were so red.

All that evening she brooded. She was wondering what explanation she could give the baron. And despite herself she was assailed by memories so sweet and so bitter that she could not help sighing. How clearly she could visualize that fine-boned head, so clean-cut that it seemed carved from alabaster—must it be so, would she never again see that pure and noble beauty, not in all her life to come? A man who had loved her so tenderly, so deeply. He could not have forgotten her—no, after five years he still thought of the lavender bed in the little garden at Linnières.

Her self-respect had not allowed her to question the boy. Yet her heart was heavy with uncertainty. Whose colors did he wear? And did not Giles of Monguoz have a pretty daughter of sixteen, Marsille? Perhaps she was tending the wounded man? And if, despite everything, he did try to see his old love again? She had no wish to burn herself twice at the same fire.

After supper the baron took her aside in the ladies' chamber, where she had been sitting in a corner on an oak chest. He did not want to scold her in public. And when he saw that they were quite alone together he asked her what she had done with her jewels. She answered that she had given them to the cathedral treasury, for the poor.

Ansiau said: "That is going rather far! You did that? Without asking my permission?"

Lady Alis immediately took the offensive. He was not the only one who had a right to give alms. She had her own soul to think of. And the jewels could not be better bestowed—God would surely reward them for the sacrifice at some later day.

The baron remained sceptical. "You can never make me believe you. Never in your life have you done such a thing. You had some reason which you will not admit."

"And what reason could I have had?"

"How should I know? No woman can open her mouth without lying. I don't want to scold you. But, blood of God! I am not such a terrible husband!—you can trust me with your secrets, I won't eat you."

"But, baron, I have told you the Gospel truth. I gave them for the poor. Furthermore, I had a perfect right to do it. I have not stolen anything. The necklace and the bracelets came to me from my mother, they are no concern of yours."

"But you should have kept them for Mahaut, when she marries. We have two daughters—if you go on at this rate, we shall have nothing to leave them."

"Since when have you been the one to complain about spending?" Lady Alis cried. "All you know how to do is mortgage things and run up debts. And because for once in a way I give something to charity, you talk to me about the children!"

"Lady, I do not believe one word of this. You did not give those jewels to the poor."

"Do you want me to swear it? You can ask Milon and Silette, they were with me."

"I shall ask them nothing. It is for you to tell me. I do not want to see you lying."

Lady Alis was frightened now. She tried to avoid her husband's searching eyes, but he held her by the shoulders and would not let her go. He was becoming angry.

"To whom did you give them? I will not let you go until you tell me. To whom? And what for?"

"Baron, keep your temper."

"Then tell me."

"Baron, let me go." Gently Lady Alis unclasped the hands which held her shoulders—she was not a woman easily defeated. At the mere touch of her fingers, Ansiau's fingers lost all their tensity, and she had no difficulty in drawing down his hands, making his strong arms close around her waist. Pressed against him, she caressed the locks on his forehead. "No, let me go, sweet. Someone might see us. No, let me go." Her voice, plaintive and tender, said something very different from her words.

In an instant Ansiau had forgotten his anger and his suspicions. And Lady Alis had only to let the game play itself out—and God knew that these sudden tempests of the flesh sometimes terrified even herself; she submitted to them because she must. He was breathing like a wild animal. She shut her eyes, and thought: "Men!"

Ansiau never reproached himself for these too-swift defeats. They were a part of the game. He saw things much more simply than Lady Alis imagined. At her first kiss he had forgotten the jewels completely. And peace once made, he would never reopen the subject.

The wedding was to take place on the first Sunday after Pentecost, and the whole house—courtyard and hall—was gay with flowers and foliage. The ladies, in their magnificent dresses, crowded into the upper chamber about Lady Oda and Lady Alis; in the turret chamber, the damsels, supervised by Lady Beatrice, were dressing the bride. The little bride herself was having rather a wearisome time—she was not allowed to sit, or raise her arms, or turn her head. Kneeling before her, Isabel and her daughter Mary were arranging her blond hair about her shoulders. "Don't move, you'll spoil everything. Huguette, hand me her girdle. Holy Virgin, how pale the child looks! She will be sick in church, I will put my hand in the fire on it!" Lady Beatrice, radiant in a white dress sewn and interwoven with gold thread, hardly dared to bend over her daughter for fear of disarranging the folds of her silk mantle. Milicent's legs were almost giving way under her and she felt like crying. She clearly sensed that she was the person of least account at this festival in her honor— the ladies were thinking of their dresses, the little girls were talking about boys and games, and she was not allowed to speak to anyone; everyone who came near her walked on tiptoe, everyone was afraid of touching her veil or her miniver-lined cloak. Her old father had often told her what a beautiful dress she would wear on this day. But she was still too much of a child to care about a beautiful dress.

At last she was led into the hall amid the shouts and acclamations of the knights and squires whom old William had invited to the ceremony. But even then she was unable to understand that it was all being done for her. Her father, taller than ever in a long green woolen robe and a dark-red velvet cloak, stood in the front row. And not even he stooped to kiss her, or took her in his arms as he always did. However, Milicent was too sharp-sighted not to notice that he was close to tears—he looked at no one but herself. Then she ran to him and buried her face in the folds of his heavy red cloak.

She soon discovered that watching a procession was much more amusing than being the center of one. Yet at first she was very much excited. The boys threw flowers and elm and ash leaves in her path, and she set herself to step on a flower every time. Her cousin Leona and Mahaut of Linnières followed her, holding the train of her dress to keep it from dragging on the ground.

As the procession passed, women crossed themselves. "God! how lovely she is! But she is terribly young."

Old William had ruined himself to provide his daughter with a wedding dress worthy of her—she was as bejewelled as a reliquary. Her gown was of white satin with a woven pattern of fleur-de-lis, her girdle was set with rubies, her bright red cloak was embroidered with golden birds among garlands of laurel. The red veil which covered her head and shoulders was held by a circlet of gilded silver encrusted with turquoises and coral. Thin and as stiff and awkward as a doll, she was smaller and younger than any of her attendants. The train of damsels—light dresses, blond or golden hair falling loose —made a charming sight. The married women followed, leaning on their husbands' arms. The bridegroom and the groomsmen had been ready first and were already waiting outside the church of St. Pancras. Here it was much noisier—there was laughter and unrestrained gaiety. Ansiet was the last person in the world to worry over fine clothes—he calmly rolled up his sleeves to show his companions the muscles in his arms.

This sacrament which bound him for life was to him merely a bargain concluded between his parents and Milicent's—a festival, a good meal, singing and dancing. Actually he had thought of Milicent as his wife ever since the day of their betrothal. During the service he thought that she looked very pale and sad and he smiled at her and whispered: "It will soon be over." She gave him her wide, trusting, timid smile, happy to find an old friend among all those splendid, unfamiliar dresses, among all those faces which had become almost as strange.

Joyously, amid shouts and songs, the procession retraced its course. The bridegroom led the bride by the hand; behind them came old William with Lady Alis, then Ansiau and Beatrice. Alis leaned on the old man's arm, secretly humiliated to find herself less beautiful and less elegant than Lady Beatrice. "Oh God!" she thought, "when a woman has only one child and an old husband who ruins himself to pay for her whims, it is easy for her to be beautiful. . . . The baron was taller on our wedding day, I think. God, how I loved him then!" And she shook her head to drive away her sad thoughts.

When they reentered the house Milicent saw the flowers in the carpet spinning and coming toward her so fast that she put out her hands to hold them away. . . . She came to herself on her old father's knees. Lady Alis was rubbing her temples with vinegar. She felt her father's beard shaking and tickling her cheek. She said: "I'm hungry."

True it was that no one had remembered to give her anything to eat. They brought her white bread and good creamy milk. Sniffling noisily, her father fed her with his own hands, as if she were a baby. "My lamb, my white flower!" And she flung her arms around his neck, caring no more about her pretty dress.

"You know, baron," said Alis to her husband, "that was a very bad omen. I don't know what we should do. Here is the boy tied for life, and I cannot believe that girl will bring him happiness. It is a handsome dowry, of course, but a dowry is not everything."

"Bah!" said Ansiau. "Girls are always fainting over nothing."

"Mahaut never fainted in her life. You'll see—the child is not strong. God! if she dies without issue, the inheritance will go to Manesier, and our boy will have lost his chance for better matches!"

Milicent had never believed that she would have to leave her father; the old man had told her so time and again, but she had only half listened. "You will be going away soon and I shall be all alone," and again, "I have not much longer to live. Soon you will be left without a father"—he had said those things to her so often that finally she had come to believe he was only saying them to make her more obedient or more affectionate. Her Ansiau was the first to make her understand that she was really to leave her home. Three days after the wedding—it was a Wednesday—he sat down beside her on the carpet where she was playing with Mahaut and began looking at her with such a serious air that she felt troubled.

"Did you ever see such fish eyes!" said Mahaut, and Milicent laughed. But the boy neither laughed nor grew angry—his face remained pale and tense, his eyes stared. Then his lashes began to tremble and salt tears welled from his lids and ran down the sides of his nose. And Ansiet neither wiped away the tears nor hid his face, he looked at Milicent's hair and her forehead, and the tears flowed faster and faster, tickling his nostrils and the corners of his mouth. And before his wordless grief the two little girls were abashed. At last Milicent put her arms around his neck and asked him what was the matter. Then he caught her by the shoulders and shook her and kissed her, and he began to speak, though his lips were trembling and his voice was half stifled by sobs. "My fair lamb, my white flower,"—without being aware of it, he used old William's words—"they have lied to me—they have made game of me—they were deceiving me when they told me you were my wife—if I had known I would have refused, I would have hidden myself—they did it to part us. What good does it do me to have you for my wife? If it were not for that, you would stay on here. I never did the old man any harm. No—I know it is he who is sending you away, my father never wanted it. What good will it do me to have you when I am grown up? I shall be dead before then, I know it."

In his self-pity he began to sob so pitifully that Milicent was frightened and said: "No, no, you will not die."

"Silly girl," said Mahaut, who had been watching the scene with the zest of a connoisseur. "That's not what he's crying about. He's crying because he's in love with you. My cousin Frahier cried just like that when I left Linnières before Trinity."

"Ah!" said Milicent, happy to have learned something new about life—she considered Mahaut the fount of all knowledge.

"Don't listen to that stupid girl," said Ansiet somberly, "she thinks everyone is in love. I'm not in love—did I ever do anything to hurt you? And besides, you're too young. Tell me—did you tell your father that I kissed you too much, is that why he wants to separate us? And if I promise not to do it any more? I won't even lay a finger on you if you will stay."

"I don't know," said the girl. "Do you think I am going away?"

He cried: "Idiot! That's what I'm saying. You are leaving tomorrow with my father and mother."

Then it was Milicent's turn to burst into tears; for the first time, her imagination conjured up her departure into an unknown world. In dreams she had sometimes seen herself suspended over bottomless abysses in a freezing wind; she would scream "Father, father!" and her father did not come. When she heard Ansiet's last words she felt the same terror.

Instantly she ran downstairs to her father, to assure herself that he had not vanished.

"My little girl, tomorrow you will not sleep under this roof. You are too young to understand what I am saying. But you must remember it for later on. I shall never see you again in my life, joy of my eyes—look at me, do not forget me, I am your old father who has loved you well. Now listen closely. In five or six months they will tell you that I am dead. My body will be laid under the ground in the graveyard, to be eaten by worms and to fall to dust —but that is nothing to grieve over, for it comes to everyone. If God has mercy on me, He will give me life and strength again after Judgment Day, so that I may go to Paradise. And there I shall see you again, my joy, my loveliness, beautiful and happy with God's saints. And then we shall never part.

"But today, my lamb, we must part, for you are a maid and a wife, and God made you to have a husband. And now I have given you a good husband, honest and loyal, and you must love him more than anything in the world. You are children still, he and you; but when you are children no longer you will see how you will love each other—it is not for me to tell you. By him you will have fair issue, and for a woman there is no greater joy.

"Milicent, my fair lily, always remember what I shall tell you now: If ever in years to come you do such things as an honest woman may not do, dead and buried though I shall be, I shall know it, you may be very sure. And then, even though I am in Paradise with the angels, I shall be more unhappy than if I were in Hell.

"There—love me always, kiss me, kiss your mother."

Lady Beatrice was crying and wiping away her tears with the end of her veil. But Milicent drank in her father's words with all her frail being: she was sure that no one had ever spoken so beautifully and so wisely. What she did not understand with her mind went straight to her heart, and she locked it away there like a relic in a shrine. She sensed the solemnity of the moment too clearly to make any show of grief.

Bruised and pale after travelling two days on the crupper of Lady Alis' horse, Milicent found herself being lifted down by the great black hands of the baron of Linnières, and it was from his immense height that she saw the courtyard, the gray stone keep, the wooden ladder, and the dark, straw-strewn hall.

"My fair damsel," said the baron, "here you are in your house, and one day it will belong to you"; and he set her down. Then Milicent saw a vast fireplace, a vast vault, vast flagstones, a vast shield hanging on the wall, and she felt crushed. The idea that she would one day be mistress of this house was so absurd that she did not even consider it. She looked around for beings of her own stature—Mahaut, or Gertrude, her little maid, or a dog. And all around her there was nothing but men's legs and women's long dresses—it was as if she were under a curse. She did not dare to raise her head because she knew that everyone was looking at her. She felt ashamed, and wondered what naughtiness had brought such a punishment upon her. And because she was proud, she did not cry, she merely gnawed her nails.

If she had been in her father's house, she would have thought that what all these strangers were saying to her was meant for praise. But here she felt sure that they were trying to humiliate her, make game of her. It was Lady Alis' big, soft white hand which extricated her from her difficulties—it took her by the wrist and led her to the upper chamber.

Behind the gray linen curtain burned a tallow candle, illuminating a paunchy red clay jug with two round handles. Between the curtain and the wall stood a great low bed made of oak. Women's clothes—light-colored dresses and embroidered girdles—hung above it. The candle flame threw shadows of the girdles on wall and bed, and the slow motion of those black shadows made Milicent afraid. Two dark girls in white shifts were lolling on the bed, braiding their hair for the night.

Mahaut, seated beside the bed on a chest decorated with wrought iron, was dipping her pretty, high-arched feet in a basin, and an old serving-woman, kneeling before her with a white towel, waited for her young mistress to deign to take her feet out of the water.

That first night Lady Alis looked after Milicent herself—she made her sit in her lap, combed her hair and did it up in two slender braids. The child was ready to drop with sleepiness and kept resting her heavy head on Lady Alis' breast, and the lady chided her gently: "I can't do your hair that way, kitten, sit up." Milicent opened her eyes very wide to keep from falling asleep. Above the curtain she could see gigantic shadows moving over the vaulted ceiling of the great chamber; she heard men's voices, bursts of laughter, and she wondered what mysteries, what strange scenes were enacted in the vast space which lay hidden behind the gray curtain.

Lady Alis' hands were so soft and warm that the mere touch of them made Milicent's weariness and tenseness vanish—she felt as if she were a tiny child again and she had only one wish, not to have to leave Lady Alis' lap. But, without knowing how, she found herself in the big bed, lying next to the wall beside Mahaut, who was taking off her shift. The two dark girls, who were in the bed too, were laughing and talking softly together. Milicent turned her face to the wall which was hung with a heavy cloth striped with red, but the shadows of the girdles, which would not stop moving, frightened her and she clung to Mahaut.

"Are you cold?" Mahaut asked. "In summer we sleep without covers. It gets very hot in here."

Milicent asked: "Where is Lady Alis?"

"In her bed."

"Is it far from here?"

"Rather far—it's in the south corner, you have to go past my Lord Girard's ladies—it is a big bed, the finest in the castle, big enough for ten girls to sleep in crosswise—I slept in it when I was ill."

Milicent only half heard her. The candle went out and the bed was plunged in darkness—but behind the curtain the play of lights and shadows continued. The dark girls laughed softly. At the foot of the bed an old serving-woman muttered.

Milicent was amazed by the vast spaces of Linnières—the upper chamber, which ran from one end of the building to the other, the great hall where the boys could practice archery, the vast court full of yellow mud which was just the thing for building castles—they all impressed her as rich and magnificent after William of Nangi's cramped little town house. She did not yet know what poverty was, and Mahaut was in no position to tell her that Linnières was merely a very humble little country castle. She did not notice that Lady Alis' clothes were made of old materials, and if the wooden table service was cruder and more worn than the one at Nangi, Milicent did not know why new dishes should be better than old.

The vast and shadowy forest, about which Ansiau had so often told her, drew her more and more. She saw it surrounding the castle on every side— dark, green, motionless—with crows drawing zigzags over the treetops and buzzards wheeling slowly in the still, heavy air. Milicent knew that it harbored stags with human voices, will-o'-the-wisps, werewolves—and she was not afraid. Her mind had seized eagerly on the dream world which Ansiau had opened to her; she felt more at home in it than among human beings. When her new aunts and cousins spoke to her she hid her face in her sleeve or ran and crouched under a bench. Only Lady Alis had been able to tame her.

Day by day Milicent discovered new varieties of living beings. The lady of Linnières was certainly the only one of her kind—Milicent quickly learned to know her warmth and her odor, her rapid step, and her loud, slightly guttural voice. She would have been greatly surprised if anyone had told her that she liked the lady of Linnières better than her mother—in her heart there were no degrees of liking. The lady of Linnières was a fire that warms, not a star in the sky. Her kisses always came straight from her heart, just like her blows.

The first days Milicent's fingers were pricked and swollen, her back was tied in knots from bending over her work. Her small hands were moist with sweat; it made the cloth greasy and the thread black, and despite her best efforts she could not manage to make two stitches alike.

"It is shameful—a girl of your age not knowing how to hold a needle," Lady Alis scolded. "Really, you are no credit to your mother. Look at that seam—it looks like a hedge of thorns or bird tracks in the snow. If you don't do better, I shall box both your ears later on."

Milicent only managed to prick herself even deeper and to make a bloodstain on her poor rumpled bit of cloth. Mahaut, who was working on the same shift, felt sorry for her.

"Here, give it to me—Lady Alis is not looking."

Her heart overflowing with gratitude, Milicent handed Mahaut her needle. But when Lady Alis saw the impeccable stitches which followed those impossible bird tracks, she frowned and looked Milicent straight in the eyes. "Learn, my daughter," she said, "that a noblewoman never cheats or lies. You are making a very bad beginning. Now you shall have your ears boxed twice instead of once! And never try to do anything behind my back again." Wide-eyed with admiration and terror at Lady Alis' clairvoyance, Milicent took her punishment without flinching. It was the first and last lie she ever told Lady Alis.

Mahaut, not wishing to get her own ears boxed too, said nothing, but afterwards she did her best to console her little friend: "Listen—when we go down to the courtyard I'll show you how to climb onto the stable roof. I often do it, with Girard and Frahier. From up there you can see the little garden and the meadow beyond the palisade. On Sunday they will let us go walking in the meadow."

Beguiled by Mahaut's promise, Milicent forgot all her troubles and dreamed so hard of stables and meadows that her needle began making enormous stitches. And Lady Alis gave up the struggle and took her work away from her.

Milicent's little new world grew wider every day; in the formless mist of strange faces a child's features would become distinguishable—a pair of eyes, a smile which she could recognize. After Mahaut came their bedfellows, Simone and Aelis, both of whom Mahaut called "cousin"; then Girard, Mahaut's brother, who was Milicent's age; and Frahier, another cousin, who was already eleven. There were Haumette's daughters, and Haumette herself, who had been Ansiet's foster mother. But above them all—immense, superb, inaccessible—towered the master of the castle. Milicent knew that, compared with him, even Lady Alis herself was only a servant—and that was saying a great deal.

One fine day after All-Hallows—the baron had just come home from Troyes —Lady Alis took Milicent on her lap, put a honey cake in her hand, and said: "My child, I have something sad to tell you. Your father is dead."

Milicent looked into her eyes, not really understanding what she meant. And Lady Alis, who loved that look, kissed her and began crying. Then the child clung to her and cried too—but only because she was fond of Lady Alis and felt sorry for herself.

On the day she had said good-bye to her old father she had accepted the fact of their separation. She knew very well what death was—her father had explained it to her. She knew that her father had closed his eyes forever, that he would be eaten by worms and fall to dust, but because she had such faith in him, all that did not make her afraid—it was only a change which had to happen before you could go to Paradise. And she knew what Paradise was, too —she had only to close her eyes to see a blaze of white and gold light so beautiful that you could spend your life looking at it; and Paradise, she knew, was even more beautiful, God had ordained that everyone in Paradise should be bathed in joy from head to foot, forever be washed as it were by living waters, forever be surrounded by birds, each singing in a voice far sweeter than the next. If her father had to go there, no doubt it was something everyone must do. She would do it too, as soon as ever she could.

"There, my child, don't cry," said Lady Alis. "Your father would not want to see you sad."

"Yes, I know," said Milicent, and again she gave Lady Alis that frank yet rather absent look. "He told me all about it. He promised me I should meet him again in Paradise."

Lady Alis reflected that perhaps old William had promised more than he could perform, but she did not permit herself to say so to Milicent.

Milicent appeared to be very little changed by her loss. She had such trust in her father's promise that he seemed no farther away in his grave than if he were still at Troyes.

And little by little she forgot him altogether.

Milicent fell completely into Mahaut's hands. Mahaut was a tyrant, but a kindly tyrant. She seriously undertook the education of her little friend, taught her songs and embroidery stitches, came to her rescue when the boys teased her, and confided her own knowledge of life to her—a knowledge which, considering her age, was rather extensive.

Mahaut was talkative and vain, quick-tempered and stubborn. She was not greatly loved at the castle; the waiting-women were always complaining of her rudeness, her aunts and cousins thought her insolent. Lady Alis, on the other hand, stood up for her child and spoiled Mahaut as much as it was possible to spoil a big girl who had five brothers and sisters younger than herself. And Mahaut, strong in the support of her mother, became more and more unbearable. Indeed, the baron was much displeased with her—in his opinion girls should be sweet and tractable. Often he said to her: "I pity the man who marries you."

Mahaut was pretty—extremely pretty—but to Lady Alis' great chagrin her hair was growing more and more coppery, which, however, was not unbecoming to her. She had the milky complexion that goes with red hair, her skin was fine and smooth and white, and she had big black eyes which would have been described as cowlike if they had not always been bright with malice or temper. Her left eye had a decided outward squint, but strangely enough this defect only added a certain charm to a face which, without it, would have been a trifle insipid; indeed, there was something arresting in those ill-matched eyes: at once piercing and dreamy, they seemed always to be seeing things beyond visible reality. However, Ansiet and Herbert, with the traditional kindliness of brothers in all ages, always said that Mahaut had "red hair and cockeyes."

Mahaut was extremely proud of her beauty, her blood, and her intelligence, and she had no hesitation in showing it—pride, in her opinion, being only an added quality in the daughter of a noble house. Furthermore, her mother consciously fed Mahaut's pride, for she knew the dangers of life in a castle only too well, and lived in terror lest her child should be exposed to the assiduities of male cousins and the younger varlets. Mahaut was destined for nothing less than a count.

If Mahaut thought a great deal about love, it was because her older girl cousins hardly ever talked of anything else and she wanted to be like them. She knew a great many things—too many, indeed—because she was curious and eager for knowledge. And who, she thought, could teach her to know life and the world better than grown girls of thirteen or fifteen? Mahaut was convinced that real grown-ups—even Lady Alis—never told the truth. And her cousins' stock of knowledge was confined to walks in the moonlight with handsome young men and gossip which revolved around the marriage bed or its illicit substitutes. Mahaut believed that the end and aim of life was making love in company with a courteous and valiant knight, but her speculations were entirely theoretical; her fierce purity revolted at the thought of even a single secret kiss, and her lovers (for she had lovers), thought her harsh and cruel. Frahier, Garnier's younger brother, brought her flowers or live birds or butterflies every day, and she accepted them with regal indifference. Her other lover, Aimeri, a boy of fourteen, son of Girard the Blond, was very scornful of Frahier's fashion of paying court, but he was equally unsuccessful.

Naturally rude and insolent with her superiors, Mahaut was gentle with children younger than herself. She loved her brother Girard, little Alette, and even William, who at the age of four was as sorry a baby as anyone might ever expect to see. Sitting in his cradle with his arms dangling and his heavy head swaying on his scrawny neck, he uttered vague bleatings and stared into space with unseeing eyes. Mahaut, good soul, would stuff his mouth with honey or stoned cherries. Or she would sing to him—"William, little Willie"—and insist that she had seen him smile. Lady Alis, heartsick, half believed her.

Mahaut became passionately attached to her new sister Milicent. In the first place, she sensed in her—and it was no small thing—an equal in blood and rank. She adored her fine hair, her long lashes, her tiny hands. And then Milicent was so ignorant, so trusting, that it was a pleasure to teach her the things which she, Mahaut, knew so well. She instinctively realized that, for all the child's apparent docility, the only way to dominate her was to begin by loving her. And she loved her—it was love in the grand manner, with vows of fidelity and exchanges of locks of hair, girdles, and bracelets. Mahaut, all fire and flame, made jealous scenes, flung away, begged to be forgiven, and Milicent, more placid, allowed herself to be loved and led without protesting—her thoughts were elsewhere. Her grown-up friend was a sort of living catechism to her; Ansiet's rather foggy fantasies were quickly dispelled by contact with the strict, dry logic of her new and terrible mentor. Mahaut despised boys—her elder brothers in particular—roundly criticized her uncles and aunts, made fun of Father Aimeri, and even tales of ghosts and werewolves lost their mystery when she told them and became almost comical. Yet she believed them.

Alis adored her eldest daughter. She adored her because of her beauty, her grace, and her cleverness at all kinds of work. She adored her because—far off—she could see the day approaching when her child would be taken from her by a stranger. She adored her because the half-grown girl was becoming her friend and her assistant. Only Mahaut felt sorry for her when her babies were ill, only Mahaut was kind to William. Lady Alis was sometimes moved to tears because her daughter's frail body already lodged a soul so brave and noble. And she flared up with anger when she heard the baron or Richeut discussing Mahaut's failings. "Gentle? Why should she be gentle? You men never look for anything else. Ah, I have been far too gentle with you, baron. And she will do well not to follow my example."

The baron of Linnières now made only brief appearances at the castle, staying for the hunting season and coming back to celebrate Assumption Day and All-Hallows. The rest of the year he wandered over the countryside with Andrew, Garnier, and Thierri, moving from Troyes to Bar-on-Seine, from Bar-on-Seine to Provins or Reims, hardly ever missing a tournament, even the smallest—his passion for the lists was becoming a vice and Lady Alis complained bitterly over having "such a jousting husband." Although he was never defeated, he spent so much on lances, helmets, and horses that they cost him all the ransom money he extracted from his prisoners. Besides, he often let a prisoner go without a ransom: a sudden friendliness, a passing moment of good humor, were enough—then he would ask nothing even from a man of great wealth. And when Lady Alis heard about it she bit her lips with rage. He would say: "Lady, I am not a merchant!" And she would think of the interest that must soon be paid to Abner.

The baron had changed greatly since his return from Palestine—four years had passed, and he seemed always to have just arrived or to be just setting out. The castle was not the place for him. He was too tall, he took up too much room, he turned everything upside down whenever he took a step or made a gesture on his own account, like a wild falcon which cannot move its wings indoors without upsetting a dish or a stool. Every time he gave an order Lady Alis found it inopportune; he brought a hunting party to stay when she was in her last month of pregnancy; dismissed soldiers so that he would not have to pay them; gave his friends the few remaining objects of value from the store which his father had painstakingly assembled; if he sent a varlet on an errand to Bernon or Hervi, he was sure to choose just the man Lady Alis needed for some piece of work at the castle.

The only places where he was perfectly at home were the stables and Lady Alis' bed. In the latter respect she had nothing to complain of—he was an extremely ardent husband, and his wife could not help feeling flattered by the fact. As a lover he made up for his shortcomings as a castellan, and Lady Alis forgave him and shut her eyes to the damage he caused on his brief and frequent visits.

He loved her—it was like a ground swell which forever brought him back to her arms almost despite himself. He did not spare his horses; sometimes, between tournaments, he went unbelievably far out of his way to visit Linnières. Four or five days later he was off again, just when Lady Alis was beginning to enjoy his presence.

He was an attractive man. Though past thirty, he still had a small waist and narrow hips, which made a rather striking contrast with his immense shoulders—that almost shrunken abdomen under that very broad chest led his friends to say that he must be always on the verge of starvation. He was so tall that he seemed to sway as he walked, and so easy in his motions that his extraordinary stature looked not ungraceful. He had not lost his Mediterranean tan, and four years after his return he was still as dark as a gypsy; and despite all his jousting he still had a full set of fine teeth. His great prowess in arms had given him such a reputation that he passed for handsome; however, he ruthlessly repulsed the women who made advances to him; he did not mean to be tempted to break his oath to Lady Alis. And at the castle of Linnières he was worshipped as if he were God.

Toward his own family he had an easygoing kindliness which made him grant every request without reflecting whether it was in his power to do so or not. If it sometimes happened that he was harsh and unjust, it was never from ill-will, and his punishments were accepted unprotestingly, with a sort of respectful admiration.

But there was one whose admiration for him was a passion which drove away sleep and appetite, and that was his little daughter-in-law Milicent of Nangi. She recognized the tread of his horse when it was still far away and knew the clink of his spurs on the courtyard and in the hall. When he warmed himself by the fire she watched him from her corner and let her work fall and did not hear a word that was said to her—you could have pricked her with a needle and she would hardly have noticed it.

Milicent was considered a rather backward child, and so she was—she was ignorant, awkward, and absent-minded. But it was as if her heart had developed too soon at the expense of the rest of her faculties. At nine she understood things which were still unknown to Mahaut for all her precocity. She could think up excuses for going to the stables so that she might glimpse the baron's leather gaiters or his mop of brown hair; and then she went wild with fear at the thought that he might raise his head and see her. She learned how to wait days and weeks for the sound of a horse's hoofs at the castle gate; she learned to distinguish a single voice from among twenty more, a single laugh, a single oath. She learned what a sweet and beautiful thing a smile could be, even when it was meant for someone else. She learned to weep at a harsh or indifferent look.

It was an unreasoning adoration, without end or aim, but it was an adoration ferocious and entire. And the child was well aware that she loved, and she took good care to hide her feelings from everyone. She did not think that she was in love in Mahaut's sense of the word—she wished she could be turned into an amulet or a talisman which he could wear around his neck, against his heart.

He did not seem old to her, because he was the measure which determined her vision of things and beings. Anyone younger than he was only a child, anyone shorter a dwarf, anyone fairer skinned was too pale—and every other man in the world had one nostril too many.

JERUSALEM

THE YEAR which followed the news from the Holy Land was the easiest and most untroubled Ansiau of Linnières had known since he became a castellan. He ingenuously believed that God was rewarding him for having taken the cross; in reality, the easy terms upon which crusaders were allowed to pay their debts counted for not a little in his new feeling of well-being. A man could breathe for a while.

The great impulse which had shaken Christendom to its foundations and filled the churches with penitents and the high roads with pilgrims had now died away. In the heart of many a crusader nothing remained but the memory of a striking act of penitence and a certain self-satisfaction. After the bad news—the worst, indeed, that could possibly be imagined—the course of events in Palestine was received with a sort of somber indifference. What was to be expected, now that Holy Cross was in the hands of the Moslems? The only hope was the Crusade—and the kings had promised to set off at Easter of the following year—the year of Our Lord 1189. Count Henry of Champagne had taken the cross between Gisors and Trie on January twenty-first—he and all the high barons of the realm. And the chivalry of Champagne had followed his example in the spring, and few were the families which did not count at least one crusader that year. As for clerks and sergeants, the multitude of them was so great that the lists would not hold them, the barriers were broken down, and the crusaders' army overran the fields and the outskirts of Troyes. Strange scenes of despair and disorder had been enacted; and in the market place before the cathedral the priests announced to the listening multitude the news of miracles which God had even now performed in Palestine and at Rome, and read messages from the Pope and the bishop of Troyes. Templars and Hospitallers arrived to tell of the sad estate of the Holy Land and to call upon the faithful to take the cross and to give of their goods for God's War.

Lady Alis herself, when she learned that the Holy Cross was in Saladin's hands and that the infidels had stabled their horses in Holy Sepulchre, was seized with such terror that she instantly took a part of her jewels to the church at Hervi "for the rescue of the Holy Land." She had never believed such sacrilege possible. She was hardly aware that Holy Sepulchre had been won by the sword less than a century earlier—that was in the days of her grandfather's grandfather, and he had not been a crusader. To her, Jerusalem was rightfully and actually the apanage of a French and Christian king, it was served by a patriarch, guarded by noble knights, it was the fairest place of pilgrimage the world had ever known. And now suddenly pilgrims could go there no longer, the Saracens disembowelled Christian women and roasted Christian children alive—worse yet, they spat on the Holy City's crosses, destroyed her shrines, and profaned her churches—and what churches! It was the end of the world, no doubt of it. After such calamities, what might not God be expected to do! Through their own fault the Christians had lost just those things which were their best warrant of God's help—why should He defend them now? Alis lived in momentary expectation of plague or famine or some incursion of infidel looters, of whom the countryside had kept alive the memory and the terror for centuries.

God punished sinners—but who is without sin? Among her own acquaintances Lady Alis knew sinners enough to people a good-sized portion of Hell—and she herself had sins to her account which were far graver than her habitual failings of gluttony and anger. But she thought that God would be unjust to punish the Christians of France and Champagne, who lived such straitened lives and could not avoid running up debts, killing, swearing, and fornicating—a man, particularly a knight, could not obey God's law short of retiring to the desert. But the Christians of the Holy Land, they who had the Holy Cross among them and trod the very ground where God had walked, they at least should have been able to restrain themselves and not befoul the holiest land on earth. And instead they had grown so wicked that they had brought misfortune upon themselves and the whole of Christendom. Alis considered the barons of Palestine traitors to all knighthood because they had so gravely compromised the Frankish and Christian cause in the eyes of God. It was beyond her understanding. She had always been told that they were brave men who fought doughtily. So it must be that God had taken vengeance on them for their sins. She was not far from holding Simon of Linnières personally responsible for the disaster, because he had had a share in it.

The baron, who had a much clearer conception of what was occurring in Palestine, was less surprised and less terrified; it had been a severe blow, but all was not lost—the kings would send a vast army which would overcome Saladin—what was needed was men and arms: too much time had been lost, that was why King Guy and his barons, surrounded as they were by infidels, had been defeated. He would not hear of the blame being laid on the vanquished, they were knights and Christians.

Meanwhile, the thing to do was to make ready—and that was no small matter. The baron had reckoned that when the time for departure came Ansiet would be seventeen and Herbert sixteen. He wanted to take them both with him. It would be a dangerous expedition, but he believed that a boy who was left at home to preserve him from perils would never amount to much afterward. Ansiet at least would be old enough to be dubbed; perhaps he was a little young, but he was tall and reasonably strong. Yes, he would see his son a knight before they left. So he must think about an outfit for him—he had already trained the new horse which was to replace Gail-lard and which he would give the boy on the day of his dubbing. The boy would need a new hauberk too, one made with a light mesh, for it was not good to put too heavy a weight on seventeen-year-old shoulders—he was shooting up very fast, it was a drain on his health. Never had his father seen him complain of fatigue or lag behind when his comrades were practicing archery or leaping. In every game, in every contest, he was admirable—steady, well-schooled, master of himself, one who goes on running with a sprained ankle or a thorn in his foot rather than drop out. And it was pre-cisely Ansiet's regal disdain for pain and effort which a little disquieted his father—the boy did not know how to husband his resources. "It is his age. At sixteen," thought the baron, "I was knighted and married. And my old father lived in dread of my breaking my neck. Fathers are all alike."

At Troyes he lodged in Manesier of Nangi's house and the boy came to serve him, dignified and humble as always; and as always his father never wearied of admiring that grace of his which was like the grace of a highly bred animal. Ansiet was not talkative now, he had little to say to his father. His life had become too complex—to tell of it would have required far more wit than he could boast; he became hopelessly confused when he tried to describe the very games he played so well, and never knew what he could safely tell his father about the rather rough pastimes in which he indulged with his comrades. (Among the more innocent of their diversions were splashing each other with icy water in midwinter and putting pitch or chalk on the robe of some wandering monk.) Ansiet knew that his father was extremely strict in regard to women, and love affairs occupied a considerable place in his life—true enough, the adventures were not his own but his brother's or his comrades'; for his part he scorned love and regarded it as an amusement for varlets or children, who had nothing better to do. But, like it or not, he was under an obligation to help his friends. Herbert especially, being engaged in a highly dangerous adventure, often asked him to stand guard, and Ansiet, like a good brother, conscientiously performed the task, even though all the next day he would be as sleepy as a dormouse.

Ansiet always asked the baron: "Is Lady Alis well? Has she had a baby?" (He seemed to think that she should have a new baby three times a year, so accustomed was he to brothers and sisters making their appearance in endless succession.) Then he would go on: "And Uncle Girard? And Mandor? And Milicent?" In the depths of his heart he still had a weakness for his little wife, the absurdly sweet and wayward girl whom he had taught her first prayers—it was as a piece of pure childishness that he remembered the kisses he had inflicted upon her one evening in the window niche on the stairs. But he would ask: "Has she grown any? Has she learned to sew, and do up her hair herself? How long are her braids? Does she eat well?" As a rule the baron was unable to answer these questions; he thought his little daughter-in-law charming, and that was all he could say about her.

This time—it was three days after Epiphany—Ansiau arrived at Troyes in rather a bad humor, for he missed his jousting more and more (tournaments had been forbidden during the period of mourning for Palestine), and it was still too early to talk about the day of departure, which had been set for Easter but about which there was still much uncertainty. "If it turns out," he said to Manesier, "that the money raised for the Crusade has to be spent against England, God was very right to do what he did to Jerusalem, for the Christians are a worthless lot." Manesier, who had taken the cross too, shook his head; he was used to hearing this sort of talk from all his land-owning friends who came to visit him, and he had ceased to react.

The morning after Ansiau's arrival at Manesier's house, Thierri told him something which increased his bad humor. Thierri was one of those people who announce the most dismaying news with as little emotion as if they were talking about the weather. He calmly told the baron that strange stories were abroad on the subject of Herbert and Manesier's wife—he had heard it from one of the kitchen boys. At first the baron was inclined to laugh— what could there be in common between a boy of fifteen and a woman who must be nearing thirty? Then he reflected that no one would ever invent such an unlikely story; if people were telling it, there must be some truth in it. And as he had no wish to become involved in a scandal, he sent for the boy, took him to a deserted corner of the courtyard, and asked him point-blank exactly what his relations with Lady Oda of Nangi were.

Herbert instantly got on his high horse. "And who told you about it?" he asked savagely.

His father said: "Answer me."

But Herbert was not listening. He gnawed his lips with fury. "Give me the name of the coward who betrayed me," he shouted. "I'll spill his guts, I'll eat him alive!" He was not allowed to go on—a blow to the jaw rocked him on his feet and sent him tumbling into the gravel. Ansiau was so furious that he would have killed the boy on the spot if there had been a weapon at hand. The admission had been categorical, and Ansiau had not believed his son capable of such behavior. If the boy had remained on the ground, Ansiau would perhaps have trodden and kicked him to death like a dog. But Herbert was up again in an instant and came at his father, rolling up his sleeves as if preparing for a fist fight. Surprised by such audacity, Ansiau gave him another blow in the face which sent him rolling; again the boy sprang to his feet, panting, frothing, his nose dripping blood. This time he rushed at his father head down. Ansiau could have sworn it was Baldwin of Puiseaux at Chaource crossroads—and it was in self-defense that he struck his third blow. A third time and a fourth Herbert picked himself up, under the astonished eyes of Manesier's sons and varlets, who did not dare to interfere in the strange struggle.

Bloody, swollen, disfigured by rage, Herbert's face was a hideous sight. But his fighting spirit had power to touch a father's heart. Ansiau caught the boy's fists and said, more gently than he intended: "I don't want to kill you.

Go wash yourself and have our horses saddled. We will talk outdoors."

Father and son rode along the Seine until they were some distance from the city. His face swollen and bruised, Herbert looked at his father suspiciously.

"Now then, fair son," said Ansiau, "I wish you no harm. Tell me what has happened and we shall see what can be done. And do not try to deceive me, there is nothing I despise so much as lying."

The boy proved easier to tame than Ansiau had expected. After some hesitation for form's sake he admitted that for two months he had been Lady Oda's lover—her only lover!—and, fatuity overcoming prudence, he began cynically expatiating upon his triumph and treating his father to a series of leers which might have been appropriate between grown men but which looked strangely out of place on the face of a young boy.

His father said: "You have lost your mind, you do not know what you are doing. There is no name for a man who sullies his lord's bed. If Manesier had caught you in the act, it would have been a disgrace to your entire family."

"He would not have caught us in the act," said Herbert somberly.

"Listen to me. Men like you are destroyed like dogs, and it is right that they should be. But you are only a boy. The woman is guiltier than you. I shall not punish you, but I am going to take you away from here."

This time Herbert was really frightened. He began pleading his cause with a lack of tact which was disconcerting. He loved the woman. He could not live without her, she would die of grief if he left her. At first Ansiau was so amazed that he forgot to be angry. "A woman of her age does not love a boy of fifteen," he said at last. "What a simpleton you must be! She had an itch you know where, and you were the only fool she could find to play her game. You ought to put all this nonsense out of your head."

"Oh, I can prove it," said Herbert. After a moment's hesitation he unfastened his collar and drew from under his shirt a woman's slipper, a girdle, a glove, three ribbons, a bracelet, and a purse embroidered with the arms of Nangi, and handed them all to his father, who was quite at a loss what to make of such a collection of feminine gewgaws.

"By St. Thiou! What does this mean?"

"She gave me every one of them. There is nothing she will refuse me."

"Hm," said Ansiau, "so it seems. The place for all this trash is the fire. And now you had better forget this woman—I shall give you a better."

"Listen to me, baron, I do not want a better. And besides, she has promised and vowed to me that when Manesier dies she will marry me."

"She!" cried the baron. "I would rather see you dead than married to a sow who seduces her lord's squire."

Herbert shouted: "I forbid you to say such things!"

The baron lost all patience; he gave Herbert a dozen blows with his whip and half stunned him. In this condition he took him to the house of his friend and cousin, Mathis of Monguoz, who lived a league outside Troyes.

He asked Mathis to shut the boy up in his cellar and give him nothing to eat but dry bread. "He has angered me beyond measure," he said, "and I mean to punish him. I shall come back for him in a day or two."

He returned to Troyes the same evening and told Manesier that he had decided to take Herbert back to Linnières and marry him—a suitable match had been proposed and he wanted to have the wedding celebrated before Lent. Manesier was much displeased. He knew that the boy had been cruelly beaten by his father that very morning and he concluded that Herbert must have refused to marry the woman chosen for him. He greatly regretted the loss of such a squire. "What a boy!" he said. "He has not his equal in all Troyes. What a fine archer! And so eager to fight! He has been an honor to me."

Ansiau said nothing and blushed very red.

"He is not sixteen," Manesier went on, "it is a difficult age, he is in the middle of his training, and 'Poor thrift to let a good blade rust.' I hope you will send him back to me as soon as you get him married."

"I will see," said Ansiau. "I do not wish to inconvenience you. In any case, I shall bring him back to Troyes before Easter."

Whether or not Herbert was laboring under an illusion in regard to Lady Oda's feeling for him, the fact remains that she appeared at supper looking very pale and with her nose and eyes red from crying. Ansiau eyed her with such scorn that the poor woman could not bear it and left the table, pretexting a headache. And the baron of Linnières wondered whether he had the right to leave Manesier in ignorance. He would gladly have warned him, but he was afraid of compromising Herbert; he finally decided that the boy was undoubtedly neither the first nor the last and that Manesier had only to keep his eyes open.

After supper Ansiet asked his father: "Where is my brother?"

"I have taken him to Monguoz, to the house of my cousin Mathis. I shall not let him come back to Troyes." Ansiau supposed that the boy must know all about his brother's love affair, but he did not want to discuss it with him because he did not want to scold him. But the boy opened wide, astonished eyes. "What! You are taking him to Linnières? Before Purification? There are going to be sports at Troyes Castle."

"You know very well why I am taking him away, you wicked boy. And he is lucky to be getting off so cheaply."

"And you took him away without letting me say good-bye to him?"

The boy looked so stern and so reproachful that Ansiau regretted having acted in such haste without a thought for his elder son. Ansiet, who was forbearing enough with strangers, could not stand to be crossed even in the slightest by his father—in his universe the baron was a sort of God whose first and foremost preoccupation was the happiness of his son Ansiet; he credited him with more than human power and intelligence, so if his father was causing him pain, it was intentionally and out of sheer cruelty. Ansiet could not tolerate failings in a father whom he wished to think perfect, and he did his best to make him realize his cruelty and injustice.

"There," said the baron, somewhat ashamed, "you will see him at Easter, he has not left you forever."

Two days later Ansiau went to Monguoz and released Herbert from his imprisonment. The boy was in a pitiful state; his face was black and blue and his lids so swollen from weeping that his eyes were almost invisible. He took his disappointment in love very seriously. He implored the baron to let him see his lady once more, "just once, before yourself and Manesier—only let me see her!" And when Ansiau flatly refused, Herbert threw himself on the ground and said that he wanted to die. Ten minutes later he was at table, giving free rein to his enormous appetite and sprinkling his roast mutton with tears.

So Ansiau carried his son off to Linnières with the firm intention of getting him married as soon as possible, and he knew whom he would choose for a daughter-in-law—Haguenier of Hervi had an only daughter of nineteen, Bertrade, who was still unmarried because she was considered ugly and her father could not give her much of a dowry. But Ansiau knew her well—he knew that she was discreet and kind and he told himself that she would make Lady Alis a good daughter-in-law. He wanted to lose no time; when they reached Hervi he resolved to make his request at once. As Herbert was not yet in a condition to present himself before a possible betrothed, he was sent to Seuroi under good guard and the baron went to Hervi Castle with only Andrew and Thierri.

His request was well received by Haguenier, and Bertrade did not dare to refuse. Too stout for her age, brown-haired and brown-skinned, she knew that the baron of Linnières' second son was an extremely good match for her. She sulked a little when she learned that her husband-to-be was only fifteen years and nine months old. But she thought of love and marriage with the almost morbid emotion of an ugly girl, and she was happy when she learned she was to be married in only two weeks. Her trousseau had long been ready and her father was more than glad to be getting her off his hands.

Lady Alis protested shrilly when she saw her boy in such a pitiable state, and at first thought of nothing but applying herbs and unguents to his face. "The very idea! You might have disfigured him for life. It is great luck that he still has all his teeth and didn't break his nose." The baron took her aside and told her why he had been obliged to bring Herbert home. Lady Alis was outraged by Lady Oda's effrontery, above all because of the peril in which she had put the boy. "Manesier would be capable of ripping out his heart if he found him in bed with her. . . . She purposely picked out a boy who had no idea what he was doing. A mother! And she looked so sweet and sensible! After this, no one can be trusted!"

The preparations for the wedding did not take much time—the baron had no money to spend on festivities, he needed arms for the coming spring. The marriage took place in midwinter and was as dreary as possible. On the square in front of Hervi Church the groomsmen shivered and rubbed their hands and noses; wearing a gray wolfskin cloak, the groom himself, with his empty staring eyes, looked like a wood owl. He had been obliged to yield to superior force and had resigned himself to renouncing his dear lady. But his vanity suffered cruelly from this botched-up wedding, the cold, the scantily decorated church, the preoccupied and annoyed faces of his father and Andrew and his uncle Girard. He remembered only too well his brother's wedding, with the splendid procession through the streets of Troyes and the pale little bride in her white-and-gold dress. And his own wedding had to be this wretched farce!—it was just his luck.

A white horse carried the bride to Linnières through the snow-covered forest, and her bridesmaids and her kindred from Linnières and Hervi followed her, laughing and blowing on their numb hands; the horses' hoofs rang on the frozen road.

At the castle the great fire in the hearth made the hall bright. The baron of Linnières dismounted and himself conducted his new daughter-in-law to the bedchamber to present her to Lady Alis; and Herbert and his young companions settled themselves in the hall by the hearth. Laughing, the bridesmaids relieved the bride of her furs and veils. Rosy from the cold, palpitating with emotion, transfigured by the expectation of the new happiness she was so soon to know, Bertrade looked charming; her features seemed to have grown more delicate, her eyes shone, and Lady Alis gave her an approving look. "She is no green fruit," she thought. "And so much the better, since the boy seems to prefer mature women."

The celebration was gay, despite everything. Everyone drank a great deal. Herbert appeared to find his young wife to his taste and pinched her thighs under the table. Abashed, Bertrade kept arranging her long black hair over her shoulders; she barely touched the dishes which were offered her. The couple was led to the bathhouse which had been heated and decorated for the occasion the great bed with its white sheets smelled of mildew and lavender, the candles spluttered, the girls bustled about Bertrade like a flock of sparrows around a blackbird.

Bertrade instantly fell in love with her young husband, her eyes followed him with a sweet look of submissive and timid admiration; and Herbert, whose masculine vanity was flattered, obligingly permitted himself to be loved. So the baron left the castle, thinking that he had settled everything for the best. He wanted to visit Bar-on-Seine before Lent—he had a particular devotion to the Virgin in the church of Bar-on-Seine. And there was more need than ever to pray to her that year, for the day of departure was almost at hand.

Herbert soon proved to be an unmitigated calamity. He was a tall boy for his age, anyone would have supposed him to be eighteen. He was handsome, but it took time to realize it because his eyes were dull and inexpressive and his features very seldom became animated. In addition, his gluttony had afflicted him with a precocious stoutness, which promised to become obesity with age. He had a fair complexion, together with a tender skin and a tendency to nosebleeds—a weakness which he had inherited from his mother. His hands and feet were small and well shaped, his eyes rather large. He had a sensual but well-cut mouth, and a veritable mane of blond, curly hair which tumbled in wild disarray over his forehead and neck. Lady Alis sometimes tried to untangle it—she was better at it than Bertrade. Herbert fidgeted and swore and stamped his feet. "God! fair son, whoever combed your hair when you were at Troyes?" "Lady Oda," the boy answered glumly, and his mother replied with a sigh.

For two weeks Herbert remained faithful to his young wife and kept comparatively quiet. Then he became unbearable. He began attacking the maids in dark corners, picking quarrels with his cousins, and rolling on the floor at the slightest provocation. Lady Alis undertook to reprimand him. Herbert loved her very much and was sorry to cause her pain, but he was always right—his cousins were his inferiors, he was not going to let them humiliate him, his temperament was such that he must have more than one woman. Bertrade no longer suited him, it was not his fault. Lady Alis silently agreed, for she did not like her daughter-in-law. But when she saw him try to rape little Milicent—and in Lent at that!—she considered that he had really gone too far and threatened to curse him. Herbert kept quiet for three days, then he began again—Lady Alis knew only too well that she could not keep using the same threat indefinitely, and after a time Herbert realized that she would never really curse him. The baron came back about the middle of Lent, bringing word that there would be no setting-out that spring. The kings seemed to have no idea of going, and Count Henry had agreed to wait for them. There was nothing for it but to plan to spend several more months in Champagne. "And God knows when the kings will stop making war on each other."

"God be praised," said Lady Alis. "I shall keep you for yet a few months. I shall not be sorry either." Ansiau shook his head for form's sake; but he was not anxious to leave his wife; she was expecting another child about Holy Cross Day in May, and since William's birth the baron had never felt much confidence in her ability to bear healthy children—at least this time he would be present to see the outcome.

Lady Alis could not but complain of Herbert. "I am convinced, baron," she said, "that one day he will be the best knight in the castellany. But for God's sake, take him wherever you will, so long as you do not leave him here; a castle is no place for him, he must be possessed by a Devil." The baron said that he could not send him to any of his friends, or Manesier would be offended. But finally, out of regard for the virtue of his nieces, he decided to take the boy to Seuroi. "Gervase is growing old," he said to him. "You shall take his place and serve as squire to your uncle Andrew."

"I?" said Herbert. "Serve a bastard?"

After which answer he was sick for several days, and Lady Alis spent two nights at his bedside putting wet cloths on his forehead and tending the wounds on his back. His huge, white, fat body seemed to her as tender and vulnerable as the body of an infant, and her heart contracted with rage and bitterness when she thought of the baron's cruelty. For once Ansiau could neither forget nor forgive his son's offense. "I'll make him a stable boy," he said, "I'll send him to herd swine, I'll have him clean privies." It was Andrew himself who begged for mercy for his nephew; he loved him dearly. "The boy is worth his weight in gold," he said. "We must not be too hard on him just for saying a foolish thing—it will certainly not be the last. Let me talk to him, you'll see he will come round."

As soon as he had recovered, Herbert had to ask Andrew's pardon, which he did with very ill grace, looking at his uncle much as one would look at a wild beast about to spring. Andrew smiled: "There! I forgive you—said and done. Let us talk no more about it—I believe we shall be good friends." Herbert opened his eyes wide, hesitating between gratitude and scorn. As he did not want a second whipping, he chose gratitude and bowed his head—which was as great a sign of good will and surrender as he was capable of giving. From that day on he was attached to Andrew's person and lived with him at Seuroi.

Ansiet was not dubbed a knight that year. Festivals and tournaments were prohibited, and the knights who were ready to set out wandered about Troyes like lost souls; they had come there out of habit and felt frustrated and deceived; even those who least wanted to go were eager for a quicker and surer decision. King Philip's portion was a constant stream of raillerie and reproach. The marquess of Montferrat, alone with a handful of men in the fortress of Tyre, was withstanding the assault of all the Moslem forces, and the Christian kings, rich in arms and money, shamelessly expended the sums raised for the Holy War. Such being the case, everyone said, Count Henry ought not to wait for the kings.

> *Jerusalem raises her moan*
> *For the help which does not come.*

His chin on his fists, Ansiet listened raptly to the minstrel's song of Jerusalem and forgot to serve his lord with drink. That year, which was to have brought him such splendid things—knighthood, departure for the Holy Land —looked as gray and ugly as the last. He was beginning to find it hard always to have to serve, always to be treated as an inferior. And a year was so long, twelve months, another summer, another winter—and before his eyes rose Jerusalem, luminous and bleeding, a vast relic for which all the prayers and all the blood of Christendom could never pay. Royal Jerusalem, crown and pearl of cities, the noblest and the most sullied, trodden by Saladin's horses, profaned by the lewd antics of Mohammed. It had been many years since Ansiet had dreamed of hidden treasures, but he was seventeen and he longed to leave all, to lose all, to give all for the great beauty which shed its light in his soul and which he now called Jerusalem. The baron's prowess paled beside the prowess of Richard Lionheart and the brave marquess of Montferrat; and ever since there had been no tournaments in Champagne Ansiet had lived on tales—true or false—of the exploits of Christian knights in Palestine.

The baron found his son even taller and thinner, and wondered if he were not in love. Not particularly handsome, with his tousled hair and his freckled nose, the boy had a body whose grace made it attractive, and his father regretted that Milicent was so young. But Ansiet still had his boyish smile. "Hasn't Lady Alis had her child yet? And Herbert—how is he? Is his wife pretty? Does he love her?"

"He doesn't dislike her."

"I thought so. I miss him very much, you know."

Ansiau looked at the boy's broad scrawny shoulders and big fists and thought that he had done well not to buy him a hauberk that year—next year he would need a bigger one.

A new worry had been added to Ansiau's usual difficulties—if the Crusade were put off until the following Easter, Herbert too would be old enough to be knighted. And Garnier, Simon's eldest son, was clamoring to be dubbed before setting off for the Holy Land; he insisted that Simon, if he were still alive, should find himself the father of a son in whom he could take pride. Ansiau had promised Simon that he would treat his children as he did his own, and he could not refuse Garnier what he was prepared to give to Ansiet and Herbert. Besides, the boy had been serving him as squire for six years, they were never apart, and a great friendship had sprung up between uncle and nephew, one of those friendships which are not expressed in words or gestures and which remain below the level of consciousness until the hour of trial comes. Ansiau began to realize that a hauberk for Garnier was as necessary as a hauberk for himself, and he racked his brains to find a way of outfitting all three boys at once.

It was a luxury which a man could hardly permit himself in normal times. But what finer gift could he bring to martyred Jerusalem than three newly dubbed knights, three crusaders? It was men that the Holy Land needed. And after many hesitations Ansiau mortgaged all the revenue of Linnières—forest, tannery, and vineyards—to the monastery of Saint Florentin for a term of five years.

It was madness, he knew—but at least he had made sure of the three boys' equipment, and the rest was not so very important. Ansiau of Linnières was far from scatterbrained—on the contrary, he looked ahead. Money, he thought, comes and goes—what matters is to make a boy into a man, and a man who is respected. His sons were his greatest wealth, and he wanted to make the most of it.

When Lady Alis learned that her husband had mortgaged fields and forest for five years she was openly indignant. Really, she had had enough of a husband who cared no more for her than he did for last year's snow, who did nothing but complicate her life—and God knew she had worries enough with the children already; he knew perfectly well that the income from the vineyards and the tannery were part of Mahaut's dowry, and that the girl was old enough to be married. And what sort of a wedding could she provide without a penny? The baron said that Mahaut was so beautiful that she needed no dowry.

"Really, baron, you are talking without thinking! Do you believe that some man is going to take your daughter out of pity? I would rather see her a nun than married to a man who will throw her poverty in her face!"

"Lady, do not be angry. We can always manage to find a dowry for Mahaut. At the moment the great need is to outfit the boys."

"The boys! You never think of anything but the boys! The girls are just as much your own flesh and blood, baron; do you want them to marry sergeants, like your cousin Claude? Better that they had died, like my poor little Ala," and at the memory Lady Alis burst into tears. "I shall never forgive you," she said. "You have robbed your daughters—no more and no less!"

She had known that she would wound her husband to the quick. And indeed it was long before he forgot—"robbed" was too ugly and too unjust a word, and Lady Alis had no right to use it. And what did she mean by talking about dowries and weddings when the Saracens were putting the Holy Land to fire and sword? However, he began to think about a husband for Mahaut; the girl was thirteen, and he could not start too soon if he was to find a good match for her.

Mahaut was growing more beautiful every day. She was as slender as a reed, and so white, so fresh. Her features seemed to be carved in white gold and her eyes shone like two black diamonds. She was full of life and gaiety and had so many admirers that she had lost count of them. Frahier and Aimeri still adored her; Hugh of Beaumont's sons fought one another for the privilege of helping her mount her horse; John, Girard the Young's youngest son, lay in wait for her in dark corners to beg her to listen to him—and Mahaut laughed at them all and at all their doings. Except, perhaps, for one—Garnier, the son of her famous uncle Simon, inspired her with a degree of respect. Garnier was not handsome, but he was always with the baron, took part in every tournament, and seemed to know a great many entertaining things. But he was so outrageously rude to her that she had come to detest him with all her heart. Whenever the baron came to the castle Lady Alis knew beforehand that she would have to intervene in a quarrel between Mahaut and Garnier, and she always took her daughter's side.

Mahaut, who never complained of anyone, overwhelmed her mother with grievances when Garnier was at the castle: "Lady, he stepped on my foot! Lady, he pinched my arm, look at the black-and-blue mark he gave me! Lady, he said that Milicent is prettier than I am." (Even her fondness for Milicent could not make her admit such an enormity.)

And Garnier proclaimed to all and sundry that Mahaut was a conceited, heartless jade, that she stole her mother's perfume, and tried to make every boy in the countryside fall in love with her. "And Aioul?" he would jeer. "Have you ever seen Mahaut with her Aioul?" Aioul was the son of a petty tenant named Frahier the Short, who served the baron of Linnières as a sergeant and had a farm on the Armançon. Aioul came to Linnières every day, sometimes to bring Lady Alis some carp or tench his father had caught, sometimes to borrow a scythe or a rake; he was so in love with Mahaut that when he saw her he stood stock-still in ecstasy with his mouth wide open like a simpleton. When Mahaut went to walk in the meadow with the other girls he followed her, sometimes touching the ends of her braids, sometimes picking up a flower she had dropped. He was a handsome boy of eighteen, and Mahaut's heart was not made of stone. Scorn him as she might because he was a vassal's son, she smoothed her eyebrows and straightened her collar and girdle when she heard his horse enter the courtyard.

It was a dreary summer for Lady Alis. Her latest child—born in May—was weak and sickly; it cried constantly, and she spent her nights rocking it in her arms. In her inmost heart there was a mortal weariness, the despairing knowledge that the child would not live through the summer. It was a boy and had been christened Henry. Henry had a round, dark head, big curious eyes, and the warm, flawless skin of an infant. Lady Alis rocked him, he cried, she gave him the breast and still he cried; he grew thinner every day. Lady Alis lost her head and sent for Flora, who had become as necessary to her in these last years as wine to a drunkard—Flora had remedies for every illness, foretold whatever she was asked to foretell; she was often wrong, but Lady Alis believed in her nonetheless. Flora said: "I can tell you nothing about him, but your next will be the most beautiful of all your children." Alis sighed, not knowing what to think or what to hope. She was so tired and had so much to do. Baby Mary was beginning to walk, the twins were growing up into little devils, and William—ah, William! God knew why she still loved him with a fierce tenderness, a tenderness which made her neglect her younger children, which forced her, sick and pregnant as she was, to get up at night to cover him or change his soiled sheets. The child could not even smile; he was over six, and plump but very weak; the more he grew, the greater became the aversion he aroused in everyone who saw him—in the baron first of all. But Lady Alis was convinced that William knew her and loved her. When he was cold he snuggled against her, and that was enough to make her forget all the suffering he caused her. The baron would say: "You know very well that child will never be good for anything, what is the use of keeping him?" and Lady Alis knew that he was right and reproached herself for being a weak mother, yet her remorse only made her tenderness the fiercer, her pity the more poignant. Perhaps the memory of her sin, which the child must expiate, had something to do with it—but of that she never thought.

King Henry of England died on September first, and the news reached Champagne at the same time as the news of the coronation of Richard, duke of Poitiers. Men hoped great things of Richard and of his friendship with the king of France. Yet the old king was regretted. With him died a whole age of wars and tournaments, of feasting and chivalry. Those who had fought in the wars in France felt suddenly much older—the days of King Henry Plantagenet were now the past. Perhaps Richard would be a better man than his father, but he would be different, and with age men cease to welcome change. At Troyes, at Reims, at Meaux, at Provins, processions wound through the streets with song and shout and blazing torches in honor of King Richard, uncle to Count Henry. It was to him more than to anyone else that men looked for victory over Saladin.

> *High to the tower mounts fair Ysabet,*
> *Leans her blond head over the parapet,*
> *The fringes of her cloak with tears are wet . . .*

The girls' white hands rose in rhythm, drawing their needles. Mahaut, who had sharp ears, raised her golden head and frowned. Then, feeling her mother's eyes upon her, she began singing again, and her heart beat faster because she heard a horseman ride into the courtyard.

> *I cry to thee!*
> *For wicked tongues have driven me o'er the sea!*

Lady Alis, whose thoughts were elsewhere, did not raise her eyes from her work. But it was not Aioul who entered the hall, and the smile vanished from Mahaut's lips. The man approached the lady of Linnières, knelt before her, and kissed the hem of her dress. It seemed that what he held in his hand must be something very strange, for Lady Alis, stared and blushed, then rose and led the messenger to the window where she could talk with him and not be overheard.

> *Ah, gentle lady mine, I know a knight*
> *Who has won praise in tournament and fight—*
> *Well would he love you, in all men's despite . . .*

sang Mahaut. Lady Alis wished that she could stop up her ears.

"Ah, God! Again?" she said. "I cannot imagine what your master wants of me, my friend. Why come here? I have troubles enough as it is."

"Lady," said the man, "my master is close by, at the chapel in the old forest, and he wishes to see you."

Alis felt her hands grow cold and damp.

"To see me? What for?"

"Lady, do not be angry. My master has asked me to speak to you for him.

He is setting out with his lord for the Holy Land before the end of the month. He has come here all the way from Brienne. He did not want to leave the country without bidding you good-bye. If you refuse to see him, he will be greatly grieved—he is waiting for you near the chapel."

"He is leaving?" said Lady Alis. "God! Why did he not come to the castle? I should have been glad to receive him."

"Because of your lord and your kindred. He is stopping with Manesier of Coagnecort, at Hervi. He says that he will not set foot in your castle again."

"That is just like him. And it happens that my lord is at Troyes. Well, my friend, stay a while. I will have you fed."

"Lady," Mahaut asked, "is it bad news?"

"Neither bad nor good, my daughter. This young man has come to tell me that the count's seneschal may stop at Hervi when he comes to hunt in the forest, and I need to see him about getting an extension of time on my debts. I shall take Milon with me, ride straight to Hervi, and see if I cannot catch him there."

Despite her haste Lady Alis spent a good half-hour over her toilet, trying now one necklace, now another, and rubbing her cheeks and lips with carnation juice. Thinking that Erard must be wanting money, she stuffed her purse with all the crowns she could find in her coffer. Then she covered her face with a heavy veil of pink muslin and went down to the courtyard, where Milon was waiting for her with the horses.

She did not know what she was doing. To see Erard was neither a joy nor a need for her—it was more like an obligation. Her head and her heart were as empty as last year's nutshells. Had she sworn that she would never see him again? The vow seemed absurd. He was leaving Champagne, perhaps forever, going to get himself killed before Jerusalem, or to die of thirst and heat—and should she refuse to render him the last service he asked of her? The Holy War had already turned life upside down and made right of what had seemed wrong—she was soon to see her husband and her sons go, and would not that atone for more than one sin, past and to come?

At the crossroads she stopped and said to Milon: "Milet, my friend, no one is coming to Hervi, neither the count nor the seneschal nor anyone else."

"Then why are we going there, lady?"

"I am not going there. Milet, I have something to ask of you: Swear to me that you will never question me about what I shall do today and that you will never breathe a word of it to a living soul."

"I swear it, lady."

"Very well, then—you take the road to Seuroi and I will take the lefthand road. I will meet you at Seuroi this evening. But if it should happen that I do not reach there until tomorrow, think up some explanation for my absence and do not be alarmed."

Milon's imperturbability seemed greater than ever. "Very well, lady." And he turned his horse into the road to Seuroi.

There was a high wind blowing, and Lady Alis wrapped herself in her cloak and held her veil, which was fluttering in her face. At the last minute she wondered whether Erard would not have wearied of waiting, if he would not be gone—patience was not his strong point.

However, he was there before the chapel, sitting motionless on his white Arab horse—a rather short man, spare and sinewy, and a little stiff. He was staring at the meadow and the brook and seemed to be absorbed in thought; his hands—Alis instantly recognized the gesture—were tearing a maple leaf to bits. He did not hear Lady Alis approaching until she was only ten paces away. Then he started and turned round, and at the same instant the wind tore off his woolen hood and tossed his long blond locks into the air—he tried to control them with his left hand. He wore a short, tightly curled beard.

It was so long since Lady Alis had seen his face that at first she did not recognize it. It was a faintly tanned, rather pale face; the features were so sharp and hard that no one would think of them as beautiful. Under the large, heavy-lidded eyes there were traces of dark rings. Alis was so startled that it fairly stopped her breath. But an instant later she was wondering why she had ever pictured him otherwise.

Erard seemed quite moved himself. He smiled and said: "Lady, I thank you for coming."

Lady Alis did not know what to answer, her heart was beating so fast that she thought she would be sick. Never had she supposed that the mere sight of him could upset her so. She wanted to give him her hand, but her fingers were trembling so uncontrollably that she could not pull off her glove. Astonished at her silence, Erard asked: "Are you angry, lady?".

Lady Alis recovered her breath: "Oh, no! No, not at all! But it gave me such a shock to see you again."

"Why? Have I changed?"

"Oh, no! Not at all! At least not much. God, God! I never thought I should see you again."

Then they were both silent, embarrassed, at a loss for words. The gusty wind tore at their cloaks and whipped his hair and her veil—over the dark forest crows traced zigzags in the air, struggling against the gale—the trees creaked and sighed. Erard proposed that they should take shelter in the chapel.

Under the little stone vault there was no more wind, and Lady Alis sat down on a bench against the wall to recover her breath and readjust her veil. Erard came in a moment later and sat down beside her.

"I tied our horses behind the trees," he said, "so that they cannot be seen from the farther side of the meadow. What weather! It's pleasanter here than outside. Ah! I was sure that you would find a way to come--true enough, old Gypsy Face is at Troyes, which makes matters easier—come, talk to me, I have hardly heard your voice."

Alis had grown unaccustomed to violent emotions; she felt broken, dull, her arms and legs were like lead. She could only say, "God! oh, God!" and press her hands over her heart to keep it from beating so.

"Won't you take off your veil now," said Erard, "so that I can look at your beautiful eyes?" and he raised his hand to take it off himself, but she stopped him with a swift gesture.

"No, my friend, not yet. You do not know. I have changed. Oh! I have grown old. I am not as I was. You will not find me beautiful."

"What, lady, will you not even give me a kiss of welcome? You would not refuse it to a stranger."

"Not now. Later," Lady Alis said. "We have time, my friend. Oh! believe me, I never thought that I should see you again."

And she threw her arms around his neck and hid her face on his shoulder. He held her close, and the touch of his hands woke so many memories in her heart that she burst into sobs.

"Lady! What is it? Are you unhappy?"

"Oh, how unhappy, Erard, my sweet! If only you knew! It is seven years since the baron came back. I have had much sorrow since. If only you knew! I am weary. Always the children, the children, and troubles hanging over me. I do not complain. But it is hard nonetheless. Since you left I have had four who are still alive, and I have buried three. And the last died on the day of Our Lady's Nativity, only two weeks ago. He was less than four months old—he smiled at me."

"Bah! You have such a brood of them already," said Erard coldly. "I am amazed that you can tell them apart."

Lady Alis stopped crying—God knew why she had expected to find Erard more compassionate than the baron. She said: "Obviously, no one but a woman would worry about such things—they seem trifling enough to you. Let us talk of something else. You have not yet told me why you are here."

He raised his eyebrows. "I thought Bertrand had explained. I have taken the cross, I am leaving with my lord—I shall be gone within ten days. I came to bid you good-bye."

"Really?" said Lady Alis. "You came here all the way from Brienne just to say good-bye to me? I shall never believe it."

"Yet it is true, lady. Naturally I told my wife that I was going to see my brother, but God knows I could have done very well without."

Lady Alis' face darkened. "Your brother? And his wife as well, no doubt?"

"Lady! Enough! Ah, I see you have not changed. Lady, sweet, take off your veil, it troubles me."

"No, not yet. Please. Talk to me. Talk to me about yourself."

As so often, he did not answer her; instead, he listened to the piping of the wind. He looked sad.

"Lady, listen to me. I have not forgotten you. You cannot imagine how many women I have tried for my pleasure, but not one of them gave me such joy as you. It has never been the same thing since. I have never met a woman like you."

"A woman you left on the third day," said Alis bitterly.

"Against my will, as you very well know."

"But you made no effort to see me again—if you had stayed at Troyes instead of going to Provins, we should have met again before All-Hallows. And at Pentecost three years ago, when I was at Troyes for my son's wedding, you knew I was there. Once your ransom was paid there was no one to prevent your coming to St. Peter's to pray."

"If you had asked me, I would have come," said Erard. "You sent me word that I was not to see you again; I obeyed you. Besides, I was in no fit state to appear before a lady."

Alis shook her head.

"You can always find an excuse. Well, I shall not argue with you any longer. Tell me about your life—do you love your wife?"

He shrugged his shoulders.

"But you have children," Lady Alis said. "Your brother has told me so."

"Yes—two little girls, Mary and Elissa. Mary will be five in May."

"Are they pretty?"

Erard gave a bright, boyish smile. "The prettiest little things I have ever seen."

Alis sighed and said nothing.

Launched on the theme of his present life, Erard seemed quite to have forgotten his old love. He took Lady Alis' hands and began explaining how the count of Brienne had managed to equip himself and how difficult it was to set off before everyone else.

"No one will help you at all," he said. "They all answer: 'I have taken the cross myself, I have my own equipment to look after.' And now it is nearly a year since we began getting ready, and our hauberks are rusting in their boxes. Even in Count Erard's own household there are men who keep putting off their preparations—one has a lawsuit, another a sick wife, no doubt they think they can promise to go later and that will be the end of it.

"Certainly, I do not blame Henry of Champagne for waiting for the kings—he is hardly more than a boy and King Philip is his uncle. God save Countess Mary—but I think she has done the country more harm than good by her kinship with the kings; she has made Champagne into a weathercock which turns as the winds from France and England blow, and God knows they do not always blow in the same direction. Taking it all in all, I preferred Henry Plantagenet to the king of France."

"Indeed?" said Lady Alis, yawning. "I have always heard that he was a valiant knight. But he was a very old man."

"He still had teeth. He would have led the army well. But you will see—King Philip will find some excuse to stay at home in the end, and it will be such a shame and disgrace as France has never known before. And why? Because he will not have money enough left to equip his men, even after laying a tithe on clerks and barons and driving the poor to beg their bread on the highways. That money will never be spent for Jerusalem, I warrant you.

"Believe me, lady, it is enough to make a man vomit—I have seen so much foulness since I took the cross that I am sick of my country and my countrymen. No one in all Champagne thinks of anything but growing rich at God's expense. Beginning with my mother's husband, the seneschal of Provins—who has suddenly become so generous that he has doubled his men's wages and gives presents to them all, and to all his kinsmen besides. Before the tithe he never carried his head so high, I assure you. Well, I have told him what I think of him. The money is spent faster than it comes in, and meanwhile the knights eat up their wages and champ at the bit. I am glad indeed to be in Erard of Brienne's service and to be leaving the country. I do not believe that I shall ever come back."

"And why not, my friend?" Lady Alis asked gently. "After all, men do come back from the Holy Land. You have been there once before."

"I will tell you, lady," said Erard, and Alis was struck by the sudden seriousness of his face, "I will tell you—but only two or three of my friends know it yet. I have decided to become a Templar."

Lady Alis crossed herself. "God! I cannot see you as a Templar. You!—become a monk!"

He laughed. "You think it a waste? You do not know me. Women always suppose that a man cannot live without loving them. But I have had such scores and scores of women that it means nothing to me any longer. It is not that I look forward to becoming a monk and shaving my head. But one of my mother's uncles is a Templar—he will help me. Better to make an end—there is nothing for me here."

"Friend," said Lady Alis, "I beg you not to do anything so foolish. You will regret it."

"I? I have nothing to regret. I have seen Jerusalem with my own eyes, and I have not forgotten it. And when I think that the infidels are shovelling horse dung on the altars of Holy Sepulchre, and buying and selling our Frankish women for their filthy harems, I want to make them pay for it—if I had a thousand of them in my power, I would have them all beheaded, knights or no knights. If I stay in Palestine to fight them, it will not be after the fashion of your cousin Simon of Linnières, who they say has grown rich serving the barons of Ultramar. I would never live as such men do—they smack too much of the infidel. It is the Templars who best resist corruption."

Lady Alis asked: "And your wife? And your daughters?"

"My wife knows nothing yet," said Erard. "She mortgaged her jointure to equip me—it was hardly the moment to tell her that I was leaving her for ever. She will know it in time, she will be free. I do not love her, I took her for her dowry."

"Friend," Lady Alis said again, and her voice trembled a little, "if you loved me you would want to come back, so that you might see me again."

"No, no," he said. "There is no use starting the same thing over again a dozen times. I came here to bid you good-bye. Ah, lady, those were happy days. Do you remember——the little hidden garden——the lavender——the crickets singing in the meadow. Now you go there to meet someone else."

Lady Alis drew herself up. "God! Who ever told you such a lie? May his tongue rot and drop from his false mouth! I have no man except my baron."

"Come now! You are too beautiful not to have a lover. No one would expect you to get along with only your Noseless. After all, it is none of my affair. You are here, and that is what matters, isn't it?" And he smiled more goodnaturedly than Alis would ever have expected, showing all his sharp white teeth. Yet she was not disarmed, for she had more than one reason to be angry. She stood up and started toward the door. The wind had dropped a little. The air was cool and damp, patches of blue sky showed above the yellowing trees.

Lady Alis turned her back on her companion and choked down tears of humiliation and wrath. Erard followed her and laid his hand on her shoulder. She put it away without a word.

"Lady, are you angry? Why are you so harsh to me?"

"Come, My Lord Templar," she said, "I do not know what you want. It is not harsh to say good-bye, and it need not take long."

"You know very well what I want."

"No, really, I do not. You have not told me."

"I want to taste your fair body once more before I cross the sea."

"I am not a woman you may take and leave at your pleasure, my friend. You won me once. But that was long ago."

"Yet I thought——come, lady, this is too cruel. Why make me suffer? I have never harmed you. I love you loyally, and well you know it."

"Go, you have already made me cry too much."

"But now it is you who make me cry. Only turn your head, let me take off your veil. Let me see your fair face."

"Very well," said Lady Alis, turning her head. "But ask me for nothing more than that."

With both hands Erard raised her veil and lingeringly kissed her lips and eyes. Then Alis gave him at least a dozen quick kisses, as if she wanted to make up for lost time.

She let her passion carry her where it would. She felt no fear and no shame—it was as if all the tender words she had suppressed for six years had risen to her lips at once. She barely listened to what Erard was saying—those words of his, at once so sweet and so shameless, which she knew so well—he must not prevent her from saying what was in her heart, she would never have a chance to say it again.

What she loved in him was his self-control—he never dreamed of plunging straight on to consummation, like Ansiau. He enjoyed talking of love and hearing her talk of it; he was not in a hurry, she knew that he would never force her, with him she was free to give herself or not, as she chose.

She had no mind to refuse herself and she said so quite simply.

"Look—the wind has blown the clouds away," said Erard. "Lady, why should we not go and look at the glade where we loved each other so well that hunting day—do you remember? I have not forgotten it."

"As you will, sweet. But the paths are very bad after rain."

"Bah! That doesn't frighten me. We will have time—it cannot be much after noon. Shall we? I'll fetch the horses."

They rode for a long time over muddy paths, Lady Alis leading to show the way. When they reached the glade Erard looked about, surprised and disappointed.

"But this is not the same place, sweet. It cannot be. You must have made a mistake."

"I know the forest, thank God!"

"But it is impossible. It is not at all like it was. The stones were much bigger and whiter. I remember it perfectly."

"They are gray after the rain," Lady Alis said. "There is nothing I can do about it. It is the same place."

"How strange!" Erard shook his head. "Are you certain? Why, there is where we lay, and that is the oak where I tied the horses. It has grown, but it is the same oak."

He dismounted, tied their horses and helped Lady Alis to dismount. "My cloak is thick," he said. "We shall not feel the wet. Let me look at you. You have changed, you did not have those lines under your eyes. I think you are thinner. Your lips are less rosy. Lady, sweet—ah, it is too sad to think that you have changed. That time when Bos saw you in church he told me that you had not changed at all."

Alis said: "Be still, be still," and closed his mouth with an eager, hungry kiss which lasted so long that she lost her breath. Erard talked, but she knew that his words were no longer addressed to her—it must be that he knew them by heart and was repeating them without thinking.

An hour later they were sitting side by side on Erard's gray cloak, sharing a piece of bread which he had found in his saddlebag. Neither spoke. Lady Alis was mending a tear in her collar; from time to time she stole a look at her lover. But he did not look at her, he was frowning, his face had grown hard.

"My dear lord, my love," Lady Alis said gently, "do you not deign to look at me? It is not courteous in you—I have not failed you."

Erard flung a stone at a flying crow and brought it down. He blinked and looked away from his companion. "I might have saved myself the journey," he said at last. "I do not love you."

"That is an ugly thing to say," Lady Alis answered, "after you have had your will of me. It should have occurred to you that I would not have grown younger and more beautiful in seven years. No more have you, my friend. It is not my fault that you are no longer twenty."

Her reproach recalled him to a sense of decency and he became more gentle. He said: "You are right—I should not have· said that. I would not want you to think me a boor. I could tell you all the things one always says—words come easily to me. But I do not like lying. And what would be the use? Better that I tell you at once how things stand—you will not love me so much and you will regret me less."

Then Alis put her two hands on his shoulders and looked straight into his eyes. "My sweet and my lord, it is very good of you to take such thought for me. But know that it will not make me love you less and that I shall regret you just as much—I do not change my heart as easily as you. If I have loved you it was not in jest. From the day when you went to fight Guian of Lorraine to please me, I have loved you and I have told you so frankly. Never think that all I cared for was your beauty and your youth and your prowess in arms. If you were old and ugly, I should still love you, because your heart is neither base nor cowardly. I think it is not your fault that you no longer love me, and you were right to tell me so and not to lie. And I, too, shall speak the truth: I shall love you until I die, for now I know well that I can never be cured of my sickness. And the least I deserve is that you should pity me and be kind to me."

Erard smiled at her and stroked her hair. "Lady, you are better than the rest. I think that I love nothing and no one now, either in Champagne or France. I long to be on a great-sailed ship—the sea air is so good, I have never yet been sick at sea. I want to have it all behind me, once at Tyre or Acre I shall take orders, and then farewell to wife, kindred, and friends. I owe nothing to anyone. You will tell me that the Templars keep a very strict discipline. But you know how wild and disorderly my life has always been. I still have time to reform and earn forgiveness for my sins, time to become a new man.

"My beloved lady, listen to me. I said to myself: 'I must have one good plunge into the pleasures of the world before I renounce everything.' God! what stupid things I did, if I were to tell you of them you would have a good laugh. But finally I reached the point where nothing amused me, nothing gave me pleasure. And I thought of you, lady—I thought that you were the best thing life had given me. And I said to myself: 'If I have her once again, it will be my last and greatest joy, and afterwards I shall want nothing more.' And now it is done, and I have nothing left to desire. And now I suppose I must go—I set out from Brienne tomorrow."

Lady Alis asked: "Then you want no more of me?"

"No. What would be the use? The first time is the best. It would just keep getting less and less. It is as if I should try to wear a pair of shoes until they fell to pieces. I am not a miser. Let us say good-bye. And try not to feel resentful."

"I will ride as far as the chapel with you," said Lady Alis. "You would never find the way by yourself."

She dreaded the moment of farewell. As long as Erard was there, she could believe that he would remain with her always. And she knew that, without that belief, she could not go on living. Outside the chapel she kept thinking of excuses to hold him. She hoped that at the last minute he would say, "I want to spend the night with you," or, "Come tomorrow, I will be waiting." The main thing was to gain time. But Erard was a man of his word if ever there was one. It did not occur to him to change his mind.

"Sweet," said Lady Alis, "I have been wondering if you might not be in need of money—on a long journey one can always use more than one has. Will you take what I have in my purse? You will need it more than I."

"Well," he said, "I will not refuse, even though I can never pay it back except in prayers. You are kind."

"And tell me, sweet—that other time, when you sent to me for your ransom, was I the only woman you asked?"

"No. But you were the only one who did anything for me."

Milon found Lady Alis in the chapel in the forest—God knows what lover's insight had guided him there; from Seuroi he had taken the long way round by the chapel and, seeing Lady Alis' horse tied at the door, had gone in. Lady Alis was sitting on a bench, her chin in her hands, motionless as a wooden statue. She was staring into space, her lids trembled a little, her lips moved. Her face was drawn, and gray with an opaque pallor.

She did not move when she heard Milon enter—she seemed not to be aware of his presence. He knelt and asked: "Lady, shall I go back alone or shall I wait for you?"

She gave him a bleak, empty look. "I will go with you. Where ought I to go?"

"To Seuroi, I think," said the squire. "At the castle everyone would be surprised to see you back so soon."

Lady Alis rose without a word. It was an effort for her to walk, her eyes saw everything double, her legs were like lead.

The next morning she returned to the castle, calmly intent upon allaying whatever suspicions her escapade might have aroused. She had wept so much that she was dulled and exhausted; she felt alone and mortally tired and had only a vague idea of what had happened.

In her heart there was nothing left but a bleak amazement. She had never forgotten Erard—that she must admit. She had not often thought of him, but once the mere sight of Hugh of Baudemant had almost made her faint. But now the memory, with all its beauty and joy, with all her pride in being loved, was gone. In its place there was a somber, painful need, an unquenchable thirst—the man was no longer young, no longer handsome, and he no longer loved her; no doubt of that whatever, yet it only made her love him the more.

She was not again visited by the fears which had followed her first sin —it was enough that she had felt them once; sin had become a thing to which she must resign herself. Her accounts with God were sufficiently complicated; she believed that she had long since imperilled her soul's salvation, and, at bottom, she cared very little. In her own eyes she had acted well—she could refuse no wish of a man who was about to sacrifice all for God. Her man—the only man in the world.

Since all the men had left with the baron, life at the castle was rather monotonous. Lady Alis was kept so busy supervising the women's work that now she never had time to hunt. The baron was expected any day, but he seemed to have taken a liking to long journeys—from Monguoz he went to Provins, from Provins to Bar-on-Aube, visiting his friends and sighing for tournaments. Lady Alis could picture him coming home with his hands full of presents for everyone and his head stuffed with miracles and news from the Holy Land. More than ever her heart swelled with resentment against him. She thought of him as a stern, callous master who managed always to be in the right. There were moments when she believed she despised him. "And why is he always going somewhere else—what does he think he will find?"

This time she had a particular reason for wanting him to come home, a reason which kept her awake nights and brought cold sweat to her temples when she thought of it by day. As she sewed with her women she would stop her work and count the days and weeks, grow hopelessly confused, begin over again. And when the baron returned, two days before All-Hallows, Alis could only give a great sigh of relief.

Never before had she supposed that any man beside her husband could give her a child. And now she was forced to admit that it could happen— and leave her none the worse. The immediate danger weathered, she could draw breath and think. The fact was too extraordinary in itself not to fill her with dread—she was certain that she would betray herself in one way or another, either through a resemblance in the child, or through some other sign which, not knowing, she feared even more. She had Flora come secretly to advise her, and Flora assured her that there were many ways of telling whether a child had been conceived in wedlock or not, but only if the husband or the husband's family took a hand in the matter and submitted the child to a test. "And that," she said, "only happens when there are serious suspicions—a lady almost never has to undergo it."

With a sort of timid distrust Alis noted the signs which revealed the presence of the stranger, the intruder who had entered into her by trickery; she exaggerated all her disagreeable symptoms and felt as if she were pregnant for the first time in her life.

She bore fruit every year like an apple tree whose boughs sink every autumn under the weight of their ripened load. But this time the normal course of the seasons had been interrupted, the laws of nature had been violated, and there was this obstinate little life, making itself at home, pushing its way into the world, and molding her to its exigencies. By dint of observing herself Alis came almost to a sense of wonder over the mystery which until now had been so natural and familiar. Had God then decreed that she and Erard should found a line together, when neither she nor he had ever wished it?

Toward the end of November Bertrade of Hervi, Herbert's young wife, gave birth to a daughter; at the baron's wish the child was christened Aelis. And Lady Alis, rather depressed to find herself a grandmother at thirty-two, washed and swaddled the little thing herself, and with her own hands smoothed back the sweat-soaked strands of hair from the new mother's face. Haggard, yet transfigured, Bertrade rested her dark, heavy head on the white pillows, so exhausted that she did not even ask to see her child. Lady Alis was not very fond of her daughter-in-law, but that day the thought of the life she herself was carrying made her pity Bertrade and treat her gently.

On the evening after the christening she told the baron that she had been pregnant since All-Hallows; he began counting on his fingers and said that the child could not be born before the end of July. "No doubt I shall be gone by then and shall not see it. Be very careful, lady—you have lost three children in four years. You must bring this one through alive."

"Don't worry," said Lady Alis, "I shall."

And she forgot the baron and sank back into her reverie. She could hardly believe it yet—her child would have Erard's eyes and Erard's mouth and Erard's hands, and she could marvel at them and kiss them unhindered, she could talk to him, tell him all that she had not found time to tell his father—God! he was on the sea, far away among the great winds and the salt waves, with never a thought for the lady he had once loved at Troyes, his rose-cheeked lady—yet he was as much a father as any wedded husband. She had but to bear his issue, to nurse it and protect it, to let it take all that remained of her youth and strength. The day he came back—it could not be that she would never see him again!—she could swear to him upon relics that he was indeed the child's father—and then perhaps he would smile, as he had smiled when he spoke of his two little daughters.

She let the candle burn on unheeded—for the twentieth time her hands braided and rebraided the ends of her tresses.

Ansiau said: "How beautiful you are, sweet. I have never seen you look so. You are different."

She started. "What? You are imagining things, baron. Why should I be different?"

"I have no idea. Can anyone understand a woman? I have it—Flora has told you that your child will be pope or emperor—if you are not thinking about him, may I be damned forever!"

Alis blushed like a woman found out, and could think of no answer. The baron laughed and began to tease her over her embarrassment: "Why, no one would believe you are a grandmother! One of these days I shall find you a virgin all over again." And because she frowned and turned away, he stopped laughing and became tender in earnest. With her he was never afraid of being weak. Over and over he repeated the few paltry words of affection which he had not forgotten during his years of travelling and tourneying. It was always "Ala," "Alette," "Aielis," "Aielot," and twenty other variations on her name. Besides, with him kisses always counted more than words.

In no mood for his sudden outburst of tenderness, Lady Alis exploded angrily: "A man your age!"

"Never too old to love you, lady! What does it matter that I am a grandfather? We shall still have ten more children, all younger than their nephews."

"It is easy enough for you to talk." She shrugged her shoulders. "I am going to put out the candle."

"No. Let me look at you a little longer. You are so beautiful tonight, sweet." Brusquely he took her head in both hands and bent it back so that the candlelight would fall full upon it—he tried to look into her eyes, but they fled him, they pretended to be heavy with sleep, blinded by the light. Yes, there were little lines on her lids, and her mouth had hardened—then how had she managed to remain so young? And why had he not noticed it before?

Alis was wondering how, with the best intentions in the world, her husband always succeeded in being so exasperating. Between his two hot hands her head seemed to be in an oven, she closed her eyes and felt a bristly beard tickle her chin and nose, a dry burning mouth cling to her cheeks and her forehead—she had forgotten that such things were called kisses and caresses. She was a block of wood. She thought of how expensive candles were—and God knew how many they had burned already for the baby's christening! A man could always spend more money than he could earn.

Midnight Mass at Hervi Church.

Tall white candles, tall red candles, spearing from the altar, from the high-hung wrought-iron chandeliers. On the company in the front row they cast a light as bright as day.

Ansiau, lord of Linnières, sat in the place where his father and grandfather had sat before him—grave and imposing in his heavy, dark-red cloak lined with fox skins. Frozen in the ritual attitude, head bowed and hands clasped, he did not look at the candles, their brightness had lost all power to amaze him. Nothing so simple could make him weep for joy now, he had forgotten his first midnight Mass at Hervi with Alis at his side. Christmas had come round eighteen times since then—always the same, whether at Hervi or Troyes or Jerusalem or in the galleys—the High Night on which the Light was born. Men might change, grow old, and die, but not a letter would be changed in the service sung through all lands and all ages, unto eternity—*Gloria in excelsis Deo.*

He, Ansiau, baron of Linnières, Curt-Nose, husband of Lady Alis, was but a little link in the chain of Christians who would hear this Christmas Eve service—as his father had done, and old Galon, and Galon's father Herbert before him; and as Ansiet would do, sitting in that same seat beside his blond Milicent and their children yet unborn—and when their children's children had long since forgotten the names of Ansiau and Alis, they too would still hear this very service in this very place.

Thirty-five was the age when a man reached the plenitude of his powers, or so said clerks and scholars. At thirty-five he ceased to grow, his muscles stopped developing, his sinews began to harden, his blood to thicken. It was the peak of a man's life, and after it he began going downhill.

That year, before the decked and shining altar, time and old age had little reality for Ansiau of Linnières—that Christmas might well be the last of his earthly life, and he had only to thank God who had allowed him to ripen so that he might give all that he had to give. True enough, he had little to offer to God but swordstrokes which would split a man from shoulder to navel, but after all no one had ever taught him anything else or ever expected anything else of him.

The great, the beautiful thing was that he was still in his prime and that he had three sons old enough to bear arms. There they were—two of them at least—kneeling behind him, tall and broad-shouldered, their hair properly clipped in a fringe on the forehead and hanging loose over ears and neck, well washed and neatly combed. Herbert's was blond, Garnier's chestnut. In ten years or twelve Herbert would be able to bend a horseshoe with one hand. In the lines of his neck, in his slightly fleshy shoulders, in his over-heavy legs, there was a certain softness and shapelessness which did not deceive the baron—he had trained puppies which at first seemed heavy and sluggish, as if crushed by a strength too great for their age, yet once they were old enough to run they had proved as fierce as the best. At sixteen and a half, Herbert was still unconscious of his strength; he seemed to take pride only in things hardly worth thinking of—his magnificent hair, his clean hands, his successes with women—not very brilliant successes, at that. He had the ruthless eyes and the hard mouth of a younger brother who could make his way only by his own efforts and who eagerly watched for opportunities to distinguish himself. But set him face to face with the infidels and the boy would be worth his weight in gold.

And Garnier—Garnier had inherited Simon's long, sinewy limbs, his thin neck and weasel slenderness. He was very enduring, very strong, and very reliable. Garnier, the baron thought, took after him far more than Ansiet and Herbert, in manner, gestures, and speech. It was more or less conscious imitation on the boy's part—he was eager to learn the art of life and he knew of no better model than his uncle—at least, of course, until the day when he should meet his father again in Palestine—for, although it seemed most unlikely, he was convinced that his father was still alive. He would say to Herbert: "I feel it, my heart tells me so." Yes, for all his roughness, the boy had a streak of febrility—a trait which he shared with his father.

It was their turn to weep for joy and to adore the Divine Child—Ansiau gladly ceded them the privilege of youth—and even Herbert, pale and expressionless, sniffled noisily when the *Noëls* and *Glorias* rang out. He was always easily moved to tears by beautiful music, particularly church music. He had a very simple faith—in the presence of God he believed that he was perfectly good, credited himself with every virtue, and rose from his knees thoroughly content with both his Maker and himself.

In the brightly lit church the young of both sexes had a rare opportunity to display their figures, their furs and embroidered cloaks and muslin veils. And Mahaut, her eyes raised to the altar, set herself to clasp her slender white hands duly and rightly and to throw her light veil back just enough to show her face, which was suffused with angelic piety. She was not a hypocrite; she went to church to be admired, she would have time enough to pray when she was old and ugly. But the boys must be made to think that she was an angel.

Yellow torchlight played over the church porch, making the heavy ranks of sculptured flowers and fruit stand out in blocks of white and black. And the knights and their families came out of the church, and before the steps a mob of beggars and village men and women crowded to see them pass. The squires came and went with their torches, patterning the crowd with light and shadow.

With his heavy cape swinging from his shoulders and his green silk tunic falling in wide folds to his ankles, the baron of Linnières looked so imposing that the folk of the countryside, to whom he was no stranger, could not but cry out their admiration. He stopped in the porch to talk with Haguenier of Hervi, and the crude, flickering light shifted over his face, revealing now his mutilated nose, now his thick, square-cut beard, and leaving mouth and brow strangely in shadow.

And Milicent, pressed against the central pillar, waited for the moments when those great black eyes caught the light and glowed; they were such open eyes, so ill-defended, that she always dreaded some accident would befall them, put out their light—they were too beautiful. She wondered if she would ever gain entrance to the world in which he lived—in that world everything must be magnified, larger than life, all his thoughts must be too beautiful for a poor little girl to understand. And though she could not hear his words she knew that what he was saying to Haguenier would have made her happy if only she could have understood it. Snuggled against her, Mahaut rubbed her frozen cheeks against the fur of her cape.

The boys came out and flung themselves on their young girl cousins to kiss them in honor of Christmas. Milicent offered her lips with the indifferent dignity of a well-bred girl; Mahaut laughed and joked, complained that she was being shoved—she knew that these Christmas kisses were a bounty long awaited by her lovers. And Christmas being the day of days for charity, she granted them their little joy wholeheartedly. Only Herbert and Garnier had not yet condescended to salute the damsels—they were standing apart, talking with Haguenier's sons.

"Really," said Mahaut in a loud voice, "I have a most courteous brother— it is easy to guess that he will be knighted at Easter. See how polite he is to ladies!"

Herbert did not even deign to look at her, and Garnier turned and said: "She thinks I can't see through her game. What a way to ask for a kiss!"

Mahaut haughtily raised her chin. "The impudence! I never said a word about him! God be praised, he is no brother of mine—I should be ashamed to be sister to such a boor."

"But you would go to bed with a boor if you could have your way," Garnier shot at her. "It is a great pity Aioul has to sit in the back row—he couldn't watch you rolling your eyes like a fish out of water." (Garnier always became very loquacious when it was a matter of insulting Mahaut.)

"Listen to him," she said, and laughed scornfully. "As if I couldn't see him scratching his back all through the service!"

"She must have seen it with her left eye," Garnier chuckled. "Get along with you, Squint-eyes!"

Mahaut blushed, bit her lips, and hurried to kiss Bertrade, who was just coming out. Garnier started for the horses. But, happening to turn his head, he had a momentary glimpse of a pale face, white under the dark hood, of a little, hard, tight-lipped mouth, and a trembling, tearful light in a pair of beautiful squinting eyes. The next moment Mahaut was laughing at the top of her voice, and Garnier took Andrew's horse by the bit instead of the baron's.

Night-ride through the forest—the torches smoking and flaming—trees looming out of the darkness, bursting into yellows and reds. The play of light and shadow on the branches overhead, the narrow road, the riders in single file.

Riding one horse, Mahaut and Milicent laughed together, delighted with themselves, with the cold, the darkness, the joyous banquet awaiting them. When the first riders swept down on the meadow before the castle the snow was beginning to fall in thick flakes—torches crackled, the boys clapped their hands at the thought of the next morning's hunting.

When the girls entered the courtyard together everything was white—the stable roofs, the ground, their furred or woolen capes, the horses' manes. The castle door stood open, letting a wide streak of light fall on the trodden snow. The baron and his cousins had already gone upstairs, their squires were leading their horses to the stables. Mahaut was looking absently at the little clouds of pink vapor issuing from her horse's nostrils when she felt a hand laid on her foot. A low, half-stifled voice, rising from the level of her knee, made her start: "Mahaut, I ask your pardon."

She bent her head and saw a pale, square face, with black blurs in place of eyes.

"Is it you, fair cousin? What ails you?"

"Forgive me. For just now. I was stupid."

"I quite agree," said Mahaut haughtily. "And I do not mean to forgive you. Let go of my foot."

"It is a sin to refuse forgiveness on Christmas Eve. My last Christmas in Champagne, Mahaut."

"Well then," she said hesitantly, "for Christmas' sake I forgive you. But you will do it again."

"I promise not. Mahaut, may I kiss your foot to prove that I am speaking the truth?"

With a regal gesture, Mahaut drew up the hem of her long dress, revealing a slim ankle clothed in a woolen stocking and a small foot shod in red leather. Garnier touched the shoe with his lips.

The great table was decked with a white cloth, the candles were lit in the great copper candlesticks; on the hearth huge logs crackled and snapped, sending up tall flames which bathed the tablecloth in a reddish, flickering light. The joy of Christmas shone in the children's eyes, in the ladies' smiles, and burst into fullest flower in the baron's broad face as, sitting in the place of honor beside his lady, he ceremoniously began to carve a fat young wild boar roasted to a turn and decked with holly.

He was an ideal master of the house on days of festivity—his gaiety was contagious and communicated its warmth, like a good fire of an evening in a room well stopped against drafts.

In a veil embroidered with crosses in red and blue, Lady Alis looked a little pale and kept blinking her eyes, yet her face wore a rare expression of gentle serenity.

The baron was thinking that no one had a finer family than himself. There at his left sat his cousin Girard, a knight, with Richeut, his wife. There at Lady Alis' right sat Andrew, also a knight; next sat the knights of the coming year—blond Herbert, with his wife Bertrade who was nursing her baby daughter, and Garnier, tall and mannerly in his blue woolen tunic. Farther down sat Claude, widow of Bernier of Beaumont; then Garin, brother of Girard the Young, with his wife; then the girls—Mahaut, an ivory trinket set with two beads of jade, her coppery red hair falling over her shoulders in close waves, and Milicent, all brightness, with her pale blond hair and her white-and-yellow dress; and Aelis, Richeut's daughter, whose cheeks and dress were of the same rosy pink.

The hall was filled with tables and benches at which the varlets, soldiers, and vassals were eating with their families.

Pomp and simplicity were never far apart at these Christmas Eve banquets where the dishes were more plentiful than subtle, and the varlets kept setting yet another roast on the table—boar, hart, mutton, venison, fowl, dressed with mustard and spices. The pleasures of the table were pleasures in which all, young and old, shared with equal gusto and equal lack of restraint—fingers were licked, girdles loosened, the cup passed from hand to hand, filled with old red wine from the vineyards of Burgundy and Champagne. This time the feast had an uncommon element of solemnity, for the castle was to send forth its men in three or four months—and who knew how many of them would ever return?

Girard, the baron's third son, now twelve years of age, was still living at Linnières because Lady Alis considered him too delicate to go into service. Milon taught him whatever could be learned at the castle, and he served as page to his father and uncles. Milicent and he were great friends. They were the same age and the same height, but Girard was stronger and darker-haired. Active by nature, he was always glad to run and fill the wine cup, and perhaps pinch some red-cheeked girl on the way, or pull the ears of a dog which had slunk up for a bone.

As he passed her, Milicent tugged at his coat. "Girard, see that I get something to drink—it's so good."

Girard said: "Come to the cask and help me draw."

Taking advantage of the confusion, the two children cautiously made their way to the tun of Burgundy around which the other squires were elbowing for places.

"God! My head is whirling—Girard, I feel so light, I shall fly away. Girard, Girard!"

"What is it? Quick—the baron is calling me."

"Girard, my fair Girard, let me carry that one cup!"

Girard laughed and Milicent threw back her hair with an air of decision: "I shall carry it—so there! Give it to me or I'll upset it."

Laughing, and trembling for fear that their laughing would spill the wine, the two children made their way to the baron's seat. The baron was talking to Andrew across Lady Alis' back.

"Here, I want to give it to him."

"No, he'll be angry."

"Let me!"

Trembling, Milicent knelt and offered the baron the cup, and the baron turned, surprised to see something like a blur of light where he had expected to find Girard's brown coat.

"What?" he exclaimed with a laugh, "does my daughter-in-law want to be my cup bearer tonight?" He took the cup, and Milicent, embarrassed because people were looking at her, hid her face with the skirt of her dress. Behind her, Girard was choking with laughter.

"Youth!" said the baron, "always laughing! My fair daughter, I drink to your loves. There!" He kissed her on the lips and handed her the empty cup. Swift as a kid she sprang up and fled to the other end of the hall. Girard followed her.

"Whew!" She dropped into the straw, between the tun and the hearth. Her heart was beating wildly. "Oh, Girard, fair cousin, why was I not born a boy? How I would have loved . . . I love all the things boys do. Tell me, do you think the baron would take me to the Holy Land if I were a boy?"

"You are too young," said Girard, considering.

"But next year will be my first-communion year. Some who will go are younger than I." She stretched out on her back. Damped by the fumes of the wine she had drunk, the noise in the hall came to her ears as music—oboes, trumpets, hunting horns. . . . Looking up into the dark vaulted ceiling, Milicent tried to realize that now the room was upside down—the floor was hollow and dark, it would swallow you if you tried to walk on it, on the ceiling there were tables, candles, people hanging head down and never falling. . . .

Yet it would be so perfectly easy and simple—all she need do was to become a boy—cut her hair, stain her face, put on breeches instead of a skirt. . . . Ah, to serve him at table, in his bed, in battle, to be with him everywhere and always—she so humble, he so great—to follow him even to the Holy Land—even to death. . . .

The girls huddled together in their cold bed—they had lain down to take a little rest before early-morning Mass.

"Milicent. Millie, tell me something. You are in love with the baron. I saw it."

Milicent blazed out: "No! It's not true."

"I saw how you looked at him."

Milicent shook her by the shoulders. "I tell you it isn't true!"

"Silly! As if I would betray you! I am your friend. Tell me the truth—you love him?"

Milicent did not answer, she merely sniffled softly. Mahaut stroked her hair.

"There is nothing wrong in it," she said. "The baron is a good knight—

it is not as if he were a coward or a villein. However, you must face it—he will never love you, because you are Ansiet's wife."

"I know," she murmured.

"I couldn't love a man who would never love me," said Mahaut thoughtfully. "Never! I would rather die. Tell me, how do you love him?"

"How?" said Milicent, lifting herself on her elbows. "I will tell you. You know there are workmen building a new tower on the cathedral—on St. Peter's Church, I mean—it's so tall that you can't see the top of it when you look up. Well, I dreamed—I thought he was carrying me up and up the wooden scaffold, and I clung to him—like that—to keep from falling. And when we came to the top I looked down, and down there it was all full of devils, with horns and pitchforks, and God! how ugly they were. And he said to me, 'Millie, I love you,' and then he threw me down onto the pitchforks—and I was happy, oh, so happy, Mahaut darling. You know—I wish it would happen to me really and truly."

Mahaut said: "You are a fool. You want the silliest things. It would make more sense if you said you'd like to sleep in his bed."

Milicent shook her head: "He would never let me—not he. He would kill me if he knew. . . . Oh! yes he would!"

"Bah!" Mahaut sighed. "With men, you can never tell. . . ."

Lying on her back with her hands under her head, Milicent stared into the darkness with wide-open eyes, too lost in her dream to speak.

"You will never, never tell anybody?" she said at last.

"I? Of course not. I swear it by my christening cross, by the Holy Virgin, by St. Anne-in-the-Forest—what else would you like me to swear by? Millie, listen. I am going to tell you something—so you will know that you are not the only one. Wake up, Millie, are you listening? Millie, I am in love. And I think it is real love. . . ."

Her voice became soft—astonished and happy.

"Who with?" the child asked placidly. "Aioul?"

"No, stupid! Can't you guess? With somebody worth bothering over. With the pride of our castle, with somebody who is going to be a knight this Easter. . . ."

"Garnier?"

"Who else could it be? Tell me I am right—he *is* worth loving, isn't he?"

Milicent said that she could not possibly love a man who lowered himself so far as to kiss a woman's foot.

Mahaut interrupted her. "Stupid! You don't understand. If it had been any other woman, he would sooner have let himself be roasted alive. He did it because he loves me." And she laughed tenderly and happily.

Now it was Milicent's turn to be sensible. "The baron will never give you to him, you are cousins."

"We'll see." Mahaut preferred not to look so far ahead. "In any case he is going away. And then—tell me—mightn't he fight so well against the infidels that the Pope would grant him a dispensation to marry me?

If he wants me he must win me—mustn't he? What do you think?"

"Oh," said Milicent, delighted, "what a fine idea! Tell him about it!"

Mahaut said: "Listen. You can do me a favor. Tomorrow after Mass we will go out into the meadow to look at the new snow, you and Girard and I. Suppose you ask Garnier to come with us. . . . Tell him I'll be there—but don't tell him that I am the one who wants him to come!"

The four drew rein a few paces from the brook and Girard dismounted and began tying the horses. The immaculate white of the meadow was broken only by the hoofprints and yellow stains of dung left by their own animals—the castle palisade, the keep, the roofs of the village with their smoking chimneys had become one with the forest and the meadow—white and still. Through the windless air they could hear the bells of Hervi ringing for terce.

Soft and clinging, the snow mantled every tree branch and even the fine spray of bushes. Milicent and Girard fell to rolling a snowball, and Mahaut went to the brook and began running over the ice, firm under its thin covering of snow. From either bank leaned willows and hazels as white as cherry trees in full flower; they met above her head, their black trunks rising from a thick blanket of snow as level as a board.

Mahaut slid on the ice, caught at the willow branches and amused herself by shaking them and bringing flurries of wet snow down on her head and shoulders. In her dark fox-lined cape and her marten cap, her cheeks rosy with the cold, her feet agile and light, she knew that she looked prettier than ever and felt so happy that she wanted to shout. She laughed and laughed, and for the first time in her life her laughter was clear and musical. She took such pleasure in hearing it that she made herself keep on laughing.

"Garnier, come here! Garnier! What a wonderful day! How happy I am! How good it is to be alive!"

Garnier slid over the ice after her, caught up with her and took her in his arms. For a few moments they slid together, tugging at branches to powder themselves with snow. Then, where the brook turned, Mahaut flung her arms around the trunk of an old willow and stopped to regain her breath. Red from exertion, Garnier bent over her—his heart was softened, he felt like a boy again. He smiled.

"You aren't angry with me any longer, Mahaut?"

Mahaut put her two hands against his chest and Garnier covered them with his own. Mahaut said: "Do you love me?"

Then Garnier kissed her on the lips and Mahaut put her arms around his neck and began kissing him quickly, like a child trying to stuff down all the cherries it can before it is caught.

In the distance Milicent's clear voice sang:

> *Let him who loves a maid*
> *And wins her love,*
> *Keep faith . . .*

"Oh, God!" said Mahaut. "You knew that I loved you?"

"And you?" Garnier asked.

She looked at him in ecstasy.

Garnier said: "I have always loved you." Never had he thought her ugly, he went on, it had made him furious that the other boys could always be talking to her, while he had to travel with the baron all the time. . . .

"But then why were you so nasty to me?"

"You know very well why," said Garnier gravely.

"No, I don't."

"Because I cannot marry you."

Mahaut pouted. "How little you know about love!" she said with a trace of disdain. "If I were a man, a thing like that would not stop me."

"You do not know what you are saying," he answered.

Instantly Mahaut flung away from him. "You talk to me as if I were a child. But I am fourteen. I know very well what I am saying. You do not love me enough, that's all."

Garnier stroked her hands. His face was grave and sad. "Mahaut, my fair love, you know very well that the baron will give you to some knight of his acquaintance. And they say that a woman cannot help it, she falls in love with the man who takes her to his bed. You will soon forget me and love your husband."

"On the contrary!" said Mahaut, laughing. "I'll be unfaithful to him."

Garnier drew himself up. "If you are, it will not be with me!"

"Now you are being nasty again. But Garnier, love, there is nothing else we can do—when people love each other loyally, it is no sin—do you want me to swear that I will never take another lover but you?"

Garnier said that he knew only one thing—he would never disgrace his uncle.

"And I, Garnier? Is it nothing to you that I love you? Garnier! Kiss me again. You know, you are the first boy who has ever kissed me."

At this Garnier looked very touched and blushed furiously. "Is that true? What about Aioul?" he said. "Didn't he ever . . . ?"

"Not even the tips of my fingers."

"Truly? Tell me, is it really true? Oh, my beautiful, oh, my dear!" He held her against the willow and covered her cheeks and lips with kisses. It was not long before he lost his head and began talking wildly.

The girl looked straight into his eyes. She seemed astonished, but her own eyes did not waver. "You mean you want me to give myself to you?" she asked softly.

"You are killing me, Mahaut."

"But I will, Garnier. I love you. I will do whatever you want, we have only three months before us."

Garnier spoke very fast, his voice was a little hoarse: "Come to my pallet tonight, to the left of the baron's bed. I will arrange to be alone."

Though Mahaut had expected this, it frightened her. She put her fingers over her eyes. "Oh, I'd be afraid to," she said. "But it will be good, won't it, Garnier! You will be my lord. Will you be good to me?"

Garnier crushed her arms and shoulders in his broad sinewy hands.

Sliding on the ice where the others had uncovered it, Girard and Milicent made their way down the brook. Little did they care for the impeccable beauty which lay all about them—their one thought was to leave their mark on as much fresh snow as possible; they rolled on the banks and threw snowballs at each other until their fur cloaks looked as if they had been dipped in flour. Far away they could hear the barking of hounds closing in on a wolf. Milicent had taken off her cap, her hair was powdered with snow. She began singing her ballad again at the top of her voice and Girard joined in the refrain:

> *Let him who loves a maid*
> *And wins her love,*
> *Keep faith . . .*

Then they saw the pair of lovers. Milicent caught Girard's hand and pulled him into the shrubbery, shaking off the snow which fell from the laden branches as they passed.

"Well!" said Girard, gasping with laughter, "well, well! . . ."

"We mustn't tell a soul," said Milicent. "If Lady Alis hears of it, Mahaut will get a good beating."

"Well!" said Girard, regaining his breath after his fit of laughter. "They certainly seem to be enjoying themselves. Shall we try it too?"

Milicent pushed him away. "No," she said thoughtfully. "It is not a game."

Mahaut and Garnier rode back to the castle side by side, wordless and grave. Mahaut seemed filled with a tranquil wonder, Garnier looked unhappy. When he helped her to dismount he squeezed her waist, then pinched her arm so hard that she cried out. "Ouch! What's the matter with you, Garnier?"

He said: "Let me be!" and fled to the stables.

The very same day he asked the baron for permission to visit his mother in Chaource for some days. He set out immediately after the after-dinner nap, but there was reason to think that he found it hard to leave, because he asked Herbert to go with him to keep himself from turning back. Though Herbert was suffering from violent indigestion after the Christmas Eve feast, he agreed to make the journey since his sister's virtue was at stake. It was not until evening that Mahaut learned they were gone.

In Milicent's arms that night she wailed over the cruel lover who had disdained her. "Since he loves my father better than he loves me," she said, "I am not going to love him either. I will love somebody else—I'll love Aioul. Garnier was always a boor. I loathe him.

"That will teach me to listen to boys! And suppose he goes around saying that I am an easy girl and laughing at me? Do you think he will?" and she sobbed with shame and indignation. "Perhaps, after all, I ought to avenge myself. He has insulted me, hasn't he? Do you think I should?"

"Of course you should," said Milicent with conviction. "He has treated you very badly."

But Mahaut felt more tenderly toward Garnier than she was willing to admit, and she soon gave up her idea of vengeance.

Mahaut's troubles were not yet over. Herbert, who never got anything straight, took it upon himself to tell Lady Alis that Mahaut had made advances to Garnier which had forced him to leave the castle. He did not mean any harm; he saw himself as an elder brother guarding his sister's honor—though that had not prevented him from consoling Garnier by saying: "Never mind, you can make up for it after she marries."

Lady Alis was quick to accuse Garnier—the older, the grown man. She forced Mahaut to confess her brief adventure and boxed her ears a few times for form's sake. But she knew that Mahaut was one of those girls whom danger and punishments make only the more daring. She knew that a day would come when some cousin's kisses would turn her daughter's head—indeed, for three years she had been living in fear of that day. She talked to her at great length about shame and dishonor, but the words had no meaning for Mahaut—she had heard them too often. And Lady Alis was humiliated by the thought that, at fourteen and a half, Mahaut, who should by rights be receiving offers of marriage from the pick of the countryside, was left without a dowry and without a suitor. And bitterly did she reproach the baron—a father who calmly planned the downfall of his daughter!

Ever since the baron had settled down to staying at the castle husband and wife quarrelled almost constantly, first on the subject of their daughters, then because of William. William slept in the same cradle with the twins and little Mary. The twins, big boys of five, were always unintentionally shoving and jostling their elder brother who lay as motionless as a log; and Lady Alis cuffed them soundly, saying that they mistreated the unfortunate child. The baron did not like to see small children hit about the head and he said: "You want to make the two of them as helpless as their brother—I can see that you do not love them." In this he was right, for the twins had come into the world during the time when Lady Alis was entirely preoccupied by William—besides which, bearing twins was something abnormal and slightly ridiculous; she had been ready to love a single child; when she found herself confronted with two, she did not know which to love best and quickly lost her fondness for both—it was William who needed her.

Despite his thin limbs and chunky body, William was physically a fairly well-developed child. He had never learned to walk and he had a big head, but the latter defect was less visible now that his hair had grown long. Sitting in his cradle all day and hardly making a sound, he gave little trouble to anyone. But the baron could never see him without feeling a sort of horror and disgust, and hearing the child's inarticulate mouthings gave him goose-flesh. He was ashamed to be the father of a monster. And the most trying thing was that William looked much like him, whereas of his other children only Mahaut took after him at all. The strange little creature was now six.

"Lady, I have been more than patient with you, but friends or strangers may come here to visit me and I do not want it known that I have such a son. It is high time he was taken to a monastery—if you wish, I will pay to have him well treated."

Lady Alis would not hear of it—monks were all hypocrites, they would take the money and let the child die by inches; besides, he harmed nothing and no one by being at the castle.

"On the contrary," said the baron, "he makes me want to vomit."

The same scene took place every morning: Lady Alis got up, took William out of bed, washed him and dressed him, set him on her lap and spent a long time happily combing his long chestnut hair and arranging it in round curls. She talked to him incessantly, as one talks to an infant: "What a naughty boy he is this morning, he won't turn his head, poor mother can't clean his ears. How handsome My Lord William will look today—mother is going to put on his pretty red shift; and then he'll eat some nice cheese and some lovely soft bread, and drink a big bowl of nice white milk; and then mother will put him by the fire so his pretty little hands won't get cold—why, they're covered with chilblains!" And when she kissed that expressionless mouth and those vacantly staring eyes the baron had a feeling of acute discomfort, as if he saw her caressing a corpse or an animal. He believed that she did it on purpose to vex him, out of feminine obstinacy. As he grew older, he had come to hold a rather poor opinion of women in general, and Lady Alis could hardly be exempt from the faults of her sex.

On the eve of a leave-taking which might well be his last, Ansiau became aware that his family life was not as happy as he had supposed. It was pleasanter to spend a week at the castle between two tournaments than to stay on there from All-Hallows to Easter. He went hunting, spent a night at Seuroi with Andrew and Herbert, or paid a visit to Haguenier, whose sons had taken the cross. At these places he felt at home. At Linnières he was so hounded by problems and duties that he did not know which way to turn. He had always thought of himself as a good father; now he saw that he had mortgaged his entire estate to set up his two eldest boys and Garnier, and that Girard and the twins were still on his hands, to say nothing of the girls—Mahaut, the redhead, the beauty; blond Alette; and little Mary. He knew that there had been something between Mahaut and Garnier—all Linnières knew it—the girl was now very strictly watched and Garnier was living at Chaource with his mother. Until now Ansiau had always been proud of his eldest daughter because she was beautiful and because through her he expected to gain a rich and noble son-in-law. And here suddenly she had become only one more burden—he had thought her too young to be dreaming of a husband, he was in no position to give her a dowry, she would soon be fifteen, and after he had gone God knew when and how she would be able to marry. And, without intending it, he became harsh to Mahaut; when the hunters came back to the castle she called to them in her abrupt, noisy way to show her the day's trophies, and her father said: "It is unbecoming for a girl to shout as you do. You'll see—nobody will ever want to marry you."

Mahaut was unimpressed; she felt sure that there was not a count or prince on earth who would not be most glad to marry her (only one had no use for her, and compared with him all the rest were varlets).

Lady Alis always stood up for her daughter. The baron, she said, had eyes for no one but Milicent; it was sinful to prefer the child of another to one's own blood—could he not see that Mahaut was worth ten of Milicent, that she was prettier and cleverer and more skillful at every kind of work? He hoped to have grandchildren by Milicent, but after all she had given him none yet; the child had still to prove herself, she lost her breath every time she climbed a ladder, she was growing too fast and coughed all winter—and Lady Alis was wondering what kind of children she would bear!

The baron sighed, for his daughter-in-law was really not very strong. He tried to reassure himself: "She is still growing." He loved the child—his heart felt at rest when he looked at her—she was gentle, he thought, a girl who would love her husband as if he were God. Her whole life lay plain and clear before her—he need not give it another thought. No, he would never have to worry about her as he was worrying about Mahaut.

At twenty-five he had left his lady and his lands with neither sorrow nor regret, joyous at the thought of serving God, eager to see new countries. In those new countries he had lost friends and kinsmen and—he could not but admit it—the love of his lady. Now, at thirty-five, he found himself on the eve of another departure, and he asked himself if he was not about to lose the little he had left, the share of happiness which he could really call his own: Alis, who would not be young much longer, and the child in her womb, whom he might never see. His sons would soon be knights, they would have their own families, their own lives—Herbert already had a baby daughter and did not seem to know that he was a father. But he, Ansiau, set great store by the little lives which Lady Alis brought into the world each year, the unfailing signs of his power over her. Formerly he had looked upon his children as his line, his heirs, the future house of Linnières. Now he had more heirs than he needed, and the babies yet to come were Lady Alis' children, children of love—he had no future, no place prepared for them, and he loved them without thought of return, as one loves useless things.

Toward the end of Lent Lady Alis had become noticeably big-bellied and was much preoccupied by thoughts of her coming child. The baron laughed at her and found it touching that she should be as emotional as a young woman. Soon he must part from her, and he had never known her to be so gentle. Left alone to manage the estates, she would do it well—since the Crusade under the old Count Henry she knew more about it than he did himself, she was made of good stuff. Nevertheless she was thirty-two and Milon of Le Cagne was never far away. Ansiau could not be jealous of a varlet; but there was an unspoken hostility between the two men—Milon was always looking meaningfully and falling into silences and dropping his eyes and making it clear that if he obeyed the baron it was in order to please his lady; he was getting tired of conditioning God knew how many horses each year for the baron's tournaments, he complained of the waste of oats, and suffered to see Lady Alis at her wits' end to meet due dates; and Lady Alis insisted on keeping Milon to serve her. "In any case," said Ansiau, "if I do not come home, in God's name do not marry Milon—the children would be ashamed for you." Lady Alis replied that she would just as lief marry her watchdog.

The day of departure neared. About the fifth week in Lent the baron summoned Garnier to Linnières and asked him to go to Troyes and fetch Ansiet—the boy must come to the castle to receive his mother's blessing, Lady Alis being in no fit state to make a journey. A week later Garnier returned alone—Ansiet had refused to come. He was too busy getting ready to be dubbed, he was spending all his time practicing with bow and lance, and in any case Manesier needed him. He sent his mother his cross and an undershirt so that she might bless them in his stead—he would always wear them. He sent his best wishes to Lady Alis, to Milicent, to Mahaut, and to Haumette, his nurse.

Ansiau regarded his refusal as the height of insolence and for the first time in his life he was angry with his eldest son. But he planned to leave the castle himself before Easter and did not have time to go after the boy. And Lady Alis wept. Her big boy, her first-born, the son she had not seen for three years—how he must have grown, his shirt was as big as Andrew's!— her first-born refused her the joy of kissing him for the last time, and who knew how long he would be in the Holy Land?

It was her own fault—she had not been able to suckle him herself, she had not been able to make him fond of her, she had borne too many other children—but he, her very first, the child she had borne before she even had breasts, before she had finished growing . . . her tears dropped on his big, white, carefully ironed shirt, and she sent it to Flora—Flora must enchant it so that he who wore it would be safe from sicknesses and arrows. During the last few months Lady Alis had spent the income from her fields for three months on amulets and charms—the baron must be protected, and Herbert, and Andrew, and Garnier, too, even though Garnier had made a fool of himself by trying to seduce Mahaut.

The day of departure neared, and with growing anxiety Lady Alis watched the preparations, saw the fever which laid hold on every man in the castle, one after the other. Sergeants from Chaource came to Linnières to put themselves in the baron's service; Aioul, son of Frahier the Short, wanted to go too, and the baron accepted him as a squire. The three boys were to be knighted on the Sunday after Easter, and the next day the army would set out. Garnier and Herbert thought only of their dubbing and spent their days on horseback in the courtyard, charging and turning, lance in hand. And Lady Alis, in the midst of her daily cares, began to feel a great, a heavy grief—grief because once again she must live without a man, once again be alone in her joys and her sorrows—and God knew that, for all his perpetual absences, her husband was a husband after all, and a good husband—the most trustworthy friend she had ever had. And even for the child she was soon to bear—the child of another man—she felt that she would miss Ansiau's tenderness and joy. Yet she knew that it was wrong to let her husband love another man's child—when the baron came back, she must find a means of keeping them apart. But now he was soon to go, and of an evening he would say: "Take good care of the child, lady." He hardly ever said anything else on the subject, but that one admonition he repeated often enough, too often indeed. One day, however, he added: "If it is a boy, name him Hélie." "Hélie? Why Hélie?" "I don't know. It is a fine name." Little by little Lady Alis herself began thinking of her future child as Hélie.

The day of farewells approached and everyone feared it. Two-thirds of the men of the castle were to leave, and nearly all the women went about with red eyes and hastily mended their men's travelling clothes and linen and tags and belts. The younger girls, left to themselves, took advantage of the confusion to neglect their work somewhat and wander about the hall and the courtyard.

Mahaut and Milicent, inseparable as always, took part in all the preparations; they chattered with everyone and asked the most amazing questions about the Holy Land and Saladin and King Philip. Mahaut in particular took great interest in the Crusade and repeated with complete conviction the phrases she had heard used by her father or Andrew; and the young men listened to her openmouthed in admiration. She had ceased to speak to Garnier, and he pretended not to see her—they both knew that the first word that passed between them would plunge them into a quarrel. And Mahaut, to salve her pride, put herself out to be friendly to Aioul.

Aioul lost his head completely and swore to her that he had taken the cross only to please her. "You shall see," he said. "I will fight so well that everybody will talk about me. I shall come back a knight."

Mahaut shrieked with laughter. "My boy, if you bring me back Saladin's own helmet and sword, I will marry you."

Aioul tossed his long dark curls defiantly.

"And I shall do it, lady."

"Poor Saladin," said Mahaut, laughing even harder. "I fear he hasn't long to live."

On the eve of the day when the knights were to take their departure—it was a mild, warm March day—Mahaut and Milicent were walking in the courtyard, which was full of puddles after the recent rains. Garnier, seeing them hesitate before a veritable pond, asked them if they wanted to go to the stables.

"Yes," said Milicent, "but we don't dare pull up our skirts so high and the water here is really deep."

"I'll carry you over," said Garnier, and he took Milicent and set her down on the farther side, then did the same for Mahaut.

"Fair cousin," said she, "you have not always been so kind to me."

"Fair cousin, you very well know why."

"Fair cousin, now I know it—you love my father and my brothers and your knighthood, and you care no more for me than for a worn-out glove."

"Fair cousin, I never wept or stayed awake night after night for an old worn-out glove."

"Garnier, you hurt me very much. See how thin and pale I have grown."

"No one would notice it," said Garnier. "Forget all this. I shall stay in Palestine with my father."

"I will not forget it," said Mahaut. "But you shall never have me."

"Do you think I want you?"

Roughly Mahaut freed herself from the arms which were still about her and fled as fast as she could run. Garnier looked after her for a moment, seemed to hesitate, then began to run in the direction she had taken—she had disappeared behind the hay barn.

Milicent went on to the stables and found herself face to face with the baron, who was on his way back to the keep.

"Well, daughter-in-law," he said, "out walking alone? Where is Mahaut?"

"My lord," said Milicent, "I wish to speak to you," and she climbed nimbly onto a great oak log which the grooms used for a bench. She was panting so hard that her voice was almost stifled. "I have something to give you," she said.

"My poor child," said the baron, "you are worn out, you have been running."

Milicent quickly unfastened the neck of her dress and drew out a little plaque of enameled silver which hung on the chain with her cross. She looked very grave. She detached the silver plaque, gave it a long look, then handed it to the baron, who seemed rather surprised. Her perch was so high that their heads almost touched.

"It is a beautiful thing," said the baron. "Syrian work."

"Put it with your medals," said the girl. "Around your neck."

"A good idea," said the baron, "otherwise I should lose it. I will give it to Ansiet as soon as I see him."

Milicent blushed painfully, opened her mouth to speak, hesitated, then brought out: "No."

"No?"

"It is for you."

She spoke so softly that he could barely hear her. He looked at her slender white throat, her loosened collar. The blood rushed to his head. He picked her up like a baby and began showering kisses on her throat, her collarbones, her thin, half-bare shoulder. At that moment he heard Thierri calling him; he set her roughly on the ground, turned on his heel, and left the stable.

"He kissed me here—and here—and here too." Milicent had taken Mahaut's hand, and at every "here," she touched it to a different place. They had long since blown out the candle. "It's strange—it is much better than on the lips."

"On the lips is better, anybody will tell you so," Mahaut retorted.

"Oh, no! Everybody kisses you on the lips, and when it is over there is nothing left. Tell me—do you think he could love me?"

"You are mad—he is too old."

Mahaut was in no mood to talk that night. She had cried so much that her eyes hurt. While Garnier was looking for her and calling to her through all the barns, she had crouched in the hay, biting her fists to keep from sobbing. She had been so angry with him that her only thought had been vengeance. And now she was thinking that tonight was the last that Garnier would ever spend in the castle, and they would never see each other again. Never. She was sure that she could never love another man.

The next was the great day of farewell.

Everything was ready—horses, arms, and baggage. They heard Mass. All those who were to leave communicated. That day was only the first stage, but it was the most painful. The red cross was on every garment, and the men looked as though they were wearing a uniform, like monks or archers.

The sobbing of the women was so loud that the trumpets and the whinnying were lost in it. Bertrade, Herbert's young wife, had fainted—the waiting-women seated her on the well-coping and bustled around her. Herbert did not even look at her; he was talking with Andrew.

The baron had laid both hands on Lady Alis' shoulders and was looking into her eyes without a word or a tear. He could not tell her how great was his sacrifice.

His wife before the priest, she who had plighted him her troth, the rightful share God had granted him in the joys of this life—and now God was taking her from him. Now he was leaving her alone with a child to bear and the castle to maintain; now he was making her unhappy, making her weep, when she had deserved so much better. All he had been able to do was to ruin her and forsake her; and never in any way could he make up for the wrong he had done her, or even repent of it, because he had done it for God. He knelt before her and said: "Lady, forgive."

Almost frightened out of her wits by behavior so unusual, Alis quickly said: "It is not for you to kneel." But Ansiau gave a great sob and buried his head against her swollen flanks. She stroked his hair and his shoulders with both her hands.

That year at Easter Troyes was so full of knights and men-at-arms that there was no more room in houses or inns, and the crusaders camped in the courtyards and outside the city. In haste to see his son, Ansiau stopped neither at the square nor the church but pressed straight on to Manesier's house. Garnier followed him, silent and thoughtful; his lips still bore the salt and bitter taste of Mahaut's farewell kiss, but he found some consolation in admiring his own conduct toward his young cousin. What other man in his place would have resisted as he had done?

Herbert and Andrew talked gaily as they rode—uncle and nephew had finally become good friends. Herbert was never so happy as when he was seeing knights and armor and weapons. As they rode through the square he amused himself by identifying pennons and escutcheons—he had an extraordinary memory and knew the arms of almost every knight in Champagne. He was glad to be back in Troyes after his two years' absence, and shouted greetings to the comrades whom he recognized in the crowd.

Ansiau had no sooner entered the courtyard of Manesier's house than he found himself face to face with his son, who was leading Gaillard out of the stable. The father gave a sudden start of surprise and delight—"the boy" was looking extremely well. Ansiau had never expected to find him in quite such fine feather; his upper lip bore a narrow blond mustache, the ends of his hair had been curled with tongs, he was wearing a freshly ironed tunic. He smiled. "Why! Good day, baron!"

"Haven't you a kiss for your father?"

Ansiet offered his lips, then straightened his collar and said rather self-consciously: "They are waiting for me at the castle."

"Then let them wait. Take Gaillard back to the stable."

The boy's face suddenly became gray and expressionless. He looked uneasily at the gate, at Gaillard, at the baron. Then, making up his mind, he said: "I am expected. I'll be back in an hour." And he jumped into the saddle and rode off without even looking back. The baron was astounded.

"What does this mean?" he asked Garnier.

Garnier shrugged his shoulders. "A woman, naturally."

The baron started. "A woman? What woman?"

Garnier said he knew nothing about it. From Manesier, however, the baron learned that since Christmas Ansiet had been infatuated with one of the Countess' ladies-in-waiting, the wife of a Gascon knight who had recently come to Troyes with the ambassador of King Richard of England. The lady's name was Oriana of Padillac; she was dark and no longer young, but was considered a beauty. The news annoyed Ansiau greatly. It was no time to be thinking of women! Really, this was the last straw: Herbert was frankly a profligate, Garnier had acted vilely toward Mahaut, and now his eldest son must follow their example! God knew why he had hoped that the boy would never succumb to love! "The blood of Puiseaux," he said to himself, remembering Baldwin's insane passion for his Irma. Like their uncle, Ansiet and Herbert must have a craving for dark, mature women. Oda, Irma, Oriana —one was as good as the other. "I'll soon set him right again," thought Ansiau. "He is too young to begin such tricks. I'll teach him to let other men's wives alone."

Ansiet did not come back in an hour, or in two. He came back very late at night, after everyone had gone to bed.

Ansiau thought that nothing would be easier than to make the boy listen to reason. He spoke to him gently—he had heard talk about a woman; well, this was hardly the moment to be thinking about women, you wasted your health and your nerves at it, and what you gained was no great matter.

"Remember," he said, "that you are to be knighted in ten days, you must keep fit."

The boy listened, staring at the floor. When his father had finished, he answered that he did not think that what he was doing was wrong, and that he felt perfectly fit.

"You are too young to judge of right and wrong," said the baron. "When I tell you something you must take my word for it. It is a waste of time to fall in love with a married woman. And even if she were to be widowed, you are married yourself and could never make her your wife."

Ansiet said that he had no such intention, since he would be in Champagne only a few more weeks.

Then his father set about proving to him that nothing was viler than lechery—lechery was something for priests and minstrels and effeminate men who passed their time perfuming themselves and sprawling on cushions. "How much time did you spend having your hair curled? Little or long, it was time wasted. A man has other things to do."

Ansiet studied his clean, square-cut fingernails; he showed no sign of being angry or annoyed; his smooth, well-scrubbed face wore the impassive expression of a man who listens to a stale sermon and is too polite to show that he is bored to death. Finally he said: "I must be at the cathedral for the service at sext."

"I too," said his father. "You shall go with me."

As they rode through the streets Ansiau's feeling of pained astonishment only increased. He studied that absent, almost nonexistent face, which neither the blond curls nor the clear complexion could make attractive. "He is a different boy!" he thought. "I ought to make that bitch pay for it."

At church neither father nor son had an opportunity to see the lady of Padillac; she was not at the service. Ansiet spent the entire time turning

around, shifting in his seat, craning his neck, and he left the cathedral looking like a man under sentence of death. When they had crossed the bridge
he reined in his horse and said that he must stop in at the castle.

"Nonsense," growled his father. "Manesier is waiting for us."

The boy caught his arm. "I must go to the castle," he repeated. "I'll be
back. I'll be right back."

The baron saw that they were blocking the street and gave in. "Very well,"
he said. "We will discuss it this evening."

He never learned the details of the adventure, for Ansiet himself remained
as dumb as a fish on the subject. Herbert said that the lady had promised
Ansiet a meeting and then kept putting it off for fear of a lover of hers, a
man of high rank who was insanely jealous. "A very beautiful woman," said
Herbert with relish. "Nice and fat in all the right places and with eyes like
two black plums stewed in honey—she has a pretty voice too—sounds like
a dove cooing—and she never swears. And very hot, apparently—always has
three or four lovers at the same time." As for the lover of high rank, even
Herbert did not know his name, as Ansiet had been a model of discretion
on the point.

Ansiau was of the opinion that a woman so fickle deserved no respect, but
the young men of Troyes thought differently. Ansiet, in any case, languished
and burned, neglected his duties, and came back from the castle each day
in a pitiable state—his father learned that he did not always manage to see
his lady even at a distance, and when he did see her she barely greeted him.

Ansiet blamed his lack of success on his enemies, on jealous gossip, on
his rivals—it was true that he had plenty of rivals—for he was convinced
that he was loved. Everywhere he saw plots against him, malicious attempts
to blacken him in his lady's eyes. He floundered in a net of intrigue and
suspicion and conjectures, each wilder than the last—one day he was sure
that his lady was testing him, the next that she was jealous, the next that
she feared for him; or a rival was threatening to kill her if she so much
as looked at Ansiau of Linnières, son of Ansiau; or she was ashamed to love
a man who was not yet a knight. And worst of all was the anguish of having
to leave Troyes before he had gained his promised recompense.

The baron talked to him of Milicent, of the Holy War, and the boy could
not understand why his father looked so far ahead—he, Ansiet, had no
future, he looked no farther than the day of departure, already so near. His
father's advice drove him to desperation by its banality—never anything but
platitudes—all fathers in all ages had always said exactly the same things
to their sons to prevent them from living as they chose.

But Ansiet was not the only one to be swept off his feet by the current.
A new frenzy for love had seized on most of the departing army, especially
the younger men. Affairs began and ended, brief and feverish, and the least
attractive ladies at the court had more suitors than they knew what to do

with. Every day marriages were celebrated in the churches of Troyes, in spite of the Easter season—there was no time to be lost, the days that remained were so pitifully few. . . .

That spring brought the first news of the siege of Acre—the first news of death and bereavement. Of the crusaders who had set off without waiting for the kings, many were already at rest in the cemetery of St. Nicholas, outside the beleaguered city. Erard of Brienne was dead, and many of his knights, and Andrew of Ramerupt, and many another less illustrious man of Champagne—so many martyrs in heaven, so many widows to find new husbands. The siege was by no means over—Saladin was to bring up fresh troops in the spring, and if the kings did not hasten, the besieging army would be crushed by sheer weight of numbers.

The kings were not yet ready, and the knights who had taken the cross began to ask themselves if they would ever be off. Many a jibing song was made on the subject of King Philip's procrastination—no doubt he wanted to give the emperor of Germany the honor of taking Jerusalem and planting his standard on Holy Sepulchre. The emperor had set out months ago and could not now be far from Syria.

Manesier's house had been transformed into a barracks; the noise and confusion were terrible. In the evening, hosts, guests, and friends who had taken the cross gathered there to listen to some traveller returned from the Holy Land or merely to some minstrel retelling scattered bits of news. Andrew of Linnières, who for two years had dreamed of nothing but the Holy War, was one of those who complained most bitterly over the slowness of the kings—he who complained so seldom had become sullen and irritable, and caustically criticized the demoralization current in France—no one there nowadays thought of anything but his purse and his comfort. And King Richard, he who had been duke of Poitiers, he of whom so much was expected, had turned out to be no better than the rest—he had been the first man in Christendom to take the cross, but he might have spared himself the trouble for now it seemed that he wanted to be the last to leave.

Ansiau, and Manesier too, did not like hearing hard words said of Richard, brother and friend of Countess Mary—if Richard seemed to be delaying, he had excuses enough. There was his father's heritage to be set in order; besides, he did not intend to equip his army without due consideration, he was not the Lionheart for nothing, he wanted his army equipped so that he could crush the Saracens at the first blow; he was said to be building immense machines, catapults, flame throwers, high enough to overlook the walls of any fortress in the world. He had sworn either to die in the Holy Land or to recapture Jerusalem. What was a disgrace in the king of France became a virtue in Richard—such was the power of a high-sounding nickname and the prestige of an arm which had not its equal in France.

On the second Sunday after Easter three hundred young men were initiated into knighthood at Troyes, at the count's castle. The three sons of Linnières were among them, and few were more joyous. After the trials and the great banquet at the count's table all returned to their lodgings through the torch-lit streets, singing and shouting "Noël" for Count Henry and the king of France. Once home, they lost themselves in contemplation of their new arms, their very own, part of themselves—consecrated, blessed, and delivered to them for the defense of God's own Holy Land. To them had fallen the honor of recapturing Jerusalem, it was their good fortune that the year of their knighting was a great year.

Ansiau was content to admire his three boys, his three knights—each so handsome, so broad-shouldered, so noble looking. He had forgotten his heart burnings, his disappointments; the three were as perfect as the angels in Paradise. Ansiet, the tallest, was smiling blissfully, Herbert held his head high with all the dignity of a bishop, Garnier looked fondly at his new sword.

Fair young oaks sprung from one root.
Fair lilies without stain sprung from one stem.
Fair, swift falcons flown from one mew, fair line of knights, men of Champagne, men of France, men of Christ.
Clear as silver, hard as iron, precious as pure gold: Ansiau, Garnier, Herbert.
Noble youths, consecrated to the noblest of wars. The war in God's defense.
The one true God, He Who has never lied.
And Who died on the Cross for our sins.
He Who prayed in the Garden of Olives.
Who was judged by the Jews and delivered unto death by Pontius Pilate.
And Who was crucified on Mount Golgotha.
Before Jerusalem.

In agreement with his uncles the kings, the count of Champagne had decided to set out in advance with the chivalry of Champagne. The kings would follow soon. So, toward the middle of May, the date of departure was finally set. And time passed more and more swiftly—everyone was weary of waiting. And under the strain of their waiting the army created a new life, a life without a tomorrow, a strange, idle life, pleasant enough in comparison with the hard life of a camp. And how many were they who felt that they would never see the Seine or Troyes again!

Ansiet took a boyish pride in at last appearing before his lady as a knight, wearing his new long tunic and white belt. His comrades, who were deeply interested in his love affair, soon had reason to believe that he had at last obtained the long-desired meeting. For, one evening, he came home with his belt on backwards, his eyes shooting flame, his nostrils quivering; momentarily he looked much older than he was, matured and hardened as by fire—

never had the baron seen him so haughty or so sure of himself. His joy was insolent and aggressive, the kind of joy which seeks out obstacles for the sheer delight of overcoming them.

But things very soon went wrong, as was to be expected, for Ansiet was not one to be satisfied with a single assignation, and the lady either could not or would not grant him another. For several days she did not appear at court, and her lover believed she was dead, murdered, ill, and almost died of anxiety himself. But when he saw her again he was little happier. Though he did not know precisely what was happening, Ansiau saw that the boy was suffering and he felt more pity than anger. "Don't fret," he said, "you will get over it. There are plenty of beautiful women in the world. At your age it doesn't take long to forget." And his son looked at him stonily, and wondered why people were always throwing his age in his face.

Came the day when they must pack, and it brought an unexpected gaiety with it. With the help of their squires, the three new knights boxed up their brand-new helmets, which glittered in the sun. The courtyard was noisy with hammers and the clash of arms. Manesier's sons were there, and several other young men of the castellany. Some sang in chorus, others struck their lances on their shields in time to the song, the youngest tried on their helmets and fought mock combats. Ansiau, Andrew, and Manesier stood in the middle of the courtyard watching them and making sure that everything was properly packed.

Sobered by the thought of departure, Ansiet worked as hard and cheerfully as the rest—he loved arms and knew how to treat them with due care, as if they were living beings. He was nailing up a chest and humming a song. His father walked over to him: "Fair son, remember to pack the shift that your mother blessed for you. You will need it in the Holy Land—no use wearing it out beforehand."

"Right," Ansiet said. "I will send my squire for it. Poor mother! To think that I may never see her again! Tell me—she wasn't too angry with me?"

The baron said: "She cried." Then he added: "By the way, I believe I have something else for you."

He took from his chain the enameled plaque which Milicent had given him—his conscience told him that he had no right to keep it.

Ansiet looked at it in some surprise. "Is it a talisman?" he asked.

"It is a present from Milicent," said his father.

Ansiet laughed and attached the plaque beside his cross. He considered it quite natural that a man setting off to war should have a sweetheart to think of him—after all, Milicent had a right to love him. A moment later he had forgotten all about his little wife.

THE GREAT ADVENTURE

W E BADE farewell to flourishing France, we entered Burgundy, and
passing the pride of the swift Rhone, the impetuosity of the difficult
Isère, the threats of the Durance, passing the desert mountains of
Burgundy, passing the stony defiles of Provence, we at last reached the city
of Marseille.

"There we found a harbor for ships: the rocks which surround it shelter
it from the wrath of the winds. Marseille owes its name to its site: *super
maris sita,* seated by the sea, or *maris situla,* bucket of water drawn from the
sea. One may read in books that it was built by the Phocaean Greeks. We
were kept at Marseille for many days, gathering weapons, supplies, and ships.
From the crest of the rocks we contemplated the uncertain face of the sea
and its motions, while we awaited a wind propitious to our sails. Finally the
sea became favorable to our vessels, there was as it were an accord between
winds and waves. We had difficulty in quitting the harbor, which is surrounded by reefs; but soon, driven on by the wind, we saw before us the
wrinkled face of broad, transparent ocean.

"When the third day dawned we saw our first island, lying to our left.
It was Corsica of the numberless rocks and angular promontories. The following morning we saw, lying even closer and also to the left, an island which
neighbors Corsica and which Sardus, son of Hercules, was the first, men
say, to inhabit—whence its name, Sardinia. From there we made our way
to Sicily, which is separated from the Calabrian mainland by a narrow arm
of the sea, difficult to navigate; on either side the reefs almost meet, between
them runs a fierce current strong as a raging stream and often upheaved by
storms. We found the island in great unrest and full of discord . . .

". . . Finally, on the thirty-fifth day after our departure from Marseille,
we saw afar off the long-desired promontories of Syria, that maritime
pentapolis long since the possession of the Philistines: Gaza, Gath, Azotus,
Accaron, and Ascalon. How many prayers had we not raised, how many tears
had we not shed, how many sighs had we not heaved in the hope that we
might see this day which now was dawning for us, and which, causing us
to shed tears of joy, showed us the land from which milk and honey flowed!
Heavenly land, worthy to be the dwelling place of those who dwell in
Heaven! Holy land promised to the saints, fount of our regeneration and
place of our redemption, mother of the Holy Fathers and nurse of the
Saviour!

"We dropped anchor not far from that famed Syrian city which the ancients called Acre and which was later named Ptolemais. Held by the enemy, it was already beleaguered by our land army and by our iron-crowned ships. Our helmets, drawn from the chests where they had so long lain captive, our swords, our bucklers flashed in the sun like the lightning that comes with thunder. The brightness of our arms, reflected by the waves, played, as it were, in the heart of the waters, the wind toyed with our silken sails."

Such is the account which Guy of Bazoches, who accompanied Count Henry, has left us concerning the voyage of the crusaders from Champagne. It was on July twenty-seventh that the fleet dropped anchor before Acre. The sun blazed down, and even after the army had landed that immense world of blue and gold still danced before their eyes, the ground seemed to rock under their feet. Thirty-five days at sea under the great sails, the creaking spars, the salt wind. Faces which had been white or pink at Troyes were now red or brown or black as the faces of the infidels themselves. With what astonishment did many a man touch that sacred ground with foot and hand, and find that it was real ground, gray and rock-strewn, bearing a sparse and sun-browned herbage and swelling into blue hills that stretched along the horizon.

Southward rose the city, a white fortress reaching out into the sea; farther southward and eastward, on the wooded hills, Saladin's camp lay outspread, tent after white tent, looking like a flock of wild geese at rest.

A crowd of soldiers and women and beggars lined the shore and welcomed the newcomers with shouts and tears of joy. The same frenzy marked the arrival of each new Christian band—so great was the people's distress, so strong their hope. The women rolled on the ground, sobbed, held up children naked and terrifyingly thin—in all the ragged, motley crowd there were few blond heads, and you would listen long before you heard a word of French.

King Guy himself had come down to the strand, with his queen and the count of Thuringia, to greet Count Henry of Champagne; followed by his uncles, the counts of Blois and Sancerre, Count Henry slowly made his way toward the camp, walking between the king and queen.

All day long squires and sergeants and sailors worked at unloading horses, munitions, sacks of wheat and quarters of salt meat, and bringing them safe to shore. The mob crowded around the military machines, children clung to the crusaders' garments and begged for bread, young women offered themselves with frozen smiles, their black eyes gleaming under their white or gray veils.

A turn in the road, and before them were the first Christian banners, the tops of the tents, then the tents themselves, red, white, of a single color or striped, and soon a whole city rose before them, multicolored, dazzling under the torrid sun, swarming with life—and high above it the king's great golden tent, pitched on the summit of a hill and facing the ramparts.

The men of Linnières felt rather lost in that sea of tents; they had never imagined that a camp could be so vast. Curiously they examined standards yet unknown and arms and garments such as they had never seen in Champagne. It was all strange to them, the heat was exhausting, their boxes were heavy, the ground was hard, the tent pegs would not hold. All together, masters and varlets, worked tirelessly to have a place to sleep that night.

It was about midday, the sun had turned toward his setting and hung over the sea and the walls of Acre. Then it was that they began to notice the smell. They had been unaware of it at first. It did not come from the latrines—heavy, sweetish, sickening, it was everywhere. It came from the direction of the city.

The three new-made knights mounted the rampart of hard yellow earth and studied the plain which lay between them and the Turkish camp. It was full of vultures with great wings and fleshy, featherless necks—sailing, circling, wheeling, dropping to the ground. Their hoarse discordant cries made a chorus most unpleasant to hear—at first the noise of the camp had smothered it, but now it became so importunate that it seemed the only sound in the world.

The plain was one vast charnel house, a single mass of corruption, crawling with flies and jackals and crows, and the vultures dove into the heap, making no distinction between carrion and living prey. Swollen and black, from a distance the corpses looked like a cloud of grasshoppers resting on the ground. There were corpses everywhere. There was no end to them—you could look neither to left nor right without seeing more and yet more. The stench which rose from them made breathing almost impossible. Here and there in the confusion of rotting bodies a leg or an arm seemed to move.

Herbert sank to his knees, then tumbled on the ground like a sack of flour.

His two friends tried to revive him, and the soldier who was keeping watch on the rampart came up and rubbed his face with wine from his gourd. Herbert opened his eyes, rolled over on his stomach, and vomited.

"They are infidels?" Garnier asked the soldier.

The man shrugged his shoulders. "Not one of them but bears the cross on his body."

Terrified, the two boys crossed themselves. Ansiet opened his eyes wide. "Our men! All ours!" It was as if he were under a spell, he could not turn away or look at anything else. "So many, so many!"

With tears in his eyes the soldier said that the finest sergeantry ever seen lay dead there because they had tried to force the Turkish camp. It was no longer ago than day before yesterday. And the king and the barons had let them be slaughtered to the last man and had never lifted a finger to help them— they had barred the entrances to the camp so that the poor wretches could not escape from the Turks. More than ten thousand of them lay dead there, and the barons were well satisfied, they had fewer mouths to feed, they had betrayed their sergeants on purpose. . . . One of his comrades hurried up to him, gesticulating—the man changed his tone, broke off complaining, and said that now that the counts of Champagne and Blois had arrived with such a store of munitions and food the siege was sure to advance more rapidly. Stupefied by the heat and the stench of the corpses, the three young knights listened gloomily—they could not understand it, the thing was too ugly, they wanted some explanation. They were ready to accept any that might be given. But the soldiers had nothing to tell except camp gossip—there was nothing to eat, the men were unhappy, the grain merchants sucked the blood of the poor and forced them to sell even their clothing. And if there was a consummate traitor in the camp, it was the marquess. He was worse than the Devil—he had sold himself to Saladin and had sworn to reduce the camp by starvation; he refused to bring food from Tyre, when he alone commanded the port and traffic along the coast. He it was who speculated on the price of wheat, and he was as rich in his own right as the emperor of Constantinople—his train when he passed through the camp on his way to the port was something to see. . . . Ansiet and Garnier shook their heads in sympathy, but they would have been very much surprised to learn that the object of these animadversions was none other than the marquess of Montferrat, who was so much admired in France.

The day was not over before Linnières lost its first man. It was Aioul, squire, and lover of Mahaut. Like most of the new arrivals, he had not known enough to beware of the sun and had worked all day pitching the tents and carrying boxes. About lauds he lay down on the ground and asked for water. His friend Guiot of Beaumont said: "I'll bring you some when I have time." Two hours later Aioul was still lying motionless on the ground. The baron called him, he did not raise his head; the baron took his hand, it was cold.

The three boys stood in the yet unfurnished tent and stared in astonishment at the humble comrade of whom they had so often made sport on the voyage. Before the regal gravity of that beautiful head with its brown curls, Garnier remembered that he had once been jealous of Aioul and wondered how he could ever have taken such childish nonsense seriously. Aioul had won—at a single throw and for all eternity. He had done better than to kill Saladin.

Despite their fatigue, the stench from the corpses, the flies, the heat made sleep impossible. The sky was still light and the camp more animated than ever, filled with songs and shouts and the clink of cups. No one seemed to remember the disaster of two days since—the count of Champagne, emissary of the kings, had arrived and would set everything to rights. Eager to admire and acclaim, the newcomers proceeded in a body to the Toron, the little hill on which King Guy's camp was pitched. The king and queen were entertaining Count Henry and his uncles in their tents that evening; varlets bearing torches lined the way like an animated hedge; from the brightly lit royal tents sounded the music of horns and hurdy-gurdies; amid the murmur of voices a woman's laughter sometimes rose, clear and light.

Where the sea lay, invisible but ever-present, stretched the black ramparts of the city; a few lights still flickered on the walls and about the castle.

That night Ansiau rested in his tent from the labors of the day. A few paces away lay the body of Aioul, with the boys watching beside it. Flies and mosquitoes, attracted by the candle, stung their hands and faces incessantly. Herbert's clear voice was saying the rosary; there were tears in his eyes. His father wondered how the boy, who had so little patience at best and who was half dead with fatigue, could yet find the heart to stand and pray over a mere varlet. The boys were still at the age when death strikes fear, they were thinking of the vultures and had not become used to the charnel-house odor which wafted all about them. Ansiau, who was more indifferent, thought principally of chasing away mosquitoes—he had almost forgotten what it felt like to be stung by them; he thought too of his nights in Champagne, of crickets singing in the fields, of his lady's warm hands. She must have borne her child by now. Hélie. He felt certain that it was a boy. A boy who would never go to Palestine—his two eldest sons were surely enough. Very calmly Ansiau told himself that this second expedition would be worse than the first.

During those first days the men of Champagne felt that they were the most important people in the camp, for young Count Henry was elected chief of the entire army until the kings should arrive; his men distributed generous quantities of meat and grain to the famished soldiers; and the knights of Champagne, with their new arms and their unspent pay, were looked up to by the poor as emissaries from God. Little by little they grew accustomed to the stench, the heat, the flies; they learned to be cautious about water and not to walk in the sun.

At first those who had never seen Syria—the younger men especially—went about admiring the motley garments, the strange arms of the crusaders from other lands, and risked excursions outside the camp to see the country. Then, like all the rest, they grew to hate that indifferent sun which always rose from behind the hills at the same hour, set always in the same spot, and never brought anything new.

A week after their arrival Ansiau was wakened from his afternoon sleep by Thierri, who said that a knight was asking to speak with him. The man who entered the tent was of middle stature, thin, spare, and richly dressed. His face was shaven, as was the custom among eastern Christians, and he appeared to be about fifty years of age. Under his sallow tan his skin was lumpy, the purple pockets beneath his deeply sunken eyes indicated poor health. Something in the man's stiff attitude, his vulpine profile, made Ansiau think of his uncle Herbert.

"How now!" said the stranger. "You did not expect to see me, fair cousin?"

"Simon!" The two cousins embraced a dozen times, then Ansiau called Thierri and asked him to bring wine. When Thierri had left them alone together once more, the two men looked at each other in silence, hardly knowing what to say. "Well," Ansiau said at last, "this country seems no fit place for you, fair cousin. You do not look healthy."

Simon did not seem too pleased by this remark. "No one would look healthy who had seen the things I have seen—and still see," he answered gloomily.

Ansiau sighed: "It seems that you were right. You remember—when you talked of Jerusalem."

"Three years!" said Simon. "Soon it will be three years, and we are as far as ever from recapturing Jerusalem. The kings are delaying too long. You, cousin, have not changed—you do not look your age. And now tell me the news of the family."

Simon listened, attentive and impassive, yet the corners of his lips trembled when he learned that his daughter Simone was married and the mother of two children. "And Garnier? He is here? Here in camp? Truly? A man grows stupid as he grows old, cousin. Well, I hope that he will behave as becomes a knight."

Simon fell silent and paced up and down the tent, lost in his thoughts. At that moment the three boys and their squires burst in, stopping short when they saw the visitor. They had entered in a paroxysm of laughter which they could not immediately stifle. Simon looked at them, trying to divine which was Garnier.

"Garnier," said Ansiau, "come here."

The boy came forward, looking at the ground and biting his lips to keep back his laughter.

"Stop acting like a fool and look at me," said his uncle. "Garnier, this is a happy day for you—here is your father. He has come for you."

Garnier's laughter died instantly. He raised his eyes. The thin, sallow man, no taller than himself, who was smiling at him in such an embarrassed way, could not have borne much resemblance to the hero father of whom he had dreamed since childhood. In any case, it must be supposed that his face expressed only a restrained joy, for Simon stiffened and gave a dry little laugh.

"By St. Thiou! The boy must have thought his father was St. Michael the Archangel in person," he said. "Come, boy, you might give me a kiss just the same."

The boy touched his lips to his father's malodorous mouth.

"Don't be offended, cousin," said Ansiau, and laid his hand on Garnier's shoulder. "He is not soft, he is no girl—are you, nephew? But, brother, you will soon see that he has not his equal."

Ansiet and Herbert stood by the door, staring in amazement at their celebrated uncle Simon. With the inconstancy of their age they had instantly shed their old admiration; and their only thought was for Garnier's embarrassment—their cousin obviously had no idea what to make of his father. And when Garnier sat down on the camp bed beside their uncle Simon, the two brothers exchanged a pitying glance which meant: "The old man looks like a hard master."

Then Andrew entered and his arrival broke the ice. The two brothers recognized each other at once. And that evening Ansiau invited his friends from the castellany to his tent—Haguenier's sons, Thibaut of Puiseaux,

Manesier of Coagnecort, Giles of Monguoz, all of whom had known and esteemed Simon of Linnières. They greeted him warmly, exclaimed over his pallor, and asked after his health. He answered that it was his shaven beard which gave him such a sickly look. His red hair, not yet flecked with gray, but from which the color seemed to have faded, fell over his shoulders in long, stiff, straight strands; in his right ear he wore a large turquoise.

At supper Simon showed that he could be pleasant company; he talked freely and well, though he had not his father's colorful imagination. He had seen much. He had shared in the battle at which the Holy Cross was captured, and had only escaped by a miracle—Balian of Ibelin, his master, who was commanding the rearguard, had extricated himself and his knights from the general affray and had fled in the direction of Jerusalem. Simon had seen Jerusalem besieged, then surrendered; he had seen Saladin himself on the day when his master Balian had gone to the Sultan's camp to negotiate the surrender of the city. The company could hardly believe their eyes—how could a man from Champagne like themselves have stood in the presence of Saladin? "If he were not an infidel," said Simon, "there is neither count nor king who would not hold it an honor to serve him. If he would be christened, he would be the first prince in the country. He has such a royal air that no one would dare laugh or even look up in his presence; no man is more generous to his knights or kinder to the poor. When Jerusalem surrendered, he paid half of the ransoms himself, and would have paid more if he had had more money, but he gives everything to his emirs. And the Knights Templars, I assure you, had enough money in their coffers to buy freedom for every citizen of Jerusalem—but they felt less pity for their brother Christians than the Sultan did."

The visitors were scandalized to hear a Christian praise the Sultan and began to look at Simon somewhat askance. But Ansiau and Andrew knew of old that Simon was frankness itself.

In fact, there was something about Simon which might well startle those who did not know him well. He smoked opium, he had a little black slave boy who followed him everywhere and fanned him and rubbed his feet with balms and aromatic oils, he spoke Arabic fairly well—above all, he looked at things differently from the crusaders. He said "people from overseas" and "foreigners" when he talked of Frenchmen from France, and his friends did not understand what "foreigners" he could mean. When he spoke of King Guy of Lusignan he frothed at the mouth—the man, according to him, had done the country more harm than Saladin, Safadin, and all their emirs together: and how dared he show himself before knights and barons after he had bought his freedom by consenting to the surrender of Christian cities? "I have met men of Ascalon who saw him brought before the ramparts, and he wept and beseeched them to surrender the town. The sultan did us no service when he set him free."

A man, said Simon, whom the Leper King never wanted as his heir and who was only made king by his wife's intriguing and the treachery of the patriarch and the Templars . . . and how could anyone respect a man who had no name, a foreigner indebted for his good fortune to a wanton woman who had become infatuated with him? "And the Leper King was forced to consent to the marriage and had it performed at the height of Eastertide— no one has ever been able to guess why."

Ansiau, whose temperament was more conciliatory, said: "What use is it to speak ill of the man? Whatever his faults, he is a crowned king after all."

"Crowned?" Simon shrugged his shoulders. "Crowned by his wife! It was the queen who put the crown on his head—the patriarch himself did not dare."

If Simon was to be believed, the camp swarmed with traitors, with men who thought solely of their own interests and settling scores. There was neither king nor commander. Count Henry was too young to hold a firm hand; the best thing would be to entrust the command to the marquess. Such views were hardly calculated to gain Simon the sympathy of his old friends from Champagne. When they talked of him they shook their heads and said that he had gone to the bad, that the life of the country had spoiled him. In any case, they were beginning to form a rather poor opinion of these Oriental Christians who had allowed the infidels to conquer God's Holy Land. What was to be expected of men who had negotiated the surrender of Jerusalem to Saladin as if it had been some ordinary city? The younger knights—Garnier especially—said that the knights who garrisoned Jerusalem should have died defending it, to the last man—and they had surrendered the city without striking a blow, Simon himself had simply paid his ransom and walked out with wife, slaves, and goods. In such a case it was no use saying that they had not had men and arms enough—there was no excuse for cowardice.

Garnier was not overpleased at having to leave his uncle and his cousins. But Ansiau would hear of no excuse—he belonged to his father, his father had come for him, it was his duty to follow him and serve him. "My boy," he said, "pack and be done with it. You would not wish your father to think that I was keeping you from him purposely, he might accuse me of double-dealing." Garnier did not want his uncle blamed—he kissed him tearfully. Balian of Ibelin's tents were pitched not far from the Toron; they were far finer and better equipped than most of the newcomers' tents. So Garnier entered the service of one of the wealthiest barons of Ultramar, husband to the queen dowager and a model "Colt." Garnier had already learned the nickname, which signified a Frank who was a native of the country, and he regretted that he was obliged to class his father among the "Colts."

At forty, Simon of Linnières was beginning to weary of a life of riding and fighting; his health was bad, but he refused to admit it. For ten years his one passion had been the land to which he had devoted himself irretrievably, body and soul. For him Jerusalem was not a place of pilgrimage, a promise of adventure and salvation. He loved its houses, its churches, its groves of oranges and olives; he loved it with its motley inhabitants, its splendor, its freedom, its crowded market places; he loved its little white forts lost in vast orange groves and surrounded by dark cypresses; he loved the Palestinian spring—hills, fields, and orchards teeming with flowers—the glory and beauty of the Chosen Land. All these crusaders, wave after wave of them, coming to gain martyrdom or to carry home a bloodstained booty and an illustrious name. . . . The crusaders inspired more distrust than gratitude in Simon. They might well leave the country more despoiled and desolate than ever the infidels had. Age and the trials of the last few years had made Simon of Linnières gloomy and irritable, inclined to blame rather than to praise.

The sudden and unexpected reappearance of his son revived the little tenderness of which he was still capable. Since the death of his father he had thought that he loved no one in the world. And this is how he had learned that his father was dead:

It was in the October of 1181 and he was at Naplouse. One night he had heard Herbert's voice giving his old hunting call: "Ho-ho-ho-hoi!" All night long the voice called, now clear, now hoarse, and Simon could not sleep. And in the morning he heard it again, calling "Simon! Simon!" and he closed his eyes and saw his father lying by a tree in a forest, and there was a wound in his face. He knew that his father was calling for help and that no one came. And that night he heard and saw nothing more, all was darkness. That night Simon shed the last tears he was to shed for many a year and prayed long and fervently. He thought that he had lost his last earthly tie. He led a comfortable life, but it was because he saw no reason for denying himself a few very modest pleasures of sense and sight—his luxurious tastes, unlike his father's, had never become a passion.

This hard-faced, stubborn boy, who wore his knightly attire with the grave dignity of a child, was a stranger to Simon. Yet he was his only son, the only one of his children he was ever to see. He never learned to understand him, but he loved him instantly and without reservations. Suddenly a whole future lay before him. He had no children by his second wife, he would make Garnier his sole heir; once the kingdom was reconquered, he could hope to obtain a fief for the boy—he had connections at court. "My wife has an estate near Bethlehem," he said, "which will bring in enough for us to live on comfortably. . . . My wife is a good woman, she will love you like a son. She is no longer young, but she will take all the better care of you. I know that you have pleased my lord, he will speak to the king on your behalf—there is every reason to suppose that it will not be King Guy. Indeed I think it would be well to enroll you in the marquess' guard at once. Though he is not king yet, he deserves to be."

And Garnier quite naturally took King Guy's side, despised the "Colts," and said that the marquess was purposely starving the army. He told his father that he would never marry because he loved his cousin Mahaut of

Linnières and that he intended to join the Templars—he knew that Simon abhorred the Templars.

Ansiet had not forgotten the ten thousand corpses which had greeted him on the day of his arrival, and his heart could forgive neither God nor his father for them. Although he knew that the baron had nothing to do with it, he blamed him because he trusted him too greatly—the baron had not protected him properly, he had left him alone face to face with that mass of corruption, with that immense slaughterhouse of spoiled meat—there it still rotted, poisoning earth, air, and water. Ansiet had never thought about death; until now, death had been a part of life, people fell ill or were wounded, received the sacraments, and were borne to the graveyard with an escort of chanting priests. And now his own eyes had seen the reality of death. An ugly thing, intolerably ugly and foul-smelling. Herbert had simply decided that he would never let his clean white body be eaten by vultures. But Ansiet could not yet detach himself from those ten thousand Christians, from those who died each day by dozens, victims of dysentery or sunstroke—he had a compassionate heart and a vivid imagination. And before his son's stern and reproachful eyes, Ansiau felt like a criminal. So far as he was concerned, the troubles of the camp weighed on him hardly at all—he knew too well what was bound to follow when once a man had taken the cross.

Toward the end of the month it was Ansiet's turn to fall ill—and so ill that no one believed he could recover. His father was panic-stricken, made vows, went barefoot, cut his hair, promised a three-pound candle to St. Nicholas, and the boy recovered from his dysentery. But no sooner was he better than he fell ill again, this time with a malignant fever which made boils break out all over his body. The heat was terrible, and at night the sick lad's bed was moved close to the entrance of the tent, where the air was less stifling. Ansiau never left his side, wrapped wet cloths around his head (they dried out in half an hour), and when his fingers touched his son's fiery forehead he wanted to die. Ansiet was delirious the greater part of the time, all his talk was of Troyes and Linnières, he spoke in a high piping voice, a child's voice strangely in contrast with his great frame and bearded lips. "Oh, baron, a squirrel! Up there in the pine, there! Quick, quick!" and again, in a tone of happy surprise, "Why, it is the Armançon! Oh, how clear the water is, you can see every fish, you can catch them with your hands!" and then, "Haumette, Haumette, I'm thirsty. Take those sticks off the fire, I'm too hot. Haumette!" After a week of fever he recovered consciousness; he was so thin that his cheekbones and jawbone almost pierced his skin, and so weak that he could not lift his arms. Nevertheless he had the good grace to smile when his father washed his face or gave him drink. But he had no sooner begun to eat again than his dysentery returned. And then, for the first time in his life, he lost heart and wept—

not because he feared death, they were tears of pure rage against the suffering which would not leave him.

Ansiau of Linnières almost went out of his mind—which saint should he invoke now? And his friends, when they saw his hollow cheeks and troubled eyes, blamed him for worrying so much over a boy who was far from being his only son. And Ansiau answered that if he had a hundred sons he would rather see them all dead than lose this one boy. Herbert, though he worshipped his elder brother, would not risk coming beyond the entrance of the tent. He could not bear the smell of sick people and he was afraid of contagion—he could not help it, he would rather touch red-hot iron than a sick man's hand. Ansiau called him a bad brother, but Ansiet, in his weak voice, said: "Let him alone. It is my wish, not his."

Ansiet's recovery was long and difficult—toward autumn he was able to get out of bed and stand, supporting himself on his father and Andrew. To everyone's surprise he had grown half an inch taller. But he was only a skeleton clothed in skin, and the stock of food brought from Champagne was exhausted and the price of wheat was rising by leaps and bounds.

Even the most sensitive grew accustomed to the ceaseless funerals which every day added new tombs or new crosses to the cemetery of St. Nicholas. After all, to die of disease was a way of gaining martyrdom too. Yet more frequent attacks on the city, men murmured, would produce deaths more profitable to the cause of God.

The Emperor Frederick Barbarossa had died by drowning, and now there was nothing to face Saladin's army on land and raise his blockade of the Christian camp before Acre. The only thing left was to wait for succor by sea, and the kings seemed still undecided whether to come. It was known that they had left Marseille and had stopped when they reached Sicily.

The shadow of the terrible marquess dominated the camp. King Guy, though he was well liked, cut a poor figure beside him. The marquess was everywhere, every misfortune was laid to his account, and every hope was built on him. From the rampart of Tyre, when the Saracens had shown him his old father as their prisoner, he had answered: "I would rather shoot him myself than yield one rod of Christian ground," or so the story went. And the camp repeated the words with a horror in which there was a spice of admiration. It was a terrible thing to say, but such was the marquess. Holding his head high, hard-mouthed and eagle-eyed, the man had a strange beauty compounded of authority and pride; his arms and his armor glittered with gold and precious stones, his gray fox cloaks were trimmed with golden chains, his gloves were sewn with pearls, his falcons bedecked with rubies. Yet such magnificence was so natural to the man that it went almost unremarked. His was a head which demanded a crown, and the fairest crown of all, the crown of Jerusalem. He made no secret of it—he wanted it as his due, because he knew himself worthy—and he was soon to have a legal claim to it: Queen Sibyl of Jerusalem and her two daughters had died during the October epidemic, leaving King Guy without heirs and with no rights to the throne except the fact that he had been crowned at Jerusalem; Balian of Ibelin and his wife, Queen Mary, had no difficulty in proving that the rightful heir to the throne was Isabel, the dead queen's younger sister and Mary's own daughter. On November twenty-first, 1190, to the indignation of the entire army, Conrad of Montferrat married the youthful Isabel of Jerusalem, who had been forcibly separated from her husband. It was no use saying that Onfroi of Toron was a coward and could never be king. That extremely handsome, almond-eyed young man, whose shaven chin gave him a strangely boyish look, had come and complained to the barons and bishops of the army, weeping like a child and begging them to have his wife restored to him. Among the petty knights who made up the bulk of the army he aroused a feeling of scornful pity, but it was pity nevertheless. He is not the man to stand up to the marquess, everyone said. Onfroi must have thought as much himself, and he soon gave in. And Jerusalem, occupied by Saladin for three years, thus found itself with two rival kings, who divided the army and became a new cause of discord.

The day-to-day existence of the camp depended on the marquess in a way which no one could fail to see. And as they shared their meager rations of beans and dry bread, the men of Linnières roundly cursed the marquess of Montferrat, which did not mean that they hated him—it was simply a habit which the whole camp had acquired months since, sergeants as well as knights—the marquess had charge of the provisioning and they were hungry. The October storms had forced his ships to withdraw to Tyre, and from the beach the crusaders watched Turkish ships calmly anchoring in the harbor of Acre, bringing supplies and fresh troops. At nightfall the wind wafted the long chants of the muezzins from the besieged city. . . . There stood the fortress, living its monotonous and savage life, and the crusaders finally grew to believe that it was impregnable. That double wall, that moat, those square, massive towers began to weigh on their hearts, to hurt their eyes— they could no longer bear the sight of them. To have nothing before them but that wall of stone and all Saladin's army at their backs—it was enough to make them despair of life. The kings wanted the best of the crusading army to perish on that accursed shore, and when they arrived they would find only a graveyard.

When it was not sickness that reigned in the tents, it was whoredom—in tents of brocade as in tents of gray cloth. The woman animal made for pleasure, with hoarse voice and bared teeth and feline odor—the daughter of famine, with protruding bones and the eyes of a whipped dog, and the madwoman, the visionary who rolled in convulsions and claimed to have slept with St. George in person—several hundred of them had come at the beginning of the siege, worn-out women who had failed elsewhere and who were only too sure of finding an easy prey in these voluntary exiles. Very few they were for that host of thousands and tens of thousands. But there were also women of the country who had come seeking protection from the infidels. The epidemics quickly carried them off, and not many came to replace them; without a burning zeal for the sacred cause, few were willing to run the risks of the Hell which was the camp.

Yet so great was the men's misery that, especially among the sergeants, the most loathsome strumpets, living and breathing corruption, were apparently still pretty enough to find more lovers than they wanted. And who can stop to think about beauty, or even cleanliness, when death stalks abroad and will not wait?

Another scourge, too, quickly became widespread, often finding its victims among the boy-squires and the younger men, even in the ranks of the knights. Herbert was the unluckiest of the Linnières troop in this respect— every day his smooth skin, which would not tan, and his curly hair brought him startling proposals, which he answered with oaths and spitting, much disgusted at being taken for a girl.

Ansiau had long known camp life, but he had not yet known what it was to live in a camp with Ansiet. He had an aversion for debauched women and frequented them no more than he considered absolutely necessary, and he did not want to see his fine boy fall into their filthy hands. And the boy was far from being willing to listen to reason. His father thought: "It is the climate." And doubtless the climate had a great deal to do with it, for it produced the same effect on the majority of the crusaders. The fact remains that Ansiet was quite capable of giving shirt, shoes, breeches, and even his baptismal cross to buy a woman, even the ugliest of women. He paid little heed to his father's remonstrances, for he was without pride and without shame—he was a man, he must do as nature demanded, it was perfectly simple. It was even too simple—he became almost sottish, and shamefully neglected his personal appearance; between weariness and carelessness, he never washed himself or combed his hair and went dressed in rags even in winter. As a result, his hands and head were covered with scabs, and he suffered from boils and malignant fevers. But he bore it all with his usual imperturbability—indeed, he seemed hardly to notice it.

Herbert, to the surprise of all his intimates, behaved much better than most of the young men of his age. He spent so much time caring for his precious person that his father became irritated and insultingly asked him what man's attentions he was hoping to attract—the fact was that Ansiau could not forgive his younger son for outshining Ansiet. And Herbert was obviously held in high esteem by his friends, the young knights of Champagne. His fine clothes and haughty air had something to do with it. In spite of the famine, he had lost very little weight, and his father suspected that he was being fed elsewhere —for which he did not blame him. Herbert's delicate skin had not been able to bear the sun, it had reddened, burned, peeled, and after that was as white as ever; but fleas, bedbugs, and mosquitoes decorated it with red blotches, which a few hours later became hard lumps. He itched constantly and scratched himself till the blood came. But he was never ill.

He seemed to have grown taller since his arrival at the camp, he was visibly developing, his expression was more assured, his voice more peremptory. When he said "Good morning" it was as if he were giving a command. He found it easy to make his comrades obey him and he exploited them to the best of his ability—he was not really liked, but he imposed respect. He appeared to know far more than he actually did, and his strength was already unusual. He had the kind of hands which clutch everything and let nothing go. He owed money everywhere, and no one demanded repayment. Under his pillow he had a strange collection of odds and ends which he had found or been given or had taken as pledges—feathers, arrows, little mirrors, ribbons, sheaths, unusual shells, laces. He kept these childish treasures carefully and used them for barter—a sensible procedure, for in this way he never had to do without anything he wanted. He was disinclined to share, and Ansiet was not demanding. Sometimes, in a burst of brotherly devotion, Herbert would give his elder brother a bit of copper chain or a Saracen arrow found on the rampart. The gift was always received as gladly as it was given. In their common universe the most trifling objects often took on magical powers, and an iron nail might be more precious than a golden pin. So little alike, the two boys became like twins when they were together. Together they still made absurd plans which they forgot as soon as they parted. They did not judge each other.

Garnier, whose duties to the baron of Ibelin kept him very busy, sometimes paid a visit to his cousins—he rode a pearl-gray Arab horse and wore a fine coat lined with black lamb skins. He was becoming accustomed to his father but he still regretted his uncle. He said: "My own father simply begot me and then abandoned me as if I were a bastard. I owe far more to my uncle, he made me a knight. He mortgaged his land to buy me a hauberk, and I shall never forget it."

"You have no cause to complain of your father," said Herbert, enviously eyeing Garnier's fine gray horse.

Garnier shrugged his shoulders: "He gives me what he has no need for."

Garnier was homesick—more than Ansiet and much more than Herbert— and when he came to see his cousins he asked them to sing him songs of Champagne; he himself sang very badly. Herbert would sit at the door of his tent, his arms around his knees, and sing in a loud, vibrant voice which made the soldiers on the ramparts turn to look at him.

Garnier had not forgotten Mahaut—he was so proud of having saved her honor that he no longer forbade himself to love her, he even told himself that if he were to see her again some day, a married woman . . . But he knew that it was only a dream and that he had missed his one chance for happiness in life. "Women are fickle," he said to Herbert. "No doubt she has forgotten me. But I know that I shall never love another woman." This did not prevent him from boasting that he had obtained the highest favors from a beautiful Greek girl who served Queen Mary. His cousins were unspeakably envious. In actual fact the Greek girl in question was far too fat and what little hair she had was black and greasy. But she was a woman, and imagination did the rest.

The winter rains flooded the tents and rotted the wheat and salt meat in the storehouses. The horses stood in water to their fetlocks and caught cold, ditches were dug around the tents and the water overflowed the ditches, the tents themselves, perpetually soaked, began to rot. It seemed impossible that there could be a dry stitch in the entire camp. They had to wear damp clothes, eat damp bread, and sleep in damp beds. Graves were no sooner dug than they filled with water, the corpses were dropped into them side by side, without coffins, and hurriedly covered with soft, sticky earth—the monstrous cemetery swallowed two hundred, three hundred every day, there was not room for them all. The duke of Swabia was dead, the count of Clermont and Baron Anséric of Monréal were dead, the losses among the poor were beyond counting—there were as many corpses in the cemetery as living men in the camp, and panic seized on the hardiest.

The troop from Linnières cut as sorry a figure as the rest as they lay shaking with fever on their soaked pallets. Ansiau had buried sixteen of his companions and considered himself fortunate because he still had his two sons and Thierri. Andrew had abandoned him to take service under the marquess and was now at Tyre—luckily for himself.

Lying side by side under a great woolen cloak, the two brothers looked more than ever like two children. Herbert had grown very thin, his lips were swollen, his eyelids red, and he tossed his head back and forth on the pillow in a way which strangely recalled Lady Alis in her illnesses—he was whimpering like a three-year-old baby: "Baron, I'm hungry! Baron, father! I'm so hungry. I don't want to be hungry." His voice grew thick for a few seconds, he lost consciousness, then he opened his eyes again and began tossing his head back and forth, faster and faster. His brother, lying with his head thrown back, was gasping painfully, his chest was full of dull rattling and plashing sounds. Spells of almost continuous coughing had exhausted him, and he was dozing. Before his half-closed eyes the open entrance to the tent was transformed into a naked, white woman who came to him and lay down beside him, soft as a gigantic flower, and then another appeared in her place and came to him and lay down, and she was even lovelier than the first and so white that it hurt his eyes; and more came, bearing armfuls of fresh fruit, ripe grapes, cherries, apples which changed into gilded cups filled with water as bright and clear as rock crystal. Then the entrance grew larger, it was the portal of a church, decorated with massy rows of flowers and fruit, not in gray stone, but living flowers and fruits of every hue—red, golden-cheeked, bowered in dark-green leaves. Then the portal drew away and simultaneously grew larger, it filled the whole tent, the whole sky, and a great cross became visible in the midst of it, luminous, as if formed of white-hot iron; above it, in the same white light, appeared a crown of thorns, and to the right a lance and to the left the rod and the sponge. The cross grew larger and larger, more and more brilliant, Ansiet closed his eyes and saw nothing but fountains of light. Very far away, somewhere above his head, he heard the baron's voice and Thierri's.

Then two hands lifted his head and something hard and cool was put to his lips.

"Drink!" He had no idea what it was—a thick, fatty liquid which filled his mouth with an unpleasant taste. Ansiet made an effort to swallow, and spat.

"What are you doing?" said the baron. "It is milk."

The boy had gone without eating for so long that he thought he was not hungry. He said: "Give it to Herbert," then added, "I have seen the True Cross."

His father crossed himself. "Speak not of that! Try to drink a little."

Ansiet had no idea what promises and threats it had cost Thierri to obtain that bowl of milk from an old Armenian women who said that she needed it for her sick daughter. Thierri was the great purveyor of victuals for the Linnières tent. No one would ever have expected such ingenuity from a man so simple and so imperturbable. Ansiau never asked him where he had found the handful of dry grapes or rotten beans which he brought back from his long excursions, but he knew that Thierri would have let himself be hacked to bits before he would have touched a single grape or a single bean.

That same day Renaud of Hervi, Haguenier's eldest son, whose tent stood next to Ansiau's, burst in on them, shaking with fever and sobbing; his brother James had just died and there had been no time to call a priest. "I have sent him to Hell. God! Do you think I have sent him to Hell? How could I know?"

"There, there," said Ansiau, "it is never too late to pray for him. After all, we are here in God's service, are we not?"

Renaud collapsed and lay on the damp ground, sobbing even harder. "I have had enough. I can bear no more. We are abandoned. We are betrayed. We shall perish."

Ansiau made him sit up and gave him a little milk to drink. "There, there, cousin, it is no such matter. The kings are sure to come in the end." But he was not so certain himself, and as he looked at the two blond heads, terrible in their emaciation against the dirty pallet, he wondered if the kings would arrive in time. Renaud wiped his wet clotted beard with the back of his hand; his troubled eyes brightened and set in a feverish stare. "Milk? You have milk?"

"Thierri found it," said Ansiau. "I cannot give you more, it is for my sons."

Renaud gasped. "Fair cousin, give me that milk. I will give you all that I own, I will serve you. I am so hungry."

Ansiau regretfully handed him the bowl—after all, his boys were so ill that a little milk would not cure them Renaud of Hervi drank it down at a draught and vomited it almost at once. He wept. Accursed country. Accursed winter. Accursed war. "Here we are, dying like dogs in the sight of the infidels, and they laugh at us. They are right. It was not for this that we left Champagne. We shall never return. Oh, God! James, James!"

Ansiau hardly heard him, his head felt heavy, he wrapped himself in his cloak, his teeth had begun to chatter. It was the same every alternate night, he had grown used to it. When he had fever he stopped feeling hungry.

For three days the younger men had been running down to the beach at dawn to see if King Richard's sails had yet appeared on the horizon. In the morning the heat was still bearable, the sea breeze played with your hair and caressed your body under your shirt; the sea was not yet quite blue, but it was very clear and very calm, and the white of the sky changed to pink. In the bay it was the hour of great activity. The short, big-waisted ships with their flag-hung masts swayed gently on the warm sea, and barges and dinghies, loaded to the gunwales with boxes and sacks and horses, moved slowly through the dark water toward the shadowy shore, which swarmed with life like an ant-hill. The only sound was a barrage of English and Gascon war cries and the "Diavolo" and "Porco Madonna" of the Genoese sailors. But in the direction of the besieged city the staccato noise of the catapults was beginning to drown out all the other noises of the camp.

Everything was ready for the final assault, the army was only waiting for King Richard. Since the king of France had arrived with his machines and his knights the siege had rapidly advanced. The city had been cut off on the land-ward side by a rampart; it was surrounded by siege machines, and the Accursed Tower, which had cost the Christians so much blood and so many tears, al-ready showed breaches and cracks that indicated it could hardly hold out for long. The moats were filled with earth and the corpses of men and horses, and the garrison of Acre, faced with the threatening waves of new arrivals, seemed on the point of surrender. Deserters from the city told of famine and discour-agement. But the terrible walls still stood, they still held firm and still show-ered well-aimed arrows into the Christian camp. And many a Christian said: "If they were not infidels, there would be no braver men on earth."

On the first of June the grave of Philip, count of Flanders, was added to the tens of thousands of Christian graves. On the same day the first English ships arrived, bringing the king's advanced guard, Queen Berengaria, the king's sister, Queen Joan, and their escort of noblewomen. Everyone saw them pass, sheltered under daïses and veils and feather fans: with their light dresses and their soft voices they seemed to beautify the white, crude sunlight; and the blue sea, of which everyone had been sick for so long, once again looked like sap-phires and emeralds.

After such sufferings there was everything to hope for. The mere name of Richard Lionheart would send the walls tumbling down and scatter Saladin's army. In all Christendom there was not a greater warrior. If he had kept them waiting for so long, it was only that he might the better comfort the crusading army—after days of rain, the sun brings all the more joy. The greater their sufferings, the sweeter would be their reward.

In the course of Saladin's last attack on the camp Ansiau had lost Thierri, and never did he forgive the Saracens for it. Disfigured and riddled with wounds, the body of his faithful squire had been carried to the tent where it was washed and wrapped in white linen. Ansiau had been unable to rescue or defend him—for the first time in his life he had failed his servant. Stunned himself by a blow from a mace which his shield had failed to deflect, he had not resisted when he was pulled from the saddle and dragged along the ground. Thierri, with the help of Herbert and Manesier of Nangi, had rescued him, and he had been able to rise and pick up his sword. But Thierri, like the conscientious squire he was, had rushed to save his master's horse, which the Saracens were leading away by the reins. Ansiau had seen him catch the beast by the bit, then fight and fall among the hoofs of the Saracens' horses. All that Ansiau and Herbert had been able to rescue from the enemy was a dead body. The hands had been cut off by Saracen battle axes; the face, half crushed by a hoof, was black and blue. Thierri was buried like a knight, with candles and chanting, but though Ansiau spent all his ready money for Masses and alms it availed him nothing, he remained inconsolable. Never had he believed that the death of his squire would come as such a blow. The man who for twenty years had not left him for a single day, a single night, was like his right hand, his eyes, his sword, a part of himself. He remembered those hellish days on the galley benches, with Thierri behind him humming a song to keep up his courage. Thierri, to whom he had never spoken a harsh word in his life. Thierri, who for twenty years had never eaten before serving his lord. Thierri, with whom Ansiau had always shared everything—even women—reserving only the first choice to himself. Thierri, twin brother and watchdog of Ansiau of Linnières, companion of his youth and his manhood. The two men had grown so accustomed to each other that they had come to be alike—Thierri, shorter and stockier, was a smaller replica of his master. But it was Ansiau who had acquired something of his squire's patience and gentleness.

And now he must take another squire, a squire who would not know his habits, who would not wake at his master's slightest movement, who would not know how to turn or bow properly. He chose Guiot of Beaumont, a cousin of Simon's on his mother's side, a good vassal, a young man of about twenty-five, intelligent enough and a capable groom. But every time Ansiau needed him he called "Thierri," and Guiot did not always realize that it was he who was being addressed. And finally the baron renamed him Thierri, and from that day on began to grow fond of him.

The day that Richard Lionheart arrived before Acre all grief was blotted out. The knights of Champagne were among the part of the army charged with guarding the camp. But, on the word of spies who said that no attack was in preparation, many of them deserted their tents and their posts on the ramparts and went down to the strand, their heads wrapped in white cloths to ward off the sun. Emerging from a luminous mist, great-sailed ships rocked on the sparkling waves, their pennons rippling in the breeze. They seemed to come no nearer, yet they grew larger and more distinct—masts, stays, rigging, broad rounded hulls painted red. The first ship, which flew the royal standard, dropped anchor in the mouth of the bay, the rest drew up, ponderous, majestic—dark shadows against the bright sea. Their every sail bore the cross. On the decks stood troop after troop of full-armed knights, bursting with color, glittering in the sun. And the Englishmen's shouts of joy mingled with the answering shouts from the shore to form one immense cry which spread through all the camp and even into the city, drowning all other sounds.

The cry swelled to thunder when the crusaders saw Richard himself leave his ship and take his place in a broad-beamed barge, between the duke of Bedford and the earl of Leicester. The barge swiftly neared the shore, the six powerful oars gaily cutting the choppy waves of the bay. Standing under the crimson daïs, towering over his companions, his right arm uplifted, Richard Plantagenet displayed his imposing figure to the frantic acclamations of the crowd. His helmet and hauberk might have been parts of his natural body, the long red-silk tunic which he wore over his hauberk was gold-embroidered with Norman lions and marked in front with a great white cross.

Some young knights and squires jumped into the water, swam to the barge and surrounded it, only too happy to risk being wounded by the oars if thus they might come near to the English king. And Philip of France, awaiting his ally on the shore surrounded by his high barons, had every right to be jealous of his vassal—there had been fewer shouts of joy on the day when he had reached the camp. Yet it was he who had pushed on the siege and restored the morale of the troops. And now Richard was come to reap the laurels.

He landed, and then there was one continuous shout, a tempest driving everything before it—no more doubt, no more hesitation—the Deliverer was come, to free the Promised Land and save the Christians. The white cross on his breast shed light and the golden circlet around his helmet glittered in the sun like a halo. Slowly he moved toward the crowd, walking beside the French king, whom he overtopped by half a head. Hands were stretched out to him, white heads and blond heads bowed to him; and beneath a multicolored line of banners and flags of every Christian nation Richard mounted a white horse, purple-harnessed, which two barons led to him by the reins. And again there was delirium, as if each new act of the Deliverer's were a new cause for wonder and joy. He rode forward, his face uncovered and his right arm raised in salute. The knights in the front row of the crowd cast their cloaks on the ground beneath his horse's hoofs. . . . And as he passed under the banners of Troyes his eyes rested on a tall, slender young knight whose face, with its great pale freckles under bared straw-colored hair, was luminous. At once broad and emaciated, with flat cheekbones and big, slightly bulging eyes, it was a striking face because of the fervor which seemed to fire it from within—those full, grave lips were lips in prayer, and the bright eyes were filled with the tenderness of a happy child. The lids dropped and the eyes filled with tears when they met King Richard's eyes, and the king smiled.

It was a smile between equals, the simple smile of the man who wants to smile and has no ulterior motives. The king made himself adored by this simplicity which did not distinguish between the greatest and the humblest, in good humor as in anger. The man was sincere even in his poses, solid as a block in his least gestures—and heavy as a block, let us say a block of pure gold. It was the quality which made his enemies accuse him of duplicity.

Joy spread like oil on water. After the king came troop after festive troop —King Guy of Jerusalem, the prince of Antioch, the count of Tripoli, with their banners, their knights with tufts of white or scarlet plumes in their helmets and wearing long, bright-colored tunics. Near and far the cries echoed, now it was the camp which was filled with shouting, little by little the crowd on the shore broke up, fewer still were those who remained to watch the English sailors unload their cargo of huge machines, catapults, and hundreds of battle horses which almost broke from their grooms and, rearing and pawing, threatened to capsize the barges.

Ansiet was in love. With a man, of course. With a reddish-blond mustache, with two green eyes shining from under bushy brows, with a face tanned by wind and sun, pale from weariness, shadowy under its golden helmet like a relic in a chase. All beauty, all sanctity were in that face. The Deliverer. The Saviour. The King.

"Did you see him? He looked at you. Yes, at you!" Herbert and Renaud of Hervi could not get over their amazement and envy. "Did you see the earl of Leicester? Did you see King Guy?"

Huge fires of logs and brush lit up the tents and the rows of men crouching or lying on the ground; there were candles and torches without number, as far as the eye could see, among the tents and along the ramparts; there were flares in the hands of varlets, who moved forward in lines, kindling ever more and more torches even in the farthest parts of the camp. The whole plain between the city and the Toron was a sea of lights, and the star-sown sky was clear and bright as if its inhabitants, too, had wanted to share in the great joy of the Christians. All night long there was singing and the music of horns, drums, lutes, and pipes. The king of England had brought many minstrels, and their presence made the camp even more festive. Wines of Palestine in huge bronze vats were brought out of the tents and set near the fires, and the cup bearers ran tirelessly back and forth filling the cups. Washed by the flames, every face looked keener, younger, eyes were deep and bright, smiles full of kindliness. Never before had the land of Palestine seemed so beautiful to those poor pilgrims, nor the sky so clear.

To say that Ansiau of Linnières, son of Ansiau, was in love would not be accurate—he was an idolater who had found his idol. After spending the night wandering about the royal encampment with his comrades and crying "Noël" and "Hail to the king," he returned to his father's tent in the morning, drunk without having swallowed a drop of wine, dead tired, happy, and with but one thought—to find some way to win another look and another smile. He felt ashamed to have received so much without having done anything to deserve it, and clearly his entire life was too little to free him of his debt, to repay that single smile. He must be first on the wall, plant the banner of Champagne on the Accursed Tower, bring back the arms of an emir, and die at the king's feet.

From that day Andrew and Simon ceased to exist for Ansiet, because he knew that they were of the marquess' party and Richard was supporting King Guy of Lusignan. From that day he began to take care of his person and send his shirts to be washed. He spoke little—rather less than usual; it was enough for him to listen to his companions vaunting the prowess of the Lionheart. Before reaching the Holy Land the king had conquered Cyprus and sunk a large Saracen ship laden with food and arms—and what might not be expected of him now? The king had his tents pitched to the north of the city, and no sooner was he settled than he sent his criers through the camp to announce that any knight who wished to serve him would receive from him four gold bezants a month. This generosity won him great praise, for the French pay was three bezants at most. Furthermore, the count of Champagne was short of money and his knights received their wage only in part and at long intervals and had been obliged to pawn their horses. It was said that King Philip had plenty of money in his coffers but that his avarice made him refuse to help his nephew. So Richard's offer was most timely. Ansiau's sons did not hesitate to take advantage of the king of England's generosity—they told their father that they wanted to become Englishmen because there was more profit and honor in serving King Richard than any other man on earth. Their opinion was shared by their uncle, Thibaut of Puiseaux, and by Joubert of Villemaur, their comrade-in-arms. Ansiau, who was short of both money and fodder, agreed with them. No, he could not blame his sons for leaving him—it was only natural that every man should seek to better himself, and a young knight must watch for opportunities to distinguish himself and show his mettle. However, so far as he was concerned, he declared that he had vowed liege homage to the count of Champagne and he would never serve another man. Even though King Richard was, in fact, the count's uncle, it would always be embarrassing to have two masters—so long as he owed service only to Henry of Champagne he knew where he stood; the count was at liberty to turn French or English or even German, if he wished.

The boys insisted upon joining Richard's camp that very day, "because," they said, "if we do not find a place there now, there will be no more room." At this their father frowned: "That is asking too much," he said. "You can see for yourselves—you are relieving me of six horses and all your squires, which will leave me only Thierri, Garin, James of Le Cagne, and James the One-eyed. You know very well that I lost my horse on the day Thierri was killed, and the one I have now is cow-hocked in front and nervous. The viscount of Provins is counting on me for the assault, and if we are ever attacked on the rampart side, Joubert of Villemaur will be gone and his father-in-law with him, and that leaves very few men in our sector. The men of Ermele are so sick that there is no counting on them. We shall make a poor showing when it comes to the attack."

The boys were determined not to alter their decision. Herbert, however, seemed to hesitate, then he said that the viscount of Provins was no brother or godfather of his. Ansiet said nothing. His face might have been wood or stone

—it was the face of his bad days, a face without expression. So he looked whenever his father ventured the least suggestion of a reproach.

"What need is there for you to change camps now?" the baron asked at last. "You will always have time to reach your posts after the assault is ordered."

Herbert said that if everyone did likewise it would cause confusion in the camp. Besides, time pressed, they must pack. Ansiau lost his self-control and called him "dog," and "son of a whore." Herbert was used to such treatment and did not even flinch.

Ansiau himself packed his sons' arms and armor to make certain that everything was in proper condition—his boys must do him credit. At heart he felt a little uneasy about them, especially about Ansiet. Ansiet's squire was a certain Hugh of Linnières, a trustworthy sergeant of forty; Ansiau took him aside and ordered him to keep good watch over the boy. "You know what he is like. If he exposes himself too much during the assault, get in front of him. I don't want him wounded. Above all, see that he doesn't drink too much and that he eats regularly. And you know that he can't digest pork fat or beans."

They left the camp of Champagne at the same time as another little band of knights. And Ansiau, left alone with his squires, felt rather sad. Garnier, he thought to himself, would not have deserted him.

Ansiet had made up his mind to think no more of women—they disgusted him. He had never distinguished between love and lust, and he wanted to be worthy of his king. At the moment his main thought was to find ways of approaching the Lionheart as closely as possible. And it was not always easy.

He seldom spoke—it seemed impossible that the same boy had seen magical herbs and talking stags in the forest of Linnières. Whatever he saw now, he told it to no one; perhaps he saw nothing. No longer did he see Jerusalem with the eyes of seventeen—it was a city to be won back from Saladin, a city which his uncle Simon and other "Colt" knights had known and lived in, and where very ugly things had happened, to hear them tell it, a city which had had a lecher for a patriarch, an intriguer for a constable, a traitor for a seneschal, and an imbecile for a king. The men of the kingdom were much more interested in recovering their estates than in freeing Holy Sepulchre. There was nothing to be gained by fighting for them. And the king of France took their side and decreed that the crusaders should hold neither houses nor land in the kingdom—the Holy Land would be given back to those who had not been able to guard it. The king of France must have been bought by the marquess and the barons of Palestine. Indeed Ansiet was amazed to hear how many men in the army had been bought by one leader or another—it was a puzzling question where the money to pay for so much treachery had come from. Not a baron of any prominence but was accused of having sold himself to Saladin or to the marquess or to Richard of England, as the case might be. Ansiet did not trouble his head with doubts or arguments—all the barons sold themselves, it was a rule of the game.

During his eleven months before the beleaguered city, sky, earth and sea had gradually lost their saints and their spirits; Ansiet no longer believed in their power, because he had too often prayed to them in vain. Now, for him, all miracle was concentrated in a single man, a man so great and so near, the new redeemer, sent by Christ Himself. The man who bore a lion on his standard, the Lionheart, the King Knight. But it is dangerous to make a god of a man of flesh and blood. Ansiet prayed in church and saw not God, but Richard seated on a golden throne. And that robust, red-faced, bearded God, clad in a heavy hauberk covered by embroidered white silk, had little to give his votary. Ansiet could not manage to win a second look from those terrible green eyes, and the wines and spiced dishes served in Richard's tents were certainly not heavenly gifts. However, they were accepted with eager gratitude. The youths who had taken the cross were capable of love. Few living men had ever been better loved than Richard Lionheart.

On June eleventh King Richard's wooden tower, which had been advanced to the walls of Acre, was burned by the Saracens. Covered with fresh cowhides, it had long seemed invulnerable. But the infidels had contrived to soak it with naphtha and throw Greek fire down on it—the whole machine had gone up in flames and many of the men inside it had been roasted alive. It was a great sorrow to the camp, for much had been hoped from the tower. Three days after Richard's arrival the army began to change its tune. The city had not fallen; the French were annoyed to see that Richard had drawn to his camp a goodly number of the Pisan and Genoese knights, as well as many of their own; the Christians of the kingdom reproached the king of England with favoring King Guy when the king of France had already granted the crown of Jerusalem to the marquess. Every hope was pinned on the long-deferred assault. And early on the morning of June fourteenth the criers gave the signal, to the great joy of the knights, who rushed toward the city with ladders and battering rams, wading through the corpse-choked ditches. They were greeted by a shower of arrows and stones and a deafening noise of trumpets and drums —great columns of smoke rose from the towers, to signal the Sultan, who was encamped on the *tells* over against the city. And so the fighting soon grew thick about the outer ramparts, and great was the confusion, for everywhere men were crying that the Saracens had entered the camp.

Straight before him in the thick of the battle Ansiau of Linnières, who was fighting beside Raoul of Jeugni, viscount of Provins, saw a Templar, a lay brother, surrounded by Saracen knights. The Templar was neither tall nor stout, but he seemed to be keeping his adversaries thoroughly occupied. Ansiau was too busy himself to help the Templar. Perched on a rearing horse, his light shield split in two, his white surcoat brown with blood, the man was fighting like a mad wolf, whirling right, whirling left, ducking, straightening up, making his short sword whistle around his head, and all with a rapidity that the eye could hardly follow. He was so beset by infidels that Ansiau lost sight of him and forgot him. But presently the Templar's hoarse, shrill voice reached him through the confused cries of the infidels. "Companions," Ansiau cried, "the friar is a man of Champagne, I hear him swearing by St. Thiou and St. Cydronius." Head down, he flung himself among the Turks. Renaud of Hervi followed close behind him. . . .

The knights of Champagne who were fighting under the banners of the viscount of Coulommiers and Andrew of Chavigni surrounded the Turkish horsemen and pushed them back toward the rampart. In this battle the man who won most praise was Geoffrey of Lusignan, the best knight in all the army, men said, a very different man from his younger brother, King Guy. The Saracens fled, leaving the earthen rampart in a pitiful state, but there was such confusion in the camp that no one knew whether to run to the rampart to ward off a fresh attack or to resume the assault on the city. And those who had joined the assault had been forced to return to the camp in all haste, for fear of finding themselves cut off and captured by the Saracens, for the panic in the camp was so great that the assault had been forgotten. Insufficiently guarded, the French king's catapults and movable towers were in flames, increasing the noonday heat, and on top of the city wall the Saracens stood jeering and laughing and clapping their hands.

Garnier had been one of the first to join in the attack on the walls of Acre. He had asked his father to allow him to go as a special favor—and an unlucky day for him it was. He was thrown from a ladder, rolled into the fosse; the ladder fell on top of him and he was so crushed and trodden by his companions in the escalade that he was picked up unconscious. He was carried to Simon's tent, undressed and swathed in wet cloths. He had no wounds or broken bones, but there were huge bruises all over his body; he did not recover consciousness and moaned incessantly. He must have suffered a blow in the chest, for he was gasping, and a bloodstained froth showed at the corners of his mouth.

Ansiau disarmed in the viscount of Provins' tent; he was tired and in a terrible humor. A fine assault, indeed! Well conducted and all to the glory of the Christians! If the king of France was no better prepared, he should not have given the signal. King Richard, men said, was so sick that he could not leave his bed. No doubt he had come to this accursed country to die. The city would never be recaptured from the infidels. . . . He was thinking these gloomy thoughts when his squire—Thierri-Guiot—told him that a man wanted to see him, a lay brother, a Templar, who had come asking for the tall knight of Champagne who served under the banner of Provins and wore a red-striped helmet. "I suppose," said Guiot, "he means you."

Ansiau's bad humor vanished in an instant. "Ah! the brave Templar!" he said. "I will see him at once."

At the entrance to the tent he saw the man of the morning's affray, still wearing his plate jerkin and his blood-stained tunic. He had taken off his helmet and was wiping his short hair darkened by sweat.

"By St. Thiou, my brother," said Ansiau, "you have well deserved a place in Paradise by this day's work."

The man looked up and stared at him in astonishment. "What!" he said.

"Is it you? Are you not the castellan of Linnières, near Hervi? Ansiau, son of Ansiau?"

"I am." Ansiau frowned, trying to recollect where and how he had met this fellow countryman. "The Devil pluck out my beard if I remember you, my brother. You cannot have been in the Temple long? I must have seen you at Troyes."

The man laughed. "You saw me at Linnières. Well, brother-in-law, you have a poor memory."

Ansiau told himself that he was under no obligation to remember the innumerable husbands of his elder sisters. "It must have been a long time ago?" he said doubtfully.

The Templar began counting on his fingers. "Eight, nine years ago, the year old Count Henry died. You had just come back from the Holy Land, I think. Do you still not know me? Erard—Erard of Baudemant, near Villemaur, Hugh's brother."

Ansiau cried out in astonishment and stared at the man with increasing perplexity. Until now he had thought that he was talking to a man older than himself, and he did not know what attitude to assume toward a petty knight whom he had called a puppy years ago. Furthermore, he remembered Erard as a very handsome young man. And from this haggard, sallow face all the beauty had been washed as by a sponge, at most a few traces of it remained in the structure of the head, in the proud lines of the neck. Only the eyes seemed to live, burning under dark lids. Doubtless Erard was somewhat embarrassed by the effect his words had produced. Perhaps he felt a little saddened by the thought that he had grown so unrecognizable. And Ansiau was embarrassed too—he had more or less forgotten why Erard had been so distasteful to him; but he remembered well enough that he had infringed the laws of hospitality in his respect, and the memory was a painful one. "If I wronged you," he said at last, "I believe that I have righted the wrong this day." And he held out his hand to his brother-in-law.

"I could not let you go unthanked," said Erard. "I came straight from the ramparts—excuse my dress."

"What!" said Ansiau, "there is no better dress for a knight! Besides, I think our bath women are the best in the camp. I hope you will disarm and bathe here, and stay with us until evening, if you have nothing else to do. Perhaps you will find some old friends."

Lying in a great white tent, the two new friends were bathed and rubbed by an old woman with a mustache and horny hands. Ansiau stretched and shook the water out of his short hair. "I know nothing better. Though certainly this is not quite up to the baths in Troyes."

Erard, whose eyes were closed, remained silent.

"Good old Berta," said Ansiau, "she knows her trade. A pity she is not a little younger, don't you think?"

Erard said that such things were no longer for him and that he must not think of them. Ansiau opened his eyes wide. "What! You are a real monk?"

"So far as possible," said Erard quietly.

Then he began explaining that all women, noble or villein, were instruments of the Devil, created for the perdition of men. "Such is the teaching of the Church and the Fathers. From woman sprang original sin, and all evil, all suffering, and all impurity. I am in a position to speak," he said, "I know something about it. I can tell you that I have known many women who passed for honest, and I swear to you that they were mad bitches, every one of them —there is nothing in their heads but sin and filthiness. To live a good life, a man must avoid them—that is my advice to you."

"You are very severe," said Ansiau, who could not help feeling a certain respect, yet remained unconvinced. "When one lives in the world, one judges differently."

Then Erard began demonstrating that there was no worse state than that of a knight who lived in the world—it was a perpetual siege of the seven deadly sins, especially anger and lust. And those two sins led straight to Hell, where you were seethed in boiling pitch, which was what happened to all men who were too hot in their earthly lives. That was just why the military orders were such a good thing, he said—there, the fires of lust were repressed so effectually that they rose to the heart and head and soured the blood, which sourness became anger, which anger turned to hatred for God's enemies. "Thus, as you see," Erard concluded, "the two gravest sins are transformed into planks of salvation."

"By St. Thiou," said Ansiau, "that is all very well, but it is not an idea which would ever have occurred to me. Did you have a vocation to enter the Temple?"

"I cannot say that I had a vocation," said Erard after a short silence. "But, after all, I have my soul to think of. I am past thirty. I have lived for pleasure long enough. And there is no joking with God—once dead, you can do nothing to help yourself, it is too late. You have to start now." He shook his head. "I do not believe," he said, "that taking the cross is enough to save a man. I know many a man here who spends his time filling himself with Giblite wine and thinks that makes him a holy martyr. Our men lead lives that would shame even the infidels. And they are properly punished for it, by God!—look at all the sicknesses which run through the camp."

Ansiau sighed. "Yes. They say the king of England is very ill. A great misfortune."

"A perfect example," said Erard. "He is being punished for his bad faith to his lord. He does everything possible to embarrass our king because it makes him jealous to see that the Christians of this country prefer the king of France. He has not been here a week, and look at all the affronts he has put on the king and the marquess. Yet he must see that everyone is tired of King Guy."

"On the contrary, he is under an obligation to defend King Guy," Ansiau answered. "They are both from Poitou, and the Lusignan family are kin to the duke of Aquitaine. And King Guy is not a bad knight."

337

Erard laughed. "King Guy is a fine man," he said, "but he is a fool. It is not his fault, he could not possibly have held the kingdom. And he has shown it clearly enough."

Ansiau thought that the king was not so greatly to blame—he owed his misfortune to bad counsellors and to the treachery of the count of Tripoli, who had deserted him in the middle of a battle. But he was too courteous to argue with his guest.

At the entrance to the viscount's great tent the two men met Herbert and Ansiet, who had come to see if their father had been wounded in the battle.

"You have not met my sons?" said Ansiau with a broad smile.

Erard raised his head, surprised: "What! Your sons? And to think that I saw them when they were two little brats who didn't come up to my knee! But they must be your sons by an earlier marriage?"

Ansiau burst out laughing at the thought that anyone should suppose he had been married before. He said that he had never had any wife but Lady Alis.

"Of course," said Erard, studying the boys' faces. "Besides, they take after your lady."

Erard was well received and acclaimed in the viscount's tent. Of the knights who were present he knew hardly anyone except Ansiau and Renaud of Hervi. Nevertheless he could barely conceal his joy at finding himself among fellow countrymen once more. He was extremely animated, ate as much as two men and drank enough for four—on the whole he produced a favorable impression. Ansiau even thought him changed for the better, more serious and more modest than in his early days. But toward the end of the meal, when the wine had produced its effect, Erard became freer-spoken, and his old offensive familiarity seemed to return. He gushed a good deal over Ansiet and Herbert, who, sitting grave and dignified opposite him, did their best to show that they were no longer the little brats Erard had seen at Linnières.

"Fine stock!" said Erard. "Why did you bring them here, brother-in-law? This is a poor place for the young. I dread to think what they will learn here. I am glad that I have no son, a soldier's life is a dirty business."

"What is to be done?" said Ansiau. "Neither you nor I can change it."

"It is a great pity," said Erard thoughtfully. "You should have left them in Champagne. What can they acquire here except vices and diseases? This life is good enough for old campaigners like ourselves, but those boys. . . . They're young, they're tender."

Ansiau thought: "What is he sticking his nose into?" and he said: "I am not going to keep them in a reliquary." He had no intention of admitting that he did not sleep nights for worrying over his sons.

"It is a pity," Erard repeated, "a great pity." And Ansiau began to look askance at him and to think that it would be better not to let the man see his sons again—he might well have the evil eye.

To change the subject, Renaud of Hervi asked Erard why he had become a Templar.

"You mean you want to know why I did not become a Hospitaller?" Erard asked. "I know that in France the Hospitallers are more highly regarded. But I had an uncle—" He crossed himself. "God rest his soul, he died on Palm Sunday. He was a Templar, a knight of the order; he entered the Temple in the first year of the Leper King, having lost his only son. When I came here he protected me, he saw that I got a good place; I serve the Friar Treasurer."

Garnier had recovered consciousness the morning after his accident, but his condition did not appear to improve. The pain in his abdomen was so intense that he screamed whenever he was touched, and his chest was almost equally painful. Simon sent for an Armenian doctor who gave the patient opium to drink. And the next morning Garnier said that he felt much better and that it was shameful that a man who was not really wounded should lie abed. He begged the doctor to cure him as quickly as possible, as he wanted to be fit for the grand assault. And the grand assault was set for the next day. And although the king of England was still ill, it was actually begun. When Garnier heard the voice of the trumpets and the ceaseless thunder of the catapults, he got out of bed and began to dress; he was alone, Simon was under the walls with his lord, and the squires had other things to do besides looking after a sick man. So Garnier put on his hauberk himself and went out to find someone who would help him lace it. His side pained him violently, but he told himself to forget it. Armed after a fashion, he managed to join Balian of Ibelin's troop. There the excitement was intense, for it was rumored that Saladin was attacking from the rear again and had already taken the rampart. Simon and the other "Colt" knights had not words enough to revile King Richard, who had refused to join in the attack and had forbidden his men to join in it. "If the assault fails," they said, "it will be because of Richard's treachery. He is sold to Saladin, he and all his men." Garnier went to his father, who was so angry and embittered that he did not even look at him. "Father," said Garnier, "I do not understand what is happening. The assault was ordered." "The assault! There is no assault!" cried Simon. "Go to the Devil!" When he learned that there was no assault Garnier felt his weakness rush back on him—his head whirled and he sank into blackness. His arms and legs were as flabby and heavy as bags of wool.

Simon despaired of ever persuading his son to lie quiet. Garnier was as stubborn as a mule. Though he was spitting blood and suffered from pains which nothing but opium would relieve, he insisted that he must get up, he wanted to go to the machines, he wanted to be with the English and Pisan knights who were preparing to storm the Accursed Tower. Simon was too busy to watch him himself, and he never had a moment's peace, for he was always wondering what mad thing his son might do during his absence. He finally decided to take the boy to his wife's house in Tyre, where he could stay until he was cured. Garnier refused to hear of it—he would be called a coward if he left the camp before the city fell. In desperation, Simon asked Ansiau to help him.

Ansiau started when he saw his nephew's gray, despondent face, the hollow eyes, the dark, cracked, swollen lips.

Garnier smiled. "It has been long since I saw you, my uncle," he gasped. "Tell my father to let me alone. He wants to take me to Tyre. It would be cowardice to go now, wouldn't it?"

"There, my boy," said Ansiau, "your father knows what is right better than you. He will never advise you to do a cowardly thing."

"He is worried about my health," said Garnier with a scornful smile. "But I didn't come to the Holy Land to take care of myself, did I?"

"I shall tell you one thing, Garnier," said his uncle, very seriously, and the boy raised his head, for his uncle never called him by his name except upon the most solemn occasions. "I shall tell you one thing, Garnier—you are a bad son. And a bad son cannot be a good knight. A son must obey his father, my boy."

"I am not a child," Garnier muttered.

"My dear boy," said Ansiau, "I promised your father that I would make you a good knight. He has a right to blame me, for I have brought him an ungrateful and vicious son who is not worth two pease. Do not bring shame on me, my fine boy."

Garnier began to cry. "Do not force me to go," he said.

"You must."

"But the city will be taken!" cried the boy. "And I shall not be there!"

Ansiau stroked his hair. "You big baby! There are many more cities to take!"

A galley belonging to the marquess was to sail the following morning, and Simon had his son carried aboard on a stretcher and went aboard himself, his lord having given him leave to spend a few days in Tyre. The sea was calm and the sea air seemed to do Garnier good. Lying on deck, under a great white awning stretched between the sails, he closed his eyes and fell into a half-sleep. The monotonous, almost rhythmical cries of the Genoese sailors, the plash of waves against the hull, the rays of the sun which, through awning and shirt, found and caressed his body—it all blended into a familiar music, a chorus of women's voices in the hall at Linnières.

Blows the wind, the branches sway,
Lover and beloved, soft sleep they...

Simon did not own a house in Tyre, but as he had been one of the first knights to take refuge in that city after the defeat, he had gone to live in a little town house belonging to a certain baron of Belmont, a knight in the service of the count of Tripoli. The baron of Belmont had been killed in the battle of Hattin and his widow had fled to Tripoli. It was a small house of white stone, squeezed between two others; the street was narrow and dark, but the rear of the house gave onto the gardens of the monastery of the Trinity, and the gardens in turn extended to the rampart, which overlooked the sea.

The city of Tyre, although overpopulated and crowded with soldiers, seemed tranquil in comparison with the feverish agitation of the camp. Sails, white or yellowed, swayed gently in the intense sunlight, the shore had the gay, animated look of a great commercial port. Poor Garnier was bumped and jostled over steep streets like flights of wide stone steps; between his half-closed lids he glimpsed windowless, whitewashed walls, striped curtains drawn over doors, stone fountains at street corners. Veiled women, their arms laden with bracelets, stood by the fountains with tall, gray clay jars; long-bearded turbaned Armenians passed, solemn and stiff; barelegged watercarriers tugged at the bridles of their donkeys to make way for the litter.

After passing through a low, dark, vaulted passageway Garnier was astonished to find himself in a small square courtyard strewn with fine yellow sand; in the center of it a rose laurel spread its dark foliage. A wide strip of red cloth, stretched between two walls, shaded the courtyard from the noonday sun; against the eastern wall a vine trailed its bunches of black grapes. Two half-naked blackamoors were busily sifting flour through a silk sieve. Three maids in white, squatting on a mat on the ground, were spinning wool. The sunlight which filtered through the red cloth bathed the little courtyard in a warm, even light which was very pleasant. Simon slowly took off his gloves and his squire ran upstairs to inform the mistress of the house that her husband had come home.

It was a thin, dark-skinned old woman, laden with jewels and heavily perfumed, who bent over Garnier. Never had he seen so much finery—from throat to waist she was covered with chains and necklaces and heavy embroidery in gold and pearl. Her olive face was framed in a white veil fastened under the chin and a circlet of wrought silver half hid her forehead. Her face was not beautiful, but her deep black eyes flashed and glittered between tremulous lashes. The old lady turned to Simon and put both arms around his neck. "Poor friend," she said, "my poor friend."

Garnier was put to bed in a secluded room. He lay among silken cushions on a soft, low couch, and black slaves rubbed his body with scented oils. Simon sent for doctors, and Garnier was turned and rolled and kneaded by their deft, cold hands, which hurt him everywhere. He was suffering, said one of the doctors, a Greek who spoke French fairly well, from internal injuries—vessels had burst in his chest and abdomen, and viscera had been stretched and displaced—the cure would take long. And Simon understood that very little could be done—how was it possible to treat internal injuries? Rest was prescribed—and Garnier should have it, he should not make a single unnecessary movement. Since his conversation with his uncle, Garnier had become very docile and did his best not to cross his father. Besides, he felt so badly that the thought of getting up no longer entered his mind. He had fever every night and breathed with difficulty.

"The journey has tired him," said Simon. "He will soon improve here, my wife will take good care of him." He spent two days in Tyre, then came to say good-bye to his son. Garnier's face was as small and pinched as the face of a ten-year-old child. Only the eyes, the nose, and the mouth stood out—lips, nostrils, and lids were tinged with brown and looked swollen.

"Fair son," said Simon, "I must go. I shall be criticized if I stay away too long."

Garnier opened his eyes wide. "So soon?" And the thought of his father's going frightened him—his companion in suffering for ten months, his only friend in that strange city, his uncle Ansiau's cousin, his own father—now his father, too, was forsaking him. He said: "Stay a little longer!" and felt ashamed of his weakness.

Tears came to Simon's eyes and for a moment he hesitated. Then he remembered that King Richard's final reinforcements were already off the port of Tyre and that the great assault might be launched at any moment. His friends would hold him a coward if he stayed quietly in Tyre with his wife on the day of the decisive battle. Besides, so far from the camp, he already felt out of things—he was impatient to know what the marquess would do, and if King Richard was well again, and if King Guy would really have his rights confirmed.

"I will be back in two weeks," he said. "Even sooner, if possible. That is, if you are not well by then—in which case you will come to Acre by yourself."

"I will come," said Garnier in a choked voice, without even thinking what he was saying. Simon kissed him, and the boy clung to his father's neck with both arms. "Father!" he sobbed. "Father! Father!" Simon attributed this unexpected outburst of affection to the boy's weakened condition and he set out with a heavy heart. Never had he dreamed that the parting would affect him so deeply. He was oppressed as by a weight of iron. He vowed that he would return to Tyre as soon as possible.

Simon's second wife was five years older than her husband. From her mother, who was French but had been born in Constantinople, she had inherited the Greek Christian name of Theodora—Theodora of Latran had been her maiden name. Thrice married, she had never borne children and she was ready and eager to mother the big French boy her husband had brought her from the camp at Acre. She was a kindly soul. With his real mother Garnier's relationship had been polite and cold. This strange lady who talked in a musical voice and breathed such a scent of amber and sandalwood drew him as the sun draws young, frozen shoots. She might be a foreigner, but she was a woman. Her gestures were calm and soothing, her fingers so light that they seemed made to touch nothing but flower petals, butterflies' wings. When she smiled her whole face broke into fine little wrinkles, though her eyes remained sad. Garnier asked her to stay near him, and she sat in a cushioned chair with a piece of needlework in her hands—an alms bag with a pattern of black birds and golden birds crossing wings and feet. Each day she showed Garnier how it had progressed—she was very proud of her work. A little Greek serving-girl sat at her feet, sewing a shirt. Garnier's bed was by the window, and the window opened onto the little courtyard. Garnier's room was the prettiest in the house—it was like a very small chapel or a reliquary. The floor was spread with bright-colored silk rugs, the ceiling was painted white, and on the south wall hung a Persian tapestry. Garnier amused himself by making out the designs in it: a flowering cherry, gazelles, eagles, hares. On the other walls were a profusion of rich embroideries, some depicting battle scenes, others flowers and crosses. And the window was framed by a broad mosaic in which white, blue, and golden stars mingled and joined. Each day Theodora brought in some new rarity— an enameled dish, a ewer of wrought copper, or an ivory horn carved like lacework. She could not spoil her stepson enough, she stuffed him with pre- served fruits and almond paste made with her own hands—but Garnier had little appetite.

He could not yet understand how he had come to be there beside the peaceful little courtyard flooded with warm reddish light, with its rose laurel, its dark grapes, and its white doves cooing all day long. Lady Theodora's perfumes, her bracelet-laden wrists, her full muslin sleeves—it was all so far from the camp, the noise of the catapults, the oaths. Never before had anyone taken such care of him. He was given a medicine which contained powdered gold—not without qualms he drank it down, but Theodora told him that it would restore his strength. "And when you are a little stronger," she said, "we will journey together to Our Lady of Tortosa, and within a month you will be well. No one has ever gone there and not been cured, Christian or infidel. And now eat a little of my rose jelly—I make it better than anyone." She combed his hair and said: "You are looking better already."

Nothing could have been more untrue. Garnier spat blood and pus inces- santly and his fever was increasing. In the evening, when the fever rose very high, he became animated and appeared to be delirious. "Snow!" he said. "Ah, snow! The snow in France is so beautiful, mother—if only you knew. All the ponds are frozen. The willow branches are white. There is all the snow anyone could ever want, all the snow. . . ."

"Don't talk, child, it will tire your chest," said Theodora.

But the boy gasped: "No, no, wait! She is so beautiful, if only you knew! My cousin Mahaut, at Linnières in the forest. Little pink lips like cherries not quite ripe—I was the first boy she ever kissed. So white and smooth, and her lovely, black squint eyes—" (For Garnier, squint eyes were an essential ingredient of feminine beauty.) "The most beautiful girl in Champagne. And she loved me. I swear she loved me!"

"Don't talk," Theodora implored. "Look—I beg you on my knees. I will cry if you talk any more."

"No, no, let me! No, you don't know. Oh! how it pains!"

Two weeks after his coming to Tyre Garnier realized that he was far from being cured. Terrified, he looked at his emaciated arms, his big hands—mere bones covered with dry, cracking skin. "Mother, tell me, shall I get well?" he asked. "Mother, I don't understand it, I don't feel any better." Then one day he did understand, and terror took him. "No, no! I won't! Not that! It is too hard. Mother, I am too young, God will not permit it."

He began to have fits of deep coughing which tore his chest, and after them he fell into a state of somnolence and prostration. He suffered so much that he had only one fear—that the horrible coughing would begin again. He preferred to feel his chest slowly filling with pus; then he strangled, and began to cough and spit once more. For three days he had eaten nothing, and one morning it was not the doctor who came to see him, but a priest.

"Oh! If I had known," Garnier said, "I would never have done it. I ought to have taken what I was offered. I am properly punished for having been too good. Go away, shaven-pate, I do not want you. You will only bring me bad luck." He wept like a child, but soon he resigned himself, confessed, and received the sacraments. Theodora and the little Greek serving-maid sat weeping in a corner of the room.

Garnier behaved quite well—he even made an effort to smile at Lady Theodora, he gasped: "Greet my father for me. And my uncle Ansiau. Everyone." Then, because he was suffering terribly, he began to scream and call: "Mahaut! help me! Mahaut! help me! Mahaut, dearest!" Then the death agony began, and, though he breathed stertorously for several hours more, he did not recover consciousness. Lady Theodora wiped the froth from his lips and nostrils. That evening he was dressed and laid on a tapestry-covered couch in a room with drawn curtains. Heavy clouds of incense hung in the still air. It was very hot, and on the cheeks and under the eyes of the bony yellow face little flecks of brown began to appear. The priest recited the prayers for the dead, and old Theodora, kneeling at the foot of the couch, wept without a sound, sniffling softly from time to time.

Simon had returned to the camp in a very bad humor, which he attributed to his disgust with King Richard's behavior. In the French ranks there was more and more talk of treachery—the king of England was sending messengers to Saladin, receiving presents, and doing nothing to advance the siege. In any case, he was always sick. And the marquess had withdrawn to Tyre, for fear, the word went, of Richard's plots. The marquess—the king of Jerusalem to those who held with him—was a leader, and without him the crusaders felt abandoned and feared the direst calamities. The catapults were still hammering the walls of the city, but all through the camp there was utter discouragement.

Ansiau came to ask Simon for news of Garnier. "He will soon recover," said Simon. "He is being well cared for. He is better off there than here."

"No doubt," said Ansiau, who was thinking that Ansiet had weak lungs and was much too thin—how would he get through the long winter rains?

"I shall go to see him," said Simon. "I believe he is becoming fond of me."

"I was sure he would," said Ansiau. "There is not a finer boy on earth. God, God! If only he recovers!"

"Andrew went with the marquess' escort and did not let me know," said Simon. "If he had, I should have asked him to go and see Garnier—I don't believe he even knows that the boy is in Tyre."

"It would seem that your marquess has bewitched Andrew," said Ansiau. "He is a different man. He has forgotten us."

"I smell a rat there," Simon laughed. "I believe there is a woman in the case."

Ansiau shook his head. "Andrew? A woman? Impossible."

"That is what I hear, nevertheless. One of Queen Isabel's maids-in-waiting, of a good family from Tripoli. However, Andrew, at his age and poor as he is . . ." Ansiau continued to shake his head—he could not imagine Andrew sighing for a maid-in-waiting. "He is devoted to the marquess, that is all," he said.

Simon began pacing up and down the tent again. " 'To the king' would sound better to my ears, though at the moment, God knows, marquess is a better title than king—everything is topsyturvy. It is the king of England who has spoiled matters—instead of Richard his name should be Trickard, for there is not a trickier traitor in the camp. And if he has come here to give the country back to King Guy, I believe he would have done better to leave it to the infidels."

Ansiau gave him a hard look. "That is no way to talk."

Simon began spitting on the floor and kneading his temples with his fists. "I know, I know. But when I see treachery everywhere, it nauseates me. All week Richard has been negotiating with Saladin—God knows about what— and receiving gifts of falcons. It was not for such japes that he took the cross."

"The marquess is doing exactly the same."

"With the marquess it is different—he does it as a matter of courtesy and to arrange exchanges of prisoners." Simon became increasingly excited. "And no one could ever accuse the marquess of selling himself to the infidels, because there is not another Christian on earth whom the Saracens hate and fear so much. Richard knows it and he is boiling with jealousy, and so he has started rumors about the marquess. Why, the English even dare to accuse the baron of Ibelin—my master—who has lost so much and suffered so much through the Saracens and who has never spared himself in battle . . .

"Cousin," Simon went on, "God knows it is wrong of me, but there is more than one man here to whom I wish a bad end, and speedily. You Franks, you come here on pilgrimage, your lands and your wives are safe in countries that are Christian. You will go back, and we shall still have the infidels on our necks. And do you think we lead an easy life? I have lived in this country for ten years, and not a month has gone by of which I have not spent a week under arms, both in the Leper King's time and in King Guy's. Even in peacetime the country is not quiet. I have been taken prisoner twice, I have been wounded in the head and leg and God knows how often in the arm. When the Saracens came it was *our* lands and *our* houses that they took.

We have everything to lose in this war. And the folk from across the sea dare to insult us and call us cowards!"

Ansiau turned very red. "What! Who has called you a coward? You must tell me their names."

"No one that I know of," said Simon, "but there are those who think it. There are those who are dividing up our lands and castles among themselves beforehand. And if the kingdom is reconquered to make Guy king, with his Englishmen and Gascons and Poitevins—may God let me die before I see the day!"

Ansiau said: "Wait until it comes. Things have not gone so far yet."

Simon sat down beside his cousin on the bed and covered his face with both hands. "God is punishing us for allowing the Holy Cross to be profaned," he said. "He will deny us the victory because of our sins. And yet He knows well enough that we are not so greatly at fault, for we fought well. It was King Guy and the Templars who ruined us and the whole country with us."

Ansiau tried to console him, but Simon was in one of his blackest humors. To distract him, Ansiau talked of Erard of Baudemant. "Another who wants to save his soul," he said. "He is Hugh of Baudemant's brother. He fights like a madman, it is a pleasure to see."

"Ah?" said Simon. "The little cur? By St. George, I know him. He is only a novice, but he makes such a show of zeal that he will soon be first assistant to the Friar Treasurer. And when that happens, someone had bettter watch the ducats. It will not take him long to slip them into his sleeve!"

"Come, come," said Ansiau. "He is a kinsman of mine."

"All Templars are alike," Simon cut him off. "They love money even better than usurers do. And he is the worst kind. He is as ferocious as a weasel—I wish you had seen him cutting off prisoners' heads and hands for sheer spite."

"It is natural for a friar to do it, since the infidels behead all the friars they capture."

Simon shrugged his shoulders. "Exactly—they think only of themselves. To hear them tell it, God created the Holy Land for the use and service of the Order of the Temple. Cousin, God keep me from loving the infidels, but I believe I love them better than I do some Christians. Ah! Lord have mercy on us!"

On July third the French king's marshal, Auberi Clément, was killed on the walls in sight of the whole army. He was mourned by Englishmen and Frenchmen alike and there was great grief through the camp. And on the second day following, the assault and all the work of the siege were interrupted for three days in honor of those who had died since the siege began. The end was nearing. The army breathed more freely, yet no one dared to believe that victory was sure, even though the cost had been so great. It was strange not to hear the noise of the machines, the whiz of arrows, the cries of the wounded—it was as if everyone had suddenly gone deaf. The camp churches and chapels were crammed with soldiers and knights, the concourse was so great that soon there were crowds outside the churches, and the archbishops of Canterbury and Reims, the bishops of Meaux and Orléans and the other prelates came out and blessed the kneeling multitude. Few were they who had not lost a kinsman or a friend during the siege. Kneeling beside Renaud of Hervi, Ansiau murmured the names of the soldiers and comrades he had buried in the cemetery of St. Nicholas, but he kept making mistakes because the list was so long. Of the twenty-five men he had brought with him from Champagne, eighteen were dead—Aioul had been the first to die, Thierri the last. Of his comrades, he had lost Mathis of Monguoz, Manesier of Nangi, Joubert of Ancis, Thibaut of Puiseaux, James of Hervi—and how many more whom he had met during the siege!

"Jerusalem and Holy Cross!" Assault on the northern and northeastern walls, a tumultuous hand-to-hand fight under the burning sun. Gray, massive, and full of breaches, the wall is covered with ladders laden with men, as a garden wall in summer is covered with bunches of grapes supported on stakes. Crouched under their shields, the knights press to the foot of the wall. The archers on the wooden towers shoot into the city. The Accursed Tower is half battered down at last, and there is fighting in the breach.

On his wooden tower which has been drawn up to the rampart, under a great red-silk baldaquin, on a camp bed spread with white, sits Richard Lionheart, his legs stretched forward, his back resting against cushions held by English and Gascon barons. He holds his crossbow with both hands and aims at the Moslem soldiers who defend the wall. The arrow loosed, his squire puts a new one in the bow, and again Richard shoots. The squire has barely time to reload, and at each shot a man falls.

Ansiau was returning from the ramparts when one of Simon's squires greeted him and asked him to come to Simon's tent. Ansiau told Guiot of Beaumont to follow him and made his way toward the baron of Ibelin's tents. He felt dead tired and half overcome by the heat, and he was limping.

In Simon's tent he found Andrew, who had just arrived from Tyre. Andrew was looking well: his shaven face gave him a youthful appearance, over his reddish-gold hair he wore a square of white cloth, fastened Turkish fashion with two gilded copper clasps. Simon was pacing swiftly up and down, swaying as he walked, like an infuriated tiger. His face was gray, and his nose seemed to have grown a good half inch longer.

"Cousin," Ansiau asked, "what is the matter?"

Simon winced and stood still. His small eyes shot greenish flames. What was the matter indeed! Ansiau—like all the rest of his tribe, Simon might say—was too thickheaded to see what was happening. Did he really not see that Richard had broken his sworn faith to his lord and was insulting him before Christians and infidels alike? The king of France was negotiating the surrender of the city, and Richard had attacked purposely, in bad faith, to make his lord appear a liar. King Philip was sick with grief over his vassal's behavior. "When we should have attacked," Simon shouted, "he hid in his tent like the coward he is. And now, when it is time to keep the peace, he attacks. Sitting there under his red-silk daïs so that his sergeants can admire him! Being a good crossbowman does not make a man a good king!"

"Enough," said Ansiau. "Speak no evil of him, I will not hear it."

Simon cried: "You are all his varlets! Because he has promised you the booty—gold, houses, horses! And because he will let you put the city to fire and sword! It was not to pillage Christian cities that you took the cross. He has bought you all, beginning with Henry of Champagne, who sold his sworn lord for wheat and pork!"

Ansiau turned and left the tent; Andrew followed him and caught him by the sleeve. "Come back," he said.

"It is no place for me."

Andrew repeated: "Come back, I have something to tell you."

He looked so solemn that Ansiau re-entered the tent. Simon, somewhat calmer, was hacking at the wooden tent post with his knife. Ansiau thought that he looked suddenly aged and shrunken—it was as if he had a pain in his back and was making an effort to stand straight. Andrew said nothing. And Ansiau wondered what the two brothers could have to tell him—despite himself he felt afraid. Simon went on cutting crosses in the tent pole and did not look up. Then at last, in a dry, broken voice, he said: "Garnier is dead."

Ansiau swayed forward, then backward, then forward again and fell his length face down on the ground, dragging his squire with him. It took two good bleedings to bring him back to consciousness.

The following morning Andrew and Simon were leaving the church of St. Nicholas, where they had attended a Mass for the repose of Garnier's soul. Ansiau was still too ill to walk and had not come. Simon was calm, but his eyelids were rather red. "I do not complain," he said. "He has gained martyrdom, I could ask nothing better for him. When I think of all the misery God has spared him, I should not protest. But how can I help it? The flesh is weak, and I had grown used to him."

"All the same, it is a pity," Andrew said. "It was not for this that God created him."

Simon shrugged his shoulders. "We know nothing about it. Better for him to leave this world pure and unstained—not to have come to be like ourselves. Yet, brother, if it is true that God judges the heart, He cannot but have mercy on me. He knows that my only love, my only treasure in this world, has been the land of Our Saviour. I may have sinned in the flesh, but never in heart."

Andrew sighed: "It is for Him to judge, He knows better than we can."

"Brother," Simon continued, "you saw it for yourself—I did not weep long for my son. But I swear to you that for Jerusalem I have wept—wept until, to my sorrow, I had no tears left. And how can a man fail to weep for Jerusalem, when Our Lord Himself wept for her with the tears of His body? Our lust and our pride have lost her, and the whole land with her. God knows whether we shall win her back from the infidel dogs—we are making a very bad beginning."

"Thierri!" Ansiau rose, heavy-headed as if he were waking from a nightmare. A pallid and uncertain dawn was filtering through the entrance slit. Ansiau heard the horses stamping in the long tent which served as a stable; in the distance trumpets were sounding, watchmen were calling to one another; the camp was gradually waking, and already a choir somewhere was singing the slow, sad music of a funeral service. Funerals, like everything else, had to be got through early, before the heat came down.

Ansiau felt very tired—if the king of France in person had spoken to him at that moment, he would not have answered. He had had enough. He would leave the camp. He would take his boys. He had given enough—let others have their turn. He was no fool—he knew that Ansiet was sick with fatigue for three days after each assault. The boy could not be allowed to go, like Garnier. Garnier, Thierri. Two martyrs were more than enough—Ansiet should not be a third, he was made for something else. He was made to be castellan of Linnières, and God would not deny it to him.

Ansiau stepped outside the tent and watched the horizon whitening above the *tells*. The whiteness spread over the whole sky; the earth was gray and colorless; on the horizon the light steadily increased—purple, red, scarlet, living and triumphant—the gables of the tents caught fire one after the other like the candles of an endless procession; the first light fell on the Toron, the banners of the king of Jerusalem were bathed in blood-red, then the streams of purple flowed over the cloth of the tents, then the whole hill hung luminous above a sea of fiery gables, from which the incandescent flags rose like beacons.

All through the camp grooms were leading whinnying, rearing horses to the water troughs; the church bells were ringing for morning Mass; the soldiers were running to the wells for cooking water.

Standing before his tent, Ansiau looked at the sky and the wheeling vultures. It would be a hot day, he thought—an inferno for the men on the machines and the moving towers. But undoubtedly the city could not hold out much longer; the Accursed Tower was so mined that it was said to be ready to topple. God! how much Christian blood it had caused to flow—enough to fill a lake. And, in their thousands upon thousands, the crosses of that city of tents seemed to move in upon Ansiau and crush him from every side—crosses on clothes, crosses on flags, crosses on crowns, graveyard crosses, church crosses. And greatest of all, the One True Cross, which must be won back, which Saladin held a prisoner in his palace—God tear out the mad dog's heart and entrails! "Lord God," said Ansiau, "I am at Thy mercy, I am Thy vassal. I shall stay because stay I must—grant only that I see not my son perish. Thy will be done. Amen."

Ansiau had thought that his sons would be sick with grief when they learned of Garnier's death. To his great surprise the news left them almost indifferent. They looked at him for a moment with staring, frightened eyes, and that was all. It was not that they lacked feeling. They could not allow themselves to pause and think. They did not want to be crippled by grief at the moment when Acre was at last to fall, at the moment the kings were to enter it and plant their banners on the wall—at the moment when the Holy Cross was to be brought back to Christian soil. They would have time to weep later. Now they were as if drunk with wine.

They had known too much of death. They had seen it too close—it could not touch them—they could not die. So much the worse for those who let themselves be caught! Ansiet duelled with death as with an equal—he was one of those who purposely sought out the most dangerous situations, who wanted as many arrows as possible to stick in their armor. He did not duck when the stones from the Saracen mangonels flew past his head; he went to the rampart without his hauberk, pretending that he was too hot. He ate spoiled meat and insisted that it was as good as any other, he forgot his hat despite the intermittent fevers from which he had suffered since winter. In short, he permitted himself an infinity of unnecessary risks well calculated to make his father lose sleep. This behavior did not spring from braggadocio or a desire to shine—he was absolutely without vanity. But he was a good gambler and the stakes were worth it.

To the king of England, his leader and lord, he felt an attachment which was gradually dying for lack of food—he needed more concrete pleasures than the memory of a look, or a glimpse of a golden helmet shining far off behind a hedge of casques and lances. He could easily have turned to women, who were more plentiful since the famine had ended. But Richard was still his God, and that made him scornful of women in general—not one of them was worthy to hold a man's attention for more than half an hour.

Detested by the "Colts," the French, the Germans, and most of the Genoese sailors at anchor in the port, Richard behaved as if he were the only leader of the Crusade and the only Christian king worthy of the name. It was as much as he would do to admit that King Philip had the right to a voice in making decisions. Yet Philip was certainly no man to let himself be overawed—despite the extraordinary independence of his too powerful vassal, he succeeded in getting his policy adopted, and the capitulation of Acre was negotiated and concluded through the marquess of Montferrat, Richard's worst enemy.

The city opened its gates to the shouting of the crusaders and the sound of drums and trumpets. The sky was clear and windless. Breached and crumbling, the ancient walls were at last to rest; the Accursed Tower, dismantled and transformed into a huge heap of rubble, looked like the corpse of a dragon. Everywhere on walls and towers appeared Christian banners—the cross, the fleur-de-lis, the lion, the bars. They rose as if by magic, and each was greeted by cheers. The marquess of Montferrat, with an advanced guard of Lombards and Frenchmen, was the first to enter the city; behind him his barons carried the royal standards. And that day there were no enemies in the camp—he was acclaimed as he passed; the sick and the dying had their beds carried to the ramparts so that with their own eyes they might see the cross rise upon the walls they had so often cursed. The emir Karakush, and Maktub, the commandant of the city, surrendered with the entire garrison and placed themselves in the hands of the Christian kings.

The days passed, day after day of heat and uproar and disorder. Victory and relaxation had gone to all men's heads, it was one long search for something good enough to recompense the pains they had endured. The knights drank in the palaces and the gardens, the soldiers drank in the streets and squares. No decent woman dared to leave her house. In the great hall of the Temple commandery, where King Richard had taken up his quarters, there was feasting every day; and, because the king loved music, troops of minstrels gathered there and gave concerts from dawn to dark and from dark to dawn. Ships laden with prostitutes arrived daily, coming from every port in Syria—there were beautiful Georgians, Venetians, Persians glittering with jewels and accompanied by their slaves and their duennas—and the lesser game as well, simple soldiers' wenches recruited among Syrian or Frankish or Jewish slaves—there was something for every purse. The whole port seethed with their motley dresses, their veils, their head tires, their bare arms. In every courtyard, in the corners of rooms and on street corners, couples sprawled, alone or in groups. The good wines of the country, which the kings and barons bestowed on their men without cost, ran in rivers both into men's bellies and into the gutter—never had such waste been seen. Stretched across the streets, drunken, half-naked soldiers prevented the passage of horses.

"Of Linnières." Ansiau had no reason now to bear the name, for Linnières was far away, at the other end of the world, buried, lost for ever. Every soldier who had been through the siege should take the name "of Acre," he thought—they had buried so many kinsmen and friends and brothers-in-arms that each of them had a good share of ground in the cemetery of St. Nicholas, below the Toron.

Ansiau no longer thought of his castle—he would not go back to it; like Simon, he would stay in Palestine. Lady Alis had a good head, she could bring up the children and manage the household. He no longer had a duty to anyone—he had made his two sons into good knights, and now they did not need him. Andrew had left him. Before him he saw nothing but camp life, behind him there were graves, grave after grave. Garnier's was the latest. But Ansiau did not want to think of that, he put aside all the memories which bound him to his dead nephew.

He was now comfortably settled in the city, in a house in the Pisan quarter which had belonged to a cloth merchant. The house had two stories and an inner courtyard which was converted into a stable. He was still followed by a whole troop of men who, though they had sworn no faith to him, acted as his vassals—as he had lost his own men, others had come to replace them. At the moment he had Renaud of Hervi, with his squires, and Sales of Jeugni—both his kinsmen by marriage. Then there was a tinker from Reims and little juggler who had lost his occupation by breaking his leg, and several masterless sergeants—in all, some thirty men. Ansiau did not choose them—they were tent mates or starving men with whom he had shared his victuals and who had stayed on. He accepted them a little unwillingly, let them drift into waiting on him, and saw to it that they had something to eat. Like the majority of impoverished knights he was unscrupulous, he borrowed and did not pay back, sold horses which he knew were unsound, and pilfered from the reserves of fodder which belonged to the duke of Swabia's Germans, who were encamped not far from the tents of Champagne.

As he served the count of Champagne directly and received his orders from Viscount Raoul of Provins, he had managed to get a good house in the city; but even so his men found themselves somewhat crowded. The rooms were small, low, and scantily furnished—a few empty chests, a few battered tables, two beds without mattresses, and a spit and two pots for cooking were nearly all the furnishings they had found in the house.

The owner of the house had died during the siege, but his widow had returned to take possession of his property and she was already settled in the house before Ansiau and his men arrived. She received them with low bows, forced smiles, and frightened looks. She spoke an execrable French embellished with "Santa Maria!" "San Giorgio!" "San Giovanni!" and innumerable *i signori*, but she talked so much that she managed to make herself understood. She swore by the saints on the slightest excuse and crossed herself three times a minute to prove her sincerity. The *signori francesi* must not think that she had hidden carpets or sheets. it was the infidels who had taken everything—she was ruined, utterly ruined, she was a poor widow. The *signori* must excuse her for serving them no better, she had not a single bezant in her coffers, they might come and see. And she swore by every saint in her pious vocabulary that she was alone, utterly alone, that she had no children, she had lost them all during the siege, they were in Paradise. . . . She was a woman of about thirty, with a swarthy complexion and a fairly slender figure. At the conclusion of the first meal Ansiau signed to his men not to follow him, took the widow out into the courtyard, and asked her to show him the rest of the house. The courtyard was very small and very dirty and smelled of dung and spoiled goats' milk; the sun fell full on the eastern wall and the stone stairway which scaled it and led to the upper story. Ansiau had drunk a little and was stifling—what attracted him to the woman was principally her dark, moist eyes, bright with fear. He laid his hand on the heavy *relievo* embroideries which covered her breasts, and the poor creature began to tremble and say: *"Signor francese, signor francese,"* but she was too terrified to dream of resisting. Ansiau said: "Your bedroom." Without a word the widow climbed the hot, sun-smitten staircase. It was a small room, so low that Ansiau could not stand upright and felt as if he were in a cage—all the space was taken up by a big square bed covered with a striped cloth; on the whitewashed wall hung a crucifix of black wood and a towel embroidered with gold. The hot air had a very strong odor of musk and sweat, the sunlight entered only through the brown curtain over the door; at the foot of the bed stood a great water jar of gray stone.

Ansiau had lived so long without a woman that the widow rather went to his head. She had little beauty—she was faded, sallow-skinned, full-breasted, and full-hipped—but she was docile. At night she would comb her long black hair with a wooden comb, humming a song; she never went to bed without saying a rosary to the Virgin and kissing each of her medals—and she had a score of them. She wore a full blue nightgown and a sandalwood necklace.

Her name was Maria Nicolai, her father was a Pisan, her mother a Venetian. She had been born in Acre and had, so to speak, never left it, and even in Acre she knew only her own quarter and hardly ventured farther than St. Anne's Church. The arrival of the infidels had forced her out of the city, and like the rest of the citizens she had spent four years of privation and hope camping in the outskirts. Now that she was back in her house again she could hardly believe in her good fortune. She submitted to the law of war without protest—so great was her fear of men-at-arms that she felt only too happy to escape being flayed alive or seared with hot irons. Two days after Ansiau and his men arrived at her house her new lord had become the idol of her worship. She had lost none of her fear, however, and racked her brains for ways of pleasing him.

The third day she burst into tears and told him that she had lied to him— not all her children had died during the siege, her eldest was still alive, a girl of fourteen, Pascaline. She had hidden her in the cellar for fear of the soldiers. She did not know what to do, she dared not keep her hidden any longer, the child would fall sick from her close confinement. Ansiau promised to protect the girl—he had, he said, a daughter of the same age himself. The widow clasped her hands in astonishment, as if she could not believe that a warrior and a foreigner could have a wife and daughters. She cried out with delight when he told her that he had two sons at Acre, in the earl of Leicester's company—perhaps, she said, they would do her the honor to visit her house, she was anxious to see them—were they as handsome as their father?

The following day Ansiau, who was in a fairly good humor that morning, gave his widow permission to present her daughter to him. "I will see her," he said, "she will remind me of my own girls." Since he had come to live in the house he had been staying in bed rather late in the morning. It was not a habit of his; but he was extremely tired, and in the sort of dovecote which he shared with Maria the mornings were cool. White ringdoves strutted on the threshold, the pillows were stuffed with down, it was good to stretch out on them. Subdued by the brown curtain, the morning light was soft to the eyes. The widow brought in her daughter, a short, slight child whose head was covered with a blond, tightly curled fleece of hair. The child wriggled and clung to her mother's skirts, meanwhile looking surreptitiously at the French lord with a mixture of fear and amused curiosity—she must have thought a naked man a rather ridiculous object. The mother, in an Italian even faster than her French, told her to stop hiding her face and to greet the French lord properly. Ansiau smiled: "Pretty hair you have, my child. Better hide it or you will find yourself in trouble." The sound of an unfamiliar language routed the girl completely; she sat down on the ground and pulled her mother's skirts over herself, to Ansiau's great amusement.

From that day on little Pascaline became the forbidden fruit of the household—the soldiers all ran into the courtyard when she showed her face at the window, and when she climbed to the roof to feed her pigeons the men crowded at the foot of the stairs to see her legs and the boys shouted and cat-called in chorus and imitated Dame Maria's voice: "Pas-ca-li-ine! Pas-ca-li-ine!" At first Pascaline cried, then she grew used to it, and in the end joined in the laughter herself. She was a vivacious and light-hearted child. Ansiau laughed when he saw her golden head emerge from behind her mother's shoulder; Pascaline had eyes as bright as a squirrel's, a sly little face, and how she could laugh! It was a joy to hear her. She seemed to find life prodigiously amusing. True to his promise to the widow, Ansiau did not allow his men to approach Pascaline—there were plenty of women of easy virtue in Acre, enough for everyone.

A man who has a tottering rock poised above his head finally puts it out of his mind and relaxes—but the fear stays alive within him, ready to be waked by the first sound, the first gust of wind. Amid all the disorder in Acre, Ansiau led the careless and idle life he had lived as castellan of Linnières, looking after his horses, attending banquets and Mass, drinking heavily, spending his nights with his Maria, and thinking hardly at all. The rock which hung over his head was in the shape of a tall, thin youth, with hair bleached by the sun and a face tanned chestnut. Ansiau encountered him from time to time, more or less by chance, in the street or at church. And each time, like a wild beast scenting the hunter, he stiffened and his heart grew heavy. His son brought him little joy—that he must admit.

Ansiet was in his twentieth year. And certainly he was no longer a child— far from it. He was tall and powerfully built, thin but muscular. He had a blond mustache which stood out against his dark skin, and a beard which he had a barber shave but which grew again too fast. His chin was hard, his nostrils too mobile. He dressed decently. With his long white woolen cloak hanging from one shoulder, he even looked extremely handsome, especially when he was praying in church—calm and dignified, hands clasped, eyes unclouded, the very image of the pious knight.

Ansiau could not grow used to the fact that his boy had quite simply become a man, a man among all the rest, a man like himself. When had he matured? Where was the dividing line? It was someone else who looked at him now out of his son's clear, vacant eyes; someone else who seemed to be saying: "You shall never have me." His father scolded him—over women, naturally. Ansiet did not listen, he gnawed his mustache and gave his father a long look in which disdain, a touch of sorrow, and a great deal of unconcern were strangely mingled. He found no words in which to answer; weary of listening, he merely said: "You are right, baron," with an expression which meant: "You know nothing about it." Women . . . the baron was old, he could not know what they meant. When they were cleanly bathed and soft and white, when they used perfumes so strong that your head spun, when they had fine, black, smooth, beautifully curved eyebrows, and great black eyes in which you saw your face as in a well! A woman's body—it was so soft and so tender, there was nothing foul or shameful in touching it. That was what God had created it for—that, and nothing else. During the siege Ansiet had seen men go with other men, even with mares and mules—it had not killed them. Life was like that. Besides, the baron's tenderness oppressed him, he had no need of it. He was no longer a child, he had no use for a nurse. Never was man prouder or more reserved than Ansiau of Linnières, son of Ansiau.

Ansiau could not bear to see his son ruining his health for nothing—finally he said to him: "We have been in the city a week now and I imagine we shall soon be off campaigning again. You have had enough of a good time, you ought to get some rest."

"Rest, baron? I should be bored to death. I cannot stay still." To please his father, Ansiet consented to spend a few days in his house. The first night he was feverish and slept very badly. In the morning he felt dizzy and could not get up. He said to his father: "I cannot stay here. It bores me. It has made me ill," and as soon as he could put on his clothes he left, and Ansiau felt as if a knife had been thrust into his heart. Keeping at a distance, he followed his son everywhere—to church, to festivals, to the port. Night and day he saw nothing but that face, pale under its tan, those trembling nostrils, those hard indifferent eyes, the eyes of a suffering man. He could not foresee what would come of it, but chills ran up and down his spine. Once more Ansiet passed him without noticing him, arm in arm with two other youngsters and two beautiful girls. The boy tossed back his long locks. He was gay, and almost frightening to look at—his expression was that of a starved wolf cub gnashing its teeth with impatience as it leaps on its prey. His eyes shot sparks, he breathed hoarsely. Not if he were to be struck dead on the spot would he give up his share of earthly pleasure! Never had Ansiau seen him so. He thought: "They have made him a different boy," and all night his head was heavy, he tossed and turned; and his good Maria, sunk in sleep, sighed and asked if it were time to get up already. The next day Ansiet came to his father and said: "I will stay with you if there is still room for me."

"You can have the whole house if you want it!" Ansiau cried. "What is wrong? Have you quarrelled with someone?"

"No," said Ansiet. "I am going to be ill. So I would rather be here than somewhere else."

Ansiau asked: "You know beforehand?"

Ansiet was very calm. He seemed tired, but he stood as straight as ever. "I have had dysentery three times," he said. "I know all about it. I want to get well as quickly as possible. I must be in shape for the campaign. Let me have a room."

Ansiau turned Renaud of Hervi out of the largest room in the house and gave it to his son. He forced Maria to give him all her bed pillows and her biggest blanket as well. Ansiet was a very tractable patient. Lying quietly in his bed under a white sheet, he kept his eyes closed and showed no sign of suffering. When colics racked him he merely drew down his eyebrows, as he might have done to chase a fly from his forehead. The doctor—a converted Jew—discovered nothing serious, prescribed remedies for the diarrhea, and said that the best thing to bring down a fever was a crocodile stone—one of his friends who was an apothecary could lend one for a few days. Ansiau sat by his son's bed all night. Toward morning the fever increased, the crocodile stone had no effect. His eyes open and staring, his lips drawn, the patient held both hands clasped over his abdomen and his head rolled slowly back and forth on the pillow, from left to right, from right to left. In a youth who always bore pain so stolidly such signs of suffering were terrifying. Toward terce Ansiau went to Mass at St. Anne's Church and vowed to give a chalice of pure gold if his son recovered—even if he had to go short on food and drink for ten years to pay for it.

And when he came back, Ansiet was already unrecognizable—his face had turned dark-gray, his cheeks had sunk in. When the Jewish doctor returned in the afternoon he looked grave, declared that little hope remained, and administered an infusion of poppy seed to still the pain. The patient was too weak and exhausted, he said; he himself could do nothing, they must call in a more skillful doctor. The fact was that he had no wish to have a patient—especially a knight—die on his hands. It was only five years since he had been baptized and he did not want the responsibility. The second doctor, a Syrian in a pointed yellow cap, said that he could do nothing before he had examined the humors and that he would come back the next day.

The infusion of poppy seemed to do good. The patient's face relaxed, he closed his eyes. Seated on the edge of the bed, Ansiau sank his head in his hands and tried not to hear the blood that beat in his ears. "Don't fret, baron, I am feeling better." The voice was only a breath, but Ansiet's face was calm. To his father's frightened look his answer was a smile—a little proud, a little sad, but very sweet. It was only the corners of his mouth which smiled—the smile of an elder brother, a smile which seemed to say, "I am sorry for your sake, but it has to be."

Ansiau of Linnières laid his head on his son's arm and sobbed aloud. He gave himself to his passion without restraint; for the first time in his life he dared to show it, never had even he believed that it was so strong. He showered kisses on his son's arms, his hands, his hair, he talked, talked endlessly, as if he believed that he could exorcise the evil by words. All that he asked, he said, was his son's life. He would take him to Champagne, where the air was so good—there he would soon recover. If Ansiet wished, he could take his beloved with him—"there is nothing to stop you—Milicent can marry Girard; as for the lady's baron, if he is still alive, I will see to him—there will be tournaments, and I have never yet failed to place my blow; and if it takes me to the Court of Peers, what do I care, so long as you have the woman you need—if she had twenty lovers, I would respect her as if she were my own mother"—furthermore he, Ansiau, had no need of castle and lands—they should be his son's, he would cross him in nothing; the others could do without, he did not care what became of them. As for himself, he would serve the count of Troyes for wages.

In his son's shadowed, unmoving eyes there was an expression of slightly disdainful pity—the baron had not changed; as usual, he was off the track. What could Lady Oriana and Linnières matter now! Toward nightfall he said: "I want to see Herbert." Herbert, who was in the house, entered the room but did not approach the bed. He was trembling violently. "Brother," said Ansiet, making an effort to smile, "I am very sick."

Herbert cried: "No! No! You are lying! They are all lying!" He burst into tears and fled from the room.

It was a hot night and the smell in Ansiet's room was so strong that he thought he would suffocate—yet Thierri kept coming to empty the basin. The window stood open, but the air was too still to enter, the curtain was a poor protection against the mosquitoes which buzzed around the candle in clouds and settled on the patient's burning face, on his neck, on his arms— Ansiau fanned him as well as he could and killed the creatures by dozens. Ansiet did not complain. He did not open his lips. His broad, thin face had become very childlike. He fidgeted, blinked, stretched his neck. He had accepted his suffering and was only trying to lessen it a little. All night he struggled and gasped, but without panic—he was like a man accomplishing a difficult but uninteresting task; calmly he said: "Baron, the wet cloth— baron, the basin—baron, I am thirsty." Then, as the window grew light, his nostrils began to open and close, he gnawed his lips. A moment later, in a voice which was low but still tranquil, he said: "Baron, I do not like to complain, but I believe I am really very sick. Send for a priest." The baron flung himself face down on the floor and said he would not—he would not even think of such a thing. Then he stood up and called Thierri.

The priest was an old, white-bearded man with deep, dark eyes, a man of

Champagne, formerly chaplain to the count of Clermont. Ansiet knew him slightly; he smiled. "It is a filthy disease," he whispered, "because of the smell. Tell me—can I communicate this morning? I drank some water."

The priest said that God would permit it in the case of a dying man. Ansiet showed his big white teeth, tried to sit up, and fell back. "Help me, baron," he said. His father sat down beside the bed, raised him by the shoulders and held him up so that he could receive the sacrament.

With his eyes wide open, Ansiet entered his last agony; his death rattle grew fainter and fainter. He seemed no longer to suffer. In a thick voice he said: "Haumette, bring a candle, it is dark," then his head fell back and he said: "I am coming up."

Ansiau watched the last traces of thought, of suffering, of life, grow dim and vanish from that clear, smooth face; the change was so rapid that his eyes could almost follow it—the hollows filled, the lines relaxed, the face appeared, frightening in its stillness, radiant with youth. The long lashes were curved, the nose stood out straight and hard like a piece of marble—the wide, soft lips were at rest.

Ansiau still held him in his arms, and when Andrew and Herbert entered the room he did not hear them. Sitting on the bed, with the lifeless head against his shoulder, he stared straight ahead and saw nothing; his jaw hung loose, his eyes were hollow—an old man. With both hands he stroked the hair on the lifeless forehead—when they spoke to him he seemed not to understand.

The women who had come to wash the body, the priest, and Andrew managed to tear him away. Then he sat down on the chest which stood beside the bed, sunk his head in his hands, and stared at the dead face. It was an intense, heavy, burning look—the stare of a madman. And indeed, as he sat there, his reason suffered a terrible onset. All that remained to him of lucidity had passed into his eyes, it clung to the ruins of that face which was already disintegrating. Of his vanished universe nothing remained but those features. Once he had known them, and he studied them to the last detail, to the last hair, to the last pore. The little brown blotches which had begun to appear on the cheeks, under the tan, were no more significant than all the rest. He believed he had strength enough to see the whole face decay and disappear. Since morning he had not spoken a word.

Three squires and Andrew squeezed Ansiet's swelling body into the hauberk which had been the only thing of value he had ever owned in his life. They laced it on. It was a beautiful piece of work, made of the finest mail, the neckpiece chased. Over the hauberk they drew the long, unbleached woolen tunic with the red cross stitched to it in front. On his knees at the bedside, the faithful Hugh, the dead youth's squire, hurriedly put the iron shoes on the stiffened feet and tied the thongs of the gaiters. Under the two hands, resting one upon the other on the breast, Andrew placed the hilt of the sword; the blade, in its sheath of gilded leather, reached to the knees.

Hard, hard to bear—this watching his son armed for another life. The mortal flesh of Ansiau of Linnières, son of Ansiau, was entering the last stage of its existence. Already the substance of it was changed, only the form remained; the big, quiet hands, with their fingers as smooth as rods of wax, crossed over the hilt of the sword, were tied together at the wrist by a silk thread. Ansiau had seen them soft and tiny, tugging at his beard or patting his cheek; he had seen them thin and dry, covered with scratches and pecked by the beaks of hawks; he had seen the first callouses form on them from the reins of the first horse, the string of the first bow. Now it was ended; it had never been. On the bed there was only this great waxen statue which had never known life. "The boy" was gone.

There in the Holy Land the dead did not wait. There could be no delaying the funeral. Ansiau had the strength to attend to it himself, with Andrew's help. He could still live, as long as there was something he could do for "the boy." He saw to decorating and furnishing the bier, he put his red cloak on it and all the poor finery of a petty knight—a silk-fringed horse cloth, a hair pillow covered with old Damascus embroidery work, a white woolen blanket embroidered with blue crosses. Trembling and hesitant, Maria appeared at the door and handed Hugh a red-silk napkin embroidered in gold—would Signor Ansello accept it to put under the head of my lord his son?—it would be most kind in him to accept it.

The side chapel in St. Anne's Church smelled of incense and burnt wax. It was a hot night—the young priest who was reading the funeral service kept wiping his forehead and neck; the candles sputtered and ran down. The bier, set high on a catafalque covered with black cloth, dominated the dark silhouettes of the kneeling men. Barely touched by the uncertain yellow light, sunk in shadows, the dead youth's face grew dim, dissolved, the cheeks and the eyes drew in, the mouth curved in a heart-rending smile which changed and changed again, vaguely imitating the smiles of living men. At dawn the face was covered with a white cloth, and the Requiem Mass began.

When it was time to close the coffin Ansiau took off his rings, the Toledo dagger he wore in his belt, the wrought-copper buckle which fastened his cloak, and laid them on the lifeless breast, below the hands. He did not know what else to give. He had nothing more. He wished he might put his sword in the coffin, his armor, his horse, his shield with the blazon of Linnières. . . .

On July twenty-eighth (sixteen days after the fall of the city), the king of France set sail, leaving his knights and his armory at the disposition of the duke of Burgundy and his place in the city to the marquess of Montferrat. Great was the sorrow among the crusaders, especially among the French and the partisans of the marquess—but the rest, too, hardly found it an encouraging example. The king was said to be sick—but if every sick crusader did as he was doing there would be few left to carry on the war. And the French said that King Philip had been forced to go by Richard's treachery, that Richard had plotted with Henry of Champagne to poison him.

The king took leave of his barons, who wept as they escorted him to the harbor. From the shore crowds of knights and sergeants watched the royal barge move away from the pier and few were they who cried "Noël!" Not since the past winter had Christendom fallen on such evil days. If the leaders forsook their men in this fashion at the very beginning of the war, how would Jerusalem ever be recaptured? The True Cross had not yet been given back, despite Saladin's promises; and the king's departure would revive the courage of the Moslems. In the city, English and Norman minstrels were already secretly singing a song about the king of France's treachery. The men of Champagne, greatly irritated to see their count calumniated by the French, jeered them, saying: "Go find the king of France! Where is he?— no one has seen him lately!" and every Frenchman who ventured into the English quarter of the city was booed and mocked for his wicked king.

Richard remained master of the field, and all hopes now turned to him. He, at least, would not leave Palestine until he had taken Jerusalem and reconquered the kingdom. But still the Holy Cross, promised by the terms of the agreement with Saladin, did not come. The army began to grow impatient. There were perpetual rumors—the Holy Cross was approaching, had reached Acre—everyone ran to the castle, to the squares for news, or rushed to the gates of the city to see it carried by—and each time their hopes were disappointed and the soldiers cursed Saladin for his double-dealing.

In the darkness which had suddenly fallen on his life Ansiau could have but one thought—to forget. His friends considered that he must have a sadly carnal and unenlightened soul to grieve so greatly for a son who had died on Crusade. He knew it himself, but he was the prey to a pitiless evil and in no state to reason. He hungered and thirsted for his son, for the boy's eyes, his voice, the locks of hair on his forehead—and nothing could distract him. He forbade his men to mention Ansiet to him; he avoided Herbert, whom he almost hated—he blamed him for not having died in his brother's stead. He had no heart to pretend or to do the conventional things. He drank heavily. And at night Maria crossed herself in terror when she heard him sighing out strings of affectionate words and calling his son's name aloud. Her nights with her Dom Bartolommeo, twenty years her elder, had been tranquil. Her new bedfellow exhausted and baffled her. "These Frenchmen!" she thought—yet God knew she was his, body and soul—but he was a creature of another species and she hardly dared touch his shoulder to ask him to lie quiet. There were times when he clasped her in his arms and said: "Lady." He would have given much to have his lady beside him— as if he believed that she still had the power to hold back the tide which was rising in him, threatening to overwhelm and drown him.

Herbert was sincerely grieved by his brother's death, but unfortunately no one would take him seriously. He rolled on the ground over a torn glove or a lamed horse; he rolled on the ground when he learned that his brother was dead; everyone had seen him do it before, and they left him to his own devices. He was told that his father was suffering too deeply, that he should stay away from him and not remind him of his dead son. Herbert obeyed because he knew his father well—he knew that his father wished that it were he who had died, and he bore him no grudge for the wish—he had never thought his father unjust. In any case, he was not, he thought, particularly fond of his father. During those dark days Andrew alone tried to console Herbert—the fat, pale youth with his indifferent eyes had a serious side which only his uncle appreciated. At night Herbert would stretch out on the ground beside Andrew's bed and talk to him of one thing and another—he was convinced that Andrew knew everything and could advise him on the most diverse matters. He often talked of his brother. "Such a good friend," he said. "He gave me all his bread when I was hungry. If I told you all he'd done for me, I would never be through talking. And all for no return! Funny—every morning when I wake up, I wonder where he is. He always used to wake me. . . .

"Listen, uncle—there were three of us—he and Garnier. and I. Don't you think it odd that they are both dead? Perhaps it will be my turn soon."

"Nonsense," his uncle said. "It means nothing. Every man has his hour."

"What I can't get over," Herbert went on, "is that I said something terrible to him the last time I saw him—it must have been the Devil who drove me. He told me that he was very sick, and I—and I," he began to gasp, "and I—said to him: 'You are lying.' Do you think he has forgiven me now?"

Another time Herbert sought out his uncle and said: "Listen, uncle—I know that the baron is angry with me because he thinks I shall gain by my brother's death. Well, I have made up my mind—tell him that I don't want the inheritance; he can give the castle and the land to Girard. As for me, I shall go to England and serve the duke of Leicester."

"It would be a shame to deprive the castellany of such a good knight as yourself," said his uncle, "and you have no right to renounce your expectations."

Herbert caught at his uncle's arm. "No, no—you don't understand. My expectations—after all, what do they amount to? The baron is not very old —he may well live another twenty years. And you think I can spend twenty years waiting for an inheritance? Twenty years! In twenty years I shall be an old man. I would rather go and seek my fortune elsewhere."

"But why do you want to leave your father?" Andrew asked.

Herbert shrugged his shoulders. "My brother would have done it too, if he had lived. We were both thinking of it. The baron—we were fond enough of him. But a brother, naturally, counts for much more—the same womb bore us and, besides, we both take after our mother's family far more than our father's. And my father does not love me. So I wish you would tell him for me that I renounce my inheritance. You see, don't you, that it might make him think better of me?"

Andrew thought it a foolish scheme, but he promised to speak to the baron.

"And, uncle," Herbert added, "tell my father that I want Rambaud, my brother's charger. Because one day he said to me, 'If I die before you do, take Rambaud.' I know the baron knows more about taking care of horses than anyone, but I think he is rather neglecting his stable just now, and Rambaud is delicate."

"I will never tell him that," said Andrew, laughing.

Andrew faithfully conveyed to Ansiau his nephew's request on the subject of his inheritance. It happened that Ansiau was in the stable, with the horses which Herbert accused him of neglecting. His son's scheme did not please him at all; he frowned and thought for a moment. "No," he said, "I will not let him go. I do not expect to go home, and the domain needs a man. Girard is only thirteen, and I do not know if he will ever make a good knight. I am willing to let Herbert remain in the earl of Leicester's service until the end of the war, but after that he shall go home."

"Why force him if he does not want to?" Andrew asked.

"He has no right to want or not want. They all do anything that comes into their heads—can a child know what he wants? If I have more sons," he said somberly, "I'll twist them like this—" he bent his riding-whip, tied it in a knot, and threw it on the ground. "I'll ride them with a short rein. I have done badly enough with the first lot." He shook his head, as if to drive away painful thoughts. "It was not my fault—I was too young. If I were the Pope, I would forbid men to marry before twenty."

Then, returning to Herbert, he told his cousin that he would not allow the boy to engage himself for any considerable length of time.

But he was still reluctant to see his second son, now his heir. Before his eyes still shone the sweet, proud face of the "other"—the cruel boy who had escaped from his love as a bird escapes from its cage, without regret or remorse. And Ansiau knew that "the boy" could reproach him with a great fault—the fault of loving too much. Hereafter, he thought, he would cease to love. He would love only God, himself, and his old comrades-in-arms. Anything else was sin and folly.

On Assumption Day a ship carrying pilgrims and French wounded was to leave the port of Acre, and among the wounded there was one of the viscount of Provins' squires. It was a good opportunity for those who served the viscount to send news to their kindred in Champagne. "You will be passing by Linnières," Ansiau said to the squire, "it is only a little out of your way. At Sézanne, you turn off to Saint-Florentin, you follow the

Armançon, and from Flogny to Linnières is only a league. You can stay at the castle, you will certainly be more comfortable than you would be at an inn. My lady will welcome you." He gave the squire a small wooden box containing a letter carefully rolled and sealed with red wax. Ansiau had spent at least two hours dictating it to the viscount's clerk.

The letter said:

"In the year of the Incarnation 1191, two days before the feast of the Assumption of Our Glorious Lady, Mary, ever Virgin. At Acre, recaptured by our forces, with God's help, from the accursed infidels.

"Ansiau, lord of Linnières in Champagne, liege man to the count of Champagne, to Alis, lady.

"Blessed be God. Dear lady, by this letter I give you to know that our son Ansiau died, by God's will, in the city of Acre, two weeks after the end of the siege. Which greatly grieves me.

"And I have further to tell you that Garnier, my nephew, is dead. And Thierri, my squire, is dead." (Here followed the names of all the men of Linnières who had died during the siege.) "They have all become martyrs.

"I ask you, lady, to send me money, as much as you can gather together. If you sell Bernon and the vineyards, you can repay Abner's loan and send me the rest. You can also pawn your lamented mother's necklace, I humbly ask you to do me this service. I am without money and my wages are pledged for three months in advance. I have also pledged my woolen cloak and I want to redeem it before Candlemas, for that is the season when this country is coldest. As soon as you receive my letter, find means to send me what you can, for I am in great difficulties.

"Herbert, our son, and Andrew greet you."

At the end of the letter Ansiau had himself drawn a cross and the first three letters of his name—L I N—so that Father Aimeri would have no doubt of its authenticity. He supposed that he would have to wait four or five months for an answer. From a sense of modesty, and to avoid filling valuable paper with unnecessary chatter, he had not asked for news of his family and household, yet he was curious to know if his child had been born alive and if it was a boy—but he assured himself that Lady Alis was intelligent enough to guess what he would want to know.

Ansiau asked Herbert to serve in the ranks of Champagne—he did not want to live apart from his last remaining son, he would look out for him; Herbert could not become an Englishman, he would be castellan of Linnières as soon as the war was over. "What about yourself?" his son asked. "I," said Ansiau, "if I do not die first, shall stay here—the country will always need knights."

"What! Stay here!" Herbert's eyes were round with wonder. "A country full of mosquitoes and snakes and so hot that your skin bursts! I would not want to spend my life here. Besides, what will Lady Alis say?"

Ansiau frowned, then threw back his head. "Lady Alis is no longer very young, she has no need of a husband," he said. "And you will hold the fief better than I, perhaps."

Through all the streets and squares of the city King Richard's criers began shouting the order to depart, but the king nearly had to set off alone with his barons, for the army was not anxious to stir—it was no easy thing, emptying houses, gardens, and taverns of those thousands of men sodden with wine, stupefied by the heat and by a month of inactivity. The king and the other leaders took the course of sending priests through the city to recall the men to their duty. Clad in their Lenten robes, the priests strode through the streets, entered courtyards, everywhere preaching penitence and the Holy War and reproaching the crusaders for their disorderly lives which would lead them straight to Hell. Some received them very badly, but most listened with tears in their eyes, eager to repent—however, so far as leaving the city in the heat of August went, everyone looked to his neighbor.

King Richard, for whom fatigue obviously had no terrors, himself went to the squares and the port, followed by a small escort of Normans; the soldiers were accustomed to him now and bore him a grudge for having failed to obtain the Holy Cross and Jerusalem from Saladin. But whenever he appeared in person he always made a great impression. He showed himself in front of the Templars' House, the cathedral, the church of St. Mark, the church of St. Andrew; he was everywhere, and the knights came running in crowds to the blasts of his trumpeters. He spoke to them humbly, courteously, as befits a man speaking to comrades-in-arms. He begged them to do their duty, not for love of him, but for love of God. Now was the time to show that God was the One True God and Mohammed a rotten straw. Jerusalem must be recaptured, the infidels must be driven from the land of God. Their friends, their brothers who had died in the siege, must be avenged. "Let them have no cause to reproach us with our sloth. For one of our men slain by the infidels, we will slay them by tens and hundreds."

Little by little, arms and armor were refurbished, the knights gathered around their chiefs once more, the courtyards were transformed into barracks. In agreement with the duke of Burgundy and the marquess, Richard decreed that no women should follow the army—the only exceptions were to be old women on pilgrimage, bath women and laundresses, for of these the army always stood in great need.

Ansiau had to leave ten of his men behind in Acre, men too weak, too ill, or merely too lazy to undergo the fatigues of warfare. At heart he was not displeased to leave his house well guarded—the fresh troops of crusaders from the West, who were still arriving in the Holy Land, should have no opportunity to steal his house and his woman while he was at war.

Red-eyed, Maria wandered through the house, unable to do enough for her Signor Ansello, who obviously had little use for her—she could neither mend arms nor curry horses, and she had long since patched and darned all the baron's breeches as well as his men's. Ansiau promised her that he would come back—he was very fond of her. "You can count on me," he said; "as long as the war goes on, no harm will befall you. And if I stay in the country, this city is where I would best like to live—here where my son lies buried. If you wish, we will live as husband and wife—I am too old to run after wantons." "Ah! Santa Maria!" she sighed. The signor was too good to her. Never could she thank him enough—for Pascaline and for all the rest. He was going far away, to fight in this heat, and the infidels were worse than Devils—had they not in their impiousness profaned the church of St. Anne? (The profanation of the church of St. Anne was, for Maria, the Saracens' foulest misdeed.) Each night she would say an extra rosary to the Madonna for Signor Ansello's health, and she would make Pascaline do likewise.

"You had better think of marrying her," said Signor Ansello. "These are unquiet times."

Maria protested—marry her, when she had almost no dowry left! It would take at least a year of sewing and stitching to supply what she lacked. Pascaline was no shoemaker's or armorer's daughter—her father had been a cloth merchant. For all her sweetness, Maria was as stubborn as a mule. She chattered incessantly and her ideas were a little hazy. Ansiau explained it all by the fact that she was not a noblewoman, and never reproached her. However, before setting off, he warned Hugh of Linnières, whom he was leaving in the house, to keep a good watch on the widow—he had little faith in women's constancy.

The Holy Cross and the Christian prisoners, promised by Saladin in exchange for the garrison of Acre, had not yet been returned, and the army began to grow restless. Men said: "We are paid with false promises." And five days after Ascension Day the rumor spread through the city that the captive Saracens had been led outside the walls—why, no one knew. An escort of Englishmen and Normans conducted them to the same hill on which Saladin's tents had stood but a month earlier.

Those who had followed to look on returned to the city a few hours later, crying that King Richard was having the infidels beheaded and that no one should miss it—it was a horror the like of which was never seen before. There they stood with their hands tied behind their backs, one by one they moved to the blocks, and the executioners cut off their heads with sabers—others were struck down where they stood, with axes. There was so much blood and so many headless bodies that even the slaughter of the sergeants had not equalled it. Some said that the infidels numbered at least five thousand, others three. Everyone agreed that Richard had wanted to avenge the crusaders whom the garrison of Acre had killed with their arrows and their machines. Yet most of the Christian soldiers were disconcerted rather than gratified by such a revenge. Then suddenly their indignation lighted on Saladin, who calmly permitted the destruction of men who had stood such a siege for him and fought so well for two long years. Saladin, the word went, had refused to surrender the Holy Cross and the two hundred thousand bezants he had promised, and gave not a thought to the lives of his hostages. It was a great sin to abandon his men in this fashion, from sheer cupidity, to avoid paying their ransom. After all, King Richard could not drag the infidels in his train, nor leave them in a city stripped of soldiers.

THE CAMPAIGN FOR JERUSALEM
(Chronicle)

ON CAMPAIGN. The heat. The sun blazing down on helmets and iron mail; shirts and bodies soaked in sweat, the skin all one sore; blood buzzing in the ears.

Pastures covered with withered grass, burned fields, olive groves—all alike, white or gray, colorless under the devouring light; only the sky a dazzling blue, dark-blue, and never a cloud. To the right the distant line of the sea. To the left, along the gray and blue *tells,* Saladin's huge army, advancing, writhing slowly on like the tail of a gigantic snake, threatening to deploy and cut the Christians' road.

The great battle. In the gardens of Arsuf, the enemy goes into action. The Turks surround the Christian army, riddle it with arrows. . . . Thirty thousand Turks fling themselves at full gallop on the Christian army, raising clouds of dust. Before the emirs march the trumpeters, the drummers, the gong bearers, shouting and screaming; were God to thunder, He would not be heard. Next come the blacks and the Saracens of Barbary, swift, agile infantrymen, armed with bow and shield. They attack from land side and sea side, in such strength that they do vast damage, especially in killing horses. Tropical heat. Horses down, men riddled with arrows. But Richard is a great general. The Hospitallers send him word that they cannot hold, he tells them to hold, and they hold. Then he goes over to the offensive . . . Whirlwind charges that sweep all before them. Baha-ud-din, who was at Saladin's side, has left a picture of the scene:

"Then the French cavalry massed, and, knowing that nothing could save them but a supreme effort, they decided to charge. I myself saw these knights, gathered inside an enclosure formed by their footmen. They seized their lances, gave their war cry with one voice, the line of footmen opened to let them pass, and they charged in every direction. One troop flung itself on our right wing, another on our left wing, a third on our center, and we were utterly put to rout. . . ."

From the Christian side, Ambrose depicts the scene:

". . . This seemed to the Turks a new thing; for now our men fell upon them like thunderbolts. Then had you seen the thick dust fly! And all they who had dismounted and were shooting at us with bows, wherewith they so harassed our folk, these now had their heads cut off; for so soon as the knights overthrew them the sergeants slew them. . . ." *

Only Saladin remains calm. He bids the drums sound, the fugitives reassemble. To avoid being carried too far by their own charge, the Frankish cavalry is forced to turn. The Saracens regain courage. "More than twenty thousand of these came, holding their maces in their hands, to rescue them that had been overthrown. Then had you seen how our men were buffeted! At those who were betaking themselves back to the host the Saracens were ever discharging their arrows; and they smote with their maces, breaking heads and arms, so that our men bowed down over their saddlebows."

After recovering breath, the Frankish knights charge once more, and the Turks flee, pursued by the Christians to the very hills occupied by Saladin. The Moslem army retreats, leaving a desert behind it.

Blood-stained rest through the long, hot night, in the ravaged gardens of Arsuf.

Then two long months in the olive orchards of Joppa, in the orange groves, among the heavy golden fruit and the dark leaves, among heavy bunches of blue or amber grapes, hot and translucent in the sun. Joppa, city of burning stone, set by the blue sea, had so many gardens that the whole army found room to camp in them, the tents were shaded by trees; good it was to rest from the heat of the sun and the heat of battle—there among the lemon trees and cool wells. Masons, native and English, helped by the sergeants, set to work rebuilding the city walls. The more adventurous knights spent their time raiding in the environs, for the country was not safe, the Moslems prowled over it in little troops, always ready to attack. Mounted on their small horses, armed with round shields and light lances, dark-faced under their white burnooses, they always outnumbered the Franks; they were fast, but easy to rout, it was enough to charge into their ranks, sword in hand—they scattered and led you far from your companions, then surrounded you, stabbed at your horse with their long lances.

King Richard went on every one of these expeditions, more careless of his safety than the meanest knight and followed by an escort so small that he was nearly taken prisoner a hundred times over. His revenge was to return to the army with Saracen heads hanging from his saddle by the dozen. And his horse, long since accustomed to the smell of blood, whinnied and trembled when it felt that load of dead flesh bouncing against its flanks.

---

* This and the following extracts from Ambrose are taken from Edward Noble Stone's version of "The History of the Holy War," published in *Three Old French Chronicles of the Crusades,* University of Washington Publications in the Social Sciences, vol. X. Slightly adapted by the translator. By permission of the publishers.

When the heat had subsided and the walls of Joppa were rebuilt, the army resumed its march. It was a few days before All-Hallows, strong winds were blowing, and the sea had changed color—it had been blue, now it was greenish-gray. Now for the first time the army left the coast and advanced toward the *tells,* which loomed larger as they grew nearer, a vast confusion of unknown, threatening heights, long, gently sloping wooded hills, behind which were to rise yet more, higher and darker. There was a battle at Yazur with the Sultan's advanced guard—after that came Rames, one-time domain of the Ibelins, destroyed by Saladin, and Lydda Saint-Georges, where the saint had suffered martyrdom; it was not far from Saint-Georges, at Mongesard, that God had given the Leper King victory over Saladin, with the help of St. George himself, twelve years earlier. There the army encamped around the dismantled fortress of Rames. Three weeks they were forced to remain there by the heavy autumn rains, and many men had insufficient clothing and fell sick. A hard winter if ever there was one. From Rames they had to press on to the Toron of the Knights, which Saladin had just destroyed, and from the Toron to Betenoble, which was but five leagues from Jerusalem. Snow storms and hail storms covered the tents and the provision sheds with a white frost which the cold wind soon turned to ice. Gusts swept into the tents, tearing up pegs and even the heavy tent posts; biscuits molded, hauberks rusted. Horses and mules died of cold; more than one fine Arabian charger perished miserably before the eyes of his desolate master, who often sacrificed his own cloak and blanket to protect his mount —a knight had no greater treasure, no more faithful companion than a good horse.

But, God knows, all the suffering was cheerfully, even joyously, accepted —because there was Jerusalem, only a day's march away. Never before had their hopes risen so high: Richard had met no obstacle on the road, the defeated infidel army had fled, the reconquest of the Holy City must follow soon. "We have reached the goal. We are close to Holy Sepulchre. God has guided us. Never again, after the day on which we shall see the tomb of Our Lord with our own eyes, shall we suffer pain or grief. They who shall now enter Jerusalem will not have lived in vain."

Christmas was a day of great joy, of repentance and forgiveness. Yet the night was dark, the mountains hemmed in the camp on every side, the wind and snow put out torches and candles even in the field chapels. But the flames were relit, and they glinted and quivered, reflected in hundreds and hundreds of tearful eyes—there was not a man in the army that night, from King Richard to the meanest sergeant, whose eyes were dry or whose heart was heavy. Losses and the lost were forgotten. The God of Heaven had not spared himself, He had suffered far greater pains to save men who were hardly worth saving. So great was His mercy. Because it was His land which was to be freed from bondage, every man would die gladly.

Christmas passed, then New Year's Eve, then Circumcision, then Epiphany, and still the king did not give the order to strike tents for the march on Jerusalem. And on the thirteenth day of January the order to move camp was given—but it was to withdraw to Rames.

It was like being hit on the head by a battle axe. Had they then borne it all for nothing, the wind, the cold, the loss of their horses, had they come from so far against such difficulties, only to beat a shameful retreat, to the joy of the infidels? Richard was not spared, and those who the day before were ready to die for him took up the old refrain: The king had sold himself to Saladin, he had been negotiating with him ever since the days of rest in Joppa, he was leading the army only to exhaust and betray it. Disgusted by the English king's treachery, the duke of Burgundy and the French barons separated from the army and withdrew to the Stronghold of the Plains, followed by the greater part of their knights. The Templars and Hospitallers, accused of having advised the king badly, laid the blame on the French; however, they were in such ill favor with the rest of the army that they, too, hastened to leave the camp. Crowds of knights, sergeants, pilgrims, sick men dragged along the roads in pitiable caravans. Their only thought was to escape the cold, to reach the plain and the sea coast, Joppa and Acre, where more than one had left a lodging, a wife, friends. Richard, who had withdrawn to Ibelin, near Rames, had kept with him only his English, Norman, and French vassals, and Count Henry of Champagne with his men. And the men of Champagne must have borne a strange devotion to the king of England to make them stay with him when they had sworn him no fealty, for never had there been such grief and such poverty in the army. "At Ibelin," says the Norman minstrel Ambrose, "lay the host, all dolorous and heavier of heart than aught that liveth. But in the morning, ere yet the sun was risen, forth went those that should go to pick their resting-places. Their tents they struck, then rode the host all armed; but never a worse day's march hath been recorded by any living man. For the journey of the day before was as nought to the journey that they made this day; through many a rugged pass they went, where their provision was lost because of the sumpter beasts that there fell down. So did God will, Who thus was trying them and proving unto them perforce that whoso will not suffer misease for His sake may never hope to be at ease with Him. And at the last they came to Ascalon, between midday and nones. And they found the city laid so waste, so ruined and so overthrown, and over such heaps of rubbish must they climb, that with sore difficulty did they enter there; thus, with the grievous travail that they had suffered that day, there was none of them that had not great longing and desire for rest. But at the last they found there rest a-plenty."

And once again, until spring returned, long days of rebuilding fortifications, of raids into the surrounding country—a life which left little time for thought. Ansiau of Linnières had no taste for the recurrent talk of treachery, he merely shook his head when his companions waxed indignant over the maneuvers of the marquess and the French. The marquess, they said, was negotiating with the Moslems, the duke of Burgundy was plotting with the Genoese to deliver Acre to the marquess, King Richard was betrayed on every hand. Ansiau had two cousins in the marquess' service and he let it be known: the man was a good Christian and a brave knight and, whatever else he might be, he could not be a traitor.

Spring covered the plain of Sephel and the hills of Judaea with a display such as was never seen in any Christian land. The fields overflowed with lilies and yellow and purple irises, the gardens and groves were red with roses; everywhere white orange trees, pink almonds seemed almost to bow under their weight of fragrant petals. The green grass must already be sprouting about the wooden cross on the grave in the cemetery of St. Nicholas, outside Acre. There was a pair of eyes which would never see this beauty. They were big, clear eyes, not blue, but gray with blue lights, and once they could open wide and grow almost round. The soul was God's, near to God with the Blessed, but the body had belonged to the father, and God had decreed that it should lie in the ground and rot until the day of the resurrection of the flesh. Far away "the boy" was living a new life free from trouble and danger, in the service of the greatest of kings—how much greater than King Richard Lionheart! And if he had loved Richard, how would he not love Him who was a thousand times better than Richard? But for a father who had loved his stock, his flesh and blood, it was a cruel blow—neither God nor the boy had taken him into account. Eight months had passed, and still, every morning when he woke, the memory that his son lay in the grave came fresh like a thrust to the heart.

But camp life and raiding did their work. The business of the day left him no time for thought. And Herbert, there was no denying it, was such a nuisance that he forced you to think of him, like it or not. No sooner did he perceive that his father showed some fondness for him than he set himself to profit by it, with astonishing effrontery and a superb disregard for anything but his own ends. He began to consider the baron's horses his own, to give orders to the baron's men, and to live entirely on the baron's greatly reduced means. It did not make Ansiau angry: he hardly noticed it. He was not going to wrangle with the boy about a little indiscretion at a time when an arrow, a lance, a fever might suddenly carry him off. But Herbert had no respect for anyone who appeared to yield to him—he became insolent. His father took him to task, but his heart was not in it; he soon forgave him for the sake of peace. Herbert was perpetually getting into quarrels or into trouble with women, and coming to his father to complain —and his father told him to go to the Devil.

Never had crusader set less store by the Holy War, Jerusalem, and Holy Sepulchre than Herbert of Linnières. Herbert had long since recovered from his childhood enthusiasms (if ever he had felt any), and thought that Palestine was a very unpleasant country full of vile people of every description. Besides, he could not get used to the mosquitoes. The crusading barons quarrelled and bickered in such a fashion that Herbert openly declared he preferred the infidels to the French. A war should be full of brilliant feats of arms, and since the great battle at Arsuf the army had wasted itself in skirmishes, in minor engagements between bowmen, in rebuilding fortifications—in short this was a war which brought profit or glory to no one. Richard apparently wanted to monopolize all the pickings of the campaign for himself—he was everywhere at once, bringing terror wherever he went, the theme of all tongues. He fell almost singlehanded on troops of Saracens, he was at the siege of Daroum, he returned to Ascalon to supervise the reconstruction of the ramparts, and at once set out again, scouring the surrounding country and bringing back bloody trophies to his deliriously admiring soldiers. Meanwhile, the war showed no signs of progressing, and Jerusalem was as far away as it had been before All-Hallows. And Richard was obliged to go to Acre himself to bring back deserters by threats, reproaches, and promises.

After Easter all the French barons left the king of England though he had implored them to remain and not dismember the army—he offered to keep them at his own expense, and when they refused he accompanied them on their way, weeping and begging them not to desert him. After their departure the army was gloomier and more at a loss than ever. There was talk that the king, too, would soon leave—he hardly stirred from his tent. Many knights of Champagne and Gascony left Ascalon, bound for Joppa and Acre—in Tyre, men said, the French were living high at the marquess' expense.

Among Richard's adherents there was always much evil spoken of Conrad of Montferrat. But when the baffled king summoned the barons of the kingdom to Ascalon and asked them to choose a chief who could press the war, they unanimously named Conrad. And the king of England had no choice but to confer the kingship on the man he hated most. He asked his nephew Henry of Champagne to go to Tyre with a small escort of knights and bring the marquess to Acre to be crowned.

Disgusted by the army's long stay at Ascalon, Herbert of Linnières seized the opportunity to enroll himself in Count Henry's guard of honor. How he had managed it, God alone knew—he rarely deigned to open his mouth, asked nothing of any man, and always succeeded in getting the best place—indeed, the man who relinquished it to him had almost to thank him for taking it! He dressed in his best, delighted at the prospect of a pleasant journey along the coast, of seeing the city of Tyre so famed for beauty, of attending the coronation, of taking part in the subsequent rejoicings—and, of course, of seeing his uncle Andrew and his uncle Simon.

A wave of joy rolled the length of the Frankish coast from Ascalon to Tyre, through the scattered garrisons and troops in Joppa, Caesarea, Arsuf, Haifa, Acre, through the settlements of Italians and Syrians, whom the mere name of the marquess sufficed to reassure—no doubt of it whatever, he was the one great enemy of the Moslems. Even those who had cursed the marquess were eager to trust him—Richard wanted him crowned, so he could not be a traitor. All was forgiven, the famine during the siege, his adulterous marriage, his plots against Richard, and even—harder still to forgive—that haughtiness of his, the sternness of a man who knew that he was superior to all men and all things. At least the Christian state would have a responsible chief—for it had been long since anyone had taken King Guy seriously.

Through the plain of Saron knights bearing the banner of Champagne rode gaily; their helmets and their horses' manes were stuck with flowering jasmine. The sky was blue over a bright sea. When they reached the beflagged and rejoicing city of Acre they stopped to rest their mounts and to hear Mass at the church of the Holy Cross.

Richard's first messengers had ridden faster than the count of Champagne, and two days after his election Conrad received the good news at Tyre, in the midst of a ceremony. He behaved with the solemnity which only he could achieve on solemn occasions—he wept for joy and raised his arms to heaven, praying God to take his life if he showed himself unworthy of the crown he had so long desired. Great was the joy among his friends, both "Colts" and Frenchmen. Tyre was ablaze with torches, and all night the illuminations on the ramparts were mirrored in the dark, quiet sea. But it was a short-lived joy—on the third day after he received the good news the marquess of Montferrat died by the hand of an assassin—he had been returning from a visit to the archbishop of Beauvais and was walking through the street without an escort—it was April twenty-eighth.

Henry of Champagne and his knights were nearing Tyre when messengers from the city brought him news that the marquess was dead. Thunderstruck, the count turned back, rode to Ascalon as fast as his horse could carry him, and from there to Daron, which his uncle was engaged in besieging.

A week after Conrad's death his widow, Isabel of Jerusalem—then four or five months pregnant—was thrown into the bed of a third husband (her first was still alive). And thus by the advice of Richard and at the insistence of the barons of Ultramar, Henry of Champagne succeeded to the rights of Conrad of Montferrat.

The marriage was celebrated with great splendor in the cathedral of Tyre. The crusaders clung to their hope—they must have a leader. One was gone, so they replaced him—perhaps the new one would be as good. When a strong man disappeared, it was as if the world fell to ruins or were suddenly transformed—the world of the present was a world without the marquess. The marquess had been like a granite pillar supporting the entire edifice—he had crumbled, and the first prop which came to hand was thrust into his place. The young count, as fine a youth as ever lived, seemed little impressed by the crown which had so suddenly been set on his head: he accepted it from a sense of duty, without enthusiasm and without fear. Of one thing there was no doubt—his bride was beautiful.

For Herbert of Linnières the royal wedding was a wholly unexpected bounty. As a member of the groom's escort, he found himself a prominent guest at a wedding—and the bride and groom were none other than the count of Champagne and the heiress of Jerusalem! Herbert had a passion for fine clothes, oriental carpets, state apartments, and festal music. He clapped his hands and conscientiously shouted "Noël!" when the bride appeared, pale and almost staggering under the weight of gold embroideries and pearls on her head, her veil, her breasts, her arms. The cathedral was white with lilies. Grave and solemn, the barons marched past, their heavy brocade-lined fur mantles swinging from their left shoulders.

During the ceremony Herbert stood with the rest of Count Henry's escort, straight as a pillar and trying not to disarrange the folds of his rather worn tunic. He was very proud to be so near the altar; he knew that he was handsome, and even as he lowered his eyes in prayer he wondered whether the queen's ladies-of-honor were looking at him. After the ceremony he went to the marquess' palace, where he found his two uncles, handsome Andrew and ugly Simon. They both looked sad and Andrew called his nephew a brainless fool. "What honor is it to our count," he said, "to wed a woman whose husband is hardly cold in his grave? This marriage will bring him no happiness."

And Simon said that he would not accuse Count Henry, but that there was no doubt the thing had been done through Richard's machinations—it was Richard who had paid the Old Man of the Mountains to have the marquess killed; the two murderers belonged to the sect of Assassins who obeyed the Old Man of the Mountains, and everyone knew that Richard had sent the Old Man presents. Herbert did not argue with him—he knew that Richard had hated the marquess. But Andrew said that more probably the Old Man had been paid by Saladin, who feared the marquess above any other Christian. "I should not say it," he added, "but I doubt if we shall find anyone to replace the marquess. God grant Henry of Champagne fame and happiness in this land, I wish him no evil."

Herbert was feasting his eyes on the beautiful damsels in the train of the new countess of Champagne. He watched them dancing in the stately hall and his eyes were bright with desire. "Uncle," he said, "I wish I would fall in love with one of them—but I do not know which to choose."

Henry of Champagne and his wife—"white as a pearl," says Ambrose—made a triumphal entry into Acre. And the same Ambrose, whose indulgence toward the young count's marriage is equalled only by his severity toward that of the marquess, thus recounts the reception which was accorded the new king: "There had you seen a noble welcoming, processions ranged in order, all the streets bedecked with tapestries, in every window and before the houses censers all filled with incense! And all the men of Acre, three score thousand or more, came forth, all armed, from the city for to meet him, so soon as they saw him. . . . The clerks led him to the minster and brought forth the relics to him and caused him to kiss the Holy Cross; and he and many more made offerings there."

It was a beautiful day, a day of high hopes. Once more Jerusalem was in every heart—there was hope of reaching it before the heats cf summer began. Henry of Champagne, with the French and Syrian barons, made his way toward Daron to join King Richard.

In Acre, at the count's palace, Herbert encountered a man of Champagne, a native of Bar-on-Aube, who asked him if he was not Herbert of Linnières. "I was told," he added, "that you look like your uncle Baldwin of Puiseaux."

Herbert said: "God! Have you news from home?"

"News I have none," said the man, "but a friend asked me to find you, or rather your father, and give him the money which the lady of Linnières has sent him."

"Praise God!" said Herbert. "We are very short of money."

Lady Alis had sent twenty silver marks in a green silk purse. Herbert took them and hastened to buy himself a fine Arab bay with a coat that shone like satin. The rest of the money he put away for the baron.

This time Andrew went on campaign with the count. Had he lost all hope of winning his damsel, or did he want to gain forgiveness for his sins by a pilgrimage to Jerusalem? God knows. In any case he did not confide his reason to his nephew. Herbert was in love with his new horse and could talk of nothing else. "What withers! What eyes! What nostrils! See how he rears!" In order not to tire his precious mount, he had it led beside him by a squire, while he himself rode his old gray.

Once more from all the coast towns crowds and caravans of men-at-arms and pilgrims moved down the plain of Saron and the plain of Sephel to join the army which was marching on Jerusalem.

And once more there was the great surge toward the Holy City, and once more the army, camped in the heart of the mountains, at Betenoble, marked time, then retreated, again at Richard's command. The crusaders were men of good will—they had lost too much to give way to discouragement; after cursing Richard, Saladin, the Templars, the "Colts," and many another, they considered the situation and concluded that the king knew what he was about and that the recapture of Jerusalem must wait for the arrival of fresh troops and fresh provisions. Meanwhile Richard scoured the countryside, winning victory after victory in skirmishes with the Saracens, who were attempting to harass the army.

Andrew had finally rejoined Ansiau in the ranks of Champagne. It was ten months since the two cousins had met. Ansiau had changed greatly; his temples were growing gray, he had deep lines under his eyes, and his face was darker than ever. Andrew found him stern and indifferent. "You remember," Andrew said, "that we wanted to exchange our vow of friendship before the Holy Sepulchre. Last time, my father's death prevented my going. But this time we shall see it side by side and together."

Ansiau sighed, remembering the thousand red candles which burned on the altars of Holy Sepulchre, and the face of the young King Baldwin, pale and puffy under its golden helmet. All that was another life—death had intervened. However, he tried to be pleasant to Andrew. He said: "I hear you are going to marry?"

Andrew laughed. "I have told you that I shall never marry. I am not a marrying man. I would not tell anyone except you, brother, but I have been acting like a fool. It was not for me, I aimed too high. And to think that twenty years ago I could have had any woman I wanted! And I wanted none of them. Do you remember Edith of Chalmiers?"

"Yes," said Ansiau. "But I do not like memories."

Andrew shook his head. "Still the most satisfactory woman I ever knew. At least she was frank. Brother, the only thing to ask from a woman is pleasure."

Andrew did not have the good fortune to see Jerusalem. He was wounded near Rames in the course of a raid on the road to Ibelin. Ansiau, his squires, and two Gascon knights were with him. The Bedouins had attacked on their flank. There were at least fifteen Bedouins, but they were poorly armed—the knights soon succeeded in putting them to flight. But Andrew's hauberk was old and worn, and a slender Bedouin lance pierced it. The lance had gone almost through his chest, between heart and stomach. Andrew was losing a great deal of blood from the wound and coughing blood as well—he could not sit his horse. Ansiau and the two Gascons dismounted him and laid him on a bed of dry grass in the shadow of a gray bramble bush. Ansiau unfastened the neckpiece of his hauberk and tore strips from his shirt to close the wound, which was still spouting blood—his clothes between his skin and his hauberk were sticky with it. It was very hot, and in the dark-blue sky vultures sailed on wide, molting wings.

Andrew began to cry. He said: "Brother, I am done for."

Andrew's beard was red and wet, and the pink foam reappeared on his lips as fast as Ansiau wiped it away. In two minutes he had become an old man, with fleshless face and long, pointed nose. He breathed laboriously. His eyes were glassy. He managed to say: "Communion."

As was the custom in desperately urgent cases, Ansiau took a stalk of dry grass and blessed it with three signs of the cross, asking God of His grace to consecrate this fragment of His creation so that it could serve as a host to comfort His servant Andrew, knight. In such cases, it was said, any Christian could act as a priest, and any bit of created matter could replace the host—not completely, but sufficiently for a man's soul and a man's faith. Ansiau humbly kissed the consecrated grass, then put it between Andrew's open lips. It seemed to give the wounded man relief. He closed his eyes, and Ansiau thought that he had gone to sleep. But Andrew opened his eyes

once more, parted his lips, and said: "Have a Mass—said for me—there—"
Then a torrent of blood choked him.

He was buried in the cemetery at Rames and was deeply mourned by his squires and Herbert. Ansiau did not have the heart to mourn—one blow more or less hardly counted. The world was growing ever emptier, ever poorer in memories—another name to commend to God in his prayers.

At the beginning of July the army again marched on Jerusalem, and this time it seemed that at last the goal would be reached. But once more Richard struck camp for fear of the heat and of thirst—the wells, men said, had been poisoned by the enemy. The French, disgusted and outspokenly indignant over a third retreat, could not find jeers enough for the worthless leader who could do nothing but shuttle back and forth between Rames and Betenoble, and who was the only man to fear dangers which the meanest sergeant was ready to embrace for the love of God. Thenceforth the duke of Burgundy and his Frenchmen remained apart from the English camp, and the French everywhere sang a song on King Richard, a song said to have been composed by Hugh of Burgundy himself, but which was so insulting that the duke never claimed its authorship.

Whether in the French camp or the English or among the Syrian knights, not a man but was sick to death of a war which neither ended nor progressed. The hot days returned, bringing mosquitoes, dysentery, and fever. A year in the field had exhausted the hardiest, and reinforcements from the West had almost ceased to arrive. The ports of Acre and Tyre were full of sick and wounded waiting for ships to carry them back to Marseille or England or Spain.

King Richard hid in his tent and every day received envoys from Saladin, and the men of Champagne and even the English began to lose all confidence and to say: "He means to leave us and go home to England. He is selling the army to Saladin." Yet Richard was not to leave the Holy Land before giving his men and the infidels the most magnificent spectacle that Palestine had seen since the day the first Frank set foot there. The men who were in Joppa that summer were never in their lives to forget what Richard Lionheart could be.

The magnificent and unbelievable adventure is told in detail by Ambrose, and it is splendid enough to be read and remembered.* How Richard, with a few hundred men, had come by sea to relieve the blockaded garrison in Joppa, how he had driven the infidels out of the city and pursued them beyond the walls—how, with two thousand men and three horses, he had succeeded in routing Saladin's entire army—those who relate these things did not themselves understand how they were done. To do them, you had to be Richard.

---

* Ambrose's full account is printed as an appendix.

Ansiau of Linnières. For the humble knight of Champagne from the castellany of Paiens, those days of heat and misery were to sweep away and consume every memory which could be destroyed. Neither while the thing was going on nor afterward had he given much thought to what was happening to him—the king thought for everyone. He remembered one incident—barelegged, barefoot, and bareheaded, he was marching through the hail of infidel arrows, without a shield and grasping his sword in both hands. Arrows stuck in the links of his hauberk, he had them on his breast, his shoulders, his arms, he shook them off when the weight of them hampered his movements. Two or three grazed his ears and his right cheek. It was very hot, everyone was shouting, he shouted too: "God and Holy Sepulchre!" And before him sounded the gongs and drums of the Saracens, their foaming horses reared under the bites of Frankish arrows.

And then an arrow came whistling so close that he had no time to duck, and it tore the flesh of his right eyebrow and, passing through the eyelid, fixed itself in the white of the eye, but without destroying it. And to Ansiau the pain that he felt was merely an annoying mishap, and he marched on with the arrow still slanting through eyebrow and eyelid, and at every step he took it swung with all its weight, causing a pang which brought tears in floods. Hemmed in by five of the enemy—three footmen and two horsemen—Ansiau did not have time to take one hand from his sword and draw out the arrow. But the tears were half blinding him. A sudden jerk of his head dislodged it—it fell, tearing eyebrow and eyelid, a stream of warm blood flooded his eye. Ansiau staggered with pain, but seeing a nail-studded mace brandished over his head, he straightened up, steadied himself on his legs, and raised his sword.

And then he realized that it was perfectly simple to move forward, driving men and horses before him, making a desert the length of his sword. He did not advance quickly. It was enough not to make a single movement to protect himself. It was enough to be ready to receive every blow. It was enough to pay no attention to anything. He made his sword sing, putting all the strength of his shoulders and trunk into it, a stroke to the right, a stroke to the left—and all was flight before him. He saw so dimly that he no longer knew in which direction to go, he took three steps to the right, three to the left—wherever in that bloody mist he dimly saw black horses and gray horses, white capes and round shields. And then he began to run, his feet torn by the arrows which littered the ground, his legs bleeding. All the plain rang with shouts: "Holy Sepulchre!" He fell over the body of a horse—its hide dripped blood, its legs stuck up into the air, its neck was twisted. He got to his knees, stood up—there was not a single infidel before him, they were far away.

And he shouted: "Holy Sepulchre!" and again: "Holy Sepulchre!" And he made his way back toward the Toron with his chance companions, still shouting.

And the sun set.

On the summit of the Toron stood Richard—huge, bleeding, a mass of arrows, his hair red in the sun, his eyes aflame with slaughter. He shook his sword in the air, he gave a great laugh, then a great shout: "Holy Sepulchre! God! God!" And one by one he embraced the companions-in-arms who clustered around him.

For Ansiau, it was a last vision—after it, there was night. And pain— God, what pain! His right eye. His whole body had become an eye, an eye seared by flame, an eye squeezed by red-hot irons, an eye which grew until it burst its socket, split his head, poisoned his blood. And then one day there was such a tearing and rending that he thought he would die, despite the hot wine mixed with opium which they had given him to drink. They were tearing the very nerves from his head and pouring boiling pitch on them. He did not die. For many hours he lay, resigned to be that hulk of screaming, bleeding flesh, without will and without thought. Then into his darkness came fever, terrible headaches, delirium—and always voices and footfalls in the dark, never a ray of light. A hand which he knew was Thierri's—not his old Thierri, alas!—held a cup of cold water to his lips. And then again came the terrible voice of the Syrian doctor, whose every word was like a hammer blow.

Then one day there was another voice, quite close, at the entrance of the tent. Ansiau's lips automatically remembered that they could smile.

"I hear the speech of Champagne," he said.

"Baron, it is I, Herbert," said the voice.

"Greetings, my son. Where have you been?"

"I come straight from Caesarea. The accursed infidels delayed us."

His father raised himself a little. "What is the king doing?" he asked.

"They say he is sick. I have not seen him."

Ansiau shuddered and sat up. "Sick? It is not dangerous? What is the word?"

"I do know nothing more—I did not go to his tent."

Ansiau lay back again, he found himself very weak. He was panting. "Then go. Ask his men. I should not be surprised if it were serious—after a day—like the other day. Hurry, what are you waiting for?" Seeing that he was impatient and irritable, Herbert went out, though it was so hot that he wished he might stay in the tent.

That evening he came back to reassure his father. He told him that the king had not been wounded but was exhausted and bruised by the blows he had received in the battle. Ansiau felt somewhat relieved. Yet he reflected that King Richard, for all his strength, was not in very good health—he spent himself too freely. Then he asked Herbert: "Fair son, there is something I do not understand—this bandage they keep on my eyes—have I gone blind?"

Herbert quietly answered that he did not think so. The doctor who had removed the right eye had said that the left must be kept bandaged until the wound was healed—the left eye had been weakened by the operation and must be spared. Ansiau sighed—he had seen cases in which a man who had lost one eye had gone blind in the other—the visual power in the brain had been affected. As he regained his strength, he found the perpetual darkness more and more irksome. He could not handle his body properly, now that it was a formless thing lost in shadows. Voices irritated him—he found it difficult to recognize them.

"When will they take my bandage off?" he asked ten times a day. "I have stood all I can. I would rather see the sun once now, and go blind afterward."

It was on a still summer evening, toward the end of August. At first he saw nothing. Then, close to his face, he saw a gray triangle, and could not make out what it was. When he stretched out his arm he saw the triangle recede and grow larger, and he understood that it was the opening of the tent, with the curtain drawn back slantwise. Then he saw his hand—huge and black—and the silhouettes of Thierri and the doctor, a stranger except for his voice. He asked to have his bed put near the entrance, where he could breathe the night air—it was very hot in the tent.

Over his head, between the black, slanting cloth of the next tent and the heavy entrance curtain of his own, hung a strangely shaped patch of sky, so full of stars that it was luminous. There were more and more stars, he had only to look closely and he saw them. Some were as big as big diamonds, others as fine as grains of gold; a patch of the Milky Way emerged from behind the curtain like a white stain. They twinkled and then grew dim—not all together, but one after the other, in turn. Never had Ansiau seen such a sight. In a new sky new stars, freshly created.

They did not speak of joy and beauty, like the stars of his youth. They were there. That was all. They knew nothing of past suffering. They were empty and simple. In a vast and empty sky.

The war was over.

The men were so weary that none of them felt sorry when the word came. Peace had been signed for three years and three months. And Jerusalem remained in the Moslems' hands. Richard was to destroy the fortifications of Ascalon and Daron, which he had just rebuilt. Henry of Champagne, a king without a crown, held the strip of coast from Tyre to Joppa. Those who had sworn the peace were, on the Frankish side, Henry, count of Champagne, Balian of Ibelin, and Onfroi of Toron; on the Moslem side, Malik-al-Afdal, Malik-al-Zahir, sons of Saladin, and Malik-al-Adil, the Sultan's brother, well known to the Christians under the name of Safadin.

The Sultan granted the Christians the right to visit the Holy Places on pilgrimage. After a war so exhausting and disappointing, the permission was an almost unexpected bounty.

How many of these men had left their homes and crossed the sea with but one hope: to see the Holy City. They had attained their goal. It little mattered how. One thing was certain—they had paid dearly for the privilege.

Knights on horseback, sergeants, pilgrims, sick men in litters and on stretchers—once again they were travelling the road to Jerusalem. They wept, they sang hymns; there was no enemy to fear now—the war was over.

Ansiau rode beside his son, his one eye gazing at the mountainous horizon, the crowded road, the slow, motley caravan of pilgrims who now were pilgrims and nothing more. Over their heads, here and there, floated banners—banners of Normandy, of Champagne, of Pisa, of Brittany—brought together by chance among the tall crosses of gilt and wood.

Near Rames, father and son halted to pray at Andrew's grave, and Herbert wept more than was his wont. But Ansiau wept little—Andrew had won to a Jerusalem far more beautiful than the Jerusalem which Saladin still held. Let the dead rest in peace—he had his life to live.

In the mountains the air was dry and keen, the north wind cold. Before the pilgrims lay the sprawling city among its outlying strongholds with their little white farmhouses, among gray or yellowish fields, woods silvery with olive trees, rows of black cypresses and dark-green orange groves. The long graying wall curved around small stone or clay houses rising one above the other, and on the square towers floated the Moslem crescent.

Vast and yellow-gold in the light of the setting sun, Jerusalem held up her dishonored palaces, her desecrated churches, for the pilgrims to see—the church of the Holy Cross, the church of Our Lady, the church of Our Lord, and the imposing dome of Holy Sepulchre, gilded by the sun.

There was the holiest of all places, and there the True Cross. It was enough; the tears of joy which were to have flowed for the freeing of the city were loosed. It was the most hurried and perfunctory pilgrimage ever witnessed. Silent, solemn, and awed, the crowd filed past, while Saladin, turbaned and sitting his horse, graciously did the honors of the Holy Cross to his Christian guests. Barefoot monks clad in frieze stood before the Holy Sepulchre, collecting alms.

From the height of their horses' backs the knights could see the Holy Cross with their own eyes, and they wept aloud and stretched out their hands to It. Those on foot, who followed them, wept too and crossed themselves, but they could see very little.

Richard Lionheart left the Holy Land at the beginning of October. He took ship at Joppa, and the crowd of crusaders on shore silently watched him go. Tears and the salt wind reddened their eyes. Richard was leaving with a broken heart, and the tears which he shed when he bade his knights farewell won him forgiveness. Yet everyone knew that he had promised to stay until Easter, and without him Saladin's presence would be far more disquieting. Whatever else he might be, King Richard was rampart and shield, the man who never forsook his comrades in the press of danger. The Saracens feared him as they feared the Devil. What he had not done it was impossible to do: he knew how to fight a war better than the knights.

The word went now that he had been forced to leave the country by the treachery of the French king and his own brother John, who had plotted together to dethrone him and strip him of his dominions. Yet despite so valid an excuse there was a feeling of bitterness among those who remained—the man had made himself admired, adored, hated, feared; he had set the world talking of him as it had never talked of any other man; yet when you asked yourself what he had done for the kingdom and the Holy War, you hardly knew what to answer. His ship, each sail marked with the cross, drew slowly northward along the coast. With cries of "Noël!" and "Long live the king!" knights and soldiers gazed after the tall, dark figure standing on the poop, one arm raised in farewell. Then the sea mist swallowed him, and the ship grew smaller and smaller without appearing to recede.

After seeing the king go, Ansiau decided to leave Joppa for Acre, which at present was easy—the coast belonged to Henry of Champagne and there was nothing to fear but highway robbers. From force of habit, Herbert had rolled on the ground on the day of Richard's departure. "He has betrayed us, sold us! He has forsaken us!" Ansiau told him that he would permit no one to say such things of King Richard, and Herbert stopped. Herbert seemed to have rather steadied down—at least for a time he was quite melancholy and meditated on death. He had lost his three best friends:—his brother, Garnier, and Andrew—and was beginning to find the world a little empty, a little ugly. And he was eighteen. Once he said to his father: "Baron, I have made a bad bargain. I did not gain martyrdom, and the war is over—I shall surely be damned."

The baron answered: "Become a monk if you are afraid of Hell."

Herbert shook his head. "That is just what I cannot do. I cannot live without sinning, I like sinning too much—I can't help it."

When he reached Acre, Ansiau went directly to his house in the Pisan quarter. It had not changed outwardly, except that the courtyard looked dirtier—there were piles of straw and manure at the doors and outside the stable. Two men-at-arms, who were sitting in the courtyard, shouted when they saw their master arrive, and Bernarde, the maid, came out of the kitchen and began calling to her mistress.

Maria rushed down the stairs and threw herself on her lord's neck. Ansiau had not expected such a reception. Sobbing, she buried her face against his chest, then she raised her head, touched his cheeks and temples, stared at him, and began to cry again, meanwhile invoking the Virgin and all the saints. "O povero!" she cried. "Poverino!" Ansiau did not like making an exhibition of himself and quickly freed himself from the widow's arms. He said: "First I must have a bath. We will talk afterward."

At table Maria served him, worrying over what wine and what sweetmeats would please him best. He noticed that she had grown thinner and paler. "And Pascaline?" he asked. "Is she married? Why doesn't she show herself?" The poor widow burst into tears and unburdened herself of her great sorrow: Pascaline had gone off eight months before with some soldiers—-men of Tours, Maria thought—friends had seen her at Ascalon. "But for three months I have heard nothing, for all the prayers I say to the Virgin morning and night! Lord Jesus, I keep thinking that it is time the Blessed Mother of Christ took pity on me. But she will not hear me." Ansiau sighed as he thought of what eight months with soldiers would have made of Pascaline, and could find nothing to say to her mother.

That evening, when he went up to the bedroom with the widow, he was surprised to find a wicker cradle on the bed; and Maria's woebegone face broke into an ecstatic smile. The signor had not yet seen her Ansellino, he should see what a fine baby he was and how he could smile and wave his hands. She took the child in her arms and began chattering to it in Italian and stroking its short black hair. It was about five months old, it had big eyes and a big mouth. Stretched on the bed, Ansiau watched the child roll its eyes and smile at its mother. That face, half hidden by a bandage, that round dark eye fixed on it, set the child crying and clinging to its mother's neck. Maria gravely told it how naughty it was to be afraid of the *babbo*. "He was born three weeks after Easter," she said. "Five months and four days ago. I had him christened Ansello—you don't mind?" And she gave the child the breast, and Ansiau laughed heartily as he watched the dark little cheeks swell and draw in and swell again.

"Well," he said, "since you are still fond of me, I shall not look for another house. Count Henry's palace is in Acre, I think I will remain in his service. I shall not leave you—I have nowhere to go."

Maria sighed and said that he was very kind, but that surely one day he would want to go back to his own country.

The following morning Ansiau went to the palace to render his homage, for he had made up his mind to enter the count's guard. But something befell him which he did not expect. He encountered a certain James of Vanlay, a squire, who had just arrived from Champagne. This James of Vanlay was distantly related to the house of Puiseaux, and he had seen Lady Alis at Troyes. "I have brought you something from your wife," he said. "Come with me, my lodging is near-by."

On the way he told Ansiau all he knew concerning the Linnières household: Lady Alis, he said, had been very ill just before Christmas, she had caught the smallpox, and all the children had been ill too, except Girard and the two oldest girls, who had been with their great-aunt Lady Hersent, the prioress. The twins and little Mary had died, "and your youngest daughter and your daughter-in-law Lady Bertrade were left badly marked, your lady told me." Lady Alis, said James, had sent her lord fifteen silver marks, a relic of St. Mamas, and a belt embroidered by his eldest daughter.

"God!" said Ansiau. "It gives me a strange feeling to know that you have seen her with your own eyes. Has she changed much?"

"She is thinner, I think," said James, "and her face is rather pock-marked, but she was lucky—it did not affect her eyes. She told me that she had not quite recovered yet and that she tired very easily. She could never bring herself to sell Bernon, and she is having trouble with the fief—lawsuits, due dates, you know what it is. She asked me again and again to tell you not to forget her and to take good care of yourself for her sake. As for your sons, I am sorry to say that I saw only your youngest—he was with Lady Alis at Troyes, a fine boy, about two-and-a-half I should say."

Ansiau listened and was conscious that his left eye filled with tears, then overflowed. "It is a shock," he said, "when you have had no news for so long." James gave him the purse, the belt, and the relic. And Ansiau stared at the old, worn purse—he recognized it—he had given it to Lady Alis one day when they were at Troyes, just after Mary was born. Mary, who had a little beauty spot under her right eye and a little mouth that was always open —Mary would have been six—and she was gone. Geoffrey was gone, Garin was gone . . . and, looking at the belt which Mahaut had embroidered, he smiled, one half of it was less neatly done than the other, the stitches were larger and more uneven—"lazy as ever," he thought, "she must have had a friend finish it for her."

That very day Ansiau told the count's seneschal that he no longer intended to remain in Palestine and that he did not wish to take service: he had seen Jerusalem, his pilgrimage was accomplished, urgent business called him home. And then he went to the cemetery and prostrated himself on his son's grave.

"I am going to forsake you," he said. "It must be—I cannot do otherwise.

"God has taken your bright face from me, and you know that to me all other faces are gray and faded.

"Never in my life shall I taste such joys as those I knew when you were at my side. Since you vanished from my sight half of my life has lain in the grave with you. May God deny me a Christian death if ever I forget you, my first-born, my lamb without stain, my only joy."

The sun was already sinking when Ansiau rose—the vast cemetery, with its cypresses, its olives, its crosses, its gravestones, already lay half in shadow, and the sky behind the city wall was yellow and red. Slowly Ansiau walked to the city and found it bathed in crimson light—the narrow, evening-shadowed streets were as animated as ever, early oil lamps flickered softly before the doors of taverns from which issued oaths in every Christian tongue. Ansiau entered the church of St. Leonard for vespers, but he hardly followed the service—his thoughts were with Lady Alis.

He saw her ill and sad, burdened by cares. All alone—keeping the house, managing the fief, borrowing, paying, with no one to help her. Three children gone. Garin, Geoffrey, little Mary. Ill, he thought. Her face pock-marked. He had seen Maria only that morning, and by now he did not know the color of her eyes. But he knew Lady Alis, he knew everything about her—the least little lines around her eyes, the texture of her skin, the small curls on her forehead. He wanted to know just how and just where the scars had marked that skin which was his. "Luckily it did not affect her eyes . . ."

James of Vanlay had seen her eyes. Ansiau saw them now—deep-set under the heavy brows, blue, small, and frank.

As soon as he reached the house he ordered Thierri and his men to pack —they would leave for Tyre in the morning. Then he broke the news to Maria. He expected a storm of reproaches and lamentations, but the widow merely sat down on a chest in the corner of the room and there remained, wiping her eyes with her sleeve and saying not a word.

Ansiau was touched, for Maria was not without charms for him—far from it. He said: "Silly! Don't you know better than to grow fond of a soldier? Life is like that in wartime—love and part. There are plenty of men in this country, you will find a better."

Maria sighed—she had not thought that her signor was to leave her so soon. He said: "Come to bed, I must be up early in the morning if I want to get to Tyre before dark."

In bed Maria recovered the use of her tongue enough to say that there could not be a better man than Signor Ansello and that his wife must be a happy woman—she must be a noble and beautiful woman too, and he would be glad to return to her, but he must not quite forget his Maria, who loved him so well.

"If you really love me," said Ansiau, "I shall ask you to do me a service. My wife has sent me some money, but it will only just pay for my journey, and I have debts besides which I can never pay. My son's grave is in the cemetery here—I don't care about the others—if after I am gone you could take care of his grave and have the prayers for the dead chanted there on All-Hallows and Christmas and high feast days, and give some alms in his name—once in Champagne I will arrange to send you what I can."

Maria sighed, for she did not like to spend money; but she said that the signor could count on her, she would do what was proper. By morning she was much more animated and chattered incessantly about the signor's long journey, storms and seasickness, and the Frankish lands where the streams are frozen in winter. She opened her clothespress and took out a woman's bodice, richly embroidered in red and gold silk, and two lengths of brocade with a woven pattern of birds and lions. "Here," she said, "this is for your lady, and the brocades are for your daughters, they can make them into sleeves. It is Pascaline's dowry, but she will be only too glad to give it up for you."

"Her dowry?" Ansiau asked in surprise.

"Yes—the poor child. You can imagine what a dowry she will need to marry now! Santa Maria, if only she comes home soon! Does the signor find these things not good enough for his wife? The signor looks displeased."

Ansiau gave a broad smile. "They are very fine things," he said. "But —well, I have a young daughter-in-law too, the widow of my eldest son— I should like to bring her something."

Maria clasped her hands. "The widow of—oh, the poor creature! You should have told me sooner. Of course I can find something for her." And thus Milicent received a gift of an ivory necklace, which, Maria said, was just the thing for a widow.

For the first and last time Maria put her Ansellino into her lord's arms. "After all, he is your son," she said. Ansiau kissed the child on both cheeks, detached a medal of St. Florentin from the chain about his neck, and handed it to Maria. "Give it to him when he is old enough to wear it," he said, "so that he may never forget that his father was a man of Champagne." Then he bade her farewell.

Herbert had not expected such a sudden departure, but his father did not like arguments. He cursed as he packed his things. "After all, you did promise to give me the fief and the castle. And now you want to go back. And what will there be for me?"

For the last time father and son visited the cemetery. Ansiau carried with him a small wrought-iron casket in which to put earth from the grave. As the body had not been embalmed he could not take it with him—he wanted at least to have this semblance of a relic of his son. He vowed to himself that he would never sleep without putting the box under his head or his pillow.

The little troop—Ansiau was taking home seven of the twenty-five men who had come with him—set out about noon. There was a strong wind blowing, and they must hurry if they were to find passage on the last pilgrim ships sailing from Tyre. At Tyre Ansiau intended to sell his extra horses and bid farewell to Simon and to Garnier's grave.

Garnier's grave was fresh and new, covered with a white marble slab and marked by a cross. A great Judas tree was dropping its last red petals on the marble. Simon had aged greatly, he was thin and yellow and his hair had turned gray. He had been hamstrung at the battle of Arsuf and he walked with difficulty. On their way back from the cemetery he accompanied his cousin to the city wall, which overhung the sea. "So," he said, and his voice was a little languid, "you have changed your mind, fair cousin? You no longer like this country?"

"I had news from home," said Ansiau. "Lady Alis is ill and is having trouble with the fief. It is time I took over for her, at least for a while. But I may well come back—too many of my dead are buried here."

Simon seated himself between two crenellations of the parapet and buried his face in his hands. "Count me among your dead," he said, "for I think there is little life left in me. I hope no one will ever see what I have seen. I accuse no one. But so many of our best knights did not lay down their lives in order that we should pray in Jerusalem at Saladin's good pleasure."

"The infidels are too strong," said Ansiau.

"We had the finest knighthood the world has ever seen," said Simon, "and what did they do with it? What is left of it? And those who survived— I with my leg, you with your eye—I accuse no one—but it is hard to think that such sacrifices were made for nothing."

"Not for nothing, cousin, you very well know," said Ansiau, shaking his head. "Every man who died gained Paradise."

"I know some who did not gain it," said Simon, his eyes burning with hatred, "some who saved their own skins and left their men to pay the price, some who came to terms with Saladin."

"Cousin," said Ansiau, "so long as I have two arms, no one shall speak evil of King Richard in my hearing. There was never a better knight. He never abandoned his men; when he came to rescue us at Joppa, he risked his life for the meanest, as a man would not do for his father or his brother. There has not been his like on earth since the days of the Holy Apostles."

"I do not accuse him," said Simon, "either for supporting the marquess or for anything else. God is punishing us for our sins, He has poured humiliations upon us, His will be done. Do you think that I begrudge losing my estate and my fortune? As if I still cared to own anything! I am old, my wife is old. I could have my other son, but I do not want him to come here— he is better off with you in Champagne. I brought no good to Garnier."

Ansiau spent two more days with Simon. Theodora looked at him and wept; she said: "You are so like the poor boy. Not in looks—it is your voice, and the way you speak. Tell your daughter Mahaut," she added, "that he loved her dearly. He called on her so often in his last hour that it is only right she should know it."

On October fifteenth Ansiau took leave of Simon and his wife. With Herbert and their squires he embarked on a broad-beamed Genoese ship, loaded to the gunwales with pilgrims and crusaders in haste to reach home before Christmas. The sky was gray, the sea the color of steel. Yellowed and dripping with brine, the great patched sails trembled and swelled in the wind, the masts cracked and squeaked. The harbor of Tyre began to fall astern, but the city stood clear against the sky, an island of walls and churches rising out of the sea; then the whole coastline unfurled along the horizon— gray, inhospitable, rocky. And as he looked for the last time at that land which was called holy and which had brought the world so much grief, Ansiau's heart beat strong—he thought of the tracks of boars and wolves on fresh snow, of sticky, yellow, swollen buds on the black branches of oak and beech, of spring green, of the walls of Linnières, of the Seine flowing by Troyes. And of his lady's soft skin.

The only wealth he was bringing home was a casket of earth. He was poor, he thought—that earth had taken his all. He was going home to a changed wife, a different son, different companions. He wondered if he had not become a different man himself.

MILICENT

LONG, WHITE, flaky clouds drifting in a pale-blue sky. Crows and kites winging over the yet leafless forest. Bushes just touched with yellow down. A cool air that urged to song and laughter. Mid-Lent.

Never was there a girl who could sing and laugh better than Alis of Puiseaux, daughter of Joceran. And now she stood before the small window from which the wolfskin that covered it in winter had just been taken down. It did not make the room much lighter, but the fresh air came in. The wall was thick and the window so narrow that you could not put your head through it. Beyond the gray stone sill, the timbers of the palisade, then the meadow, and the stream—its banks were already green, Easter fell late that year. The notes of the crows carried spring, and the cluckings and flutterings in the poultry yard told of God knew what vanished childhood days. The girls chattered as they bent over their embroidery—a great altar cloth for Our Lady of Hervi, to be offered in thanksgiving for the baron's return.

It was three months since he had come home, bringing with him Herbert, the fair white falcon. Every night for three months he had lain, hot and heavy, in the great bed, bathed in God knew what sweats, shaken by God knew what fevers. Always the iron casket under his head, and Thierri stretched at the foot of the bed. His temples were streaked with gray now, and there were white hairs in his short, curly beard. The first night he had wept; Alis had held his weeping face, his wet beard had touched her shoulder, above her left breast. God! how heavy her breasts were now—two bags of flour—with long nipples as hard as buttons; but it was only to be expected—there, low in her belly, the new burden was already growing heavy, giving her nausea, pains in the loins. As year had followed year, the symptoms had become a habit; there had been three years' respite, and now it had begun again.

The baron was a good lord and master. Alis, being a woman, could not but be beguiled by fair words. Even if you were thirty-six, when a man stroked your cheeks and arms and tickled you and said, "Aielot, sweet, sister"—the blood began to run hot. Her coy days were long since over— what if he did have no right eye, what if, under the bandage, there was a sort of hollow filled with scarred and broken flesh, and nothing of an eyebrow but a few bristly tufts of black hair? Did any woman ever cease to love a man because he was wounded in fair battle? And then his colics, his fevers, his sour sweats, his troubled sleep—what woman would put up with them, except she who had known him as a rosy-cheeked, beardless boy? "There,

there, my friend, never mind if my face is pock-marked, don't begin hankering for a girl, she would not know how to take care of you."

Her pock-marked face. From her sleeve Alis drew a lead mirror no bigger than an egg and furtively raised it to the level of her eyes. Her skin was soft and smooth, a trifle yellow in color, on her cheeks there were round scars like little holes, and on her nose three more, which turned red on frosty days and after meals. How light her eyes were—the color had all faded out of them; and her eyebrows were as thick as ropes. But her mouth was still good to kiss, full and soft; and her teeth were yellowed but firm. There were still men who would pay dear to have the lady of Linnières behind a barn or under a tree. However, she had no idea of playing that trick on the baron —not after all he had suffered, poor dear. Milon should not lay a finger on her, even if he were dying. It was the baron she wanted now—anyone else could go to the Devil!

There was only one thing amiss. The baron might have lost an eye, but he could still see well enough, and the countryside was full of fresh, smooth-skinned, rosy-cheeked girls—would to God that they had all caught the small-pox, Mahaut always excepted, of course.

From the courtyard rose a volley of soldiers' oaths, the splash of hoofs in the mud—and what a peaceful pride it was that set her heart beating faster! Soon they would be in the hall—starved, muddy, scratched by branches, and smelling of the woods. Her two lords, the dark and the fair, her husband and her son. The women stopped chattering to listen to the men's voices in the court. But Mahaut and Milicent went on whispering to each other—about boys, of course! Lord have mercy on us! Mahaut was in full, dainty flower, turning the heads of all the young men at Linnières and Hervi—and still she was not engaged. What a curse it was to be pretty and have no dowry.

The foot of the ladder creaked under a weight which was not a varlet's. The baron had acquired the habit of spending his afternoons in the bed-chamber, among the women; Lady Alis had no objection, she was always glad to see him, and he was fond of Hélie. But each time she heard him coming up the ladder something plucked at her heartstrings—her breath failed her, she parted her lips and listened. When she was young and pretty the baron had preferred to spend his time with his uncles and cousins. It was true that all his old friends were dead now.

She must do him the justice to admit that he always came directly to her. He stooped to pass under the rope from which the curtain hung, stepped over a group of children playing with a dog, and advanced toward her—tall, bony, his sleeves rolled up, his hair uncombed. His face was red from climbing the ladder too fast. Quickly she hid the mirror in her sleeve and turned away from the window.

His lips drew apart; his teeth were big and white. Without bending over, he put his heavy, rough, calm hand under her veil, plunged his fingers into her hair, turned up her face—never was man's hand more apt at disarranging, rumpling, tearing to bits. . . . "Glad to see me, eh?"

"In Lent!" Reproachfully Alis turned away her eyes. And the baron burst out laughing—like a man who once and for all has won the right to do as he pleases, Lent or no Lent.

Before the Crusade, she thought, he had never taken such liberties in front of her women—he had become too accustomed to prostitutes—at his age! "Will you stop, baron!" And, as it happened, he stopped quickly enough—he wound her hair around his wrist and roughly pressed his lips to her mouth, which automatically opened. "There, lady, I will leave you in peace. Bring me Hélie, and be quick about it—I have not seen him today. How is his foot?"

"The swelling has gone down," said Lady Alis, rearranging her veil.

Hélie was so beautiful that Lady Alis felt almost frightened—for she swore to anyone who would listen that he was the image of the baron, yet God knew the only resemblance between them was that Hélie had two eyes, a nose, and a mouth. She brought him. He was two years and ten months old— blond, warm, and heavy; his little cheeks were red because he was too hot in his long unbleached woolen dresses. A child's face was a sweet thing, bright and new; yet already those lips—too small for the face, too firm for a baby—those deeply sculptured nostrils, were hard and insolent. And the child was as spoiled as only a youngest child can be. "Come, heart of mine, say good morning to the baron before you go back to bed. Tell him if your little foot is better. Stop looking so cross at your mother."

The boy put both arms around the baron's neck and conscientiously kissed his beard. Then he began trying to take the bandage off his right eye. Gently the baron pushed away the two little hands and kissed them, one after the other. "Give him back to me, baron, you are tiring him. There, my white dove, there, my little flower, come and let me wash your pretty face." But Hélie turned away his head and frowned.

"What, damsels!" said the baron. "No laughing this evening? No singing?" There they sat, quiet and orderly, in their simple, tight-sleeved woolen dresses, damsels and waiting-women, some fifteen in all—those who had children had no time to spin after lauds. The presence of their master inspired respect; not one of them dared speak without his permission. Brusquely the baron stopped in front of Milicent, picked her up by the armpits, sat down on a chest by the wall and took her in his lap. "Well, daughter-in-law, show me the fine piece of work you are doing. I knew it— there's a bloodstain! You should have been born a boy, child—I would take you tourneying."

"I would like that," said Milicent dreamily.

"I should think as much. Soldier blood! You will bear fine children one of these days. Does that not make you happy?"

"No, my lord."

"Child! How old are you?"

"Fifteen."

"Then you are old enough to be thinking of such things." He yawned. "No, stay here. Sing me something."

"Every day," thought Lady Alis. "That great bean pole—she ought to have been married long ago. She is not pretty, but if she keeps on rubbing herself against him—true enough, she is as cold as a frog. But if I catch the two of them at it, her being an heiress will not stop me!" No, indeed, it was no time to let the baron be taken from her—if he began looking at a young woman now, he would never come back to an old one. No—old she might be, yet where would he find a woman more passionate and more courteous than Alis of Puiseaux? But men were fools.

Lady Alis still felt a vague motherly fondness for the sinewy little man whose blue eyes and fair words had seduced her—he was somewhere in the depths of her heart, with her other buried children—fantastical, unhappy, mischievous, and so near to her, so forgiveable. She was not in love with him—her love had melted like snow on the day Hélie was born. At all costs she had to forget that Hélie was in fact a bastard, that he had neither the same father nor the same rights as her other children. Hélie had been a delicate child, there was always the doubt whether God had not punished him for being a child of sin, always there were vows to make, offerings to promise—she had come to love him as if he were an only son. At last she had resigned herself to letting Girard go into service at Bar-on-Aube, she had sent Mahaut and Milicent to stay with the baron's aunt, the prioress of Saint Catherine's over toward Tonnerre. For the girls—Mahaut especially— had begun to develop narrow waists and saucy breasts.

And then the hard days, the poverty, the bad news from Palestine, and finally the baron's letter—how many widows that letter had made! Ansiet, her first-born, the manliest, the mildest, the son who would not bid her good-bye—had she been a bad mother to him? No, not a bad mother, but so busy, so tired—her babies, her pregnancies, the housekeeping, and a faithful husband, a demanding husband—God alone knew how demanding! And the child who never complained, who asked nothing, had been so easily overlooked, especially since he was his father's favorite. Haumette, his nurse, had wept as much as Alis herself, perhaps more, but neither could take time to weep long.

And then there had been money to be raised for the baron, borrowing and more borrowing, and bargaining with Abner and swearing him oath upon oath. At the castle their only food had been game, and when the hunting was bad there was nothing to eat—the wheat had been sold, rye had done badly, plain bread tasted as good as honey cake. And after Christmas had come the smallpox, and the little bodies laid in a single coffin, wrapped in a single shroud. The long winter evenings when she had sat by the fire, too weak to work, shivering with cold, unable to bear the slightest draught, her face riddled with red spots, her eyes so watery that they kept running over.

And the faces in the fire, little Mary's and the twins'—red with fever, then blue and unrecognizable. And then Ansiet's and Garnier's and Thierri's, and then the baron's and Herbert's, God only knew where they might be, perhaps they were martyrs too. . . . William and Alette had recovered, but they were weakened and sadly disfigured—and who would marry a girl with an ugly face? Then hunger again—no meat because there were no hunters. To be alone, perhaps for years—Girard was only a child. Finally she had sent for the girls. Mahaut was cheerful and good, adored Hélie, and seemed to pay no attention to boys.

And after that had come spring and her journey to Troyes with Hélie, who had just turned two. The inn at Chaource, where there was no place for them to sleep but in the open barn, on straw. The warm night, the crickets singing, the new sour wine they had drunk. Milon had kissed her ankles and the toes of her shoes, and that was the first time he had ever besought her—she had let him stay with her, between two bales of straw, until morning, and had watched him sleeping at dawn when the birds were piping in the fields and dew formed on his hair. After that day she had ordered Milon to live at Seuroi and to see her as seldom as possible—she must preserve her honor. Yet it had been hard to live so, knowing that he was there, only a league away, longing for her—knowing that she was actually his, his wife in body and will, varlet though he might be. She had made up her mind to marry Milon if the baron did not come home—but she had been sure that he would come.

At Troyes there had been an argument with Lady Beatrice, who wanted to take Milicent back because the child's husband had died. Alis had stood firm—the child had been entrusted to the baron of Linnières, and it was for him to dispose of her, he owed the girl a husband—Ansiet was dead, but the baron's younger son was still free. "It is not right," she had said to Lady Beatrice, "that we should have borne the burden of the child for nothing. I have her, and I shall keep her. It would seem that you are not the person to look after her, since her father did not want to leave her in your charge." To tell the truth, she had been thinking less of the girl than of the dowry, but Lady Beatrice was even less concerned about her daughter—she had a husband up her sleeve for Milicent, a handsome young squire, her latest lover, whose services she wished to reward. So Milicent and her dowry had remained the property of the baron of Linnières.

He had come home just before Christmas—gloomy, disfigured, aged. The dead had been mourned—God knows that Alis mourned them sincerely, for the house of Linnières had become her own flesh and blood—she mourned for each of them as she would for a brother. The baron and Herbert spent their days hunting and brought back enough meat for the spits and for salting. "Only wait, lady," Ansiau had said, "at Pentecost I shall go to Troyes, and I am sure to take some prisoners in the tournament—that will help us to pay Abner." And Lady Alis had leaned her head against his chest and thought how good it was when there were two to put their shoulders to the wheel.

Milicent was as tall as Mahaut now, she was fifteen and Mahaut seventeen. Mahaut had long legs, full hips, and breasts as big as apples and so firm that they did not tremble when she ran; her waist was so narrow that she could put her two hands around it—she had tapering fingers and slim feet and her neck was long and white. When she looked at herself in the rain-water tub she saw a face so finely carved, so clear-skinned that she was lost in admiration—there in the depths of the tub were the two black diamonds, lively and squinting, shadowed and caressing under their ivory lids. And she remembered that Garnier would never see her beauty with the eyes of the body. He would never see, never know—"if I had been there," she thought, "I would have cured him. And what use have I for my beauty, O my fair love, if I must waste it on another?" Yet she loved to look at her hands and her hair and to make herself pretty with embroidered ribbons.

The summer after the crusaders left had been hot and monotonous. The damsels, well guarded of course, went down to the Armançon to bathe, and afterwards rested on the green bank, in their white shifts and with their hair down. Among Hugh of Beaumont's sons there was a certain Aimeri, a youth of twenty with a fine brown mustache—he had managed to catch Mahaut behind a coppice and give her at least a dozen kisses. It made her very angry, and she let him kiss her again and again—she told Milicent that it was because she pitied him, she was sure he would kill himself if she refused him. Lady Alis heard of the matter and sent Aimeri back to Bernon. After that, Frahier, Garnier's younger brother, also tasted Mahaut's lips, for she was beginning to take pleasure in the innocent game. Lady Alis, seeing her come into the hall every day with her cheeks on fire and her eyelids trembling, decided to take her to Saint Catherine's Convent, where the baron's aunt was prioress.

At the convent the days were long—long and still. Mahaut and Milicent yawned, bending over their needlework and listening to the chatter of the nuns. Nothing but arguments over a scanted bowl of soup, a rosary told too fast, gossip, interminable tales of miracles in which the saints played parts which were often unedifying. And some of the nuns told of things so obscene that even Mahaut, accustomed as she was to life in a castle, stopped her ears for shame. Except for the priest and two night watchmen, the girls did not see a man all year long. Old Lady Hersent was very strict and switched her little nieces for a botched piece of needlework or an insolent answer. Mahaut was not particularly pious—during the services she amused herself by watching the flies and spiders on the chapel ceiling. But Milicent prayed with her whole heart and made all sorts of vows for her lord's health. One day she told Mahaut that St. Catherine had told her to pierce her hands with thick needles; she was sure that if she did not obey, harm would befall the baron

"Silly!" said Mahaut. "What good could it possibly do the baron?"

"I don't know," said Milicent. "What harm can it do me? It will not kill me. Don't you ever think of what he must be suffering there in Syria? Our Lord let His living flesh be nailed to the cross to save us. And am I, a worthless girl, to be afraid of hurting myself to save my lord?"

"In the first place, he is not your lord," said Mahaut sullenly. "Ansiau is your lord."

Milicent said: "You know nothing about it." She still remembered the kisses the baron had given her the day before he set out. "If a man kisses a woman's shoulder and the back of her neck, it must be because he desires her—he can't be doing it out of politeness."

"Then what, silly? Even if he loved you?"

But Milicent shook her head: "That is all I ask. I shall never breathe a word of it to him, believe me. I come of too good a house."

And that winter a man from the castle had come to the convent to ask Lady Hersent to pray for the dead of Linnières. The girls were in the courtyard, feeding the sparrows and pigeons which were fluttering and strutting over the new-fallen snow. The Lady Prioress sent for Mahaut, the elder and stronger of the two. "You can best break the news to your little friend," she said. Mahaut had lost a brother, Milicent a husband—to Lady Hersent, the latter was the greater loss. Yet it was Mahaut who was the most stricken. But it was not of her big brother that she thought—the brother whom she had loved with the peevish, half-humorous affection a girl feels for the boy who pulls her hair and calls her "Squint-eyes." She had not seen him for six years. But the other—the other—Mahaut had not even waited for Lady Hersent to finish what she was saying, she had fled to Milicent, who was waiting in the cloister.

"Millie, Millie, it is not true, I will not believe it, I cannot believe it, do you hear me? Come!" She took her friend's hand and dragged her to the cell where they slept. She was trembling, her eyes were dry. "Millie, I will not believe it, Millie darling, I know—they made it up so that I will stop thinking of him, they are lying, he isn't dead, he isn't dead, do you hear me?"

Milicent understood to whom Mahaut was referring, and tried to quiet her friend. Mahaut had thrown herself on the bed and was gnawing her wrists. "Oh, I know them! And I know better than they do! I'll go to Syria myself! On foot, with a staff, I'll disguise myself as a minstrel, I'll sing. Millie, Millie, I am mad, I don't know what I am saying. But you know what I mean—in the ground, under the ground, in a wooden coffin. And I laughed! And I let trifles stop me! Millie, darling, how can I find him now? What can I do? Help me!" And she had begun to sob and whimper like a baby.

Milicent put cold, wet cloths on her forehead and eyes. Toward evening Mahaut became somewhat calmer and decided that the only way to be with Garnier was to die and go where he had gone. "I will not kill myself," she said, "for I should be damned, and he is in Paradise. Better to let myself die of hunger. Oh, I know he would say I was right!" Milicent thought it an excellent plan, and the following days she helped her friend to hide her food and then give it to the dogs. But after four days of fasting Mahaut fell sick of a fever and was delirious, and when she recovered she said no more about starving herself to death.

The two girls had each lost a dear friend. To say that Milicent was not saddened by her loss would not be true—she had too happy a memory of the big boy who had taught her to pray and to think, for her he was like a big brother. But she had so nearly forgotten him that she could not visualize his face. However, it is hard to find oneself a widow at fourteen—she had thought her future was settled, and now all was to do again. Would she be forced to enter a new family, with a new mother-in-law and a new husband, who, this time, would be a husband in fact as well as in name? The prospect terrified her. "Mahaut, fair friend, I do not want to live away from you."

Mahaut sighed: "That will be as the baron and Lady Alis decide."

Mahaut had grown quieter and gentler. She prayed much, and in her bed at night wept with her lips on Milicent's. "Do you think the dead know everything?" she asked. "Do you think they can see us? Lady Hersent says that they can see everything from where they are. He is so good, and I am so wicked—if he sees me he cannot be very proud of me." For a time she thought of becoming a nun, but living in the convent for fourteen months had thoroughly disgusted her with monastic life. She was very happy when her mother came to fetch her. She wept as she kissed Lady Alis' poor, withered cheeks. "God, my lady, you who were so beautiful! Your sweet rosy cheeks! You shall see how I will love you—I will let no one speak a word against your face!" Home at the castle she became gay again and ran and sang as before. But there is reason to believe that she had not forgotten Garnier, for she would not let a young man come near her and insisted that she would never fall in love.

That spring Milicent had implored Lady Alis on her knees to keep her at Linnières. "I don't want to go to my mother's. She does not love me. Until a husband is found for me I ought to stay here with you."

Lady Alis kissed her on both cheeks. "There, there, kitten," she said, "your father gave you to the baron, and I shall not let you go. If the baron is willing, you can marry Girard in place of Ansiau and stay at the castle." Milicent thought that this scheme for replacing Ansiau was not a bad one— she was fond of Girard, she was sure that they could live happily together.

In three years the man seemed to have aged at least ten. There are wounds so painful, so secret, that they cannot be touched without sacrilege. The naked soul of Ansiau of Linnières had clothed itself, armed itself, withdrawn behind a wall, impelled half by modesty, half by a lingering love of life. The thing must be forgotten; he forgot. Life must be lived; he lived. Life had its pleasures. Even the thought of his son now aroused in him only a purely automatic sorrow—tears rose to his eyes and overflowed.

He had reached thirty-eight. He was rather heavier and had lost some of his quickness. His skin was tanned black, his face often looked ashy from fever and the pains in the bowels which still tormented him. A strip of black cloth covered his right eye and part of his forehead, and his left eye often blinked and hurt intolerably on days when the sun was bright or snow covered the ground. Yet that face which was only half a face still had a strange charm, all the stranger because it proceeded from a youthful smile which exposed two rows of strong white teeth.

When he had reached home Ansiau's world was still the gray and faded world he had known ever since the death of his son. In the muddy, littered courtyard he had been received by sad women shaking with cold; they all had red noses, frost-bitten cheeks, and tearful eyes. That big hussy whose cheeks looked like a ploughed field must be Bertrade, Herbert's wife—that spare old woman with black pouches under her eyes was Richeut—that red-haired, bony bean pole in the long brown cape was Claude of Linnières. Lady Alis stood in front of them, her hands were clasped and strained. She wore a white coif which covered her neck and shoulders. And her face—Ansiau had feared to find it disfigured, ugly. But though the scars which covered cheeks, chin, and nose had hollowed and hardened the skin which had once been so smooth, her face still had all its old nobility. Older and thinner, for Ansiau it had changed so little that he saw it as he had known it, and could believe that he had never been parted from her. She was so much the same that he could almost have foreseen the astonished, tender, suffering eyes with which she looked now at him, now at Herbert. Hesitantly she stood there—from the instant he had entered the courtyard he was master once more, she his servant. And he took her back as a man returns to his native country, to his mother. He reflected that they were both old now and that they had too beautiful a past behind them—that broad, gentle face with the flat cheek-bones and freckled cheeks, that head of wild blond hair, that big, pure-hearted boy, the fruit of their first loves.

He was amazed to find that the castle held children and young girls who, instead of fading, were flowering like apple trees in April. Time appeared not to touch them. In Hélie's case it seemed less extraordinary—Hélie, the unknown, the fresh, the innocent. He was there, and Ansiau accepted him. Hélie was a flower of his flesh and his seed who asked to be loved, and he loved him. But the girls, whom he had known so well before he set out, and who still lived their gentle, furtive, little life, their life of embroidered girdles and birds and songs and whispered secrets, as if nothing had ever happened—they amused him, he found them charming.

Mahaut was the prettiest, and Lady Alis was in despair because she was still unmarried. Seventeen! Her beauty will soon be faded." But Milicent ran no such risk yet, and Ansiau admired her unreservedly. She was not pretty, and Lady Alis never missed an opportunity of saying so—it was admitted that she had a big mouth, a nose like a duck's bill, eyebrows that were too pale and irregular. But at fifteen she was in perfect flower. Flaxen and blond as a baby, she had very fluffy hair which curled a little and fell in long sunny locks about her face—behind, it was braided and hung over her shoulders. She had a very smooth skin, cheeks which readily colored to a very pale pink—her large eyes were gray with golden lights. She had a wide smile, very simple and very sweet, which made people think her unintelligent, but she was far from stupid. And if her features were not regular, she had a very beautiful figure—tall, slender, delicate, airy, sloping shoulders, a slim waist, the grace of a young blooded filly. And Ansiau could never remember without sorrow that his boy had loved this child, that he had wept over her, and God knew how seldom he wept. Sometimes, watching the girl bowed over her needlework, he said to Lady Alis: "Don't you think she looks like the boy?" Lady Alis knew that for the baron there would never be more than one boy, she did not need to ask which one. "I don't see it, baron—what an idea!"

At first Milicent would redden and hide behind Mahaut when her father-in-law looked at her; but he finally tamed her. He would take her on his knees and kiss her cheeks and tell her that she must not be afraid of him—a child did not fear its father. Milicent turned away and dropped her eyes. Later she said to Mahaut: "I was wrong, he is not in love with me."

"And a good thing," said Mahaut indignantly.

"He is in love with Lady Alis, that's what it is. She knows how to go about it—perhaps she has some spell."

"See here, my beauty," said Mahaut, out of all patience, "what is it you want? To be his whore?"

Milicent crossed herself. "God, no! Idiot! I want nothing. If he would kiss me again the way he did before he left, I think I should be happy for the rest of my life."

At Easter, Girard came from Bar-on-Aube to spend a few days with his parents. On the day he arrived Lady Alis put on her red dress and the embroidered bodice Maria had sent her and rouged her cheeks—she had almost a lover's fondness for her third son, her spoiled child; she was distressed at the thought that he might no longer find her beautiful; she perfumed her hands and temples and put on her rings. She ordered roast goat stuffed with dried mushrooms, Girard's favorite dish. "How he must have grown! Fifteen! Catherine, see that the bathhouse is well heated, the child will be dead tired after his journey."

Girard galloped into the courtyard, his two varlets could hardly keep up with him. He sprang nimbly to the muddy ground, strode across the puddles, splashing a kitchenmaid who was carrying a pail of water, and in two bounds had climbed the wooden ladder which led to the hall. Lady Alis was waiting at the door for him, her lips were trembling. He almost knocked her over, rumpled her fresh veil, shook her by the shoulders, kissed her a dozen times. Then he flung himself on the baron's neck.

Whatever he might be, he was not respectful. . . . The baron said: "What manners!" and laughed nevertheless. And he studied his third son's face, searching for some resemblance to "the boy."

Girard promised to be tall—he was thin and gawky, his movements were bold and quick. Less blond than his two elder brothers, he had hazel eyes and round rosy cheeks with no sign of beard. No—he did not look much like Ansiet—the smile perhaps, the wide eye sockets, his way of tossing back his hair like a restive colt, a trick which all the boys had inherited from their father.

Seated in the place of honor between the baron and Herbert, he leaned his elbows on the table, sank his teeth into a thigh of the goat, and smeared his face with sauce like a child of five—there was even sauce on his forehead. He felt happy.

Girard looked at his father and his brother with awed wonder—two crusaders home from the Holy Land, two men who with their own eyes had seen things of which he, a child, had only dreamed—the sea, ships, infidel lands, foreign cities—Girard thought that they must despise him, a little boy who had never travelled farther from home than to Bar-on-Aube.

The baron did not know what to say to this son of his who was neither child nor man. The after-dinner nap concluded, he made the boy jump and shoot and stand on his horse's back at a gallop. Eager and agile, Girard did well because he was excited. And Herbert, sullen as always, said: "At his age I could do better." He was jealous because Lady Alis was lost in admiration of his callow young brother. At nineteen years of age he was not going to let her stroke his cheeks and chin, he was not going to lay his head in her lap—he would have liked to, but three years as a crusader had given him a new reserve, he was stiffer, more dignified—he felt closer to the baron than to Girard.

On the night of his arrival Girard learned that he was to marry Milicent to fulfill the promise of his dead elder brother. Girard turned very red—it embarrassed him to hear talk of marriage and love—he said that he did not want to marry until after he had finished his service, his friends would laugh at him if they knew he was married. However, he found Milicent very pretty, and that night he slipped over to her bed to talk to her. The girls screamed and chased him away, and Milicent trembled and cried all night in Mahaut's arms.

"But you like him, don't you?" said Mahaut.

"I feel afraid, Mahaut dear—I don't know what is the matter with me. Of course I like him, but I don't want to sleep in his bed. I should feel too ashamed."

"Silly, you will get used to it."

Girard spent the next morning playing blindman's buff and other games with the girls and the children. He kept trying to catch his betrothed and pinch her, but Milicent slipped out of his hands. At last he caught her by the braids. She turned and looked into his eyes, and so many shared memories—games, escapades, punishments—rushed into their minds that they forgot their two years of separation and burst out laughing. "Tell me," Girard said at last. "Are you in a great hurry to marry me?"

"Not at all," said she. "And you?"

"I'm not either." They laughed even harder. "We can wait," Girard said. "We will tell the baron that we are too young."

Milicent kissed him on both cheeks. "I love you very much," she said.

That evening the two children, tittering and nudging each other with their elbows, proffered their request to the baron. Ansiau laughed. "True enough," he said, "you are too young. I will wait until you have ripened a little—and I am afraid that will not be before next Easter."

From the second day of his stay at Linnières, Girard felt that there was no longer a place for him at the castle. Yet Lady Alis adored him, the baron was fond of him, he found his sisters charming. The trouble was that he could not stay in the hall—the hall had become Herbert's territory, on the days when Herbert did not go hunting he stayed there from morning to night. It was a kennel, a mew, and a tavern. The baron let his son do as he pleased—in the first place because he shared his tastes, and in the second because he had given up scolding a grown man, a proved soldier, his companion in the Holy Land who was to be his heir. He had resigned himself once and for all to putting up with him, and the two men got on well together. Herbert turned up the maids' skirts in dark corners and behind benches, and Lady Alis complained bitterly. But the baron had seen worse things during the Crusade, and age had made him more tolerant—he remarked that Herbert was a lord's son and need not deny himself—let him amuse himself to his heart's content, so long as he left his girl cousins alone. And his cousins prudently kept to the bedchamber and never went through the hall except in groups of three or four.

Herbert was the father of two children—Aelis, who would soon be four, and Haguenier, who was nearly three. He was heir to the fief of Linnières, heir too, through his wife, to Hervi, for Haguenier's two sons had died in Palestine and the inheritance would fall to Bertrade. Herbert knew it better than anyone and coldly said that when Bertrade died he would marry another heiress and thus become the richest castellan in the countryside. And he behaved like a rich castellan. All his talk was of dogs and blooded horses, he made Father Aimeri write letters and keep accounts for him—he wanted to sell the pelts of the beasts he killed, exchange puppies for lengths of cloth—yet God knew that people who lived in the country seldom thought of keeping accounts. But Herbert had a good head for reckoning. He even managed to learn his letters and to read in the good father's missal. And he was so determined the world should know he was the son of a lord, that he could not make a motion by himself—his squires had to fetch him his riding whip, buckle his belt, turn up his sleeves when he ate, bring him his horse ready saddled and hold his stirrup; and if he did not approve of the fit of saddle or bridle he threw his whip and gloves in his squire's face.

At noon, after dinner, he settled himself on a bench by the hearth—in his shirt sleeves, his collar unbuttoned, and his arms half bare—and amused himself by teasing a big black dog, thrusting a stick between its teeth. The dog growled, Herbert laughed. The baron sat down beside him, and Herbert pulled his shirt together over his fat, hairless chest, and ran his fingers through his long, bristly hair. His quiet hawk eyes expressed as much good humor as they were capable of expressing. "Well?" he asked.

"Well?" said the baron, with his wide, automatic smile. Their conversation hardly ever proceeded beyond that one word—it was when they did not speak that they understood each .other best.

Herbert showed such sternness to Girard that Lady Alis felt afraid. He never actually hurt him, but he pursued him with raillerie and ironic remarks and malevolent silences, and made him feel that he was nothing but a little brat who had better not raise his voice in the presence of his brother who was a knight and a crusader. And Girard, spoiled, high-spirited, and insolent, was not accustomed to disdain. He wept and complained to the baron —the baron called him a milksop: "A boy who can't stand being teased!"

Lady Alis reproached Herbert, who flared up indignantly: "What do you expect? I have never laid a finger on him. I will say what I please. I am his elder brother, and I have a right to put him in his place if I feel like it."

On Palm Sunday Girard left the castle, his heart full of rancor against his brother. Lady Alis filled his pockets with cakes made of fine white flour and cried as she kissed him. "He is your brother, it would be a sin to bear him a grudge. Forget all this, my fair falcon—when Haguenier dies Herbert will have money of his own and he will spend three quarters of the year in Troyes."

After Palm Sunday the meadow in front of the castle sprang into flower and the forest grew green once more. Ansiau had long since forgotten what spring was like. The crowing of cocks, the plash of water in the ponds, the warm breeze ruffling his hair—everything said: Life is good. And he knew that he was far from old. The first warmth of spring drew him toward Milicent as the force of gravity draws ripened bunches of grapes toward the ground. Without even being aware of it, he followed her everywhere, sent for her when she was not about, searched for her. When he rested after hunting, Milicent was always at his feet or on his lap—blond and warm, speaking seldom (and he did not like chatter), and as affectionate as he could wish. Lady Alis was not at all pleased by her husband's intimacy with his daughter-in-law and said that it was high time she was married—her being a widow and an heiress was ruining Mahaut's chances. And the baron was in no hurry to have the marriage performed and said that both she and the boy were too young. But Lady Alis was so insistent that at last he agreed, and toid her to tell Milicent that she was to marry Girard before St. John's Day. And that very evening Milicent came to him in tears and begged him not to make her marry. "Do you mean it, my child?" he asked. "Do you want to become a nun?"

Then Milicent answered that she would not marry Girard because she loved someone else. The announcement was not calculated to please Ansiau. He called her a hussy and sent her upstairs, then asked Lady Alis who could have had the insolence to infringe on Girard's rights. Lady Alis had no idea—Frahier seemed to be in love with the girl, and there was a young falconer of the count's who was often in Hervi and stared at Milicent when she came out of church. "In any case," said Lady Alis, "she deserves a good whipping, and if I were you I would pay no attention to her nonsense."

"I think she is fond of me," said the baron, "I will talk to her tomorrow and find out the fellow's name—if it is anyone in the castle, I had better send him away."

The next day was a very beautiful one, warm and bright, and all the girls and young men went out to dance and run in the meadow. The baron himself went to the brook to escape the heat, and as he had it in mind to question Milicent, he sent his squire to fetch her.

They sat on the grassy bank in the shade of a willow. Milicent, whose heart was beating rather fast, kept her eyes on the ground and plucked petals from a great bunch of buttercups she had gathered—her white dress was yellow with them. "Well, my fair daughter-in-law," the baron began, "you see that I am not angry with you—you are young and Girard is far away. But you have given me your promise and your oath, and I do not intend to release you. The time has come when you must keep your father's promise—you must obey me and marry Girard."

Milicent bowed her head and said: "I have reconsidered, my lord, I will marry Girard."

"Spoken like a good girl! And now, my daughter-in-law, you must tell me the name of the man who has pleased you—you can understand that I do not want to see my son a cuckold."

Milicent looked at him with terrified eyes and shook her head.

"I will do him no harm," said the baron. "I will simply send him away. Come! It is someone in the castle, I suppose?"

Milicent did not answer, she continued to stare at him with wide-open eyes.

"I know how to make you tell," said Ansiau. "Look me in the eye. I shall name every young man hereabouts, and your face will tell me which it is. Well, is it Frahier? No. Garin the Blond? Aimeri? Geoffrey?"

And gradually he forgot all the names he meant to confront her with, and gave himself up to watching those great gray eyes slowly fill with tears. Then suddenly he threw her on her back on the sprouting grass and kissed her eyes, her forehead, her hair. It was a new face he saw, there so close to his, diaphanous, pink and gold against the grass, in the sun-dappled shade—never had he known that she was so beautiful. She was radiant. She had red lips and very deep eyes.

The rest of the day was delirium. She had escaped from him almost at

400

once and rejoined her cousins at their games. But he knew that she was ensnared as if she had been bound to him with cords—in the dances and rounds she missed her turn, let herself get caught, and saw nothing with her great dazzled eyes. From far away he felt the tremors that ran through her body, and her laughter and her singing were all a cry to him.

The wind blows strong, the branches sway,
Lover and beloved—sweet sleep they . . .

He could not make himself leave the meadow or stop following her with his eyes. He prowled around her; and always she fled, vanished, lost herself among the other girls—but he knew that she could not escape him.

He saw her enter the sun-bright courtyard, surrounded by her companions. Her hair was loose and aflame, her dress had turned to gold, she was luminous and triumphant, like a queen among her ladies. He was standing at the door of the keep and she dared not enter. She turned back, he followed her. Still she backed away, not daring to take her eyes from him. She passed the stables, stopped in front of the grain barn, leaned against the wall, not knowing where to go next. He picked her up like a feather and carried her into the barn. She closed her eyes and did not stir.

Not very long afterward all he saw beside him was a poor little girl, blond and pale, lying in the straw. Her beauty had vanished. She looked frail and sickly, but very sweet too, with her lips pouting like the lips of a weeping child. Ansiau was not the man to forget the value of what he had just obtained. He gave her a broad smile of surprise and tenderness and satisfied vanity, and wanted nothing but to see her smile too. And as she remained inert he tried to cheer her up by tickling her under the chin; but instead of laughing Milicent turned away and burst into tears.

"My poor girl, it is too late to cry now," said Ansiau. "There, don't spoil your pretty eyes. Stop being such a child!"

Milicent buried herself in the straw and sobbed even louder, and the baron reflected that after all she had no reason to be particularly happy. "There," he said, "turn around, look at me. Do you think I wish you harm? You lost your head—it can happen to anyone. You have nothing to fear, I will arrange everything for the best."

Milicent slowly turned to him and, in a small, frozen voice, asked: "You want me to marry Girard?"

"Why, I see nothing else to do. You are my godfather's daughter, I cannot leave you in this condition. I shall have Girard come home at once, and you shall be married before the month is out."

She did not move again, she lay tense and stiff, hardly daring to breathe. It seemed to her that she no longer had the right to make a gesture or a movement without the baron's permission—he made her afraid. And he sat there, staring at her with his one round, dark eye—an eye she had never seen. And he was no longer laughing.

Standing by the bed, Mahaut unbraided her hair. And Milicent, sitting on the edge of the bed with her head bowed, seemed not to want to undress, and the candle was almost burned out. "Have you gone to sleep?" said Mahaut. "Do you want me to help you undress?"

"No," said Milicent, terrified. "Don't touch me!"

"Why, Milicent!" said Mahaut. "What is the matter with you? Do you feel feverish?"

"Mahaut, have pity on me. Listen. I think I have done something wrong."

Mahaut looked straight into her eyes and went very red. "What!" she cried. "With a man? With the baron?" She was trembling with shame and indignation. "Strumpet! Strumpet! Here's what you deserve!" and her swift little hand showered a dozen light, resounding smacks on Milicent's cheeks, and Milicent, her face raised to her friend, did not even try to defend herself —as a man crushed under a rock does not notice that squirrels are throwing nuts at him. A thin stream of tears ran down either side of her nose. Amazed by such submissiveness, Mahaut stopped.

"Millie!" she cried. "What is it? Are you ill? Millie, my dear, stop looking like that! Millie, my life, my heart, forgive me!" She knelt by the bed and began caressing the girl's bruised cheeks with both hands. "Poor little pigeon," she said. "To think that I have made you sadder when you were so unhappy already! Now, tell me what the trouble is, and we will see how best to get you out of it."

"He wants me to marry Girard," said Milicent. Instantly Mahaut looked relieved.

"A very good thing," she said. "He knows what he is doing. Silly, it is the best thing you can do, since you have to marry him anyway."

Milicent lay down and closed her eyes. "Oh, God! He says so too. And the very thought of it makes my hair stand on end. I don't know what it is, I would rather die."

"Of course, since you love somebody else," said Mahaut understandingly.

"I don't know if I love him any more. I don't know anything. It is too ugly. Mahaut, my fair friend, never give up your virginity—you will be better off."

Mahaut was rather put out to hear a sermon from some one younger than herself. With a look of great wisdom, she said: "You aren't used to it yet, that's all."

Milicent did not answer; she stared at the dark ceiling. Everything was dark —night, day, the sky, the walls, the flame of the candle. "Mahaut, my dear, I would like to leave him my dowry and become a nun. Do you think I can?"

Mahaut kissed her and tried to comfort her. "You are not going to ruin your youth for a man, are you? He is not worth it, even if he is my father. There is not a man on earth who is worth it."

"I don't know," said Milicent. "Do you think he will tell Lady Alis? If she finds out, I will kill myself."

The following morning the baron, as was his custom, sat down on his cushioned bench in the upper chamber, close to the women who were spinning by the windows. But that day Milicent did not raise her eyes from her work. "So," said the baron in a loud voice, "my fair daughter-in-law does not love me today? She will not come and scratch my head as she always does?"

"I am ill this morning, my lord," said Milicent. "Mahaut can do it as well as I."

He grew angry. "Who said anything about Mahaut? Come here, you scamp, if you don't want me to send Thierri to bring you."

Milicent rose and came to the baron, who made her sit on his right knee. "You bad girl," he said in a low voice, "I shall make you pay for this later —what a way to look at me!"

She said: "Let me go. Lady Alis is looking at us."

"Let her look. Listen—I have things to say to you that I cannot say before everyone. Come to the stable later, I will be waiting for you."

Lady Alis frowned and tried to catch what they were saying, but they spoke too low for her to hear.

As soon as Lady Alis had gone down to the hall to order dinner, Milicent left her wheel and slipped into the courtyard, then to the stable. She dared not disobey. The baron's reproach had cut her to the heart—she was afraid to hurt him. But she had the feeling that she was marching to her execution and she imagined that all the varlets were looking at her and laughing slyly. In the stable—the door being open, it was light inside—the baron was sitting on an old saddle perched on a stool; he was working over a broken bit. When he heard her enter he turned his whole head—a trick he had acquired after he lost his eye. He smiled, showing all his teeth. "Come closer. I want to talk to you. Are you very angry with me? That is not what I meant to say. I thought about it all night. Oh—it is hard to say. I am mad about you. Otherwise I would never have touched you."

Milicent's mouth had grown hard. "You do not love me."

"I? Stupid! You don't understand. I adore you. I want you so much that I cannot sleep. You don't know what it is, you could never love so."

"You want to give me to somebody else," she said stubbornly.

He answered gently: "Do not forget that it is Girard. I would not have done as much for any other woman. And I do it to my great regret, you may well believe."

"Then why do it?"

"What else can I do? Your father entrusted you to me. I do not want to ruin your life."

"It is ruined already," Milicent murmured; tears of self-pity welled into her eyes.

"Of course not! What an idea! You are fifteen. You will forget. Fifteen! You don't know what that means."

Swiftly he began unfastening the neck of her dress and the white shift which hid her breasts—she threw a distressed look toward the squire who was brushing Assolant. "Never fear," said Ansiau. "He will not betray us. How beautiful you are! I have never seen a woman so beautiful. Will you come to the barn again? I am not forcing you, I am begging you. I will be your varlet, I will do whatever you wish. What do you want me to do for you?"

For three days Ansiau of Linnières struggled against the new madness which had seized on him, but still he put off sending for Girard. On the fourth day he ordered his horses saddled—he must go to Troyes, there were debts which must be paid before Pentecost. And the same day Mahaut saw a pale and gloomy but very resolute Milicent come to their bed, still breathless from running. Mahaut asked: "What is it, my friend?" But her friend did not answer, she opened her clotheschest, took out a piece of gray cloth and spread it on the ground. Then she began emptying the chest and throwing her things into the cloth by handfuls—shifts, girdles, sleeves, buckles, phials of perfume, gloves, braid—everything was furiously thrown down, overflowing the cloth and spilling on the floor. Sitting on the bed, Mahaut watched her with growing terror—never had she seen her with such bright eyes and such a set mouth. "Have you gone mad?" she asked at last. "What on earth are you doing?"

"I am going to Troyes," she whispered. "He is taking me."

Mahaut leaped to her feet. "The baron? Say it again. He is taking you? You are letting him? You? You?"

Milicent did not look at her. "He is taking me to see my mother."

"You lie, you lie!" Mahaut cried. "You lie! He is taking you to be his— you very well know what. And you are letting him! Like a shepherdess! Do you not see that it will bring shame upon us all?"

Milicent bowed her head and muttered: "I am not of your blood."

"Fortunately!" Mahaut shot at her. "And Ansiau, my dead brother? And Girard? And I—am I not your sister? Have you not slept in my bed for seven years? Does that mean nothing?"

Infuriated, Milicent drew herself up, her eyes shot yellow flames like the eyes of an angry cat. She roared: "Out of my sight!"

Mahaut, straight and slender, her cheeks blazing, held her ground, magnificent in her anger. "You disgust me," she cried. "I spit on you! Whore! Baggage! Baron's doxy!"

Milicent bent and caught up an iron casket which lay in the bottom of her coffer and whirled it around her head. Mahaut gave a scream and fled.

Milicent let the casket fall and looked at her hands in disgust. Of her anger nothing remained but a vague terror and the consciousness of being the vilest of wenches, the whore of whores. She could not touch Hélie now without soiling him, she could no longer show her face before Lady Alis. Her conviction was so absolute and so desperate that Milicent bowed to it—she tied the four corners of the cloth together and ordered Sebile, her maid, to carry it to the courtyard. Then she went down to the stable, where the baron was waiting for her.

And Mahaut ran into the hall and threw herself on her mother's neck with great sobs. She had done very wrong, she had concealed gross treachery, she had known of it and had not told Lady Alis because she pitied her friend. It was not enough for the baron to have seduced Milicent, now he wanted to dishonor her completely. Lady Alis must prevent him, or she was lady of Linnières no longer.

Lady Alis was not blind and she had seen that something was going on between her husband and her daughter-in-law, but she had reassured herself with the thought that the baron was no seducer and that Milicent was a cold girl. Her reaction to Mahaut's revelation frightened Mahaut even more than Milicent's anger had done. Lady Alis threw herself down and beat her forehead against the straw-strewn flags, saying that nothing remained for her but to die with the child in her womb, since her lord had put such an affront upon her. Richeut and the other women gathered around her and tried to lift her. "Lady," said Mahaut, sobbing, "I did not tell you this to cause you pain—but if you want to stop them, hurry, they are in the courtyard now."

Then Lady Alis rose and ran to the stables. She had not had time to reflect. Her principal concern was the affront which had been put upon her and the proper thing to do in such a case. And the affront was terrible because she had a ruined face and Milicent was fifteen.

At the stable door she found the baron and Milicent tying a great bundle to the saddle of a mule.

There was a rather painful scene. Lady Alis talked of tearing out her rival's eyes and cutting her open and washing her face in her guts. Milicent was terrified and took Lady Alis' threats perfectly seriously—and so did Lady Alis. But the baron, in a towering passion, ordered his wife to hold her tongue— he would not permit his godfather's daughter to be insulted in this fashion in his own house. She was his daughter-in-law, he had a right to take her to Troyes, Lady Alis had nothing to say in the matter—he and Milicent had never done anything wrong together. Then he swung the girl into the saddle, mounted himself, and together they rode across the courtyard and stopped before the gate while the porter drew back the heavy wooden bars.

Milicent wished that she might sink into the earth, but she sat straight and stiff in her saddle, with a proud look. Lady Alis called to her: "Farewell, fair daughter-in-law. And give my compliments to your mother because it was not from me that you learned to make love to married men on the highroad!"

Slowly the gate opened, the planks were thrown over the moat. The baron rode across, Milicent followed, then the baron's two squires, and Sebile, mounted on a mule.

The road through the forest was muddy and the horses made slow progress. The baron said nothing—he was in a bad humor. Lady Alis had failed in courtesy toward him—he had not wished to put an affront upon her, God knew; he had not said an unkind word to her. He had trouble enough on his hands as it was—what was he to do with Milicent? And Milicent saw a broad brown-caped back swaying in front of her, and the words of Lady Alis and

Mahaut still rang in her ears. So this was what it meant to be a whore. And to think that only four days ago she was as much a virgin as any of the girls.

When they came to Seuroi Tower the baron stopped and shouted: "Hola! Milon! The gate!" A wide plank set with cleats was lowered from the great tower gate and steadied at an angle which allowed the horses to enter. "Tell Milon to make up the best bed he can," the baron said to Sebile, "so that your lady will be comfortable. Have him use all the pelts in the tower and spread a cloth over them. And you go over it and get rid of the fleas." Then he asked Milicent to take a walk with him to Rainard's Grave. Milicent walked with bowed head, wondering what humiliations yet awaited her. And Ansiau looked at her light, fluffy hair and her golden neck, and was amazed at possessing such a treasure. He saw that she was unhappy and laid his hand on her head. "You shall see, my beauty," he said, "how well I will guard your honor. Not a man in the countryside shall dare to say one word against you."

Milicent murmured: "It makes no difference now."

"Of course it does," he said. "You should not think such thoughts. I can always make things smooth for you. If you will love me truly, you shall have everything—I will make you the most beautiful woman in Troyes—I will take prisoners, I will borrow, you shall be dressed like a countess."

In the single great room in Seuroi Tower the fire burned in the smoke-blackened hearth; to the left of the entrance was the stable, with soldiers grooming the horses and filling the mangers. In the middle, before the hearth, were the benches and old pelts which served as seats, beds, and tables for the squires. To the right was a wide worm-eaten bed, covered with pelts and woolen rugs. The only daylight came through the door. Milon, a big, stocky, powerful man, with a wide, flat, brown face, came forward to greet his master. It was impossible to divine what Milon was thinking, for his face was always stony. But one thing is certain—he did not look pleased. He gave the baron and Milicent his place by the fire and brought them a bowl of pea soup flavored with garlic.

After dinner the baron clapped his hands and called: "Off to bed now, you women, and be quick about it—I am sleepy."

Sitting on the bed in the darkness, Milicent unbraided her hair, which looked red in the dying glow from the hearth. Her feet were icy. She was afraid to be alone with him for so long. A whole night—her anticipations went no further. She was not accustomed to him yet; she felt awkward and weak. She could conceal nothing from him, she felt rather like a woman stood up naked in a blinding light; there was no darkness any more, no shadowy corner in which she could hide and weep. And she was not ready to show herself to him, she was so young, so foolish. And now he had come again— to shake her, urge her, reproach her—she was making him miserable on purpose, he would wait no longer. Milicent could not bear it, she turned on him —how could he think that she was doing it on purpose? He should not say such things. He took her around the waist and threw her on the bed. She was to hold her tongue and obey him. "You women!—will you never have done?"

The baron's broad black body hid the last red glow from the hearth, the shadows on the walls, the whole room.

When Milicent woke in the morning it was almost light—daylight flowed in through the doorway, a pot was boiling over the fire. Milicent felt a large, curious eye looking at her; she pulled the covers over her shoulders. The thought that the baron had a body had always frightened her—there it was, big and hairy, much whiter than his face and hands; the fleece of brown hair on his chest made her want to close her eyes. He said: "Tired, eh? You can rest as much as you like here. It is not like the castle. You are not afraid now? Do you love me?"

She said: "Oh yes!" and hid her face for shame. A moment later she had recovered from her embarrassment and gravely reviewed the chain of medals which hung at her lover's neck. Little by little, she began to frown and look unhappy. "You did not keep my medal," she said at last.

"What medal, my heart?"

"The one I gave you—copper with blue on it."

"You never gave me a medal," said Ansiau, shaking his head.

"You know very well I did—the day before you left. I gave it to you, and you kissed me, here, and here, over and over."

"I? Impossible," said Ansiau. "I would never have done such a thing. You must have dreamed it."

"But I know I didn't dream it." Milicent was on the verge of tears. "It was a medal of my father's. With a cross in blue enamel, from Syria. Don't you remember—we were in the courtyard, I got up on a log outside the stable, and then I gave you the medal and you put it on your chain."

"No, my beauty, I do not remember it."

"And you picked me up and then you kissed me. For a long time."

"Why do you keep insisting—God, yes! now I remember. I gave your medal to Ansiau."

"To Ansiau? Why?"

"I thought you meant it for him."

Milicent believed that her heart was broken for ever. And Ansiau was annoyed with her for crying over a lost medal—when he had lost so much more. Still, she was only a child, and he ought not to be angry. "I will give you another medal—three if you want them. There, stop crying, I love you. Kiss me. Don't make your eyes all red."

The hoofs of a horse sounded on the road outside the tower. A strong, ringing voice called: "Hola, Milon! Is the baron there?"

"Yes," Milon answered from the stable.

"Baron, I want to come in," called the voice.

Ansiau jumped up and stretched. "It is Herbert," he said. "We must get dressed."

Milicent hid her head under the covers. "I don't want to see him. I feel too ashamed."

"Don't be afraid, pigeon. Stay where you are. I will tell him not to come in."

He hurriedly pulled on his breeches and went to the door, barefoot, his cape thrown over his shoulders. Herbert had dismounted and was prancing and snorting with impatience. "Have the plank let down, I want to come in."

"Milicent is not dressed yet," his father said, "you would embarrass her. I will have grain brought for your horses presently."

Herbert's face was set and angry, he looked furtively at his father. After a short silence he growled: "Lady Alis sent me."

"What for?" the baron asked.

"Well, it was about Milicent."

Ansiau folded his arms on his chest. "Very well, my boy. And I have something to tell you on the same subject. Anyone who talks about her will have his ears cut off, I swear it by the True Cross. You know me. And tell Lady Alis, and everyone at the castle, what I said."

Herbert scratched his chin. "So far as I am concerned, I say nothing. But there is the dowry."

"Go to the Devil. I want to be left in peace."

Ansiau turned his back on his son and went into the stable.

Ansiau was more captivated than he had expected to be. For a week he sincerely believed that there was no joy in the world except the love of a beautiful girl. True, some of the things she did were rather a nuisance. Yet there was a charm in all this astonishment and modesty and ignorance. "She is a lady," he thought, "so naturally it does not come easy to her. But she will soon grow used to it." One thing, however, made him rather uncomfortable —she was his godfather's daughter and it was becoming difficult to provide for her future—when he was dead, what could she do, with no relatives and no friends? A man of good blood would never want to marry her.

Yet Ansiau's conscience was at rest, for he felt sure that God could not be angry with an old crusader—after all that he had lost, he could certainly permit himself the poor little pleasure of making love to a young woman.

Milicent had thought that she would die of shame and grief when she learned that she alone had cherished a memory which had kept her dreaming and longing for three years. A man who could have forgotten such a thing could not love her—he wanted to enjoy her, as if she were a light woman to be taken and left at will—yet the fault was hers, not his. But as she was perhaps even weaker than she knew, she soon let herself be comforted. "Truly?" she said. "Really and truly? You want me?" He always had an answer ready: "I? I cannot live without you." For him it was perfectly clear and simple, but Milicent wanted to hear more, he would never have believed that she could ask so many questions. How long had he loved her? How much did he love her? Was he sure that he did not despise her?

And Ansiau gave good proof that he needed her, for day after day he put off their journey to Troyes—on his own land he was freer to love her. At Troyes they would have to hide and lie, and God knew that the baron of Linnières did not like constraint. In the tower it was dark, the air was heavy; the lovers spent their time outdoors, on the edge of the forest of Hervi, beside the stream, in the glades. The days were sunny, the tall grass was still green, and in the morning the dews soaked Milicent's feet so that she had to take off her red leather shoes and hang them on twigs to dry. She ran a great deal, swung from branches, quickly grew tired. She loved to be carried with her eyes shut and her head snuggled against the baron's neck—when he stopped and laid her on the ground she opened her eyes, and each time she was astonished to find herself there, to see the sky and the trees and her lover's face. Each time was like an awakening, she felt giddy—and she excited herself on purpose so that she could have the same sensation over again.

She could hardly understand what he called pleasure, joy, and the other usual names. But she so loved to see him happy that she accepted everything cheerfully. A girl lost her honor only once—she had mourned for hers, she was not going to spend the rest of her life in tears. "Since you want me," she said, "I care nothing for Lady Alis and the others—let them say what they please." She had become gay, with a rather feverish gaiety, she laughed constantly, sang, teased the horses. Ansiau no longer recognized his little daughter-in-law, she was so vivacious and changeable. She cried out when she saw a butterfly or a dragonfly, clapped her hands to frighten hares, and soon found that she had a real passion for flowers. She gathered them by armfuls; then, tired and pale from stooping so often, carried them to the baron, threw herself on the ground, and began separating her flowers and arranging them in bouquets. She knew the meaning and virtue of every flower and gravely explained them to Ansiau: "This one cures a wound from a stag's antlers, this one makes ewes give milk, and that pink there is unlucky because the ends of the petals are like little saws—it is a good thing to put in an enemy's bed. And buttercups bring gold. And that big red flower—I do not know its name, but I think it is the one that reveals hidden treasures, Ansiet told me about it. And forget-me-nots keep a lover faithful—and here's a yellow primrose, if a girl gives it to you it means she has never loved before," and she filled her lover's hair and collar and beard with primroses. "Even when I was still at my father's house I loved you. Didn't you know it? I thought you knew everything." When she saw that he had fallen asleep she amused herself by twining their hair in one braid and laughed wildly when he could not raise his head. "We are bound," she said, "we are tied, now you can never leave me." Or she took his hand and amused herself by pinching it or pricking it with the point of his hunting knife, to see if he could bear it without flinching. And he smiled to himself and heartily joined in the game, which cost him a rather deep cut in the palm of his right hand. He said: "What a child, what a child!" He considered her a little vicious, because even in her youngest days Lady Alis had never had such absurd ideas. But a mistress was not a wife, and he did not criticize her.

Then one day he made up his mind to set out for Troyes—he had business, he could put it off no longer. As was usually the case with the baron, the thing was decided in an hour—she must pack at once and dress for the journey, the horses were already outside. Milicent was afraid to go—how could she look her mother in the face, how could she hide her wild love? Sebile helped her to lace herself into her tight gray dress. "Sebile, I am afraid of Troyes—he will have so much to do, he will forget me."

The baron came to tell her she must hurry.

"But can't you see that I am hurrying, sweet? My lord, why are you looking so angry? Your face is all hard!"

"I? Not a bit of it."

"Yes, yes, you are angry with me. You are ashamed of me. I can see it."

"Sweet, you are dreaming—I do not know what has come over you."

"No, I am not dreaming. You don't want me to go. I will not go." She threw herself on the bed and hid her head under the covers. Ansiau was surprised and touched. He sat down beside her and comforted her as best he could. Of course she must go—he could not do without her. He would never let anyone scorn her. She would be happy in Troyes at her mother's house, he would come every day, he would bring her beautiful presents, she would see fine tournaments, minstrels and jugglers—little by little Milicent dried her tears. "How are we to behave?" she said, hesitantly. "People will speak ill of us."

"So long as I live, no one shall harm you, my beauty. Listen well—I have taken you, and you are my godfather's daughter. I have done you a wrong. And I swear to you that I will never forsake you and that I will watch over you as long as I live. All that I can do for you, I will do. I have spoken."

The baron did not return to the castle until toward St. Andrew's Day, at the end of November. It was a cold, wet afternoon. In the courtyard the yellow and gray puddles were covered with little dancing drops of winter rain. The rain poured down the angle of the keep, and the water butt, long since full, was overflowing. The water made channels in the brown, sticky mud; the horses' hoofs sank to the fetlock in it. In the hall a great fire was burning, lighting the vaults. Herbert, who had just come in from hunting, was warming his hands, two varlets were pulling off his muddy shoes and gaiters. Lady Alis was standing by the hearth, giving orders to the cook. She looked pale and thin. Two months ago she had given birth to a boy; she had named him Joceran, after her father, to vex the baron. God knew that the child gave her little joy—the sight of him was enough to bring back the memory of a difficult pregnancy, of long nights spent gnawing her arms for rage and shame. What was the use of having a son who was a knight if he could not even revenge you on a viper who had stolen your husband? Herbert had said: "I know the baron—if he is not crossed, he is as mild as a lamb. If you are gentle with him, he will do whatever you wish." But how was she to be gentle with him when she never even saw him? When he was at Troyes, spending his ransom money on that hussy?

He had not come back in September to learn if the child had been born alive, and Alis bitterly regretted that she had not died. She was not a woman to be silent or to resign herself. She loudly complained of her husband's treachery, and mourned each time she gave little Joceran suck. "Poor orphan, poor fatherless child! Poor innocent, better that you had died, and killed me with you!"

When she heard the baron's voice in the courtyard Lady Alis was obliged to have the door opened, like it or not. She would gladly have left her husband to freeze in the rain and mud, but Herbert would not allow it. "He would never forgive us," he said. "Wait until I am master of Hervi, I shall know how to talk to him."

Huge in his soaked cape the baron entered, and behind him came a frail girl, walking with bowed head and holding her gray rabbit cloak closed with both hands. Behind her Sebile and Thierri carried a big chest. The baron seemed ill at ease. He took off his cape and ran his hands through his wet beard. Despite himself, his eye fixed on Milicent's capacious cloak and trembling hands.

Lady Alis stood motionless, her eyes narrowed, her lips drawn. She was thinking that the wench did not look very proud of herself—her lewdness had profited her little. And the baron seemed very uneasy and did not even notice the hard looks Lady Alis shot at him.

"Come, lady," he said at last, "can you not take your daughter-in-law upstairs and help her to bed? You must see that the child is not well."

To which Lady Alis answered that she hoped to see her even less well, she hoped to see her dead for her sins. "And if I saw her fall into the fire," she said, "I would not lift a finger to pull her out."

Ansiau's only answer was a scornful oath, he picked Milicent up and began slowly climbing the ladder. Lady Alis spat on the ground and cried: "I hope it breaks under you! Do you think I cannot see she is pregnant?"

Milicent fought against her nausea and giddiness and thought that she would die at every step the baron took. At last she felt hands taking off her cloak and she was laid on the bed. Ansiau felt embarrassed—only his anger against Lady Alis could have driven him into such indecorous behavior—it was not for him to push past the girls' curtain and stand beside Mahaut's bed. Mahaut herself was sitting on the chest at the head of the bed, as stiffly and sternly as Lady Alis herself. She stared at her father with one wide-open, reproachful eye—the other, as usual, was dreaming. Little Alette had already gone to bed and was hiding under the wolf-skin cover.

The baron wanted to revive his sweetheart's spirits by kind words and caresses. But he did not dare—he merely stroked her hair, and Milicent turned her head on the pillow so that her soft warm lips clung to his hand. Gently he drew it away. "I must go," he said. Because of his daughters, he tried to keep the tenderness out of his voice.

Milicent opened wide, beseeching eyes. "Ansiau."

"Yes, my beauty."

"You will not forget?"

"Never fear. Rest now. I will come tomorrow."

When the baron had gone Milicent let Sebile undress her. But she was so sick and inert that the maid could not get off her woolen dress, too tight for her now. Mahaut rose without a word and came to help. Milicent saw that her face was red and tearful. And little Alette, from her corner of the bed, looked suspiciously at the bedfellow who had come home after such a shameful adventure—the sight of that belly, swollen like a goldbeater's bladder, made her shiver with disgust.

"Quick, into bed with you!" said Mahaut in a voice which she tried to make hard. "The three of us will soon warm each other. Poor girl! What a state you are in!"

Milicent did not listen, she gnawed her lips and tried to look calm; then suddenly she threw herself on the pillow and began tearing it with her teeth and sobbing like a madwoman. "No, I cannot! No, I cannot! No, no, no!"

"Poor thing, what is it?"

"I cannot. It is too hard. I shall die. He must be in Lady Alis' bed this minute. I cannot, he ought never—he promised me!"

"Fool! Lady Alis is his wife, you have nothing to say about it."

"I would rather die than know he is with her."

"Then you are more wicked than I thought," Mahaut said seriously. "You ought to spend the rest of your life weeping for the wrong you are doing my mother."

"It is she who is wronging me," said Milicent, hard-eyed.

"It is a sin to listen to you." Mahaut blew out the candle and slipped in beside her friend. Milicent was calmer; she wept, sniffling softly. Then suddenly she took Mahaut's hand and laid it on her belly. "There," she said, very low, "he is moving. There it was again. It is strange. So strange."

Mahaut sighed. "When do you expect it will be?"

"The first week in Lent, I think. I am so frightened, if you only knew!"

"And what will you do with the child?"

"I don't know. He wants it. He wants to keep it."

Mahaut stretched and slowly shook her head.

"And you still love him after what he has done to you?"

"My poor innocent, you don't know anything about it. It gets worse every day. When I don't see him, I die. You know—before, when I was still with you, I thought I loved him. And it was nothing. Now it is worse than hunger."

"What about him? He loves you, I hope?"

"He?" Milicent laughed happily. "How he loves me! He is mad about me. I think he would caress me all day and all night if he could."

"Oh, but you mustn't let him," said Mahaut. "He would soon tire of you."

"It is easy for you to talk. I have tried it. You don't understand . . . what he wants, I want. Anything." And she added somberly: "If ever he gets tired of me, I will kill myself. He knows it too."

Lady Alis felt mortally sad that night, she was discouraged and closer to tears than to anger. After six months away, the baron did not even deign to ask after her health and her new baby. She had been a fool to think that he had come back from the Holy Land to relieve her of her burdens—all he had done was to run from one tournament to another. Everyone knew what men back from Palestine were. Steeped in lust and dead to shame—that was what they were. They had lost all desire for their wives, they wanted young, pretty women. Enguerrand of Coagnecort had no sooner come home than he shut his wife up in a convent—ostensibly for adultery—and married again three days later. And James of Ermele had been living with a serving-wench for three months, under his wife's very eyes. And there were others—too many to count. A woman of thirty-six, whose face was ravaged by smallpox, who had borne fifteen children, had better not struggle to keep a man of the baron's age.

The baron had lain down in their bed without a word, because he felt that he was at fault. But Alis, in her mood of humility, took it for a sign of scorn. She gave little Joceran the breast, laid him on her pillow, and began combing her hair. She wondered if the baron would speak to her, but he remained silent. Then such a wave of self-pity swept over her that great tears began to fall on her breast and her arms.

"Listen to me, baron," she said. "We are neither tied nor glued together. Perhaps I had better leave you a clear field and go into a convent. If you love the girl, you can marry her—it will save you a sin and you will have her dowry."

The baron had raised himself on one elbow and was listening attentively. His one eyelid blinked. "Lady," he said. Lady Alis trembled when she heard his voice; she knew then that she would be able to soften him. With the knowledge, her self-pity only increased: She was a noblewoman, she could not bear to be insulted; she had loved him too greatly, she could not see him with another; she would rather become a nun—she would take Hélie and little Joceran with her, she would pray to God for her sins and his—which was no small thing! Before she had finished she pictured her life in a convent so vividly that she dropped her head on her knees and sobbed aloud. Then she blew out the candle and lay down under the covers. Ansiau said nothing, but the sound of his breathing told her that he was touched.

At last he spoke. "Lady, I shall not turn you out because another is young and pretty. A man who does such a thing is the lowest of dastards. I will never do it."

"Lord have mercy on me, baron! I would rather go into a convent, I would rather beg my bread on the highroads, than see you bring shameless bitches to the castle and caress them before my eyes."

Ansiau said: "You know very well that I did not do it until I had to. We have been in Troyes, in Provins, we even went to Meaux. I had to bring her back because her belly had begun to show."

"A girl like that ought to be whipped and locked up in a convent," said Lady Alis. "And it runs in the family—I have heard pretty things about her mother, but I will not repeat them to you—there is reason to believe that she is not even old William's daughter—in any case, your godfather was very old when she was born."

"There is no proof," said the baron. "I promised her father to watch over her, and I must do it. It shall not be said that I dishonored a girl of noble blood."

Lady Alis began to hope. "And what do you intend to do with her?"

"That I do not yet know, lady."

Instantly Lady Alis forgot all caution and gave free rein to her anger and her jealousy. Of course she knew that the baron could not love the girl—she was ugly—"a very different girl from myself at fifteen, as well you know—a worthless slut—a vicious creature if ever there was one. And I brought the wretch up as if she were my own daughter!" Naturally she did not blame the baron, any man would have done the same; if what concerned him was saving her from dishonor, a way could be found. They would marry her off—with her dowry, it would not be difficult.

Ansiau was weary of listening. "Lady, what are you saying? There can be no question of marrying her."

"And why not, my friend?"

"Enough, lady. We will see what can be done later."

Lady Alis did not dare to insist, for she sensed that her husband was in a bad humor. But she promised herself that she would find out the facts in the morning. She learned nothing from the baron, who considered it indecent to discuss his love affairs with a woman. But from Herbert she learned that her husband wanted to keep Milicent for himself, that he intended to let her stay at the castle until after the child was born, and then would send her to Seuroi to live. Poor Alis had to gnaw her fists in silence, for the baron was irritable and impatient. He did not like to admit it, but his separation from his beloved made him unhappy, and he did not dare to visit her because she was strictly watched by Richeut and Mahaut.

For everyone in the castle, Milicent was suffering from an upset stomach—they all knew better, but Milicent was of noble blood and must not let anyone see her in her present condition. She seldom got out of bed, and never left her corner of the bedchamber. It was so dim there even by day that she learned to see in the dark like a cat. At night Mahaut came with her bit of candle and a heated stone which she put in the bottom of the bed. Richeut told her to eat, to eat plenty because she was eating for two—and Milicent never felt hungry and gave her milk and her meat to Sebile. It was hard—the long days in bed, the fleas, the smell of mold and sweat, the freezing air that stung her as soon as she took her nose from under the covers. It must be warm over there by the fire—but just let her show herself at the hearth, where Lady Alis and the women were spinning and singing!

Her face blotched with yellow, her lusterless, greasy hair falling over her cheeks in grayish strands, Milicent was a sorry sight. But she hardly cared— the baron never came to see her. He sent word by Richeut that she must take good care of herself for the child's sake. And, for her, the child was only a malignant swelling which prevented her from living and loving. Always she imagined her lover in Lady Alis' arms; Lady Alis knew everything and could do anything, she would always be the stronger.

Sometimes Milicent found the courage to drag herself as far as the curtain— through a hole in the cloth she could see, there beyond the pallets and the chests, the group of women sitting on their benches, the reddish light from the fire. The baron seldom came there by day; at night he passed through, immense and black, holding a candle—and the swaying motion of those broad, set shoulders took Milicent's breath away; she wanted to press her lips on that mutilated nose, on the ragged flesh where the eye had once been, on those great calloused palms which the years had darkened. And he did not even know that she was looking at him.

Mahaut had almost quarrelled with Lady Alis over Milicent. She knew that everyone despised her friend, and that was enough for her. She said that the blame lay entirely on the baron and that, furthermore, the child had harmed nobody—so long as it remained unborn the mother should be well treated. It made her curious to feel that little living soul growing so close to her, and she often asked Richeut: "Will it be a girl or a boy?"

"A boy," the old woman answered, "because it lies forward. Look—her belly is almost pointed—when I carried my boys. . ."

Milicent crossed herself. "God grant it is a boy! The baron will be angry with me if I give him a girl. Oh," she said, "what a thankless task! Holy Virgin! Do you think I want a child, Mahaut, my beauty? I shall not know what to do with him."

"But a baby is such a sweet thing," said Mahaut, "so soft—you'll see."

Milicent turned to her with a surprised and dreamy look. "Why, you are talking just like he does! Even your voice—that is how he says, 'You'll see.' He wants the child, I tell you. He wants to make a knight of him, and all the rest. Oh God! all the things he said to me the day I became sure. You know, I wanted to kill myself for very shame when I knew how it was with me, I almost strangled myself with my girdle."

"God, what a sin!" Mahaut crossed herself. "But it must be sweet to carry a little baby inside you."

Milicent shrugged her shoulders. "That is what people say who know nothing about it. There is nothing worse."

Mahaut sighed, for her thoughts kept turning to a little Garnier whom she saw as a warm pink ball lodged in the pit of her stomach. More and more often she thought of her age. She said: "I am eighteen. At my age my mother already had three children. Ah, I am not what I was!" She ran both hands over her broadening hips. "And look at my wrists, how thick they are! And my eyebrows are getting bushy. If I don't marry this year, no one will want me." It was sad to be a girl with no dowry and nothing to inherit; since the Crusade there was a dearth of men, and so many girls had become heiresses because their brothers had died—Mahaut, the beauty of the countryside, attracted only married men and varlets. "If my father gives me to a squire, I will not refuse," she continued thoughtfully.

"I would rather die!" Milicent was indignant.

"Who are you to be so proud! Do you think he won't give you to a vassal when he tires of you?"

"Never," said Milicent, "never."

"You do not know men."

All that autumn Garnier, lord of Buchie, had come to Hervi for Mass and two or three times he had ridden on to Linnières to buy grain. He was old, he had a big red nose which hung down over his gray mustache, but he was still sound and vigorous—his hard yellow eyes undressed you and made your cheeks and ears burn. Mahaut knew that he came for her sake, and she loathed him. "Fortunately he is married," she said to anyone who would listen. "I wish his wife a long life." But when she said it she felt rather embarrassed and laughed very loud.

It was an extremely hard winter. During the three years of the Crusade, the wolves had multiplied to the point where they were not afraid to hunt through the village by daylight, in packs; they circled around the cottages, waiting for someone to come out; they leaped into the castle moats, danced around the palisade, and howled when they smelled the stables. The baron and Herbert finally gathered every man in the village and the castle for a great drive. The peasants armed themselves with forks and scythes, the castle men took their spears and hunting-knives. On a snow five days old, tracks by the hundred crossed and recrossed, followed the stream and the paths—the wolves had long since grown perfectly fearless and had forgotten all their ruses. Bait was set at the crossroads and along the edge of the forest, all the way from the castle to Rainard's Grave. The hounds pricked up their ears and tremulously sniffed the air, their tails between their legs—they knew that they were the weaker.

The hunt lasted a week. Exhausted and joyous, the men of Linnières returned to the castle, bringing pelts enough to make covers and rugs for everyone, and scores of wolf heads which the varlets impaled on the palisade with cries of joy. Herbert had cut off so many heads that he had learned to do it in two movements—in default of a war, it was an exciting game. And in Herbert's manner of directing his troop of peasants, Ansiau recognized long-forgotten features and tones—Herbert the Red's harsh voice, old Ansiau's bushy brows. Ansiau thought: "I must keep an eye on him. There is not room for two cocks in one henyard."

Nothing troubled Herbert. He even gave an impression of indolence; the fat was already creeping into his neck, his shaven chin, the heavy lids of his big blue eyes. When he gave an order he did not turn his head or bother to look at the person he addressed; when he was angry his face sharpened and his round eyes burned with green fire. "He needs to be ridden with a short rein. The men are already afraid of him." Back from the hunt in which he thought he had behaved so well, Herbert found himself being bullied and called a wastrel and an oaf. "The boy thinks he is master in the hall," the baron said to his wife. "Give him his head and there will not be room for him in the house."

"It is not his fault, baron, if you have left him to fume and fret here for six months, with neither arms nor money."

"After I am dead," said the baron, "he will have all the arms and money he wants."

He thought: "The fat swine will have all of Hervi, and Linnières into the bargain, and Bernon, and God knows what more, for he will never be content with so little. He will send his brothers into service at Troyes or Tonnerre and marry his sisters to varlets—I should be a fool to stint myself for his sake."

Every night Lady Alis talked of Mahaut and Alette. Mahaut was overripe; as for Alette, they must look ahead, the child was twelve, and with her pock-marked face she would at least need a large dowry.

"Enough," said the baron. "In six months the five years will be over, I will redeem the forest and the vineyards. The vineyards will go toward Mahaut's dowry."

"And where will you find the money to redeem them?"

Ansiau sighed. "Abner will lend it to me," he said, without conviction. He knew very well that Abner would lend him nothing more, except upon sufficient security. That year there had been less money to be made at tournaments than before the Crusade; and he himself, one-eyed and slowed by age, was not as good a jouster as he used to be. He had been obliged to borrow again and to humble himself before Abner, and since he could not pay back the loan at once he would have to pay three times the sum at Pentecost—and it had all been for Milicent, all because he wanted to see her wearing silk shifts and turquoise earrings. It was a nuisance to have daughters to marry when he was in love. "Mahaut is pretty—if Garnier of Buchie were a widower he would take her with no dowry but her shift. But poor Alette—it looks as if she would have to marry a vassal, if not worse. With her face, who would love her?" Yet Milicent loved beautiful stuffs and little mirrors and wrought rings, especially after she had become pregnant and thought she had lost her beauty—she never asked for anything, but she laughed like a child over every gift he gave her.

God knew that he loved her as well and better than his daughters—and with a very different love, no doubt of that. She was defenseless, she had not a soul in the world except himself. She trusted him. Naturally she did not have Lady Alis' virtues—she was frivolous, he thought, untidy, feather-brained, rather too fond of pleasure—an unbecoming thing in a noblewoman—too jealous besides; it did not flatter him to inspire such a wild passion, but he was willing to excuse it: "It is her age, youth will be youth. What she needs is a baby—they are all a little wild until they have a baby."

Lady Alis said: "We have too many children of our own to load ourselves down with bastards." But what she said did not count. The baron knew her so well that he had forbidden her to go near Milicent—it was Richeut who took care of her. And more than once Lady Alis had asked Richeut: "Friend, could you not mix her milk with a drug I will give you? If she has a miscarriage at her age, no one will be surprised. The baron could never accuse you."

"It would kill her," said Richeut.

"No more than she deserves. Girls cannot steal other women's husbands."

Richeut shook her head. "No, truly, I cannot. After all, she is one of God's creatures. I will not take it upon myself."

Milicent knew that Lady Alis wished her ill, and she feared her. She had lost her longing to be delivered, so great was her terror of the dreadful day which steadily drew nearer, drew nearer far too fast—she felt as if she were carrying a mountain, she did not think that she could ever bring her child to birth. She had heard of children taken living from a belly cut open, and she saw herself lying dead, her belly split like a soused pig's. One night, two weeks before Lent, she woke with a great cry; a knife was being thrust into her vitals and slowly turned; she shook Mahaut: "He is hurting me," she said. "I don't know what it can mean. Call Richeut, for the love of God." Trembling with cold and emotion, Mahaut ran to fetch Richeut; it was dark, she stumbled into benches, on the hearth red embers still lighted the flagstones and the andirons.

At dawn—the sky was still a dirty gray over the forest—Ansiau was pacing up and down outside the bathhouse into which women kept running with jugs, basins, and linen. Again and again the door slammed; he thought he was seeing dozens of women; in reality they were always the same— Sebile, Berta, Claude—and he did not dare to ask them what was happening. Toward terce, when the sun had already risen, Richeut came out looking deathly pale, and ran upstairs to the hall. "Lady, friend," said Richeut, "your daughter-in-law is in great agony, you can hear her screaming. In your chest there are herbs which soothe pain—have pity on her, give me some!"

Lady Alis, who happened to be sitting on that very chest, stiffened and clutched at the lid with both hands. "I will give you nothing," she said. "Let her die of her sin. I will not help her."

"Lady," said Richeut, "she is a pitiful sight."

"It is her own doing," said Lady Alis. "I would rather give my herbs to a sow. Enough!"

A little before noon the child was born, and it was a girl. When he learned that Milicent had been delivered the baron went upstairs to the chapel to arrange for the christening. He was much disappointed. Of course the little hussy could never do anything properly—what need had he of a daughter? Claude of Linnières was to stand godmother, Thierri-Guiot godfather. When Father Aimeri asked what he wanted to name the child, Ansiau said "Alis"—not because he wished to honor his wife, but because he considered it the only real woman's name. Claude went to fetch the baby, but Milicent, for all her submissiveness, declared that no daughter of hers should ever be named Alis—she would not let the child go until the baron had promised to find another name. To humor her, the baron sent word that he would name the child Milicent, but Milicent considered it a common name, she wanted something more beautiful for her daughter. For some time she hesitated between Eglantine and Blancheflor, and finally chose Eglantine. Claude picked up the baby just as it was, wrapped in a woolen cloth, and hurried up to the hall, for the wind was icy. The baron was waiting for her outside the chapel curtain; he said: "Hurry, the candles are half burned down."

After the ceremony Claude presented little Eglantine to her father. "A fine baby, after all," she said. Ansiau took her and carried her to the window, over which a pig's bladder was stretched—in the dull, yellow light he made out a long head with brown hair. The big eyes blinked from deep sockets, turning from side to side. Little Eglantine looked like her father— the cruel likeness of a newborn infant which has not yet had time to acquire a face of its own. Brown-haired and brown-skinned, Eglantine was Ansiau in miniature except for a beard; and Ansiau made a wry face and thought: "She will never be a beauty." Yet he was touched, for he had never believed so close a likeness possible. For a long time he watched the big brown eyes open and close; already they were burdened with involuntary thought. He scratched his nose and almost reluctantly handed Eglantine back to Claude. "Take her to her mother now," he said, "she must be wild with thinking that you are never coming back. And tell her that I want to see her, and to hurry up and get herself ready."

Ansiau was not allowed to enter the bathhouse until very late that afternoon—each time he came to the door Milicent sent word begging and praying him not to come in, and called out herself: "Not yet—I'm not ready yet." She made it a point of honor to look beautiful in her new rôle. It was not easy to accomplish. She was very weak, the maids had to bathe her, change her shift, put fresh sheets on the bed, spread a carpet beside it. Above all she insisted on having her hair done—it must be washed and perfumed and rolled on rods to make it curl. "You ought to be resting, my poor child. Go to sleep," said Richeut. Her eyes bright with a touch of fever, Milicent would not listen to her. "Oh God, Berta, you are pulling my hair. Ouch. No, I feel all right. No, tell him to wait, my hair is not dry. He can wait as well as I could." Sebile arranged the little pleats in her pink muslin shift, and Berta put rings in her ears and disposed the long wavy tresses, light as combed flax, on either side of her face. Milicent was so exhausted that she had no more voice. "Yes, let him in. No, not yet. How shall I hold my hands? Pull the sheet up higher." The sheet was a beautiful red which would bring out the whiteness of her hands, and Milicent laid them quietly on her stomach, one beside the other, and closed her eyes.

She had not miscalculated in arousing the baron's impatience. When he entered—at last!—he was half angry, half touched; he wiped his forehead to keep himself in countenance and because it was hot—the bathhouse had no windows in winter, the air was heavy and rank with perfumes, candles sputtered by the bed.

He stopped and gasped. For a long time he could not move. That translucent face between the shining strands of hair, a pool of light against the red pillow with its darkened gold embroidery—he had never seen it before. For the first time in his life he noticed that her face was faultless; her eyes, dark under half-closed lids, burned with a flame as gentle as candlelight, her lips were open in a tired, peaceful smile. She was so clean, she smelled so good—Ansiau hardly dared breathe, as if he feared to disturb that miraculous beauty—and under her timid, questioning, childlike look he sniffed noisily, blew his nose onto the carpet, and sat down at a little distance from her, on a bench, and bowed his head. After he had sat for some time without looking up Milicent said, all in a breath: "Ansiau. Come here. Come."

He obeyed, docile as a child; he sat down on the edge of her bed and stared at the red sheet, the little white hands, so thin, and as flawless as flowers. The slender, pink-tipped fingers closed on his left hand and slowly moved it until it rested in the hollow between her breasts; and he felt ashamed of his huge body, stinking of wet leather and manure, ashamed of his broken-nailed black hand—how out of place it looked on her pink muslin shift!

He quickly forgave Eglantine for being a girl. He forgave everything. Milicent was a saint. He was not even angry with her because she had no milk for her child—at her age it was only natural. He spent half his time sitting on her bed, or at the foot of it, gazing at her as if she were the Blessed Sacrament. He hardly dared to touch her before her churching, and seldom spoke; he laughed with a vacant look and now and again said such things as "It's a fine day," or "It's raining," or "Do you feel better today?" In short, he was like a lover of twenty. He adored Eglantine. "Just my luck," he said, "a child takes after me for once, and it has to be a girl! And with such a pretty mother, too!" But at heart he admired his little daughter because she looked so much like himself.

Milicent soon grew stronger and found herself once more enjoying life. She was glad that she was not nursing Eglantine—she would be freer. She was happy that she was to leave the castle; after her churching the baron would send her to live at Seuroi, there she would have maids and varlets, like a lady. She was continually surprised by her lover's great love for her—it almost made her think that she was an important person.

Her churching took place on Shrove Tuesday in the midst of the holiday festivities. After passing through the chapel with her candle and her *sou,* she took her old place at the high table, where she had not sat for nine months.

Taller and thinner, but strangely beautiful, she drew the eyes of every guest. No longer did she bow her head. Mahaut said to her: "You bold hussy, you have nothing to be proud of."

"Mahaut, my beauty," said Milicent, "when I was so sick and thought I should die, Richeut asked Lady Alis for herbs to ease me, and Lady Alis would not give them. I shall never forget it. God grant that you may never suffer so much. And I am happy in the love of my lover, and proud of it."

Mahaut instantly got on her high horse. "I was a fool to pity you. You are nothing but a common wench. It makes you happy to be getting my dowry money out of my father, eh?"

Startled, Milicent lowered her eyes. "Your dowry? I have property of my own."

"My dowry. And Alette's dowry. You know it perfectly well. I never thought you would enjoy wallowing in filth like a sow. I shall be very happy when I have seen the last of your dirty face."

The following morning all the inhabitants of the castle, clad in Lenten garments, their hair uncombed and strewn with ashes, did penance in Hervi Church. Men and women, beginning with old Haguenier, filed past the priest and the deacon, who struck them with a switch on the back of the neck as a symbol of penance. The baron of Linnières and his lady also knelt to receive the obligatory stroke, but he knew that he would return to his sin that very night, and she knew that she forgave nothing.

Milicent's eyes wandered as she followed the service. She felt certain that she and her lover were the very outcasts and reprobates of whom the priest was preaching that day, and she calmly accepted the fact that she was damned. However, she had to bite her lips to keep from answering: "Amen."

Two things had made Ansiau fall into the girl's power—her beauty and the mortal boredom which always came over him during those long weeks of Lent when winter drags on and on, when the winds have an odor of spring, fray a man's nerves, call to far places. Burdened with so many dead, he found it good to lie close to a little girl who knew nothing and had no memories, a beautiful body which he must guard and protect. She had developed in the last months, she had grown taller—indeed, she promised to be really tall some day; she still had her absurdly small waist, but her limbs were long, her joints strong and a trifle heavy. Such was the sweetness of her adolescent body that its very faults were so many beauties; its awkwardnesses always suggested the jaunty elegance of a blooded colt. Despite its thinness, her body was white and warm and soft as only a child's body can be; childish too were the hollows between shoulder and neck, under the collarbones, on the hip—they were what touched Ansiau most. Merely remembering them, he lost his head.

The fairest ornament of Auberi Charron's luxurious house was assuredly Lady Beatrice when, white, blond and rosy in her goffered dress, she made her appearance in the hall. A circlet of gold on her golden hair, a golden chain about her neck, her whole person seemed a beautifully wrought jewel, her great eyes sparkled like spring water, her little mouth was always fixed in a smile which carved dimples in her cheeks.

Auberi Charron liked to make a show and he had the means to do so. But the apartments in which he and his household lived were small and dark and low-ceilinged; he himself slept on dirty, grease-stained, patched quilts, his household slept on straw on the floor; the only light was a bit of tallow candle, and under his fine red tunic and his sable cloak Auberi wore a shirt full of holes, and his body was covered with fleas. He had been a rich man for less than ten years. Beatrice, whom he had married to satisfy his vanity, had transformed his fortune—gained at God knows what risk of everlasting damnation—into dresses and jewels and gifts for her lovers. Auberi despised her, but she was a noblewoman and he never reproached her, partly because he still had the timidity of the newly rich, partly because he was tired. He would have been greatly surprised if anyone had told him that the house of which he was so proud brought him nothing but trouble and unpleasantness.

Beatrice perpetually entertained a mob of friends and kinsmen, who lived at Charron's expense and ingenuously scorned him. Auberi detested them, but his parvenu's vanity made him put up with them and he could not help being humble and obsequious when he spoke to them.

One of these parasites was none other than Ansiau of Linnières, whose troubles over money did not permit him to maintain his four varlets, Milicent, and two waiting-women at his own expense. Ansiau did not like Lady Beatrice, he held it against her that she had married a villein, he knew that she was wanton and hard. But he was glad to profit by Charron's hospitality.

Lady Beatrice was about thirty and did not look twenty-five. Milicent was her only daughter; but by her second husband, Enguerrand of Bourgneuf, she had borne two sons who were living with their father's family. Enguerrand had been killed in the Holy Land. A lecher, a gambler, and a drunkard, he had been the worst of husbands, and naturally Beatrice had adored him. Widowed, her own parents dead, deeply in debt, hated by her husband's family, she had lost her head and let her brothers sell her to Auberi Charron —and dearly did she make the cloth merchant pay for her loss of rank.

No one in Troyes thought it unusual when Milicent appeared there with the baron of Linnières—he was a mature man and known for his propriety, and the girl was the heiress to a fine estate—if her father-in-law had brought her with him, it was to borrow money on her land and make her stand surety. Lady Beatrice believed it too. However, the second spring, when she was confronted by a daughter taller than herself (and so lissome, so jaunty!) she could not help making a face—more than one young man would laugh when he learned that she was the mother of that great bean pole! "She has certainly changed in a year, the minx!" Insolently Milicent took a place at her new father-in-law's table—elbows on the cloth, eyes defiant, tousled hair like a burst of sunshine around her head. In spite of herself, she had acquired a haughty look—no doubt because she always felt in the wrong; she pursed her lips and held her head high, she wore light-colored dresses, bright necklaces, and laughed in a most provocative way. And it happened that Lady Beatrice's lover at the moment was a young man of nineteen. The baron of Linnières was planning to marry Milicent to his son Girard, and Lady Beatrice would have liked to have both daughter and dowry in her own power.

It was not long before she guessed the truth, and it was Milicent's own fault that she did so. Milicent had a way of flinging her arms around her father-in-law's neck and kissing his hands and sighing, which aroused her mother's suspicions. She took her aside and questioned her. Milicent admitted everything: she was her father-in-law's mistress, she had a child, and she was not ashamed because there was not a better knight in all Champagne than Ansiau of Linnières. Lady Beatrice was consternated, as might have been expected. "The deceit of the man!" she said to Charron. "Doing such a thing to force the child to give him her dowry! This way he is perfectly safe. But if he still wants to marry her to his son, I will teach him that he can't hunt two hares at the same time—either the girl or the dowry!" Charron advised her to take it to Court. But Lady Beatrice's brothers, the barons of Chesley, took their niece's side—the baron of Linnières, they said, must be forced to repudiate his wife and marry Milicent. "A fine piece of advice!" said Lady Beatrice. "Do you want her to have heirs who will do us out of the dowry? A girl like that has lost her right to marry." Lady Beatrice was thinking that the girl might die young and thus frustrate the baron's scheme.

Ansiau and Milicent had to leave Charron's mansion and go to live in the house of an armorer whom the baron had known for many years and who consented to lodge them on credit. Ansiau was much annoyed—he had foolishly supposed that his adventure would remain a secret and that no one in Troyes would ever know of it. He accused Milicent. "You can do nothing right," he said. "Just like a woman! You ought to have your tongue cut out. Why did you tell your mother?"

"She guessed it," said Milicent. "I had to admit it."

"Fool! You should have denied it. She has no liking for me, she will tell everyone that I raped you. What will I look like?"

"What of it?" said Milicent, throwing back her hair. "Do you think I care what people say about me? I am proud to have people know that you love me—many a woman will envy me. If you knew how I stood up to her! She was furious! What right has she to reproach me? I know she sleeps with her priest, and her page Raoul, and others besides."

"Silence!" said Ansiau. "That is no way to speak of your mother."

"You are my mother," said Milicent, rubbing her cheeks against his knees. "You are the only mother I want."

Ansiau stroked her hair—she had a rather exasperating habit of catching his hand and kissing it and holding it against her forehead. He said: "My hand is not a relic."

"Oh, but I love it so! I think if I were ill you would only need to put your hand on my forehead and I would be cured."

He sighed: "Well, I have never been able to cure you of your wildness."

"Wildness? You mean I am wild?"

He laughed. But at heart he was worried about her. He was no longer young, he might die, and then who would protect her, who would look after her? She would be at the mercy of the first comer. And there was Eglantine. "If I die," he had once said, "you must give Eglantine to Lady Alis, she will bring her up properly."

"I would rather drown her with my own hands," Milicent had answered.

The baron thought her a bad mother. She paid little attention to her child—the most she did was to half-stifle it with kisses every second day. That was not Lady Alis' way—not at all! Women nowadays were a worthless lot, he thought—yet how he loved his wild girl!

Whenever she walked through the city or strolled among the fair booths with her cousins of Chesley, Milicent boasted that her father-in-law would buy her anything she asked for. Her cousins were virtuous young ladies and Lady Beatrice had not failed to tell them why Milicent's father-in-law was so generous; but Milicent was so charming that they remained her friends. And Ansiau spent his prisoners' ransoms, sold their arms and horses, which he would rather have kept for himself, and yet only managed to sink more and more deeply into debt.

It was his nature—he could not refuse her when she asked him for a gift. And to think that Ansiet had been so undemanding! He had asked for nothing because he was content with so little; during the last years especially—when his father gave, the gift was for himself, the boy remained aloof, smiling and courteous, and so far above anything his father could do or dream for him! Milicent had none of his superiority—she had learned to see a new proof of love in every gift, and had become insatiable. She did not know that her lover would have done as much for any woman, even a woman with whom he was not in love.

At the armorer' house they lived in a very small attic room; its only furniture was a bed and the chest which Milicent had brought from Seuroi. Gauchère, Eglantine's nurse, slept on the floor, Eglantine on Milicent's pillow. In the evening, after vespers, the room was still light; from the open window there was a view of barns and stable roofs. Milicent would light two candles under the crucifix—the combination of candlelight and twilight amused her, she said it was like night and day at once. She sat down on the floor in front of the chest and tried on all her finery, piece by piece, and Ansiau lay on the bed watching her. How could anyone say she wasn't pretty? She knew how to make the best of her charms—she gravely explained that she needed black ribbons to make her hair look blonder and her skin milkier. She had bought a pair of black sleeves embroidered with gold, she fastened them to a white dress. Then she returned dress and sleeves to the chest and put on a long, violet silk shift. It was very full and had innumerable pleats, and the violet threw such lights on her face that it looked like a flower. "Do you like me in this?" she said. "Look at my hair against the violet, it looks like white gold. I like violet better than blue. Do you? Do you like me in this black veil? I think it makes my shoulders narrower."

"You know very well that I like you best naked," said Ansiau, laughing. And Milicent bit her lips in vexation.

"How can anyone be so ignorant!"

Milicent was to find herself in trouble again, and again it was her own doing. She took it into her head to tell the baron that a certain young man, a friend of her Chesley cousins, was paying her court. She had meant no harm by it; she had laughed as she told him, because she felt flattered to have someone sighing for her. "He is not bad-looking," she said. "He's eighteen, and blond like Herbert. If you knew how funny he is—he cried when I told him that I had a lover already."

To her great surprise the baron did not seem to find it in the least funny—he almost choked with rage. "Tell him that if he speaks to you again I will spill his brains over his armor," he said.

Milicent crossed herself in terror. "God! What for? He has done nothing wrong."

"Nothing wrong! He wants to sleep with you—isn't that wrong? What an idea! In my time women thought differently." He said not another word all that night, but the morning was even worse. He insisted on learning the young man's name—he wanted to talk to him. Was he handsome? Did he come of a good family? What had he said to her? Had he touched her where he should not? And what had set him talking of love? Obviously, Milicent must have encouraged him.

The poor girl was completely bewildered. Never before had she seen the baron angry with her. "But why do you care?" she said, weeping. "I had nothing to do with it—I never wanted him to."

"Of course you wanted him to. No one has ever courted Lady Alis—and she was quite as pretty as you are. It is not for me that you put on your necklaces and sleeves and false hair—I don't need your switches to make me love you!"

"But you don't understand—every lady wears one. It can make no difference to you. If every man in the world loved me, I would only laugh. Geoffrey is a puppy—you are worth a hundred of him."

He said: "I do not like being flattered. I have only one eye left, but I am not blind. I should have been on my guard—like mother, like daughter, and who your father was only Lady Beatrice knows. You are a worthless wench. You did not deserve a husband like my son."

Milicent listened, her eyes staring with terror. Then, in one swift movement, she caught up his knife, which was lying on the chest, and pointed it at her throat—she wanted to drive it in, but she was afraid, her hand shook, and she only scratched her neck—and then the baron had the knife out of her hand. "You are stark staring mad! People don't play with knives!" Milicent sank onto the chest and sobbed aloud—she could bear no more, she wanted to die, the baron no longer loved her. Ansiau was terrified and ready to promise anything to quiet her. It was the second time that she had tried to kill herself; he thought that her mind was a little unbalanced, but he felt touched nevertheless. They made it up. But from that day forth Milicent had no peace. Ansiau was busy all day, he was at Abner's, or at Mathis', or at the count's castle, and when he came home at night he questioned Milicent, Sebile, the varlets. Where had she been? Whom had she seen? Had she talked privately to any young man?

"But how can you say such things?" Milicent asked. "You know that I love you."

"You must take me for a fool," he said. "I may well be jealous of you—at my age and with my face! There are plenty of handsome young men in Troyes. And I am away all day."

"What do I care for handsome young men? If Count Henry himself came begging to me, I would say no. It is you I want."

Ansiau shrugged his shoulders. "That is what all women say. Meanwhile, you let them talk to you."

"But why shouldn't I, when I always tell them no, when I always tell them I love someone else?"

"Wanton! That is how it always goes—today you say no, tomorrow you will say nothing, and the next day you will let them have their will of you."

"Oh!" Milicent began to sob again. "What have I ever done to you? Why do you talk to me as if I were a whore?"

"How should I know that you are not? You gave yourself to me quickly enough, I think. I did not even have to ask you."

"Because I loved you so."

"A fine reason! Presently you will be loving them too. All I know is that you didn't protest very much. Lady Alis put up far more of a fight the first time, and we were married!"

Milicent finally spent the days from dawn to dark in her little room. It was very hot there and she felt stifled. She soon tired of her dresses and jewels—she had tried them on too often. She spent the day in a shift, too careless even to fasten it at the neck and wrists; she yawned, and played with Eglantine, and looked out the window. Eglantine was becoming pretty, she had fat pink cheeks and a ready smile. She was fonder of her nurse than of her mother, which saddened Milicent, though she felt no jealousy. She nudged Gauchère: "Tell her to smile at me. Why won't she smile at me?" And when the child deigned to expose her little toothless gums her mother trembled with gratitude and pride. "You are really mine," she said. "Strange —I cannot make myself believe that she is my child." She was never wholeheartedly a mother—often sad thoughts came to her, and she would pace up and down the room like a caged beast, then fling herself on the bed and try to sleep. On other days she would suddenly remember Eglantine and kiss and hug her until she cried. Then she became aware that she was pregnant once more, and it was a hard blow. This time she did not try to kill herself, but a great chill seized her heart and numbed her limbs, she stretched herself on the bed and closed her eyes. She did not cry.

She felt so ashamed that she wanted to scream, to sink her teeth into her arm. It was not shameful to love a goodly knight—of that she was certain now. But to swell, to become shapeless, to howl and yelp like a beast being flayed alive—and every year, year after year—that was shameful—no rag of pride could cover you when people were looking at you as if you were a mangy bitch. Eglantine was sweet and Milicent was not too sorry to have suffered for her—but to bear another child, and a third, and a fourth—mysterious strangers, children who must blush for their mother—no, no! she would not. Besides, she knew that the baron would not look forward to a second child as he had to the first. And she was right—Ansiau scowled when he heard the news. "This time," he said, "you will have to go to Seuroi. I cannot ask Lady Alis to take you in again. That sort of thing can only be done once. Hereafter you will have to make different arrangements."

"Do as you will," said Milicent. "So far as I am concerned, I hope it dies before it is born."

The heat and her condition made her irritable; she often cried. She slept little, ate badly, and had a fever every night. About the beginning of September the baron decided to leave Troyes and take his mistress to Seuroi. Before setting out he took her to Abner's, for she had to be present in order that he could borrow money on her dowry. Milicent had to swear that she would pledge her land to no one else and that she would pay the interest as it fell due. She scrawled a cross at the foot of the written promise which the Jew's clerk had drawn up. "Do not make me perjure myself, too," she said to Ansiau. "I know nothing about these things. You have my property now."

"Does that trouble you, pigeon?"

"Me?" Milicent's eyes shone. "Have I anything of my own? Burn my vineyards, if it gives you any pleasure."

The little square window in Seuroi Tower had been made expressly for Milicent, just at the height of her head. And God knew how many mornings and afternoons she had spent at it, watching for the baron's horse to appear around the turn.

She laid her face on the sill—she had felt hot, but the cold stone sent a shiver through her whole body. Her eyeslids smarted, the breeze made her sweat-soaked shift cling to her body. It had happened—her baby girl was dead. She had lived only twelve days. Yet twelve days of such suffering were too long. After four sleepless nights Milicent could bear no more.

Never again to hear that dry cough, that gasping breath against her breast, in her heart, in her head—it was too much. Now there was silence. Milon might speak to the horses, Gauchère might scold the children—they could not break the great silence into which Milicent had entered with her baby daughter. . . . They had laid the little body on the bed, swaddled and stiff; under the bonnet the little face was blue, almost black.

This pain in her eyes, her breasts, her legs—what could she do to end it? Juliana—such a pretty name, so sweet on the lips. The Emperor of the Romans, Julius Caesar. The baron had said: "Another girl." Now he could be happy. And it was all his fault. It was all because he had not had a priest come to Seuroi. He had taken the child to the castle to be baptized. Because he had been refused Communion at Hervi, he would not call a priest. And Father Aimeri, the old swine, must have plotted with Lady Alis. The child had been born healthy. A strange baptism they had given it! Milicent felt a spasm contract her heart, and a flood of hot tears rose to her eyes—her baby daughter, defenseless and alone, and all those looming figures, those hard, strong people, gathered to do her harm, to bewitch her—Milicent no longer knew who "they" were, "they" had no faces—"they" were Lady Alis, Father Aimeri, Herbert, Flora, Richeut, God and the Devil. And a sob of anger rose in her throat. A baby—what had her baby done to them, to any of them. To make a baby suffer so! Such suffering! Above all, she must not let the other two leave the tower—harm would befall them too.

The baron had not come for nine days—but now he was sure to come. And the thought gave Milicent a sort of somber joy—it had taken this to bring him, he had not troubled over anything less. Ah! Now to hold him, not to let him go back to Lady Alis! Lady Alis—she never sat twiddling her thumbs, she always nursed her own children, she knew how to mix hot wine, to make his bed, wash his hair, mend his shirts—you did not hire me as a seamstress or a bath woman—but for love of you . . . I have kept my word, I have loved you, I have borne you three children, I have given you my youth. I am still beautiful, my lord, if only you would look at me—I still have the pointed breasts you love, and my hair is as blond as ever. It was not my fault if she was a girl—as if Lady Alis had never borne a girl! That she should have suffered so—a little thing that knew nothing—pain so terrible that she writhed and rolled her big eyes and almost stifled with screaming, Juliana, Juliette. My beautiful.

The baron came with Herbert and Father Aimeri. When she saw them swing around Rainard's Grave, Milicent left the window. She went to the bed to arrange her hair. But she could not find her comb, and her eyes fastened on the little oblong bundle which lay on the pillow, covered by a cloth. She knelt by the bed and drew aside the cloth. Cold and hard, an infant Jesus in gray stone. "It is your poor mother's cheeks that are too hot, my Juliette." A fly buzzed and circled about the little black lips. Milicent felt as if she were imprisoned in a leaden bell, she was suffocating, and every sound was at once very far and very near—the men's voices were like hammer blows on the bell; her ears rang.

When she raised her eyes Milicent saw three giants standing by the bed—she knew that the one nearest to her, broad and bearded, was the baron—that monstrous face which had but one eye and one nostril, as she had but one mouth, did not move—only the short, ragged lashes trembled above the bloodshot eye. Slowly the right hand rose and made the sign of the cross, then the man knelt beside the woman and bowed his forehead on his clasped hands. The two other men, one pale and fat, the other dark, thin, and tonsured, looked down at her with the sort of indifferent pity men feel for a crushed animal—but Milicent thought she saw hatred in their eyes and lips, they were bursting with hatred; she closed her eyes and bent over her dead child.

And then she saw the little blue lids open, the mouth tremble like a rabbit's. It was over in an instant.

Milicent sprang to her feet, with a scream so excruciating that the two little girls, Eglantine and Andrée, asleep in their cradle, woke with cries of terror. The baron rose and held her by the shoulders. She struggled, spat in his face. "You killed her! It is your fault! I told you! They poisoned her! They poured toad spit on her when she was baptized! Turn them out! Send them away!" Still she struggled, jerking spasmodically, almost involuntarily, her voice hoarse from screaming.

"No one wants to harm you," said Ansiau, holding her firmly. "Calm yourself."

But she kept repeating: "Send them away! Send them away!" And when Father Aimeri bent over the child to say the prayers for the dead Milicent screamed: "No! Not him! Not him!" She wrenched herself free from Ansiau's arms, and the good father thought it prudent to retire.

Milicent rolled on the bed in convulsions which twisted her arms and legs until it seemed that her bones would be torn from their sockets; her breath came in gasps. She did not see the child carried away. Her women talked of taking her to Hervi Church to have her exorcised, but she was in no condition to make the journey. She would let no one come near her but the baron, who finally persuaded her to drink a decoction and put her to sleep by stroking her temples. He had not even been able to leave her for the funeral; however, he did not much regret it—a baby's burial hardly counted, there were so many of them in a man's lifetime, and in any case the child was a girl and a bastard. Milicent must really be a little mad. . . . Lady Alis—and hers had been legitimate children!—had never made such a fuss. And Lady Alis was a good mother.

Milicent would not let him go—each time he rose she began to whimper. He stayed with her. His boy had never whimpered or cried and had not wanted to be protected. And Milicent asked nothing else. Sometimes he imagined that she was Ansiet.

Three years—and how she had changed! She was tall, thin, and bony—

old William's blood was beginning to tell. In a year or two her beauty would be gone, already she was very different from what she had been at fifteen—her cheekbones and jawbone showed sharply, the skin of her face and neck looked drawn and dry, like a case too small for such big bones. The poor child. Life had been hard to her these last few months—pregnancy, childbed, a sick baby. "I'll fatten her up," he thought, "she will get well."

He was not too pleased with her, because she had cost him a public affront in Hervi Church. Abbot Bernier had refused to allow him to approach the altar at Easter Mass, ostensibly because he was living in adultery. It had done him no good, afterwards, to prove that he had taken no one's wife, that Milicent had been married to his son only in name, and that in any case she was a widow. But just try to prove you are right to a churchman! They could always accuse you of more sins than you could ever atone for—he had given five francs of the revenue from his vineyard for the poor of the parish, and really he could give no more—he was so deeply in debt that he was considering exchanging his fief for a cash wage. The abbot of Hervi talked of having him excommunicated for three years if he did not leave his concubine—but how could you leave a girl who loves you and who swears she will kill herself if you abandon her? Only a man with no heart could do it. Ansiau had resigned himself to staying away from Hervi Church—and it was a sacrifice, for he believed that the sacraments dispensed by Father Aimeri were far less effective than the abbot's.

Certainly, he thought, Milicent would never have made a success as lady of Linnières—but what could you expect from a daughter of Beatrice's? She was disorderly and lazy—and demanding as well. Seuroi Tower was ill kept. Milicent left her clothes lying anywhere, began needlework which she never finished, let her women rob her—and then she reproached him whenever he spent a day or two at the castle. Yet she had no reason to be jealous, it was not often that he wanted Lady Alis. Milicent said: "What I know is that in the three years you have loved me she has had two children and two miscarriages"—as if he had ever promised her not to touch Lady Alis! Why should he put such an affront upon a woman who had served him loyally for five-and-twenty years? Well, it was something Milicent was incapable of understanding. One day he had said to her: "You ought to wash Lady Alis' feet and kiss the ground she walks on, to atone for the wrong you are doing her." And the little fool had burst into tears—she cried far too often—and said: "You love her more than you love me." As if she did not know how much he was still in love with her!—but her sulkiness and her angers were spoiling everything.

In the middle of the night Milicent woke with a great cry, and the two little girls, roused from their sleep, began crying and Eglantine screamed for her nurse: " 'Auc'ère, 'Auc'ère!'"

Milicent was shaking all over.

"There, there, my sweet, I am with you, be a good girl. You have frightened the children, you will make them as wild as yourself."

"Ansiau, listen to me. I am afraid. Something is going to happen to me."

"And why should you think so?"

"Listen—I had a dream—they were there, Lady Alis and Lady Beatrice and Father Aimeri and . . . the others—and then"—she was gasping—"they took the baby and they cooked it and ate it, there in front of me, and then they ground its bones into a powder and made me swallow it—and then I screamed."

Milicent always made up her nightmares, but as she told them she found herself believing them. Somehow she must soften the baron and explain her fears to him. And he talked to her as if she were a child: "Nonsense, dreams have no meaning. You are sick, that is all."

"Ansiau, listen. I know they did something to me just now, they put some spell on me. Sebile tells me that Lady Alis is using twice as many candles as before—what else could she be doing with all that wax? I feel so afraid."

"Afraid of what, my pigeon? I will protect you."

"Listen—I am damned."

Ansiau smiled: "You are too young to think of such things."

"For love of you. For you. And I am bringing you to damnation too."

Ansiau had a hard time putting her back to sleep.

Lady Alis was rocking her last-born child, Henry, and humming to herself. She was hot and wore only a blue shift fastened by a girdle. Her long, somewhat tarnished chestnut hair hung down her back in two loose, thick braids—since her illness she had lost so much hair that she no longer braided it tightly. She had narrow eyes—very narrow eyes—between wrinkled lids, and her heavy eyebrows joined over the bridge of her nose, as old Joceran's had once done. She had acquired a crafty look of late—she pursed her lips. It was because she was playing a cautious game. She would soon be forty—which was saying a great deal.

The baron had not left the castle for a month. Ah, the hussy at Seuroi must be tearing her hair—well, let her tear it until she was bald! "And I held her on my lap, here—and I combed her hair—and I bathed her—and she was always sweet and affectionate, I never supposed . . . but looking at an egg won't tell you if there is a snake inside it. An ugly girl. A girl who had nothing but her viciousness and her youth. If that! Let me see—she is eighteen now. She must be pretty well faded—the baron has seen to that! Sebile told one of the washwomen that her arms are thinner and she is getting potbellied. In five years there will be nothing left of her. But the baron will certainly not wait five years."

Lady Alis knew very well that she had not played fair. When the baron had come to the castle for Ascension Day she had sent a fourteen-year-old girl to him in the bathhouse—and Gay had orders not to open her mouth if the master squeezed her. Not a proper thing to do—but when it was a case of curing a man of such a foul disease, any remedy was legitimate. The remedy had proved effectual—the baron had stayed at the castle. And the little fool who put on such airs, and thought he loved her for her beauty and intelligence—she would sing a different tune now! Gay had broad hips and heavy breasts, like the peasant she was—Lady Alis sickened with shame and disgust when she saw the girl cross the courtyard. That mop of hair, those filthy feet! But she consoled herself with the thought that Milicent would certainly hear the whole story.

Flora vowed that Milicent would die before the year was out, but Lady Alis was not too convinced. Every year Flora promised the same thing and burned a handful of the hussy's hair combings, a bit of ribbon she had worn—and Milicent was still alive and every year gave birth to a living child—her last had died on the twelfth day—well enough!—but the girl was pregnant again and might yet bear a son. At heart Lady Alis did not wish her dead. The pains of Hell were a dim, distant sort of punishment; it was on earth that she should be made to pay—ugly, scorned, naked and trembling in the dirty paws of drunken soldiers—Lady Alis could not always think up punishments bad enough for her rival.

Milicent was solely responsible for all the misfortunes which had befallen the house of Linnières—and Lady Alis was willing to except her own sleepless nights, her fevers, the sheets she had torn with her teeth. God! The meanest wench in the henyard had the right to a man of her own, and she, a lady, was deprived of her husband by that hussy—but that was a separate account, she was willing to forget it. The thing that tore her heart was what the hussy had done to the children. The baron did not care—he loved his bastards—even at the castle it was: "Eglantine can say 'bread'." "Eglantine can hold her own bowl." "Eglantine's hair is as long as my two thumbs." And he would find a dowry for Eglantine, if she did not die first. And here was Mahaut, twenty and over, a great girl with breasts as big and hard as a wet nurse's, her nose was growing long, her hands becoming calloused from spinning. When the baron was not at home—he was almost never at home—Lady Alis took her daughter into her own bed, it was safer. The baron had no idea what life was like for a girl who had no suitors—and the day the child made a misstep, he would be the first to punish her! Old Garnier of Buchie came to Linnières every two weeks, talked of grain and horses, and Mahaut looked at his equine profile and sighed and wondered if his wife would live much longer.

And then there was Alette—fifteen, and so blond and sweetly built—her face was ruined, but what of it?—she would not pass it on to her children. The man who married her would be happy—but first he must marry her. And who would take her without a dowry, if Mahaut, with all her beauty, was still unmarried at twenty?

Then there were the boys. The baron had loved only Ansiet, but Herbert was his heir nevertheless, and old Haguenier stubbornly refused to die. Herbert said: "I have had enough of this—I shall repudiate Bertrade and look for a wife whose father is dead," but he did nothing—it would be a pity to abandon an inheritance which was nearly in his hands. The baron had spent so much on Milicent that now he had to pawn even his clothes and his arms —which meant no more tournaments. And if Abner was still an indulgent creditor, the banker Renier had powerful protectors and was threatening to bring an action before the bishop of Troyes. Ansiau had got into trouble enough with the abbot of Hervi over Milicent—he had better not find himself excommunicated for debt! Lady Alis knew that Herbert and Girard detested their father and particularly Milicent—in that at least they agreed. Herbert complained over wasting his youth hunting wolves, but he was beginning to age and he was not the man to give up substance for shadow. He was willing to bide his time, sure that one day he would be the stronger. But Girard, who had never been used to reprimands, wept for rage and threatened to leave the country, to become a knight errant, to join his uncle Simon in Palestine. Meanwhile, his dubbing was farther away than ever; he had come back to the castle because he had found himself in trouble at Bar-on-Aube, a quarrel in which he had struck too hard. Threatened by the parents of the man he had wounded, he had been obliged to take refuge at Linnières. He had been the last to learn that his father had carried off his betrothed—he had never been in love with Milicent, but he was used to thinking of her as his property, and then one day he learned that she had two children by the baron. His reaction had been instant scorn and hatred—she had deceived him, she had lied to him—he almost thought that he had loved her. And then, his father owed him a hauberk—and not only did he give him nothing, he had done him out of a fine dowry and was spending the money on the very woman he had stolen from him. It was all very well for that great bull Herbert to be indulgent—he had lost nothing. In fact he was glad to see his brother poor.

Ansiau found life at the castle restful after the sobs with which he was greeted at Seuroi. And then, just before Ascension Day, he had again experienced what a girl of fourteen could be—even a serf girl with dirty feet. Gay, whom he met in the bathhouse and the grain barn, was very submissive and did not fear Lady Alis. She was unresponsive, too—and he preferred that—she was merely a thing to him, he thought, an animal; with her he did not need to restrain himself as he did with a woman of noble blood.

On the day when he felt homesick for Milicent's complaints and Eglantine's smile, he set out for Seuroi without a word of farewell to Gay. But, riding through the forest, he wondered why she was so cold—it puzzled him—did she by any chance have another lover?

He expected reproaches—well deserved for once. But this time Milicent did not come to meet him as usual. He strode past the curtain and found her lying in bed. Her hands under her head, she seemed to be asleep. But at the baron's approach she started, opened frightened eyes, and rose with an effort. "It is you," she said. "Good morning, I am not properly dressed—excuse me." She spoke quickly, she was gasping, she did not even look at him—never had he seen her so indifferent. And certainly she was not properly dressed—she had on nothing but a dirty gray shift, open from throat to waist; her uncombed hair straggled around her cheeks.

"Not glad to see me? Are you angry with me?" He put his hands on her arms and thought he had touched a stove, they were so hot. "Well, at least you are not cold," he said.

Milicent freed herself with a shudder. "Stop. You are hurting me." She gave a little cough—it was hardly a cough, it sounded more like the wheezing of an old dog, it seemed to come from the bottom of her chest, effortlessly, with a strange, hollow sound. "I am stifling," she said, and went to the window. Ansiau followed her. There in the light he could see her better. She had changed greatly. Her collarbones, her jawbone, and the bones of her forehead protruded and were underlined by hard, angular shadows. Her eyes were abnormally large, burning, and bright—there were two red spots on her cheeks. Her mouth was half open, her translucent, reddish nostrils throbbed convulsively. Ansiau was so struck by her look of ill-health that he could not speak. But Milicent, a little revived, quickly grew animated and fixed hard bright eyes on him. "Now you see," she whispered. "You would never believe me. I told you often enough. Lady Alis made a wax image of me and melted it in the fire, she and Flora. You would never believe me. Look." She raised her hand and showed him her wrist—the big, yellowish bones looked as if they would pierce her skin. "Touch and feel how hot I am. It is a fire, I tell you, making me melt and burn inside. It did not come of itself. And you let her do it. You will be happy when I have melted away, your troubles will be over."

"Sweet, what are you saying? You are too young to die."

Ansiau was used to seeing her cry, but this time her eyes were dry and her voice hoarse. He did not want to show his anxiety, and growled: "You are madder than ever. I have done nothing to you. You are ill—go back to bed." She dragged herself to the bed, coughing her wheezy cough and spitting. She must have been spitting a great deal, for the straw beside the bed was wet and sticky.

"Look," she said, "it is my whole body, it is all melting away. My chest is all hollow. . . . If I touch it, it echoes. I am stifling here. It is too hot." She drew her hand over her forehead, as if trying to remember what she wanted to say, then went on: "Yes, you will be very happy. Lady Alis lets you sleep with young girls—that is just what you like. But I tell you one thing—I will not leave you Eglantine and Andrée. They are mine. Lady Alis shall not have them."

"My poor child," said Ansiau, "you are out of your mind. You need a nurse. You don't know how to do anything right. It is not surprising that you are ill if you never have yourself bled. It is your blood working in you, that is all."

Milicent raised her head with a hesitant smile. "Truly?" she said. "I ought to try it."

Milon was more accustomed to bleeding horses than men, and men than women. Afterwards, Milicent's lips and hands were blue and she shivered all night. All night she tossed in her bed and gasped—the bedding was soaked with sweat. And in the morning she went to bring the baron water, and fell her full length on the flags before she had taken three steps.

Ansiau was frightened and thought that there might really be witchcraft in it. He told Milicent that he would send for Father Aimeri to exorcize her. She said that she was afraid of Father Aimeri—he had already killed Juliana. Then Ansiau, with a sinking heart, resigned himself to going for the abbot of Hervi. He went down on his knees and begged the abbot to come and exorcize his mistress, for he believed that someone had cast a spell on her, and the spirits were making her languish and fade away. The abbot flatly refused—he would have nothing to do with a debauched woman. Ansiau supposed that he wanted to please Lady Alis and Herbert. He returned to Seuroi crestfallen. Milicent clung to him: "Well? Wouldn't he come? I knew it. You should not have humiliated yourself for nothing. I know—they all hate me because I love you. But I will never stop loving you."

In default of a priest, Ansiau called in a "wise woman" from Chaource—very well skilled, it was said, her patients always recovered. This woman, whose name was Joan the Tortoise, made Milicent plunge up to the neck in a tub of cold water and gave her iced beer and milk to drink, to put out the fire which was burning her internally. But the fire refused to go out—with flaming cheeks and parched mouth, Milicent spent hour after hour stretched motionless on her bed; from time to time she had brief spasms of hollow, dry coughing, which exhausted her so much that she almost lost consciousness. And Joan the Tortoise complained to the baron—it was a hard illness to cure because it was caused by witchcraft, and besides Milicent was pregnant, and it was always difficult to treat a woman who carried two lives. "I don't know what to try—the child spoils everything."

Milicent was only at the beginning of the fourth month. She ate nothing, suffered from pains in her stomach, and hoped for a miscarriage.

Mahaut came from the castle to see her old friend. The baron was on bad terms with her and received her surlily. "You have no reason to see her. I know—all of you have been wanting just one thing: to see her dead. She has lived without you, she can die without you."

But Mahaut wept. "She is my sister," she said. "I shall never sleep again if she dies without my seeing her."

Her father said: "Very well. But do not tire her."

"Millie, my sweet Millie, forgive me." Stretched on the bed beside her friend, Mahaut held her in her arms, as she had done for seven years in their maiden bed. Besides Mahaut's long but plump face with its soft lines, Milicent's face looked even more emaciated. But Milicent was calm; it was Mahaut who wept.

"Mahaut, my beauty. I love you dearly. How you have changed. Listen, I wanted to tell you something, but I have forgotten what it was. Oh, yes.

435

Your dowry. If I own anything, I leave it to you for your dowry—see to it. There are things that can be sold. I must atone—only don't be angry with me. I did not do it on purpose."

Mahaut cried: "Millie!" then stifled her friend with kisses. "Millie, you are mad—do you think I shall want a dowry after you are dead? I shall die too, or become a nun. You cannot believe that I will still think about men. . . . No, no—I have had enough of life, Millie.

"I have thought a great deal, Millie. And I tell you life is a small matter. It is death that counts. Always the best die young. And babies go straight to Paradise. When God loves someone, He calls—those are the wheat, the rest are chaff."

"God certainly does not love *me*," Milicent said. "Yet you see my state."

"He will forgive you, Millie—they say that the sin of love is the easiest to win forgiveness for. Just because a filthy priest at Hervi insulted you—no, my poor little wounded fawn, my little pigeon. To think that your beautiful eyes will be darkened, and I must go on living. I don't want you to die, Millie!"

Milicent was overwhelmed by self-pity. "What a life I have had, Mahaut my beauty! Oh, I don't want to say anything against her to you, but Lady Alis is the cause of it all. It is she who is killing me. She put a spell on me, she and Flora."

"I think so too," said Mahaut after a short silence. "You know, Millie, I am so tired of the castle and my brothers and my whole life. If I were a man, I would leave, I would go to the Holy Land. I would pray on Garnier's grave. I love Lady Alis, but I hate her because of you. And the baron—God! I cannot bear the sight of him."

"You are wrong," said Milicent. "No man could be finer."

"You know," said Mahaut gravely, "you make me sick talking like that. Look at yourself—in your state it is time to stop thinking of love."

With Mahaut's coming, Milicent appeared to regain strength. Mahaut was a good nurse; she seemed determined that her friend should not die. "You'll see," she said to the baron, "you'll see—she will get well." With the baron Milicent whimpered and pouted like a child, but Mahaut could make her eat and drink decoctions of herbs. "When she is a little stronger, baron," she said, "you shall take her to Langres and expose her in front of the cathedral of St. Mamas. I know that Lady Mary of Blaiguecor was cured that way."

Despite the heat it was decided not to defer the pilgrimage. Feverish and more animated than she had been for months, Milicent tied her girdle, drew on her gloves. "Gauchère, take little Eglantine's embroidered dress, she can wear it on the holiday. Put this pillow in the cart too. Here, Mahaut my dear, take this girdle, and this necklace, and these black sleeves—take whatever you want. And this white dress, if it isn't too tight for you. I don't need anything—I would gladly wear plain linen if only I can be cured. Baron, are you ready? He is never ready—always talking to Milon. Mahaut, my sweet, I bid you good-bye." Mahaut hid her face on her friend's shoulder. "Don't cry," said Milicent. "I shall get well. My beautiful! God give you a good baron and fine children. Think of me." The baron tore them apart and carried Milicent to the covered cart in which Gauchère and the two little girls were already waiting.

The road. The jolting. Every turn of the wheel was a blow in the back, in the heart. Through the cloth canopy of the cart the sun burned suffocatingly; it streamed through the cracks, made her eyes smart, parched her tongue. Her two little girls, red as beets and bathed in sweat, cried irritably, setting her nerves on edge. Flies clung to their noses, their bare arms, Gauchère had not time to drive the creatures away. But there had been no question of leaving the children behind—not with Lady Alis only two leagues from Seuroi Tower.

Half-naked on the damp, hot pillows, Milicent kept shifting her body, hoping to find some position in which her heart would pain her less. Sometimes she moved the linen curtain aside a little to watch the green and gray foliage, the trunks of oaks and birches glide slowly past—if only the jolting did not shake her so, make her vomit six times a day. And hardest of all was the thought of that useless child, that child which would never be born and which tortured her and robbed her of her last strength—as if she were not in agony enough without it.

At night the heat lessened, the jolting stopped, but rest did not come. Gauchère brought milk for the children. Flies buzzed about it. The milk smelled horrible. The children smelled horrible too—a sharp, sweetish smell that nauseated her. The baron raised the flap and bent his big brown head over her. His breath was so heavy and strong that it seemed to drive away all the air under the canopy. His voice, though he tried to make it soft, split her ears. "How do you feel, my beauty?" (As if she could feel anything but terribly ill!) His eye feigned grief, but his firm, tanned, bearded face seemed to say: "It is a beautiful day and life is beautiful." "And for me?" Milicent thought. "For me? For me everything is ugly. He is waiting for me to die. He will be free." She answered nothing. She closed her eyes. And he said: "We are only three leagues from Langres. Tomorrow noon we shall see the towers of the cathedral." She said: "Tomorrow noon I shall be dead," and her own words frightened her. It was as if, for the first time in her life, she realized that death really existed.

She did not close her eyes all night. She did not think sad thoughts— it was merely that the heat, the mosquitoes, and her coughing kept her awake. Opening the flap, she saw a field, haycocks, stars. It was all so calm and wide. Over toward the inn soldiers were snoring, dogs growling in their sleep. Close by, right at her feet, she heard the fast, gentle breathing of her two little daughters.

And at dawn, the road again. The air was still quite cool. Toward terce— the sun, which was already high, cast long shadows of riders and cart on the road—Milicent said to Gauchère: "Have the horses stopped. I am done for."

The baron rode back and asked her what was the matter: "It will not be much longer, we must not stop before the heat begins."

"Ansiau," Milicent said, "I am suffocating, take me out into the air."

He dismounted and took her in his arms. Her face was earthy, her eyelids brown. He thought: "It is the end." He was not prepared for it—he had counted on St. Mamas. He stood there in the middle of the road—lost, not knowing what to do with his burden, which grew heavier minute by minute.

"Lay me on the ground, anywhere," Milicent whispered; she seemed to pity him in his embarrassment.

Gauchère spread a blanket over new-mown hay.

"I am better," said Milicent. "I am better. Ansiau. Come here, close to me. Do you remember—the hay—the hay barn?" She smiled and laid both her hands on his forehead. "I have loved your love. It was so good. If I must give it up, I would rather die."

The big, round black eye was bathed in trembling tears; they overflowed and ran down beside the mutilated nose. "You are mad," said Ansiau. "You want to kill me. Why do you say such things to me? It will make me miss you too much."

Milicent stroked his temples. Her eyes were bewildered, staring, her lips fixed in a smile. She had to make an effort to speak. "Listen. Give the children to Lady Alis. I forgive her everything if only she will be good to them. And never let her tell them that their mother was a whore. Make her promise."

"She will," said Ansiau.

"I want to be buried in Langres," said Milicent. "Don't drag me all the way back in that cart—with the children. Pray to St. Mamas for me." She raised her head a little, seeking the baron's lips. "There. Hold my head. There. Closer—harder." Her head thrown back in the hay, Milicent received the last forbidden kisses she was to taste in her life. Then a gray shadow crept over her face. Her nose shrank. Her whole body pained her. If only the baron could hold her, hold her so hard that she could not escape. And then, she could not feel his arms.

Milicent did not even make a beautiful corpse—she was as gaunt as a skeleton. Flat-chested and frail, her belly already protruding, her hands wasted to the bone, she lay dead in the cart, and at every jolt in the road the blond head bounced, the eyelids half opened. Gauchère covered the emaciated face with a white cloth, and the two children, huddled in their corner, chattered and quarrelled and paid no attention to the corpse. However, Eglantine, who was two and a half, was surprised at her mother's lying so still.

When they reached Langres, Ansiau had a grave dug in the great graveyard, beside the cathedral. To the priest who officiated, he said that Milicent was his daughter-in-law and gave no further explanations. As she had died without the sacraments, he had Masses sung for the repose of her soul, made offerings, and promised to make more. He had little money with him and the expenses of the funeral were heavy. He sold his cloak, his rings, the few jewels that Milicent had brought. It kept him so busy that he had no time to think.

From a mason he ordered a slab of gray stone, to be carved with a square cross and the name of Milicent of Nangi, wife of Ansiau of Linnières, in full: MELISANDA NANGI ANSELLIS DE LINNERIIS UXOR ANNO DOMINI MCIVC. He promised to pay the second half of the agreed price at Christmas, when he would come to see the stone in place. Before he left Langres he took Gauchère and the two children to the new grave. Sitting on the yet damp ground, the little girls spread their fingers in the sun and bent their heads so that it would fall on the backs of their necks. Eglantine dreamily watched an earthworm gliding between two pebbles.

Kneeling before the grave, Ansiau could not make himself believe that Milicent was indeed there, lying in that yellow earth, in a wooden box— black and putrid and crawling with worms. His little girl. His wild, mad girl. His youth.

TRUNK AND BRANCHES

IN THE CITY of Châtillon-on-Seine, between Langres and Tonnerre, on the edge of the great forest, the corpse of a baby girl named Andrée was laid in a little coffin and lowered into a grave, to become earth, sap and roots. The reason was the heat. The return journey had been hard; at the inns the milk was brought in dirty basins. Both children had been ill. But Andrée was only a year and four months old—from one day to the next she had become another child. Her face was shrunken, there were dark rings around her eyes; she hiccuped convulsively, bringing up her food in feeble jets which dribbled out the left corner of her twisted mouth. The last night she screamed—long, heart-rending screams.

There was nothing to be done—she was dead. Ansiau had watched the little plump shoulders, the little red, chapped buttocks, the little gray, almost transparent cheeks fill with lead and harden. Swaddled like an infant, prone and stiff, she looked taller than before; already her face bore the resigned sadness of those who have suffered much.

Weak from dysentery, Ansiau dragged himself to the graveyard in the stifling heat—if only Lady Alis were there, he thought, to see to everything—she knew more than he did about burying children. He could not even have the little body embalmed—all his money had gone for Milicent's funeral; there was nothing for it but to leave Andrée where she had died—there at Châtillon.

It was inescapable: these children, born outside the law, were under a curse. God refused them life. Gauchère, who loved them, shook her head and calmly said: "They will go where their mother has gone," or "Their mother is calling them." Feverish and pale, Eglantine tossed and shivered on the pillow which served her as a mattress. When he came back from the graveyard Ansiau lay down close to her, his head touching hers. They were spending the night in a miserable inn; the straw and the walls stank of urine. Not a breath of air. Gauchère brought water, and it was warm. Ansiau reflected that perhaps it was better for Eglantine to die and go to heaven than to live without a mother. But all night the child clung to him, deluging him with the acrid odors of warm sweat and diarrhea—she could not lie still, she was suffering. She whimpered softly, and half unconsciously patted her father's cheek with her little damp hand—tenderly, as she would have caressed her doll, as if she were trying to reassure herself. And Ansiau's heart swelled—now he had but one thought, to keep the child at any cost, and he wondered what more he could promise to God for Eglantine's ransom.

Ah! God and Our Lady and St. Mamas and St. Columba and all the saints of Champagne must know that he was as poor as Job on his ash heap. He could not pay for a pilgrimage, he could not give to good works—the child was a bastard, and God had no reason to take pity on her.

In the morning, seeing that Eglantine was still paler and thinner, Ansiau went to the church, summoned the priest and deacon, and vowed to give Our Lady a chalice of wrought silver before a year was out if he were granted the life of his child. His promise written, sealed, and sworn, he returned to the inn. Eglantine had fallen asleep and was gnawing her lips. Flies lit on her nostrils and eyelids. Gauchère was sitting on the floor with her head in her hands, weeping as if her " 'Glantine" were dead already. Ansiau drove away the flies and made the child comfortable in his left arm.

To leave Châtillon, he was obliged to sell the cart and blankets and two of his horses. Gauchère rode pillion behind Thierri-Guiot, and Ansiau took Eglantine on his saddle. She was still rather pale, but was rapidly regaining her strength, as children of her age often will. She prattled and turned her head from side to side like a linnet. And Ansiau proudly bent his big, tired eye on the child whose redemption had cost him so dear, and he thought: "My little squirrel, my white ermine. My little fawn. Playing as if she had never been ill." Eglantine tugged at the horse's mane with both hands and squealed: "Gee-up, gee-up!"

During the night they spent at Laignes, Ansiau saw Milicent in a dream. Pale and thin, in a coarse shift, barefoot, her hair unbound, she was sitting on a rock. She wept and said: "Foul traitor, stinking villein, may your belly swell and burst, may your tongue rot, may the Devil make you swallow needles and knives. Was this your care for my child? Did I leave her to you to die? It was Lady Alis who killed her, and you say nothing. You want to kill Eglantine too." And then she began to weep, and her sobs and little moans were so pitiable that Ansiau was touched to the heart, and he said: "You are as mad as ever. Come here, you stubborn child, come to bed." And suddenly she was dressed in a transparent lavender shift, and between the pleats her body showed through the cloth—white and round as before she bore Andrée. And then he laid her down and held her by the elbows, and kissed her throat, and the hollow between throat and shoulder, and the back of her neck—and she clung to him and thrust her hands into his hair and said: "See! I am not dead, I am alive. Can't you see, can't you see? . . ."

And from the bitterness of his awakening he knew what he had lost. He almost longed to go back to sleep and never wake again. Then he felt remorseful. A dead woman was a dead woman—to be left in peace. Poor Milicent must not yet be at rest in the ground, or how could she come to him with lustful desires? He promised himself that he would have Masses said for the soul of Milicent of Nangi, his daughter-in-law, who had died without the sacraments and in a state of sin. But the dream had left the scent of his beloved, the touch of her soft, warm hair on his lips and arms. "I must find a girl who looks like her," he thought, "a thin blonde." But where was he to find hair so golden, a skin so white? It would have to be a noblewoman.

When he reached the castle he said nothing to Lady Alis. She understood. And she, too, said nothing—she was happy at being rid of her rival at last and did not want to feign grief. Mahaut sobbed like a madwoman and tore her cheeks with her fingernails.

Ansiau said: "Lady, I know, you had a right to be angry, she is dead, it is over. The little girl has done you no harm, be good to her."

"You have servants enough," said Alis. "Keep your bastard at Seuroi or somewhere else. She is nothing to me, I have children of my own."

Ansiau shrugged his shoulders and set Eglantine on her lap. "I shall know it," he said, "if you are not kind to her. If she is ill-treated, you shall answer to me for it."

Alis sullenly pushed away the child's hands, which were already reaching for her necklace. And then she saw that there were scabs around the little thing's mouth, and dirt in the corners of her eyes, and lice in her hair. She said: "A pretty state you keep her in!" and sent for water, a comb, and salves.

She wore her heart on her sleeve—no sooner had she washed and scrubbed and cleaned the little orphan than she loved her dearly. Obviously, Eglantine was not much of a child—her legs were crooked and her belly swollen; she was skinny, her head was too big, and she had an ugly face—well, that was nothing surprising, Milicent had always been ugly, her only beauty had been her blond hair, and the child unfortunately would be a brunette. Certainly Lady Alis would not have felt proud to produce that little clinging, whimpering thing—but it was the best Milicent could do. Nevertheless Eglantine came of good blood, she was not like a bastard borne by a servant, she must be saved from humiliation. Then, too, the little thing talked so well and seemed intelligent—she could be taught to obey and keep herself clean. It did not take Alis very long to find many excuses for adopting her.

That night she put Eglantine to bed in the big cradle, beside Joceran, who was her elder by six months. Joceran was fat, blond, and pink, and when Lady Alis saw the two children lying side by side she felt very proud. She thought to herself: "Baron, you are very fortunate to have such a wife as I, who treat your bastard like my own beautiful legitimate children."

Ansiau did not seem to be aware of his lady's kindness. He looked at the two children in their cradle and said: "See what beautiful long eyelashes she has, and what delicate eyebrows. Yes, there is something wonderfully delicate about that child." Then he added: "Andrée had blue eyes."

And Lady Alis thought: "So she had blue eyes. And how well you know it, baron! And you do not know the color of my new baby Garin's eyes. And you did not weep much when our Ibert died last winter." But she said none of this to the baron, for she had long since ceased to tell him her thoughts— she had lost the habit of it. She said her prayers and went to bed in silence. It was strange—she no longer felt any joy over Milicent's death. A poor silly girl—a good girl nevertheless—but so weak. Well, she was certainly neither the first nor the last to let herself be seduced by a man who had full power over her. Of the two, the baron was most to blame.

And that night Ansiau tried to speak. He said that it was hard. He said that he was sad. He said: "Lady, if you knew. She was sweet." He was ill and weak, he wept on her shoulder. And she rocked him and stroked his hair, because she could not do otherwise.

Eglantine of Nangi was a person to be reckoned with. When Eglantine cried, it was always somebody's fault—usually Joceran's. She always cried with her mouth wide open, shaking her head in fury and despair, and little round tears welled up and scattered in all directions and her cheeks dripped with them. And every time Ansiau saw her cry, it staggered him—he said: "I cannot help it—it gives me the strangest feeling, it wrenches my heart," and one thing was certain: Eglantine must never cry. He took her up and kissed away her tears. He had honey cake brought for her, he forced Lady Alis to give her Joceran's toys. He said: "She has no mother, I must protect her." When he went hunting something gnawed at his heart: Eglantine was crying, Eglantine was being beaten, pinched, bitten by a dog perhaps, or starved—no one cares what happens to a bastard. And he thought of his return and his heart beat faster.

When she saw her father Eglantine gave a shrill cry, as if something were hurting her, and stretched out both her arms, then half threw herself, half tumbled from her bench—to be caught and brandished in the air. She laughed aloud for joy, with little happy gurgles, and her eyes beamed such tenderness, such trust—it bewildered him. What could he have done to provoke this angelic joy?—he could not believe it. And already Eglantine was pulling his hair and his beard and biting his nose.

Ugly, he supposed, she would some day be, because everyone said so. She had dark-golden hair, which would turn brown, and irregular features. A baby-bird's head—nothing but two huge, black, bulging eyes and a big mouth, which was always open to laugh or cry or chatter. Her father thought: "She will have beautiful eyes." For the time being they took up too much room, they rolled, and blinked with lovely curved lashes, they opened wide in wonder and shone as bright as stars, they were almost like two beautiful creatures with a life of their own; and her mouth yawned and laughed, and gaped like a beak, it was so mobile that no one knew what it would look like at rest. Ansiau could never find tidbits enough for that mouth, and Lady Alis said: "You will give her a stomach-ache." Which is what happened. But Ansiau had his own ideas: if the child ate, it was because she was hungry; if she was ill afterwards, it was because people wished her harm.

Eglantine had little arms that clung and held, and a slender neck with a hollow at the nape, just like Milicent's. She had dimples on her elbows, the soles of her feet were pink—Ansiau could not see them and remain calm. Twice a day—at "Good morning" and "Good night"—he devoured her with greedy kisses, a lover's kisses, and the child laughed like a maniac. Lady Alis said: "It is bad for her, she will not sleep well." Lady Alis meant what she said, but Ansiau thought it only a stepmother's jealousy.

Eglantine was not easy to bring up. She was nearly three and had begun to talk. She was intelligent, but as dirty and disorderly a child as ever lived. When the baron was not present she received her share of cuffs and slaps. She never protested; but whenever her father was there she became nervous and complaining and cried over nothing. One day he asked: "Tell me, little one, does Lady Alis beat you when father is away?"

"Yes, father."

Ansiau frowned. "And who else beats you?"

"I don't know . . . Joceran." (Joceran was the great enemy.)

"And Lady Richeut? And Mahaut?"

Eglantine kept answering "Yes," without much thinking what she was saying. After that day Eglantine was never beaten again. Joceran still sometimes pulled her hair and took away her toys, and that was all. And Lady Alis would scold him: "Let her alone, you scamp, the baron will be home tonight."

Garin, Lady Alis' latest-born child, was not doing well. He vomited his milk and grew thinner and thinner. To lose a child seven months old was hard. Lady Alis kept sending for Flora—now a thin, aged witch—and dipped the child in baths of spring water mixed with snake's blood; she hung a toadstone around his neck to ward off spells, and twice a week exposed him at the door of Hervi Church. Nothing availed—Garin was buried on Martinmas Day beside his other dead brothers and sisters. Lady Alis was expecting another child by Palm Sunday. "I don't know how it is," she said to Mahaut, "but I have a feeling that this one will not live either. Since Joceran I have lost every one—Ibert and Garin and the two who miscarried." Secretly she hoped that, being past forty, she would not conceive again.

Mahaut did not answer. She had changed greatly in the last months, she was gloomy and sad, and wept often. At Christmas she and her father set out for Langres to pray at Milicent's grave. Father and daughter were not very fond of each other—days went by without their exchanging a word. But the long journey in each other's company finally brought them somewhat together. Mahaut caught a chill on the road and fell ill, but went on nevertheless. At Tonnerre, in an inn crammed with pilgrims, Ansiau settled her on a bench by the fire, after a hard tussle—not being able to pay for such a comfortable seat, he had to obtain it by force. However, everyone soon felt sorry for the pretty, shivering, coughing girl. Ansiau was anxious; he brought her a bowl of clear soup, but she would not touch it.

"Fair daughter," he asked, "why do you dislike me?"

Mahaut fixed her right eye on him. "Millie was my sister," she said.

When they reached Linnières she had to go to bed. Lady Alis nearly went out of her mind. She called her husband a murderer and said so much that she felt afraid afterwards. She upbraided him with Baldwin of Puiseaux,

Edith of Chalmiers, William, his debts, their dead children, Milicent's dowry, and finally his bastard. She said: "I have suffered too much through you, baron. I can bear no more. If my child dies, I shall leave you."

Mahaut soon recovered. But Lady Alis cherished a great bitterness against her husband, because of all the hard words she had said to him.

After the spring thaws old Garnier of Buchie came to Linnières to tell his neighbor that he was a widower at last. Still weak and pale from her illness, Mahaut served him at table, kneeling to hand him the cup. His face was ruddy but gaunt—his nostrils almost touched his upper lip, his long nose curved over his short gray whiskers and always received a share of his meals. Mahaut knelt with a heavy heart. The man took the cup from her hands and kissed her on the lips, Mahaut felt him stiffen and tremble, and her hands and feet went cold.

"My fair daughter," Lady Alis said to her that night, "do as you will, I shall not force you. The baron wants it, and I should not be sorry to see you married to him, for he is a good knight and of good blood. You will soon be twenty-one."

Mahaut was shaking so violently that she could not braid her hair.

Lady Alis was brought to bed on Palm Sunday; and two weeks after Easter Mahaut was married. The wedding was held at Buchie—which was contrary to custom, for Mahaut was an eldest daughter and it was her father's part to bear the expense of the festivities. But the whole countryside knew that Mahaut had no dowry except her virtue—"if that!" the gossips said, "at twenty-one!" Garnier of Buchie had grown sons, who, in their rage at being given a stepmother, whispered that Mahaut had borne more than one child and that she dabbled in witchcraft with Flora. Old Garnier did not care—for three years he had wanted the girl, let her be what she might. He took her to his house and gave her his dead wife's finery; he put up a swing in the orchard for her and made his youngest sister wait on her. He had her guarded like a sack of gold pieces. A month after the wedding Mahaut was pregnant and thought of nothing but the little Garnier to come.

After Mahaut's wedding Ansiau went to Troyes. He had nothing with which to pay Abner, and counted on being granted more time. He needed money again—this time for the chalice he had promised to give to the church in Châtillon. Melting up his few remaining buckles and chains had produced only half the silver it would take to make the chalice—and if the promised gift were not ready in time, who knew what risks Eglantine might not run? He had not wanted to be parted from the child for so long and had taken her with him. On the road he sank into gloomy thought—the child could have inherited her mother's dowry if only he had married Milicent to Girard four years ago—once her mother was married, they could never have proved that he was the child's father. And now Milicent's dowry had gone to Lady Beatrice and her brothers of Chesley, and he could only hope that he would not have to repay Abner the money he had borrowed on it.

At Troyes he had a long argument with the Jew: Milicent of Nangi, his daughter-in-law, had been a widow and a free woman; she had borrowed money on her estate; she was dead. Her debts passed to her heirs. But, said Abner, Lady Beatrice had refused to pay back a sum she had never received; and Ansiau of Linnières had stood surety for his daughter-in-law—the debt was therefore his. And Ansiau answered that he had stood surety for his daughter-in-law for so long as she should be the owner of the estate—on her death, however, the estate had gone to her mother and her uncles.

Abner, now old and bent and tremulous, became angry and pretended to whine: "It is always the Jew who pays. I do not know what settlement may have been made between my lord knight and Mistress Charron. One thing is certain, I lent the money, and the estate yields nothing—the late lord of Nangi long since laid it fallow for hunting."

"And the vineyards? And the hives?" said Ansiau.

"My lord knight knows very well that Mistress Charron received the vineyards in fief ten years ago."

"And you know very well, you dog of a Jew," said Ansiau, and his hands were in Abner's beard, "that Charron is even richer than yourself. Make him pay. I have nothing. Do you want my shirt and breeches?"

He had been dealing with the man for twenty-five years. He used him as one uses a machine that is both useful and dangerous—a sort of box from which you could draw money but which had a way of taking money out of your pockets if you were not careful. He knew, too, that the Jew had a fond memory of the elder Herbert, and he had exploited that weakness as long as he could—but if you keep pulling the same string it finally breaks—and the string had broken.

And Abner, whom the lady of Linnières had used and abused all during the Crusade, had lately grown less indulgent. He was tired. Before his eyes—the eyes of an old eagle—year after year these Franks had passed, so many of them, so eager for money, men and women—a bloodstained and shameless race, all alike, easy-come-easy-go, not a brain in their heads, fists like hammers. Abner scorned them from the bottom of his heart, and God knows that he had a heart and a rich fund of scorn. Yet his voice became even more honied—only his eyes hardened.

Ansiau pounded his fist on the table, swore, threatened, and said he would rather be excommunicated and thrown into prison than pay a single penny for Lady Beatrice's land. In the end he paid—at least the interest on the loan—because he must have money for the chalice and Abner would not lend it to him under any other conditions. This time he pledged his youngest son, Joceran—if the money were not repaid before Christmas, Abner should keep the boy a prisoner until the debt was settled. Ansiau, of course, planned never to bring the boy to Troyes, and he was sure that Abner would not come to Linnières after him. But Lady Alis, when she learned of it, was never to forgive her husband.

That year—Ansiau was still in Troyes—Countess Mary and Count Thibaut and all the chivalry of Champagne and the good folk of the cities heard mournful news: Count Henry, king of Jerusalem, had died in Acre. It was an accident, he had fallen from a window of his palace. He left two infant daughters, whom the bishops of Troyes and Reims, at the Pope's command, declared illegitimate and their inheritance forfeit, for Count Henry's marriage had caused great scandal in the West. Thibaut became count of Champagne in his brother's place. And already in Troyes there was talk of a new Crusade; since the death of Saladin his brother Safadin was threatening the kingdom, the Moslems had recaptured Joppa, and the word went that pilgrims were ill-treated in Jerusalem—all was to do again.

From Troyes, where he felt that he had become a stranger, Ansiau went to Chaource and from there to Hervi to visit old Haguenier, who—obese, gouty, and half deaf—spent his time weeping for his sons and receiving his kinsmen. There Ansiau found Manesier of Coagnecort, Hugh of Baudemant's sons, Joceran of Puiseaux (son of Baldwin), and his own son Herbert who, bored at Linnières, had come to pay his court to his old father-in-law. Strangely enough, old Haguenier, who knew very well how Herbert treated Bertrade, was very fond of his son-in-law and was forever saying to him: "When you are lord of Hervi," or "When the house is yours." And Herbert sighed and said to all and sundry: "God! Shall I ever see him dead?"

At Haguenier's there was talk of Count Henry, the Crusade, the Holy Land; and Manesier of Coagnecort asked Ansiau if he expected to take the cross a third time. Ansiau shrugged his shoulders and looked down at Eglantine who was leaning against his knee and playing with a ring; when she looked up, her father smiled at her timidly, as he always did when there were other men present.

"Can I abandon that little slip of a girl?" he said. "She has no mother. I shall not leave the country until I have married her—not for ten years at least."

My husband beats and beats me—why?
Husband, beware!
I have not wronged him—no, not I—
In deed or word, or may I die!
What if one day when none were by
I kissed my lover's hair?
Husband, beware!

My husband beats and beats me—why?
Husband, beware!
"Revenge is sweet," say those who try.
Before the sun has left the sky
In my sweet lover's arms I'll lie,
All bare, all bare!
Husband, beware!

"Lady," said Mahaut, "I do not like that song."

"Some dislike one song, some another—people sing them all."

"I tell you one thing, lady: I shall never take a lover, since I could not have whom I loved."

"All the better for you," said Lady Alis. "There is little profit in it." She raised her head to thread her needle. She sighed. "All the better for you. A woman with stepsons like yours should take no risks. You are thinner than you were at Christmas."

"I feel well, though."

Mahaut shook her handsome head and threw back her long reddish braids. In two years she had grown thinner and lovelier and looked more than ever like an ivory saint—her fine, full eyes, set like jewels in the delicate folds of her lids, had a steadier brightness and darted flames no longer; she had been married to Garnier of Buchie for two years. "And I wish I didn't feel so well, God knows! I tried the remedy you gave me—nothing helps."

"Still nothing? I am surprised. Your stepsons must have put a spell on you, or I am not lady of Linnières. Here is another thing you can do. Make with your own hands a stew of boars' testicles mixed with an herb I shall give you, and serve it to your baron just before bedtime—but above all see that it is on the night of the new moon, for night conceives the moon anew then, and it is the favorable day for conceptions. God knows, I never had to count days or use herbs. Look at me, I am in my fifth month, and I would ask nothing better than to put you in my place."

Mahaut looked at her enviously. "It is his fault, not mine," she said. "He still sleeps with that Guillette, and she is not pregnant either. He says that my organs were ruined last time—as if he knew anything about it, the old, toothless dog!" Her lower lip trembled and contracted, her hands dropped on her needlework. Nine months after her marriage she had given birth to a child, and in such agony that her tongue had dried up and her eyes almost burst from their sockets—and the child had been born dead— strangled by the umbilical cord, all blue . . . a boy, a fine boy. And since then—nothing, just as if she were a virgin. And still she put up with old Garnier three times a week. And Lady Alis, who was well past forty, was still fruitful—this one must be at least her twentieth. That was what happened when you had a husband older than your father.

"My fair daughter, do you know that Herbert is going to marry again in the spring?"

Mahaut yawned: "Much good may it do him! I shall not stop him. And who is the unfortunate girl?"

"Aelis, daughter of Ansiau of Bercen. Her sister died of smallpox last year and she is her parents' only heir."

"Not a bad piece of business, then," said Mahaut.

"It is bad," Lady Alis said, "because Girard wanted her too. He asked her father for her through Joceran of Puiseaux, my nephew. And her father will hear of no one but a knight. Then Bertrade died. And Herbert sent gifts and a ring through James of Vanlay, without a word to me or the baron. Ansiau of Bercen accepted and sent his cousin Bernier to us to arrange the betrothal. A nice position for me to be in—when I wanted her for Girard!"

"But, lady," Mahaut said, "Ansiau of Bercen has every right to prefer Herbert. Herbert is rich. He is a grown man. He has been to the Holy Land."

Lady Alis' face hardened. "It would have cost Herbert nothing to leave the girl to his brother. He will always be able to find a wife. Girard had a chance of succeeding—I believe the girl liked him."

"As if a father ever cares what his daughter may or may not want!" said Mahaut with a short dry laugh. "And Girard is furious, naturally?"

"Indeed he is."

At twenty, Girard was handsome, though less handsome than he had been at eighteen. Slim and tall, with a long neck, sparkling eyes, and flushed cheeks, he always seemed to be at top pitch, in the thick of battle; when he sat down, it was like a bloodhound stopping to sniff. Back from hunting, he pushed past the servants, bounded up the ladder four steps at a time, threw himself on Lady Alis, kissed her eyes. "Lady, I had good hunting today, I got the old Bernon werewolf—Guion will bring you his head presently. Mahaut, my fair sister, welcome!" He sat down on the floor, and Lady Alis began twining his long chestnut curls around her fingers.

"You are all out of breath. Why do you run so fast? You are no longer fourteen."

Girard stretched and sprang to his feet. "No, thank God! But it makes me furious to think that the fat swine had his spurs at seventeen. He has plenty of money. Why don't you tell him to equip me?"

"I have told him."

"Then you went about it wrong. Lady, listen—" He paced up and down the hall, hands behind his back, head forward, "this is what I shall do: I shall go to Bercen by night and carry off the girl. Afterwards they will have to marry us."

"God preserve you!" Lady Alis said. "Herbert would kill you."

"No—I shall do it," Girard insisted. "In fact, I shall do something better. What do I care about her dowry? I will take my pleasure of her and send her back to her father—then he can do as he likes with her. We shall see if Herbert will still want her."

"Where is your common sense?" said Lady Alis. "Go and rest. Eat something. I had a piece of kid saved for you."

"Lady!" Again Girard rumpled his mother's veil and kissed her faded cheeks. "Lady! I love you! You know how much I like kid. Lady, you are kind and good. Listen—when I am rich, I will give you a veil with so much gold embroidery that it will hide the cloth."

Despite herself, Lady Alis smiled. "Hurry downstairs, featherhead—your meat will be cold."

Girard vanished as quickly as he had come.

Mahaut was sitting on the chest beside her old bed, unbraiding her hair; her sister Alette knelt beside her, saying her rosary. Their cousin Hersent of Beaumont yawned as she undressed.

Lady Alis came to the curtain and quietly pushed it open—she had on a long shift and was carrying a candle. "Mahaut, my beauty, the baron is not here—you may as well sleep in my bed, you will be more comfortable."

Mahaut shook her head. "Oh, lady, it is so pleasant here. I am so fond of this bed"—she laughed happily—"and the chest, and the water jug. Why, it is as if I had never left home."

Lady Alis set the candle on the floor and sat down on the chest beside her daughter. "You left it of your own free will," she said. "I did not force you."

"It had to be. Oh, beloved lady, take me, keep me, never let me go.— Lady, do you remember, when Auberi asked for me, you refused—you had him driven out of the house. Perhaps I should have loved him better than I love Garnier of Buchie." She hid her face on her mother's shoulder and sobbed. "Why, lady? And Hugh, Aioul's brother—why? What have I done, lady!" Alis held her close and rocked her as if she were a child.

Alette had finished her prayers and was sitting on the floor, staring at them with her calm gray eyes.

Lady Alis' anger against Herbert was justified, for he would never have thought of Aelis of Bercen if his brother had not asked for her. Since his father-in-law's death Herbert had been living in Troyes and only came to Linnières for the hunting season. By pure chance he learned through his Vanlay cousins that Girard hoped to marry Ansiau of Bercen's daughter. Instantly Herbert was jealous—the girl must be a good match if Lady Alis wanted her Girard to get her. He gave Bertrade a few more kicks in the stomach than usual, and the poor woman never got up again. She lasted three more weeks. Emaciated, with great chestnut blotches under her eyes, she writhed and howled hour after hour. Herbert stopped in from time to time to see how long it would take her, and then went back to his occupations. When she sent for her daughter Aelis (young Haguenier was already in service far away), Herbert came too and asked her forgiveness for form's sake. Bertrade gasped: "I curse you!" Her head fell back, she swallowed her tongue, turned blue, then white. Herbert had her buried and sent his presents to Aelis of Bercen.

The woman who had greatly loved and greated hated him, his wife for ten years, passed out of his life and he was hardly aware of it. She had been a rather annoying clause in the contract which made him master of Hervi, he had no further use for her, he had put her out of the way—what mattered now was the new one.

Sure of being accepted, he had his wedding clothes made in advance, and went to Bercen in person to spend the third Sunday in Lent. Ansiau of Bercen had his guest's shield hung in the place of honor and ordered his nephews to hold Herbert's sleeves during dinner. He was a grave and pious gentleman who delighted to honor crusaders—he had lost his eldest son in the Holy Land.

"You will be as a son to me," he said to Herbert. Herbert said: "I ask nothing better," and ate as much as he could in Lent. The after-dinner nap concluded, he made the customary inspection of the manor, like a man who intends to know what he is buying. The fine old man proudly said: "Here is the stable, here is the larder." Herbert looked at him covertly, counting his white hairs, judging his breathing—the quick breathing of a man well on in years—trying to calculate how much longer he would have to wait.

As for the daughter, he hardly looked at her—a girl of fourteen! With a nice white skin, of course, not like a girl who worked in the fields. However, he conscientiously sent the old woman who scratched him every night to the ladies' chamber, with orders to procure all possible information about Aelis— her health, her complexion, her cleanliness, any good or bad signs which she might bear on her body. Herbert did not intend to marry blindly.

The next morning the old woman told him that Aelis was a great beauty, slender and willowy and firm—"you couldn't pinch her even if you tried— she is bursting with good sap, and warm, and white. And between her breasts there is a round black mole no bigger than a pea."

"A mole?" said Herbert, and the next day he looked at the girl more attentively—from a distance, for she was always with her mother. A little girl with long chestnut braids and a pretty, soft-lipped mouth. Impossible to discover the little black mole under her coarse woolen dress.

Herbert returned to Troyes after arranging that the wedding should take place on the second Sunday after Easter. He made the old woman tell him Aelis' beauties all over again, and the black mole stayed in his mind.

He had a whole harem and certainly did not look to marriage to satisfy his appetites—and suddenly that little black mole, no bigger than a pea, had come to upset everything. "Is it a natural mark?" he asked the old woman. "Was she born with it? Is it a good omen?" He could not sleep for thinking of the second Sunday after Easter.

Herbert would have been much surprised to learn that his betrothed was not at all happy at the thought of becoming mistress of Linnières and Hervi.

All that autumn and winter Girard had been coming to Bercen with his cousin Joceran of Puiseaux. He came because he was bored—Linnières was too gloomy. At Bercen he always found good cheer and a warm welcome (Joceran's wife was related to Ansiau of Bercen). The men spent hours at the table, fought cocks, watched wrestling matches between two boys smeared with dough and honey, listened to bagpipers and horn players. Joceran, who was a good storyteller, amused the company with tales of war and bawdry—Girard knew his cousin's stories by heart and went to the corner where the ladies were spinning and embroidering behind a tapestry-covered bench. He sat down on the floor, exchanged a word or two with the mistress of the house, scratched his head, stood up, bent over one or another of the young women to see her work, then went as he had come. Each of the young women was sure that he came for her. And Aelis was the surest of all, because her maids told her so.

Girard could make his beautiful golden eyes laugh and weep at will, or sparkle with malice or glow with tenderness—he had the Devil in him—he did it automatically as soon as he saw a pretty girl, merely for the pleasure of seeing her blush. He sincerely believed that it hurt her as little to blush as it hurt him to wink.

He was too old now to be amused by little girls. But one day he saw Aelis alone in the mew, just as she was tying her falcon to the bar; the mew was divided from the kennel by a wicker trellis, and Girard stopped and watched the girl through it.

Aelis turned and said: "My young lord, are you fond of falcons?"

"I like to snare them," said Girard, laughing.

"And then what do you do with them?"

Girard winked. "Fine things. If you would come to the orchard with me I would show you."

She laughed: "I am not a falcon." But she was as red as her hair ribbon.

Girard made his eyes look tender and said: "Do you know that you are very beautiful?"

Not long afterward Joceran of Puiseaux, who had a knack for arranging assignations and marriages, said to him: "It looks as if Aelis of Bercen were in love with you. You should try to get her."

Girard was not softhearted—a wife, to him, was a dowry, the means of equipping himself and being dubbed at last, either at the count's court or elsewhere. He fell to thinking.

He saw the girl again through the trellis and told her that he was dying for love. She promised to tell her father that she wanted no one for a husband but Girard of Linnières. However, when Joceran questioned Ansiau, the old man said: "Not before he is knighted." And then came Herbert's offer, and there was no more talk of Girard. And Aelis wept.

Easter was hardly celebrated at Linnières that year—there was not money to do it. The hunting was bad, and the cow barn held only three scrawny cows and a calf which Lady Alis resigned herself to roasting for Easter Sunday. The house was half empty—the widows of the crusaders had remarried elsewhere, the younger boys had gone to serve near-by barons. Girard the Young had died about All-Hallows at the age of sixty—Richeut had not yet recovered from the blow; she wept continually and was beginning to go into her dotage. Lady Alis could no longer count on her for help in the housework. And the plate had to be polished and the house set in order for Herbert's wedding. "He could have had the banquet at Hervi," she thought. "It is nearer to the church and he has plenty of servants." But Herbert insisted upon being married in his father's house. He promised to furnish the meat for the banquet, and hangings and wine and presents for the guests—since

Haguenier's death he had lived like a man of high rank; his old father-in-law's hoard was long since spent, but Herbert was lucky at tournaments and dicing.

There was only one table now in the great hall, and that was not full. Of the baron's children, only Alette and Hélie ate at the high table, Joceran and Eglantine were still relegated to the women's corner. In the middle of dinner Eglantine would slip between her father's legs, climb into his lap, and snatch the bone he was picking. He would laugh, and Eglantine would laugh back and pound the bone on the white tablecloth and watch the grease spread over it. Lady Alis pursed her lips and Richeut sighed. Ansiau said, "Enough, my little flower, my pigeon," but she heeded him no more than if he had been talking to a wall.

In his father's presence Girard became as dismal as an owl and stayed in a corner sharpening knives or mending harness. Lady Alis hated to see him unhappy and usually found some way of persuading the baron to go down to the stable—such and such a horse had gone lame, another had scraped his nose. Ansiau grumbled, rose, stretched his huge, bent shoulders. "I'll see to it . . . Come with your father, pigeon, we'll go and see Roussin."

When his father and Eglantine had disappeared, Girard said: "The little whore!"

Herbert arrived four days after Easter, with varlets, hawks, poultry, and dogs—the noise was enough to wake the dead. The baron of Hervi climbed the ladder and entered the hall red-faced, hot, and panting—he was always too hot. He threw off his fur cape, which his squire instantly caught, unbuckled his belt, unfastened the collar of his woolen tunic, and wiped his forehead. Lady Alis went to greet him, touched despite herself at seeing him again, and humbly waited for him to recover his breath. He planted two long, loud kisses on her cheeks. Ansiau, who was sitting by the fire, raised his head and said: "So the bridegroom has arrived." He smiled, for he was glad to see his grown son, but Herbert thought that he was making fun of him and said: "The bridegroom! Why, you married Mahaut off when Garnier of Buchie had been a widower only six weeks."

Herbert behaved toward his parents as if they were backward countryfolk, and had his own varlets wait on him. He had the bathhouse heated, lay there being rubbed and perfumed for six hours, and ate his dinner there. "He thinks the wedding will be tomorrow," Girard snickered. In fact everyone in the family laughed at Herbert's passion for baths. He returned to the keep very late in the evening. His damp hair, blond and shining, hung in little golden ringlets beside his clean, pink face. Lady Alis sighed as she thought that her son left it to others to wash that beautiful hair which she would so gladly have oiled and rubbed with her own hands. No, he needed his mother no longer. Not even to wait on him.

He was handsome, she thought. Not as handsome as Girard, but a very handsome man nevertheless, his mother could be proud of him. He had reached twenty-five. He was as tall as the baron and almost as broad-shouldered. He was extremely fat. Shoulders, chest, belly, and thighs bore layers of fat which only his magnificent frame saved from being repellent. His skin was as white and smooth as a woman's; his small, fat, ring-laden hands had square fingers and long hard nails. His naturally pale face, which was always well shaven, was broad—a series of rolls from his eyelids to his double chin. His round blue eyes, already swamped in fat, had a heavy, intense stare. Alis could not grow used to the thought that so much flesh had come out of herself—how small and thin she looked beside him, a mother sparrow with a cuckoo's chick.

Naturally, the two brothers could not live two days together under the same roof. The quarrel broke out the morning after Herbert's arrival. Herbert was pluming himself on his betrothed, and Girard was foolish enough to interrupt: "Aelis of Bercen! She is nothing to be proud of! I could have her without marrying her, if I liked." Herbert went red and called him a pewling puppy, and Girard threw a knife at his face. Herbert ducked, but his right ear was scratched. Lady Alis rushed between her sons, Herbert caught her by the shoulders and flung her against the wall so hard that she cried out with pain. Herbert retreated, ashamed, and Girard, enraged to see his mother mishandled, ran to his brother and struck him in the face with his fist. Again Lady Alis had to cling to Herbert's arm. The baron, when he heard of the affray, ordered Girard to saddle his horse and go to Seuroi and remain there until the wedding. And that evening Herbert complained bitterly to Lady Alis: "You always stand up for him against me, I am always in the wrong. He cut my ear and hit me in the face, and you will not even let me revenge myself."

"He is a child," said Lady Alis. "And why should you call him a pewling puppy?"

"He might refrain from saying obscene things about my future wife."

"While we are on the subject of your future wife," said Lady Alis, "I think you might have refrained from asking for her when you knew that I wanted her for Girard."

"There you are! Everything for Girard and nothing for me!"

Lady Alis' heart bled when she thought of her Girard shut up in Seuroi, humiliated, fuming with rage. However, she threw herself wholeheartedly into the preparations for the wedding. Despite the badness of the roads Herbert had sent enough cattle and wine to feed a garrison. At Troyes he had bought fittings for the nuptial chamber, and Lady Alis, lost in admiration of the beautiful stuffs, the silken tapestries and fine linen sheets, thought only of displaying them to the best advantage. She even dispatched two varlets and a seamstress to the lady of Bercen to find out what flowers and colors Aelis liked best, and sent her a talking blackbird and a set of laces which Alette had embroidered. She found places for twenty white wax candles in the nuptial chamber, sprinkled the bed with holy water, put dried wild-parsnip flowers under the pillow, and under the mattress a stone extracted from the womb of a magical hind which Flora had lured by her incantations—the stone had the power to make a newly married couple love each other and produce children. Marriage was no light matter—Lady Alis had not forgotten that Herbert's first marriage had been unhappy.

On the Thursday before the wedding day Herbert of Linnières, accompanied by his groomsmen, rode to Bercen to bring away his betrothed—he intended it as a mark of special honor. He cut a fine figure. As he stood on the flower-strewn carpet, a sable cap on his golden hair, a red linen tunic falling in broad folds over his huge body, his chin up, his gloved hands clasping his gilded belt, you would have thought him at least a count or a duke. Ansiau of Bercen could be proud of such a son-in-law.

His groomsmen stood about him: James of Vanlay, Garin of Linnières, his cousins, his friend Aimeri of Le Barnage, and his younger brother Girard, all serious and stiff in their green or blue tunics; beside the imposing groom they looked like children. Herbert did not see his betrothed that day, she did not appear in the hall. Ansiau of Bercen had assembled all his kindred, and kept his future son-in-law at the table all evening. Many a cup was emptied to the health of the bride and groom, many a song was sung in their honor. Girard sat silent with bowed head and drank a great deal—he felt like crying.

He did not know that Aelis was standing by the trellis in the mew, waiting for the kennel door to open. Her mother and her aunts looked for her and called to her everywhere. She did not move; she clung to the trellis, and her heart beat strongly and slowly, then for an anguished instant stopped, then beat again. She was found at last and taken to the ladies' chamber, washed and rubbed and stuffed with apples and cheese and milk, then—for the first and last time in her life—put to bed alone. And then her cousins and the girls who had been her companions bid her good night, one after the other—she must make a vow, she must remember what she dreamed, she . . . Then, to her great grief, they left her to herself.

In the morning there was a Mass in the castle chapel, and then the company set out and rode at an easy pace to Puiseaux; it was a warm day with occasional showers, all along the narrow puddle-strewn road the fields were growing green; the woods were bright with anemones and snowdrops. Joceran of Puiseaux entertained his relatives for the night, Aelis slept in the bed with his daughters. It was a Friday—the men drank only beer and went to bed early. It rained all night, the water ran down the angles of the walls in torrents, the stables were flooded. Girard hoped that the bad weather would hold for three days at least, but in the morning the sky was clear; sparrows and pigeons pecked cheerfully among the puddles.

They had to ride slowly, or all their finery would have been drenched with mud. The bride rode beside her father on a led palfrey. Muffled in her capes and veils, she sat on her white horse as motionless and silent as a saint in procession.

Saturday night Herbert of Linnières received his future father-in-law and his kinsmen at Hervi Castle, greeted them ceremoniously and put them to bed on fresh pallets in the dining room; the ladies went upstairs and Herbert's waiting-women prepared baths for them in big wooden tubs.

Then came the great day—the church and the candles, the bride led in pomp over a red carpet—her dress was so covered with embroidery that it was impossible to see the cloth; her veiled hair fell in long curls on either side of her face; her cheeks burned, her lips were slightly swollen; she looked very much a child as she sat beside the immense frame of her husband. Under his hungry eyes she lowered her own, and all he could see was her little rounded lids.

At Linnières Aelis was received by her new relatives: her father-in-law, a dark, one-eyed giant; her mother-in-law, a thin, pock-marked woman, obviously pregnant, with pale eyes and full, sad lips; her sister-in-law, pretty Mahaut of Buchie with her old husband; Richeut, an old, old lady; and Alette, blond and sweet, charming despite her ruined face, who thenceforth became the bride's first maid-of-honor. (Lady Alis had dressed Alette in her prettiest ribbons and her last blue silk dress, in the hope that one of the men would find her attractive.)

The long dinner began. The men, who had already drunk something, talked very loud and praised the bride's beauty; roasts, carried in on spits, and the other dishes soon filled the high table. Solemn and stiff in the place of honor, the bride and groom smiled and bowed in answer to the toasts.

Ansiau came and went, saw that the wine was brought up, led the minstrels to the middle of the hall; he was gay because he loved festivals—they reminded him of old times—yes, it was a fine wedding. It touched him to see the handsome couple under the shields of Linnières—Herbert so big and strong and blond, Aelis so little and so rosy. To the notes of a hurdy-gurdy, the musicians sang a beautiful old song:

> Now April comes and Easter brings in fee,
> Flower the woods, the meadows all grow green,
> Soft in their beds murmur the flowing streams,
> From dawn to dark the birds sing merrily.
> Ye lovers all, forget not whom you serve,
> Keep well your faith with hearts that never swerve.
> Long have they loved, Aigline and Baron Guy,
> Aigline loves Guy as Guy loves fair Aigline.

"Come, minstrels," said Ansiau. "No more of that! Sing it with their names, and it will sound better."

"Long have they loved, Herbert and Aelis . . ." sang the minstrels.

Herbert put his hot, fat, shaking hand on hers, and Aelis bent her head very low.

Girard, as was the first groomsman's duty, served the bride and groom with wine. When Aelis took the cup from his hands, she burst into sobs, which caused some uneasiness among the ladies. Her mother ran to her, shook her, wiped her eyes, and said that the girl was tired. Mahaut, who was a little drunk, dropped her head on the tablecloth and wept audibly.

Lighted by twenty candles, the nuptial chamber looked like a chapel decked for a holy day. The two fathers, both drunk, talked of Palestine and former times—each of them had left a son in the cemetery at Acre, and it drew them together. And Lady Alis had so much to do that she quite forgot she had spent her own wedding night in this very room—all that was dead and buried, now she had to think of Girard, who was so unhappy, to get the guests back into the hall, to find places for the ladies to sleep that night. . . .

Decked with wreaths of anemones and violets and dressed in white shifts embroidered with red, the bride and groom at last found themselves on their couch with their backs against the pillows. Lady Alis brought the cup of wine which they must drink together; then little by little the room emptied. Ansiau went out last, locking the door behind him.

Very late that night, light could still be seen seeping under the sill of the bathhouse door. Girard, who was drunk, had thundered at the door and shouted: "Hi, you great swine, let me in—I can do it better than you." His friends dragged him back to the courtyard. It was raining, the wind blew out their torches. In the castle bedchamber Lady Alis, stretched on a pallet beside Mahaut, tried to quiet the starts of the child in her womb.

Mahaut was crying. "Lady! Why? I can bear no more. He cannot expect me to put out my eyes. He says that I look at varlets. You will see—as soon as we get back to the castle he will beat me again because there are knights here. It makes me want to . . . I could easily, I have only to say the word."

"Don't do anything foolish, my poor child," said Lady Alis.

"No, lady, I shall not, I only talk about it. Lady! I am wasting away. I am stifling. I don't sleep all night, bleeding is no help. Lady! I want a child! Lady!"

Herbert had found the little black mole and kissed it, and the breasts between which it lay, a hundred times over—he was proud of having a wife with such a charming mole. Nor was that all, of course—Herbert was well versed in the mysteries, never had the countryside seen such a man for turning up women's skirts. He would have paid dear for the girl if he had been buying her—and not only had he not needed to buy her, he was receiving a handsome dowry with her and the reversion of an estate. It was a good piece of business. But the little mole was the best part of it.

He woke in the morning softened and tender—a thing which had never happened to him before—and went to the tannery, which was not in use at the time, to be bathed and rubbed. He sat on a bench, and two squires poured buckets of rain water over his back and chest and struck him with willow branches—Herbert shook himself and stretched and splashed water on everyone around him. He had not been there half an hour before he was impatient to see his wife again—he almost ran to her naked as he was.

Meanwhile the ladies of Linnières and Bercen were examining Aelis and giving her fortifying potions—she had almost fainted and could hardly stand. Lady Alis took her to the keep and put her in Alette's bed, with cold compresses on her head and a hot stone at her feet.

The newly married pair spent ten days at Linnières, then Herbert ordered his men to pack—he wanted to take his young wife to Troyes for the Ascension Day festivities. Before he left, Girard sought him out and said: "Fair brother, I hold nothing against you, neither your marriage nor anything else. If you will buy me a hauberk, a saddle, and a good horse, I will serve you loyally—for ten years if you wish."

Herbert said: "I want nothing to do with you."

Girard threw back his long chestnut locks and raised his chin: "I can well believe it. You are afraid you will find yourself a cuckold."

Herbert turned crimson. "Pewling puppy!" he said.

Girard shouted: "Stinking boar! Do you think I want your wench? One wink and she would come running to me like a bitch."

Herbert threw up his sleeves and stepped back for a swing. Girard had not time to raise his hands.

The crack of bone on bone split his head, and his mouth filled with a warm liquid—stunned, he staggered and fell into the mud of the courtyard.

Usually the baron sided with his elder son, but this time he was furious: Girard had four front teeth broken and his lower lip almost split in two. Herbert must ask his brother's forgiveness and offer him reparation. Lady Alis wept and told Herbert that she would never speak to him again. Faced with this domestic storm, the huge baron of Hervi scratched the back of his neck, puzzled and ashamed. Finally he went to see Girard.

Girard had fever. Lying on the edge of his father's bed, with a wet cloth around his head, he moaned and from time to time leaned over to spit out the bloody saliva which flooded his mouth. Herbert hardly recognized him—all the lower half of his face was swollen; his bleared, feverish eyes seemed to see nothing. Lady Alis sat beside him with her head on her knees, weeping. Herbert thought: "What a fuss over a few broken teeth," and cleared his throat and said: "Girard!"

Lady Alis started up: "What do you want here, you murderer, you brute! You have killed him. He will die. You can see that he is dying." And she wept harder than ever. Herbert left, and returned the following morning with the baron. Girard had spent the night in delirium; now he was exhausted and whimpered in his sleep.

The baron said: "Girard, fair son, wake up—your brother is here and wants to talk to you." Girard made an effort and opened his eyes.

"Girard," said Herbert, "I ask your pardon. I will give you a horse and a jerkin with copper plates and a white woolen tunic."

Girard did not seem to hear him. He said: "A hauberk."

Herbert said: "I cannot ruin myself for you."

And Girard repeated: "A hauberk."

Herbert said: "Take what you are offered and be thankful. It was you who provoked me, and it is I who must pay."

Girard closed his eyes and murmured: "A hauberk."

Lady Alis said: "He is delirious."

Herbert left the next morning after assuring the baron that he would send the things he had promised. "With those," he said, "he can take service under the count or elsewhere, and in time he can earn himself a hauberk."

It was a sight to see Herbert leading his young bride across the hall—he was like a victor carrying his enemy's arms, his eyes modestly cast down and his breast swelling with pride—or like a nurse showing off her baby's first steps and never taking her eyes from him for fear he will fall. Aelis said farewell to her father-in-law and mother-in-law (she would rather have stayed with them, for Lady Alis had been kind to her). Then Herbert picked her up and carried her down to the courtyard, biting at her breasts and belly through her dress.

Despite Lady Alis' forebodings Girard was up after a week's illness. He was thin and weak and had a scar on his lower lip. His caved-in mouth changed him greatly and when he smiled he was a pitiful sight. The smaller children, Joceran and Eglantine, said: "Oh, Girard is an old man now!"

"Beauty, my son," said Lady Alis, "is not what makes a man. Your father had his nose slit when he was eighteen, and he has always been considered handsome. And your grandfather Joceran, my father, had his face split from forehead to chin, and no man ever had more women."

Girard said: "They had their teeth. They were knights." At first he found it difficult to speak, he mumbled. Later he grew used to it.

Then one evening, three days before Ascension Day, when the baron was at Seuroi, Girard came to Lady Alis and told her that he wanted to speak to her alone. She took him to the chapel, sat down on the bench by the wall, and waited, trembling. Girard stood twisting the end of her veil in his fingers. At last he said: "Lady, listen. I did not want to tell you, but I cannot help it. I have to tell you. I am going away."

"Where?" Lady Alis cried. "When? Why?"

"Tomorrow at dawn. I shall take my horse from the stable, put what I need for the journey on his saddle, and set out."

"Where to? Troyes?"

"No . . . I don't know. Anywhere. But not to Troyes. I did not want to say anything, so that the baron would not send after me. But you won't tell him, will you?"

"But why go away?" Lady Alis asked again. "It is madness. You cannot go without knowing where you are going."

"Perhaps I shall go to Acre," said Girard. "Or Cyprus. Or Constantinople."

Lady Alis cried out: "Girard! For God's sake!" He said nothing. "No, no," she said. "You are saying it for spite, you will never do it. In the first place you will need money for your journey."

He said: "There are always kind people to be found in a Christian country.

I am young, I have hands and arms. I have prepared everything: a little lance, knives. I am sure to find a knight bound for the Holy Land, I will take service under him, he will feed me."

"No, no," said Lady Alis, caught off her guard. "That is no way to travel—there are brigands on the roads, they will see at once that you are a nobleman's son—surely you do not mean to beg—and, besides, it is too dangerous—the sea, there are storms and pirates—your father rowed in a Turkish galley for eight months, it was a miracle that he ever escaped. You are too young, you do not know what is in store for you."

"No, lady, I shall always manage. You will see." Sitting on the ground, Girard fondled his mother's trembling hands.

But she went on: "Besides, besides—in the Holy Land you will die of sunstroke, it is too hot. My brother Thibaut died that way. And you know how your grandfather died—the infidels flayed him alive and cut off his head and threw it into a stinking latrine—that is where it was found. And your brother Ansiau. And Garnier too. The country is under a curse."

"I am not afraid," said Girard. "Those who died there are martyrs."

"No, no," said Lady Alis, "no, my fair son. You must not do it."

"Lady," said Girard, "I cannot stay here. You love me, I know. But that stinking swine is the ruler here. The baron lets him do just as he pleases. I know that he has two hauberks, one for battle, the other for tournaments. And he has squires and horses and a squirrel cloak and three swords—he has everything! I humbled myself, I promised to serve him—and I would have done it, lady, I swear. I would have served him well. He would not have me. Because of the wife he stole from me, because he was jealous. It is not my fault that I am handsomer than he is. . . . And now he has disfigured me. I should be ashamed to show myself hereabouts with no teeth in my mouth, the girls would laugh at me. But once I have won my spurs in the Holy Land, I will come back—he'll see. Yes, he'll see. And he shall not laugh at me again."

"My child," said Lady Alis, "do not say such things. He will change his mind, I warrant you, he means no harm. He will make you proper amends."

"Never," said Girard. "I will accept nothing from him. Why, even you are defending him. And naturally—he is rich, he is the master, he spits silver and pisses gold. He is a crusader, he has seen Jerusalem—for what it may be worth to have belonged to an accursed mob who never could take Jerusalem and then came home to boast of what they had done! Is it my fault that I did not take the cross? I was too young. The baron robbed me of the whore of Nangi, and I could say nothing; now Herbert has robbed me of Aelis of Bercen, and I said nothing either—you saw it yourself. I have had enough. I will owe nothing to either of them. I am going away, the world is wide; I am through with rotting in this filthy forest, this filthy courtyard—I cannot bear the sight of them for longing to be gone. Lady! Tomorrow I shall be on the highroad, tomorrow I shall be on the road to Tonnerre. Next day I shall be at Vézelay."

"And your mother, Girard?" Lady Alis said. "Does it mean nothing to you to leave me?"

"Indeed it does, lady, it makes me sad. And leaving Hélie too, and my cousin Joceran. But go I must—there is no room for me here."

"I will talk the baron into doing whatever you want," said Lady Alis. "Girard, my sun, my life, you will see—I will manage everything. You shall have what you need. Only stay!"

But Girard clung to his idea: he must leave the next morning at dawn. "If you keep me here by force, I will kill myself," he said. "I will not stay in this castle another day, another hour. It makes me vomit. I am stifling here."

Lady Alis wept. She said: "Have pity on me at least. Wait until I am delivered—it is only three months. You will kill me." But Girard cared nothing for her child, and he could not conceive that his mother would ever die.

Lady Alis stayed up all night. She took the relics of St. Fiacre and St. Mamas which she had always worn on her chain and sewed them into her son's clothes; she had no money, but among his things she put an embroidered girdle which he could sell—she would embroider another for Alette. For the last time she combed his long hair, buckled his belt, laced his gaiters. Then she knelt before him, pressed her head against his thigh, and wept noiselessly in little gasps.

"Lady," said Girard, "stand up—they will guess."

She rose and wiped her eyes. "Come here," she said, "come closer, I want to bless you—they are not looking. There—your hands and your forehead and your chest—above all, beware of cold winds. I will look for you every day. Girard, if you loved me, you would not go!"

Girard kissed her fervently. "But I do love you! You will see—I shall be rich. I shall be famous in the countryside. I shall take you to live with me, and the baron and Herbert will have to swallow it—you'll see. Lady, I bid you farewell. And tell the baron that I am at Puiseaux. In a week you can tell Alette all about it—and tell her that I will bring back a fine knight from the Holy Land to marry her."

The old house was even emptier and more silent after Girard left. When Ansiau learned what had happened he shrugged his shoulders and pretended to regard the matter with contempt. But at heart he felt remorseful—he had not been just to his younger son; Girard had been such a gay, lively boy, and so tractable if you took him the right way. "He will come back," said the baron. "He will be home before Assumption Day. Certainly before winter. And I will teach him not to make his mother cry." Lady Alis was brought to bed before Pentecost—the child lived only three days. But she was too weak to mourn for it.

She knew that a new blow awaited her—Hélie's departure. And, as soon as she had recovered, she devoted all her energies to her beautiful boy who was to leave her. For four years it had been settled that Hélie should go to the monastery of Saint-Florentin to learn Latin and the Mass and the Offices.

Hélie was nine. When he was four, he fell and broke his leg for the first time. He had been well cared for, the fracture had healed quickly; then, three months later, he fell again, and broke the same leg and his left arm. Afterward he broke the other leg too, in two places. He was a very active child—he climbed every ladder and every roof and always wanted to ride the most spirited horses. Then one day he broke his hip bone and had to lie in bed for three months.

The baron felt uneasy, for none of his other children had been so brittle-boned. "It is because he was born forty days early," he thought. And Lady Alis, who knew very well why he was born forty days early, told herself that nothing could be done. God was punishing the child for being the fruit of an adulterous union. And each time Hélie had an accident she only bowed her head lower and hardly dared to complain for fear that even worse was in store.

Sure that such a delicate child would never make a soldier, Ansiau decided to consecrate him to God. "He will be strong enough to say Mass and write on parchment. And at least the monks will make him stop running and climbing roofs."

Lady Alis thought it an excellent plan—Hélie was taken to the church of St. Florentin, dedicated to God, and shown to the abbot of the monastery. The abbot wanted to take him as a novice immediately, but Lady Alis insisted upon five years' grace, for she feared that Hélie would sicken with grief if he were parted from his mother.

Ever since then, Father Aimeri had been teaching Hélie to read and write.

At nine Hélie was tall, very thin, and very blond. He was rather pale, because he did not often go outdoors and, even in the courtyard, stayed in the shade—he was subject to sunstrokes and had bad headaches. Enviously he watched the young varlets running along the stable roof—he could never do it again, his right leg had knitted badly and left him with a limp, and raising his legs too high gave him pains in the back.

As a small child he had been irritable and violent: he hit his playfellows, scratched Alette and Herbert's daughter Aelis, he was capable of crying and stamping for hours on end when he was refused a toy—he could still remember those days. Then he had found himself forced to lie in bed for weeks, with his leg strapped between two boards—how it had hurt when he tried to move! He was so happy when he recovered, he went back to his games, turned somersaults in the courtyard, and—bang!—all was to do again, again a leg or an arm was strapped between boards; it swelled, the skin became dead and gray, was covered with boils and scabs. Hélie did not even want to cry—it did no good. He held his mother's cheeks tight in his wasted hands when she came to bless him at night, and asked—as if he were asking a riddle—"Lady, can I get up tomorrow? Lady, suppose I could get up tomorrow after all?" And when he got up he found he could only limp slowly and painfully, it took him a long time to recover his strength. And when he was strong enough to go into the meadow and pick flowers he was as happy as a king, he laughed and clapped his hands.

After that his great joy was his letters. In the first place, he had been very proud of knowing them because Lady Alis had told him that you had to be better than other children to learn them—"It shows that God loves you, or he would not let you learn." The baron himself could barely read his name, and Lady Alis did not know *a* from *b*. Hélie had been frightened in the beginning, then he had seen that it was easy enough; each letter had its own face, there were beautiful ones and ugly ones, good ones and bad ones. In his dreams he saw *s* and *i* fighting, and armies of *m*'s marching against a huge *D* decorated with horns and tendrils. It was even finer after he had learned words: *Dominus, miles, eques, puer, ara, ave*—Father Aimeri took his hand and guided it over sand strewn on the chapel floor. Hélie could hardly believe it when at last he could write a word himself; he did not know what the words meant— explain as Father Aimeri might, Hélie could not believe him—clearly those written words were something so beautiful that Father Aimeri could not bring himself to tell a little boy like Hélie about them, and so he simply said that *dominus* meant lord, and *avis* bird. And what Hélie loved most of all was the *Ave Maria:* the *A* at the beginning and then the three words ending in *a*'s one right after the other—*Maria Gratia Plena,* like three lances beside three round shields—and then *Dominus,* like a harrow, and the shorter *Tecum,* like a double fork—and presently the three words with *a*'s became three beautiful ladies lightly stepping a dance, and *Dominus* was a church with vaults and columns, and *Tecum* was the choir; and, farther on, *Benedictus* had a sound of little bells and vibrant voices—when he copied it Hélie always hummed— he had a pretty voice, and he was the only person who did not know it. As for *Ave,* he always made it too big, he took it for a bird spreading its wings. And how he loved the *a*'s and *b*'s which he could curve and bend at the joints and draw out at the narrow places. Father Aimeri was amazed at the beauty of his letters—he did not know that the child saw flowers and stars in them.

Hélie had a straight, very delicate nose with full, translucent nostrils, very cleanly-drawn lips, and eyes that were big and very blue. Father Aimeri, who adored him, said to Lady Alis: "The face of an angel! The grace of God is upon the boy, never was there a child in the countryside so beautiful." And Lady Alis dared say nothing, for she saw in him a treacherous likeness to a certain brother-in-law of the baron's. Erard had died in Palestine—that she knew; and, strangely enough, she had felt almost nothing when she learned of it; but friends of his might come to Linnières—Manesier of Coagnecort, for example—and Erard's face was not easy to forget. And she combed Hélie's hair back from his forehead, because Erard had always worn a bang.

Lady Alis could hardly contain her pride each time she saw her little boy perched on a stool and spelling out the Latin words in the great Missal that lay on the high wrought-iron lectern. Sometimes she turned the pages at random herself, to make sure that he was not simply repeating something he had learned by heart—and her mouth fell open and she caught her breath when she saw him read without hesitation wherever she opened the book. And the baron liked to display Hélie's learning to his guests, he shook his head and said: "A fine thing. A gift from God. He will certainly be an abbot or a prior." And he rubbed his single eye and his nose.

Hélie was a charming boy and everyone loved him. He was sometimes angry and impatient, but how could you blame a child who could neither run nor bend suddenly without turning white for pain? He was so used to it that he always smiled when it happened, as if he were asking to be excused. He had a mocking turn of mind and loved to invent nicknames for everyone and everything. His world contained a Lady Longnose, a Lady Rosary, a girl named Nose-in-the-Air and another named Goosefoot, then there were the grooms, Cherry and Freckles and Sleighbell—the big stable was the barony because the baron spent so much time there, the cow barn was the dairy, the well was Magpie Tower because the kitchen maids gathered there to chatter. One evening Hélie gleefully said: "Lady, I have found names for fat Garin and my cousin Joceran—I shall call Joceran Swarthy, like our black mare—he looks like her, doesn't he?" He laughed shrilly, and Lady Alis said: "What nonsense!" Sometimes Hélie's laugh made her shudder—she saw Erard sitting at her feet, with his head on her lap, at Troyes . . . he was so young then. Hélie was not like Girard—he was less stormy, more intelligent—but they were both very affectionate sons. However, in Hélie's case Lady Alis felt a little jealous, for he was very fond of the baron too, and of Alette and Father Aimeri—he sought caresses as a little lizard seeks the sun—he clung to the baron and rubbed his face against his belt, to Eglantine's great annoyance.

Then, too, there were Hélie's loves—all the little girls in the castle were his loves, Eglantine included. But his favorite was Marguerite, a granddaughter of Lady Richeut's (Lady Longnose, as Hélie called her). Marguerite was eight, her hair was almost white, she wore a blue dress, and because she loved to run in the meadow she had tanned cheeks and a sprinkling of freckles—her face was all pink and gold. When Hélie was able to go into the meadow it was usually Marguerite with whom he played "bride and groom," they wove wreaths of leaves and flowers for their heads and sprinkled each other with water which Hélie had solemnly blessed, saying: *Vobiscum tecum quidquid benedictus spiritus,* while Marguerite opened her mouth in wonder. Then they lay on a bed of grass by the stream and Marguerite's little playmates threw flowers on them, and then they kissed each other again and again.

But when Hélie said to his mother: "When I grow up I shall marry Marguerite," Lady Alis turned away and sighed.

"And then I shall marry Perronnelle and Eglantine, too," he said dreamily.

"Silly! Eglantine is your sister."

"But she is pretty—I like to kiss her eyes. If only she weren't so young."

"Besides, you can't marry three wives," said Lady Alis, laughing.

"Then I will be a priest and write it on paper that a man can marry three wives. And even four, because I want Sleighbell's Gillette too."

Hélie had to be told that one day he would go to Saint-Florentin to stay. Lady Alis explained to him that it was a place where there were beautiful big books all full of painted pictures, and that the chanting was much lovelier than at Hervi, and that the monks had a garden and an orchard and a fountain with stone statues of the Virgin and St. John, all painted with gold and the prettiest colors—God knows what other wonders she conjured up to prove to Hélie how happy he would be in the monastery. Hélie stroked her cheeks with his gentle hands. "Very well, lady," he said; then, wheedlingly: "So long as you will be with me." Lady Alis had not the heart to tell him that she would not stay with him at the monastery.

The baron, however, was not anxious to part with Hélie. He felt uneasy about him. "The monks will beat him," he said. "He is not strong enough yet. We will wait until next Easter." And then, just before Assumption Day, Hélie fell as he was running and struck his head so hard against a corner of the wall that for several days he hovered between life and death. He had such violent convulsions and vomited so much that everyone was amazed so weak a child could survive it. In her desperation Lady Alis said to her husband: "It is because we have tried to cheat God. Let us vow to take him to the monastery as soon as he recovers—then perhaps God will be merciful." So the vow was taken, and Hélie gradually recovered. His parents dared put off his departure no longer—as soon as he could walk, the baron had horses saddled and Lady Alis packed her son's belongings.

It was only two hours' ride from Linnières to Saint-Florentin. Riding pillion, Hélie clung conscientiously to his father's belt and looked now to one side, now to the other. The road followed the Armançon. On the farther shore beeches, birches, and hazel copses were reflected in the rippling water; the coolness which rose from the river made Hélie's nostrils dilate with pleasure, he drew the air deep into his lungs and blinked his eyes in the sunshine. The high grass on the bank swayed and trembled under the sun's hot rays; where the river turned, the water was shot with flecks of light—it hurt his eyes to look at it. The baron's back was warm and smelled of leather. In the monastery fields, on the other side of the road, grasshoppers chirped and rasped, and, listening to them, Hélie wanted to go to sleep and never hear any other sound. He was a little tired, but happy. Lady Alis rode just behind him, he had only to turn and she would smile at him.

The prior of the monastery was well acquainted with the baron of Linnières and his lady; ever since their land had been mortgaged, he regularly sold them wheat and fodder; Ansiau could never pay cash, was hopelessly in arrears, and sent his varlets to work for the monks. Nevertheless, the relations between the two men were amicable. The baron of Linnières was courteous and affable; since the death of his concubine he went to church and received the sacraments, and no one could say a word against him. Hélie was well received. The prior—corpulent and dressed in an ample maroon habit, with a silver cross on his breast—patted the boy's cheek with his heavy red hand. Hélie clung to his mother's knees. "He is as pretty as a girl," said the prior. "I have a little niece who looks much like him, her name is Agnes. Our sacristan will look out for him. We have six more boys of the same age, one of them is the son of a viscount." Then he began talking crops and hunting with Ansiau. Hélie put his arm around his mother's neck and tried to think of a nickname for the prior.

Then Lady Alis said: "Hélie, Joceran has a stomach-ache. I must go and take care of him, I feel very uneasy about him. I will go home to Linnières and come back tomorrow if everything is going well."

"And if it isn't?" said Hélie desperately.

"Then I will come back day after tomorrow. Be a good boy and don't make me ashamed of you."

She said good-bye to him so cheerfully that he suspected nothing. He was in ecstasies, he stammered with delight. "Lady, you will see, there are such beautiful things here. Father Odoul showed me his book and he will show me the chapel tomorrow. And tell Father Aimeri that there is a D here with St. Lawrence inside it on his grill, and blue stars and red flames—and I am to see the sacristy when my turn comes." He was so sure that he would see his mother on the next day that he hardly noticed it when she left.

Home at Linnières once more, Lady Alis paced up and down the great bed-chamber for a long time, not knowing what work to take up—she always had more work than she could get through, but today everything seemed useless. Of all her children, only Joceran and Alette were still with her—Joceran, whom she loved less than any of the others, and Alette, who had been with her only too long—the girl was nineteen now. Her grandchildren, Aelis and Hague-nier, were one in Troyes, the other in Normandy in the service of a high baron of the dukedom—Herbert did not deign to bring up his children as his father and grandfather had done before him.

That evening she quarrelled with the baron—over Eglantine, naturally. Eglantine was a difficult child. Recently she had begun waking in the middle of the night with piercing shrieks, sobbing and saying that she felt afraid. She had to be taken into the big bed and rocked and soothed—the baron could manage it better than any nurse—then she would chatter and sing and not fall asleep again until the night was far advanced. At first the baron thought nothing of it. Then it began happening almost every night, and the child became more and more difficult to soothe. Sometimes she would feel frightened in broad daylight. She said that she saw the Devil. Then the baron lost his head, talked of witchcraft—and naturally Lady Alis was the first whom he accused.

That evening Eglantine had been more frightened than ever before, so the baron was in a terrible humor. He said: "What have you done to my little girl?"

"Nothing, baron, as you very well know."

"What have you done to her? How have you bewitched her? You can see that she is not what she used to be. She is fading away. You have sworn to be her death."

"You wrong me," said Lady Alis, "you know that I treat her like a daughter."

"I know that you killed her mother," said the baron, "and Juliana and An-drée. And you want to kill her as well."

"I swear to you, baron, that I have done nothing. When I have sent for

466

Flora, it has been to cure my babies—and for Mahaut, too. May God afflict me with leprosy if ever I wished the child harm."

"I know how you received her when she was born," said the baron somberly. "I know how much good you ever wished her mother. Tell me—have I ever insulted you or beaten you? Have I ever harmed you? Do you remember asking me if I wanted to repudiate you and marry Milicent? Did I do it? I could have. I should have kept her dowry and Eglantine would not be a bastard. And I would not do it. You have found a strange way to repay me!"

"What do you expect of me, baron? I do what I can. If the child was born with a weakness, it has nothing to do with me."

"I tell you that she was not born as she is—someone has ruined her. You and Flora have ruined her."

Lady Alis expected an outburst of anger, but she heard the baron's voice grow hoarse and sink into a rhythmical groaning that sounded like the baying of a dog—on the pillow beside her she felt him torn by such violent sobs that the mattress shook—she touched his shoulder, he pushed her away. She wanted to comfort him, to caress him as if he were a child. But she was tired and sleepy, she shut her eyes.

The next morning she said that she had dreamed of Mahaut and wanted to visit her; she had horses saddled, took Milon and Silette with her, and set out for Buchie.

Alis found it strange to be the mother-in-law of a man ten years older than herself. Garnier of Buchie was past fifty, but he bore his years lightly. He hunted the stag, went to tournaments, and spent his days in travel and visiting his estates. But this time Lady Alis found him at home. He was receiving his bailiffs and drawing up the accounts of his wheat and barley harvest—when Lady Alis learned of it, her first thought was to borrow two or three sacks of wheat. The baron of Buchie was courteous—he led his mother-in-law into his castle with many a bow and ordered his daughter Marsan to have a bath and a change of clothes prepared for her.

Lady Alis found Mahaut lying pale and languid in her bed. "God bless you! Are you ill?" she cried.

Mahaut shook her head and kissed her mother on the lips; she seemed preoccupied. "No," she said, "no, it is nothing. . . . Lady, it was so good of you to come! Tell me about home. How is everybody? What is Alette doing? And Hélie? . . . But don't tell me now—I could not listen. I did not mean to tell you, but—I think everything is all right!" Her little pale face shone—in the shadow of the bed curtains it looked as if illuminated from within.

Lady Alis said: "God keep you! Are you certain?"

"Not yet. Oh, I am so afraid I may be wrong. That is why I am lying down—I told Garnier that I have lumbago. I think it was your last remedy that did it." She let her head drop on her mother's hands and rubbed her forehead against them as she had done when she was a child. "Lady, it will be so good.

I am even afraid to speak of it. I will not say a word to anyone before the fourth month—otherwise his sons would soon put a spell on me. And I am so afraid!" She pressed her hands to her temples. "I am so afraid that they will do something to me. Yet they know very well that no child of mine will inherit the fief—but they are wicked. Thomas (he is the eldest) would like to have me sleep with him—that is why he persecutes me—and his wife is jealous and sends her children to piss on my clotheschest, they have ruined it."

"When do you expect it?" Lady Alis asked, and again Mahaut's face was lighted by a beatific smile.

"Hush. Not a word! In May, I think—not before. You will come, won't you? You shall be first godmother."

On her way back to Linnières Lady Alis stopped at St. Anne's-in-the-Forest and burned a candle for Mahaut. When she reached home she felt a little less sad.

On the fourteenth of September—Holy Cross Day—Herbert came to Linnières with his young wife, who was pregnant—he was sure that no one could take better care of her than Lady Alis. They were quite a devoted couple. Herbert was swollen with pride, his thick lips and double chin seemed on the point of bursting—he strutted about his little Aelis, covered her shoulders with a shawl, felt her wrists and kissed her on the mouth every few minutes —it was nothing but "My wife this," "My wife that"—he seemed to think his parents did not know that Aelis was his wife. Aelis was docile and affectionate to her husband—she leaned on his arm and smiled back at him. But deep in her eyes there was fear.

Herbert hoped to be a father about the end of January.

"I leave her with you, lady," he said to his mother. "Take good care of her. I have business in Troyes, but I shall come back after All-Hallows. And make very sure that she is not left alone with young men, eh? If you see anything, give her a good beating, but not on the belly because of the child."

Ansiau did not know what to do: he had taken the child to Hervi and Saint-Florentin and Bar-on-Seine to be exorcised and he thought she was cured—and then, on the day of the Nativity of the Virgin, she had come to him crying and said that a Devil was lurking by the ladder to make her fall, she did not dare go down into the courtyard. Her father tried to soothe her—there was no Devil, he saw none, nobody had seen one, she was imagining nonsense. But the child insisted: "He is all hairy. And covered with horns. And eyes. He is yellow all over." Ansiau had taken her in his arms and carried her down to the courtyard—as they went through the door, Eglantine had given a piercing shriek: "Ouch! he pinched me."

Then Ansiau sat down at the foot of the ladder and put his elbows on his knees and his hands in his hair.

Eglantine first became acquainted with the Devil when she was five and a half. He was of all sizes, in every shadowy corner, in the water, by the hearth, above all in the dark. She did not know what he looked like, his face was always different—sometimes he had only one eye, sometimes a hundred. At night in her cradle beside the sleeping Joceran, she passed the time by conjuring up his different forms before her closed eyes: snouts, swollen tongues, bloodshot eyes, flayed cheeks, a belly with horns, ears on his arms; and then the things she imagined set her crying. She could think of nothing else. And when she was taken to one church or another to be cured of the Devil she had only to stare straight before her and she saw him coming out of the priest's mouth or slipping from behind the altar; she said so aloud, everyone crossed himself in horror, and then she said it again because she was proud of frightening them.

She did not herself know how it came about that she thrashed her feet and hands and screamed and gritted her teeth—it was not by her own will. When she did it her father held her very tight to keep her from moving, and with him she became calm; everyone else only made her scream the harder and go into convulsions.

For her, the world was the baron, and the baron ought to give all his time to her. Otherwise she was lost, she did not know what to make of anything —he kissed Hélie or Joceran—it must be to annoy her, what pleasure could he take in kissing Hélie or Joceran? And when he talked to Lady Alis or Milon she wanted to pull him by the sleeve—why did he do such horrid things? Eglantine and the baron spent their time together doctoring horses, training dogs, and she really believed that she worked as hard as he did, though most of the time she sat quietly on the ground with her arms around her knees. And afterwards she would say to Joceran: "I bandaged Courante's legs." For which she was called a liar.

When the baron was not there Eglantine wanted to be like other little girls. She loved to run and wade in puddles and dance rounds. Yet when she tried to play with the others, she was usually beaten and put out of the game— there she stood, her mouth wide open with indignation—if only her father knew how cruel they were to his Eglantine! She was not aware that she always took the best place and jostled the others, she loved them all, she asked nothing better than to be nice. Then gradually they began flinging ugly names at her: liar, cheat, uglyface, bastard. And she answered: "Uglyface yourself! Bastard yourself!" And as soon as the baron came back she suddenly remembered how she had been insulted and began to cry. And when the baron was there the Devil came much oftener. She did not do it on purpose—but when her father was near she felt so little, so weak, the Devils were so strong, she was so sorry for herself.

And when Ansiau learned that his child had been called a bastard he went into a black fury and told Lady Alis that he would not allow the word to be spoken in Eglantine's presence—whoever did it again he would chastise with his own hands.

"Father," Eglantine asked, "what is a bastard?"

"Nothing, my pigeon—it is just an ugly word."

"What can I do?" he asked himself. "What can I do?" The child was ill, she had been ruined—he no longer accused Lady Alis, but his suspicions were not disarmed, he searched for some hidden enemy. Meanwhile, Eglantine did just as she pleased—her illness excused everything. As the years passed she was to lose her fear of the Devil. But she never lost her habit of crying and saying that she felt afraid, because she knew that it was a legitimate way to make her father do whatever she wished.

Herbert came back after All-Hallows, bringing news that the king of England was dead. Ansiau lay down on the ground and said that he too wished to die, he would not outlive the best knight in Christendom. "Why did I not enter his service?" he said. "I would have thrown myself in front of him, I would have received the arrow which wounded him. He must have been ill served, he must have been betrayed, I know that there are no men so devoted to him as his old comrades of the Holy Land. Why did I not follow him? We all preferred our houses and our wives, we all forgot the man who saved us. We have been well punished. Never shall we have joy on earth again, for he is dead."

"He had to die one day," said Herbert.

"Well spoken, fair son—he had as many years to live as I, neither more nor less, and I am still alive. And I tell you that never shall I know joy in my lifetime again, for I am alive and a man a thousand times my better is dead. Know, fair son, that the land of France is poorer by his death than if it had lost a hundred thousand men. Never again, until the end of the world, will Christendom see such prowess and such courtesy."

1209.

Lady Alis was fifty-two, her husband fifty-four. Of the children born to them after Joceran, only one had lived, a girl of five named Mary. God! Those ten years which had passed so heavily, so emptily for the baron, how full of life they had been for Lady Alis! She had no time to be bored or to drowse. Now, when she thought back over them, she shook her head and wondered when and how she could ever rest.

Hélie, so ill that she must visit him every week—that was her great worry at present. Her heart sank each time she saw him coming toward her along the cloister—the tall, thin figure in the maroon habit, the uncertain, limping gait, the stooped shoulders—and that golden hair cut short and tonsured. . . . In the beautiful, over-delicate face, she recognized the sharp folds of the nostrils, the chiselled lips, the curve of the beetling eyebrows, the beautiful head of the fair knight who had loved her—and now she did not even remember it, she did not remember that he had loved her, he was Hélie's father, and that was all; and Hélie's face was marked with their sin, and he did not know it, poor boy. No one knew it—for who now would remember the face of the beautiful Erard of Baudemant?

Hélie had a very pure smile which brought long dimples into his cheeks and filled his eyes with malicious gleams; he had a gay wit, he always found something funny to say; he was the spoiled child of the monastery. For ten months headaches and pains in the back prevented him from working; he could hardly attend the services—it was a great pity, the prior-said, for Brother Hélie had a gift for writing, already he was entrusted with the finest pieces of parchment, he could have become a good illuminator too. Long ago Father Arnoul, who painted the capitals and the first pages, had let the boy look after his paints. Hélie could mix them better than anyone. Then he would take a piece of spoiled parchment and try to draw letters and forms, to understand why a particular red went with a particular blue and what colors harmonized and what colors jarred with each other. At night he lay awake for hours, thinking about the folds in the Virgin's robe, or the curls and strands of an angel's hair, by day he tried to sketch surcoats and hands and leaning bodies—and he could not always draw the lines he wanted—it almost made him weep with rage.

Then one day Father Arnoul looked at the swarming lines and colors on his papers and exclaimed: "Praise God! Who taught you this?"

"You, Father."

"That is not how I work. A heavenly angel has guided your hand, my child—this is very beautiful. One day you shall work for the glory of God and our monastery. I must show this to the prior."

And Hélie spent his days and nights among flowers and stars and the robes and crowns of saints; the colors he mixed were so pure that even the least instructed brothers came to admire them and shook their heads and said: "It is Paradise." But for Hélie it was a labor, and he soon wore himself out. Now he could no longer sit with his back bent—lying on his trestle bed, he opened his eyes wide and, against the wall of his cell, he saw great letters decorated with beasts and fish, S's made of snakes, winged lions, birds with women's heads, St. Peter and St. Paul, Adam and Eve. Frowning, he tried to clarify the lines, to intensify the colors—sometimes he panted because the effort was so great. But he had neither parchment nor brushes, and all his visions slowly faded, and he forgot them. Yet he was sure he had never put anything so beautiful on paper.

And Lady Alis thought that there was room in her heart for no one but Hélie, her sick child. Yet when she returned to the castle, there were her grandchildren, Herbert's children, and little Mary—one was constipated, another had fever, and she was panic-stricken, she said her rosary, prepared herbs, and her heart grew even fuller, even heavier, she could bear no more. . . .

Ten years of life. When she had passed forty she thought that there was little left for her to do in this world. Her children married, or gone from home, or dead, her husband occupied elsewhere (he had concubines among the maids, above all he had Eglantine), she had thought of herself as free and useless. She had even called Milon back to the castle; Girard and Mahaut were no longer there to chide her—she was weary and alone, she needed a friend. The heart played strange tricks—she did not love Joceran, her youngest child. Milon had a head like a boar's, but Alis, who had known him for twenty years, no longer noticed it. He was a demanding and jealous lover—it was as if he wanted to make up for lost time. He was four years younger than Lady Alis, and now it was her turn to be almost afraid of losing him, she was very jealous. She usually managed to send the baron to Seuroi or Saint-Florentin or Hervi, and then she had the big bed for herself and Milon. Milon was silent and solemn as the Pope—he had his pride as an old servitor, he would not accept the smallest gift, he turned to stone at the least reproach, he was very jealous of the baron, and Lady Alis had a real battle each time her husband came to pass a night in the great bed—usually he slept somewhere else, holding that he was the master even if he lay on straw. He was never afraid of compromising his dignity. He had a sweetheart named Brune, who every year produced healthy bastards, to Lady Alis' great humiliation. Her own babies did not live. She had finally ceased grieving over them; she spent her time mending Milon's clothes or laying out clean ones for him or treating his wounds—he was such a reckless hunter! Even so, she had to beg him to accept these small services; he said: "You do not need to pay me." Lady Alis laughed at his foibles, but it was because she was fond of him; she had become calm and placid, she was growing a little fat, she drowsed through the hour after dinner, which she had never done before, and sometimes found time to walk in the meadow with her women. Her work did not suffer, on the contrary. It was restful—a man who had two eyes and two nostrils, who was not tormented by fevers—a man not burdened with Mahaut's unhappy marriage, with Girard's departure, with Alette's lack of a husband, with Milicent and her two dead daughters—a man who had no cause to reproach her and whom she had no cause to reproach. She bore two children which she believed were Milon's, one of them lived eleven months; when it died Milon's eyes were red for three days.

The baron, of course, suspected nothing—he thought that his wife was too old. Besides, he was Ansiau, baron of Linnières; he had been famous through the countryside for thirty years—no one would steal his wife, as no one would steal his old sword from the place where it hung beneath his shield. Wife and sword alike could serve but one man.

The excessive intimacy between Lady Alis and her steward had been accepted in the castle without surprise, almost without blame—Lady Alis was so respected that her people behaved toward her as if she had received permission from the Pope to live with Milon of Le Cagne. No one talked of it, but everyone was sure that for Lady Alis there was neither law nor sin—better than anyone else she knew what she might and might not do.

Then in time Mahaut learned of it. Mahaut was a great lady, now that she had disposed of her stepsons; after little Garnier was born she had wheedled the old baron into turning his sons out of the castle. Now she reigned there, and varlets and vassals trembled before her. She had arrived at Linnières clad in marten fur and fine Flanders cloth and riding a Persian palfrey as coppery as her own hair. She had run to Lady Alis, caught her by the shoulders, held her and shaken her: "Is it true, lady? Is it true? And Herbert has not killed the man? Then I shall kill him. *You*, lady!"

Lady Alis had sworn that she did not understand.

"People are talking. Lady, send Milon away, I do not want him to stay here."

"My daughter, I shall never send away a man who has served me for more than twenty years—he rocked you on his knees."

"Then I will tell the baron. I will tell my husband, and he will kill him. I loathe him!" She dropped her head on her mother's knees and wept. The next day Milon returned to Seuroi, and Lady Alis saw him only two or three times a month.

After little Garnier, who had lived, Mahaut had no more children and wanted no more. Garnier was all beauty, nothing could equal him, any other children she might bear would be only little abortions, she saw them lifeless and cold; Garnier had taken all that she had to give, she could not believe that she had ever brought forth such a miracle. She wanted him to be a prince or a duke, and he was not even heir to Buchie—but she knew how to go about getting that for him at least, she was not the beautiful Mahaut of Linnières if she could not make her old husband obey her. She had already persuaded him to send a petition to the bishop of Troyes: his first wife, it set forth, had been related to him in the fourth degree, his sons by her were therefore bastards, he wished to have his youngest son Garnier recognized as his sole legitimate heir. However, Mahaut's stepsons were of no mind to be proclaimed bastards, and she was perpetually going to Troyes, where she appeared in court, lost her temper, argued with clerks and advocates, beat her fist on the table, did what execution she could with her beautiful eyes. Back home at Buchie once more, she wept with rage. Then, too, little Garnier was delicate, at four he looked like a child of three, he often cried and flew into wild rages. And every month Mahaut sent a messenger to Lady Alis at Linnières—she must come at once, Garnier was not well, Garnier was wasting away. Lady Alis lost her head and arrived at full gallop, with her horses winded and her dress splashed with mud. Mahaut, lying on the floor beside Garnier's cradle, would be beating her head against the flagstones. "Lady! If he dies I will kill myself." Lady Alis took the child up, rocked him, caressed him, and always succeeded in curing him. Then she would go home, for she always had things to do at Linnières. But the little boy was never out of her mind—he had bow legs and there were dark blotches under his eyes, but otherwise he was pretty, the image of Mahaut. When he was five Lady Alis persuaded her daughter to make a pilgrimage with her and present little Garnier to Our Lady of Vézelay—after that he seemed to do better.

Then a husband for Alette appeared—a squire in the service of the viscount of Bar-on-Seine. Alette was twenty-three at the time, and Lady Alis had given up all hope of seeing her married. And then the fool of a girl had said that she would never marry!—she had the greatest respect for her parents, but the marriage state was not to her taste, she preferred to remain single. The baron had shouted, Lady Alis had wept, Alette had remained calm and smiling, but as decided as ever—in marriage there was nothing but sin and grief, she was happy in her present state. The baron overrode her refusal, and it was settled that the wedding should take place on Low Sunday. And the night before, Alette disappeared, leaving her shoes, her woolen dress, and her girdle lying on the bank of the river.

For three weeks the baron scoured the countryside with his men, but he found no trace of his daughter. Presumably she had drowned herself in the Armançon. But Lady Alis was certain that she had not, and every time a pilgrim or traveller stopped at Linnières she asked if he had not seen a tall, blond, pock-marked damsel. Often the answer was yes, but closer questioning showed that the damsel was not Alette.

That summer the woodcutters and poachers who haunted the forest of Traconne, near Sézanne, some fifteen leagues from Troyes, began finding crosses everywhere—crosses made of twigs, carved in bark, cut in moss, big and little, on the paths, at the edge of the forest, in glades. And one day in a glade a herdboy who was looking for a stray cow saw a beautiful damsel with blond braids—barefoot and wearing a white shift, she knelt before a tree from which hung a great cross made of branches and decked with flowers. The boy had thrown himself on his knees in adoration, and there the damsel stayed, motionless as a statue; then the boy had run away, and had found his cow almost immediately. No one saw the damsel after that, but there was much talk about her; some said that she was a saint, others thought her a madwoman. However that might be, the legend of the damsel who lived in the forest of Traconne spread through the region, priests had come from Sézanne and Nogent to see the strange girl who strewed the forest with crosses. Clearly the bears and wolves did not touch her, for new crosses were always being found. And toward Christmas a woodcutter coming out of his cabin stumbled upon a woman in a faint. She was barefoot and wore a white shift, and she was suffering less from cold than from hunger. Taken to Montgenest Castle, near Villenauxe, she was received by the baron himself, who was proud to offer his hospitality to the famous recluse of the forest; but when the girl stubbornly refused to tell him who she was, he became angry, called her a madwoman, and turned her out. She went to the village and asked for bread, offering to work in exchange—she could neither grind grain nor make soup, but she was a good seamstress. She was advised to go to the city. At Villenauxe she found no work and she would not beg— she travelled to Nogent on foot. There she fell ill and was taken in by the prioress of the convent of St. Nicholas.

All that the prioress could learn from the girl was that she had sworn to tell her name to no one. The mysterious stranger spent her days on her knees, praying before a crucifix; as soon as she recovered she worked in the convent workroom; she was an excellent workwoman, she was humble and quiet, and the nuns thought her feeble-minded because when they spoke to her she answered only with smiles and nods. Then one day the prioress learned that a certain baron of Linnières, whose castle lay in the forest country of the castellany of Paiens, had for eight months been looking for a daughter of his who had run away on the eve of her marriage—the damsel of Linnières was described as thin, blond, and pock-marked. Only then did the prioress and her ladies notice that there were pockmarks on the mysterious stranger's cheeks—they had not seen them before. The girl's face was thin, emaciated, not pretty, but with a modelled or sculptured quality, clean and restrained in line. But now the pockmarks were unmistakable, and all the ladies of Saint Nicholas were disappointed that their protégée was only a country damsel who had run away from home. They asked her if she was really Alette of Linnières; she refused to answer. Then, toward Lent, the lady of Linnières came in person, and Alette threw herself on her neck with a great cry: "Lady!"

Lady Alis kissed her child's rough hands and horny feet, for a long time sat silently beside her on her low wooden couch. Then she said: "Do you know what you have done to me? I might have thought you were dead."

"Forgive me, lady," said Alette. "I am wicked. But do not make me go back to the castle. I am happy here."

"Was I a bad mother to you?" asked Lady Alis.

Alette said: "I do not want to marry. Lady, the day that I am to be given to a man, if I cannot run away, I will cut off my nose and my hair so that no one will want me."

"My daughter, it is shameful for a damsel to remain so long unmarried. I have worn out my hands on my rosary praying to God for a husband for you. It is against nature not to want a husband and children."

"There are many girls who are nuns and pray to God their whole lives long," said Alette. "And God must love them best. They are like the angels."

Lady Alis said: "You know nothing about it. They are always the ugly ones or the ones who have fallen—but you, my lamb, have nothing to reproach yourself with. Alette, look at me—my hair is all faded, my face is wrinkled, I am growing old, I have had sorrow enough through all of you. Why are you so unkind to me? Have you not hurt me enough already?"

And Alette obeyed and went home to the castle, and was gentle and kind to everyone. But soon she fell into such a languor that it was Lady Alis who persuaded the baron to send her back to the convent of St. Nicholas.

Lady Alis took her to Nogent herself, and blessed her and promised to visit her. Then she left, bowed under her heavy fur cape—it was cold, it was raining, she felt so lost on that unfamiliar road, she could not take her eyes from the long gray walls behind which her Alette was imprisoned.

And that year she gave birth to Mary, who lived.

Once more the years were marked with the sign of the cross, once more the chivalry of Champagne was armed and ready for the great departure, once more gold-fringed oriflamme and red cross were borne through the streets of Troyes and along the Vézelay road—young Count Thibaut was leading the Crusade in the names of the kings and barons of France and England. For Alis, as for so many other women in Champagne and France, in Provence and Aquitaine, in England and Brittany, the red cross was but a vast cross of fire and blood, clouding their sight when they raised their eyes to the banners and the hauberks. Every woman trembled for her flesh, son or husband; each had lost more than one man. Herbert had gone. Poor Herbert—he was so fat, heat tired him and he loathed the Holy Land. But he could not help it—the wave of blood and lust and exaltation bore him along with the rest. And he remembered his brother and Garnier and all those sun-smitten cities along that too blue sea—and the color of Saracen blood.

Herbert had returned a rich man, and the baron, though his sight was growing dim, devoured his son with his single eye—he was more corpulent, hardened, older, but in those empty eyes hung some reflection of the glorious city he had helped to sack, Constantinople. There had always been little enough that could rouse Herbert to wonder—now there was nothing. Were he set down in Paradise, he would say: "I have seen better places." Champagne, with its chalkstone castles, its palisades and square-towered churches, was rustic and poor. He had brought back such a booty of splendid stuffs and cups and ewers and jewels and church ornaments that Lady Alis could only suppose he had looted Constantinople single-handed. And Herbert, a boy's boastfulness rising to his tongue after thirty years, shrugged his shoulders and said: "Oh, there was twice as much for every soldier."

Since his return Herbert had been living in Troyes in great splendor—Lady Alis never saw him dressed in anything but miniver and blazing with chains and rings and ear pendants; every month he gave presents to all his vassals and friends, of whom he had a houseful; he held lavish festivals, kept four concubines, whom he covered with jewels enough for a queen; his horses were all either Persians or Arabians. By his second wife, whom he still loved almost as much as ever, he had four children, and he insisted that they should live at Linnières—he was sure that no one could bring them up as well as Lady Alis.

The year of Herbert's return, Lady Alis at last heard news of Girard. A German knight, returning from pilgrimage, went out of his way to visit Linnières. He told Lady Alis that her son Girard was at Venice, in the service of the Doge. He had been dubbed a knight at Acre, by old Balian of Ibelin, lord of the late Simon of Linnières; from Acre he had gone to Constantinople, but had not stayed there long because the emperor did not like the French; he had rejoined the crusaders at Venice and, needing money, had entered the Doge's service. He had served through the Crusade, but had not tried to make contact with the troops from Champagne—which annoyed Lady Alis not a little. The German brought her all sorts of good wishes and respectful greetings from her son. But, strangely enough, he was surprised to learn that Girard's father was still alive. "He only spoke of his mother," he said, "I thought you were a widow." Lady Alis wept—she had a habit of weeping now, she hardly noticed when she did it—and asked the German knight to stay at Linnières for at least three months: "I will think you are he," she said. "You shall sleep where he slept, and I will wash your feet and your hair as I washed his." The young man stayed. His name was Frederick of St. Ulrich, he was blond and placid; Lady Alis grew fond of him and wept again when he took his leave.

Slowly but surely the baron was going blind. Little by little he gave up hunting, riding, hawking; he spent whole days sitting on his bench, he was putting on fat and aging. Lady Alis found that he had become capricious and irritable; he forced her to serve him as she had done in their young days; no one could cut his corns and scratch his fleabites like Lady Alis, she had to be with him always, it was all he would do not to send for her when she was in childbed. He often entertained neighbors and travellers, it was his great diversion; well skilled in hunting and horses, he talked of them with relish, slowly, like an old man, and was never done. His listeners finally fell asleep; he did not see it, and went on. Lady Alis said: "It is time you called for wine, your guests are thirsty."

When guests were being entertained Eglantine always stood beside her father's chair, dignified and a little stiff, her eyes lowered. She wore a string of wooden beads; under her dark hair her cheeks were as fresh as a well-sunned apple; her linen dress clung to her insolent breasts, her muscular abdomen. Then came the day when Eglantine no longer appeared in the hall beside her father—at thirteen she had a miscarriage after too long a ride. It had happened in the forest, during a hunt, and the only witnesses were one of her girl cousins and a young squire; they both promised to say nothing. However, Eglantine was brought back to the castle in a faint, and Lady Alis soon found out what had happened. The culprit, a little groom of sixteen named Peter, had his throat cut and was thrown into the Armançon—with matters of this sort the baron allowed no trifling. Fortunately for herself Eglantine was very ill and nearly died, and the baron did not punish her. However, he no longer dared to show her to his guests as he had done, and he ceased to speak to her—her behavior hurt him too greatly.

In the high, warm grass beside the path, her back against an old wooden cross, the girl waited. Before her lay the forest of Hervi, behind was a glade scattered with little pines and bushes and withered herbs, and then the barley field of Linnières. Her gray dress looked white in the bright sunlight, and tawny sunbleached strands of her dark hair hung over her forehead and into her great black, round eyes. Golden, too, was the blond, tanned rider who stooped from his Cordovan saddle to her, and Eglantine stepped up on the bank and raised her arms and put them around the rider's neck; she felt dazzled, she opened her eyes wide, she drew in her breath, she gave a great, quiet sigh, like someone who feels too well, who can bear no more of such perfect well-being. When the man dismounted she was there against him, her eyes devoured even the tiniest wrinkles in his skin: he was handsome, he was tall, he had broad shoulders and curly hair. He did not stay to be stared at, he unfastened her girdle and threw her down in the tall grass—once more she sighed with happiness and closed her eyes.

His name was Thierri of Chassericourt, he was a huntsman in the count's forest of Hervi, they had loved each other for a week, and it was so beautiful that Eglantine forgot all the danger and all the shame. True enough, Thierri was not the first, and he knew it—the first had been Peter, whom the baron had killed after Eglantine was so ill in the forest. She had quickly recovered, she was as hardy as a bramble. Afterwards the boys at Linnières had not dared to go near her, but at Hervi Church she often saw huntsmen of the count's, and there were handsome men among them. There had been Eudes of Montmartin, who had taken her during a check among the high bushes near Rainard's Grave—she had not wanted him to, he had caught her by a trick, but afterwards she loved him dearly. But he had gone to Reims two weeks later. Then there had been James of Vanlay, cousin to her big brother Herbert. James was not young, he had passed thirty; he met her in corners, behind beds, was always in a great hurry and afraid of being caught; but he awed Eglantine because of his age and his being a knight. And now there was Thierri. To see him she had to slip out of the castle during the after-dinner nap, exchange clothes with Bone, Gauchère's daughter, and walk half a league along a woodcutters' footpath.

Thierri of Chassericourt had seen Eglantine at the festival at Hervi Castle on the day of St. Peter-in-Prison. He had won the archery contest and had offered his prize—a bunch of flowers on a long stick—to the damsel who had seemed most approachable. She had laughed like a child. Learning that she was the baron of Hervi's bastard sister, he had risked rather daring speeches, and that night a little maid had come to tell him that he was awaited under the briar bush in the orchard. The damsel had received him with the fervor of a little starved animal; she was very closely watched, she said, she was not allowed to see men. As he was to remain in the district for some days, it was decided that they should meet in the forest of Linnières. Never had he known a girl who laughed so much and was so caressing. He had no scruples, he loved life. He asked nothing better than to laugh a little. When he mounted his horse to leave, he kissed Eglantine's great shining eyes and promised to come back the next day. He knew that he would never come again.

Burrs on her dress and grass in her hair, Eglantine slowly retraced the path along the field, while before her eyes everything dissolved in a red, glowing mist. The sun burned her arms through the sleeves of her dress, branches snapped in the forest, the grasshoppers shrilled till her head hummed, the voices of the reapers sounded as if they were close by. Doubtless Lady Alis was already looking for her all through the castle. Little did she care. Even if they shut her up, she would always find some way to come back to the forest tomorrow and meet Thierri. The thought reassured her; she stretched out on the ground, tried to watch the sailing clouds, and fell asleep.

Against the cleanly whitewashed wall of the hall, the great shield of Ansiau of Linnières hung over his long sword in its sheath of gilded leather. The shield, which had not been repainted for four years, was rather the worse for wear, the dampness had darkened the red background, and the two blue wolves looked dim. But the sword, in its rich sheath, was in perfect condition, and sometimes, as a special favor, Ansiau showed it to his guests —he had it brought to him by two squires, then he drew it slowly from the sheath; he always washed his hands before he touched the guard. In the guard, which was ten inches long and very thick, there were relics of St. George and a stone from the Holy Sepulchre. And the blade was clean and shone like a double mirror of steel.

It was hard—still to have so much blood in his veins and such strong nerves, and yet to be unable to use his body. Ansiau did not like staying in the hall, he went down into the courtyard and sat on a stone bench by the well—there he spent his days. He had a little canopy put up there to shelter him from the sun and the frequent rains. He smelled the familiar odor of the stables, the odor of blood and fresh meat that clung to the hunters when they came home at night, and the warm odor of maids going to the well for water. When he opened his one eye he saw little moving threads of blood, a red net which grew now wider, now narrower; with a great deal of effort he managed to see beyond the red net and distinguish dark shapes, patches of light—to recognize a face he had to stare for a long time, and afterwards his eye pained him and his sight was gone for hours. It was the fault of the snow. One sunny day when there was snow on the ground Ansiau had ridden from Linnières to Troyes without stopping. Afterwards it had happened— red-hot needles in his eyeball, and spots, spots everywhere, and minutes when he saw nothing but red. He had never recovered.

His almost permanent dysentery, the tertian fever which had come and gone for nearly twenty years, had no more effect on his body than mould has on the trunk of a tree. His hair and beard were still thick and curly, his temples were gray, but there were almost no gray in his beard; under his woolen sleeves his muscles swelled like the muscles of a wrestler or an archer; his teeth were as strong and white as ever, but he seldom showed them.

Eyes closed, back bent, hands clasped between his knees, he could sit there hour after hour without a word or a motion. He felt the sun through the cloth of the canopy, the coolness of the well, sometimes a fitful gust of wind, he heard the leaves rustling in the great linden ten paces away, he sensed people coming and going, warm, heavy things, shapeless and faceless. Voices and laughter—to him they were as meaningless as the rustling of the leaves. Sometimes he thought he caught the noise of a lance on a shield, the grinding of iron on iron, distant voices shouting "Holy Sepulchre!" Of all his dreams, that was the one he dreamed most often; sometimes, too, he thought that Garnier sat beside him, he heard his grave, warm voice— "Yes, uncle." And then again: "Holy Sepulchre!" Sometimes he even said it aloud himself. It was only a habit. He thought of nothing.

Time had passed so quickly that he had not even been aware of it—from Easter to Pentecost, from Pentecost to Assumption Day, from All-Hallows to Christmas—the year went by in leaps and bounds, impossible to tell last Christmas from Christmas two years ago; the only thing that changed was the girls—if only God could prevent them from growing up—ah, how and why had he let himself grow fond of anything so frail as a little girl?

On sunny days his eye hurt, it was better not to open it too often. Then he felt thirsty too, he itched, he felt a weight in his stomach, there were flies. Then it was good to have his lady there, close beside him, because her hands were gentle, her fingers healed. Only—even she could not drive away the sad thoughts that would come into his head, that turned and turned in his mind. To kill a groom who had abused his daughter was what any man must do and would do. But there were moments when Ansiau wanted to kill every man on earth—otherwise he would never be at peace. A blind man was easy to trick. Eglantine had only one thing in her head—it was not her fault, her mother had been the same. As for shutting her up, it was easy to say—but she could not spend her life in a cellar.

He thought that he was ready to forgive her everything, every day he thought it, and every day when he saw her he felt the blood rise to his head and he could not say a word to her—or at most a good morning or good night. Then one evening he learned that Eglantine was not at the castle. Lady Alis said: "No one saw her go out, I cannot understand it." Then the baron turned red and had to loosen his collar; he sent three men on horseback into the forest to search for Eglantine. "I will kill her. I will cut off her nose." He strode up and down the hall, knocking against everything he passed.

Eglantine woke. Her eyes were heavy, her legs limp, she felt stiff all over, she wanted to turn on her other side and go back to sleep—it felt so good there among the mint and the marjoram and the tall dry grass. And then suddenly she saw that the sky over the forest of Hervi was yellow-gold, was turning red, and the clouds were like flocks of blazing wool. The reapers had left the field. The bells of Hervi were ringing for vespers.

Eglantine's first thought was what awaited her at the castle. The baron's anger, Lady Alis' whip. The laughter of the children. The cellar, dry bread.

No one liked to be humiliated. Eglantine rolled over on her stomach and began rubbing her face with mint leaves. Whenever she got back it would be soon enough. Here it was so pleasant, she felt so at peace. Yet a little fear would wrench her heart when she thought that, sooner or later, she must go back. Indeed, Eglantine was not at all sure that this time she would get off with a whipping and the dark closet. What if the baron ripped out her heart or cut off her tongue? Or tied her to the tail of a horse? Or stood her naked in the stocks, because she had dishonored her lineage? She shook her head. Anything was possible. Better not to go back—certainly, if she went back so late, she could never meet Thierri again the next morning. Better to wait for him in the forest.

Immediately her thoughts were off on another track. Thierri—it was so good to be with Thierri, he was warm and shining, a great sun—even the memory of him put sunshine in her blood. He was good. When he came she would ask him to take her to his own part of the country and marry her. It was so simple. Thierri was a squire with no money, but Eglantine was sure that where he lived—over toward Nogent—life was not the same as at Linnières. Thierri had a castle all painted white, with a red-and-gold shield over the gate; there were bright carpets on the floor, bright tapestries on the beds, painted windows like the windows in churches, and so many candles that night was as bright as day. And he took Eglantine's hand and led her to his bench under the shields and put a wreath of flowers on her head and a golden ring on her finger—it shone like a great star. Eglantine closed her eyes. Where could she summon the courage to wait for hour after hour, to wait all morning? How could she be far from Thierri when she had the love of Thierri in every drop of her blood? Eglantine wiped away her tears, raised her head. Night was falling.

Lying on her side, with her eyes wide open, her heavy braids thrown back, she heard the forest waken to its nocturnal life—hares bounded into the glen, stags went to the stream to drink, an owl wailed from the other side of the field. Eglantine felt no fear—the relic of St. Columba which she wore at her throat would protect her from all harm. Besides, wolves and boars were not what troubled her. "For a girl of noble blood, there is nothing viler than this accursed heat in the blood"—how often they had said it to her over and over, all of them, Lady Alis and Father Aimeri and Lady Richeut. Eglantine knew it without their telling. But what then?

Ugly, a bastard, a liar—that was what she was. She had not known her mother, but even so it was not pleasant to keep hearing "Like mother, like daughter." "A whore like your mother and your grandmother"—that was what the baron had said to her after he found out about Peter. She had thought that she loved the baron. Then everything had changed, because of Peter—how could she have known?—she was young and ignorant, Peter too—they had not even known that those things would bring children. The baron had killed Peter—when she learned of it, her hands and feet had gone cold, she had not opened her lips. The baron had not beaten her, she was too ill. But never had she believed that he could be angry with her—he too; he had said foul things; his eye had turned all red, his beard had trembled and shaken on his chin. . . . Then Eglantine had understood that he did not love her and she began to fear him.

It was not her fault if she grew so rosy with delight when a handsome young man looked at her—she did not do it on purpose—she was so calm and so happy, she felt so safe when she was close to a man who pleased her. It was Paradise. And they wanted to force her to live without it. No— better to die!

When she woke it was broad daylight. Eglantine rubbed her eyes and stretched with delight at the thought that she was free and no one could prevent her from meeting Thierri at noon by the wooden cross. She was soaked with dew, she felt fresh and cool, her wet hair twisted in little spirals over her forehead. She undid her braids and shook her head; her beautiful heavy hair, wavy and alive, clothed her in a lovely brown mesh. And she laughed because she knew that, call her ugly as they might, she was beautiful when she wanted to be—and Thierri knew it, for he loved her. The sun cast long, pale, slanting rays, the shadow of the forest darkened half the field. The reapers came back with their scythes and sickles, their swaddled babies and their clay water bottles. Eglantine hid behind the bushes, then began walking down the path, picking flowers for a wreath. She had no fears because she saw life only until noon—Thierri would caress her in the high grass behind the cross. That was all. There was nothing else. Little did it matter whether he took her away with him or not—at heart, Eglantine knew that he would do no such thing, she was only amusing herself by imagining it. Let him come—that was all, she wanted no more.

The sun was sinking toward Bernon Wood. Eglantine sat at the foot of the cross with her head on her knees, weeping—she was hungry, her head whirled, her legs hurt—oh! never would she have believed that Thierri could be so cruel! He had promised, and it was only to trick her, to laugh at her. He had never meant to come, he had stayed away on purpose. How she hated him. How ugly the sun was. How ugly everything was.

When Raoul, the old squire, found her at the end of the path, she quietly let him put her on the crupper of his horse. She had to drain her cup to the last drop, no miracle came to save her—the return to the castle, the looks of the serving-women, the smiles of the varlets, and the silence which greeted her at the door of the hall. Lady Alis was standing by the hearth, bolt upright, her hands on her girdle. The squires and the kitchenmaids had dropped their ladles or their bellows on the floor and stood motionless; and there was that fool of a Joceran, making a face, as if he never did anything wrong! "Eglantine," said Lady Alis, "come here." Eglantine crossed the hall and fell on her knees. Lady Alis took her by the hair and pulled her up. "You will have plenty of time to kneel—first let me take you to your father so that he can see what a pretty state you are in. He is over there under the window."

There he was. Motionless, his hands on the arms of his double chair. Never had a man looked so big; his shoulders filled the whole width of the chair; seated, he was as tall as Eglantine as she stood—his old brown woolen tunic seemed to have grown too small for him, his chest rose and fell rapidly and jerkily. The great brown-and-red face, framed in graying hair, the closed eye, the tight mouth, were a single huge scar. The neck and ears grew deeper and deeper red.

The baron was silent. At last, in a hoarse, strangled voice, he said: "My collar." Lady Alis loosened his collar and held a thick key against the vein in his left temple to cool his blood. He drew a deep breath and slowly opened his swollen eyelid. Eglantine's strength failed her, her legs went limp, she sat down on the floor and bowed her head, like a cornered beast awaiting the finishing stroke. She knew that it was no time to sit on the floor, but she no longer cared. She did not dare to raise her eyes, for fear of seeing something too terrible. She wished she could go to sleep.

She heard the baron's rapid, whistling breathing. "Trollop, with whom? where?" Then came a roar: "Answer me, bitch!"

Eglantine heard herself answer: "I was lost in the forest."

"With whom?"

"With no one."

"Girl," said the baron, "I will kill you."

Eglantine said nothing and bowed her head even lower, her unbound hair spread out at the baron's feet. She would gladly be killed. That man there had betrayed her—she had thought him good, and he hated her, he was her worst enemy, he so big and strong, she so weak—better to die than to live imprisoned.

He repeated: "I will kill you. Do you hear me?"

Eglantine sniffled and said: "Yes, I hear you."

"You have sworn to drive me mad. Stand up, and say something else." When she heard the softened tone of his voice, Eglantine remembered how her father used to scold her when she stole apples, and, without wanting to, she began to cry and say: "Father! Father!"

Then a strange thing happened—he did not kill her, he took her on his knees and tried to comfort her. "I frightened you, little one. You are mad. Did you believe that your old father would kill you? Little fool. There, lady—I will talk to her, you need not trouble over her now."

Lady Alis shrugged her shoulders and walked away.

Through the trembling threads that ran across his eye Ansiau tried to distinguish the child's face—the dull, bloodshot eyes, the swollen lips, the cheeks smeared with tears, the long unbound strands of hair—yes, bad as his sight was he could divine her face; there were the freckles on her little snub nose, there was the golden down on her cheeks. He did not speak; already his eye pained him, it was filling with tears, tears of pain or of grief, he could not tell. Still he stared, blinking his eyelid. The child was sniffling and rubbing her eyes with her fists.

"Little one," he said, "I shall not kill you. It is you who will kill me."

Eglantine did not understand—it was too absurd. There she stood, awkward, motionless, not knowing yet what her father had in his mind; the day was passed when she believed that he wanted whatever she wanted; she was on her guard.

He said: "Listen, little one. When an egg is broken, it is broken. That is the end of it. It is good for nothing. And it is the same with you—you are good for nothing. You are not a virgin. A nothing, a broken egg, that is what you are. Not a pretty thing."

She sighed, listening to catch the low, broken, but fond voice of her old father—she had long known that she was good for nothing, and she did not care.

"I always meant," said her father, "to marry you to a knight. I was proud of you. When you fell the first time I almost went mad with grief. It was not your fault, you were too young. Now you have begun again. It is a disgrace to me. What do you want me to do?"

Eglantine did not answer. What did she want? She wanted Thierri of Chassericourt.

"I shall send you to a convent," he said, "so that you will not disgrace me. You will be with your sister Alette, you will be well watched, you will commit no more follies."

Now Eglantine understood—so that was what he wanted! He had pretended to be kind only to deceive her the better. From a convent there was no escaping to run in the fields. And it was for life. And it was almost upon her, no doubt of that, it was the baron's will—she! for all her life! prison! at fifteen! Her whole body went cold. She gave a piercing scream: "Kill me—I would rather! Hang me, throw me into the well, then I will not disgrace you. I know you hate me."

She was going to throw herself down and sob her heart out when something stopped her; she saw her father go pale and then red, he was trembling so violently that his teeth chattered. Frightened, she looked at him under her lashes. Then he collapsed, his head on his knees, his arms hanging loose—with a roar, a groan like a wounded bear. Eglantine shook him: "Father! Father!"

He said: "Go away."

She would not go, she kept repeating: "Father!" He was weeping.

She knelt before him, and he rested his head on her shoulders.

"You have said something to me, little one, that I shall never forget. By my beard I swear to you: You shall not go into a convent. So long as you live, you shall stay here, no one shall harm you. I will protect you. They shall not laugh at you. It is my own fault. I shall not punish you for my sin. Your mother had an old father too—but he is dead, thank God—I did not respect her the more for it. What has happened, I deserve. There—we shall find a way; you will not be unhappy. My little briar rose. You will not say that your old father hates you?" Eglantine stroked his cheeks as she had ten years before. She felt that her feet were on solid ground again, life was good, and her father had not deceived her.

Her father was to keep his word; she was not punished for her escapade and appeared at table, well washed and well combed, beside her cousin Huguette of Beaumont. Looks of surprise greeted her. But she held her head high, sure of her rights. Never was girl's face more open and more dignified. From his place at the head of the table, the baron searched through the dancing chaos of dark blurs and light blurs for Eglantine's blue dress; he found it, and winked his one eye. And when he divined a smile on her rosy cheeks, he forgot pain and shame.

But that evening, after he had drunk three cups of good Burgundy, he felt uncomfortable and asked Lady Alis and Thierri to help him—he could not climb the ladder alone. And no sooner had he reached the bedchamber than he became heavy and fell.

It was a huge weight—it took five men to raise the leaden body which seemed bigger than ever. "Bleed me. Quickly. Bleed me. Leeches."

As always, Lady Alis knew what must be done—she helped to undress him as he lay on the bed, she found a basin for the bleeding, but she did it all unconsciously. There was a great chill in her heart. That red, purple, puffy face framed in tousled, greasy hair—it was not the face of her beloved who had loved her. She did not know him. How could life have changed him so? It was not true. A man did not change like that. A man did not die like that. "Baron, brother, if you believe that I wished your death, it is because you know nothing. Baron, friend, I would rather die, I am too old to marry again. I care nothing for Milon. Bleed him, and quickly. There is the black blood spurting into a red bowl. Our blood, baron. Do not forget it, do not leave me."

Lady Alis sat out the night on his bed, saying her rosary. On the chest by the bed sat Joceran, fretful, pale, and heavy-eyed. Little Mary was there too, asleep on her nurse's knees. A puny child, Mary, scrawny and always covered with pimples and scabs—she shivered and puckered her little lips in her sleep. "Born of too old a mother," thought Lady Alis. "O God, why so long fruitful, why bear children no one needs? Has he ever given a thought to his little Mary? Does he even remember that she exists? The other—she took it all for herself, the trollop, with her youth and her beautiful body—who hasn't a beautiful body at fifteen? And for the trollop's child he has forgotten his lawful children. And now it is she who is killing him, the bitch—it was to be expected, he had to be punished for his sin one day, it was not for nothing that the girl was born vicious. And it serves him right! But only let him live, let him stay with me, he has been punished enough."

"Lady!" At the foot of the bed stood a tall white figure with two long dark braids. Of the face, Lady Alis saw only three black blurs arranged in a triangle, the two eyes and the open mouth.

"This is not the place for you. Filthy baggage," said Lady Alis. The other would not hear her. "Lady. Punish me."

"A fit time you have chosen!"

"Then you will not?"

"Go away."

Eglantine did not go; she sat down on the edge of the bed and gently wiped her nose. Then she put her arms around her knees and listened to her father's whistling breath. After that there were always voices and footfalls in the room. Old Father Aimeri came and shook his head—the baron was lying on his side, his neck was less red, his face calmer, but he still could not understand what was said to him.

"Another bleeding," said Lady Alis. "And hot stones at his feet." Thierri ran downstairs to heat the stones. Lady Alis looked at the huge animal head on the pillow. With its swollen tongue and dull, half-open eye, it was less human than the head of a corpse; on the red neck two huge leeches swelled and grew round. Eglantine could see nothing from where she sat, she only heard the stertorous breathing coming from the great bed. Thierri jostled her as he passed, Father Aimeri's long robe flicked her face. Then Thierri lay down on the floor again and went to sleep.

It was a long night. Lady Alis lit a second candle. The girl was still there at the foot of the bed, her chin on her knees, her arms around her legs. It was strange, Lady Alis thought, she could not hate the girl, though she had reason enough and more. But on Lady Alis' knees, in her arms, there was still the memory of a little, warm, trusting Milicent, a clumsy Milicent who was always pricking her fingers, always using blue thread when she should have used red, always singing the wrong verse in a song—that clumsy Milicent had known how to make people love her. Eglantine was like her only in her frankness—real or feigned. Yet there were times when Lady Alis wanted to call her kitten and take her on her knees—the great gawk was too stupid to know what she was doing.

Noiselessly Eglantine came to Lady Alis and sat down at her feet. "Lady."

"What, stupid."

"Lady. Tell me. When someone does that, must she be punished?"

"Certainly," said Lady Alis, "she must."

"Always?"

"Always."

"Is it God's will?"

"It is God's will."

Eglantine sighed. A moment later Lady Alis saw that she was gone.

She soon came back. But when Lady Alis raised her head she was frightened—she did not know who stood before her. A boy, it seemed. Ansiau become a young man again. The heavy dark head bristled with short, ragged curls, hastily hacked through with a hunting knife. The big eyes shone.

"There!" Triumphantly Eglantine threw back her head. "I have punished myself."

Lady Alis breathed a great, silent "oh!" and crossed herself—never had she seen anything so shameful—how could she dare to go to church or a festival with a girl so dreadfully disfigured? Such things were all very well for servants!

Eglantine turned the serious face of a good child toward her. "And now he will get well?" she asked in a little voice that was at once timid and confident. "Lady, may I stay here? Lady, may I look at him?"

"Yes, but do it quickly."

Eglantine knelt by the bed and clasped her hands. She could not understand. She felt afraid. Was that her father? It was to punish her that he had changed like this—without eyes, without a mouth, without a face, a thing incapable of understanding. It was too cruel. Yet she had punished herself enough—what more did he ask? She cried: "Father, it is I! Father! Father!"

The baron's left eyebrow moved and his mouth gaped open. Lady Alis clutched Eglantine's shoulder. "Call him, call him again!"

And again the girl cried: "Father! Do you hear me?"

Again the eyebrow moved. "Lady! He hears me! Me! Me! He did hear me! Lady!" Her cries waked Joceran, the nurse, and Mary.

Lady Alis was trembling. "Go," she said to Eglantine, "go quickly before anyone sees you—at least put something over your head."

Forgetting all respect, Eglantine smothered her with kisses. "Lady, is it true? He will not die?"

Lady Alis said: "God grant it."

"Lady! It is because of me! Don't you see? I knew it."

"Hurry off to bed, addlepate."

Eglantine kissed her father's hand and ran to her bed. Lady Alis looked after her and shook her head.

Now she was tense, her eyes fixed on the man's eye, his nostril, his lips. "Baron, baron, move, don't make me wait like this!"

The heavy blood-laden eyelid stirred, trembled, a great tear filled the eye, and the eye opened wide, sad and resigned like the eye of a wounded horse. With an effort the lips moved. "Lady." Lady Alis understood without hearing. His mouth had barely opened, as if it were full of glue.

Lady Alis screamed: "Ansiau!" and fell with her head against the baron's arm, panting and hoarse. "Only let me keep you—I will go to Rome on foot!"

Ansiau did not know what was the matter with him. He felt the leeches on his neck and heard noises, loud noises. He was accustomed to seeing nothing. Eglantine's voice called to him from far away, plaintively: "Father! Father!" He thought she was four years old, and thanked God for having made her a child again. He wanted to say, "I am coming," and could not. Then, opening his eye, he began to distinguish patches of light and saw a woman in a shift sitting beside him on the bed. Her head was uncovered, and her two braids hung down over her shift like two ropes. It was strange that this bareheaded woman with her hair down should be Lady Alis. This ordinary woman in a shift open at the neck. Now he could distinguish the grayish strands of hair which fell into her face, the little wrinkles under her eyes. An old woman. Simply an old woman like the old women who mended clothes, who sat by the hearth spinning, who told their beads.

He could not remember the time when she was not with him. This great bed, this room, this house—they were she. Life in the castle was she, the world was she. He was sick, he knew it now, he was sick and she was with him. With her, he was sure to recover. He wanted to raise his right hand, and it was so heavy that he could not move a finger. The other hand was more alive. He raised it and slowly set it on Lady Alis' hand, there on the coverlet.

Eglantine was somewhat reassured now that she was again in a world which held a father. Lying in her corner, she buried her face in her pillow and sobbed, thinking again of Thierri's golden lashes. "My hair! Oh, my hair! Oh, my beautiful hair!"

Herbert reached Linnières four days after the baron's accident—a varlet whom he bribed had sent him word that the old man was dying, and Herbert had come for his father's blessing and to step into his inheritance. But when he arrived he found that his father was not ready to die. He felt almost disappointed—he had made the journey for nothing, the heat had been stifling, and he had business at Troyes.

His entrance into the castle was as noisy as ever. He brought his wife, his concubines, and his boon companions James of Vanlay and Aimeri of Le Barnage, in addition to two knights of Troyes. (He had assembled a petty court of men whom he fed and clothed and condescended to treat as equals, he called them his friends. As the years passed, these satellites became dimmer and dimmer, grayer and grayer, they had grown so much alike that it was almost impossible to tell them apart. Herbert moved through the circle like the sun among clouds.)

When he entered he took up the whole hall. He was obese—or, rather, square in all directions, enormous. Children could never manage to see his face—from below, all that they saw was the long, loose skirts of his coat and the rounded slope of his huge, broad, protruding chest. His head, surmounting massive and rounded shoulders, was always thrown back to leave room for his carefully shaved double chin. His features were big—big nose, big mouth, big eyes; even the pouches of fat on his cheeks gave an impression of strength, not softness. His faded blond hair was nicely curled, he wore it in a smooth roll around his neck.

At thirty-six Herbert looked forty-five; no chair would hold him, he broke benches by his mere weight, and it was hard to mount him. He usually travelled in a two-horse cart. It was difficult for him to stoop, and Lady Alis wondered how she could reach up to kiss his pale, wrinkled cheeks. She laughed, and he grunted like a boar. He had forgotten how to laugh and did not know how to show his pleasure—he loved his mother.

"Come to see the old lady?" said Alis. "How did you know that the baron was ill? I sent you no word because I did not want to make you uneasy. It is nothing serious."

"I thought he was dying," said Herbert, "or I should not have come. When an old man falls ill one never knows. . . . The blood goes to the head, and the next thing is a Requiem. It happens even at my age. I am hot-blooded, you know. See how red my neck is."

"You would do better not to wear furs in summer," said Lady Alis with a sigh. Herbert did not answer. He was always too hot and never left off his cloaks of squirrel or marten—he was vain and loved display. His forehead was always beaded with sweat, he radiated heat like a stove, and smelled as strong as a spice chest with his rare, heavy perfumes. Whenever he came to the castle Lady Alis shut all the young women and girls into the servants' bedroom in the attic.

"Well, I am glad the old man is going to recover," said Herbert with a sigh. "I should have felt it if I had never seen him again. We fought well together in the Holy Land. He was a good comrade."

Lady Alis said: "You may see him. He does not get about much. Thierri has to help him when he walks. His right leg drags a little. But you'll see—he will live another twenty years."

Her son said, "Hum," and calculated that in twenty years he, Herbert, would be fifty-six, which was a little late to inherit the fief. Lady Alis was not interested in such considerations—she was sure that no one could wish for anything but that the baron should live. Even Herbert must wish it—his old father was no trouble to him, after all.

"I have him sit by the window," she said, "he gets a breath of air, and he can see the courtyard and beyond—it keeps him occupied. You will see, he is perfectly well now. I make him drink herb waters. Tomorrow I shall give him a chicken."

She looked younger and more animated than she had done for months. She took Herbert to the armchair where the baron was sitting comfortably on wolf-skins with his feet on a cushion. He was asleep. On one arm of the chair sat Eglantine, her head covered by a white veil; she was sewing a shift.

She raised frightened eyes to Herbert—usually, the first feeling Herbert aroused was fear—and laid her work in her father's lap. Then she rose and greeted her brother with a respectful bow. Everyone at the castle already treated him as the master; everyone knew that, once he was baron of Linnières, he would not easily forget past insolence; and Eglantine knew that a bastard sister was often less than a servant.

"Well, my beauty, not married yet?" said Herbert. "And she hides her hair like a nun! By the bones of St. Peter, she is pretty. A pity you are my sister, little one."

Eglantine blushed and hid behind her father's chair. There were tears in her eyes.

The baron snored.

Lady Alis touched his hand.

"Baron, baron, we have visitors today."

Slowly he stretched his shoulders and neck, then raised his left hand. "Where is she?" he said in a voice that drawled a little. "Little one! 'Glantine!"

She returned to the arm of his chair and scratched his gray temples—he was gasping slightly.

"Little one—where were you? I don't like this. You are deceiving me. I sleep too much. Yes, that's it. I sleep too much."

"She only just got down to greet Herbert," said Lady Alis. "Baron, here is Herbert come to see you."

Ansiau made an effort to open his eye. He hardly understood what his wife had said. From the tone of her voice he divined that a visitor had come, that there was a man with her. Herbert—he searched his memory. "Yes, Herbert. Herbert the Red, my uncle. He is dead. It is Herbert my son. Greetings, son. Come to see if I'm not dead yet? After I die he will let his knights do as they will with the little one. But I shall last a while longer. Herbert will not be young on the day he succeeds me. A fine boy, Herbert. Strong as a bull. In the Holy Land he was never ill except once—that winter when we were so hungry. Father, I am hungry—I am so hungry."

Lady Alis thought that her husband had gone back to sleep and she said: "You are tired. Herbert will come to see you again tomorrow."

"No," said Ansiau, "no. Welcome, son." He made an effort to see. Before him stood a mountain. Warm furs, hands laden with rings. Herbert knelt. When he was on his knees his breadth was greater than his height—he panted. Painfully Ansiau peered at the foggy face, the unfamiliar face of a man growing old—he could hardly see it, he found none of the old features. He remembered a stout, blond, white-and-rosy boy with two round blue gems for eyes. It was a stranger who was looking at him, he did not know what to say. He turned his head to the window.

Things at a distance he saw more clearly. Behind the palisade the forest of Linnières stretched still and motionless, dark and warm. The sky was yellow Kites sailed over the treetops.

Lady Alis sighed and sat down on a stool beside the baron's chair. She was tired. Taking care of that great, heavy, immobile child was hard. She thought of William, who had become so big those last years, so heavy that she could no longer pick him up—he too slept in the graveyard at Hervi, and no one had wept for him but she. She had borne so many children for whom no one else had wept. Now it was over; she would not bear another. She would not give suck again. Her heavy breasts were already drying up, and their long, hard, brown nipples, which had fed so many mouths, which had been so sucked and drawn and bitten, would rest forever.

But her heart would never rest. It would always beat wildly each time a stranger arrived, because in its folly it would believe that there would be news of Girard, it would bleed every Sunday in the parlor at the convent of Saint-Florentin, it would grow heavy as a millstone each time one of her grandchildren fell ill.

She shook her head and rested her cheek on the baron's shoulder.

A huge red sun set behind the forest.

APPENDIX

JOPPA RETAKEN
(July 31—August 5, 1192)

. . . "Meanwhile the host returned to Acre all heavy and disconsolate. All thought now to depart and were going straight to their vessels. King Richard himself had now taken leave of the Temple and the Hospital and had looked to his galleys that they might be well preserved. And on the morrow would he go on board to proceed to Beirut and besiege it. Now came a barge full speed toward Acre. And they who came forth of the barge hastened to the king, and they told him that Joppa had been taken and our folk besieged on Toron, and if these were not succored by him they would all be destroyed and slain. And the king said: 'In sooth will I go thither!' But in no wise would the French obey him. Nevertheless many Templars and Hospitallers and many other good knights made ready and gat them to horse and journeyed by land straight to Caesarea. And the king went in galleys on the sea. Richly had he and his armed themselves. There was the earl of Leicester, and there were Andrew of Chauvigni, Roger of Saci, Jordan of Hommet, Ralph of Mauléon, (who bears a lion on his banner), Auçon of Faï, there were they of Priaux and many others. These were going in God's service, with them of Genoa and them of Pisa. . . .

"They that were going by land to Joppa, and who thought to go all the way thither, had rested at Caesarea; and scarcely were they come thither when it was told them that Saladin was causing the roads to be guarded, so that they were so good as besieged there; it was the Assassin's son, who lay between Arsul and Caesarea. And on the sea our people were held back by a contrary wind—both the king and the rest that were in the galleys—so that for three days they lay off Caïphas nor moved thence. And the king cried: 'Have pity, O God! Wherefore holdest Thou me here? For 'tis on Thy service I am bent!' And God in His bounty sent them a wind out of the north, which bare him with all his fleet to the port of Joppa on a Friday, late in the night; and on Saturday, at nones, would the truce be expired. Then had the Christians been in evil case and doomed to death and dole, had not God delivered them through the king. . . .

"The brave king and his illustrious men had lain in their galleys through all the night of Friday even until the morning of Saturday; then he armed himself, and his men did likewise. Now shall ye hear of the warrant whereby the safety of the city had been warranted, and of the treachery that the Turks had contrived against them that thought their safety warranted by the bezants which they had promised. The Saracens demanded that they should pay in the morning, and in the morning they began to make their payments. But even as they made them, the Saracens cut off their heads one by one. And they thought that they were acting very cunningly; but fie upon the faith of a cur! Already had they slain seven and cast them into a ditch, when they that were on Toron perceived it. And they that were there said that then might ye have seen a very pitiful sight upon Toron, before the tower, because of the fear which they had that they were now doomed to death. Then had ye seen many folk weeping, kneeling down and praying, making confession, reciting their *mea culpa*; whilst they that were without gat themselves within, into the great press of people, that they might put off their dying as long as possible. For every creature, when death close pursueth it, seeketh a little season of respite and delay. . . .

"Then did the Turks perceive the galleys which were already in the harbor. All down to the strand they came, until the shore was so filled with them that they could scarce abide there. Bucklers they bare and targes; and they shot at the barges and clean over to the king's galleys. They that were on horseback hurled themselves into the sea, shooting at our men to keep them from getting to land.

"But the brave King Richard drew all his vessels together, for to speak to his company. Then said he to his chivalry: 'Ye gentle knights, what shall we do? Shall we go hence, or shall we get us to land? Or how shall we be able to do this?' Certain ones there were who answered that to their mind it were of no avail to gain the shore or to seize the port, for all thought that surely were the people of the castle already slain. Whilst they were yet enquiring whether they could get them to land, lo, the king of England saw a chantry priest leap suddenly from the shore into the sea, who came a-swimming straight toward the king. And him he took into his galley. Then quoth the priest: 'O gentle king, perished are the folk that here await thee, an God and thou have not compassion on them!' 'How, good friend,' quoth the king, 'are any yet alive? Whither are they gone?' 'Yea, sire, before yonder tower are they all assembled, awaiting death.' And so soon as the king perceived that this was so, no longer did he tarry, but straightway said: 'God hath caused us to come hither for to endure and suffer death; and since it now behooveth us to die, then shame on him who will not go yonder!' Then he bade the galley draw near to the shore and, with his legs unarmed, he leaped into the sea—by good fortune, only up to his girdle—and came apace to the dry ground, the second or mayhap the first to land; such was his custom. Geoffrey of the Wood and Peter of Préaux, valiant companion of the king, and all the others leaped in after him and went against the Turks with whom the shore was filled and attacked them. And the brave king in his own person slew many with his arbalest; and his people, bold and ready, pursued them all along the strand. The Turks fled before the king, whom they durst not confront; and he laid hand to his brand of steel and went running after them and pursued them in that hour so hard that they had no leisure to defend themselves. They durst no longer await him nor his well-proved company, who were smiting them like folk gone mad. And so did these smite and press them that they cleaned the shore of Turks and drave them all back; and after this they took tuns and timbers and great planks and old galleys and barges, and therewith builded they a bulwark across the shore betwixt them and the Saracen folk. And there the king put knights and sergeants and arbalesters, who skirmished with the Saracens. The infidels howled and hooted, but they withdrew perforce in their own despite. Then the king went up by a winding stair which leadeth to the House of the Templars. There entered he the first of them all and gat him by force into the city, and he found there more than three thousand Saracens who were despoiling the castle and carrying away all that was therein. Then Richard, the bravest king in all the world, so soon as he was on top of the walls, caused his banners to be displayed and to be lifted up until the beleaguered Christians saw them. And so soon as they espied them, 'Holy Sepulchre!' cried they all. Their weapons they seized and did their armor on, nor tarried any longer. Then had you seen the infidel host assailed with fear when they beheld our men descending! Then had you also seen full many a Turk laid low, whom the king struck down to earth. None durst await his stroke, lest his life be lost thereby. Then were our folk come clean down into the midst of the streets. So was the town delivered and the Saracens put to great shame.

"The king went out of the city after them, who had already wrought such prowess that day. Only three horses had he; nor ever, even at Roncesvalles, did any man, young or old, Saracen or Christian, acquit himself in such fashion as he. For when the Turks beheld his banner they trembled on every side. There had no coward cared to be; for never hath God made snow or rain to fall thicker or faster, even when they fall most grievously, than the bolts and arrows which rained down in the midst of the Christians. Then was the news brought and told to Saladin that his people were thus assailed; and he, the accursed infidel, who was worse maddened than a wolf, waxed feverous with fear. Nor durst he tarry longer there but caused his pavilions to be struck, and his tents, and to be carried back into the plains. And the king and his proud and valiant men followed and pursued after them, smiting them and treading hard upon their heels, with their arbalesters shooting at them and slaying their horses. And so close did they press the Turks and so sorely did they wound them with their arrows that they retreated full two leagues. Then straightaway the king caused his own tent to be pitched in that very place where Saladin had not dared await him. There encamped Richard the Great.

"When that two days' fight was ended and when the host of the Turks had retreated, then was that host abashed and sore ashamed because they had been driven back by folk on foot, who had but a little force against so great a multitude as they were; but God had put forth His hand that His people might not come to harm. Then, lo, Saladin called together his Saracens and

495

Turks of highest estate and asked of them: 'Who pursueth you? Is, then, the whole host come back from Acre, that it hath thus put my folk to flight? Are they on foot or horseback, they that came down upon you?' Then up spake a certain traitor who knew the matter and had seen the king: 'Sire, never a beast have they with them, neither horse nor mule, save that the king, that doughty warrior, found three steeds in Joppa; so many are there or can be—not another one! And if there be any one here who would fain undertake the thing, then could he seize the king's person with scarce any pains; for he lieth all alone in his tent.'

"Now it was on a Saturday (according to the history that I am reciting to you) that the city was recovered and delivered from the Saracens, who indeed had wrought marvels there which shall always be spoken of: for they had taken Joppa a second time, and had put to death the sick Christian folk that they had found there, and it was proved of a truth that they found so many swine in the city, which they killed and destroyed, that the number thereof was infinite; for it is in sooth known that they eat not the flesh of swine and are therefore very fain to kill them, nor hate they more any other earthly thing in their despite against the Christians' faith. So they had mingled and laid side by side the dead folk and the swine. But our people, being moved by God to do this thing, took up the bodies of the other Christian folk and laid them all in the earth; but the Saracens that they had slain on the Saturday they cast out together with the dead swine, which stank so that our folk could no longer endure it.

"Then did the king bid them toil on Sunday and on Monday upon the wall of Joppa, and on the Tuesday also, wheresoever they saw it broken; until in the end they had reared it anew so well as could be done without lime or mortar, so be it there were any need of defense. But the host abode without in their tents, where they must needs keep straiter watch. . . .

"Lo, in a galley came Count Henry of Champagne from Caesarea, he and his company. For the host had come to Caesarea; but there, despite itself, had it been stayed by the Saracens, who were watching the streams and passes so that the king might get no succour. Nor had he any, of all their company, save only of the count his nephew. Nor had he, for to carry him through that day's fighting which had been prepared for him, more than fifty knights, or at the most three score, with sergeants and arbalesters brave and skillful in their business, and men of Genoa and men of Pisa who had offered themselves there in God's service, and other folk about two thousand. Nor even then, after he had rescued the city, had he full fifteen horses, good and bad together; such lack of these had he thereafter that his people had surely perished and been undone if God had not protected him against the Turks and their designs.

"Now shall ye hear a great marvel, whereat all the world marveleth; for certainly had all our people been taken on Wednesday through that complot whereby the enemy thought to seize the king, had not God taken care of him. That night, about the hour of matins, the Saracens mounted and drew up their ranks, then they laced their aventailes and rode forth by the light of the moon. And then did God perform one of His glorious acts of mercy; and when He doeth such a kindness, fitting it is that it be recounted. Behold them, then, riding adown the plain in serried ranks. Then the Lord God Himself caused a dispute to arise betwixt the Kurds and the Mamelukes, whether of the twain should dismount and await our people on foot so that our men might not be able to retreat into the castle and find shelter there. And each company said: 'Ye shall dismount!' 'Nay, ye shall!' 'Nay, ye yourselves; that is but right, for we are the better horsemen!' So came they, quarrelling among themselves; and the strife of each with the other endured until they saw the daylight clear, even as God had purposed. And the king was yet asleep in his tent.

"Now listen ye to the high adventure of a certain Genoese who had arisen and gone out upon the heath at the very peep of dawn. And as he was turning about to go back he heard the Turks coming and saw the glistening of their helmets. Then straight he bowed his head, but lifted up his voice and cried to our people to do their armor on and all rush to arms. And the king was wakened by the cry, albeit he had labored hard that day. Forth of his bed he leaped upon his feet and donned, I ween, an hauberk white and tough and stout. He bade his companions instantly awake; nor is it any marvel if, in so sudden a surprise, they had much ado to clothe and to arm themselves. And I can well assure you that they had such haste, both the king and many others beside, that with legs unarmed, bare and uncovered save by the shadow of the clouds—yea, some even naked and unbreeched—they fought perforce that day, receiving many blows and wounds; and 'twas their state that troubled them most of all.

"Now whilst our folk were arming themselves, the Saracens were drawing ever nearer. Then the king mounted, and he had with him not more than ten men on horseback. And the history telleth us clearly that Count Henry of Champagne was there on horse with his company; and there was the earl of Leicester, Robert, who was worthy to be there; and Bartholomew of Mortemer was there, mounted, I ween; and there was Ralph of Mauléon, who never had his fill of fighting; and there was Andrew of Chauvigni, stout and valiant in his saddle; and there was Girard of Fournival, on horseback with the king; and there was Roger of Saci, sitting on a sorry nag; and there was William of L'Étang, who had a foundered horse; and there was Hugh of Neuville, a sergeant bold and noble. And Henry Le Tyois bare the king's banner in the midst of their band.

"And now behold our people drawn up in order against the cruel infidel host, and ranged by battalions, each with its own command. The knights were on the left hand, along the shore, over toward St. Nicholas' Church, fronting the Saracen folk; there was it meet that they should be, for thitherward moved the more part of the Turks, beating their drums and yelling. And before the gardens were set folk of diverse nations; there were Pisans and there were Genoese, nor were it now possible to tell or to recount the assaults that these suffered of the hated folk. The Turks began to shoot their arrows, and to hoot and to shout and to yell. There had you seen marvellous fighting and our good folk hard beset. They kneeled upon their knees, setting their targes and their shields upright before them, their lances in their hands. And the king, who was well skilled in arms, caused to be hidden under all the targes, betwixt two men, an arbalester and a man for to bend his bow and give it back to him when he had bent it; and by this means was the host well defended. Thus were they ordered.

"But it must not be doubted that they who were in such jeopardy, opposed to the multitude of Turks that they saw, had fear for their own heads. But it is so true as that you are now here that the king went amongst them, encouraging them and exhorting the knights; and John of Préaux went with him, likewise preaching to them. And they said: 'Now will it soon be shown who will strive to do valiantly so long as God preserveth his life. For now is nought else to do save to sell our lives dearly and to await our martyrdom, since God hath so decreed for us. Now are we in the right way, since He of His bounty giveth us that which we came to seek. Here is found our true recompense.'

"Then the ranks stood fast, and the squadrons of the Turks came on. And our folk ever kept their legs planted in the sand and all their lances in rest, ready to receive them. Then advanced the battalions of the false Saracen folk with such impetuosity, with such clatter of hoofs, that an our folk had moved at all, the Turks had broken through their line; for there were, an I err not, a thousand in each battalion. But when they were hard upon our men and saw that they moved not, they turned and rode close along our front. Then the arbalesters let fly, and the Turks durst not await them; for they hit both their bodies and the bodies of their horses and overthrew them. But presently back came the squadrons, and yet again were they drawing near, stopping short, and wheeling them about; and thus did they many times. And when the king and his men saw that even though they were so many and were on horseback, the Turks would not do otherwise, then with lance head lowered, each man thrust himself with all his might full into the great press of misbelieving enemy folk; and so violently did they assail them that all the ranks trembled, even unto the third line. Then did the king look about him, and yonder on the left saw he the brave earl of Leicester fall, who had been stricken down from his horse, though valiantly had he fought; but the brave king went and rescued him. Then had you seen so many Turks come charging straight toward the lion banner! Then, lo, was Ralph of Mauléon led off captive of the Turks; but the king put spurs to his noble steed and gat him out of their hands again. Mightily wrought the king in the midst of the press against Turks and Persians; never in one day hath any man, be he weak or strong, performed such deeds of prowess. For he charged into the midst of the Turks, and clave them to the teeth; and so many a time did he charge them, and so many blows did he deal them, and so wore he himself with smiting, that the very skin of his hands cracked.

"Then came a Saracen pricking, outstripping the other Turks, riding a courser swift and mettlesome. This was the valiant Safadin of Arcady, he that wrought such deeds of prowess and bounty and largess. Spurring he came, as I have said, with two Arab steeds which he delivered to the king of England, praying and beseeching him, because of the king's prowess which he knew and the great valor he possessed, to mount them; with this understanding: that if God brought him safe and sound out of this pass wherein he saw him now, the king would grant to him some guerdon. Thereafter had he rich reward for this. The king was, very fain to take them; and he said that many another such would he right gladly receive from his most mortal enemy, an ever again he were brought to such straits as he was now in.

"Then hotter waxed the fight; never was its like seen before. All the ground was covered with the arrows of that folk perverse, which men gathered up by armfuls. So many wounded were there to see, that the rowers fled back into the galleys whence they had come forth. He that fleeth in such an hour greatly dishonoreth himself! Then arose a cry from the city that the Turks were coming thither in a body, thinking to take our people by surprise both in the front and in the rear. And the king, with two other knights, rode thither, bearing his banner. And so soon as he was entered therein, in the middle of the street he met three Turks in costly harness; he smote them like a king and gave them so rude an encounter that he straightway gat him two other horses there; and the Turks he slew.

"And the other infidels drave he by force out of the city. Then passed he on and caused the gate whereby they had entered to be stopped from side to side and from top to bottom, and he set guards to guard it. Straight to the galleys then went he, whither his people had gone in great fear and distress. And Richard, son of prowess, brought back courage to them all and caused them to row again to land, and he gat his people once more together, so that there remained only five men in each galley. And with the rest back came he to the host, which had no repose. Then made he that adventurous charge—none other such was ever made! For so deep he charged into that heathen horde that they swallowed him up, nor could any of his own folk longer see him. And it lacked but little that they had followed after him, breaking their ranks; then had we all been lost. Howbeit, the king was not dismayed; but he smote before him and behind until with the sword that he held he had made him a highway there, whithersoever he would go; were it man or horse he smote, he cut them all down. There, at one stroke an I mistake not, he clave off the arm and head together from an emir in iron armor, sending him straight to Hell. And after this stroke, which the Turks beheld, so wide room did they make for him that he came back, thanks be to God, unharmed. But his body, his horse, his trappings—all were so covered with arrows which the swarthy folk had rivalled in shooting at him that he resembled a hedgehog. So came he back from the battle, which endured all the day long from morning until eventide—so cruel and so fierce a battle that if God had not sustained His people, ill had it gone with them. But in sooth was He with us—that saw we, when never a man had we lost there that day, save one or two only [?]. But the Turks lost more than fifteen hundred horses, which were lying on the hills and in the vales, and more than seven hundred men also, who all lay there dead. Nor for all this their travail did they carry off the king, who before the eyes of their hated folk had wrought his great feats of knighthood; so that they were all dumbfounded at the prowesses which they saw performed by him and by them that were with him, who put themselves in jeopardy of death.

"When God had thus of His bounty delivered the king and the Christian people from the infidel folk and the host had departed, then were told the words that the Sultan Saladin had addressed to the Saracens in his bitter anger at his discomfiture. 'Where,' asked he, 'are they that have taken the king? Where is he that bringeth him hither to me?' And a Turk from a far country made answer: 'Sire, I will tell thee, nor in aught will I lie. Never yet hath such another man been seen—so valiant, so cunning—or one better proved in arms. For every need will he be found ready. Greatly have we travailed and mighty blows have we dealt, but never have we been able to take him; for none dareth to await his stroke, so bold is he and so dexterous.'

"My lords, think it no fable that the Turks knew him right well, or that they would have taken him that time but for God's help and his own great cunning. For so many prowesses wrought he that day, and such travail had he and the other brave men that were with him, that they fell sick—being yet nigh to that folk whom may God curse!—both from the labors of that day's emprise and from the carrions wherewith the city was so defiled; and so was their natural strength broken that it lacked but little that they had died—both the king and the others that were there.

"Now whilst the king lay sick and in sore misease, Saladin sent him word that himself and his Saracens would come and take him where he lay, so be it he durst await their coming. And straight the king sent word back to him that Saladin should know and be assured that he would await him in that very place where he now was; nor ever, in any place, so long as he could stand upon his feet or raise himself upon his knees, would he flee one single foot for him. Thus was taken up the gage of war. But God knew well how little ease he had the while he spake thus nobly. Then did he send Count Henry (so saith the tale) back to Caesarea for the French who had come hither afore, and for the other folk that were there, to come now and defend the land. . . ."

(Ambrose: *The History of the Holy War*)

MAPS

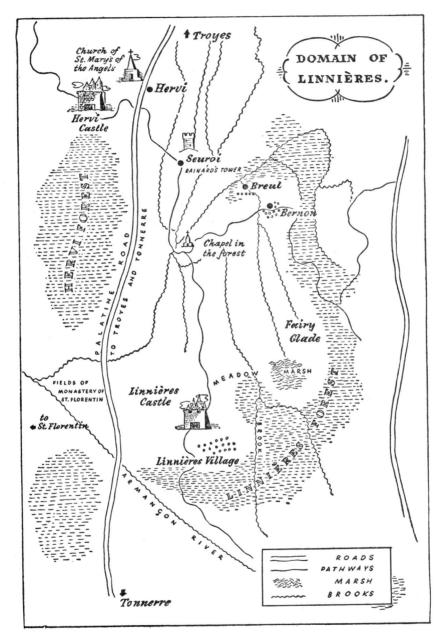

DOMAIN OF LINNIÈRES.

↑ Troyes

Church of St. Mary's of the Angels

● Hervi

Hervi Castle

HERVI FOREST

PALATINE ROAD

TO TROYES AND TONNERRE

● Seuroi
RAINARD'S TOWER

◉ Breul

◉ Bernon

Chapel in the forest

Fairy Glade

MARSH

FIELDS OF MONASTERY OF ST. FLORENTIN

MEADOW

LINNIÈRES FOREST

Linnières Castle

to St. Florentin

BROOK

Linnières Village

ARMANÇON RIVER

↓ Tonnerre

	ROADS
	PATHWAYS
	MARSH
	BROOKS

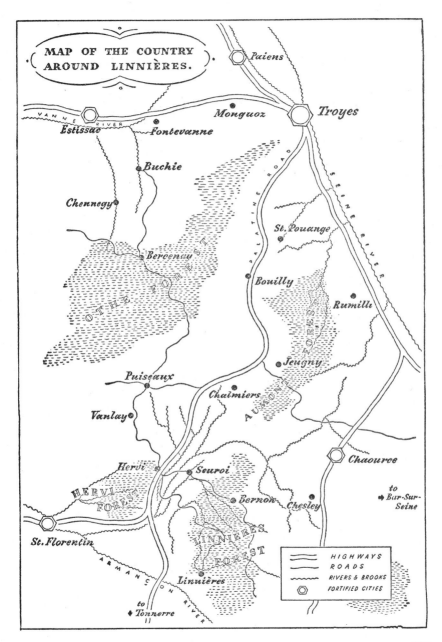

MAP OF THE COUNTRY AROUND LINNIÈRES.

Paiens

VANNE RIVER

Estissac

Monguoz

Troyes

Fontevanne

Buchie

PALATINE ROAD

SEINE RIVER

Chennegy

St. Pouange

Bercenay

O THE FOREST

Bouilly

Rumilli

AUMONT FOREST

Jeugny

Puiseaux

Chaimiers

Vanlay

Hervi

Seuroi

Chaource

HERVI FOREST

Bernon

Chesley

to
Bar-Sur-
Seine

St. Florentin

ARMANÇON RIVER

LINNIÈRES FOREST

HIGHWAYS
ROADS
RIVERS & BROOKS
FORTIFIED CITIES

Linnières

to
Tonnerre

505

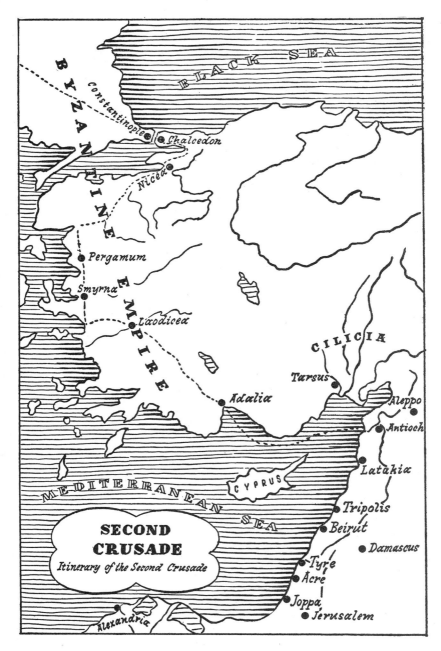

SECOND
CRUSADE

Itinerary of the Second Crusade

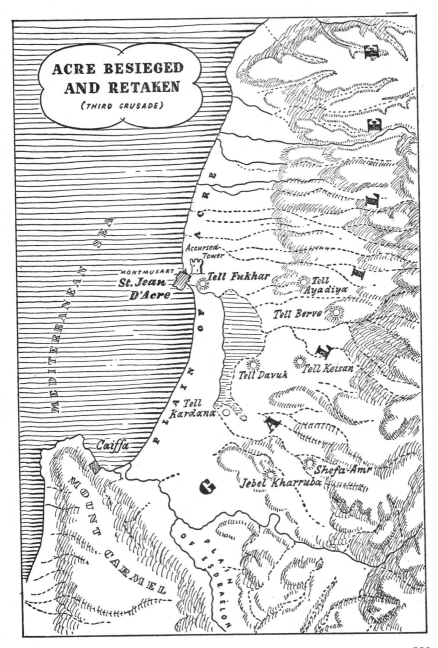

ACRE BESIEGED
AND RETAKEN
(THIRD CRUSADE)

MEDITERRANEAN SEA

ACRE

Accursed Tower

MONTMUSART
St. Jean
D'Acre

Tell Fukhar

Tell Ayadiya

Tell Berve

Tell Keisan

Tell Davuk

PLAIN OF ACRE

Tell Kardana

Caiffa

Shefa-Amr

Jebel Kharruba

MOUNT CARMEL

PLAIN OF ESDRAELON